D0850543

A
Garland Series

VICTORIAN
FICTION

NOVELS OF FAITH
AND DOUBT

A collection of 121 novels
in 92 volumes, selected by
Professor Robert Lee Wolff,
Harvard University,
with a separate introductory volume
written by him
especially for this series.

UNDER WHICH LORD?

Eliza Lynn Linton

Three volumes in one

Garland Publishing, Inc., New York & London

1976

PR 4889
.L5
U5
1976+

Bibliographical note:

this facsimile has been made from a copy in the
British Museum
(12625.m.9)

Fiction
Linton, E
.U5

Library of Congress Cataloging in Publication Data

Linton, Elizabeth Lynn, 1822-1898.
    Under which lord?

    (Victorian fiction : Novels of faith and doubt ; 35)
    Reprint of the 1879 ed. published by Chatto & Windus,
London.
    I. Title. II. Series.
PZ3.L658Un15 [PR4889.L5]   823'.8   75-482
ISBN 0-8240-1559-2

'Only the neighbour and the gentleman is recognised in this house.'

Under which Lord?

BY

E. LYNN LINTON

AUTHOR OF 'THE WORLD WELL LOST' 'PATRICIA KEMBALL' ETC.

IN THREE VOLUMES

VOL. I.

WITH TWELVE ILLUSTRATIONS BY ARTHUR HOPKINS

London

CHATTO & WINDUS, PICCADILLY

1879

'Because we have found not yet
  Any way for the world to follow
    Save only that ancient way;
Whosoever forsake or forget,
  Whose faith soever be hollow,
    Whose hope soever grow grey

Monotones : Songs before Sunrise

CONTENTS

OF THE

FIRST VOLUME.

CONTENTS

FIRST VOLUME

LIST OF ILLUSTRATIONS

TO THE

FIRST VOLUME.

UNDER WHICH LORD?

CHAPTER I.

CROSSHOLME ABBEY.

CONTRARY to all expectation and the father's prophecy, the marriage had turned out a success. It had looked doubtful enough when it was made, having in it almost all the elements which lead from hope to disappointment and bring bitter fruits after fragrant flowers. Unsuitability of worldly position; that intensity of youthful passion which is so sure to cool down into a maturity of prosaic indifference; parental disapprobation, even when all active opposition was withdrawn—and parental disapprobation always carries a curse with it—yes, it was certain to turn out ill, said the world, adding up the crooked sum diligently and seeing only sorrow as the result, as it has so often seen the like before.

And if nothing else were amiss, they were too young

to know their own minds. Indeed this might be taken as the foundation of the whole sorry super-structure. A romantic girl of seventeen and an easy-going young officer of just twenty-one can hardly be expected to understand what is needed for solid happiness or the best development of their own natures ; and, married at that age, the chances were that they would grow apart as they grew older, and that when they came to be real man and woman they would find themselves thinking differently on every subject under heaven. And without mental sympathy, where is the true joy of home?

Why the chances were greater that they should grow apart rather than together, and come to mental discord rather than to harmony, the prophets of evil did not explain. They only said that it was so, and that the thing was certain ; and assertion to some people is as conclusive as proof.

Then, the money was on the wrong side.

Richard Spence, though emphatically a gentleman, had only his pay as a lieutenant in the army, while Hermione Fullerton was an heiress entitled to look among the aristocracy for her husband, had she been wise enough to wait and make use of her gifts. Young, exceptionally beautiful, amiable, wealthy—there was no state nor place below a throne to which, in her father's estimation of chances, she might not have reasonably aspired. Had she cared to marry a Roman prince she might have chosen among the proudest ; had she been content with an English earl, she might have found one to her mind and many to her hand. Instead of either she fixed her affections on a mere nobody—a handsome, clever, well-conducted, good-tempered nobody if you like —but no more what she had the right to expect than if he had been the blacksmith or the shoemaker. So said her father in his wrath ; and his friends echoed his displeasure.

Being however a weak-willed man if an angry, and having always indulged her every wish, Mr. Fullerton suffered the girl to take her own way; and before she had reached her eighteenth birthday the great heiress of Crossholme Abbey was married to her penniless subaltern of nowhere, to the indignation of her other suitors and the general dissatisfaction of the county.

Mr. Fullerton did what he could to neutralize the commercial disadvantages of the match by making things safe for his daughter and unpleasant for the man of her choice. Every farthing of her own fortune, inherited from her mother, was settled on herself : and though

Richard had given up his profession, with its Indian appointment and contingent possibilities, at her instance, and therefore might have reasonably expected a certain provision without being considered a fortune-hunter, yet he had not even a life-interest in any part of the property ; and if his wife died before him all went to her children ; or, failing these, to her next of kin. It was submission to these terms, said Mr. Fullerton grimly, or no wife. He might choose which he would, but he had to choose one or the other.

As the young fellow was sincerely in love, money or no money, and felt that his life with all its grand inheritance of thought and feeling would be in vain if Hermione did not share it, he submitted—hard as the terms were ; and gave up his profession and independence as the sacrifice that he too made for love's sake. He was not afraid that Hermione, loving and generous as she was, would ever make him regret his trust by the humiliation which it would be in her power to inflict. He knew that he was throwing himself as a dependent on her bounty, if she liked to make it so; but he was magnanimous enough to rely on the magnanimity of another, and, faithful for his own part, he believed in faithfulness as probable from most—from Hermione as certain.

Fortunately for the young people, Mr. Fullerton died about four years after their marriage. While he lived he made life hard enough for the young fellow whose union with his daughter he never forgave, and whose sonship he never acknowledged; and it took all Richard's sweetness of temper and practical philosophy to bear with patience the petty insults and galling annoyances to which he was daily subject at the Abbey. But all things come to an end, and the elder man died just as Hermione came of age ; and even she felt, through all her natural sorrow, that the one sole danger to her happiness had been removed.

The first clause in his will provided that the young people should take his own name, and be thenceforth Fullerton. He would not recognize the husband even so far as to allow his name the penultimate place. The others made Hermione his heiress, with the same provision for her children or next of kin as in the marriage settlements ; all benefit being denied to Richard, save such as came to him through the fact of his marriage and consequent sharing in his wife's possessions.

It was the hardest legal instrument that could be devised, and was like a blow in the young man's face from the dead. But it had just the contrary effect to

that intended. Still so young—the love between them
as fresh and fragrant as when they stood in the garden
together on that memorable day, and Hermione, like
Corisande, gave Richard a rose—the birth of their little
daughter Virginia having been but an additional bond
of union, and the death of the boy who came after
drawing them as close by sorrow as this by joy—
Hermione felt less the grateful daughter than the outraged wife ; less the proud possessor than the reluctant
heiress ; and vowed amidst tears and caresses that nothing
should ever make her act on the provisions of a will so
unjust as this, or accept the undeserved place of superior
assigned to her. Richard was her lord, as all husbands
should be to loving wives; and what she was in name he
should be in fact.

She placed everything unreservedly in his hands, and
kept nothing for herself. Her first act of mistresshood
was to give her husband a power of attorney to deal with
all as he would. This was the utmost that she could do,
according to the will ; but both felt that, poor weak
instrument as it was and revocable at pleasure, it was as
firm and sure as if it had been an Act of Parliament
duly signed by the sovereign. From cheques to leases
all was in his hands, and she would not even learn what

he did with the land and its revenues, nor how he exercised the manorial rights and privileges standing in her
name. She was a woman without much reasoning.
faculty and with no sense of property ; but with an
overwhelming power of obedience and self-abnegation
which made her the docile creature of the man whom
she loved. And this sacrifice of her fortune, this transfer
of her rights to the husband from whom they had been
so jealously guarded, pleased her more than power
would have done.

Her reward lay in his love. Passion, romance, and
mental exaltation were her life ; and in relation to the
saying that human nature cannot live at high pressure,
and that passion wears down into sober sense by use, she
was the exception that proves the rule. She could have
lived for ever at high pressure ; and her romance would
never have worn itself out by use, if only it might be fed
by the daily renewal of vows and caresses—the daily
repetition of the sweet follies of the courting-time. What
she dreaded most was the prosaic dulness of the commonplace—what she most esteemed, perpetual mental excitement. If her husband would be always her lover
living only for her, and if her marriage might remain an
unending courtship, she would ask no more of God or

man. But she was not one with whom duty would ever
take the place of emotion, or the quiet security of home
stand her in stead of the unrest of romance.

If this was a weakness, it was an amiable one ; and
for the first four or five years Richard met her more than
half-way, and made her life, as she used to say, like one
long poem. But as time went on and his love con-
solidated by very habit, he became, after the manner of
Englishmen in general, less assiduous than content ; less
the lover than the friend ; no longer suing for something
not bestowed, but holding in such inalienable security
that neither doubt was possible nor prayer needed.
Besides, after Mr. Fullerton's death and his appointment
as his wife's irresponsible agent, he had other things to
do than sitting at her feet, or she at his, while he read
aloud the last new novel or the latest poem—her cheek
against his knee and his hand among her golden curls.
Truth to say, like all men who have anything in them,
this Armida's garden which in the beginning he had found
so satisfactory, so seductive, had somewhat palled on him.
He wanted something beside the love without which,
however, he could scarce have lived at all.

He loved his wife—no man better ; no man with
more faithfulness, more trust, more devotion ; and

just in proportion to the depth, the reality of his affection, seemed to him the value of quiet acceptance and the uselessness of incessant demonstration. The thing was a fact; and facts when once established have to be taken for granted. What was the good of always repeating what was so well understood? The time for love-making had passed, and that for loving in deep and tranquil trust had come.

The time too had come for graver duties and deeper studies. He must take his place among men; exercise such moral influence as his mental powers entitled him to exercise; make up his mind on certain speculative matters which had begun to trouble him and to importune for a settlement; and when his mind should be made up, then his action would be clear. It was the natural development of youth into manhood; and he would not have been the fine fellow he was had he not gone through the process. Love is the first heaven of the young man; but then comes his life as a citizen among citizens;—passion preceding thought, unrest giving place to calmness, and pleasure lost in work and found in knowledge.

But to a certain class of women this gradual development is never accepted with philosophy. They would

keep their men always boys and never let the lover pass
into the friend ; and they resent the law of nature which
crystallizes that which was once fluid and transforms into
quiet certainty the love which was once so delicious
in its unrest. Hermione was one of these women; and
though she was too devoted to complain—having indeed
nothing tangible of which to complain—she felt the
nameless difference that crept by degrees into her life,
and suffered as much as she had once been blessed.
Where her husband, suspecting no dissatisfaction and
conscious of no want, lived in supreme content and
happiness, tranquil, secure, but a little abstracted, a
little pre-occupied, she began to silently eat out her
heart, and to recognize that her life had a void of which
she knew neither the name nor the remedy.

Her husband? No woman could have one more
tender in all essentials, more devoted, more faithful. If
he spent long hours away from her, he had, as he said,
his local duties to attend to which must be fulfilled.
And she could scarcely grudge him the dry studies to
which he had devoted himself, and for which she had
no aptitude, though he found them more enthralling
than art or poetry or love. Biological science and ecclesiastical history ?—she cared neither for cells nor pro-

toplasm; neither for the crack-brained subtleties of sectarian doctrines nor for the horrors of the Papal rule; nor yet for philological accuracy, and whether all the words in the Bible were rightly rendered or no;—in all of which matters Richard had cast his line, hoping to fish up Truth as his reward. No, she could not share his studies; but she had not therefore the right to interfere with them; and though she silently resented the time given to them as time stolen from her, she was wise enough to keep silence, and not to let him know that she was jealous of his microscope and wished that all his books on science were burnt in the fire.

On his side indeed he might argue that she had her child, who was naturally to her what his studies were to him—her little Virginia growing up in docility and sweetness unsurpassable, and lovely enough to justify even a mother's idealizing admiration. She felt all this, if she did not put it into so many words; and she used to ask herself—with health, fortune, a faultless husband, a sweet and interesting child, and the faculty of loving and rejoicing as fresh as when she was herself a child—how could she have a void? What was it? Why did she feel so lonely, so bereft as she did?— for in what blessing did she fail?

She could not tell. Nevertheless, there it was ; a fact
as true as the rest. She used to sigh when she read
those tender bits of poetry, sang those yearning songs
which once expressed her own condition, but which now
seemed pictures of a land that she had lost, of a home
whence she was shut out. Tears were often in her eyes
as she looked at the golden sunset, or watched the
changing clouds, or wondered at the mystery of the stars.
She did not know what ailed her ; but there was so
often that aching at her heart, as if her life were empty
of some sweetness that it ought to have ! The quiet
security of her very happiness oppressed her with a
sense of dumbness and sleep. It was all so monotonous
and commonplace—all so unexciting ! Days passed one
after the other, and all exactly alike. Had she been
poor she would have been forced to exert herself ;
forced to think and contrive and do ; as it was, there
was no need for any exertion whatsoever ; and the neighbourhood afforded no pleasures of such brilliancy as to
make them distracting and enlivening. Everything in
her life was sleek and quiet and sleepy. The hours
were fixed, their habits punctual. Richard gave all the
morning, much of the afternoon, and often the best part
of the evening, to his studies and pursuits ; and when

he wanted to amuse her told her some facts in natural history or the more recondite positive sciences, of which, not having the context, she did not understand the bearing and wondered at the importance which he assigned to them.

If it were for things like those that he neglected her, she used to think, she wondered at his taste, and thought him both blind and cold. He was neither, as she knew; but it pleased her to believe him both, that she might have cause for the small thin thread of bitterness which was beginning to weave itself into the golden garment of her love. And when she looked into the glass and studied what she saw, that thin thread grew broader; for she knew that, thirty-eight as she now was, she was as beautiful as when she was first married, even if the fashion of her beauty had changed, as needs must, with the passage of time. Still, if she were always lovely, Richard was no longer her lover; and of what use her charms if he had failed to see them?

Sometimes she thought this secret pining of hers came from an unregenerate heart and the want of vital religion. True, she went to church; but for form's sake and because it was expected of her as the duty owing to her position and to Virginia—not for spiritual need and less for spiritual comfort. She supposed that some things which she heard there were true ; but she did not realize them, and she more than half doubted the rest. In the state in which she was, religion was rather an irritation than a support, and the Bible perplexed instead of strengthening her. She did not know what in it was true, nor feel what in it was elevating. If there were such a thing as the Divine Life, the present vicar of Cross-holme, sleepy, indolent, " unawakened " old Mr. Aston, could not lead her to its knowledge ; and at home she was even farther from help or guidance. Her husband's studies had led him into the opposite camp, and he had become a pronounced free-thinker—agnostic he called himself ; infidel he was called by others. He had placed science in the seat of theology, and his life's endeavour now was to weaken the hold of the Christian faith on the minds of men :—not by reviling the creed and its pro-fessors, but by showing the contradictions which exist between nature and revelation, Genesis and science, by substituting knowledge for superstition, reason for faith, and history for mythology.

Not to give umbrage to any one, and especially not to Mr. Aston, whose age demanded consideration if his character was unheroic, by using for his secular lectures,

with their heterodox tendencies, the schoolroom where
missionary meetings and the like were held, Richard had
built just outside the gates of the Abbey park a working-
man's reading-room, which he had stocked with a good
library, of anti-religious character, and where he himself
gave lectures and held classes, chiefly scientific and
historical—whence he trusted that his audience would
draw conclusions favourable to free-thought and hostile
to the domination of the Church. His opposition was
always good-tempered and impersonal, even when most
unmistakable ; always courteous and founded on elemental principles, not on the practice of professors ; the
opposition of a gentleman and a fair opponent; but it
was as strong as if it had been brutal, and all the more
telling because it was so calmly reasoned.

As his studies grew in extent and deepened in
character, he became more and more confessedly a free-
thinker ; more and more convinced, he used to say, that
modern Christianity is a string of errors founded on part
falsehood, part misapprehension;—the Bible history a
conglomerate of myths;—the influence of the Church
the consolidation of intellectual darkness;—that belief
without proof is folly, and faith as opposed to reason the
superstition of savages and children;—that the highest

duty of man is that which he owes to the community—
his bravest act of spiritual manliness the confession of
his spiritual ignorance.   Mr. Aston, too old and self-
indulgent to trouble himself for other men's souls, indifferent to all that was done in the parish provided he
was left undisturbed, and liking both Hermione and her
handsome husband, infidel as he was—more the pity!—
too much to quarrel with him, received these shafts of
modern thought on the broad shield of established position.   Here was the church and here it would remain.
Christianity had been argued out to the dregs, and
proved divine by all the tests that could be applied ; and
what Tillotson and Blair and Chillingworth and Newton
had believed he was not ashamed to accept. He had not
seen yesterday's sun ; and if any madman chose to say
that it was not there because he had not seen it, why let
him.   What did it signify ? and who was the worse for
a fool's folly ?

This was his stock of arguments; and of what vital
good were such to a soul seeking for light in the darkness
or wishing to be convinced of salvation in the midst of
doubts on immortality ?

So stood matters at Crossholme Abbey when Virginia
had passed her nineteenth birthday by just two months ;

at which date this story opens. Her father—happy, busy, contented with his lot all round, giving his main strength to educating certain men, young and old, into such knowledge of science as should lead them to the rejection of both Christian dogma and clerical influence ; loving and affectionate to his own family, but not living much with them and still less in society—was a grand and glorious figure in this life, truly ; but he was not her companion ; and at her age, with her nature, she wanted religion, not philosophy; faith, not scepticism ; adoration of God and the angels, not critical examination of verbal forms and isolated facts in natural history.

Her mother, outwardly happy because calm and uncomplaining—of what had she to complain ?—inwardly withdrawing herself more and more from her husband, and secretly disposed to find things with him wrong which once were right—neither religious nor irreligious—feeling that it would be better if she could believe more faithfully and live more earnestly than she did, but as she could not—why, she could not !—always conscious of that dull aching void and suffering from her nameless yearning, but unable to kill the one or satisfy the other—was even less a guide, less a companion than her father might have been ;—and she herself, pale, sweet Virginia

beginning to ask herself restlessly the meaning of life—
beginning to realize that it ought to contain more than
the mere routine duties of a pleasant, peaceful, objectless
home.

Pale, pure Virginia ! the most like a human lily to be
seen anywhere !—the most of a saint out of canoniza-
tion ! No sweet sad legend of maiden courage could
show a more perfect ideal of the virgin-martyr than she
was ; no child's dream of an angel could have found
a truer impersonation. Tall, with abundant hair—not
golden like her mother's nor chestnut like her father's,
but of the true flaxen hue, and like heavy hanks of spun
silk; with blue eyes, large and mournful, but light where
her mother's were as deep as sapphires and her father's
were dark grey; all her lines long and slender; her manners
full of unconscious grace and of unconscious modesty ;
indifferent to physical pleasures and averse from social
gaiety ; devoted rather than expansive ; thoughtful rather
than observant ; conscientious, truthful, ever eager to
confess a fault, but more silent than communicative and
seldom speaking of herself or her feelings—she was a
natural nun ; and had she been a Roman Catholic her
vocation would have been assured.

As it was, what was her place ? what her rightful functions? She had no more of the romance of love in her nature than she had of care for dress or pleasure in dainty food ; so that marriage did not seem her fitting lot in the future, though it might be almost necessary because of her wealth and position. Indeed, the idea of marriage when associated with her, seemed sacrilege rather than the fulfilment of a natural destiny ; and a commonplace courtship would be an impossibility. Her mother used to think that her own life would have been brighter had her daughter been different. It would have been so interesting to watch the dawn and progress of a pleasant love affair between her and some charming youth—such as Richard was before he had taken to mythology and protoplasm, and when he was still a lover, ardent, poetic, and uncertain of her full response. Assisting at her child's young dreams would have renewed her own ; but alas ! there were none at which to assist. This fair young saint moved through the quiet shadows of her life as if she had been a second Una or the modern high-priestess of the Vestals. When the men who had fallen in love with her sincerely and for her own sake—like Ringrove Hardisty, for instance— looked unhappy, and pleaded only dumbly with their eyes, she was sorry to see them sad. But when they said they loved her and asked for her love in return, then she shuddered and took refuge with her mother, as a child frightened by some strange monster. When her father, true to his belief in liberty, laid before her the offers for her hand which came to him, and the "requests for permission to address" her—with a grave smile if the thing were socially or personally absurd, with tears in her eyes if it were possible, she begged him to refuse ; and, laying her hand on his shoulder, would say tenderly : "I want to love no one but you and mamma. If only I could *do* something for you !—if I could work or sacrifice something to show my love !"

No one had as yet stirred her heart or warmed her imagination in the smallest degree ; not even Ringrove Hardisty, who was of a kind that need not have sought far for a response, and who was backed in his hopes by her father's wishes and her mother's desires. But the life for which Virginia longed—that unknown, undesignated life of spiritual exaltation, of the realization of God— was the farthest possible removed from human love or physical enjoyment ; and neither Ringrove Hardisty nor any other man had touched her with that fire which consumes and withers as much as it vivifies and beautifies.

This was Virginia Fullerton at the age of nineteen ; and such as she was, she was the true product of her parents, though so unlike each. Her mother's need of romantic emotion and personal excitement was mated with her father's passionate love of truth for its own sake ; and both together gave her the possibilities of that exalted and unselfish devotedness which once made martyrs and still makes zealots. If she had only known how and where, she would gladly have given herself to the service of humanity, or have dedicated her life to the perpetual worship of God in Truth. But, rudderless as her mother was, with no insight for her own part and no message for others—mentally isolated and content with the denial of dogma and the assertion of material fact as was her father, finding in intellect all that she sought in spirituality, in science what she yearned for from God—to whom could she turn for help? what could she believe? how learn what was true and divine in this world of ours, and what false and human only? And, above all, what could she do to utilize her powers for the good of others?

Yet surely some nobler kind of existence was to be found than in this smooth, calm, self-indulgent life of a home like theirs, where their very charities cost them

nothing—not even the self-sacrifice of a little trouble—
and where their main duty was to be happy and to enjoy.
And again, surely there was something spiritually greater
than this dry knowledge of a few scientific facts—this
sweeping denial of all that could not be touched and
seen! So many men and women had not lived and
died for a mere dream, nor yet for an impossible lie.
The religious life must have something in it, if only she
knew what it was! Girl as she was, day by day she
became more sorrowfully if still only dimly conscious
that this was not her fitting sphere; and that lying for
her elsewhere were work and peace of a far different
kind from these lady-like occupations of no earthly good
when done—from this sleek happiness through the mere
absence of disturbing sorrows—such as made up the life
of home. But what? and where?

Once, when she was reading *Butler's Lives of the
Saints*, which her father had given her to show to what
mad excesses superstitious fancy can lead mankind, she
laid down the book with a sigh.

"If only all this were true, mamma!" she said, raising
her eyes that were as full of unanswered yearning as was
that mother's heart.

"Yes," said Hermione, echoing her sigh; "but you

see it is not, my dear ; and your father says the whole thing was hysteria where not falsehood or imposture."

"I think there was something in it beside disease ; and these were not the people to deceive or impose," returned Virginia.

"It is possible—who knows?" answered her mother vaguely; and the conversation dropped, as all their conversation always dropped, because the one had nothing to teach and the other had all to learn.

But the wish to know and share the mystical passion and rapt enthusiasm of the old-time saints remained; and the longing to find the real meaning of life and to fulfil some high duty toward God or man deepened and grew with Virginia till it became an ever-present pain, and the uselessness of her days an ever-sharp reproach.

CHAPTER II.

MEASURING THE GROUND.

GREAT events were not frequent at Crossholme. At Starton, the county town some five miles away, more was stirring; and feuds and love-makings, deaths, marriages, and new things generally were of constant occurrence. Here at quiet Crossholme the great flood rolled more sluggishly, and history had but little to record. The death then of the old vicar, which happened rather suddenly at this time, was a matter of supreme importance; and who was to be his successor, and what he would be like, filled men's minds with speculations as grave as if the question had been, to the Romish Church, the consecration of an immortal pope—to the United States, the election of a life-long president.

It was a question of supreme importance even to Richard Fullerton; though standing for his own part so far beyond the outermost pale of the communion as to have neither sympathy of thought nor personal interest in anything within. All the same, the matter touched him nearly; more nearly indeed than many others whose minds had never wandered an inch beyond the fold. So far as things had gone hitherto he had been unmolested in his doings, and had not come into direct collision with any one. True, he was called an infidel, and people pitied his poor wife for the certainty of eternal separation that she must foresee, when she, it was to be hoped, would go to heaven and he would be inexorably consigned to the clutches of the Evil One; and his lectures were considered a "pity" and non-sensical—for what did village carpenters and wheel-wrights want with chemistry and astronomy, physiology and history? It was only filling their minds with things quite out of their sphere; making them conceited with a little knowledge, and doing no good anyhow.

But if the vicar and the resident gentry had not upheld, neither had they opposed; and Mr. Fullerton's reprehensible craze had been given fair play and its full swing.

Would the new vicar be as tolerant, and content himself with now a Shakesperean quotation, and now a Biblical, expressive of his contempt for the rabble and the inutility of casting pearls before swine? If he chose he could make things unpleasant enough for the iconoclast of the Abbey—as unpleasant, in another way, as his father-in-law had done. He could embarrass his relations with his men—as he called his little band of regular hearers—and either compel him to silence or commit them to social ostracism; supposing that he got the ear of the place and used his power tyrannously. Starton was quite near enough, and communication between it and Crossholme frequent enough, to render this latter independent of local handicraftsmen; and a man of influence could, if he chose, starve out an obnoxious villager living by the goodwill of others. What if the new man did so choose?

These thoughts had come to Richard with painful vividness when he heard of Mr. Aston's sudden death; and now they were renewed, more vividly and more painfully, as he thought of his successor, the Honourable and Reverend Launcelot Lascelles, who had read himself in last Sunday, and on whom he and Hermione had been discussing at breakfast to-day the propriety of a welcoming visit. Knowing the new vicar by repute as one of the most advanced of the ritualistic party, with clear and well-defined views on the power of the priesthood and the submission of the laity, he felt that he must prepare himself for the struggle that was sure to come. The days of neutrality were over and those of strife were at hand. A man holding the most extreme doctrines as yet formulated—one who, assuming quasi-divine powers as part of his functions, preached confession as absolutely necessary for the health of the soul and priestly absolution as integral to God's forgiveness —who exalted the worship of the Virgin into a religious necessity, and taught the value of invocation to the saints and the pious need of priestly prayers for the souls of the dead—who was a Roman Catholic in all save name and obedience, being his own pope and college of cardinals in one; absolute by right of ordination, and owing no submission to the heads of the Church whereof he was an inferior member, nor to the laws of the country whereof he was a citizen, should either displease him—one who was contemptuous of modern science, sceptical of modern progress, and opposed to all forms of mental freedom—such a man as this at Crossholme, where the unthinking majority was careless and the thoughtful minority unbelieving! Yes, that meant a struggle, and Richard realized the position.

"But my men will not be warped," he thought, as he lifted his head from the microscope through which he had been looking—thinking rather than seeing ;—for indeed the moment was grave. "They know the truth now, and the falsehood of all those fables which no man of sense can believe if once he dares to examine them by the light of reason. No priest will be able to get hold of them, trading as they all do on ignorance of scientific facts, on hysterical emotion, and on sensual impressionability. If he threatens them however with loss of work?—and is able to make his threats good? That is possible, and what I fear more than all. Well, if he does, my income is large enough to bear even a severe drain, and I will help them as much as he hinders. Poor fellows! they shall come to no worldly loss for the sake of the truth, so long as I have sixpence to share among them."

It was characteristic both of his trustful temper and unselfishness, that Richard thought of his men only, not in any way of himself or his own house; characteristic of his circumstances, that he thought of *his* income, *his* power to do such and such things and deal as he thought best with the Abbey lands and revenues. He had been so long accustomed to supreme administration as to forget that in reality all belonged to Hermione, not to him, and that he was only her agent, to be dismissed at her pleasure and having no real power over what he had held for so long in undisputed pos- session. To have reminded himself of this would have been either a folly, as one who should make preparations for the end of the world, which yet is a great fact that has to come, and might any day—who knows?—but will not; or it would have been an act of *lèse majesté* against the best, truest, and most loving heart that ever made mortal woman precious to man.

Good, faithful wife! How thoroughly at that mo- ment he realized her steadfastness, her loyalty; and how warmly he recognized his own good fortune in possessing her! His thoughts went back to those first days of his youth; and like a picture the whole thing passed in one rapid moment before his mind. He saw her as she was when they first met at the county ball, the prettiest creature whom he had ever beheld; he remembered how his passion grew and grew, though he never dared to hope for a successful issue, because of her wealth and her father's known ambition. And yet those dark- ened eyes; that blushing face; that tell-tale sunny smile when they met; and those maddening tears when he told her that he was going, and she turned away sobbing, struggling vainly with her pride, overpowered by her despair!—and then he remembered how the floodgates of his own love opened; and the girlish joy that took the place of all this sorrow as she smiled up in his face "I love you!" and kissed the rose which she picked to give him as her token. He had that rose yet in his drawer. It was sacred to him, withered and faded as it was. Then all that followed:—her father's opposition and her own steadfastness; the marriage and its hard financial conditions; his life of small humiliations and her sweet cheerful love as his reward; the little one that came to bless and that remained—that other which came only to sorrow, and that left them; and now his calm, useful, busy life; her divine content; Virginia's sweet unsuspectingness of sorrow or of sin. How happy he and they were! There was but one evil that could touch him, and that was Death. But, *absit omen!* That dreamless sleep was far from either, and years on years of love and peace lay before them. They would see their silver and their golden and even their diamond wedding, he thought, smiling to himself; and carry on their tottering knees Virginia's golden-haired grandchild. They were so happy! no one in the world more so! He wanted nothing, absolutely nothing; save perhaps that dear son whom he had so earnestly desired and so sorely regretted. But Ringrove Hardisty would one day be his son; so he hoped; and he believed as he hoped. The only difference was that the family would be continued in the female line; and that his daughter would inherit the property which had come to him through her mother. Yes; everything was right, and everything would go on as it had been for all these years.

And then he turned to his microscope again, and studied afresh the monad whose " life history " he too was recording as his contribution in a certain controversy raging among scientists with some unphilosophical warmth. Ah, this was something worth living for ! The Honourable and Reverend Launcelot Lascelles was forgotten as if he had never existed. His love poem with Hermione faded as if no sweet echo had ever thrilled the fibres of his brain, the chords of his memory. Virginia and the lost son; Ringrove Hardisty and his hopes; his men and their possibilities of trouble—all were merged in the eager closeness with which he marked the changes from a line to a sac, and from a smooth sphere to an irregular figure of no denomination, of a transparent little creature not to be seen at all save under a magnifying power of some hundreds of diameters.   And of what use pray, when seen ? the unscientific world asks with a sneer.

And while he was studying and noting, absorbed in his work, the servant came into the room to tell him that the new clergyman, Mr. Lascelles, was in the drawing-room ; and his mistress said, would he please to come when convenient?

"Directly, John, directly," he answered, not looking up. "Tell your mistress I will be with her in a moment."

But the moment lengthened out into rather more than an hour before he came ; for time flew fast with him and memory stopped still, and it was only when all his observations were made for the day that he remembered his wife's message, and that the new clergyman was waiting for him in the drawing-room. And all this time Mr. Lascelles had been sitting alone with Hermione, whose soul he had been probing and whose weak places he had been finding out with the skill of a man accustomed to read character, to deal with opposition, and to convince ignorance.

He had found out certain things already. One was that she was weary—with that worst of all weariness, idleness ; and that she would hail anything that gave her a new interest and new occupation. Another was that she was impressionable, and, he should judge, weak; affectionate—but is it affection only, or is there not some admixture of vanity as well, which makes a woman amenable to a man's flatteries judiciously offered? And Hermione was amenable to flattery; else why that sudden flush, that bashful quiver of the downcast eyelids, when he, preparing the ground, spoke to her of the help in his great schemes and hopes for the parish which he expected from her, the Lady of the Manor, and of such sweet and noble repute as she was?

As for her husband, Mr. Lascelles ignored him altogether. When Hermione, woman-like, wife-like, put him forward, claiming first his permission before consenting to this plan, that proposal—or, sure that he would never allow her to do this, to commit herself to that—the clergyman set him aside with a kind of lofty high-handedness, as if wifely submission were an old wife's tale unfit for a reasonable woman to hold, and for a Lady of the Manor, a lay rector, unseemly—considering all things. Had those things been the other way, and she the infidel, Richard the believer, perhaps his argument would have been different. But that was not the present question ; and Hermione had not skill enough to see that certain principles are like chameleons which change their colour according to the ground on which they rest.

The first two things which the new vicar had it at heart to do were to parcel the parish out into districts —of which the ladies of the place were to be the visitors—and to organize a small surpliced choir. The first would give him the influence over the women, the second over the boys ; and both would necessitate much personal intercourse between him and those of his flock whom it was most essential to win over into personal attachment and moral submission. The more advanced methods would have to wait. They would come in time ; but the time was not yet ripe ; and, bold as he was, he feared that he might frighten some of the more timid and put the cautious on their guard, were he to unfold the whole of his programme at once. Besides, of what good to say " I intend " or " I wish " when you cannot do ? Why call the world to criticize the house of which even the stones are not yet quarried ? For the present he must be content with the beginnings, of which to gain first the confidence and then the obedience of this pretty, sensitive, well-endowed woman was the most important.

Already, even in their first short interview of one hour, he had made some way with her. He had got her to promise that she would use her influence with her husband should he oppose her wish to support the two new schemes—which were all that he exposed to-day—of district-visiting and the surpliced choir. He had got her to confess that, though she was the happiest woman in the world—quite the happiest; repeated with suspicious fervour—life at Crossholme was rather dreary, and religion without ceremonial fatally poor and unsatisfactory. He had put the words into her mouth, and he made her assent to them. She had not known that it was an advanced ritual for which her soul had been hungering all this time; that she sighed when she looked at the sunset for want of candles on the altar, and processions round the church; or that tears came into her eyes when she sang certain sentimental old songs because the saints' days were not observed and they had no harvest-home thank-offerings. Had she confessed truly, she would have said it was quite another thing; but as he had told her with a sweet smile, courtly, kind, and patronizing all in one, that he could read her like an open book—"an open book of goodly print and fair illuminations," he added, thinking flattery like everything else lawful that should win power to the Church—why, she had smiled and blushed and said that his penetration was marvellous; that he was very kind; that she would be glad indeed to see his views established; and that in fact she would help him to the utmost of her ability:— which was about the best hour's work, looking at things from his point of view, that the Honourable and Reverend Launcelot Lascelles had ever accomplished.

"I can scarcely say how happy it has made me, to find you so ready to put your hand to the good work," he said with just the right amount of enthusiasm and gratitude. More might have startled her ; only so much warmed and animated. "And you yourself will gain so immeasurably in happiness—happy as you now are— when you feel that you have brought such a glorious duty into your life."

"All duty helps one's happiness," said Hermione, rather vaguely.

"But duty to God through His Church the most," returned the vicar with impressive gravity.

She raised her eyes to his as he spoke. His tone half frightened her. If she wanted a new excitement, some fresh emotion, she did not want to be put all at once into religious fetters ; and, like so many, she mixed up gloom and religion as inseparable. He seemed to read her thoughts with that quick perception of his which was like another sense.

"And in the Church," he said quietly, "there is such ever-varying interest, such a wide and healthy and affectionate companionship, that all the best human instincts are cultivated at the same time that the work of faith is being carried on. We are a world in ourselves— the most cheerful, the most united, and the happiest to be found anywhere :—a band of brothers and sisters all working towards a common end, and emulous only in doing good according to the directions of the Church, through the Superior."

His picture re-assured her.

"I have always thought that I should like to belong to some kind of organization," she said. "It must give one such a feeling of support."

"Yes ; as you will prove," he answered.

"But my husband?" she objected timidly.

He smiled. "We do not come between husband and wife because we wish the services to be well performed, and the authority of the Church acknowledged

by the laity!" he answered soothingly but with a touch
of sarcasm. "You need have no fear on that head, Mrs.
Fullerton. The sole chance of collision between you
and your husband is, if he refuses to allow you free
exercise of your own conscience—and your own means.
From all that I hear he will not; and from all that I
see"—gallantly—"he could not, if you exert your influence over him and win him to consent."

"He is very, very good," she answered; "but he has
such a dread of the whole thing!"

"He will be won over," returned Mr. Lascelles with
a cheerful smile. "He is a candid person—so says
report; and though now notoriously astray, yet, believe
me, God will not leave him always in error—and you
will be the chosen instrument to bring him into the
light of truth."

She sighed.

"I should be very glad," she answered; but she did
not kindle at the thought. She knew the ground too
well to believe in what was well-meant encouragement,
truly, but futile, because founded on ignorance of the real
state of things.

Then she was silent, and a certain change passed
over her face as she caught the sound of her husband's

footsteps through the hall. He opened the door just as Mr. Lascelles was saying in a perfectly natural voice :

"What a magnificent view you have from this south window. It seems to me the most perfect I have seen."

"Oh, Richard, Mr. Lascelles," said Hermione, with an unusual nervousness in her manner. Then, as if recollecting herself : "My husband," she added, looking at her visitor.

The two men met; looked at each other fixedly; and shook hands. So do men before the fight which may end in the death of one of them. They knew that they met as foes, and they mutually measured their strength and took the ground in that first searching glance. Absolutely unlike, they were yet well matched. They were of the same age ; both handsome, well-educated gentlemen ; both entirely sincere in their convictions ; both positive that they had found the truth and ready to defend their principles to the death. Mr. Lascelles, tall, courtly, graceful ; with a high forehead and smooth-shaven face ; thin lips closing in a firm and colourless line, but mobile and full of expression when in speech ; a high thin nose, the transparent nostrils of which easily quivered and dilated ; a narrow but high

head, and short coal-black hair already thinning about
the temples ; a nervous organization betokening a nature
full of hidden fire and restrained eagerness ; with
manners of singular grace and courtliness, but through
all their polish the pride of the aristocrat and the scorn
of one who holds himself intellectually superior to the
mass, and spiritually illumined where others are dark,
breaking out in every look and feature ;—was ecclesiastic
to his finger tips.

Richard, with curling hair as thick and luxuriant now
as when he was twenty, but with more white in it than
chestnut ; a bushy beard and moustache veiling the full
kind mouth but not concealing the bright good-humoured
smile that so often came on it; his dark grey eyes, speculative, mild and calm ; his manner not so courtly as the
other's, but more genial ; his latent energy as great but
less nervous, less impatient ; for the irrepressible pride
and sarcasm of the conscious superior substituting that
subtle deference, that patience with ignorance which
shows the man to whom humanity is sacred—looked in
his turn what he was—a philosopher untouched by personal sorrow or spiritual disquiet; glad of such light as
he had found in proved fact, and for the rest content
with darkness till full illumination should come.

But, deep as was the antagonism between them, the beginning of things was trivial enough.

"You have not been long here, I think?" said Mr. Fullerton in his rich voice and rather slow utterance. "We were talking of you at breakfast this morning, and arranging when we should call."

"Thank you," said Mr. Lascelles with a slight smile. "Your visit to my sister will be welcome, when she has arranged her home affairs so as to be able to receive you. That will be social; this of mine to you is functional. I am making acquaintance with all my parishioners, as their priest—not as a householder just yet."

"Priests are not much in my line," said Richard, quite simply and as of course. "The vicar is a neighbour, and so far one of ourselves; but I make the distinction between the man and his office."

Mr. Lascelles raised his eyes. They were not handsome in form or colour, but they were keen and searching. He had the habit of keeping them for the most part lowered, with the taught and artificial humility of the Romish priest, but he used them with effect when he did look up. He raised them now, suddenly, swiftly, and looked full into Richard Fullerton's face.

"A distinction without a difference," he answered. "A priest is always a priest, and does not put on his character with his surplice."

"Only the neighbour and the gentleman is recognized in this house," said Mr. Fullerton, with the same kind of simplicity of truth, but perfectly urbane.

"Yes, I have heard something of that," said Mr. Lascelles, even more urbane than his host. "But," with sudden frankness, "that is not my affair."

"No," said Richard, "it is mine."

"What is my affair," resumed Mr. Lascelles, as if he had not heard him; though Hermione had flushed and looked across at her husband uneasily—why flourish his flag so aggressively, so obtrusively? she thought— "and a serious matter too, is to get the parish into good working order and the service into decent condition. I find everything in disorder—everything neglected. The church services are disgraceful—the choir nowhere— the whole thing deplorable; and I must appeal to my parishioners for support. The first thing that I have to do is to divide the parish into districts, of which I must ask the several ladies of the place to be my visitors. I came here to-day to secure the services of Mrs. and Miss Fullerton."

"My wife and daughter will, I fancy, scarcely join you in your church-work," said Richard with a tranquil smile. He felt so sure of his own!

"No? Not to do kindly services to our poorer brethren?—not to help a struggling woman, say, with a friendly word in season?—not to show those who suffer that we sympathize with them and understand their needs?—not to comfort them in their afflictions?—aid them in the dark hours where friendly sympathy can do so much? You, who are said to feel so much zeal for humanity, can scarce refuse that!"

Mr. Lascelles spoke with fervour; his eyes glittering with the heat of the struggle that had begun so soon, and on the issue of which he based so much of the future; but he was entire master of himself and his methods, and took the tone which he thought most efficacious to his purpose. Then turning to Mrs. Fullerton, he said appealingly:

"Mrs. Fullerton, your woman's heart will plead my cause and the cause of the poor with your husband. Wife and mother yourself, you know that I am asking from you the duty owed by one woman to another, and I feel sure that you cannot refuse me! What do I pray of you?—to take a certain district and to look

to the poor dwelling within its area as your special
care, so that when they are sick you will visit them,
when in sorrow comfort them, when in want relieve
them.   Can you refuse?"

"Indeed, Richard," said Hermione shyly, "I, and I
am sure that Virginia too, would like to have a district
to look after.   It would be something to interest us
as well as doing good to the poor," with a faint sigh
which Mr. Lascelles caught and her husband did not.
"And we ought to do some good in the parish," she
added.

"You do already, my dear, a great deal of
good," said Richard with surprise.   "You have your
working   women   and   your   old   pensioners   and
your soup kitchen—why! it seems to me that you
do an immense amount of kindly work among the
poor."

"Not under organization," said Mr. Lascelles.

"Which is just what I object to ; church organization is the leaven that ruins all, in my mind."

"Surely not !   It is order that saves the world
from chaos and destruction," cried Mr. Lascelles ; "you
must allow that, Mr. Fullerton, standing every inch on
your own ground.   Sporadic activities are of no value

anywhere. It is the closely serried phalanx that carries all before it."

"And this is a phalanx of which I do not wish any one belonging to me to form a part," said Richard, rather more slowly than usual.

"Not for the good of humanity?—the simple relief of physical misery?—and you the friend of man!" Again Mr. Lascelles fixed his bright keen eyes on the face before him; and, looking at it, smiled. "This is no question of doctrine," he said, as if coaxing a child to look behind the screen where some ugly phantom had been thrown; "it is merely one of kindly practice; and I think we both see that your wife wishes it."

"My wife would do nothing against my wish," said Richard, turning to her with a confident air. Mr. Lascelles also looked at her, his eyebrows slightly arched.

"I do not think there is anything in this to pain you, dear," said Hermione gently; "it is only to visit the poor."

It was rarely indeed that she ever held her own against his desire. Her worst show of displeasure against him had never been more than the childish pettishness, the half-innocent waywardness of a pretty

woman who thinks herself unappreciated—of a loving
one who thinks herself unduly neglected. But now her
promise to Mr. Lascelles compelled her; and indeed
Richard was unreasonable to object, she thought; there
was nothing wrong in having a district and going about
among the poor !

Her husband's quiet face clouded for a moment
with perplexity rather than displeasure. The shadow
passed as quickly as it came.

" You are the mistress of your own actions, my
dear," he said pleasantly; " if you wish it, by all
means."

" Then may I count on you and Miss Fullerton?"
the vicar asked in a matter-of-fact way, looking down
as he took out his bulky pocketbook and made an entry.
His voice was clear, but his nostrils quivered. He had
gained the first victory, and he accepted it as an omen.
Holding his hand where he had written her name, but
not looking up at Hermione—"yourself and your
daughter?" he said again.

She turned to Richard.

" Do you object to Virginia's joining me?" she
asked in quite her own manner of sweet submission for
love's sake : the manner which, with her rare untouched

MEASURING THE GROUND. 47

beauty, made her like a great girl more than a matron
with a marriageable daughter.

"The daughter goes with the mother," he answered
gently. "What you think right for her is right."

He was a man to do things handsomely if at all,
and not to skimp his grace in details; but Hermione,
womanlike, almost wished that he had made a stand
and refused his consent altogether for both; for all that
she had just mentally accused him of unreasonableness
in objecting; and a sharp pain struck her heart as she
thought: "He cares so little for me now, he does not
even forbid me to do what he does not like."

Mr. Lascelles, like many of his class, was a man of
consummate tact when needed, and of as much boldness
when boldness was the better policy. He understood
how far he could go, and felt his ground with the skill
of a practised pioneer, and rarely made a blunder. The
question of the district-visiting settled, there remained
that of the choir, and he thought it better to bring this
forward at once. He saw that he could count on
Hermione, at least for the moment; but he could not
be sure of her stability; and he saw that her husband
was true to his principles of liberty and self-assertion,
and that she could do, with a little pressure, what she

wished. It would score something considerable for him
to have the Fullerton name at the head of his subscription list ; and in the uphill fight before him he disdained
no advantage that he could get. His work would be
heavy enough with every advantage. There was the
dead weight of long-time indifference and the custom
of generations to pull against, as well as the active
opposition of those to whom an advanced ritual would
be naturally abhorrent—fraught with mysterious danger,
no one could exactly say what ; and to gain the public
support of the confessed free-thinker of the parish, the
richest man in it—if rich only by right of his wife ; and
one of the most respected in all save his diabolical
opinions—diabolical enough, however saintly his life
might be—to gain the name and aid of Richard Fullerton
would be a step of incalculable value. Wherefore he
took the leap now at once ; the iron was hot and would
bear a second blow, he thought.

"Now," he said, his thin lips relaxing into a smile
which did not reach his eyes; "now you must help in
the formation of a properly trained surpliced choir.
The present state of things is simply disgraceful, and
must not be allowed to go on."

"No, no," said Richard; "that is impossible. Do

with the services what you like, and what the parish will
bear—that is your affair and theirs—but do not ask me
to give you a farthing of my money or a helping hand
any way."

"If not you—I can understand and respect your
opposition ; it is fair and consistent—but if not you, then
Mrs. Fullerton," said the vicar with his courtly air.
"But let us argue the question on its merits. What
reasonable objection can you have to this ? There are
certain fixed musical passages in the service which now
are sung abominably ; what danger can you see in a well-
trained choir, with a distinctive dress, doing that well
which now is done ill, but which, well or ill, has to be
done somehow ? "

"It is the thin end of the wedge," said Richard ;
"and I cannot lend my name to any part of a system of
which I disapprove all the parts alike."

"The thin end of the wedge ! Surely, Mr. Fullerton,
you are not the man to cherish a superstitious fear or
indulge in a baseless fancy ; and what is this but a
superstitious fear ? Are you all to be Romanized—which
I suppose is your special *bête noire*—because the Nunc
Dimittis and the Te Deum are sung in tolerable
time by a trained choir, instead of being, as now,

bawled out in all directions and with more false notes than true?"

"I know all these arguments so well; so did Reineke," said Richard. "They are always the same; the innocent beginnings of the fatal end."

"Then I must appeal again to Mrs. Fullerton," said Mr. Lascelles, a sudden flush on his pallid face and his keen eyes flashing. "She is the Lady of the Manor; and the lay-rector to whom rightfully, and legally, the care of the chancel belongs; and I appeal to her sense of justice and propriety whether things are tolerable as they are, or whether she will not give her assistance to make them if only decently creditable."

Hermione looked distressed, but the vicar's reasoning seemed to her both just and unanswerable.

"Things are certainly very bad," she said in a low voice and as if apologetically; "they ought to be improved, Richard. You see, you do not go to church, and do not know how carelessly the services have been performed, nor how excruciating the singing is."

"Thank you, Mrs. Fullerton," said Mr. Lascelles quickly; "I shall count then on your subscription."

For the first time since her marriage Richard Fullerton's wife wished that she had kept some part of her income in her own hands. Hitherto she had never desired more than she had had for the asking. She was an indolent woman in every-day affairs ; and as the housekeeper kept the books and overlooked the trades-men's accounts on the one hand, and the milliner supplied her with all that she wanted and sent in the bill on the other, and her husband paid everything by cheques, she had no need for more than the few loose shillings wanted for her visits to the poor ; and she had not the trouble or responsibility of keeping a purse, which she was always losing or mislaying. Now how-ever she wished that she had money to use as she liked with or without her husband's sanction.

" My name shall not go to help any scheme of the kind," repeated Richard, a little more slowly and a great deal more emphatically than his wont.

" But Mrs. Fullerton's ? "—asked the vicar, em-phasizing the title.

" Mrs. Fullerton thinks as I do," replied Hermione's husband.

" Surely not," cried Mr. Lascelles. " The Lady of the Manor—the lay rector—refuse to help in the decent ordering of the church services? Forgive me, Mr. Fullerton—you ought to know best, of course—but

I should have thought Mrs. Fullerton too true a woman to sanction the present disorder, and with too lively a sense of her position in the parish to make it possible that she should not see where her duties lay."

Hermione flushed. How he insisted on her rights! But, after all, she was what he said—she was something more than Richard's wife. She was the actual proprietor of all; and had she not her duties? He had insisted on those duties in the conversation which they had had together—insisted on them strongly, and as if they were too patent to need subtlety or delicacy of handling.

" Oh, we settled that long ago," said Richard, turning to his wife with a smile. " We revised the old Latin speech, and made it after our own pattern. Where she is Lady, I am Lord."

" You refuse then?" Mr. Lascelles asked quickly; also turning to her. " You wish the present disgraceful state of things to continue, and throw the weight of your influence and your name into the scale of disorder, neglect, and artistic unloveliness? You must remember, Mrs. Fullerton, that, right or wrong—I am not here to argue that part of the question—the Established Church is a fact which cannot be got rid of. The question then is:—Shall it be an elevating, refining, and ennobling fact, or one that does more harm than good by its want of decency and artistic truth?"

" Things are very bad at Crossholme, certainly," said Hermione; " and indeed, dear Richard, I should like to see them improved! I should like to subscribe to the choir. In my position, it is only right."

" You must act according to your sense of right," her husband said, after a pause. " In my position" ran in his ears like some strange speech of which he had not the key. " You know my feelings, but I do not coerce yours, nor forbid your action."

"Whatever your private feelings may be, the fact is simply this, that the musical parts of the services are at present very inharmoniously rendered, and that it would be better to have them well done, if only for the sake of good art," said Mr. Lascelles, arguing the question on its evident merits.

" That is only reasonable," put in Hermione; "and, after all, Richard, what possible harm can come of a well-trained choir?"

" The game usually begins with a well-trained sur-pliced choir," said Richard; "the game that ends in the denial of all freedom of thought, and the substitution of the most monstrous superstition for truth."

"Do you scent Romanism and the Inquisition in a dozen linen surplices to cover the ugly and not always decent jackets of so many school-boys?" asked Mr. Lascelles with open sarcasm.

"Richard!" cried Hermione in remonstrance. She thought it so ill-bred in her husband to insist on his dislike to Christianity in the presence of a clergyman, and one like Mr. Lascelles!

"My opinions on this subject are not new, and they are well known," said Richard very slowly. "I understand the whole thing only too well."

"I am sorry to find you so bitter," Mr. Lascelles answered with perfect temper; "and, as I must think, scarcely fair to yourself. But the question presses for a settlement, and I have already trespassed on your time more than I ought to have done. What am I to do then?—consider you as opponents to my choir, or put you down as subscribers?"

"I am an opponent," said Richard.

"And you, Mrs. Fullerton?"

"No; I cannot call myself an opponent," she answered, looking down.

"A subscriber then?"

She turned appealingly to her husband.

" Do you wish to subscribe, Hermione ? " he asked.

"Yes," she answered in a lowered voice. " I ought to do so."

" You are mistress of your own actions," he said as he had said before; but only after a moment's silence. He was a little bewildered and scarcely knew how things were. " Subscribe if you will, my dear," he added more naturally. " How much ? "

" Twenty pounds," said Hermione, ignorant of the value of money.

" So much ? You are more than generous," said her husband, looking disconcerted. " I should have thought five, or even one, sufficient."

" As Lady of the Manor ? " sneered Mr. Lascelles, always touching the same chord.

" Not too generous, surely," pleaded Hermione. " You see, dear, I ought to do more than any one else."

" Twenty pounds be it, then. Shall I write the cheque now ? "

" Thanks," said Mr. Lascelles. " If you please. I shall not have to inculcate on you the duty of obedience," he continued in a peculiar voice, when he and Hermione were alone. It was a voice rasped with sarcasm, for all its honeyed words of praise. " You are the model of

conjugal submission, and I foresee will one day be as
dutiful a daughter of the Church as you are now a wife."

"I have always tried to do my duty," stammered
Hermione, feeling that he was mocking her, and that he
disapproved while he commended.

"And even more than the strict lines of duty. You,
the owner of all, cannot even write your own cheques—
cannot even subscribe for the well-ordering of your own
property—without the permission of your husband, whose
life you have made?—Admirable! but almost too admirable!"

"We have always lived like this," said Hermione.

"The doctrine of perfection carried out to its ultimate, but in a wrong direction," returned Mr. Lascelles,
below his breath.

Then Richard came back, and soon after the new
vicar took his leave.

"The thin end of the wedge, indeed!" he said to
himself, as he walked down the park road, and drew his
breath hard. "The thin end of the wedge, and soon
the thick!—when the power of this accursed infidel will
be split asunder, the Church delivered from a formidable
foe, and the souls of a now lost household saved."

CHAPTER III.

THE WORK TO BE DONE.

ALL the land round about Crossholme had once belonged
to the Church. In the Abbey grounds were part of
the cloisters and the remains of a grand east window
overgrown with ivy, where the owls made their nests
and the bats found their resting-place, and whence fragments of fine old carving were still at times turned up
from beneath the soil. Indeed, had any one cared, it
would have been easy to have traced out the whole
ground-plan of the monastery by the fragments which
were left and by the plates in early county histories
before the ruins had become so shattered as they were
now. But the place had come into the possession of the
Fullertons before archæology was in fashion, and the
ruins were—just ruins, which had given the stones for the
new house when it was built some hundred and fifty
years ago, and out of which the builder had also made
capital lime for mortar. Still, there it was—Church
property self-determined; and the names which still

clung to other places in the neighbourhood bore evidence to the former ecclesiastical character of the estate, if indeed further evidence than the old title-deeds were wanting.

Churchlands, where the Molyneux family lived, had been an old farm leased by the Benedictines to a far-away ancestor of the present proprietor, who had bid for the holding when the Dissolution was ordained. This ancestor, one Beaulieu, was by no means in the direct line, and on the female side if at all; but the last Molyneux had traced the stream, at least to his own satisfaction, and if he had had to make hypothetical bridges across unquestionable gaps, why, all genealogies show the like, and he was no more daring than his neighbours.

Monkshall, the property of young Ringrove Hardisty, had been a kind of offset of the Abbey, where were lodged with more or less of pomp and hospitality those strangers whom it would have been inconvenient to receive in the monastery itself. The very name of the parish, Crossholme, was entirely ecclesiastical; and Mr. Lascelles felt like a man unlawfully dispossessed—a son unjustly disinherited—when he looked round on the beautiful country and well-favoured land which the

Church had once called her own, and which was now held by usurpers and heretics. For to him the National Church as it is had lapsed greatly; and he, like all his party, had vowed himself to do his best to purge it of its sin of Erastianism, and to restore it to its supremacy as in olden times.

Mr. Lascelles was not in any sense a hypocrite—not one of those pious mountebanks who pretend the faith which in their secret soul they despise. On the contrary, he was earnest and ardent to 'fanaticism; but he was insincere just so far as this—that he disdained no weapons by which he thought he might deliver a telling blow; and he knew so well how to make himself all things to all men, that he could even feign liberality and the allowance of private judgment when talking with unbelievers whom he thought it worth while to conciliate. He was thoroughly alive to his good gifts of person, birth, and manners, which he counted on as aids and auxiliaries, as a man reckons up his various sources of income when he is laying out his expenditure. He knew that his intellect was clear and keen; and that his knowledge of books and men was greater than that of most. He even understood that a romantic name like his—a name savouring of chivalry and knighthood and sentimental romanticism, and thus uniting the splendour of man with the religious authority of the priest—was a small point in his favour; at least with women who need to have their imagination warmed as much as the average man demands that his reason shall be satisfied. And he understood to the fullest the value of women as helpers as well as subjects. Their sympathies, and the submissive activities of young men still in the first ardour and fervour of their age and while retaining something of the feminine element in their zeal for faith and their abhorrence of doubt, were the allies to which he trusted. For men of mature judgment and independent thought, reasoning, cool, far-sighted men, he left them alone—so far.

His avowed work here at Crossholme was to bring the services of the Church into conformity with a more advanced ritual; his secret dream to get back some of the forfeited property if he could so far work on the consciences of the present holders. From being one of the wealthiest monasteries in England, Crossholme had been carved down into one of the poorest livings, fit only for a man of independent means to hold. If, then, he could so win over to the truth any of those now possessing unlawful lands—he must always insist on the spiritual sin of their possession—as to induce them to restore to the Church what rightfully belonged to the Church, he should have done one good deed in his life, and fulfilled to some extent the purpose to which he had dedicated himself.

The work that he had set himself to do was hard, but, perhaps for that very reason, all the more attractive. A trial of strength was of all things that in which he most delighted, essentially a fighting man as he was, though his weapons were only mental. When he reckoned up his chances they were not so entirely desperate as they seemed at first sight. True, there was Richard Fullerton in his way—the most formidable adversary that he had. A man of large means, of local influence, of blameless life, and universally respected—yes, he was a formidable adversary indeed, in appearance. But looking nearer? Mr. Lascelles, knowing the world, knew that a man openly professing rationalism—which Christians take to be high-polite for atheism—is a man having no solid foothold in English esteem. He may be as virtuous as Marcus Aurelius, as truth-loving as Socrates, as great as Plato, but—he disbelieves the Seven Days, the handful of clay, the rib and the Tower of Babel; he denies that the sun and moon were ever stayed; he proves by anatomy that Jonah could not have been swallowed by a whale; he doubts the cruse of oil and the ravens that fed the prophet; and he asks how all the kingdoms of a sphere could have been seen from the top of any mountain in Judea or elsewhere; and it is therefore supposed that he is capable of every crime that can disgrace humanity, and that if he have not committed himself hitherto it has been for want of temptation, not for want of will to yield, should that temptation come. No; Richard Fullerton's position was impregnable to look at; but there were weak places in this brazen tower, and it was his business as a priest and a teacher of truth to find them out, and bring down that man of sin to destruction.

If the wife could be gained, he knew that the husband would neither make a party of opposition nor be able to head it to any serious result if made ; for if she could be won over, Mr. Lascelles, who had learnt all about his parishioners long before he took the living, knew that he would have carried the key of the position. Without money what could Richard Fullerton do? and was it not in her power to revoke her former deed of resignation and take back her lapsed rights? Could she be won so far as this?

Young enough still to feel the want of some passionate interest in life, Hermione was at that age when a woman begins to long for new emotions. Her husband has become by now only her friend, and any romantic impulse himward is stale and dead, if not ridiculous, and sure to be repulsed. Her children, if she has many and is strongly maternal, may certainly supply all her mental cravings, by love, by occupation, by the constant interest of their ever-changing development. If she has only one—a daughter, say—she may renew her own youth by sympathy with her girl's fresh feelings and new experiences.

But there was nothing of all this for Hermione. More a natural nun than a likely wife, yearning for what neither father nor mother could give her, and indifferent to all that the world had to offer, Virginia was as little sufficient for her mother's happiness as mistress of her own; and Mrs. Fullerton was therefore, as Mr. Lascelles partly knew and partly divined, un-occupied ground waiting only the hand of the tiller. What then might not be done with one whose life was rusting for the want of using? Religious enthusiasm, all the more potent because new; the constant occupation given by the Church; the pleasant fluttering of the female spirit, found in submission to a new direction, a

new influence, a new love if you will, which the conscience approves and which neither the husband nor
society can condemn; the excitement of assisting in the
development of a stately ritual in her own church, and
the natural human pride of being pointed out as the
beneficent donor, the generous benefactor; the pressure
brought to bear by an organization of which she had
made herself part; all this would give her the new interest,
the passionate life that she needed, and make her his
plastic instrument. Could he reach her? He thought
he could. He had seen enough in that one visit to
have proved her amenable to his influence and to be
touched by an appeal to her conscientiousness, her
vanity, and her sentiment all delicately interwoven. If
he could hold her securely, he could destroy her husband's accursed influence in the place and bring back
to the Church—or banish from the place—the souls
which he had warped and led to ruin.

And for the rest? There were the two young
Molyneux's—Cuthbert and his sister Theresa, living
with their aunt Catherine at Churchlands. Cuthbert
had just returned from Cambridge, where he had taken
only a moderate degree—not disgracefully low, but
not honourably high—and where he had distinguished

himself by his romantic Ruskinism, his enthusiastic desire to do good and serve God, rather than by his zeal for science or his devotion to lectures and the classics. He was thus far a convert ready made, and Mr. Lascelles anticipated here an easy success. His young sister, Theresa, was enthusiastic like himself, warm and devoted; their Aunt Catherine was good, gushing, weak, and with no more reasoning faculties than a child;—Churchlands was a rich property; and the outlook was bright.

Young Ringrove Hardisty, at Monkshall, was not so promising. He was the ideal of one kind of Englishman, but not the kind which goes readily into ecclesiastical excesses. He was commonly reputed to have been tainted by Richard Fullerton's diabolical influence and to be nearly as great an infidel as himself. He was not a man of science like Richard, but especially a man of action—one of the born rulers of a country society. He was a tall, powerful, handsome young fellow of nine-and-twenty, with the traditional blue eyes and curling, short-cut golden hair of the Saxon race to which he emphatically belonged; a man incapable of meanness, of cruelty, of subterfuge, or of cowardice, but also incapable of mysticism or of spiritual intoxication; and though generous and noble more likely to be a benevolent despot in his dealings with others than a submissive son of the Church, or a husband whose wife held the reins. From all accounts, Ringrove Hardisty was not a likely subject for manipulation. The only hold on him came through his known love for Virginia Fullerton. She gained, with her mother, he might be brought within the fold of the dutiful children, as wild elephants are cajoled by the tame ones.

Going on, the Nesbitts at Newlands offered only pretty Beatrice as in any way likely for his purpose. Mrs. Nesbitt was a sweet kindly-natured woman, loving and soft truly ; but she was not *désœuvrée* like Mrs. Fullerton, nor gushing and weak like Miss Catherine Molyneux. She had a family of ten children to look after, of whom the eldest was Beatrice—called familiarly Bee when not Beata, or sometimes more irreverently Belva, on account of that curly head of hers, and broad natural fringe, which some one said was like a pretty little wild bull's. And naturally such a mother as Mrs. Nesbitt finds in her family that kind of healthy and absorbing occupation which leaves a woman no time to dream or to regret, occupation which taxes all her strength to do the duty lying plain before her without the need of casting about for that which is irrelevant and adventitious.   Mr. Nesbitt himself, bred a lawyer and now the county court judge of the district, was a shrewd, hard-headed man, with an Englishman's dread of ecclesiastical domination, and certainly not likely to make one of the new vicar's vanguard.   But he was a Conformist; and if the whole parish were swept into the ritualistic net, in all probability he would find himself too among the meshes.   Nevertheless, he was one to be handled gently, and to be craftily blindfolded while led.

The Campbells and the Stauntons, the Davidsons and the Lawleys, were people of that uncertain quality on whom no man can count.   They were of the second set, and would either follow implicitly as their social superiors led, or oppose them openly for the sake of making another party of their own.   He could not foresee which way it would be, but he thought the chances were in favour of the former.   If the latter, he believed that he should be able to make them feel excluded from the parochial aristocracy, not that they had excluded him and his.

And truly things ecclesiastical had fallen into a sufficiently bad state at Crossholme to justify a sweeping reformation.   The wave of church restoration, which has

swept over almost all England, had not stirred the sleepy
shallows of Crossholme, nor washed away the unsightly
dust that had accumulated through many generations of
neglect and indifference.　The pews were still like cattle
pens, of all shapes and sizes and heights, where the
congregation stood in all positions, and where comfortable corners and high baize-lined backs still afforded
snug sleeping-places out of the preacher's sight.　The
choir, such as it was, sat in the raised seats at the
end ; the school-mistress played the harmonium which
was always out of tune and of which she was notably
afraid, while the more daring lads played marbles or
gave shrill whistles when they were kneeling, and the
more timid girls only giggled and passed lollipops from
mouth to mouth.　The chancel was large and bare.
There were only a few backed benches in it for the
servants of the Abbey, Monkshall, and Churchlands ;
and the Tables with the Creed and Lord's Prayer, so
old and time-worn as to be almost illegible, were the
sole ornaments on the white-washed walls.　The whole
condition of things was haphazard and neglected, so
far as the church went; but the village was wonderfully
moral, and "Mr. Fullerton's men" were a splendid set
of fellows, who did much to give a tone to the whole

place. They were men against whom slander itself could find nothing to say, save that they too disbelieved in the Seven Days and the staying of the sun and moon; and they did not come to church, but went to Mr. Fullerton's scientific lectures instead; and that they held the modern doctrines concerning evolution and the origin of species. But of what good is it that working men should be moral, sober, thoughtful, and in every way respectable and well-conducted, if they do not believe in verbal inspiration and the power of one man to bind or loose the sins of another? The Church wants obedient sons, not moral infidels; and between the brigand who believes and the atheist who passes his life in charity and welldoing, she has most pleasure in the former and least hope of the latter.

All the same, things were atrociously neglected. Granted a church at all, Mr. Lascelles had not only his work cut out for him, but there was a crying necessity for beginning that work now at once.

Holding to the celibacy of the clergy as one of the strongest purchases over women and men alike, Mr. Lascelles knew the importance of feminine aid extra to active district visitors and devoted church servitors. The mother is wanted as well as the high-

priest, and the Vicarage without a mistress would have
only half its influence.   Therefore he brought with him
his eldest sister, a woman of about forty whom a sentimental godmother had insisted on naming Araminta,
but who, a few years ago, had taken Saint Agnes as
her patron saint, and had adopted her name in token
of her special dedication.   "Sister Agnes" she called
herself officially; but all the same she never quite forgot that she was the Honourable Miss Lascelles condescending to humility.

   She had once been a showy, handsome-looking girl,
and was even now well-favoured and singularly well-
mannered; with that same fine aristocratic flavour running
through her voice and air and gestures as ran through
her brother's.   Some perhaps would have said that
she was a trifle too slow and sweet, and what irreverent
folks would call silky, or even sickly, in her words and
ways; but when a well-favoured woman gives up the
pomps and vanities of the world for simplicity and
religion, who is there that dare throw stones?   You
can but prove your faith by your works; and she had,
so far, proved hers.

   In person she was tall and thin, with a slender
waist and flexible spine, and a long throat bearing a

small neat head. Her black hair, touched here and there with grey, was braided close and smooth under a white muslin cap trimmed with a narrow plaited frill. She always dressed in black alpaca, with a white collar and cuffs—her gowns made short round the instep, and without train or trimming. Her walking-dress was a large black cloak and a black cottage bonnet with a long black veil; and she wore neither gloves nor boots—only thick-soled high-low shoes. Her sole orna- ment was a large black cross which was suspended from a bead girdle round her waist. She was a mem- ber of one of the Anglican Sisterhoods, but she had received permission from her director and the superior to accompany her brother to Crossholme for a time, that she might aid him in his work and lend her strength also to the conversion of a parish which, moral as it was, they regarded as little better than heathen.

When Mr. Lascelles came back from his first sur- vey of his parishioners, his sister met him in the garden.

"Well?" she said with her customary smile; "you have sped well?"

"Beyond expectation," he answered. "I shall carry the parish in time; I have already got a footing in the Abbey."

"That is good news indeed, Launcelot. Did you find Mr. Fullerton so plastic?"

"Yes, and no. He does not thwart his wife; I can influence her. She is eating out her heart in her present mode of life. Church-work will save her from herself, and give her a new interest altogether."

"She will not be let rust in idleness if she gets into your hands," said Miss Lascelles with a demure smile.

"No," he answered; "there is so much to do here, that all who will work will have to work."

"Are they nice people, Launcelot?"

"Very; of their kind; which is bad enough at present. Mrs. Fullerton is charming, and the young daughter, whom I saw only for a few minutes, seems singularly sweet. You must undertake her, Agnes; she must be one of your lambs. Poor child! as things are she is but a lost one, I fear."

"I will do my best for her, and I hope that I shall do her good," returned his sister. "But Mr. Fullerton—what is he like?"

"Pleasant and well-bred enough, but an outrageous infidel; one of those presumptuous fools puffed up with a little pseudo-knowledge who think themselves capable of settling every subject, and who boast that they believe in nothing which they cannot see and touch— a rank materialist, living without God in the world. As a man he is well enough, but as a soul he is as much in the clutches of the Devil as was ever Judas. I feel that in fighting against him and his diabolical influence here I am fighting against Satan in bodily form."

The vicar spoke warmly; had he not been a sacred man, it might have been said he spoke with undeniable temper.

" And you are," said his sister. " I hold all infidels to be possessed. They are the emissaries of the Evil One, and this so-called modern science is the means by which he works. But you will conquer in the end, Launcelot. The Church is stronger than the Pit."

"By God's grace," answered Launcelot; and then they both went into the house, glad that the good work had been so far begun.

CHAPTER IV.

SISTER AGNES.

OF the ladies in Crossholme, Hermione was the first to call on the new vicar's as yet unknown sister, because the first to be told that the house was now so far in order as to render it possible to receive visitors; and told in a manner that conveyed a special and intentional grace. In all his intercourse with Mrs. Fullerton, which somehow he managed to make of daily occurrence—though he never saw her husband and not always Virginia—Mr. Lascelles gave her to understand that she was his first thought, his principal social care; and that both for herself as a human being—" the most interesting woman he had seen for years," he told her once, " uniting the simplicity and innocence of a child with the experience and strength of a woman"—and on account of her position here as the lay rector—how he hated those rights of hers !—the largest landed proprietor of the place and the Lady of the Manor, she was the one who ought to be most considered.

He was never weary of thanking her for what she had already done for God and the parish, while drawing vague but gorgeous pictures of the future when she would do yet more. And somehow he always contrived to convey the impression that he and she were allies against her husband; but this was only an impression, and so craftily suggested that Hermione never found the moment when to protest against it. She used to ease her conscience by speaking warmly of her husband's goodness when these uncomfortable little shadows were cast; but after a time she was obliged to give up even this not too ardent advocacy, and content herself with wifely loyalty carried in silence. Something in Mr. Lascelles froze the words on her lips, and made her ashamed to bear testimony in favour of her infidel lord. It was the only subject on which he did not agree with her, and where he was not eager to bring his assurance of sympathy. For the rest he was her sworn friend and knight ecclesiastic. Had he not been a celibate clergyman, with so high a standard, the profane would have been justified in imagining that he was flirting with the wife of Richard Fullerton;—he said such soft things to her, and pressed her hand with so much tenderness—fatherly, of course; but tenderness all the same. It was long

since the pretty woman had heard herself so delicately
flattered—and ah ! how pleasant it was ! What a pity
that Richard was so dull and heavy and absorbed,
instead of being alive at all points like Mr. Lascelles !

By this time, comparatively short as it was, a good
deal of ignorant gossip concerning both the vicar and
his sister had been set afloat in the place, and monstrous stories passed from lip to lip as to their lives and
actions. Many said that they were Jesuits in disguise,
if such transparent masks as theirs could be called
disguises at all. And some of the more hostile and
imaginative among the men prophesied the loss of all
parochial liberty, and a time of ecclesiastical tyranny
almost as severe as in the olden days when the Abbot
was lord of all and the whole population were his serfs
forced to obey his will on pain of worldly loss and
spiritual excommunication. Some said they were mad;
some curled up their lips and said—no, not mad, but
bad. Few believed in their real goodness ; fewer still
in their sincerity—for all that the outer ordering of their
lives, by which their faithfulness might be considered
best tested, was simple almost to poverty and strict
to partial asceticism. They were like foreign birds of
strange plumage settling down among the barndoor

fowl which gathered round them, wondering what they were and indisposed to give them welcome, simply because they were strange ; and for the first few weeks scarcely a voice was raised in their favour.

Then the vicar, as the vicar, was much disapproved of. He cut up the services into distinct "offices," as he called the various parts ; demanded uniformity of position—and that the eastward—at the Creed ; and every Sunday gave out some novelty at which his hearers gaped and wondered where things were going to. Now it was Wednesday and Friday morning prayer; now a Saint's day to be observed; now a startling bit of doctrine; and now "early celebration." His sermons were of only twenty minutes' duration ; he preached in his surplice and he began his discourse abruptly, without the usual prayer and with only the invocation "In the name of." He bowed and knelt and inclined at strange places in the service; and openly expressed his disgust with things as they were and his intention of changing them radically. And if that was not enough to set a sleepy old conservative parish against its new vicar, what would be ?

But Hermione Fullerton stood out boldly from the rest, and spoke of Mr. Lascelles warmly and with thorough-going commendation. Where others sniffed jesuistry and proclaimed hypocrisy with all the tale of vices given by ignorance to novelty, she made herself his liberal-minded champion and maintained that he wanted only what was right and good for the parish, and that this prejudgment was un-English and unfair.

So it was ; but looking at things from the conservative point of view, these innovations were unpleasant, at least in the beginning and until men's minds had become attuned to novelty. And again, looking at things from his own special anti-clerical point of view, her husband had some reason on his side, if also some bitterness, when he one day said to her quietly, after a rather passionate harangue :

" It may be unfair, my dear, to assume that a particular snake of a venomous kind will sting you, and in this belief to kill it as it lies. Still, common knowledge of the breed leads you to suppose that it will if it gets the chance ; and you kill it if you can before it has time to kill you. And a knowledge of what priests of every religion have been in all ages, and still are—what they have done to oppress and enslave the minds of men and still do where they have the power—warrants wise men in resisting their first endeavours to gain influence."

"But a clergyman ought to have influence in his own parish. Why is he here, if every ignorant ploughboy is to judge of religion as well as he?" said Hermione, with unusual warmth and acerbity.

"The law gives him more power than is good for him or the people as things are," said Richard. "We need not strengthen his hands by extra grants. For remember, wife, every inch of ground gained by the Church is so much lost to freedom, truth, and science."

"Richard! how can you be so unjust? I have never known you so bad as this before," she cried almost passionately. "The Church has been the best friend of man for all these ages; and you speak like this!"

He laughed his pleasant good-humoured laugh.

"So bad as this before?" he said. "Am I always so bad then in your eyes, my wife? And when was the Church the best friend of man? When the Huguenots were massacred? when the auto da fé was a common institution in Spain? when Servetus was burnt? and when Romanists and Protestants lighted the fires in Smithfield in impartial alternation?"

"You uphold liberality in principle," said Hermione, not answering him, but going back to her personalities which interested her more than did his historical remi-

niscences; "and you are just as illiberal as any one else
when you speak of what you happen to dislike. It is
really too bad of you, calling Mr. Lascelles a snake!—
your own clergyman, and so good and kind and well-
bred as he is! I wonder at you, Richard."

"I know the tribe, my dear, better than you do;
and granting them all the private virtues to which they
can lay claim, I dread them as mental guides — as
spiritual leaders—as much as I should dread that
obnoxious snake, which offended you, if he came to coil
himself about your throat or mine."

"I will not discuss the subject with you; you are
too unreasonable," said Hermione loftily.

"Do not be vexed with me, for a matter that cannot
touch either of us personally," he returned kindly. "Mr.
Lascelles may be privately good or bad; that is not
our affair; and for the rest, his influence will never
invade our house, and so what is it to us? We are one
thing, he another; and there is no reason why we should
dispute about him between ourselves, is there?" He
leaned forward to pat her flushed face, while she turned
away from him. "Don't, Richard!" she said pettishly,
in a parenthesis. "If you like him, dear," her husband
continued, rather astonished at her petulance, but sup-

posing it was nothing, and certainly not of so much importance as to be noticed; "I will not annoy you by saying that I do not. But in truth, wife, I do not, and," more gravely, "I should be glad if you saw him and the whole subject with my eyes."

"That I cannot do and do not wish to do," said Hermione, still peevish and unlike her usual self. "I do not hate religion as you do, Richard. I believe in God and the Church and a future life and the value of prayer; and I see Mr. Lascelles as a devoted clergyman—a good high-minded Christian gentleman: and you see him as some monster."

"No, not á monster, only a priest; the consecrated enemy to truth and freedom; the barrier *ex officio* to progress," he answered, finding that roll-call of articles of faith a little difficult to digest.

"Truth!" retorted Hermione disdainfully. "How do you or any of us know what truth is?"

"We may all know what it is not, if we choose to use our reason," he said. "It is not a collection of old-world fables, current at a time when science was nowhere, when the laws of evidence were not understood, and when men were so ignorant that they could be made to believe the most monstrous lies which the

imagination could invent ; just as the Breton peasantry
of our own day are made to believe in trumped-up
miracles."

" I suppose, though you do think so hardly of our
vicar, you do not object to visit him ? to my calling on
Miss Lascelles ? Of course I am your wife and have to
obey you ; and if you refuse to allow me to go, I cannot
and will not. But I suppose I may ? I have your permission ? " said Hermione, shifting her ground suddenly
and speaking with a disagreeable air of false submission
as unlike her usual self as was indeed all the rest. " I
suppose your insane hatred of the Church does not go
so far as this ? " she continued ; " your dislike of the
Bible does not include ill-breeding and want of hospitality to a gentleman and lady, because they happen
to be our clergyman and his sister ? "

He laughed again. Her ill-humour with him was
patent, but it was so childish that he could not choose
but smile at it. She had never been so petulant as this ;
and Richard was too philosophic and easy-going to cross
swords readily ; especially with a woman, and that
woman his wife, so trusted in, so beloved.

" No," he said. " Call on them by all means. Ask
hem to dinner here if you like, and as often as you like.

As neighbours, my house is open to them ; it is only the priest to which I object."

"And you ? " she said, not noticing his permission. Somehow it grated on her more than it pleased. " Will you not call with me, Richard ? "

" No; take my card; that will do as well, or per-haps better. Mr. Lascelles and I have not much in common, and I do not wish to break through my habits of not giving up the afternoon for a man whom I do not specially affect. You and Virginia can go ; and my pasteboard."

"Well, I will do as you wish, of course," she an-swered with a sigh. " I think you are very wrong, Richard, very unjust and illiberal, and not acting well ; but you are your own master, of course, and I will make your excuses."

" Give me a kiss after all that storm," he said, half tenderly, half playfully.

She turned away her eyes. She was still ruffled and heated, still unlike herself altogether, and in no loving mood anyhow.

" Don't be so foolish," she said again ; and went out, leaving him with a certain numbness rather than pain, like a person startled and amazed. He did not often

ask for a kiss in these days; and never before now had
she refused a glad response to his tenderness when it
had come. Now something seemed to have stolen into
her heart that had hardened it, at least for the time.

Mother and daughter made a strange contrast to
the vicar's sister in her severe dress and studied absence
of all grace and ornament. Hermione in a light grey
silk delicately touched with pink, and small grey bonnet
also with the same light touches of pink to give it life
set among her golden curls; her wrists clasped with
bracelets; her neck in a broad gold chain; her whole
attire luxurious, rich, elegant, and in the latest fashion
of cut and pattern;—Virginia, in the traditional maiden
white, with more simplicity but as much conventional
elegance as her mother;—and Miss Lascelles in her
Sister's dress, plain, black, and eloquent of her renunciation of the pomps and vanities:—yes, they were
indeed strangely contrasted!

The house too which the Fullertons had left and
that to which they had come were as unlike as themselves. There everything was costly and luxurious;
everything was beautiful in itself, but upheaped, over-
crowded, and so far failing in perfect taste—the central
idea, if ever there had been one beyond the upholsterer's

notions of things handsome and necessary, having got overlaid by excess in the parts. Here in this drawing-room of the Vicarage the furniture was almost oppressive in its severity, and the general expression was cold and insufficient. The table was deal, with heavy, plainly-squared legs and a plain, unornamented "autumn-leaf" table-cover ; the old oak chairs were stiff, hard, and straight-backed, and there was not an armchair, nor a lounge, nor a sofa anywhere. The cold grey walls were hung with a few pictures—all sacred subjects ; some in oils, copies from the Old Masters, and some of the Arundel Society set in plain white frames, without even a gilded edge. A few flowers in grès de Flandres vases gave the sole signs of living life there were ; but these were only on two brackets which flanked the feet of a large carved ivory crucifix—an antique—that hung against the wall. A Mater Dolorosa was on one side, an Assumption on the other; and below was the hollowed side of a pecten shell. It was a room which suggested more than it expressed, and which was as utterly unlike the ordinary drawing-rooms of society as Sister Agnes herself was unlike the ordinary ladies of the world.

" I am glad to see you," she said with extreme sweetness, coming forward to meet them when the Fullertons were announced, and giving a hand to each. "My brother has told me of you, and I have been longing to make your acquaintance."

Her manner was gracious and cordial, but it was not the grace nor cordiality of society. It was a strange manner altogether, and unlike any that Mrs. Fullerton had ever seen. It was, and was not, condescending; friendly and yet not social; somewhat the manner of an official superior, with a certain false kind of fraternity as if to encourage his inferior. The Honourable Miss Lascelles and Mrs. Fullerton of the Abbey were social equals, and their first meeting would naturally have been one of more or less stiffness; but Sister Agnes, high in the order of grace and Church enlightenment, was in the foremost ranks of a hierarchy where this pretty, well-dressed heathen was but a stranger at the gate—a Gentile in the presence of one of the Chosen. She was as a child needing encouragement and teaching, and Sister Agnes, half unconsciously, treated her as one; patronizing her by the very sweetness and disregard of social formalities with which she had received her.

"You are very good," said Hermione, a little taken aback and yet flattered. "I am much interested in

your brother—in his plans," she answered, half awk‑
wardly.

"Yes, he is a very pure creature; so devoted, so
thoroughly in earnest! Our dear Mother Church has
no more dutiful son, no stronger champion," said Miss
Lascelles smiling.

"He seems to be so," said Hermione, not in the least
understanding the worth of what she said; but she knew
it was something to which she ought to assent.

"He hopes to do much here," Miss Lascelles con‑
tinued. "Things have been fearfully neglected, and it
will take some time to bring them into order. But we
have courage and the consciousness of a good cause and
Divine help;—and we count on your support," with a
charming smile.

"I shall be happy to do what I can," said Hermione.
"I feel the truth of what you say. Things have been
neglected. Mr. Aston was old, and no one"—she hesi‑
tated.

"No one cared to fan the embers which he allowed
to die out." Miss Lascelles finished the broken speech
neatly. "Now, however, all will be changed. We must
get the parish into good working order, and the services
of the Church better organized. And everyone must

help. You, dear Mrs. Fullerton, and your child among the foremost." She took Virginia's hand and looked tenderly into her face. " It is such as you young innocent creatures whom the Church asks to give the first fruits of your strength and life to God; and to you," turning to Hermione, "bountiful woman of means and energy, that she looks for her true support."

But she turned back to Virginia. She knew that Hermione was already somewhat entangled and assigned as her brother's special charge, while the girl was to be hers.

" I shall be very glad to have something to do," said Virginia with quiet intensity, involuntarily clasping the long thin hand held in hers with more fervour than she knew of. " It will be so happy for me to know what to do."

" And you do not now?"

" No," with a half sigh.

" You shall not be long without guidance," said Miss Lascelles. " You will have your district assigned you very soon. The vicar means to speak to you about it to-day, and that will give you an interest beyond what you can imagine now. Then, I am going to establish a Church working society, to meet here at the Vicarage two or three times a week. We want vestments, altar-cloths—

everything! I can show you how the things are to be done. Will you make one of us, Mrs. Fullerton?"

"With pleasure," said Hermione.

"And you, my child?"

"Yes," said Virginia, her face brightening; "I will do anything you wish me to do."

This was a large promise for Richard Fullerton's daughter to make; he who characterized the clergy as snakes, and who was devoting his life to the destruction of their influence and the substitution of knowledge for faith—science for religion. But already Miss Lascelles had touched her;—and if here was to be found food for her starving soul?

At this moment Mr. Lascelles came into the room. He smiled when he saw Hermione sitting there with his sister; but quietly, with reserve—not hilariously, as a man unconsecrated might; and came forward with that kind of tender courtliness, of grave eagerness, which sits so well on a handsome priest.

"So glad to see you!" he said with finely subdued cordiality, pressing Hermione's hand gently as he spoke.

The blood rose up into the pretty woman's fair face. How young she looked! In her light colours, with her fluffy golden hair, fair skin, and flushed cheeks, she did

not look more than five-and-twenty. Grave, pale, if no
less beautiful, Virginia might have been her sister rather
than her daughter.

"Thank you," she said simply; but she was glad
to see his evident pleasure.

"Now come with me into my study, and I will show
you how I have mapped out the parish. I want your
opinion also on the restorations which I have resolved
to make in the church. The chancel will be your care,"
smiling. "No, you need not bring your daughter. My
sister will take care of her."

Mr. Lascelles said all this with perfect courtesy and
good breeding, but in the tone of a man accustomed to
be obeyed and who did not anticipate refusal now.

"If I can be of use," said Hermione rising; with an
odd fluttering at her heart as she left the room, giving to
another man than her husband the same unquestioning
obedience, the same womanly submission that had
marked her life with him. How strange it was to have
this new authority over her—shadowy, subtle, vague, as
it yet was! but it was pleasant in spite of its strangeness.

"And now, child, tell me something of yourself,"
said Miss Lascelles to Virginia, drawing a low stool
close to her own chair. "Come and sit at my knee, like

my child, which you are to be in Christ, and tell me of
your life."

"I have nothing to tell," said Virginia, raising her
eyes, always so full of secret yearning, of nameless
melancholy, to the smooth, satisfied face bending down
to hers. It was so evidently the dark seeker and the
enlightened finder—the unsatisfied life and that which
was fulfilled.

"No sense of God's grace; no consciousness of sin
and pardon?" she asked.

"No," answered Virginia confusedly. "I have no
religious life at all. I wish I had, but I have not. I do
not know what to do or what to believe."

"Poor child! poor child! but you shall have now
what you want. You are seeking for Christ, and you
shall find Him. I, by our Holy Mother Church, will
lead your first steps, poor wandering darling, and my
brother will consecrate you to the true life. You do
not know what happiness is in store for you, child, nor
what a load of misery and heaviness you will lose! I
can see it all in your face—the yearning, the blankness,
the want, the seeking, and the darkness;—all to be supplied from the Everlasting Fountain! Do you say your
prayers?"

"Yes, sometimes," said Virginia, tears in her eyes. "But they are not answered; light does not come, though I ask for it."

"It will," said Miss Lascelles. "You believe in the goodness of God, and the influence of the Holy Spirit?" with a reverent movement of her head and hands.

"Yes," she replied; "for some perhaps, but not for myself."

"Do you believe in the power of the Church to enlighten and absolve?" the Sister asked.

"I scarcely know which I believe, Miss Lascelles!" said Virginia, laying her arms across the elder woman's lap; she would not have done so to her own mother. "All is so confused at home! Papa is so good, so good, but he believes in nothing at all—neither in God nor a future life—and mamma seems not to know what is true or what is not. We go to church; but then we do not keep Sunday as Sunday at home, and we never have prayers or anything of that kind. And it seems to me that if religion is true at all it is the one thing to live for, and that it ought to be made one's whole life. Or else let us disbelieve it entirely, as papa does."

Miss Lascelles gave a little shudder.

"Dear child, you don't know what pain it is to

me to hear such an awful alternative from those young
lips, which should repeat only prayers and praises!
Do not say such a thing again. Do you know what it
means?"

"No," said Virginia, a little scared.

"It means that you place before you the alternative
of worshipping God or the Devil." She made the sign of
the cross as she spoke, and rapidly repeated the Lord's
Prayer.

"Papa says there is no devil," said Virginia. "He
says it was an invention of the Jewish priests to frighten
the people, and borrowed from them by the Christians."

"Pray to God, my child, that he does not find it to
have a reality," said Miss Lascelles solemnly. "But I
do not care to discuss your father's religious opinions—or
rather want of them—with you. My object is to save your
soul, not condemn his. Yours must be saved, and now
it is—lost!"

Virginia shuddered and turned pale.

"I feel lost," she said in a low voice.

Miss Lascelles bent over her with a tender smile—the
smile of a mother to her grieving child.

"All will come right, dear one," she half whispered.
"God is even now calling you. He has sent me to be

your salvation. But first—do not call me Miss Lascelles; call me Sister Agnes."

" That would be a liberty," said Virginia, blushing gravely.

" No, that is my name in the Church and by which our dear Mother Mary knows me. Saint Agnes is my patron saint, and I do her work, and obey her wish when I call myself by her name."

" Her wish?—do you believe in the saints? " cried Virginia with irrepressible surprise.

The Sister smiled.

" Do I believe in the sun and moon and stars? " she said. " Of course I do! The dear saints and our blessed Mother Mary are half the good influence of religion, half the foundation of the Church."

" If I could but believe in the saints! " cried Virginia. " But papa says that it was part imposture and part disease; and I have never dared to let myself believe in the things that I have read of them. How I wish I could!—and how I wish I could feel as they felt! "

" Child, I must make this stipulation with you—do not bring your father's authority between us. He is a good man, I have no doubt; but he has trusted to his own strength, and God has abandoned him and given

him over to destruction. I will believe that it is only
for a time; but for this time, to quote him, when I am
teaching you, is like one of your own rustics objecting
to be taught how to spell properly, because his father has
always written heaven with two v's. What a joy it will
be for you, darling child, if you are made the blessed
instrument of bringing him to the light of God's knowledge !"

Miss Lascelles spoke earnestly, but with perfect
temper, when she mentioned this obnoxious father. He
was horrible, dangerous, devilish ; but she wished to convey the impression of a fine Christian liberality which
could find room for even such a sinner as he.

"Ah!" said Virginia, raising her face with a certain
rapt look like sunlight stealing over it. Then it clouded.
"But I must first be enlightened myself," she said
sorrowfully, the tears starting.

Miss Lascelles kissed her forehead.

"Good, dear child ! Now I have your soul," she said
fervently ; "now I know that my saint has heard my
prayer, that the Blessed Mother will be gracious, and
that you are to be counted among the beloved and the
saved. You are one of the lambs to whose salvation I
am consecrated, and through God's grace and with the

help of my dear saint and the Blessed Mother, I shall be permitted to save you ! "

Silently, quietly, but with a strangely abrupt motion, she knelt by the girl's side.

" Kneel with me," she said softly ; and Virginia knelt, not abashed, not confused, not uncertain, as would have been natural to her an hour ago, but rapt and overcome, part in pain and part in ecstasy. Had she then at last found that home for which her soul had been seeking? and should she be admitted, if indeed this were that home?

Sister Agnes made a prayer. It was short but fervent, and was addressed to the Blessed Virgin Mary, the Mother of God, beseeching her for her special grace to this lost child who was seeking her and whom now she brought to her beloved feet. Then there was an invocation to Saint Agnes, reminding her that she was the special patroness of young girls, and how this girl above all needed her care and protection. When it was over she kissed Virginia again on the forehead ; her eyes bright with tears. Virginia's were overflowing.

" This is the first act of your consecration, my child," she said softly. " Ah, how good the dear Mother has been to me to give me this blessed work as my first fruits in a strange land ! "

" How good you are ! " murmured Virginia, leaning against her bosom while she threw her arms round the Sister's waist. She felt more mothered on that breast than she had ever felt before.

" No, Saint Agnes is good, the Blessed Mother is good, and our dear Lord and our Father. It is they who have given you to me. I am only their instrument. Through me you hear them. Now I want you to wear this for my sake and theirs, to remind you that They have called you and that you have promised to obey. Wear it under your dress, and keep it as a secret between Heaven and you. Your spiritual mother gives it to you."

She took off from her own neck a small silver crucifix which she wore on a slender elastic thread concealed under her collar. She kissed it, made the sign of the cross, and whispered a prayer as she placed it round the girl's throat.

" Never take it off," she said ; "wear it as the sign of your first consecration, till my brother or I give you another. And read in these books and pray from them," she added, lifting up her apron and taking from a large pocket in her dress two small books of devotion—one of prayers, with those to the Virgin and Saint Agnes specially marked, and one of exhortations and obedience to the Church and her ordinances. "We will talk again," she added, as she heard steps through the hall. "Come to me whenever you feel the need of comfort or advice. Remember, I am your spiritual mother, and you are my child whom God has given me."

Then the door opened, and Hermione and the vicar entered.

The mother and daughter did not stay long after this. Both were excited, both moved. Mr. Lascelles had been discussing with Hermione his project for the restoration and embellishment of the church, and had insisted both plainly and strongly on the duty which lay before her of undertaking the chancel at her sole cost. When she hesitated and said that she did not think her husband would consent, he had told her, still with the same plain if so quiet speaking, that she owed a higher duty to God than even to her husband; and that this was for the glory of God, which ranked before servile submission to a professed atheist, let his relations to her be what they would. She must make a stand, should Mr. Fullerton object. The money was really hers, and she would be called to account for its use on that Great Day when a woman's

fears would not save her soul. And even, setting religion
side, for the decency of the parish the thing ought to
be done; and she, as the lady of the manor and the lay
rector, ought to bear her part nobly. She therefore was
silent on the way home. Her heart was full of perplexity,
and the new and the old were warring together; an
aroused conscience and a love, though irritated by no
means dead, were jostling each other through the mazes
of her tangled thoughts, and she could not find comfort
in the meaningless nothings which made up her usual
conversation with Virginia. And to the girl herself
silence was also necessary; she held that sacred link
between Heaven and herself as a holy secret which even
her mother must not share; and the cross stood as a
barrier between them. At last the girl said, lightly touching her mother's arm:

"Mamma, she is an angel! She is Sister Agnes, not
Miss Lascelles, and she says that I am to call her Sister
Agnes. She believes in the saints, and all those beautiful
stories are true."

Hermione as lightly touched her daughter's hand.

"Gently, gently, dear," she said with a sudden impulse of caution. Between wishing to make the church
beautiful in an artistic sense and to see something like a

religious feeling in the place, partly as a good thing for the poor, if also in part as that form of personal excitement which makes a handsome clergyman very precious to a woman nearing forty—between this and believing in the lives of the Romish saints was a wide step. "You must not believe all you hear, nor all at once," she added.

"I believe in that because Sister Agnes says so," answered Virginia, all her soul in her eyes. "And oh, mamma! so will you some day!—and so will papa."

Hermione's face fell.

"Your father will never be brought to believe in God, still less the saints," she returned with an odd kind of sad impatience. "If he will allow me to do as I think right, I can hope for nothing more."

"Oh, papa is so good, so kind, so noble, he must believe in time!" said Virginia fervently. "He wants only to know the truth to follow it."

"He thinks he has the truth now," she answered hopelessly; "and he is too old to be convinced. To him a bit of dead matter is God:—and what can be expected from him—hating the clergy as he does? No, dear, we must look for nothing from your father; but he will probably be just to us and will let us act as I think right for us both."

Virginia touched the place where the small crucifix hung. It was like a talisman to her, potent enough to work the miracle of reclaiming to the Church even one so set in his own way and so convinced of the rightness of his views as was Richard Fullerton, her father, a professed agnostic for his own part, and the ardent teacher of denial and infidelity to others.

CHAPTER V.

THE FIRST TESTIMONY.

" HERE is Ringrove, wife," said Richard some days after that memorable visit, during which time more intercourse had been going on between the Vicarage and his woman-kind than he knew of or would have liked had he known. " He will stay to luncheon if you ask him."

The young man followed his host into the drawing-room, his handsome face beaming with pleasure. Ever since she was a girl of fourteen, Virginia had been the feminine ideal to his highest self ; and for the last two years he knew that he loved her as a man should love the woman whom he longed to make his wife. He was waiting now until she should ripen into love for him in return. She had given no sign that way as yet ; but he was always hoping that it would come. Her very reti-cence and virginal modesty, her quietness of speech and manner, her sweet unconsciousness of self or sense, her absolute freedom from all kinds of girlish vanity—those very qualities which made her cold to him as to all other

men, and indifferent as yet to his love, attracted him
more powerfully than would the most beautiful woman's
most voluptuous, most enticing charms. Not that he
would have been insensible to these last. He was young
and an Englishman, and by no means an anchorite ; but
he would not have made even Aspasia his wife. He
must be the first, last, and only one to the woman whom
he should marry ; the magician armed by love to awaken
the sleeping and give form to the formless ; and the
honourable name confided to the keeping of another, he
must feel assured would be held as sacred as the life of
her child is sacred to a mother, or the holiest symbol
of her faith to a devotee. He was a man to whom
purity in a woman was an essential; and he loved
Virginia more because she was pure than because
she was beautiful. Venus as Anonyma would not have
enthralled him, but he would have given his life to be
Endymion to Diana.

For all his bright good humour and carelessness of
certain conventional forms, Ringrove Hardisty was both
proud and arbitrary; and with the possibilities of jealousy
if once aroused that made him as potentially formidable
as he was now lovable. Like so many of us, he had the
double nature of good and evil in almost equal power ;

and it would depend greatly on the facts of his life which gained the upper hand.

In things spiritual he was just the average strong man in the full vigour of youth and life, who was content to live honestly and not give himself much trouble about them.   He would maintain the Church as it was, because it was English and national and helped to keep the poor in order ; but he would have it strictly subordinate to the State, and he had a healthy horror of priestly domination.   He had not reasoned the thing out from its elements like Richard Fullerton, but to a certain extent he had accepted the results to which the elder man had come.   He stood on the neutral ground of supposing that something in religion was true, but not half so much as was made out ; and he supposed that the future would see some modification in the present faith so that it should be brought more into harmony with scientific truths and modern enlightenment.   This, however, was not his affair ; and meanwhile, his duty as an English landed proprietor was to uphold the existing order of things as socially valuable, and to oppose with equal zeal dissent, fanaticism, clerical encroachment, drunkenness, immorality, and pauperism.

This was where he stood ; and on the whole Richard

'*Now, I want you to wear this for my sake and theirs.*'

Fullerton was satisfied with his position—recognizing, as he so often said, the need of crutches for the lame, and that while men and women are mentally so weak as to require the aid of external authority, they had better have it. But he gave his life to make them strong enough to do without it, and he would not have been sorry had Ringrove done the same. He went with him who said that he would rather see England free than sober ; and if in pulling down the power of the Church other things were lost beside the superstitions that it held—well, those other things would grow again all the more luxuriantly for the loss of these superstitions, like flowers when the wood is felled.

That with such a nature as this of Ringrove's— strong, wholesome, pure, manly, but entirely without spiritual enthusiasm—Virginia should have much sympathy, seemed by the very necessity of things unlikely, and as matters stood between her and the Vicarage, more so than ever. The only chance in the question had ever been—would his own strong and honest love, his fine moral qualities, the social fitness of things—not to speak of his personal beauty, which perhaps would not weigh much with her—warm her into the life of love? or would her natural disinclination to marriage carry the day over all other considerations whatsoever? This was the question which Ringrove had set himself to resolve, though he did not put it in that form. His blunt but no less true thought, was: " I love her, will she ever love me? If she will, I will make her the happiest woman in the world, as I shall be the happiest man."

But he knew no more than Richard Fullerton what was going on at the Vicarage; he no more than the father suspected the strong hold which Sister Agnes had already got over the girl and was daily increasing; or knew of the "consecration" which had claimed her as one of the lambs of the Sister's patron saint, and turned her yet more with her heart towards heaven and her face from the world. As yet everything was concealed; for the time for public profession had not come. When it should, no one would be more bold in confession than Sister Agnes and her child; but meanwhile the best policy was the quietest.

" I hope you do not think me a hungry nuisance, Mrs. Fullerton?" said Ringrove, with his frank laugh and clear carrying voice.

" No; I shall be very glad if you will stay—if you are not too hungry. I cannot undertake to supply you with an ox roasted whole," said Hermione pleasantly. She liked him, and would have been glad had Virginia liked him too. At one time she had done what she could that way, but lately she had rather forgotten him. " Where have you been?" she asked. " We have seen nothing of you lately. But you have been away, have you not? "

" Yes, I have been in town for the last month," he answered. " It was so hot and stuffy ! I was glad to get home again, I assure you."

" I should think so. I should not like London at this time of the year when the country is at its love-liest," said Hermione. " Would you, Virginia ? "

Ringrove turned to Virginia sitting pale and quiet at her own special little table, embroidering a strip of white ribbon with coloured silks.

" But you do not care for London at all, do you? " he asked.

" No, I never did," she answered; " I wonder who could ! "

" And have you been well and gay since I last saw you?" he asked with that strange awkwardness of a man speaking before others to the woman whom he loves and who does not love him.

" Quite well, thank you," she answered tranquilly.

" Gay !" said Hermione uneasily. " Are we ever gay at Crossholme ? "

" What pretty work ! What is it for ? " he asked, touching the ribbon in her hand.

" Yes, it is very lovely," she answered evasively.

It was a marker for the lectern Bible; but Sister Agnes had told her not to tell its purpose, if she could conceal it without positive falsehood. This doctrine of reserve was one of the girl's greatest trials. If not communicative she was entirely candid ; and to evade a question was as difficult to her as to tell a falsehood.

" What are those things ? " he asked again.

" Roses," she answered.

" Oh ! heraldic fellows."

" Conventionalized," said Virginia, who knew her lesson.

" I like them better when they are more natural," said Ringrove. " These are so stiff, they are not like roses—they are like geometrical figures."

She handled the work as if considering whether she should assent or not, but in reality because she did not want to continue the conversation.

" Why, Lady-bird! I did not know that you could

do anything so smart as that! Show it to me again," cried Richard who was standing at a little distance from the two, looking at them with paternal pride and satisfaction, and feeling sure that in time things would come about as he desired. But only in time. There was no hurry. Virginia was but a child yet; but when the times were ripe he should like this better than any other match that she could make. He knew Ringrove, and could trust him with his darling's happiness. A strong man of character—honour—what more could he want?

Virginia rose, and took her work over to her father reluctantly.

" I have never seen you do such as this before," he said. " What is it for—a pair of braces? If you have no special use for it, give it to me, lassie. I shall prize it as my little girl's first handiwork of the kind."

A look of pain and perplexity came on the girl's transparent face. She loved her father dearly, but if the cross had stood between her and her mother, how much more was it a barrier against him!

" I am afraid I cannot give it you, papa," she said.

" No? Well, make me another like it," he said

tranquilly. " Who is your first favoured—Ringrove? " with a little laugh.

Virginia looked at her mother. Hermione—never quick at an excuse and less apt at subterfuge, at a loss how to direct herself in moments of difficulty and utterly unable to help another—looked down and made no response to the mute appeal. Her daughter must get out of this little tangle by herself : she foresaw thorns enough for both of a sharper kind than this of a promised strip of embroidery.

" No, not Ringrove; it is for Sister Agnes," said Virginia, with the courage of sincere youth.

" And who may Sister Agnes be, my love? " her father asked.

" Miss Lascelles, papa."

" Are you so intimate as that already?" he asked again. " Do you call her by her Christian name and make her presents ? "

" Sister Agnes is her real name, and the one that she wants me to call her; and this is a marker for the new lectern Bible," said Virginia.

" Did they ask you to do it?" said her father with a shade of displeasure in his voice.

" Yes, papa," she answered.

"Are you going to belong to their fantastical school? to be made a new light?" he asked with a certain forced merriment that meant uneasiness.

She looked at him with tender reproach. She loved him well; who would not, who knew him?—but though she loved him she was bound by a higher law to think him wrong, and to show him that she did not agree with him.

"I only want to do what is right; and that is all which they want," she answered gravely but gently.

His face took almost a woman's softness as he put out his hand to take hers, so cold and white.

"You are always right, my lassie!" he said tenderly. 'My little one never gave any one any trouble since she was born, and never will!"

"We are all going to be shaken up and put in our places with a vengeance, if all I hear is true," laughed Ringrove, ignorant of danger and the lay of the land within the Abbey walls.

Hermione flushed with displeasure; Virginia looked down, and her pale face became rather paler than usual. It was as if a man of sin had touched the ark of the anointed with the one; and the other resented the presumption of this mere youth who dared to laugh at the doings of one who seemed to her the most notable, the most splendid man she had ever seen.

"Mr. Lascelles hopes to do much good in the parish," said Hermione coldly. "Things have been so disgracefully neglected in Mr. Aston's time; it is only right that they should be put in order now."

"Yes, if he does not go too far," said Ringrove carelessly. "I do not think that Crossholme will bear very much, and these ritualistic fellows go to such extremes!"

"Please not to speak of Mr. Lascelles with disrespect in this house," said Hermione. "He and his sister are not people to be laughed at."

Virginia raised her blue eyes, full of gratitude, to her mother. How glad she was that she spoke so openly! It would have been impossible for her to have defended them; but mamma was able in every way; and how well she took their part!

"Do you know them, Ringrove?" then asked Hermione, holding her head a little stiffly.

"Not yet. I have seen them, but I do not think that I shall care to know much of them at any time. I am not in their line, and they are not in mine."

He spoke quite good-humouredly, but without mincing the matter. At all hazards, he too must stand faithful to his side.

"Then how can you judge of them, if you do not know them?" She spoke with a severity rare in her at any time—though less rare of late than it used to be; but still unusual. "Is it fair to prejudge people in this manner? I am tired of all this illiberality! One would think that a sincere Christian were really a monster, and a clergyman who wished to do his duty a criminal, for all that has been said of Mr. Lascelles since he took the parish."

Ringrove looked at her for the moment aghast. She spoke with so much warmth and bitterness, it scarcely seemed to be Mrs. Fullerton speaking at all.

"These ritualistic parsons have some kind of spell over women," said Richard, turning to Ringrove, half smiling and half disturbed. "Here are my wife and little girl bewitched at sight!"

"I am sorry for it," said Ringrove gravely. "I do not think the clerical influence, carried too far over women, a wholesome one."

"It is not being bewitched to see how good and faithful Sister Agnes is, papa," said Virginia, touching the crucifix beneath her dress as she spoke, and gathering courage from the contact.   " If you knew her as we do, you would see for yourself how good and noble she is !"

"And it is not being bewitched to see that things are disgracefully neglected, or that they might be improved," added Hermione coldly.

" But improved, how? With what will prove to be a rod of iron," said Ringrove.

"What rubbish, Ringrove ! How can you talk such nonsense ? " she said tartly. "In common fairness and good feeling it seems to me that all you who hate the Church and religion might wait till Mr. Lascelles has done something outrageous before you condemn him as you do. As far as he has gone yet, he has proposed what every one in the world must agree to ; he has wanted nothing extreme."

"Well, here is Jones, and luncheon is ready," returned her husband, as the man-servant came into the room. " Do not let us discuss these new-comers further. I confess it somewhat amazes me to see the readiness with which you have given in to them ; but you are your own mistress, dear, and you will come all right."

" Thank you," said Hermione disagreeably, as she

took Ringrove's arm, the father holding Virginia's hand
while they crossed the hall into the dining-room.

The luncheon was dull and heavy. Ringrove did
his best to bring a lighter spirit into them all; but he
had gone too far on the wrong track to be able to set
himself right; and he felt that he had hurt his cause both
with Hermione and Virginia herself more than he should
be able easily to heal. Hermione was irritable and uncomfortable, especially to her husband, whose temper she
seemed to do her best to ruffle; looking at him with
eyes full of provocation that turned to tenderness which
was akin to tears, and these again quenched themselves
in anger. Virginia was pre-occupied and Richard was
troubled, but in spite of her advocacy and in spite of
her temper, less for his wife than his daughter. That
good Hermione was fixed as a rock, he thought—
settled in loving obedience to him, in oneness of heart,
in perfectness of marriage. He had but to exert his
authority and he would be obeyed—as he would if
things went too far. But Virginia was young; plastic;
her character was still to make; and he dreaded this new
influence more for her than for her mother. He had
not the hold on her that he had on that mother;—what
father has? and she might be warped, his child though

she was. He must speak to his wife. He must remind her that she was the natural guardian of their darling's discretion, and that religious enthusiasm carried to excess and Church devotion to zealotry were not discreet in his daughter. He imposed no authority on any one. His method was to convince by reason, not to forbid or command; still something was due to him as the head of the house, and it was scarcely fitting that his child, still educable, should be trained in a manner so directly opposed to his views.

Wherefore, the three chief personages being each so full of thought and care, the meal, usually pleasant enough, was silent and dull, and Ringrove felt as if something had come into the house, or had gone out of it, since he was there last.

While lounging in the drawing-room yet a little time before leaving, doing his best to bring back Mrs. Fullerton to her usual smiling graciousness, and to make Virginia's sweet eyes look tender or her grave mouth relax into a smile, as he told now a plaintive story and now a merry one, visitors were announced; and Mrs. Nesbitt and her eldest daughter, the pretty, soft-eyed Beatrice, came in.

They too came partly to discuss the new order

of things beginning in the parish, of which Mrs. Fullerton was openly said to be the chief supporter. And it was such a strange bit of contradiction that the wife and daughter of the confessed infidel of the place should be quoted as the ardent disciples of an advanced ritualist, that Mrs. Nesbitt and Beatrice hesitated to believe it until assured by word of mouth.

The three girls of Crossholme, Virginia, Beatrice Nesbitt, and Theresa Molyneux, were all good friends enough; but Virginia was less intimate perhaps with either than were Beatrice and Theresa with each other. She was more reserved than they, and she did not care so much for the natural pleasures of youth as they; hence they found her a shade cold and unconformable, and she found them a shade frivolous and uninteresting. Still they were intimate enough for Beatrice to be able to say in an under voice :—

"Virginia, dear, it is not true, is it? that you and Mrs. Fullerton have promised to support Mr. Lascelles in everything he wishes? They are saying so everywhere."

"I do not know what that means, Bee," said Virginia. "I can only say that I have made no such vague promise, because I have not been asked for it; and I am sure mamma has not either."

"Everyone says so," repeated Beatrice.

"People always say a great deal more than they know," said Virginia, unconsciously copying a speech which Sister Agnes had made to her. "Whatever Mr. Lascelles and Sister Agnes have asked us to do we have done, because they have only asked what is good and right; and so I suppose it will be in the future."

"But he is half a Roman Catholic," said Beatrice, opening her big brown eyes. It was as much as if she had said he was half a dragon or a sea serpent.

"He is an Anglican Catholic, which is not quite the same thing," answered Virginia again, repeating her lesson.

"But Miss Lascelles wears a cross, and the dress of a nun," insisted Beatrice, as if she had found the weak spot now, and one which there was no getting over.

"She only wears the dress of her Order; and no Christian can object to a cross, surely, Bee!"

"That is just it. She is of an Order, and we have none in our Church," the other said.

"Yes, we have indeed—a great many—and Sister Agnes belongs to one of them."

"You are so intimate with her as to call her by her

Christian name already!" cried Beatrice, as Richard
Fullerton had said before her.

"She is Sister Agnes, just as much as a man is a
captain, or you are Beatrice Nesbitt. That is her name,"
answered Virginia. "When she was in the world she
was Miss Lascelles, and now that she has given up the
world she is Sister Agnes."

"Well! I cannot understand it at all," said Beatrice,
full of perplexity.

"Nor can I," put in Ringrove. "The new vicar and
his sister may be charming people on their own account,
but I am sorry they ever came here."

"Oh, don't say that, Ringrove!" cried Virginia,
carried out of herself. "They are the salvation of the
place!"

"I don't think we wanted so much salvation," said
irreverent Beatrice, taking Ringrove's part, as she always
did.

"Bee! don't!" she answered, really distressed.
Then her angel's face became more angelic even than
usual, as she said with a kind of concentrated enthusiasm, looking at Beatrice first and then at Ringrove:
"You must not say now what you will be sorry for
hereafter; you will both come to the truth; and Sister

Agnes will be your spiritual mother, Bee, as she is mine!"

"I don't want any mother but mamma," said Beatrice; "and I do not think that I could let any stranger come between me and mamma."

"A spiritual mother does not interfere with our earthly mother," said Virginia gravely. "My mother is just what she always was, but Sister Agnes has led my soul into the way of truth."

"How dreadful all this is!" thought Beatrice. "She talks cant as if she had been used to it all her life. It is all too true, and she is more lost to us than she ever was."

"You are always so good!" said Ringrove, finding this one of the most difficult moments of his life. "But indeed you must be a little on your guard against too much enthusiasm for those new people. We have to know them first before we can trust them so thoroughly as you and Mrs. Fullerton seem to have done."

"I want no more than I know now," she said. "We do not want to learn more than the sunlight. It shines; and that is enough."

"Poor Ringrove!" thought Beatrice. "It is all over with him!"

She raised her dark soft eyes to him pitifully. She was his confidante, and had heard again and again the whole story of his love for Virginia, and walked every step of the way, now of hope and now of despair, and ever of suspense, that he had trodden for the last two years.

"True for the sun," he answered ; "but not for the application. I will wait a little longer before I think our new vicar such a lord of life as this."

"Do," said Virginia in the simplest good faith. "And you will be rewarded."

Mrs. Nesbitt found no more satisfaction in her talk with Hermione than Beatrice had done with Virginia. Her half-apologetic disclaimers—sorry to repeat such foolish talk, but thinking it due to her old friend to tell her what was said—had been met with indignant acceptance. Hermione had defended not only her own adhesion, but the vicar himself, stoutly; had maintained the worth of all that he was doing here at Crossholme, and the crying need there was of more religious life in the parish and more decency and beauty of service in the church. But, as Mrs. Nesbitt said when she repeated the conversation to her husband, it seemed so odd that Mrs. Fullerton of all people in the world should go on so

about religion and all that, when it was her own husband
who had done everything he could to make the people
as great infidels as himself, and when every one knew
that up to now she had never given the subject a
thought!

As it was, however, Hermione had reason to a certain
extent on her side; and as no unreasonableness of
excess had yet appeared and the new vicar wanted only
what was just and right, she carried her colours out of
the discussion and left Mrs. Nesbitt without an argument, but unconvinced all the same. She used so
far her woman's privilege, that, while obliged to assent
verbally to all that Hermione said, she kept still that
central point untouched which she expressed by : " I
cannot argue with you, but I feel that you are wrong."

From this day she could not deny that her friend
Mrs. Fullerton was the new vicar's right hand and supporter, and that both she and Virginia had been completely won over. And how Mr. Fullerton would bear
it, was now the question beginning to be asked by the
community of Crossholme.

CHAPTER VI.

AT THE VICARAGE.

WHAT might be called the personal part of the parochial management of Crossholme went actively forward; but as silently as actively. Working parties at the Vicarage were organized for three afternoons in the week, where Sister Agnes was the clever teacher of all sorts of beautiful embroidery for church purposes, and where sometimes the vicar came in and read while the ladies stitched. He generally read such books as Wiseman's "Fabiola," or Newman's "Apologia;" but always beginning with milder portions of the "Churchman's Manual," teaching them when to bow their heads in the services, and how to stand and kneel, with certain other observances in use among the ritualists. But he was cautious in this and went softly; knowing, as do all his sect, the value of a judicious reserve and the safeguard of silence, and how it is necessary to lay well the lines before drawing in the net, if at times a bold haul is the best and safest policy. There was much to do, and he had time before him; this was only preparing the way of the future.

Yes, there was indeed much to do before the church services would be made even outwardly decent according to the Lascelles idea; still more before the parish would be as well in hand and as spiritually submissive as it was intended to make it. Altar-cloths—which were always called frontals—of various colours and patterns according to the ecclesiastical season and the special service, had to be embroidered; stoles and copes, also varied; eucharistic emblems and linen for the communion; banners for the processions which had to come;—there was no end to the work in hand, but the true meaning of what they were doing was kept from most of the workers.

Sister Agnes, like the vicar, trusted to the love of women for beautiful things to ensure that amount of diligence which was necessary for the purpose; and to their pride in seeing their own handiwork publicly honoured and admired for their active partisanship should a time of collision with the men arise. What comes from afar and from unknown sources may be dangerous, like clothes that carry the plague; but the roses and lilies and sacred monograms and interlaced

scrollwork which our own Susan and Sukey have
embroidered can surely contain no secret spiritual
poison; and Susan and Sukey defend their own artistic
stitches.

All this the brother and sister understood to perfection; and they knew also that if they told too much
prematurely, in all probability their Crossholme Susans
and Sukeys would become frightened before their time,
and would strike, leaving the work half-done to be
finished by strangers. And they had it at heart to make
the ladies of the parish commit themselves, first by their
co-operation and then by their certain desire to see what
they had done utilized and appreciated.

The most constant in attendance and the most
useful, each in her own way, were Hermione and Virginia
Fullerton, Theresa Molyneux and her Aunt Catherine.
The first two were the deftest embroiderers; Aunt
Catherine laid the straightest hem and sewed the neatest
seam; and Theresa, who had everything to learn, practised her future art on the rougher kinds of material
and the simpler patterns, which it would have been a
waste of strength to have given to proficients.

Other ladies of the parish also attended, but as they
are of no special value to this history, they need not be

particularized. They made up the numerical strength of the society; helped to swell the fast increasing number of female adherents to the new order of things in the way of bowing, position, lowly inclinations, and the like, during the service; and they ensured a certain amount of work accomplished and of animation among the workers. And here their value to us ends. Among them however, was neither Mrs. Nesbitt nor Beatrice. Mr. Nesbitt did not approve of any scheme, how innocent soever in appearance, which might end by giving undue influence to the Church.; and, unlike Richard Fullerton, he allowed no exercise of free-will in his family, but ruled his household as he thought best. And above all things he held to the belief that a woman's duty lies at home and a wife's honour in submission to her husband. On her own side, Mrs. Nesbitt felt that she had too much to do for her family to give her strength to ecclesiastical æsthetics; and Beatrice followed her mother in this as in all other things, and assented to the truth of what she said, as if no second reading were possible.

When Sister Agnes proposed that they should join her working parties, Mrs. Nesbitt set the matter at rest then and for ever after by her frank straightforwardness, which was in no wise offensive—quite the contrary—but also in no wise to be mistaken.

"Why no, thank you, Miss Lascelles," she said; "Mr. Nesbitt would not like my leaving home so often; and Bee and I have really too much to do for the little ones to make it practicable."

"Power comes by the use," Sister Agnes argued with a bland smile; "the time given to the service of God takes nothing away from your family."

"I don't see how that can be," said Mrs. Nesbitt in perfect simplicity of good faith. "You see, there are only eighteen hours of the working day, and if every one of them is filled up, as it is, and as much is done as can be got into the time, I do not see how doing more will make the days longer. I have as much to do now as I can get through, and if I were to undertake new duties, I should simply have to drop some of my old ones."

"Try it," said Sister Agnes with the same bland smile. "Try it, and prove for yourself that the same power which fed the multitudes from a few loaves and fishes can also help you, and that what you give to the Lord is never lost to man."

But Mrs. Nesbitt shook her head.

"I do not believe in present miracles," she said.

"And if I take two hours in the afternoon three times a week for church work, I cannot do for my children what I do now. If I am here, I cannot be there ; and if I am embroidering linen I cannot be walking with them or my husband, or doing the same amount of work in the house that I must, to keep things straight— that every woman must, who is her own housekeeper."

"Perhaps you do too much, Mrs. Nesbitt. You are rich, with servants and governesses and all the usual aids and helps to mothers. There can be no need for all this active superintendence, still less for your daughter's assistance."

"I assure you I find that there is," said Mrs. Nesbitt, with undisturbed equanimity. She thought it odd in the vicar's sister to lay down the limits of her domestic activities ; but then, clericals are odd and take liberties which no one else would dream of. "And I do not think that any woman whatsoever, with so large a family as mine, can find time for more than her home duties and the social intercourse which must be kept up."

"Like Martha, encumbered with much serving," said Miss Lascelles with half a smile and half a sigh, deftly concealing a well-bred sneer.

"Yes, if you like to say so," answered Mrs. Nesbitt

simply. " But I keep my dear children well and happy.
I do not let them get into bad habits for want of my
care, nor be made unhappy by others ; and I do as my
husband wishes. And then you know, Miss Lascelles,"
she added smiling, " I am of the old-fashioned school,
and hold to the value of a wife's obedience to her
husband and a mother's superintendence over her
children."

" In short, you are as obedient as Mrs. Fullerton."

Sister Agnes spoke so quietly that no one could say
whether the words were sarcastic or simply assertive ;
and Mrs. Nesbitt was not the woman to find out sneers
or hints unless very patent.

" I hope so," she answered cheerfully. " I am
thankful to say that in Crossholme we have no unhappy
marriages and no disobedient wives so far as I know.
We are very fortunate in that way, and give no cause for
gossip. I do not know one unhappy household—not
one ! "

" I congratulate you," said Miss Lascelles, a little
coldly, " and yet—there is something greater and holier
in life than domestic peace."

" No, no ; there can be nothing better ! " cried Mrs.
Nesbitt warmly. " There can be no real goodness where

there is discord at home; and the woman who neglects
her own family, that she may give her time and energies
to a cause, is doing wrong whatever that cause may be."

"Softly, softly, Mrs. Nesbitt," said Sister Agnes, with
her superior smile.   "Do you carry your theory of
obedience so far as to think it right to deny your God
and your Saviour should your husband be an infidel?
Is a woman justified in caring only for the physical
comfort and happiness of her own children, while
letting the wretched poor starve? in ensuring their
moral purity while the abandoned thousands all around
are claiming Christian care, and the lost souls are crying
to be saved?   Does your creed go as far as this?"

"No," answered Mrs. Nesbitt quietly; "nor would
any woman's.   But there is no question of all this here
at Crossholme."

"There are degrees even here at Crossholme," said
Sister Agnes.

"I do not allow that my joining your working parties
belongs to them if there are," she answered.

"So be it," returned the Sister.

And then the conversation dropped.   The Nesbitts
were not gained; and, on the contrary, a certain feeling
of antagonism to the whole thing rose up in the good

staunch loving heart which could never quite forgive the vicar's unmarried sister for speaking slightingly of that which made her own happiness through the sense of love and duty fulfilled, and which she held should make the happiness also of every other good and virtuous woman. Between embroidering silk and linen for the church and seeing that her children were happy and good, she thought no true mother should hesitate for a moment as to where her real duty lay; and no argument that could have been used would have shaken her. When she repeated the conversation to her husband her concluding remark was:

"If poor Miss Lascelles had ever been married she would have thought differently, because she would have known better;" and she pitied her for her ignorance of the best things of life as much as Sister Agnes pitied her for her sensuality disguised as instinct and her practical paganism calling itself conjugal obedience and maternal duty.

All this new occupation, these new interests were making in a sense new creatures of the four chief workers. Aunt Catherine—Miss Molyneux—a good, kindly, weak soul, with more imagination than common sense, and like clay in the hand of a potter who had

clear insight and a strong will, had gone down helplessly
before the new vicar and his sister, who had known
exactly how to touch her. She had been won over by
that St. Catherine, Virgin and Martyr, whose namesake
she was, and whose life of mystical ecstasy she was
exhorted so fervently to imitate. She might attain to it
if she would, they said—if she would strive and obey. And
as the steps of her *scala santa* were of no more difficult
practice than (for the present) working in coloured
silks on linen and satin, bending at certain parts of the
service where she had not been used to bend before,
attending Early Celebration, and going to church on
Wednesday and Friday mornings, she was by no means
disinclined to take the sainted Alexandrian as her model
in obedience and belief, and to dream that perhaps
some of the same grace might be shown to her as was
vouchsafed to her antitype.

She might therefore be counted on as a sure
adherent to the ritualist party. Her imagination had
been fired, and so indeed had her vanity—or what shall
we call that need in women of a certain age to renew
in fancy the dead facts of the past?—the need which
makes some of them go into spiritualism, when at least
the spirits who come about them do not regard their

wrinkles or grey hairs?—which makes others find in religion as much excitement as they once did in love, and with some, not very different in kind?

Theresa, a slender delicate hysterical girl of about twenty-two, had also been won over as quickly as her aunt. Her life, which hitherto had been spasmodic and fragmentary, for the first time found concentration and direction. She had wandered about in thought a good deal. At one time she had been an ardent patriot, emulous of such fame as that which hung about the maid of Saragossa—the apologist of Charlotte Corday, and the worshipper of Joan of Arc; at another she had wanted to make herself a hospital nurse that she might go out and nurse such wounded soldiers as the peace of Europe required for its victims. Now she made a night school for ploughboys, but after a fortnight she broke it up; they were too hopelessly stupid, she said, and their hands were so dirty! Then she took to visiting the sick poor, but the cottages were close and she always managed to stumble on inappropriate chapters. She was full of enthusiasm and activity, as yet wasted; and now—it was utilized.

But Theresa was not one of Sister Agnes's lambs. She left that to Virginia, who was as devoted to her spiritual

mother as if she had been indeed the saint who was
her shadowy patroness. Theresa carried her enthusiasm
to the vicar—straight to head-quarters—and thought that
if the world could but be ruled by such kings of men
as he, there would be no more doubt or sorrow—at least
for women. He was to her a clerical God ; but it
would have seemed to her almost blasphemy had
any one desired to be the Semele to his divinity. So
at least she thought ; and for the present her thoughts
were true.

Virginia was perhaps the happiest of the whole
group. She was devoted to Sister Agnes, who, all
things considered, treated her tenderly, and led her
quietly along the devotional path designed for her. Of
late however, she had begun to impose small penances
for omissions of duty which she got the girl to confess
to her as a spiritual lamb to her spiritual shepherdess,
in preparation for the more important confessions to
be made in due form to a director. Thus, she would
forbid her to sit in her accustomed seat near herself, and
would send her over to where Catherine Molyneux was
turning her hems and maundering about her patron saint
and the Divine marriage as she worked. And this was
about the severest task that could be set the poor girl.

For to Virginia, grave, still, shy, the babble and gush
of this silly creature were distressing beyond words;
and only her loving loyalty for her spiritual mother
enabled her to perform a task which was indeed so
essentially a penance. But it was difficult to find any
punishment for Virginia. It was part of Sister Agnes's
management that the lambs should be every now and
then gently chastised; and as no one is in want of an
excuse when he wishes to flog for error, cause for that
chastisement had hitherto been always forthcoming.
But this, so easy with others, was difficult with Virginia. She was so gentle, so obedient, so entirely in
earnest and so lovingly desirous to do as the Sister
wished, that it was hard to find the flaw, even in the
exaggeration of confession; and harder still to punish
it when found. She had no senses to subdue and no
vanities to chasten; but the Sister knotted out of her
very virtues the cord that was to be her discipline, and
though the strokes were gentle, they were effectual
for their purpose—the still more complete establishment of her spiritual supremacy, and the still more
complete subjugation of Virginia's will.

On her side Hermione, although occupied and
interested more than she had ever been, was restless and

uncertain ; her temper, once so placid, was breaking daily ; she was tart and snappish to her husband as she had never been before, and then again hysterically loving ;—he to the one opposing his unruffled sweetness which she called indifference—meeting the other with his calm serene devotion which made hysterics unnecessary, and which she also took as indifference. Thus, either way she was thrown back on herself, and whatever he was she wished that he had been different. She was variable with Virginia :—now forbidding her to go into the excesses which she said she saw were at hand—now herself taking her to the Vicarage out of the ordinary course of things. The vague disquiet which had once been gentle was still as vague but becoming less restrained ; and once or twice she wept bitterly where formerly tears had only gathered in her eyes but had not overflowed. Life was busier with her now than formerly, yet it was blanker. Her husband seemed to have drawn farther and farther from her : and it was as if every effort that she made to reclaim him only separated them more. She did not recognize that she had gone from him, not he from her, and that what she needed for her happiness was trust, not effort.— She was beginning to hate actively the pursuits to which she had never given ardent favour and to feel them out of place in *her* husband. Mr. Lascelles spoke to her so continually of the iniquity of free-thought, and the futility as well as the presumption of modern science, that it was not to be wondered at if she grew into less tolerance where she had never felt sympathy or admiration. And as he spoke also as continually of the duty which she owed to herself, the truth, and the parish, because of her position, she, who had never been anything but the loving wife glad to live in her husband's supremacy, began now to feel that she had done foolishly in her sacrifice of power, and that he had acted ungenerously in his acceptance of that which she had forced on him ; and that Mr. Lascelles was her best friend— the only one who recognized her worth and wished to see her in her right place.

Cuthbert Molyneux was sometimes allowed to attend these working parties, and given the office of reader, or as Sister Agnes used to call him the lector—when the vicar was unavoidably absent. He was the only "man-body" admitted to the coterie ; but then he was such a poor creature and so little like an ordinary man that he scarcely counted. Tall and thin and reedy, with a small head and narrow sloping shoulders, long thin hands and

a conscience that was always awake while his reasoning
faculties were deliberately placed below "feeling," "conviction," "realization," "faith," he was one of the born
believers of the national creed whatever it might have
been—a subordinate priest, governed by his more intellectual superiors and doing their will with the unquestioning fidelity of a slave. He was a very woman in
this—in that he felt the need of a director or a superior;
and he, like the women of whom we have spoken, had
found what he wanted in Mr. Lascelles—Father Lascelles
as he once or twice called himself to the young men, as
if in joke, though he said that his favourite title was
Superior—the Superior of the little band which though
not conventual had some of the qualities of a community apart; and it was just these qualities which he
intended to enlarge and consolidate when the days were
ripe.

For the rest the meetings were pleasant enough taken
as mere social gatherings; and neither the vicar nor his
sister wished them to be other than genial and interesting.
Their line was not gloom, though it was discipline; and
when they fished for souls the bait was bright if the
hook was sharp. Sister Agnes knew how to make
herself agreeable to each in turn, as a clever well-bred

woman always does. She talked domesticities with the wives, and advised them on the management of their babies and the conduct of their servants. She tried neat little personal arrangements of their hair and dress with the girls, taking them to her own room and showing them practically how much better they looked with simple braids and without fringes or fluffs; how bright colours warred with their complexions, and how far superior greys and neutral tints were to every other. She allowed light blue as the Virgin's token; but no other positive colour at all. She wished to bring her own special band into a certain conformity of simplicity which should show them marked with the same sign even to outsiders; and she intended that next Lent they should all, at her suggestion, wear black;—and she would have gained enough influence over them by then, she thought, to make them obedient to her will;—the thing was worth trying for.

To Virginia she was, even when the giver of penance, secretly the tender mother, the holy guide; and made the girl feel that she was her favourite lamb in all the flock; the nearest and the dearest, and dear to Saint Agnes and the Blessed Mother also. Day by day Virginia's submission increased and her love grew—a love which associated Sister Agnes with the angels, and made her feel that in obeying her she was obeying Christ—in loving her she was loving God.

With Aunt Catherine, Miss Lascelles was as a sister worshipper of sister saints—the two standing hand in hand in heaven as they the devotees stood at times on earth. Sister Agnes made a little sketch of Saint Catherine, with the Divine Heart and her marriage ring— Saint Agnes, with her lamb. They were floating on pink clouds, embracing each other like two Christian Graces ; and when she gave her the sketch, the Sister placed Aunt Catherine and herself in the same positions, saying:

" See, we are now just as our patron saints are in heaven."

She knew that this would kindle the fervent imagination of the weak creature whom she had undertaken to bring over to ecclesiastical domination, body and soul, and make her doubly zealous for a Church which gave her a saint as a godmother and a prototype—for the Sister declared with her sweet smile and in her softest voice that Miss Molyneux when she was young must have been very like the pictures of Saint Catherine. And she was not disappointed ; spiritual vanity is as true a fact in human nature as personal pride, and people like to feel that

they have guardian angels and patron saints who give
themselves a host of trouble in protecting from physical
dangers and listening to the prayers of miserable sinners
of no more value to the universe than so many tadpoles
in the water or harvest mice among the corn. The position was too pleasant for Aunt Catherine to abandon it;
and one of the happiest strokes in a game made up of
happy strokes was that which fitted Catherine Molyneux
with her patron saint, as well as gave her nephew Cuthbert his, and offered the mystic Spaniard as the exemplar
and guide of her namesake Theresa.

Mr. Lascelles too did his part, and he did it well. He
let no one feel neglected, but he made each lady believe
herself his special charge. To Hermione he was all
things—gallant as a man of the world would naturally be
to a pretty woman; respectful, as in some sense an
official inferior—for had she not the great tithes as lay
rector where he was only the humble vicar?—fatherly
and reassuring as the spiritual guide leading her from
darkness to light, and from the famine of ignorance to the
rich pastures of grace. To Theresa he was quite as
assiduous and even a little more paternal in the way of
a certain secret familiarity, as if the tall, thin girl of
twenty-two had been a child not half that age. He

made her feel that of all the souls to be saved in Crossholme hers was the most precious to him and heaven,
and the one for which he gave himself most concern.
He saw her power of passionate self-surrender ; and he
traded on it for the good of the Church, if also as a
"student of human nature" for the sake of psychological
vivisection.   And as Theresa was a girl not to be directly
influenced by women, but only to yield obedience to a
clever man who knew how to mould her, it would have
been of no use to have turned her over like Virginia, to
the special care of Sister Agnes.   Of herself the Sister
would have had no influence ; only as the sister of the
sacred vicar.   Of warm imagination and an hysterical
temperament, Theresa must always have some admixture
of human love to keep her steady to the point, and these
attentions of Mr. Lascelles supplied just what she wanted.
It was perhaps a dangerous experiment, seeing what she
was ; but he had been successful in the like before now,
and why not again?

As for all the rest he was grave to some, bright to
others, bland with all.   He laid himself out to make
those Vicarage parties as pleasant as if they had been so
many fashionable *soirées* : and he succeeded.   There was
not a woman who belonged to them who did not look

forward to them with enthusiasm, and not one who was not more than half in love with the handsome, well-bred, well-mannered vicar. But he, to do him justice, had but one thought and one aim—how to advance the interests of the Church : and to his way of thinking every method was lawful that should attain that end. It was not his fault, he thought, if women were sentimental, weak, and silly; but it was his duty to utilize their very follies for the strengthening of the Church and the advancement of religion : and if in the process his humanity became dearer to them than even his doctrine, that was their folly as it would be their punishment. He had power enough over his own passions to keep himself free from all trammels—and he never denied how far better he held celibacy for the clergy than matrimony. But he never said openly that he himself would not marry. Only, in speaking generally, he said it was better. Still, other High Church clergymen have said the same thing before now;—but the hour has come, and the woman ; and might it not now again here in Crossholme?

CHAPTER VII.

THE THIN END.

SELDOM twenty-four hours passed without some intercourse between the vicar or his sister with Hermione
or Virginia. If no Church work was going on at the
Vicarage—of which by the way they were the main
support—there was sure to be some question of importance which could only be solved at the Abbey ;
and as, after that first afternoon, Richard never appeared, the spiritual excitement which had to be kept
up at fever-heat suffered nothing by his interposition.
Day by day Hermione's religious convictions increased
and the vicar's influence grew ; and day by day she
was more discontented with her husband and more
variable in her feelings :—now petulant, repelling, fault-
finding—now tearful, clinging, hysterical ; but always dissatisfied both with herself and him, whatever her mood
or his response. If he were good-tempered and patient
when she was irritating, he was insulting in his indifference ; if he were grave, he was beginning to hate

her:—she saw it and knew it too well!—if he returned her caresses gently, as was his wont, but without the sweet follies of the dear old fervid time, she bored him and he treated her like a child, giving her a kiss for a sugar-plum just to pacify her; if, thinking all this excitement unhealthy, he tried to calm her, she was repulsed as no woman but herself could bear; and it was trying her too far!—for all her love for him there was a point which even he could not, should not, overpass.

The whole armoury of feminine unreasonableness was ransacked for her weapons of self-torture secret and shown; and she knew no kind of peace save when she was with the vicar or Sister Agnes. They seemed to supply the buttress of authority which was wanting to her own conscience. Her conscience indeed, as taught by them, was satisfied as things were; but her womanly feeling went against her new convictions; and between the two peace and happiness were lost, while feverish excitement and unrest remained. And yet— she could not call herself unhappy. That feverish unrest in which she lived was in some sort the kind of life she loved. If only there had been no haunting shadow in the background!—no vague sentiment of present wrong and future remorse—if only she could make her husband as bad as she wished to believe him! But he was always so sweet and calm and reasonable, that she could find no weak spot in his armour anywhere. Even after she had tried him most with her temper she found him just the same as ever when she came back, and as little likely to resent her petulance as he was to reply to her provocations. She would have preferred that he should have done both. His calmness irritated her at times almost past bearing. And she wanted a cause against him. Like all people who are discontented with their conditions, she wished to justify her dissatisfaction by some potent fact of wrong-doing or ill-usage; but she searched for her justification in vain.

One day, the vicar came to the Abbey full of a new project for which he wanted money. That section of the Church to which he belonged always are wanting money, and make no scruple in asking for it. It is for the Church, working through, if for, the needs of man, and why should they not?

The vicar's special object to-day was twofold—on one side a thing to be done; on the other a root to be struck and a hold to be gained. The Order of the Mother of Dolours to which his sister belonged, from "Penitents" had extended its work to invalids, and now wanted a Home in the country where it could send its convalescents. And as all kinds of work and organization tell for the establishment of ecclesiastical influence, the vicar was glad to have the Home here at Crossholme. When minds are enfeebled by sickness and hearts softened for gratitude, impressions can be made which, once made, may perhaps be rendered permanent; and Mr. Lascelles had found before now the wisdom of the rule which subdues the mind by ministering to the body. This Convalescent Home would be a tower of strength to him here at Crossholme; and who can object to a work of pure charity and benevolence? But he wanted money for it; and Hermione must give it.

"I should be glad if you would help me," he said, after he had detailed his plan. "The Knoll, up there at the head of Squire's Lane, is exactly what we want— a fine healthy but sheltered situation, where the poor creatures will have all the sun but be saved from the north and east winds."

"It is the exact place," said Hermione, her kind heart kindling at the project. "The long walk in the garden is quite like the south of France—so at least Mrs. Parsons used to say when she lived there, and she was fearfully delicate."

"Yes; I see all its capabilities," he answered; "but of course it must be arranged specially for our purpose, and furnished ; and the garden must be put somewhat to rights—at present it is a mere patch of weeds; and all this will dip deeper into the funds of the Sisters than they can or ought to afford. Will you lend a helping hand? I am sure you will!"—with his sweetest smile, his best air, claiming her aid by the right of his friendship as well as by the natural instinct of her own character.

"With pleasure ; as you know," said Hermione. "I will ask my husband for the money; he never refuses me."

"May I speak to you frankly on a very delicate subject, Mrs. Fullerton?" said the vicar suddenly. "I have no right to interfere in your private arrangements— believe me I feel that—keenly." He sighed, and his sigh made Richard Fullerton's wife quiver. It meant —What? "Nevertheless I feel that you *are* in a sense my own," he went on to say with a sudden eagerness. "You are—my spiritual child and I am your ghostly father," he added in a different voice and manner, as

Hermione blushed and turned her large blue half-frightened eyes from his face to the floor; "and I feel responsible myself for your soul's health."

"Yes," said Hermione, catching his tone. The Child and her Father pleased her; she was to blame to have been startled.

"This scheme proposed by the Sisters of the Mother of Dolours—in which you are to help—must pass as their own. You are not to appear as having helped. We do not publish all and everything to the world; and we are content to labour for Christ and His Church without the reward of man's applause. We give to our Orders the glory which they give to God."

"I see," said Hermione with an earnest face. "It is beautiful—true—holy!" she murmured to herself.

"I like your range of epithets," said Mr. Lascelles with gentleness. "It is the true course for all souls to take! But to go back to our theme. You must not ask your husband for funds for our Convalescent Home. It must be established here as by our Order, with my sister as the Superintendent and me as the Chaplain. You must give to the Church in secret what you wish to give at all. How can you do that when you have no private fund whence to draw these gifts to the Lord?"

"What can I do?" said Hermione distressed. "I have never had the control of my own money. As you know, when I married I gave it all up to my husband, and there has never been the smallest difficulty between us on this matter."

"Nor must there be now," he answered. "And to keep your domestic peace unbroken you must avoid, what else, with Mr. Fullerton's disastrous views, will become a serious cause of dissension between you— namely, your noble aid given to our church work—by having your own private income with which he shall have nothing to do, and over which he must not have even the right of supervision. I want you to ask your husband to make you an allowance;—no! I will not put it in that way," he added a little warmly. "You must take part of your own money into your own hands—such an amount as will enable you to serve God without praying the permission of one who denies our Lord and is the sworn enemy of His Church."

"But what will my husband think?" said Hermione, looking down in extreme trouble; "though indeed," she added with perilous frankness, "I feel now that it would have been better if I had kept back some for myself, and not made him so entirely the master."

"You are right; and now is the time to assert yourself. Mr. Fullerton will respect you all the more for your determination," replied Mr. Lascelles, preaching peace where there was no peace. "This arrangement is simply due to yourself as the inheritor of your father and the proprietress of the estate. Wifely obedience is a virtue—granted; no one holds it higher than I do; but this complete effacement, even to the power of doing good, is an offence to God. It is placing the creature before the Creator, and a secondary virtue—a virtue of circumstance—before one that is elemental and integral to your own soul. It must not be, Mrs. Fullerton; you must reclaim your lapsed rights—at least to this point of a private source which you can deal with as your own."

"My husband will do what I wish—I am sure of that," said Hermione as his advocate. "It was my own doing that gave him the supreme control, but I have only to ask for an allowance and I can have it. Of course, it was very silly of me to do this—but I was very young then, and knew nothing of life; and the

idea of managing this large estate frightened me. Perhaps," she added with the finest dash of temper, for this
wish for a private fund was not born to-day, and had
been growing long enough to have become bitter;
"perhaps he might have done this of his own free
will. I think indeed that he ought! It would have
been better than making me feel that I have to thank
him for what is really my own."

"Forgive me for saying so, dear Mrs. Fullerton, but
had he been a man of true delicacy, of true generosity,
he would have done so. He would not have waited to
be asked."

"I think so; but he did not mean it. He has
been very very good to me!" said Hermione with the
vacillation of feeling that was only too frequent with
her now.

"He could scarcely have been anything else," said
Mr. Lascelles with his courtly sneer. "The wife who
has given him all, could scarcely be other than
cherished." Then he added suddenly: "And has your
daughter no allowance, such as most young ladies
have?"

"No; we have never had the keeping of money;
neither she nor I. My husband pays all the large bills

by cheques. We have quarterly accounts, and the question of expense and payment is never discussed. Indeed, I know nothing of our affairs at all. He has the supreme control."

Mr. Lascelles slightly shook his head, and smiled as at the confession of a fault which at this moment was not to be too gravely rebuked. It was a fault; no doubt of that; but he let it pass for the time under protest, and Hermione understood his by-play only too clearly.

"It would be as well to accustom your daughter to the keeping of money and dealing with it of her own free will—under judicious direction," he said. "She is of an age now to learn practically the things of life; and sooner or later she must deal with large sums. Let her begin now. When taking out your own share let me advise you to claim a fitting portion for her. You do not object to my presuming to advise you? In our relative positions it is my duty and my privilege."

"No! no! indeed I do not object! I am so much obliged to you; it is like a new life to me, having a friend who cares for me and wishes to see me righted," cried Hermione. "I think you are very kind to take so much trouble for me."

"Nothing can be a trouble that helps you in a difficult and delicate path," answered the vicar gently. "I know what you have to bear already, and I fear that your burden will become heavier and your way yet more thorny. For such a woman as you, so humble-minded, so sincere, so desirous to learn the truth of God and to follow as the Church directs, to be the wife of a professed atheist!"—He shuddered. "What an awful union of good and evil!" he half whispered, lifting his eyes to heaven.

Tears stood in Hermione's eyes.

"If I could but bring him over!" she sighed, feeling herself at the moment a martyr for truth's sake.

"Yes, if you could!" he answered, echoing her sigh. "And who can say that it may not be? Moses smote the rock and the living waters gushed out, and Divine Grace may break down the pride and blindness in which your husband has encased himself and allow the light of truth to come in. Who would dare to limit God's power or to circumscribe His grace?"

"It would be a miracle if he were changed," she said.

"And such are still wrought; if with such a one as he, seldom," he answered.

Had anyone told her twenty years ago that she would have held such a conversation as this, with a strange man, about that beloved husband of hers—had anyone told her even ten or five years ago, or less, that she should have taken the attitude towards him of now an impatient and now a sorrowful contemner—she would have cried out against that prophecy as an impossible transformation—a miracle that no power in heaven or earth could accomplish in her heart. But it had come; and sitting there with Mr. Lascelles she felt that here was true wisdom as well as her own true friend, and that Richard was blind and dark for the one part and her slightly ungenerous exploiter for the other.

All that day Hermione turned and turned this proposal over in her mind. She was a gentle creature in her inner nature, not one to wish to hurt—even a husband; and she knew that this sudden disturbance of old ways would pain hers. She knew that she was entering on an unacknowledged warfare with the man whom, up to now, she had loved so tenderly, and had only blamed in the secret recesses of her heart because he did not show with sufficient warmth the love which she knew he had for her. She knew too that she was unjust to condemn him for his want of orthodoxy. She had borne with his agnosticism for the last fifteen years in perfect tranquillity of conscience—her utmost remonstrance having been no more severe than an " Oh Richard ! " said with a smile when he was more than usually audacious, more than commonly broad; and to pretend to herself now that she was a martyr because the wife of an infidel was trading on her own changed feelings with scarce the full measure of honesty towards him. But through all this dim and vague self-communing ran the distinct desire for independence—as much to punish him as to gratify herself. He had not cared to keep her by the perpetual renewal of a lover's courtship, as she should have been kept ; and he had lost her, to a certain extent, in consequence. She had escaped like a bird from the hands of one negligent of his prize, and he was to blame if she was miserable. But the only step as yet contemplated for the attainment of this coveted independence was that private allowance on which she had now set her heart—such a mere piece of justice as it was, and so unjust as it was of him not to have done it long ago !—a private allowance which was to be her own, and with which she could deal as she wished, like a sacred bit of soil fenced round against his intrusion, and which she could consecrate to the Church through Mr. Lascelles.

Meanwhile, pending the demand, she asked Virginia if she too would not like to have an allowance of her own—it would be good for her.

At first the girl said no, she would rather not ; but on her mother reminding her that if she had money of her own she could help Sister Agnes in her plans, and that then she need not trouble papa for all that she wanted, she took back her negative and said yes, she should like it; as perhaps it would be better for papa not to know always everything, unless he could be brought to love the work with them.

"But it is not deceiving him, mamma, is it?" she asked anxiously, as the natural honourableness and transparent quality of her character broke through these later spiritual sophistications. "It is only pre- venting his being vexed and fancying all sorts of things about Sister Agnes and Superior "—this was the vicar in his intimate circles ;—Superior of the little band of "Church-workers," as they called themselves;—"things which are not true and which would annoy him? It is not deceiving him, is it?"

"Certainly not," said her mother. "Superior himself

advised it, and would he and Sister Agnes, so good and high-principled as they are, advise anything that was wrong?"

"No," said Virginia warmly. "What they advise *must* be right!"

It was one of the sweetest of our English evenings —a rich warm August evening when the beauty of summer and the wealth of autumn meet in flower and fruit, in the unthinned luxuriance of the foliage and the first washes of gold and crimson over the earlier-changing trees. Dinner was over. It had been more than usually silent, and it was never noisy—for Richard was thinking over his lecture to his men; the monthly lecture due the day after to-morrow—Hermione was considering what she should say and how word her request—and Virginia was lost in a dreaming kind of reverie picturing to herself the peace and blessedness of the conventual life, as she imagined it to be; so that no one found much to say, and no one wished that the others were more communicative. Now they all went into the verandah for coffee; and Hermione's hour for opening fire had come.

How sweet the evening was! Richard looking at

that fair expanse of country, where cornfield, wood
and meadow, farm and cottage, and the winding stream
that gave life and increased picturesqueness to it all
were his—felt a glow at his heart as he thought of
the moral influence which such a property gave him.
In his own mind it was like a green and living island
of truth in the midst of a desert of falsehood; the
deep and real fountain of life where all the rest was
the mere mirage of things—vapour playing over sand.
All this was his; and all this represented the cause
of light and knowledge and science against darkness,
ignorance, and superstition. While he lived he felt
that he was the keeper of an impregnable fortress which
would never fall into the hands of the enemy. He
and his little band would make headway here, and no
one should overcome them; and, man for man, he
pitted his influence against the new vicar, and was
not afraid of the issue.

But there was that lecture on the Duty of Man as
a Member of the Community waiting for him to arrange.
He must swallow his coffee and go. The sunset glow
tempted him to remain—for it was a singularly beautiful
sky, a rarely perfect evening; but he must tear himself away and finish his preparation for one of the

boldest and most outspoken lectures that he had yet delivered.

He turned with a smile to Hermione.

"Well, good-bye for the present, wife. Coming to give me a kiss before I go?" he said, moving in his chair.

Hermione laid her hand on his arm.

"Oh, don't go yet!" she said a little nervously. "Do stay with us a little longer, Richard! You are so seldom with us now, and the evening is so lovely!"

"You think that you are lovelier to me than the evening, you mean?" he laughed.

"By your habits we might both be witches, Virginia and I," she said with a smile. "You avoid us as much as if we were."

"If I am not much with you it is not from want of love, my wife," he said. "But, as you know, my life is full and I can give but little time to pleasure."

"I do not see why your wife and daughter should always be the most neglected." She put on a pretty pout, raising her soft blue eyes from under her brows as she lowered her head. It was a girlish trick revived; or rather it had never wholly died.

"Do I neglect you?" he asked pleasantly. "You? —the best-loved she in England!"

"Am I? Poor things—if I am, how I pity the rest!"

He laughed. His feeling of their absolute oneness was so strong, so deep, so interwoven with his very life, that in spite of the small disturbing currents which of late had set across that halcyon sea of his faith and trust, he could not choose but accept such a declaration as this as so much womanly play. Besides, though she meant what she said, she spoke as if she did not.

" You pity them for their smaller portion? Well, perhaps you are right. They are to be compassionated," he said.

"No, I do not look at it quite in that light," said Hermione, suddenly grave. "Nor in your secret heart do you. But never mind all this," she went on hurriedly, as he was preparing to protest. "I have a little matter of business that I want to talk to you about. So please attend, and let us be serious."

"All right, wife—what is it?" he asked.

"I want to have a private account of my own at the bank," she said with a plunge.

She was not gifted with the faculty of diplomacy, and with Richard she had always found the directest course the best. He was slow at taking hints and he

was especially a man with whom anyone could be
absolutely straightforward. He was not likely to be
offended by either frankness or boldness ; but crookedness and burrowing were unpalatable to him.

"What do you want with a private account?" he
asked after a little pause. The proposal had taken him
by surprise ; and he did not wish to show how much.

"For many things," she answered.

"But why disturb present arrangements, wife? You
spend what you will and I make no objection to
paying."

"It would be rather odd if you did, considering all
things," said Hermione, remembering what the vicar had
said.

He passed his hand over his forehead. What did
her allusion mean? What did it all mean? If he had
administered the property was it not his duty as the man
—the husband—the head of the house? It was their
property, for they were one; and he as the man was the
holder for their joint benefit. Why did she remind him
that legally it had been hers, and that he had once
been the recipient not the owner? He never thought
for an instant that he was still only the recipient, and
not the owner.

"Dear wife," he said, "I scarcely understand you. I cannot see what need you have for a private or separate account. What are you likely to buy that I should object to pay for?—what are you likely to do that you would not care for me to know?"

"It is not pleasant for any woman to have to go to her husband for every farthing that she wants," said Hermione with an injured look and tone.

"And how many years have you taken to find that out?" he asked.

"That is not the question, Richard," she replied, a little less amiably than hitherto. "I have found it out now—surely that is sufficient."

"But why should things be different from what they have been?" he urged. "I feel, perhaps foolishly, that a certain vague cloud of distrust would creep in between us, wife, were you to separate yourself from me even in so small a matter as this;—you and I who have always lived in such unbroken harmony, such devoted love! This must not be, my life! Whatever else may happen to us we must go down to the grave as we have lived through our youth, hand in hand, heart to heart, one in a perfect and flawless life-union."

He leant forward as he spoke, looking into her face

with a certain loving pathos, a certain pleading passion that went to her heart. Oh! why was he not always like this! she thought—why had he become so cold and indifferent to her, and put all other things in life before her and his love for her!

"We have been very happy and will be always," she said falteringly. "We are not going to quarrel, Richard, because I should like to have a little money of my own to do with as I like,"—attempting a smile that somehow failed. "It will be better for everyone, and for Virginia too. I should like her to have an allowance. She must learn the use of money, and she knows no more about it now than a child—than I do!" again forcing a smile.

"You have no need to learn the use of it, dear," he answered. "While I am by your side, have you not always a faithful custodian?"

"Yes, dear, I know; but still—I should like it," said Hermione.

"I cannot understand why." He spoke with the same reluctance that he had shown throughout.

"It is not so very difficult to understand surely!" cried Hermione, piqued at his opposition, which she had not expected would be so tenacious. "I am not a baby to be managed for ; and, after all, papa left me absolute mistress of everything. It is only my own at the worst ! "

The next moment she would have given worlds to have re-called her words. The sudden spasm of pain that crossed Richard's face told how deeply she had wounded him ; and though she felt bound to obey the vicar's will, which indeed had become her own, she did not wish to pain her husband—unnecessarily.

" It scarcely needed that reminder, dear wife," he said gently, when he could speak naturally and without self-betrayal. " If I have administered your fortune it was because, being the man of the two—the two so perfect a one !—it came more naturally to me to attend to the details of business than it did to you. I have not wished to invade your rights nor to keep back that which is your own. Always remember that, my wife ! "

" Asking for an allowance to be placed in the bank in my own name need not distress you so much as it seems it does," said Hermione uneasily in feeling, but playfully in manner. " I never knew you stingy before, Richard ! you, who have everything, to grudge poor me this little portion—for shame ! "

He shook his head. Her forced playfulness did not

impose on him, nor heal the wound which had been made.

"How much shall I put into the bank for you, wife?" he asked suddenly but quite gently. The suddenness was in the complete and unconditional surrender of all opposition—the gentleness was his natural manner.

"I would like to have two thousand a year," said Hermione also gently.

"Is this to include your milliner and all other personal expenses?" he asked. "I ask you, dear, because the outgoings of our house just match the incomings, and I want to know what this sum taken yearly—you said yearly?—is to include, that I may calculate."

"Yes; I will make it sufficient for myself and Virginia," she answered magnanimously.

"So—good! And you like the idea of an allowance of your own, Ladybird?" he asked playfully; anxious to show that the fact once established was to be no sore between him and them.

"Yes, papa," she said going over to him and kneeling down by his chair lovingly.

"And what will my little girl do with it?" stroking down her long silky shining hair.

"I will try to do good, papa," she answered gravely, lifting up her sweet face, so like an angel's, to him.

"You are always good, my Virginia," he said.

"No, papa; I am only trying to learn the will of God, and to follow it in the least bad way I can," she answered.

His fingers still stroking down her hair, caught in the elastic string round her neck, and the little crucifix was pulled out from its place of concealment.

She took it in her hand reverently.

"This is my sign," she said; and kissed it.

Again that look of pain over his face. The veil was lifted just at the corner, and with bitter anguish he saw the shadow of the truth within.

"Are you sure that all which you take to be good and godly is so in fact, my Virginia?" he said, holding her hand and looking steadfastly in her face.

"Yes, papa," she answered. "The Church is the voice of God on earth—oh papa! papa, if you would but hear it!"

"I hear a better," he said; "the voice of science, and of that true humility and courage which can confess ignorance yet not be disturbed. But tell me, child, who has got hold of you? Is the new vicar tampering with her, wife?"

"I do not call it tampering," answered Hermione. "Both he and Sister Agnes saw that Virginia needed religious instruction; and they have given it to her—as was indeed their duty in their position."

"I shall be sorry if she is made zealous for orthodoxy," said Richard slowly. "It would be painful to me to have my daughter join hands with the school which I give all my strength to destroy."

"Conscience must be supreme with Virginia as with others," said Hermione. "I cannot forbid her in a matter of this kind. What she thinks to be right that she must do."

"Still, our daughter is but a child; and direction in this case means conviction. It is the direction to which I object."

"And which makes my true life, papa!" said Virginia fervently. "I would rather suffer martyrdom, like any of the early Christians when they were persecuted by the Romans, than give up Sister Agnes and all that she has taught me—all that she is and has been to me."

"Virginia was pining for some kind of religious

conviction," said Hermione. "You do not know her as well as I do. The coming of Mr. Lascelles and his dear sister has been her salvation."

"Oh papa, you do not know how happy I am now!" cried Virginia, clinging to him while still kneeling by his side. "I have wanted so to tell you all! I know now what to believe—I am no longer wandering in the dark—I have found God in the dear dear Mother our Church! I could not go back to that miserable time when I did not know what was false and what was true —when we had no daily services, no right teaching, no earnestness in religion, no guide, no teacher! I would rather die than give up what we have now in dear Superior and Sister Agnes."

"All this is a bewilderment to me," said Richard, looking from his daughter to his wife and not exactly taking in all that she had said. "I feel somewhat in a fog. Have you too, my wife, gone *tête baissée* into the new system like the child?"

"I am older and less enthusiastic perhaps than Virginia," Hermione answered with a certain reserve.

"Still you have gone the same way?" he persisted.

"I do not like to answer you as if I had committed a fault—something to be afraid of," said Hermione a little stiffly. " I confess to having found immense spiritual comfort from Mr. Lascelles and his dear sister since they came."

" And you wanted this comfort ? "

" Yes ; sorely."

He was silent for a moment. All these revelations bewildered him.

" I had no idea that you were in want of comfort of any kind," he said slowly. " My belief was that you were perfectly happy—both you and the child—as happy as I myself. If I had known that you were pining for any pleasure—any change—I would have given it to you without remark or remonstrance. I would have preferred any distraction to this."

" It was not pleasure that we wanted, papa," said Virginia ; " it was faith—it was God ! "

" Things might have been different, Richard, had you not been always so dreadfully occupied," said Hermione half in tears. " You know what kind of life you lead and how entirely you absent yourself from us. If you had cared to keep us more with you, perhaps we should not have been so ready to accept all this new life."

" Don't say that, mamma ! " cried Virginia. " It was not for want of excitement or mere occupation—not that

—it was because we were both wandering and now we have found our rest ! It was not because we wanted papa—dear as papa is—but the Father whom we have found !"

"If this is true, my wife," returned Richard, not noticing Virginia's more thorough partisanship, more enthusiastic confession, " I would have given up all—all that I most loved and valued—to preserve you from this dreadful blunder—this fatal bewilderment. Oh, why did you not confide in me, my wife ? you whom I trusted so entirely, and love so devotedly !"

"After all, Richard, are we not making a great deal too much of—what ? " said Hermione, suddenly changing her tone. Virginia's passionate advocacy a little frightened her, and did in a certain measure chill. And then she saw how heart-struck her husband was, and she did not want to hurt him too much ; they had once been very happy, and he did not mean to be disagreeable to her. " We have a new clergyman here in the parish, and Virginia and I like to assist in the parish work. This is the whole of the matter from beginning to end ; and it is not one that deserves either your pain or our hysterics. Virginia has been greatly taken with Sister Agnes—girls of her age often are with clever women like

that ; but we are all making too much of it !   Don't
look so grave, Richard !   I have always been loving and
obedient to you," she went on to say, warming with her
own words and talking herself into a new mood ; "and
I always will be, unless "—smiling sweetly—" you want
me to do what my conscience disapproves.   And I am
sure you are too good and liberal for that."

"I want no other assurance than that, wife !" he
answered, going over to her as she sat on her low chair
opposite.   He stood by her and turned up her face
with one hand, laying the other on her shoulder.   "Let
me keep the conviction of your unbroken faith to me, as
mine to you, and I can meet the whole world !"

She looked up at him and met his eyes—those dear,
mild, honest eyes in which she had once seen all her
hope and found all her bliss.   Memories of the old days
came over her, softening and warming her heart and
turning back her love to him as if she had been a girl.

"Richard !" she said impulsively ; "if it pains you,
dear, I will give up all—even——"

"Mr. Lascelles," said the servant ; and the vicar,
close at his heels, passed into the verandah like one to
whom the house is free.

"I thought I might catch you, Mr. Fullerton, if I

came at this hour," he said blandly, showing neither disappointment nor vexation; though he had not expected
to see him, and was annoyed to find him on the ground.
"I have just received the Faculty from the Bishop, and
should like to consult Mrs. Fullerton—and yourself—on
the restorations to be made in the church; and to which
she, as the great tithe owner and the chief lady of the
place," graciously, "will have much to say. Are you at
leisure? May I show my plans?"

"If you wish it," said Richard gravely, feeling that
his enemy was in his camp, but holding a flag of truce
that meant treachery.

The vicar's evident familiarity with the house, the
kindling of Virginia's face when he came in — that
dreadful crucifix on her bosom!—and Hermione's flush
and embarrassment coming on her request for such a
strange alteration in their old relations — all had impressed him; and it seemed to him that his proper place
was truly here, as the head of the house watching over
its weaker members when danger was by.

But he was too late; the roots had been struck, and
the tree had begun to grow;—was it the Tree of Life or
the upas?—that which would give salvation or bring
destruction?

CHAPTER VIII.

THE WHOLE DUTY OF MAN.

THE most notable of Richard Fullerton's "men" were John Graves the tailor, Tom Moorhead the blacksmith, and George Pearce the carpenter of Crossholme; and, notable in another way, Adam Bell, that clever, reckless, shifty fellow who kept the chandler's shop at the far end of the village.

Apparently, to judge by the ease with which he could talk of methods and handle various sorts of tools, Adam had practised every kind of handicraft not requiring special breadth of shoulder or development of biceps—and some others that needed sharp wits more than deft fingers. No one could make out exactly what he had been, but everyone gave him credit for having been a great many things; and it was even said that he must once have been a play-actor. Certainly no one sang a better comic song, or spouted with more fluency, or gave imitations of the various best known actors with more facility;—there were no experts among the

critics of Crossholme to determine whether the imitations
were exact or no ;—they seemed to be so, and that was
enough. When in the vein too, he could go through
whole parts of wild melodramatic plays, such as are
given in barns by strolling companies and at "Richard-
son's" in fair times—plays full of poison and death and
love, and with a large amount of high-falutin' and impossible virtue to balance the as impossible vice. And, as
those who discussed him argued, shrewdly enough, it
was scarcely likely that he would have taken the trouble
to learn just one character and no more in so many
pieces—though he knew scraps of the rest—if it had
not been for business and his slice of bread. And the
shrewd wits had probability on their side.

As Adam was a stranger at Crossholme, coming out
of the clouds one murky winter's morning and with no
clear track to his last place of residence—conjecture
was free to make of him what it would. And conjecture had a fine time of it ; for he neither volunteered
any precise information about himself in the past, nor
gave cause of suspicion by resenting it when asked.
He never by any chance mentioned where and what
together. The nearest that he said was : "When I was
down south I picked up from a yokel an old watch for

two shillings that I sold afterwards for a matter of twenty pound."—"When I travelled the eastern counties I collected some rare old coins of the Roman times."—"Once when I was up in the far north I was lost in a snow-storm."—"When I peddled Cornwall way."

This was the nearest that could be got out of him :—He had peddled : first for a master and then for himself; and now, tired of wandering, he had resolved to cast anchor and make himself a home ; and Crossholme fitted him to a hair. But where he was born and where schooled; what he had done when a lad, and who were his father and mother—it being to be supposed that he was not born peddling—no one knew more than he knew what his great-grandfather had been doing this day a hundred and fifty years ago. He had come to the place quite suddenly ; opened a chandler's shop much wanted at the time and traded in a very small way at the beginning—but having his character to make, and knowing how it is best made for the long run, he took care to sell good stuff of fair weight and at reasonable prices; and thus, by degrees which were neither slow nor long, he won the confidence and custom of the place and was now doing well. So far things were not in his disfavour; and no one has the right to imagine spectres which are neither seen nor heard.

Restless in all things, of a prying and excitable kind of intellect, if Adam had curbed his nomadic blood so far as to settle quietly in one house for the last six years, he had not put his brain into harness; and the inventions and discoveries of which he was the father, and which would revolutionize society had he but the money to work them, were as many as there were objects on which he laid his long thin supple fingers. He had invented an electric locomotor, and an automatic printing-press; and he had a torpedo—on paper—which, if put into material, would blow into sky-rockets aught ever laid in the sea; and he had a steam-engine that would pump out a mine in less than half the time of the best in use now—still on paper; a plan how to regulate the boiler so that a blow-up should be a mechanical impossibility : and if he were to be believed, he had the whole re-organization of practical dynamics on that dusty old shelf in the little back parlour behind his shop. Such as he was—talkative but not confidential, bragging but never committing himself to provable statements—he was a character in the place; personally liked by some because amusing and superficially good-

natured, but gravely doubted by the better sort, partly
because of that ill-natured insular prejudice of ours
which doubts a stranger *quâ* stranger, and partly because
of that clever shiftiness of his which gave one the feeling
of instability and consequent untrustworthiness. It held
off such men as John Graves and George Pearce; and
rough Tom Moorhead even more than they. Yet Adam
was one of "Mr. Fullerton's men;" and the loudest
in his admiration of the doctrines which developed him
from a jelly-fish through the common progenitor of
himself and an ape, and which denied the personality
of the devil or the existence of hell. But though he
professed himself to be an enthusiastic disciple of the
new school of thought, and a loyal partisan of its
expounder here—the master of the Abbey—when with
those who really believed in the religion of humanity
and the saving grace of science, yet he was not backward in clever parodies and nonsensical exaggerations
when with those who had not taken up the thread; and
his humour was never so broad as when he was demon-
strating to his hearers that they were no better than
so many tadpoles, and were just the "gorillas of the
future."

He never quite conquered Richard's instinctive distrust of him, as he never quite conquered that of the three men already named. He did his best to get over the master, whose custom at his shop counted for much; but the kind heart was united with a clear brain and an instinctive perception of realities; and though the one part of him hoped all things from all men, the other believed in none short of proof, and gave little heed to protestations that looked well and rang false.

For the rest, John Graves was elderly, quiet, thoughtful, and noted for the pathetic patience, the philosophic dignity with which he had borne the heavy sorrows of an exceptionally sad life. His unbelief was his religion, as it was to Richard himself; and he denied Christianity because he believed in science. Tom Moorhead, a man in the prime of life, was an ardent Radical and the Boanerges of the group; and George Pearce, about thirty, was more after the pattern of John Graves, whose only surviving child he had married, and whose quiet thoughtful temperate nature he took as his own model with the reverent love of a true son.

Tom Moorhead had a daughter too; and people laughed as they noted how often keen-witted, sharp-featured Adam Bell was at the forge when the shop door was shut and every man's servant was now his own

master. But there were few who dared hint to Tom
at the possibility of such a suitor as the like of him
for pretty Janet. He of all the group most doubted
this clever intellectual acrobat, this foretime pedler who
had wandered here out of the clouds; and would as
soon have thought of marrying his girl to a soldier or
a tramp as to Adam Bell of no known antecedents and
not of this parish.

But Adam thought that he could work his way in
time; with the help of money if all else failed. Every
month he was putting by a little matter, which would
soon make a tidy sum; and with a good settlement to
offer, fathers-in-law are not difficult game for lovers to
bag. He had had a good deal of experience in life, he
used to say; and he had brought out of this experience
one strong settled conviction—that every man has his
price and every man his power, if only you can hit on the
one and find how best to utilize the other.

Only one thing more need be said at present of these
men :—John Graves and George Pearce, his son-in-law,
were tenants of the Molyneux family; Tom Moorhead's
house and forge belonged to the Abbey estate; but Adam
Bell's shop stood on part of the small bit of glebe that
had been reserved for the Vicarage. The village was a

long straggling irregular place; the estates were as irregular as it; and odd corners had been bought and sold till it was almost a topographical puzzle to know where Churchlands ended or the Abbey began, or why this little croft should belong to the Vicarage and that half-acre of wood by its side to Monkshall. So however it was; and no one at Crossholme thought it strange or wished that it were otherwise.

More besides these men went to the reading-room, both when Richard gave his monthly lecture—which was of a stronger and more speculative kind than the weekly —and in the evenings and at noon, to read, to play a game at draughts, or to take a hand at "spoiled nines," or " three-card lant." This allowance of card-playing had been made into a nine days' wonder when the rules of the reading-room had first been drawn up; and the neighbourhood had objected to it strongly and canvassed it severely. Indeed it had been raised into a crime by the more rigid; and to hear them talk it would seem that Richard Fullerton had organized his pretty, half Gothic little Institution to become a very sink of iniquity. But as he said, when those who spoke against him and his ways behind his back most unreservedly, approached the subject to his face with greatest discretion :—" I treat men like men, not like children ; and if it pleases them to have a game at cards, why should they not as well as others? I trust to their developing tastes for a higher kind of recreation than gambling; but if they have that desire—many men have ; it seems almost instinctive— they had better gratify it in a place where public opinion goes against excess, than in the public-house where they drink till they are inflamed and lost to all self-control."

And as he was the owner and master, and had the right to arrange his own rules, he carried the day, as he intended to do ; and the Institution allowed cards, smoking, and beer, as well as giving other things of a higher class. The members numbered about fifty—all the available men in the place indeed—but those spoken of were the principal, and all with whom we have to do in this story.

The lecture to-night was on the duties of men as members of a community. In contradistinction to the theological view of rewards and punishments, of pleasing God and saving our own souls, duty was set forth as self-respect on the one hand and the good of the community at large on the other.

" All is bad or good as it affects the well-being of society, or let us call it humanity," said Richard. " There can be no intrinsic evil, no positive sin, where there is no community to be harmed by your acts."

He brought forth the old argument of the desert island and how a man could not sin by himself. If he could do no ill to others he could do no ill at all;—spiritual wickedness, self-generated, self-destructive, and offending God only, being a myth and an impossibility. This was naturally utterly opposed to the theological view which makes sin a thing in itself between a man's own soul and God, and in nowise because of its action on the community;—which sees in it primarily an offence against Heaven even when it is a crime against society—damnable because disobedient to divine command rather than to be punished because of its evil handling of man's body and property. "This latter is allowed to be morality if you will," he went on to say; "but the deeper crime, according to theologians, is the spiritual wickedness of disobedience of God's command—not because such command is good for man, but because it is God's." "The only laws that we know," he said, "are those which we are slowly finding out for ourselves in the positive sciences, and that educated and still to be educated sense of justice, equity, and respect for humanity, which we embody in codes and call concretely conscience. It is

childish to talk of a devil who tempts us to do evil—
humiliating to common sense and manhood to fear
eternal punishment if we have done evil—and what
grosser superstition has the world ever seen than the
Christian doctrine of God incarnate in man that we might
all have a better chance of heaven?—a better chance,
mind you ; not a certainty—and the whole universe disturbed that we might be less unfairly handicapped ! No !
no, my friends ! man is only a part of the whole—a unit
of the sum ; and there is no more value in his life than
there is in the life of a fly, or an ant, save such as he
makes for himself by his higher intelligence.   What we
have to cultivate is the sense of justice to all, ourselves
included ; loyalty to the best interests of the community
of which we form a part ; reverence for humanity at
large ; love of truth for its own sake irrespective of the
conclusions to which it leads us ; while ourselves personally, and what advantages us one way or another, is a
consideration which comes nowhere in the school of a
wise and elevated philosophy.   We have to live for
humanity, not for our own souls.   Never let us forget
that.   Our duty is here—our work is here ; we know
nothing but life—can prove nothing but matter—and
to waste our strength in vague speculations on things

that are unprovable is the sorriest use to which we can put it."

Was this strong meat given as food to babes, and poison rather than nourishment? Richard did not think so; nor did some of his hearers; if others felt a certain uneasiness, a certain kind of mental droop and collapse at the thought that it was not regarded by a Higher Power whether they did well or ill—just as weak and paralyzed limbs suddenly taken out of irons would fall helpless to the ground. Some felt a certain relief in the idea that if they kept clear of the police here they had nothing to fear hereafter, and were free of the devil who else might have had his word to say to them for fleshly indulgences, or faults of mind and temper which broke no human law and hurt none so that they should cry out; but others again, took the doctrine as it stood, and found it ennobling and heartening. The doctrine of self-respect, and of the duty owing to the community, was one which seemed to them to strike a true chord, and to be a higher phase of thought than that grovelling Eastern personal fear and purely selfish endeavour which are expressed in such phrases as fleeing from the wrath to come and saving your soul alive.

After the lecture was over the usual discussion followed,

when the men spoke out their minds and asked questions or expressed dissent. This was always the most inte resting part of the evening, and the most important. The doctrines set forth in the body of the lecture were then more clearly demonstrated and more directly urged.

John Graves was generally of Mr. Fullerton's way of thinking. There was a certain sympathy of nature between the two men which made their minds in unison, and rendered the teaching of the one acceptable to the other. To-night he gave his unqualified assent to all that he had heard. It was not wholly new ground to him, for Mr. Fullerton had gone over it before with him in private, though this was the first public lecture in which he had put forth these doctrines. It was his view of things, he said, put into scholarly language and cleared out. But Tom Moorhead had a word to say against duties to all the members of a community as at present constituted. He would render no tribute to Cæsar because he denied the rights of Cæsar, whether called absolute or constitutional, emperor or queen ; and what he denied to the sovereign he was not minded to give the aristocracy. He was hostile to it all, and wished that Mr. Fullerton had touched on that head

in his discourse, and limited the right to demand
and the obligation to pay.

Tom always dragged in that shock-headed repub-
licanism of his whenever he had the chance ; and when
he had not he still made his friends and hearers
understand that there was his *bête noire*, standing in
the shadow outside the door and waiting for the first
opportunity when he could thrust his ugly muzzle into
the thick of the fray.   He was an impetuous, unreasoning, one-ideaed kind of creature ; but he was trusty and
honest ; and truth, like falsehood, can work with different
materials and by various tools.

George Pearce boggled not a little at the doctrine
of sin being impossible save such as refers to the well-
being of the community.   He was a tender-souled
young fellow with the possibilities in him of zealotry
if set on the track, and he cherished the belief in an
inner life which the scalpel could not lay bare nor
the spectroscope analyze, nor the crucible reduce to
its ultimate essence.   "A man is conscious of a certain
sort of a something," he said modestly, " that has nought
to do with what others may know or not know, nor
with what harm may or may not be done to those others
in consequence. He could not argue well," he said, " but

conviction and consciousness were facts which everyone could prove for himself."

"A man is convinced of many things which we know do not exist," said Richard. "A spiritualist believes in the materialization of ghosts, and an African in the incantation of his Obi man. Private and personal convictions have ruled the world for a long time now, George, and you see into what a morass of folly and superstition they have landed us."

"These were things, sir ; but what I mean is states of feeling—thoughts which only a man's own self knows and can realize."

"Like the ecstasies of nuns, the visions of hermits. You would not put them as solid bases of conduct, would you? Save as physiological facts to be dealt with by medicine they are contemptible ; and as philosophical arguments inadmissible. Conscience and consciousness are mental conditions varying according to health and education. They have not even a claim to consideration by their stability or uniformity."

"It makes life a little vague, sir," said George, who was somewhat off the line of the lecturer's meaning.

"No !—Why should it? There is just this difference between us and the orthodox—that we would educate

a man's conscience for his own self-respect and his
duties to other men ; while the Church says that the
welfare of the human family is not the end of life, but
rather the cultivation of your own spiritual graces—
chiefly humility and faith. We are not without a guide
in conscience ; but we have the civic and human, not
the theological—that which refrains from evil-doing for
justice and self-respect, not for fear of consequences.
I am not speaking against conscience as a fact, but
against the direction given to it by the Church."

"You come down pretty square on the Church, sir !"
said Adam Bell. He could never keep silent for long,
and he was beginning to consider within himself the
value of keeping open a line of retreat. He had a
shrewd idea of how things would go presently in the
parish, and he thought holding an even balance no
bad test of skill.

"Not more strongly than justly," said Richard.
"The Church has always been the source of ignorance
because its power is founded on pretensions that cannot
be proved and which science destroys."

"They make things difficult for plain men like me,"
returned the chandler. "I have been to the old place
these last Sundays to hear what the new vicar has to

say. They are talking of nothing else down town; and it is queer to hear a gentleman like him tell us that we shall all be burnt in flames for ever if we do not think as he bids us, and then to come here and find that there is no place for hell in all creation, and that the Church which pretends to know everything and to teach us all is no better than a nigger pow-wow man."

"What has the Church ever taught that has been of the smallest permanent or real good to man?" said Richard. "Every scientific truth by which society has been revolutionized and man's knowledge of nature and morality enlarged, has won its way after a fight with ecclesiasticism. Astronomy, geology, and now biology have had against them the Church with all its power of persuasion, all its force of negation; and it has only been when further denial was impossible that she has sullenly admitted the new truth and set herself to prove that it told nothing against her omniscience after all! To make it plain that Genesis demonstrates the truth of geology, and that no Christian scientist need trouble himself about the physical cosmogony of the Bible, is now the great endeavour of one section in the Church. I prefer, for my own part, the greater thoroughness which sneers at science in the interests of Moses and the prophets, and declines to sit on two stools of different heights and strength.'

" Like our new vicar," said Adam smartly.

" Yes ; he at least is uncompromising," said Richard. " So far we know where we are ; for the fight has begun here at Crossholme, though everything looks so fair and smooth. You will be sought to be gained over to the Church by the attractiveness of the services, by the zealousness of the minister, by the tears perhaps—the solicitations certainly—of your wives and daughters who will be won without difficulty ; and it will be a hard thing for you to make a stand. But if you go over you will lose the best birthright of your manhood ; and the price that you will pay for your reconciliation with falsehood and mental oppression will be your freedom and your intelligence."

He had seldom spoken so strongly ; never so directly in personal and local application ; and Adam Bell took notes. If there is a chance of the ship going to the bottom, are not the rats wise to swim ashore betimes ?

Soon after this the discussion came to an end ; and Ringrove Hardisty, having to speak to Richard, entered the reading-room ; when the two left and walked by the side path through the park and so on to the house.

Ringrove had come to consult his elder friend on the advisability of offering himself as the churchwarden chosen by the parish. The election was not far off now; Cuthbert Molyneux was to be the vicar's nominee; and Ringrove wished to be the parochial "sidesman," to match the other in local weight, and surpass him in personal intelligence. The one a gentleman, so must be the other. It would never do to pit against a landed proprietor, and such a thorough-going partisan as it was known Cuthbert Molyneux would be—seeing the direction in which he was going—anyone who should not feel himself equal to both him and Mr. Lascelles combined.

"I am glad of that idea of yours, Ringrove," said Richard heartily. "You and I, my boy, must do what we can to stop this new madness, and keep the parish from being overset and destroyed. I am too deeply committed to opposition and denial to be able to be churchwarden at all, in any interest; but you will do all that I would were I in your place, and without rousing the animosities that I should have done."

"I am glad you think it the right thing to do," said Ringrove. "I feel it to be so. I should like to see the Church decently kept up and all that, but I do not want to have Mr. Lascelles or any other priest in the saddle here at Crossholme; and I will do what I can to prevent it. The Church belongs to the English people, not we to the Church; and I will do my part in making the distinction very clear."

"He is working mischief swiftly enough," said Richard; "and I fear that he has touched my child. You know what my hopes have always been, Ringrove, but I have been a little out of heart for the last day or so. I was pained more than I can well say to find a cross round Virginia's neck the night before last. Sister Agnes—as they call Miss Lascelles—has evidently got hold of her; indeed her mother confessed as much; and the child is just at the age when impressions are most easily made—and unfortunately, unhealthy ones even more easily than the healthier. I am troubled about it, Ringrove!"

"Oh! don't be troubled!" said Ringrove boyishly; "she is an angel and will come all right! But just as good and sweet and lovely as she is, are they wretches who would play on her best feelings and make her as much of a hypocrite as they are themselves."

He spoke with warmth, and naturally with injustice ; giving neither Sister Agnes nor Mr. Lascelles credit for the sincerity of faith which was as real with them as their very lives.

"At least she has a thorough-going champion in you, my boy," said Richard smiling.

"And shall have to the end of my life," answered Ringrove fervently.

As he spoke a moving light in the Abbey attracted his attention. It was Virginia walking across her room. She put the candle at a distance and came out on to the balcony that ran round the bay window—standing there, looking at the moon and stars. It was strange how ethereal she looked under the transforming light of the moon. She might have been a spirit or a creature of another race and kind than ordinary gross humanity, for the subtle beauty, the supersensual kind of purity that seemed to inform her whole being. And so simple, so purely unaffected as she was! Here were no æsthetic poses borrowed from pictures and intended to represent saints or goddesses—no artificial ecstasies, nor conscious assumption of rapt reverie.

Apparently it was just an innocent, beautiful, fair-haired girl looking with natural awe and admiration at the starry splendour of the sky; but beyond this was also that unconscious something which touches the imagination of men, and which calls forth their highest feeling towards, and their truest worship of, woman.

"I can understand how men came to worship the Virgin Mary," said Ringrove in a low voice and with a lover's reverence.

"Yes—such as that," the father returned with a certain sense of awe;—she looked so like—what? One who had died and had now re-appeared for a moment, showing herself to sorrowful hearts for their comfort in the old place where she had once been their joy? But no spirits were in Richard Fullerton's universe, and death with him was—death—and no return. And in like manner in his world of faith was no plan of holy angels coming down on earth from heaven—no revelations possible of other spheres, of other lives. He did not know what it was that caught his breath and brought something that felt like tears to his eyes, as he looked at his daughter standing there on the balcony in the bleaching moonlight. He wished that she would speak, or stir!—but when it grew too painful, he himself broke the spell.

"Good-night, my Ladybird!" he called out from below.

"Good-night, dear papa," she said, turning her sweet face downward with a smile that was more sad than merry.

"Good-night, Virginia," said Ringrove Hardisty, his voice not quite so full or cheery as usual—rather hushed and subdued.

"Good-night, Ringrove! sleep well!" she answered him back, her serious face still turned downward.

"Ah!" said Richard with a sigh; "we lose some beauty out of life, my boy, we who go in for plain truth, and matters of fact not fancy. I have never understood the belief of men in angels so well as since Virginia came to me—if I believed in heaven at all I should say, direct from heaven!"

"She is worth a man's dying for!" said Ringrove passionately.

"Yes; or better still, living for," returned her father. "Well! come to breakfast to-morrow, my boy. It is too late to ask you in now—I see the household making its nightly stampede to bed."

"Thanks, yes," he answered, pressing Richard's hand; "you are always so good to me!"

" Well, you see, I look upon you as a kind of son," said his friend pleasantly; " and in any case as the young fellow for whom I have the most respect of all known to me."

CHAPTER IX.

FOR THE SAKE OF CONSISTENCY.

To no one was the new order of things likely to be more unpleasant than to Jacob Ellis, the head-gardener at the Abbey. Hitherto he had had things pretty much his own way; and provided that he supplied the house with timely fruit and vegetables, kept up a good show of plants and flowers for the hall and dwelling-rooms, and took care of the lawn and walks, he was neither required to cut his best blooms nor to account for the grapes or peaches in the margin. But since the new vicar and his sister had come, he had had another family to supply as well as his own, he said grumbling; and, my word! but they must have the best of everything, and what was good enough for his own master's table was not for them! The best of the stuff must all go down to the Vicarage; and if things went on like this, he would give up his place; that he would; and be off hot-foot. He could not stand two masters; and though he thought the worlds of his own, the new-comer was not in his line.

If he had grumbled like this at the things which had been done in the green wood, what were his feelings at those which came to him in the dry, when it was not the question of a dozen of peaches, or a few bunches of grapes done up in a basket of vine-leaves—just what would be enough for two people with a snack over— but of cartloads and barrowfuls, for the decoration of the church at the Harvest Festival?—when the green-house was ransacked of every show flower; and the choicest of the fruit taken pell-mell like so many pig potatoes?—when boughs were cut down by wholesale, and the place that knocked about, he said, as would take years to get the better of?

He was sullen enough as Ringrove rode in to break-fast with the master the morning after the lecture, as invited; superintending the loading of a cart with branches of trees, armfuls of ivy, choice flowers and plants, and the best of his wall fruit. Virginia and her mother— the former dressed as for a walk—were at a little distance, standing by the door of the conservatory; Hermione pointing out such and such plants as she wished should be taken to the Vicarage direct, and others that were to go to the church.

No lady in the place was more popular with her

servants than was Hermione. She neither scolded nor interfered with them; was always gracious in manner and kind-hearted in fact; and her housekeeper, catching her tone, made life pleasant for her subordinates and did not pack up unnecessary burdens for them to carry in needless pain. And as for little missy—so they called Virginia among themselves—she was the general property of the household, and the darling of young and old alike. The timid among them only feared that she was too good to live; but while she was alive she was their treasure and their angel. But not even the popularity of the ladies could reconcile Jacob Ellis to the new ordering of things, nor give him patience on the day of parting with his best growths; nor, truth to say, make this sudden invasion of his department in any way acceptable to him. Wherefore, ladies or no ladies, he was sullen out of all likeness to his usual self, and his under-gardener had a hard time of it.

"You are busy this morning, Jacob," said Ringrove, as, seeing Hermione and Virginia by the conservatory, he rode up to where the gardener stood with two men loading the cart with his precious growths.

"Yes, sir," said Jacob shortly, working viciously at his job.

'I'd rather have seen them given to pigs.'

" Where are all these going?" he asked.

" For the Harvest Festival they call it, sir," returned Jacob, still sullen in temper and viciously active in deed. " Have a care, Jim—there's my best gardenia a-standing lopsided ; and look out for these Chasselas ! "

" The Harvest Festival? where? whose?" asked Ringrove, who had not attended closely to the announcement last Sunday and now had forgotten all about it.

" At the church, sir. It's a sore thing, Mr. Hardisty, to see one's best going down to rot and mildew for a mere child's play like this ! I'd rather have seen them given to pigs, I'd go bail I would, than go like this, and never a man the better for it !"

" So !—to the church, are they!" cried Ringrove, who had by this time dismounted. " Faith ! they will make a good show ; but, as you say, it seems a pity; only I dare say the vicar will take some of them for his own private use, and very likely give the rest away," he added, remembering the old story of Bel and the Dragon and the tell-tale feet, which he had no doubt was as true now as it was then.

And with this he turned away and strode on to the conservatory.

"You are early!" he said to the two as he came up to them. He was a true Englishman in the way in which he usually began a conversation by stating a self-evident fact.

"Yes," said Hermione a little demurely; "I wanted to superintend the things we are sending for the decoration of the church, and Virginia has been there already."

"It will be so lovely, Ringrove!" said Virginia, looking somewhat less ethereal in the morning sunshine than she had done under the moonlight, but always with that far-away kind of look in her angel's face which people have whose lives are more inward than outward, and whose best affections are not here.

"It ought to be pretty with all that you are sending," he said; "and with your taste for arranging," smiling.

"You ought to come, Ringrove," said Hermione.

"Oh! you will!" added Virginia, turning to him and raising her eyes full to his.

"Weekly services are not much in my way," he answered with embarrassment. If Virginia should take it in hand to proselytize him, he felt that denial of her prayer would be the most difficult task ever set him by consistency and principle to learn.

"Not yet, but they will be," returned Virginia, still looking at him with her sweet, frank, pleading eyes.

Had she been the most finished mistress of the art of seduction she could not have touched Ringrove more deeply than now by this loving care for his soul, this pleading with him for what she thought the better thing, though he neither agreed with her nor wished to follow her direction. Still, that she should desire to direct him was in itself happiness unspeakable to the man who was waiting with so much patience for the lighting of that little spark of love which gave no sign as yet of kindling. He made a greater effort over himself than she knew not to yield on the spot. But, in love though he was, he had also some regard for that same consistency which manly men prize so highly ; and he did not want to be quoted as one of the vicar's adherents when heart and soul he went the other way.

"We must learn things by degrees," he said with a lover's instinctive hypocrisy. "Meanwhile, what I have come for," turning smiling to Hermione, "is breakfast, if you will give me some. Mr. Fullerton asked me last night."

"He did not tell me—indeed, I have not seen him

since dinner yesterday; but I am glad to see you, Ringrove, as you know," said Hermione graciously.

She was naturally hospitable; and by reason of her husband's studious habits, also not a little because of his objectionable opinions, had only too few opportunities of showing her liking for society.

" You are always the pleasantest and sweetest hostess in the world ! " cried Ringrove enthusiastically.   He did a great deal of love-making to Virginia through her mother.

She smiled and brightened even more than before, and she was her brightest self this morning.   Ringrove had always been a great favourite with her, and until the new order of things in the parish she had given herself no little trouble about him and his affairs, and had done her best to warm her daughter towards him by the frankness of her own liking.

" I think breakfast must be ready now, Virginia—do not you ? " she said, turning to the girl whose eyes were roving over the stands, looking if there were not more and more stately plants that might be taken down to the church, for all that Jacob had vowed and protested, half in tears, that he could not spare another stick or leaf, and that he had given too many already.

"Oh, yes ; I am sure it is," she answered, looking towards the house.

She was not hungry nor thirsty nor wanting physical comfort in any way; she was satisfied with things as they were, and could have gone all day without more nourishment than that which she drew from her excitement and devotion ; but as breakfast was a fact that had to be accepted and got through, she was anxious to have it over that she might go down to the church again. And indeed so was Hermione. To both, the church, the vicar, and his sister were the whole for which they lived —all that made their happiness and their occupation.

They were fairly fascinated ; as were others in the place ; but if to Virginia it was true spiritual exaltation, wherein human love, strong as it was for Sister Agnes, counted only as the medium not the end, to Hermione it was somewhat different—though she honestly deceived herself and believed that to God was given all, while to man was paid only the rightful tithe which the priest may justly claim. If men like Mr. Lascelles did not allow women to thus deceive themselves, when they do not more actively hoodwink and mislead, their power would not be what it is now. But sex when most ignored is oftentimes most potent; and the priest is no less the man to his female devotees because he offers himself to them as a saint.

"Well ! there is the gong ; let us go in," said Hermione. "We have a hard day's work before us, Virginia and I, and we must make haste."

"Good morning, my wife; out so early !—and my Ladybird armed *de cap en pied* before breakfast ! " cried Richard, holding out his hand to Ringrove. He met them all in the hall as he came from his study when the gong sounded. "What has called you out so early, my wife ? " he asked pleasantly, taking her hand on his arm and looking at her with laughing eyes.

"I have been in the garden," said Hermione.

"So ! that is good ! You are looking as blooming as a flower in consequence," he answered back with playful malice. Hermione's indolent habits and late hours in the morning—never getting down to breakfast till half-past nine or ten—had always been a little source of half-loving half-earnest discussion between them ; and Richard meant to remind as well as to compliment her.

"I never saw Mrs. Fullerton look better," put in Ringrove.

"Are you going to adopt my suggestion at last, wife ? —and see the sun rise on occasions ? " asked her husband.

"I do not know about adopting your system," she said smiling. "I have been into the garden to-day because obliged."

"Yes? why? What were you doing, dear?"

"Superintending the removal of the plants and flowers for the Harvest Festival to-morrow," she answered, looking into her plate.

"What Harvest Festival?" he asked with surprise; and then, as Ringrove had done, he added: "Whose and where?"

"At the church," she answered, trying to speak with indifference.

"And is that what you have been doing, Ladybird?" he asked of Virginia.

"No, papa. I have been to matins—early morning prayers," she added in answer to her father's look of surprise. "We are going down after breakfast to help in the decorations. To-morrow is our festival, and the church must be decorated to-day."

Both she and her mother had been told by their respective spiritual directors that no concealment was to be attempted with the husband and father concerning the part which they had taken in the autumn festival of the church. He was free to learn so much to-day of how

things stood between them and the church to the de
struction of which he had devoted himself; in general,
by their advice, he was left in total ignorance of their
movements and feelings; lying by the suppression of the
truth not counting as a sin where that truth might prove
too weak for success in battle.

"But I thought that it was the people who had
benefited who gave their thanks," said Richard. "How
is it that we, who hold no land in our own hands, and
therefore have nothing to do with the harvest, should
supply the thank-offerings?"

"It is our duty. We are here to set an example,"
said Hermione. "And if others will not do as they ought,
we must."

"Is not this vicarious?" he asked.

"You may call it what you like," she answered,
flushing; "but it is our duty."

"Still, it sounds a little like a cheat—buying a substitute on the one side and supplying it on the other.
No argument can make the Abbey fruit and flowers a
true thank-offering from those who are assumed to bring
their tribute because they have cause for rejoicing," said
Richard, with a smile. "This is altruism that goes
beyond even me."

"It is gratitude to God and paying honour to the Church, whoever does it," said Hermione a little stiffly.

"And the second clause, my dear, is the dragon which eats up the first. Surely you are not so far touched with superstition, wife, as to imagine that it pleases the great First Cause, the Force which you call God, to have a handful of fruits and flowers hung up in a place called a church because the sun has shone at a favourable moment for certain growths, and a few men have stacked a few measures of wheat in good condition! We are going back to fetishism at lightning speed indeed if these degrading absurdities are to rule our minds and actions."

"Richard! how can you talk so wickedly? It makes my blood run cold to hear you!" cried Hermione with displeasure.

"Because I do not think that the Power which expresses itself by this great universe is to be mollified like an autocratic barbarian with offerings—pleased, like a child, with gifts? Keep to the sway of the church as your argument, if you will. I can understand only too well how the clergy should teach these silly superstitions, and how weak and ignorant folk still believe in them; but do not bring them gravely forward here, where we have no need of subterfuge."

" I bring forward what I believe and am taught," said Hermione.

"You believe that your God is to be propitiated or thanked, or whatever you like to call it, by a few apples and pears, and a bunch or two of corn and hops? Hermione! my wife! what has come to your reasoning faculties?" said Richard.

"What it would be as well if it came to yours, Richard; a little humility and a little faith," she answered tartly.

" If you are humble, dear, what is that which pretends to teach you?" he said. "A body of men declaring themselves infallible—the possessors of eternal and immutable truth, affirming an intimate acquaintance with the secret counsels of God, to use their own phraseology—and the mappers out of heaven and hell as if they had been over both with a measuring tape; and all quarrelling among themselves; and none of them knowing so much as we others of the world around them in which they live. Do you not see that you are being traded on through your very virtues? that your humility is the pabulum of their insolence? your faith bolsters up their presumptuous assertions, and makes their monstrous falsehoods possible?"

"No! and I do not wish to see anything so blasphemous," said Hermione.

"I am sorry for it, wife; there ought never to be the time when we do not wish to see the truth," he answered gravely.

Virginia leant forward and put her hand in her father's. This was the first real dispute that her parents had ever had in her presence, and almost the first that they had ever had at all; and though firm to her own view of right as Sister Agnes had taught her—had she not the little crucifix to tell her how to stand and where to go?—she was distressed all the same.

"Dear papa," she said very quietly; "is it not all in that very word? You think one thing true, and mamma the other, and—and——" she hesitated.

"And my little Ladybird's cool hand comes in between as peacemaker; is that it?" he answered smiling, half ashamed of the heat that had been stirred up in the talk, though he himself had been so far less excited, so far less angry than Hermione. "But has the father no word to say that should be listened to, my lassie?—no authority of guidance? Does this belong only to a stranger? And is he who loves best and sees most to be set aside as one having no voice in things?"

"If you had not set yourself against the Bible and the Church as you have done, you would have been listened to, and things would have been different, Richard," said Hermione. "But what is to be done as things are? You believe in nothing at all except your horrid old bones and senseless bits of jelly; and your opinions are really too shocking for anyone to listen to —and before Ringrove and the child, too! I wonder how you can say such awful things, Richard! If I were in your place I should expect the roof to fall down on me!"

"No, dear; that is just what you would not expect if you were in my place," he said quietly.

"If you were anything of a Christian—anything of a believer—and not such a fearful materialist as you are, I would obey you gladly in all things," Hermione went on to say, not noticing her husband's characteristic little disclaimer. "But while you abuse the Church and the Bible as you do, and deny the very existence of a God, or the life after death, both Virginia and I must disobey you. We cannot help ourselves; and it is your fault, not ours!"

"And the religion which brings strife where there was peace—dissension where there was love—and all this hysterical and unwholesome excitement where there was calmness, security, rest—that religion seems to you holy and true?" he asked, as much amazed at the fluency as he was at the openness of her opposition. It had never come to this point before.

"Christ said He came to send a sword," said Hermione.

"Are you going to draw it, wife, against me?" he asked, his eyes growing dark and tender.

"You have drawn it yourself," she answered, turning away her head, and in so low a voice that he did not hear what she said.

"Come down to church, papa; come with us to-day to help us with the decorations, and to-morrow to the service!" said Virginia by way of making peace. "You and Ringrove both come!"

Poor Ringrove, who had felt keenly the humiliation of this quarrel—for what else was it?—between the two people in whose perfect union he had believed as in the sun, and who had not known where to look nor what to do during the time that it had been going on, was so pleased, so relieved by this diversion made by Virginia, that he gave in at once—at least to the first part of her plan.

"Yes," he said in his cheerful, pleasant voice; "I shall be very glad to go with you to-day, Virginia, and help you with the decorations."

"Good boy!" cried Hermione impulsively; while Virginia, smiling, radiant, and feeling sure now of this upright, honest, but unenlightened soul, looked up into his face with such gladness, such tenderness in her eyes, that Ringrove felt himself grow as it were dizzy, as if he somehow lost his balance.

"And you too, papa," Virginia urged.

He shook his head, smiling and calm, but grave, and as if not to be stirred even by her sweet prayers.

"Yes, do, Richard!" said Hermione, turning to him with a total change of manner; all her anger gone, her rigidity melted into tenderness, her coldness into yearning, her opposition into beseeching. "You will make me happier than I have ever been in my life, darling, if you will only come with us to-day or to-morrow. Richard, dear, dear husband, do come with me, if only for this once and never again—but for this once! Do, darling!"

She left her place at the table and went over to him, taking one hand in hers while she laid her arm round his neck and bent down to look the better into his face. Not once since Mr. Lascelles had come into the parish,

nor for long before, had she looked like this; not once
turned back so thoroughly to the tender lovingness of
the old, old days.

"My wife," he said fondly, "for your dear heart I
would do much—you know that too well for me to need to
say so—but do not ask this. You would not have me a
hypocrite? Even to give you pleasure, Hermione, would
you have me false to myself?"

"No, no; not a hypocrite," she said. "But come
with me to the church to-day or to-morrow."

"I could not unless I were a hypocrite," he said.

"You will not do this little thing for me, Richard?
Yes, I am sure you will! Husband darling, do come!"

"Do not ask me, wife; do not look at me like that.
Those dear eyes that have been my happiness, my very
life—do not look that prayer through them! Ask me
for anything else, my darling, but not for this one thing
in which my self-respect is bound up—my loyalty to my
flag, my loyalty to truth."

"But what a truth!" she said. "And I ask so little
of you!" she went on hurriedly; "only to help us
to-day. We have the service to-morrow. All I want is
that you should come with Virginia and me now, just to
see the decorations; only to see them, Richard. You

need not stay; but come with us! You see Ringrove is coming."

"Ringrove acts according to his conscience, so must I according to mine," he answered gently.

"If I could but induce you to come!" she said again, tears starting to her eyes. She raised the hand in hers to her lips and kissed it passionately. "Come with me, Richard!" she cried again; "come with me to church! Oh, if you would only yield!"

Neither he nor she herself knew what dim unspoken fear, what dumb thought inspired the passion, the fever, the yearning with which she spoke. It was all so much the more pain to the heart of the man who loved her, but who had cast his conscience and self-respect on the other side. He had to choose between the two—between Hermione and the truth, love or manhood.

"Blessed, good Hermione!" he said, taking her to him; "I would that you had asked me what I could do! This is not possible, my life; anything but this."

She turned away with a sob, let his hand fall out of hers, and drew herself from his arms. Then, swift as lightning, her mood changed. She looked back at him over her shoulder.

"Never forget," she said in a strange voice, "that I

once prayed you, Richard, to be with me in my new life. Whatever happens, never forget this."

She went back to her place, and a silence, frozen and dead, fell over them all. Ringrove was the first to break it.

" I will do duty for you," he said to Richard awkwardly. " I will go to the church as your representative."

" Thank you," said Richard abstractedly; " take care of my dear ones, and do not let Virginia over-exert herself. My wife will take care of herself for my sake," he said, looking at her tenderly. Hermione did not answer, save to say to Virginia hurriedly :—

" Come, my dear, it is time for us to be going."

" Oh, papa, how I wish you had ! " said Virginia, her eyes wet with tears because of his obduracy, as she went up to him to wish him good-bye ; while Hermione left the room without speaking to or looking at him ; not flouncing, not tragic, nothing but simply cold and as if a death had fallen between them.

When she came down she was flushed and excited, and with a certain reckless kind of air and manner that even the servants noticed as unlike herself. She kept so far terms with appearances as to nod a careless good-bye to her husband, who was standing in the hall waiting to put her into the carriage, but she did not look at him; she was buttoning her gloves. Her heart was sore against him, feeling as she did that she had asked him to help her in a moment of peril, to shield her against herself, and that he had refused. Now she might go headlong where and how she would. She was free from blame; and on his head be it. But nothing of all this was clear to Richard; nothing indeed was clear anyhow as he sat by the table in his study, his head resting on his hand; neither reading nor noting, neither examining nor testing; too much disturbed for philosophy to help him, too much at sea for science to enlighten him.

CHAPTER X.

THE HARVEST FESTIVAL.

NEVER in Crossholme within the memory of man had there been such a festival as this Harvest Thanksgiving, which Mr. Lascelles had arranged and the ladies of the place had carried out according to his ideas. And never had the old church looked as it looked to-day. It was like a bower of greenery interspersed with fruits and flowers and miniature sheaves of corn and barley, and was true fairyland to the women and children—a seductive illustration, as Mr. Lascelles wished that it should be, of the beauty and pleasure to be found in the way of religion as the Church directs. For religion without the Church was, according to him, only climbing over the wall like so many thieves and robbers; and the Master of the Orchard would give no sacks full of fruit to such bold breakers of the law. If the people wanted material beauty as well as spiritual safety and eternal life they must come to him as the dispenser and interpreter of it all; and to-day was an earnest of, a kind of preface to, the real thing behind.

And truly the old place had been made fair enough
to the eye.   The dirty whitewash of the finely modelled
freestone pillars was hidden by twisted wreaths of laurel
and ivy ; the reading-desk and pulpit, the pew-tops and
altar-rails, the line of the noble Norman arches—all were
marked out by borderings of laurel and laurustinus mixed
with scarlet berries and snow-white flowers.   The altar
was like a conservatory, heaped up with pyramids of
hothouse fruits and greenhouse plants ; and the bare
walls of the chancel were covered by a trellis-work of ivy
with floral ornaments of crosses and crowns, trefoils,
triangles, and doves among the interspaces. A magnificent
cross of gardenias on a ground of scarlet geraniums formed
the centrepiece.   It was Hermione's own work and her
special gift ; and it had cost Jacob Ellis not a few angry
tears and a volley of bad words for the ruthless destruction of his best blooms which it had entailed.   It had
cost Theresa Molyneux also many tears.   She had
petitioned so earnestly for this place of honour ! She
would have spent pounds and pounds for the most
splendid flowers that could be bought if the vicar would
but have allowed her to be so distinguished ; and when
he had refused, saying that Mrs. Fullerton had already
petitioned and been accepted, she had wept with more

passion and despair than the occasion of itself seemed to warrant. It had been one more lifting of the veil to the man who had already divined what lay within; and though he was sorry to see her suffer, her suffering only confirmed him the more in his intention of asking Hermione to supply this grand central ornament as the public expression of her dutiful affection, instead of allowing Theresa to confess therein her passionate desires. To her, however, he gave the two secondary designs—the three triangles interlaced and the trefoil which flanked the central cross, and which, made as they were of blue salvias, early yellow chrysanthemums and purple dahlias, completed the chord of colour.

Already the walls of the church had been enlivened by boldly illuminated texts which to-day were framed in leaves; and from the capitals of the pillars floated banners of ecclesiastical meaning which helped to give a still richer flood of colour. Lights were on the altar, which it would have been worse than bad manners to have called the communion table as in the old days of darkness; and the musty smell of dust and dead air so familiar to the congregation, had given place to the fragrance of nature mixed with the lingering scent of incense. It was a transformation in truth, complete in all its parts ; and the ladies had worked well and deserved the praise that was given to them.

Everyone was excited and almost everyone enjoyed the show, though some sturdy old Protestants shook their grizzled heads at the patent Popery of it all. Still, that did not prevent their taking their fill of the pleasure which the Church spread before them so liberally as the lure that should bring them over to attendance at her services and acceptance of her doctrines as well as of her decrees. It relieved their consciences to shake their sapient old heads and grumble behind their bandana neckerchiefs ; but it gratified their senses to join in the crowd and gape and sniff with the rest. And after all, the church was their own; and a bonny sight is always a bonny sight when the cost of it does not come out of one's own pocket,

Presently the harmonium sounded a few opening chords with a bold vibrating touch. No frightened schoolmistress was the performer to-day, but the High Church organ-builder who had come down to take the dimensions of the gallery where the magnificent instrument was to stand when the restorations should be completed. The congregation rose, led by the ladies as the fuglemen who knew their lesson and gave the note of

direction ; and then came in the procession of choristers
and clergy, closed by Mr. Lascelles in shining white satin
vestments, embroidered in gold and many-coloured silks,
as the culminating point of interest. He was preceded
by several strange " priests " and " brothers," in vestments
of various symbolic meanings, who had poured in from
London to give greater dignity to this, the first stately
festival in his Crossholme kingdom ; immediately behind
him, his eyes bent on the ground, came Cuthbert Molyneux, solemnly swinging an incense-burner as if he believed in the lurking demons who were to be put to flight
by means of its scented fumes ; while before the strange
priests and brothers, and heading all, marched the choir
in white surplices over red, carrying candles, crosses, a
banner or two, and the crucifix as the unmistakable sign
of the party to which they belonged. Some of the lads
rather spoilt the solemnity of the show; for, not yet broken
into due decorum, they nudged each other slily and
giggled and blushed like girls when they caught the eyes
of their mothers and sisters fixed with pride and exultation on them as they paraded the church round the side
aisles and up the nave.

The men of the village looked at each other doubt-
fully. This kind of thing was new to them and they did

not approve of it. But as it was not Sunday they let the banners and the crosses and candles pass as part of the raree-show. It was a kind of religious play-acting to them; and being a work-a-day matter made all the difference. Had it been Sunday, now, they said to each other, some by look and some in whispers, it would have been a crying shame and a burning sin, and nothing short of profanation and Sabbath-breaking; but week-day mountebanks are lawful, and their foolishness is not to be too gravely considered. All the same they thought it taking liberties with the Constitution, the Church as by Law established, the village and the old building itself; and each Tom and Bill wished that some other Tom or Bill would have the boldness to speak to the vicar and give him the mind of the place; while all shirked the task for themselves. Mr. Lascelles was not an easy man to deal with, as they had already found; and it is ill work plucking nettles with bare hands.

This was the general feeling of the benighted commonalty; but the ladies who had worked the banners and become familiarized with the vestments—the stole was Hermione's own work; every stitch put in, as she believed, purely for love of religion and Church observances—the ladies who had made the wreaths and crosses and all the

mystic emblems, were delighted with the results, and congratulated themselves warmly on their good fortune in
possessing such a vicar as Mr. Lascelles.

How grand he looked in his beautiful new vestments
symbolizing rejoicing and gladness !—how saintly, how
divine, and how handsome !   More than one heart beat
fast as he passed with his slow and stately step, the very
ideal of a well-born, well-bred High Priest, the incarnation
of godly functions and goodly manhood !   Theresa,
flushed and feverish with excitement, hysterical for want
of sleep and insufficient food, felt as if an archangel were
passing by when she heard his measured tread, and
caught the mellow notes of his well-trained voice chanting
the processional hymn; and when he ascended the altar
steps and stood there with his arms outstretched in the
form of a cross, for a moment she was faint and dizzy
with the passionate ecstasy that swelled her heart and
drew the mist across her eyes like a veil—that ecstasy
which made her realize the supreme bliss of a soul
possessed by the Divine.

The burning love that shone in her large bright eyes,
her rapt look of personal adoration, startled Mr. Lascelles
himself, used as he was to the passionate love of women
disguised as religious fervour—to the personal adoration

of so many before her, whom, like her, he had spiritually
seduced for the good of the Church. It discomposed him
for the moment. It was flattering, truly, and marked her
as his own possession—and the possession of the Church
through him ; but it was also a little terrible ; and he felt
for the moment rather the peril of her devotion than the
glory of her conversion. He must manage her carefully,
else there would be trouble, and though he could meet
them boldly enough if they came, he was naturally
anxious to avoid all such scandals.

Then he looked at Hermione's face—animated more
than usual—with a certain reckless air in the pose of
her head—affectionate and even something more, as she
stole one of her shy girlish glances at him ; but it had
not in it the possibilities of danger from excess that were
in Theresa's. The one was an instrument which would
yield to his touch when he chose to awaken its response,
and be passive and uncomplaining when he saw fit to
leave it mute. The other would respond—yes, without
question respond ! but the strength of the echo might
break it to pieces, and the wail of those rent chords
might sound too far and wide for the dignity of his office
or the honour of the Church. Yes, Hermione was the
safer of the two, as well as the more profitable both

socially and pecuniarily; but Theresa was the better subject for vivisection—to be conducted with caution and his hands well protected.

All this flashed in one formless thought through his mind as he stood before the altar in the attitude of a High Priest, symbolizing the cross and blessing the people, while Theresa knew the supreme bliss of spiritual ecstasy—that ecstasy which though spiritual is also sensuous; and Hermione, with darkened eyes, thought what a charming thing it was to be religious, and how happy she was in her new life! For the moment Richard, her late trouble with him and her marriage, altogether had ceased to exist, and she was now simply one of Mr. Lascelles' congregation—and the favourite member.

Perhaps Virginia was really the happiest of all. She was not quite so pale as usual, and her gentle face had even more of that tender peace which had come into it since she had known Sister Agnes, as she fixed her eyes on the white cross above the altar and prayed to Mother Mary and Our Lord to make her worthy of her privileges. And ah! what a treasure of pure love was in it as she looked over to Sister Agnes in her nunlike dress standing in voluntary

humility by the pillar in the free seats, and said an
Ave as her act of thanksgiving for the gift of her
spiritual mother.   Then she looked at Ringrove, who
was looking at her, and her eyes shone if her lips
were still—glad, grateful, as she was that she had been
able to bring him here, according to the command laid
on her by the Sister.

That look was poor Ringrove's reward for the
violence which he had done to his truest self in
coming here to-day simply to please her; and, being
in love, it made him think :—

"Perhaps after all such women as these are right.
Perhaps they do see more clearly than we coarser and less
pure men, and we might do worse than listen to them !"

It was a concession to have got so far as this ; what
if Virginia should care to lead him to the end?

Aunt Catherine near Sister Agnes, also ostentatiously
in the free seats, was mysterious and beatified but
fluttered and half coy to-day.   The ladies had all come
in their brightest dresses to do honour to a festival
which was in its intention joyful and a thanksgiving ;
and Aunt Catherine was in white, with a strangely
bridal character about her veil and bonnet that looked
odd enough on a rosy-cheeked, apple-faced, round

little dumpling of a woman past fifty as she was. But she had dreamed last night of certain heavenly espousals by which her imagination had been more awakened than usual—and it was never very drowsy; and thinking a ghostly bridegroom better than none at all, and a marriage made in a dream a witness of sealing here which shall be proclaimed and solemnized hereafter, she had come in what she meant should express bridal array; and the meaning of which she would explain to Sister Agnes and Superior when mass was over.

For the rest, pretty Beatrice and her younger sisters were here, shame to say, in part as at a show; not having reached that state of ecclesiastical grace when the Church is the same as God, and a week-day service, with decorations like a fair, as sacred as the Sunday prayers without. She glanced often at Ringrove Hardisty; her brown eyes full of mild surprise to see him standing there, tall and superior-looking, in his pew. For she was an unconverted kind of creature ; and, though thoroughly good and gentle and whole-some, had not in her the makings of a zealot—besides having no great admiration for the man who was now the great god Zeus of Crossholme. Ringrove had been always her ideal of what a strong good man should

be ; and especially had she taken delight in his quiet
resistance to the new vicar. And now he was here in
church on a week-day, and assisting at a service that
was just a Roman Catholic mass and nothing else !
How odd it was, and how strange these contradictions
were ! And how strange too were these differences of
feeling ! Here was Bee Nesbitt sorrowing secretly over
her friend's weakness, while Virginia's soul was elate
with holy joy to think that this pleasant, good-tempered,
honest-hearted sinner, known since her childhood and
liked always if never loved, was so far on the road to
salvation that he might one day be looked for among the
saved—turned into a new path by the means of a
handful of incense and a few barrow-loads of flowers !
It was a very little matter on which to build up hope
or fashion fear ; but life is made up of small touches—
and Ringrove was in love; and when men are in love
there is no miracle that may not be expected, no transformation that may not be wrought.

Even Mr. Lascelles allowed himself to draw bigger
conclusions than the premiss warranted. As he said to
Cuthbert Molyneux in the sacristy—there was no vestry
now-a-days—Virginia Fullerton's influence was evidently
blessed. She had brought Mr. Hardisty to the service

to-day, as she had brought him yesterday to assist in the preparations; and, tainted as he notoriously was by the diabolical principles professed by Mr. Fullerton, it was an immense deal to have accomplished. What a gain it would be to the Church should he be won over by the means of this dear young saint, this sweet child of grace and natural piety united!

To which Cuthbert had assented warmly, so far as Virginia was concerned—but in the matter of Ringrove's possible salvation, somewhat tamely. He wondered at the time why he was not able to feel more Christian and fraternal exultation at the possible gathering-in of a notorious outsider like Ringrove. It was not like him not to hail the probable salvation of a now lost brother with effusive sympathy; yet, he would rather that Superior himself, or say his own Aunt Catherine, had been that vessel of grace by whose influence the master of Monks-hall had been won. He was not in love with Virginia ; not in the least, as wholesome-minded men count love ; but he was glad to be the only male sheep in the flock which held her as its most precious lamb; and he dreaded the introduction of another masculine saint, especially one so self-assertive and strong as Ringrove Hardisty. He was a good young man ; a very good young man indeed ; but he had rather mistaken his vocation in being a man at all, and if he had some of the virtues of women, he had many of their faults and not a few of their foibles.

But now the procession and the processional hymn were ended ; the Wicked Man and the opening exhortation had been intoned in a high-pitched key by one of the strange priests ; and then the ladies dropped on their knees in the abrupt automatic manner practised by this school, which makes manner of as much account as matter, and holds it for testimony when human beings are enabled to make themselves look like marionettes jerked by a string. Virginia knelt close behind her mother in their big pew, which was soon to be cut down into an open seat in conformity with the rest. Theresa, her burning hands clasped nervously together, repeated the clauses of the Confession, while the inevitable reaction from that moment of ecstasy having set in, the hot tears of what she thought was penitence and Mr. Lascelles knew to be hysteria, streamed down her face ; and the service went on in great volumes of voice and music such as they had never heard at Crossholme before, and did not know what to make of now when they did hear.

Still it was fine and heartsome. Even those most hostile could not deny the grand effect of it all, while those most committed were enraptured; and of the *tertium quid*, halting between two opinions, some were won over by the brave show and thought that there must be something in it all, and some were terrified at the papistry which now seemed to have thrown off its disguise, and would never stop until it had got its foot on their necks, and made them slaves without a voice in the disposition of their own souls.

And then, in its right place in the service, Mr. Lascelles, in his surplice tied round the waist with a cord, and with a small cap or berretta on his head, went into the pulpit, and after his usual formula, " In the name of—" crossing himself rapidly as he spoke, abruptly began his textless sermon of thanksgiving.

No pains of hell, nor penalties for sin, informed the vicar's discourse to-day. It was all jubilant, hopeful, inspiriting. It spoke much of the gratitude which we owe to the Divine Father who gives us all these good things, and who leads us so gently through the thorny ways and guides us safely over the burning ploughshares; who cares for us as His children and does not allow a hair of our heads to fall without His will. It spoke much too of the peace which comes to souls that are reconciled to the Church, and by the power of the Church made free of divine grace and eternal forgiveness ; and it extolled the beneficence of the Creator who had given us grain for our food, fruit for our refreshment, and flowers for our delight. He might have made all these things painful to us, but He made them pleasant instead ; wherefore, praise be to His Name.

He left out of sight the other side of the question— the side which might put forward, as a plea for the rights of man, the elemental fact that, being here, we must live ; and as by the law of our physical constitution we live by eating, we must therefore have something to eat. Also he left out of sight the possibility that the Supreme Intelligence which he assumed to magnify, was degraded by rhapsodies of wonder at necessary consequences of certain conditions—as that the earth should bring forth food when all organic nature has to be fed; or that the Benevolence which he assumed to honour was insulted by rhapsodies of gratitude in that life is not rendered more terrible than it is already to so many of us ; and that, born as we are without our own consent into a world of suffering and death, and set in the midst of circumstances which we have not shaped and cannot control, we are not punished yet more severely than we are for the sinless ignorance of our forefathers and the innocent helplessness of ourselves. Nothing of all this was so much as hinted at; and save Ringrove Hardisty, who did not pay much attention to what was being said at all, there was no one in the congregation acute enough to form these thoughts in his own mind, still less to give them utterance. So Mr. Lascelles had it all his own way, and his sermon brought comfort to some and conviction to others, and seemed to all a rational and faithful method of stating the main facts of human life.

Then the vicar ended as abruptly as he had begun; his last words being an exhortation to the people to show themselves worthy of their privileges and grateful for their blessings, by following the commands of the Church in all things :—beginning with punctual attendance at daily matins, and, for such as were fitted to receive the grace, reverent attendance at weekly Early Celebration. Then the rest of the service went on; and the offertory was the largest ever made at Crossholme.

CHAPTER XI.

IN THE SACRISTY.

WHEN the service was over Mr. Lascelles gave notice
that any of his parishioners who wished to speak to him—
about their souls—would find him in the sacristy for an
hour from that time, or for so much longer as he might
be wanted. This too was a fitting occasion for the thin
end, and he wished to gently insinuate it before he
drove home the wedge with what he meant should prove
to be irresistible force. He knew human nature so well!
and he knew that when the senses have been stirred, as
now, hearts are softened, consciences are awakened, and
the reason is sent to sleep with fear, caution, and distrust.
And as he intended to establish confession as a practice
of faith and duty, he thought he might as well begin
with the alphabet to-day.

He had already told Hermione and the Churchlands
family what he intended to do, so far as receiving his
parishioners in the sacristy after service went; but he
did not say even to them that he intended this as the

beginning of weekly confession. He had merely asked
Theresa to come in to him when service should be
over ; and to Hermione he had said, with friendly
meaning and a graceful kind of partiality:—

" Do you come the last of all, dear Mrs. Fullerton.
Wait until the rest have gone and then come in."

The prospect of this private conference had a little
disturbed the devotions of both these ladies. Perhaps it
would be better to say, it had heightened their fervour
but distorted the direction. The vicar and the Almighty
were getting sadly entangled in their minds, the one for
love and the other for authority, and to obey Mr.
Lascelles was to both perilously synonymous with obeying God; which was exactly the state of mind that he
wished to produce.

The first however to go into the quondam vestry,
and present sacristy, was Adam Bell, the sharp, keen-
witted chandler of the village. He went, he said, in
great mental distress and some perplexity. He could
not rest, he continued, drawing down the corners of his
mouth like a man who has a secret grief which he is
about to disclose, until he had discharged his conscience and told the vicar how things were going in
the parish ;—also, until he had confessed manfully his

own share of the blame in having gone to hear one
whose teaching was so outlandish and full of harm.   He
then gave a clever but inexact account of Mr. Fullerton's lecture the night before last ; which he translated
as an invitation to men to take life easy and make the
best of the sunshine when it comes, and not bother
themselves with the idea that this is wrong and that disallowed by God, for there is no such thing as right or
wrong anyway, and God is only a name put forth by
the priests to frighten folk into submission.   And then
he professed himself uneasy in his mind, and indeed
he might say penitent, for having listened to such
blasphemy.   So long as Mr. Fullerton had confined himself to telling them a few plain facts about stones and
gases, bones and crystals, he said, he had been glad to
listen to him and learn from him ; but when he touched
sacred things, then he, Adam Bell, parted company with
him, and would go no more to hear him.

The keen eyes glancing here and there restlessly,
furtively, never looking straight into the face that looked
straight enough at him, told their own miserable tale,
and condemned the would-be penitent as a renegade, as
he had been a spy from the beginning.   Mr. Lascelles,
no longer looking down with that affected humility, that

artificial reticence which was one of his professional
tricks, but fixing his eyes boldly on the mean and crafty
face before him, took the measure of the man who thus
offered himself for his service, and appraised him at his
true value. The vicar was not one to be easily deceived,
however smooth in speech and careful he might be not
to show distrust. Men whose object in life is to use
others and to make all things subserve a settled plan,
seldom are easily taken in. But Adam Bell's treachery
and ratting pleased him as a sign of what he at least
thought of the way in which things were going, and what
was to be the dominant rule of the parish. It was a
straw; but straws are good indicators of the quarter
whence the wind blows; and the Crossholme chandler
served this turn as well as any other.

He showed nothing however of the contempt that
he felt; but thanking Adam gravely for his information,
said a few words of priestly exhortation, perhaps more
friendly than priestly, and then ended the interview a
little abruptly. The farce was too transparent to need
lengthening out; and Mr. Lascelles, though he did not
disdain to use his office as a lever, did not like to degrade
it by humbug that was confessed and palpable—besides
having the disdain of the gentleman for the trickiness of

a cur. He could do dishonourable things on his own
account when need be, but he was always the gentleman even when he did; he was right then to disdain
the trickiness of a cur !

When Adam Bell went, Aunt Catherine came in with
the story of her dream; wanting dear Superior to confirm
her in her belief that it was a true vision—an actual
spiritual occurrence—and that henceforth she might look
upon herself as Chosen and a bride. But Mr. Lascelles
would not go all the way with her.

" Before confession and absolution?" he demurred ;
"while still so young in the practices of the Church?—
not having attained the counsels of perfection?   I should
be inclined, dear Miss Molyneux, to accept it rather as a
picture of the possible future when you shall have taken
still higher rank in the world of grace, and have learnt
more thoroughly the mind of the Church and how to
obey her ordinances."

It was a hard blow to the poor little woman. Religion
had been to her a very charming and a very flattering
drama wherein she had her part to play, with saints and
angels and Divine personages all round for her comrades.
She had no idea of creeping painfully up steep places
and walking humbly on the lower levels. She held to

sudden conversions and souls snatched up, like so many Elijahs, straight from earth to heaven, without the necessity of middle terms of striving and discipline. She cried a good deal when Mr. Lascelles blew down her house of holy cards, and made her understand that she was still in the dark ages of comparative ignorance, and still had much to do and far to go before she should be accepted as she believed she had already been.

But tears or not, it was what he had to teach and she to learn. For though his object was to excite and warm the imaginations and affections of his people to the wildest extremes, they must all be under discipline —all be under the guidance and control of the Church, without whose permission there could be no visions or spiritual marriages, no dreaming of divine dreams or spiritual camping out in high latitudes. Aunt Catherine had gone too fast. She must be checked; taught the duty of humility and obedience; and sent to the bottom of the class, with hope only, not fulfilment.

"Learn the will of God through the Church; practise faithfully your duties, dear Miss Molyneux; and what has been only a vision now will become a reality. But you have something to learn yet, and something to do; and one of the first necessities for such grace as your loving soul desires is confession—with priestly absolution to follow. There are many, many more essentials ;—works of corporal mercy to perform ; works of spiritual mercy to fulfil ; fasting, abstinence, and absolute obedience ; counsels of perfection to attain. Heaven is not won by a *coup de main*, dear lady, and the strait gate which leads to the narrow way is not to be carried by assault. I am sorry to distress you, but my duty as your priest bids me destroy your hope."

"I will obey you in all things," sobbed poor Aunt Catherine in her humiliation. "Nothing will be too hard for me to do if I can but make my dream of last night true. Oh, it was so good to feel safe and accepted !"

"Take it as a prevision—a state to be attained after diligent endeavour, and something for which to live and strive," said Mr. Lascelles.

And Aunt Catherine, with a crushed mien and a sore heart, said "Thank you" gratefully, and still weeping left the vestry, a poorer woman by many degrees than when she entered.

She was not the only penitential Niobe whom Mr. Lascelles received in his sacristy this day. Theresa, broken with hysterical emotion, in the depths of

spiritual despair—because of what?—her realization of
sin, she thought to herself, poor innocent girl of twenty-
two ; she, who had never done harm to human being, nor
even come to the knowledge of the forces which stirred
her !—feeling lost and abandoned by God and all good
angels, and only yearning to be taken into the arms of
some strong Saviour who should guard her from herself and from evil alike—poured out her flood of self-
accusation, of self-betrayal, as she knelt at the vicar's
feet and wept out the passion of her love disguised as
sorrow for her soul's sin.

He understood it all. He was forty years of age, and
he had not made the study of the human heart, and
above all of the female heart, his chief care in vain.
He read her like an open book, as he had read some
others before now; and smiled at the poor little transparent subterfuge with which she hid the truth from
herself and turned it full to the light for him. Here
was no need of grave admonition to curb the too
ambitious flight of a vain and somewhat silly spirit ;
here were needed precious balms that should heal, not
caustic that would eat out the proud flesh starting so
mischievously to the surface. But they must be balms
administered gently and sparingly ; balms that should

soothe but not nourish—that should still keep the sight enchanted as with the old-time dwellers in fairy-land, but not give the power of showing to the world that she had the right to see and the claim to speak.

"God is calling you, my child," he said gently. "In your tears He is speaking to you; in your yearning, your despair, you are feeling for Him. He will not abandon you; trust to me, your pastor, me, sent to be your guide and leader. Lean on me, child, and I will carry you to the foot of His throne, to tne presence and the knowledge of Eternal Life. The Church can oo all things, and the priest has power to absolve, to teach, and to save."

"Can I ever be saved, I who am so wicked?" cried Theresa, burying her face in her hands. "I am so full of sin, so abominable altogether."

The faintest smile crossed the vicar's thin lips.

"If you repent and turn away from your wickedness," he said gravely. "Grace is never denied the penitent and faithful."

She lifted her tear-stained agonized face to the light, her large dark feverish eyes looking full into his.

"Can I ever be assured of salvation?" she cried; "shall I ever know the feeling of acceptance?"

He took both her hands in one of his, and with the other smoothed her hair.

"Trust me," he said with grave tenderness; "I will be your pastor in the secret and divine sense, as well as openly by my office. You shall be my soul's care, my child in the Church, my spiritual beloved. Will you not trust me, child, your director and father appointed by the Church to lead you?"

The touch of his long, white, scented hand seemed to act as a charm on her ; the word "beloved" sank down like sweetest music into her soul, but music that calmed while it inspired her. The flush did not fade from her cheeks nor the feverish brightness from her eyes, but her tears no longer flowed, and the poor parched lips, pinched and strained before, relaxed into a smile like that of a child in sleep. She looked so tender, so confiding, so innocently impassioned, so slight of frame, so frail of health—there was something in her that was so appealing, so eloquent of suffering and sincerity and love—that the vicar might have been forgiven had he forgotten his priesthood and remembered only his humanity and that marriage is an honourable estate. But he did not. What she felt he knew well enough. He had seen it too often before not to understand

every sign of it now; and he meant to make his account
of it now as he had done before; but he himself was
neither moved nor warmed, neither disordered nor
elated. He was only the vivisector studying phenomena
and interpreting symptoms; only the priest binding his
victim to the horns of the altar; the fisher of men haul-
ing in his net with his prize.

The moment had come when he could clinch all this
excitement, and with one blow make it serviceable to
his purpose. In a grave and tender but eminently
priestly manner he told her what he wished her to do,
and framed her answers of confession to his questions of
inquisition. Oh, how sweet it was to be thus questioned
by him! to bare her secret soul before him! to kneel
there at his feet and lay her innermost being without
veil or disguise in his hands! to give him that greatest
gift which a woman has to bestow—the gift of her
spiritual freedom, her self-respect, her reticence, her
reserve! There was no evil deed done of which she
had to make shameful confession, as there was no hostile
influence at home or in her own heart which he must
set himself to overcome. It was only her soul that she
had to declare—only her selfhood that she had to yield
into his keeping. He questioned her of her waking

thoughts and nightly dreams ; he probed now the yearning and now the suffering, to which she gave fancy names
that disguised the truth from herself but not from him.
When she looked up with her feverishly bright eyes, and
said how ardently she longed to realize Christ and feel
Him always with her, he stooped his head low to hers
and whispered a few words which seemed to give her all
she wanted ; and when she spoke of her spiritual darkness, her loneliness by reason of her consciousness of
sin, he assured her of the divine companionship because of the divine love that was around her. Then he
gave her absolution, and imposed a few light precious
penances—such as prayers and fastings and observances
to be followed rather for the sake of the good which lies
in acts of obedience than as punishment for her sins.
And then he lifted her gently from the ground and
pressed her to him—paternally.

Her heart was throbbing wildly, her blood was all
on fire, her brain was dizzy with excitement. He was
as calm and cool as in his quietest moments.

" You are very, very precious to me," he said tenderly, but with the same priestly intonation as before.
" You are my child, consecrated to my care."

She clung to him confidingly.

" Thank you," she said simply.

He stooped his head and kissed her on the forehead.
Were not the elect sealed there ?

" Now you know," he said, " how dear you are to me—
Theresa."

It was the first time that he had called her by her
name; and had anything been wanting to complete her
deep sense of blessedness it would have been found in
the sweet and holy familiarity of this splendid high-priest
in the Church of Christ.

" And now you must be good, my child, and show
me that you deserve my love, my pastoral care ; that
you profit by my ministrations, and will not falsify the
hope of my heart.   We must have no more tears, no
more sorrow or hesitation.   Your pride has been broken
down, and your heart turned to God once and for all
time ; now, cheerfully and hopefully, follow on the way
which the Church marks out, as one of her dearest and
most dutiful daughters.   Doubt of acceptance, so godly
in the beginning—so necessary until you receive grace
and pardon by absolution—may become doubt of that
grace—disbelief in that pardon; which is a tempting of
the devil and to be resisted as much as overweening
pride.   Do you understand me, Theresa ?"

He said these last words gently, caressing her with his hand.

"Yes," said Theresa, in a low voice.

To stand there encircled by those holy arms, resting on that divine breast, was enough for her, so far. She was calmed, consoled, soothed. He had given her the assurance of divine acceptance; why then should she doubt or weep? Was not he her friend? Was not God her Saviour? This harvest festival would stand for ever in her mind as the epoch whence she should date her personal happiness and spiritual peace; and she must for ever connect this beloved priest with her hopes of salvation and her assurance of acceptance.

She lifted her face to him, softened and less disordered than when she had entered. His kiss had been both the seal of her blessedness and the charter of her acceptance. It had transformed her from Magdalen the sinner to Magdalen the saint; but whether sinner or saint, Magdalen the woman who loved. And when, to study the effect for a second time, the vicar pressed her to him as tenderly as before, and again laid his cold thin lips on her forehead, she felt as if she had been taken bodily into heaven, where some supreme archangel had received her.

All life had a different significance for her, all human feeling other issues than she had ever known before, as she left the sacristy and turned into the church still redolent and glowing with the offerings of the time. How cold and tame and meaningless all her other loves had been, she thought, compared to this her love for the Church and religion! She cast herself on her knees before the altar and prayed with a very passion of yearning, a very ecstasy of thanksgiving, that seemed to draw her soul away from her body and fill it with divine light and life. Heaven seemed to open to her—the majesty and mystery of the Divine were revealed as in a painted picture above the altar. With eyes strained upward, hands clasped and body rigid, she realized one of the ecstatic visions of her namesake, Saint Theresa; and when the sacristan, who was once the clerk, came to do something with the flowers, he found young Miss almost gone; as he told his wife in a voice of awe; and if so be as Madam Fullerton had not been closeted with the vicar, he would have called him out to help; he did not add—to look at his own sorry work.

And now there was Hermione with whom Mr. Lascelles had to deal. She was both more manageable and less dangerous than Theresa—more profitable, too;

though he hoped to make the Churchlands family profitable enough to the cause before he had done with
them; but she had to be handled in a different manner
from that which best suited the girl. It was more subtle
play with her, and an enemy to be fought through her;—
another set of feelings altogether to be manipulated, and
love to be craftily gained for ulterior ends, not love
already gained to be soothed for fear of danger. What
a sense of power all these women gave him! How weak
they were! how contemptible, and yet how interesting!

Mr. Lascelles was gracious, courteous, unexcited,
but tenderly alive to the grace of this visit and the
social importance as well as the personal charm of the
visitor—as much the gentleman as the priest—when
Mrs. Fullerton came in, as he had desired, the last of all.
It was late now; long past the usual luncheon-time at
the Abbey—that house of unbroken regularity and
monotonous sameness of habit—but Mr. Lascelles was glad
that again to-day the antagonism between himself and
her husband should be shown clearly, and that Richard
should see for himself which was the stronger of the two.

At first Hermione, still in her wilful, reckless mood,
had also been glad to put this little affront on her
husband. He deserved punishment at her hands and

she was not sorry to humiliate him—so far—and to show
him that she cared no more for him than he for her; and
that if he did not think it worth while to strain a point
for her pleasure, neither would she inconvenience herself
for his.   But as time wore on she began to relent.   Opposition, like independence, was so new to her, so
foreign to her nature—and she had loved Richard so
much, and she once believed that he had loved her also
so much, before he had become a philosopher and a
sceptic!   She did not want to hurt him really ; and she
knew that this break in the home habits, for such reasons
as she had to give, would hurt him.   Besides, she was
getting hungry for her own part ; and she was annoyed
that Theresa Molyneux had stayed so long with the
vicar.   It was not nice, she thought; and she wondered
at Superior—whom however, being annoyed, she called
mentally Mr. Lascelles—for allowing this long interview
which was a kind of slight on her own claims.   So that
altogether she had somewhat veered in her feelings since
the benediction, and came in looking a little sulky and
undeniably dignified.   At a glance Mr. Lascelles took
in the change, and understood the ruffled state of her
feeling for him, which of course meant corresponding
smoothness towards her husband.

"I am so sorry that you have had to wait so long," he said with his best breeding, placing her in a chair opposite to him.

No kneeling penitent pouring out her love as confession of sin was this fair creature—as yet—but just a lady of the parish consulting him, the vicar, on parochial matters.

"It is very late. I do not know what they will say at home," said Hermione gravely.

"I will not keep you long, but indeed I must have a word with you to-day," said Mr. Lascelles more gravely, looking at her intently.

She looked up half frightened at his air and manner. What was amiss? What had he to say that called forth a tone so full of menaced danger?

"I am afraid that I shall have to mar the per-fectness of this blessed day to you, Mrs. Fullerton," he began; "but the cross laid on us to bear must be carried at all costs, and there is no happiness in a false peace."

"What has happened?" she asked, turning pale.

"More than I dare trust myself to speak of, save in generals," he answered. "But I must tell you so much: that your husband's lectures, dear Mrs.

Fullerton, are simply the scandal and the sin of the parish."

"I know how dreadful his opinions are!" she cried nervously. "But I can do nothing! I am helpless to prevent them! He will not listen to me—I have no influence over him, and he will go his own way, whatever I may say!"

Mr. Lascelles, still looking at her narrowly, thought to himself: "How much will she bear?"—he must feel his way cautiously, if boldly.

"He is the curse of the place," he said solemnly. "He is the direct leader of souls to hell."

Hermione shuddered.

"It is dreadful," she said helplessly. "It breaks my heart, and always has, to know that he holds such awful opinions; but what can I do?"

"You cannot stop him?" he asked. "If I were to tell you what he said the night before last, I think you would be ready to take almost any steps that I might recommend to check this awful flood of blasphemy and sin which he pours out in that place of yours. To men too ignorant to understand even his few paltry facts in natural science he preaches license to sin—for there is no God and no hereafter and

laughs at all but human law and human knowledge,
ridiculing justice and mercy together—denying God and
Satan in one. It is an awful state of things, Mrs.
Fullerton, and the responsibility rests on you as well
as on him; for, though you are his wife, you are the
owner of the estate."

She did not quite take in his meaning.

Tears gathered into her eyes.

"Yes, I am his wife," she said; "but he is the
master. And though I know how wickedly he thinks
on matters that are dear and sacred to everyone else—
yet he is so good in himself!" she added; her heart
turning back to him as her consciousness of his faithful
love and noble intentions compelled her to defend
him. She acknowledged his blameworthiness; he
was an infidel, a sinner, the denier of all that
she held dear—but "he is so good," was the truth as
well.

"How can you call that good which is in direct
hostility to Christianity and the Church?" said Mr.
Lascelles more sternly than he had ever spoken to
Hermione Fullerton before. "This is indeed preferring
the creature to the Creator—saying to evil, 'Be thou
my good!'"

"I do not think he means to do harm," she said apologetically, frightened at the vicar's manner.

"And he succeeds in doing more—of greater extent and of graver consequences—than any man ever known to me in person," he replied. "Not one of the most infamous men of history—not Voltaire, nor Rousseau, nor Paine—not one of the whole tribe of Judas, crucifying Christ afresh as they did, was a more blasphemous infidel than is your husband, or did more awful mischief to the immortal souls of the men with whom they came in contact."

"What is to be done?" she cried in a despairing voice.

It was hard on her to have the brightness of the day darkened by such a terrible vision, such a fearful parallel; and poor Richard, wicked as he was, had once been so sweet and dear!

Mr. Lascelles, still looking at her, thought again: "Is the time ripe?"

"You are mistress. Your husband is only your agent," he said slowly.

"He is master in reality," she answered. "I have no power."

"You can have it if you will," he said, still watching her.

She sighed. "Things have gone on too long as they are, and I could not change them now even if I wished," she said. "I should like to have some things different from what they are ; and yet—I could not do anything to really hurt him—angry as I am with him !" she added ; her old love for him overmastering her for the moment.

Mr. Lascelles was silent. His nostrils quivered and his thin lips curled, but he put force on himself and said nothing. No ; the time was not yet ripe ; but it would come. As sure as to-morrow's sun would rise it would come, and that Dagon of sin and infidelity would be overthrown. After a time he spoke, quietly and almost monotonously in voice and manner, but with what he wished her to understand as disappointment and sadness.

"In this case you must come out publicly," he said. "You must let it be patent to the world that you do not share your husband's blasphemous enmity to revealed religion—his diabolical hostility to the Church, that ark of man's salvation. You must separate your action from his, and show the world that you are faithful if he has made himself a castaway."

"That is only my duty," said Hermione relieved.

"Tell me how I can best prove to the world that I am a Christian, and I will do it," she added fervently, a little carried out of herself.

"I will tell you," he said in his high-priestly manner. "It is not difficult;—Undertake the restoration of the whole church in your own name. This will do something to neutralize the fearful mischief worked by your husband in the parish and on your own estate."

She gave a little gasp.

"That will be costly," she said.

"About ten thousand pounds," he answered with indifference. "We might get it done for eight, but I think it will come to ten if it is done as I wish."

She looked distressed. She was the most generous woman in the world by nature—and the least conscious of the value of money; but she was startled at the sum named—for her husband's sake not her own.

"I scarcely know if Richard will consent," she said in extreme embarrassment.

"I do not see that his consent is necessary," said Mr. Lascelles, holding his head high. "You are the person to be consulted, not he. You are the Lady of the Manor, the lay rector; you receive the great tithes which ought to belong to the church, and hold the estate which was once the church's property—taken from God for man. It is your affair entirely, and I do not recognize Mr. Fullerton's share in the matter."

"Yes, I know," she said, looking down, embarrassed, ill at ease, set between two fires and burned by both. "But if we cannot really give so much money? When I asked for my allowance a little while ago, Richard said that our income and expenditure exactly met, and stipulated that I should pay my own milliner; so that if there is not money enough, what is to be done?"

"For the sake of God's house and His glory, cannot you make some little personal sacrifice?" asked Mr. Lascelles eagerly;—"put down a carriage?—a horse or two?—a servant here and there?—or, if necessary sell your jewels, your silver? Or, cannot you make your husband close that devil's shop of his, that reading-room built on your own ground and maintained at some cost, as we all know? Say the restoration of the church will be ten thousand pounds;—that is five hundred a year given to the Lord and snatched from the propagation of infidelity. I cannot believe that you will hesitate, Mrs. Fullerton."

The vicar spoke sternly and strongly. It was like a heavy hand laid on the pretty gentle creature's shoulder.

"If only my husband would!" she sighed again, looking up, appealing against his strength in mercy to her weakness.

"Then take back your lapsed rights and deal with your own property according to your own sense of duty," he cried irritated.

She drew back.

"He is my husband," she said with a frightened glance to the door.

"Well! you must use your own discretion—perhaps wifely caresses and cajolings will do what you desire," said Mr. Lascelles with almost brutal contempt: "and if these fail"—he shrugged his shoulders expressively— "one means of grace will be shut off from you and one occasion of testifying! I shall not be the sufferer, nor will the Church," he went on to say with a certain indifference of manner that galled her more than all the rest. "I have asked your co-operation first, as my inclination and the respect due to your position in the parish prompted, but if you cannot or will not!"—he shrugged his shoulders again and beat his finger-tips lightly on the table. "The chancel is your own property, and that you must restore," he continued; "and what else you refuse the Molyneux's will accept. They have asked to be allowed to make liberal restitution to that House of God which their ancestors defrauded and despoiled. And I have promised to give them all that you reject."

"At least the chancel is my own property. They cannot interfere there," said Hermione with a deep flush.

"Of course, I know that; have I not just said so?" he answered unpleasantly. "To restore it in harmony with the rest of the church is not only your duty, but your obligation—your legal obligation," he repeated. "What I wanted was that you should undertake the whole of the church, leaving to us the windows and organ. It would be cheering to me personally if you came forward prominently, unmistakably, as one of my supporters here in this uphill fight. And what joy it would be to my soul to think of your name as handed down in everlasting protest against the sin which else is committed under its sanction and upheld by your fortune— sin which is indelible here and hereafter, and which will be brought against you, as the accomplice, at the Last Great Day!"

She shuddered.

"If only Richard would!" she repeated quivering.

He rose from his chair, and stood towering above her.

" You make your marriage idolatrous," he said sternly.
" Your infidel husband, whom you should spurn from
you as a viper—as a child of hell—stands nearer to you
than your God, than your Saviour. This is not love, it is
idolatry ! " he repeated.

There was nothing of the courtly courteous gentleman about him now. He had risen to the height of his
office and was the inquisitor who probed, the priest who
condemned, not the admiring friend who now flattered
and now consoled, now gently directed and now fervently rewarded. Never in her life before had she been
spoken to as now. She, the petted plaything of her
father, the tenderly adored of her husband—if once passionately and now gravely, yet always tenderly !—she to
be held as it were by a torturer, a master, an executioner! Appalled, terrified, she shrank within herself
at the stern voice, the attitude full of spiritual menace,
the words that passed so terrible a sentence on her.

" Have I no power consigned to me by God?" he
went on to say, speaking more rapidly but no less
severely. " Have I no authority as your priest, your
spiritual director? You know that I have ! You dare
not look up and defy me. And here, in this holy place,
I command you in the name of God to obey me. I

your priest, order you to undertake this work as your
tribute to the Church, your offering to our Lord ! Let
it bring what discord it will into that unblessed house
of yours—that is not my affair, nor should it be yours
in the face of your greater duty. What is mine is to
enforce your obedience; what yours, to give it !"

Hermione sat there paralyzed, overcome with terror
and dismay. It was like some terrible dream—some
awful vision. She did not recognize the man whose
grace and subtle flattery had touched her imagination and
stirred the long-stagnant waters of romance. He was a
new impersonation; but something still more compelling,
still less to be resisted than the former.

She turned away her face sobbing with terror. They
were sobs that had no tears in them, but were just in-
articulate cries of fear. The vestry seemed to grow dark
as night; the radiant earth and help of men to be shut out
from her for ever; God was no longer a loving Father
to be approached with gladness, trust, love, but a stern
and implacable Judge, denouncing and condemning her
by the mouth of this his high-priest. The vicar's form
seemed to dilate to more than human stature, his eyes
to burn into her soul as if they had been flames of fire.
All the foolish sinful thoughts that had ever passed

through her mind, all the foolish sinful things that she had ever done in wilfulness or ignorance, came back on her memory in one great flood of spiritual remorse and shame. She felt as if the man standing there before her could read the whole unsatisfactory story of her life, which terror and exaltation exaggerated into crime, deepened into spiritual apostasy and wickedness that could not be forgiven.

"Have mercy!" she sobbed, shrinking together in her fear.

Did she pray to him or to God? She could not have said which; for at that moment the two were one, and the vicar was God impersonate.

"Kneel!" said Mr. Lascelles in a deep voice, lifting her from the chair as he had lifted Theresa from the ground, but instead of taking her to his arms forcing her to her knees. And scarcely knowing what she did or where she was, the wife of Richard Fullerton, the free-thinker, the pronounced enemy of the Church, the confessed agnostic knowing nothing where others formulate all, knelt at the vicar's feet, and led by him made her first broken pitiful confession.

When she arose from her knees she had promised three things :—one that she would publicly defray at her sole cost the restoration of the church; another that she would obey all the rules of discipline which he, the vicar —her Director now—might enjoin on her—her husband willing or unwilling; and the third that she would confess to him weekly, here in the sacristy, to be directed according to the will of the Church and for the best welfare of her own soul. But this last matter was to be kept as yet a profound secret from every one. In return for all which promises he gave her absolution, and assured her of eternal forgiveness and his own deep sympathy, affection, and esteem.

CHAPTER XII.

DEFEATED.

THE vicar had been some months now at Crossholme, but he had accepted no social invitations of
ceremony; nothing beyond a family dinner at Churchlands when they were quite alone, or a quiet cup of
afternoon tea with other favoured members of his
flock. Invitations to formal dinners had poured in as
matters of course, but all had been refused,—and—notwithstanding the relations existing between the Vicarage
and the Abbey—with as much stiffness there as elsewhere.
Perhaps indeed with more; breaking bread with an
infidel of Richard's uncompromising type not being
much in the line of a man who, whatever else he might
be, was at least as sincere in his faith as he was unscrupulous in his methods of obtaining influence.

He had said this one day with bold disdain when
Hermione had asked him timidly why he would not
come? Of late his disdain had been getting even bolder.
As his power over the wife increased, the thin film of

consideration that he had had for her husband—for policy—grew thinner and thinner; and once he said, speaking generally, that he looked on an infidel as a kind of outlaw, one who had put himself as far beyond the pale of personal courtesies as he was beyond that of the Christian communion, and whom it was lawful to fight with any weapon that might lie handy.

A short time however after the Harvest Festival with its memorable results and unfinished dramas, the vicar said to Hermione pleasantly, that he wished she would ask him to meet General Sir Angus and Lady Maine. Sir Angus had just been appointed commandant to the garrison at Starton; and Lady Maine was his superior officer. "She might make a grand affair of it if she liked," he added still more pleasantly, and in the way of one conferring an obligation. "He would like to meet the Maines first under her roof," he continued, "feeling for her what he did. Others he knew were preparing to make up dinner-parties for this purpose; but would she not take precedence?"

Mr. Lascelles had the oddest way possible of taking little liberties of this kind with his friends. He held his flock as a band whereof he was the head; a little knot of holy communists whose goods he could administer

and whose actions he could command in his quality of
Superior. And acting on these assumptions he said what
from others would have been unwarrantable impertinence
so frankly, so simply, with such a lofty unconsciousness
that he could possibly give offence, such a pleasant faith
in human kindness, so much trust in the loyal docility
of his chosen band, that no one thought of being
offended ;—and women indeed liked his small freedoms ;
received them as spiritual caresses ; and thought themselves favoured in proportion to the extent to which he
carried them. Even had not Hermione begun her life
of absolute submission in confession she would still
have accepted this proposal as a proof of friendship and
goodwill. As things were it was a grace for which she was
bound to feel grateful.

Her face brightened with joy as she said prettily :

"I am so glad—thank you, Superior !" then added
—"I will ask my husband what day will suit him ; and
I will write the notes this evening."

Mr. Lascelles smiled. It was not quite the same
kind of smile as before. That pretty woman's foolish
obedience—idolatrous submission rather ! he thought
angrily—to that infidel husband of hers still so strong
in her, despite his own undeniable influence over her,

always irritated him when shown. It was a delicate thing for a Director, a priest believing in St. Paul, to teach wifely rebellion ; but this obstructive loyalty to an atheist, this habitual deference to a son of perdition, was unrighteous ; and, come what might, it should be broken down.

"You are without exception the most obedient wife it has ever been my lot to meet," he said with that unmistakable touch of sarcasm in the voice by which words of praise are made into sentences of condemnation. "You are the perfection of conjugal submission ! In general the lady of the house manages all these little social matters by herself, without consulting her husband, and often without heeding his convenience. It comes hard sometimes on men who are greatly occupied; but to one like Mr. Fullerton, without engagements or outside duties, it would not much signify. The greater marvel of self-effacing sweetness, the greater perfectness of conjugal submission in you ! "

"I know that I am very weak," said Hermione with a nervous laugh and heightened colour; "but it has grown into a habit. It would seem quite strange were I to arrange anything whatever without first consulting my husband."

" I can understand that, married so young as you were," said Mr. Lascelles, with a certain grand air of liberality and comprehension which he was accustomed to put on when he meant to give a blow; "and yet," smiling, "you have already broken through your habit of deference in one or two things of late. I fancy he has not been consulted on that question of confirmation for our child, of which we spoke yesterday; and I am sure that he understands nothing of the place which you hold with me—and I with you. He does not know that I am your Director and that you are my penitent and precious charge."

"Of course not," said Hermione a little confused. "He knows nothing of my religious life, nor shall he. He would only exasperate me by his infidelity, and make things difficult for Virginia."

"And the free will, under direction, which you have exercised in one thing it would be better on all accounts if you carried into others," said Mr. Lascelles. "Witness that private income which was one of the first matters on which I advised you—and witness the divine peace that has come to you since your reconciliation with God and your acceptance into the living body of the Church."

" Yes," said Hermione in a low voice, her eyes filling with tears.

She did not feel much at peace, but if Superior said she was, she supposed that he was right; still, if she were really so happy as he said, why those ready tears ?

" You see, dear Mrs. Fullerton," he continued, drawing a little nearer to her, and taking her soft small hand in his ; " you have now by your side a daughter—our sweet child—whose mind you have to train in part, and for whose soul you are chiefly responsible. Is it well, think you, for her to see this complete self-effacement of the mother in favour of the father—the mother a believer and the father an infidel? For her sake you ought to show more character and stand out against the tyranny of your husband with more boldness of protest. The effect of things as they are cannot be quite wholesome for her."

Hermione looked down disturbed. She was discontented with her husband—truly—but after all, more superficially than openly, so far at least as things had gone. What they might grow into was another matter. And she was strongly, powerfully fascinated by Mr. Lascelles; displeased with the infidelity of the one and out of sympathy with the main direction of his character,

while led away by the doctrine and authority of the
other. But between displeasure, more vague than positive, and taking such independent action openly as would
lead to pain and trouble at home, was a wide step; and
she did not feel quite strong enough for it, yet. She was
glad to be flattered personally and petted spiritually by
Mr. Lascelles; to confess and be absolved; to complain
and be soothed; to be reminded of her dignities and
condoled with on her undesignated wrongs; to be made
to feel that she was a suffering saint for truth's sake, and
an oppressed wife whose very virtues had been turned
into weapons of offence and causes of humiliation; to
be idealized to herself and set in graceful poses before
a moral mirror. All this was delightful, and gave her
life new colour and her days a new romance. But to
openly affront her husband was not in the programme,
and would only complicate matters. Still, Mr. Lascelles
had a strong will; and she had given him the one hair
which was to be his purchase over all the rest.

He saw her hesitation.

"Forgive me," he said with a rapid change of
manner—a manner that conveyed the impression of
being wounded by her want of trust, and a determination not to cross the boundary line again; to be never

anything more than the priest and ghostly director. His personal friendship was not appreciated, and for the future he would know how to guard himself from rebuff. Reticence was easier to him than undertaking an ungrateful task, and so she should find. "Forgive me. I ought not to take it upon myself to advise you in temporal matters. It is only my deep sympathy with you—my sorrow for the undeserved trials and sufferings of your life—my desire to see your wrongs righted and your noble nature allowed free scope; only my intense admiration and deep affection for one so cruelly circumstanced and so deserving of all homage, that makes me overstep the barriers of conventional restraint. But I will not do it again. It displeases you."

"No, no, indeed not, dear Superior!" said poor Hermione warmly. "I am more grateful to you than I can say for your advice. It is always so good and wise. It seems to me that you are the only sincere friend I have ever had in my life. You are what my brother would have been if I had had one!"

She looked at him with innocent lovingness.

"I am more than that," he answered fervently, kindling at her glance, and pressing her hand more warmly. "I am your father in the Church," he added in another tone, drawing himself away and letting her hand fall, while he loosened the band round his throat, as he saw the fair face flush and the pretty dark blue eyes droop like a girl's. "Am I not your Director?"

"Yes," said Hermione, after a pause. She felt as if she had just had a shower-bath. And she did not like shower-baths.

"Then you do really wish me to be your worldly adviser outside my spiritual functions?" continued Mr. Lascelles, after another rather long silence between them, again taking her hand.

She raised her eyes to his face. "Yes," she said, with a certain controlled intensity that let him see into her heart. "You are the only disinterested friend that I have, and it is my duty to obey you."

"You are right!" he said passionately. "Right in your obedience, and in your belief in my pure disinterestedness of affection. I am your friend and your only one! Well!" more briskly, as if shaking off a dangerous feeling; "let me continue in my pleasant task of advising you in all things; and let me begin with the little affair of the dinner. I am to dine with you to meet the Maines? Good. Now, say when. You know quite well that it is your duty to make these arrangements. Now," raising his hand playfully, "no excuses. Exercise your own free will, your own right as mistress of the house, and say now at once when it shall be. I tell you frankly, I will accept only your invitation. As I said once before to you, no power on earth should make me cross the threshold of the Abbey were it not that it is your house. The place where the enemy of the Church weaves his accursed plots for the ruin of men's souls and the destruction of our own dear Mother is no place for a minister of Christ!"

"I can understand that," said Hermione dejectedly. "It must be dreadful for you!"

"No, not while you and our child are there—not if I go by your own sole invitation. You see, I look on you as the personage and your husband as your unfortunate appendage; you are the substance and he is the accident. But this is reversed if you put the power over everything into his hands, and make him the chief while you are the subordinate. Then indeed I could not accept the Abbey hospitality! Do you not understand me, dear child?"

"Yes," said Hermione, flattered but inwardly frightened.

"Good again! When then shall our grand dinner come off?" he asked laughingly.

" When you like," she answered. " Fix the day your-self; all are alike to me."

" Let me see—to-day is Saturday," he said musingly.

" Shall I say next Friday?—but that is scarcely a long enough invitation," asked the graceless creature.

He smiled.

" Friday?" he repeated, arching his eyebrows. " A fast-day? I never go out on Friday!"

She blushed in confusion.

" Of course not! How stupid of me to forget," she said, as if Friday fasting had been part of the ordinary consideration of her life. " When then?" nervously.

" Not Friday, because it is fast-day; not Saturday, because it is Sunday eve. Next Monday or Tuesday week," he answered.

" Let it be Tuesday," she returned innocently. " Monday is Richard's lecture night."

Mr. Lascelles suddenly stiffened. His lips went into a thin straight line, and his nostrils quivered like those of a fretted horse.

" I am afraid this is the only day that I can give you," he said coldly. " Now that I think of it, Tuesday is impossible. It must be Monday or not at all."

" But what can we do about my husband's lecture?"

asked Hermione in genuine embarrassment. She was beginning to find her new master's hand a little heavy.

" It is simple enough," said Mr. Lascelles with cold contempt. " He must choose between his duties as a host and a gentleman and this lecture—from the blasphemy of which it would be a mercy that the misguided men who listen to him should be saved if only for once ! "

" Yes, it would," she answered helplessly.

" Then I am to consider myself engaged for Monday week, provided the Maines and the rest can come ? " he asked, his eyes glittering.

" Certainly ; with pleasure," answered Hermione, hers drooping and her heart as heavy as lead though she did her best to speak cheerfully.

He smiled his superior smile. " What a weak, pretty creature it was ! " he thought ; but all the more valuable for his purpose. She was the battle-ground on which the duel *à outrance*, that had already begun between himself and that godless infidel, had to be fought out :— and so far he was content, for so far he had had the advantage.

" And you will write the notes this evening—without taking counsel of your husband ? " said Mr. Lascelles.

She hesitated, and turned helplessly in her chair.

" I count on your fidelity to your promise and attention to my wishes. Remember what I have said. If Mr. Fullerton were to ask me to his house I would refuse to go. It is as your guest only that I consent to appear—only because this dinner is yours, not his. You understand, my child?" He spoke quietly but strongly. He wanted her to feel that he was in earnest.

" Yes—I will do as you tell me; I promise," said Hermione, yielding finally to the pressure put on her. " I will arrange it as you wish, dear Superior. Perhaps it will be better after all ! "

" You are very sweet and good—you are the per-fection of the kind of woman whom men most appreciate!" said Mr. Lascelles with more warmth of admiration than he had hitherto shown ; and Hermione, blushing like a girl, felt half ashamed and half elated at the praise of this handsome man, her spiritual Director.

Soon after this, Virginia and Sister Agnes came into the room where the two were sitting, skirting so cleverly by dangerous places, like skaters shooting over thin ice. They came from the Sister's private oratory, where the girl had been making her simple " statement of thoughts and feelings" which the Sister was careful not to call confession, and receiving advice which she was as careful not to call spiritual direction; but which advice included, among other things, a recommendation to be very sweet and even tender to Ringrove Hardisty whom it was essential to win over, and very sorrowful and reticent, and even cold, to that father who must be beaten with many stripes till the offending Adam was whipped out of him;—for the good of his immortal soul tortured in his humanity through his paternal love, that his spirit might be cleansed and redeemed. These confidences and directions from the Sister were in preparation for the graver confession to the vicar, which, with public confirmation, had to come when Virginia and Hermione should be judged strong enough in the faith to take an independent line without wavering—trusted to stand out publicly—the one against the father and the other against the husband. As yet —the wife, at least—was not to be wholly counted on.

Hermione rose as the Sister entered and went to meet her with a certain conscious confusion and rather excessive affectionateness. She had walked up from the church with Mr. Lascelles after weekly confession to him in the sacristy—the fourth now ; and she was a

little fluttered, as is natural, when a woman has been
saying in secret to one man what she would not repeat
to all—when a wife has been receiving praises and
assurances of friendship and sympathy which she would
not care that her husband should know of—and when
one whose life should be clear as crystal and informed
by duty rather than sentiment, has been mingling religion and romance, secresy and spiritual philandering in
one sweet dangerous cup together. These weekly con-
fessionals were fast becoming the charm of Hermione's
life :—Had Mr. Lascelles not been a priest, one might
have said the probable ruin as well as the present
charm. As it was, her fair face was flushed and her blue
eyes were softer, darker, more humid than in general
as she caressed the Sister in voice and manner with
the instinctive hypocrisy of one who wishes to disarm
suspicion and divert attention.

"Superior has been kind enough to promise to dine
with us on Monday week," she said, holding the cold
thin hand warmly clasped in hers.

Sister Agnes looked at her brother with a charming
smile.

"He does not often go into the world," she said.
"You ought to think yourselves specially honoured ; "

—that silky smile on her face still fixed and un-changing.

"Yes," answered Hermione, having nothing else to say, but saying this prettily and looking at Mr. Lascelles with docile eyes; while Virginia, stealing her arm round the Sister, pressed her waist lovingly, proud and happy at the prospect of seeing, on a fixed day more than a week hence, this spiritual Zeus whom she knew that she should see every day in the interim, as had been the rule for some time past now. But, then, this spiritual Zeus was *her* brother; and Virginia was essentially in love with the Sister, and was happy, failing the sub-stance, in the shadow.

The girl had to do penance for this little bit of effusiveness. Sister Agnes was a secret kind of person, and did not approve of "showing one's feelings," as she used to say. And she was an extremely cold woman as well, and easily bored by demonstrations of affection. She was sweet and caressing in manner—or rather in the tone of her voice, in the turn of her head, in her smile; but it was only manner. It went no farther than voice and smile, the bending of her small head and the curve of her long thin throat; and more was repulsive to her. So when next the Fullertons went

to the Vicarage to work for the Church, the Sister placed
Virginia by Aunt Catherine in the window, and enjoined
on her sympathy with that silly creature's spiritual experiences—which a profane person might have called
senseless maunderings.

It was not a pleasant moment for Hermione when
she had to tell her husband what she had done. In
spite of all the dissatisfaction which had been growing
steadily, if silently, for some years now—though she
had diligently cherished a deep displeasure against him
since his refusal to join in the Harvest Festival—and
notwithstanding the influence which Mr. Lascelles was
gaining over her and the strong fascination that he had
for her—the habit of love for her husband was a
powerful element in her life still, and she did not
enjoy the thought of paining him. And she knew that
this arrangement, meant as an affront to him as it
was, would pain him. He would reason himself into
tranquillity again after a time ; but the first moments
would be bitter, and she dreaded giving the wound.
But it had to be done. She herself had feathered the
arrow, and now she herself must plant it.

"Richard," she said, when they were alone in her
dressing-room that evening after the maid had left her

dressed for dinner, while waiting there, as they always
did, for the gong; "we ought to ask Sir Angus and
Lady Maine to meet Mr. Lascelles. We ought to give
a large dinner-party."

"I suppose we ought," he said with an involuntary
sigh.

There was a wound deep down in his heart which
the vicar's name chafed. He would not acknowledge
to himself that the fight between them was being carried
on in his own house, with his wife and daughter for
the stakes. He insisted in his own mind that it was all
impersonal and on purely intellectual grounds; and
that if Hermione had become a little warped and
Virginia somewhat too warmly won, it was only a
passing phase with each—and that the wife would
come back to her best self again soon, very soon, and
would bring her daughter with her. Yet the wound was
there all the same; and he was like one beginning to
stir in an uneasy dream to a painful wakening—not
wholly asleep nor fully aroused—only dimly conscious
of distress now and of anguish to come.

Hermione flamed suddenly, as one whose sacred
image is touched with a profane hand.

"Why do you sigh in that manner, Richard?" she

asked hastily. "You are not overburdened by society; least of all by that of Mr. Lascelles."

"It was nothing, my wife. Did I sigh? Perhaps I am tired," he answered patiently.

"We have not had the vicar once yet to dinner. You need not look at this invitation as such a tremendous infliction!" she said, returning to the charge as her best defence.

"No, no; do not mistake me, dear. I do not make it an infliction," he said. "Of course we have to ask him—of course—naturally; we could do nothing else. When shall it be?"

"Monday week," said Hermione with a plunge. How her heart beat!

"You forget, my dear; Monday is impossible," he answered. "Monday is my lecture night, and a *dies non* with me at all times. How came you to forget, sweetheart?"

"You must give up your lecture," she said with a false air of calm conviction.

He looked at her in frank astonishment.

"I could scarcely do that," he said quietly. "For ten years I have never once failed my men, and I should scarcely like to do so now for no better reason than choosing this night, of all the nights in the week, for a dinner-party at home."

"If you have been so regular for all these years, you can afford to disappoint them for once," said Hermione, taking one view of the question.

"Or, put it that if I have accustomed them to rely on me so implicitly, I am not justified in failing them for a caprice," he answered back, taking the other.

"But the vicar has no other night. If he does not come then he cannot come at all," said Hermione, her colour rising.

"In that case it had better not be at all," said Richard coldly. "Ask the rest on some other evening, and let Mr. Lascelles come when he can. I am not disposed to give up my duties that I may conciliate his fancies."

"I think you might consider ·what is due to the clergyman of the parish," said Hermione stiffly.

"Dear wife, are we to open this unprofitable vein?" he answered very gravely but very gently. "As a clergyman Mr. Lascelles stands nowhere with me—you know that as well as I do! As a neighbour and a gentleman only is he recognized in this house."

"Pardon me, Richard—Virginia and I see him as

something else," said Hermione, flushing to the roots of her hair. "And I think that both as her mother and the mistress of the house I have some right to consideration—and some right to my own way too. I do not often ask for it."

"You have every right to your own way, my wife; and you have never been refused when you have asked for it," said Richard, speaking as he would have spoken any time these twenty years past, had such a discussion as this been possible before these sadly disturbed later days;—that is, speaking with the sense of masterhood— a masterhood that was his by right of mutual love and perfect sympathy, and no more to be questioned in its righteousness than that the sun should shine and the earth bring forth her fruits in return.

"You give me my own way when I ask it! You are generous, certainly; considering all things, very generous!" said Hermione with a sneer.

And then her heart smote her. She tried to laugh off her words as if they had been said in jest.

"I mean to be so," said Richard gently, keeping his eyes lowered.

"And now you must give me my own way in this," cried Hermione, passing from her odd ill-temper to the caressing voice and ways which, in spite of everything, came to her more naturally than any other when speaking heart-open to her husband.

He looked at her smiling.

"How can I, wife?" he said. "I will not fail my men for such a ridiculous reason as this. Make your dinner-party on some other day which can include Mr. Lascelles and will not interfere with my arrangements."

"I cannot," she said. "Mr. Lascelles himself fixed Monday week, and I cannot change it now."

"So! it is already arranged?" he said with a sudden flush. "In this case there was no need to consult me. If you have acted of your own free will, wife, why go through the form of asking my consent?"

"I do not think I did ask your consent," said Hermione quickly, up in arms at the word. How sudden her transitions! how uncertain her mood nowadays!

"No? What was it then?" he asked, trying to smile.

"I think I only told you of the fact," she answered with dignity. "As the mistress of the house I surely have the right to ask my best friend to dinner without the formal consent of my husband. It is a thing which every other married woman does; and I tell you frankly,

Richard, I will not submit to your tyranny any longer !"

He did not answer. Indeed for the moment he could not.

"There can be no discussion between you and me, my wife, on your rights," he said, after a troubled pause. "If it pleases you to ask this man—whom you call your best friend, and who is instead your worst enemy; yours and mine and our child's—to ask him every day in the week, you have the right to do so ; and if it pleases you to do this without consulting me you have also the right. Our life of harmony and oneness has not been tyranny on my side and enforced submission on yours, but so perfect a welding together that our two wills have been one, needing only one voice to express and one action to embody. And that voice and action have naturally been mine, because I am the stronger man while you are the weaker and less experienced woman. As soon as there comes to be a divided will—as now by some strange fatality there is—yours has all right; and you will find me the first to recognize it. But this arrangement is not your will—it is Mr. Lascelles' ; and to this I do not feel disposed to submit."

"You must, Richard," said Hermione hastily.

" No, wife, I will not," he answered gravely, taking her hand in his. " You have your rights ;—Exercise them. Ask Mr. Lascelles when and as often as you will ; but I also have my duties—rights if you like to call them so—and I will not disappoint my men for the mere whim of one who is the confessed enemy of all that I hold most dear, as I am also the enemy of all that he represents and believes ; one who," he added sorrowfully, " has been the occasion of the only serious dissensions which we have had together for the whole of our married lives."

" Then you ought not to hate the Church and religion so much as you do ! " said Hermione with a sob, breaking away from the point. " It is your own fault for being such an awful infidel as you are ! How can a clergyman be anything but your enemy, especially one so sincere as Mr. Lascelles ? If he is true to his own faith, he must abhor yours ! "

" Do not let us discuss this part of the question," said Richard quickly. " That would indeed be waste of time."

" Then give way for my sake," she pleaded.

" Do not ask me, dear love. It is not for your sake ; I know that too well ;—but to flatter a man whom I dislike, on an occasion which, contemptible as it is, he has chosen as the test of his power. Come ! dry those dear eyes. I do not like to see them full of these strange tears. We are not going to quarrel about Mr. Lascelles as we did about the church decoration," he said, with contempt and sorrow mingled. " He is scarcely worth that sacrifice ! Let the thing stand as it is. Ask him for Monday—if indeed that is his only day —and have the other people on another day ; or put off the whole affair till Mr. Lascelles can come on any day in the week but a Monday evening."

" I cannot," said Hermione, yielding to the sudden candour of helplessness. " The notes are written and sent ; and if you disturb the arrangements now, you will put a public affront on me ; and I think I scarcely deserve that at your hands, Richard ! "

He turned away and walked to the window. It was a very little matter and intrinsically unimportant in the face of the greater tragedies of life ; but it staggered him as if it had been a really grave and serious declaration—as if it had been physically the blow that it was morally.

She followed him shyly, but penitently, with her eyes. Now that it was done, she was sincerely sorry and wished that she could have prevented it. Yet how could she help herself? It was dreadful to have to hurt him like this ; for, after all, he was her husband, and she had once loved him so passionately—before he had grown so stupid and abstracted ; but Superior, of course, must be obeyed now. He was her Director—her father in the Church—and she had no alternative ; but she wished that he had not laid this thing on her to do ! It was an awful test ; how sorry she was ! Poor Richard ! and how sorry he was too !

She went up to him and put her arms round him as he stood by the window looking out on the dark evening sky, but not seeing what he looked at. He was conscious only of pain and bewilderment, and the feeling that he had to accept personal humiliation at the hands of the wife whom he so tenderly loved and so implicitly believed in.

" I am sorry if I have vexed you, Richard," she said sweetly, laying her curly head against his shoulder as she stood behind him with her arms round him. " Don't be vexed with me, husband darling ! I could not refuse the vicar when he put it to me as he did. I did not like, too, to seem such a baby that I have not a word to say in my own house ; but I did not like to do it all the same. I cannot bear to think that I have vexed you ; have

I vexed you, Richard?"—all said in the sweetest, softest, most coaxing tone and manner, while her pretty pink fingers wandered up to his face, and her round white arms pressed him to her lovingly.

He turned round and took her to him.

"Not vexed me, sweet wife. Just a little surprised; a little wounded," he said gently, crushing down his bitterness of pain for the sweeter pleasure of forgiving one beloved. "Let it pass. The thing is done, and we will say no more about it."

"How good you are!" said his wife tenderly.

"Who could be anything else to you?" he answered back. "The vague cloud that has come between us sometimes of late is not of your making. I know that, sweet faithful heart! And are all these years of truth and love to be forgotten for a slight misunderstanding that will pass like the morning mist on the mountain tops? My Hermione! do I not know you!"

He kissed her and she clung to him girlishly.

"Oh Richard!" she said, her fair face raised to his : "if I could but make a Christian of you!"

He smiled.

"Never that, my life!—but always your best and truest friend—your defender from all sorrow and evil;

and, if you will let me be so, your guide to truth out of
the dark regions of superstitious error."

Hermione shuddered visibly and drew away from her
husband's breast. " The leader of souls to hell" sounded
in her ears, and she seemed to feel the vicar's hands
dragging her bodily away. That breast had once been
her dearest home where she had been her best self and
her happiest ; now she was frightened and felt almost
sinful in being there at all.

But habit is strong, and with a sudden revulsion of
feeling she turned back to him passionately, and clung
to him with a nervous, almost convulsive grasp, like one
who had lost and now has found. Then they went
downstairs, she still clinging to his hand—which once
she furtively kissed when Jones was not looking that
way.

They were so happy, so bright and cordial together at
dinner, that Virginia was in a certain sense ashamed, and
bewildered as well. She was full of her instructions
from Sister Agnes to be very sweet and sorrowful but
unmistakably cold to her father ; to let him feel that she
held him as a sinner with whom she was bound by her
loyalty to a higher law not to associate familiarly, though
all the while she loved him as his daughter who would—

should he repent and be absolved—return to her natural
obedience when he entered into the way of grace.   And
she knew that her mother had been set on the same way
by Superior.   And now she had come in with papa,
laughing and talking as they had not talked together for
ages, as it seemed to her; and when she herself had
become interpenetrated with the sorrowful strength of
his partial excommunication !   It was perplexing; but
she had the sincerity of her youth and knew no disobedience to the law by which she had undertaken to
live.

Her coldness however passed for some time unnoticed
by Richard; save as temporary dulness of spirits, due as
he supposed to temporary indisposition.   When she
smiled so faintly at his fond follies and did not answer
when he looked for a playful response, as in the days of
what was substantially now another life :—when she would
not promise to take that long-talked-of early morning
ride with him :—for how could she when she went unknown to him every morning to eight o'clock matins at
the church? and telling falsehoods even in fun was not
much in her way :—he was sorry for her evident depression and a little anxious, but he supposed nothing
wrong.

Hermione however, who understood the play, was secretly greatly annoyed.

"Girls have no sense," she said to herself. "They never know when to relax;" meaning that if she herself had relented for a day, and had turned away from the new creed to the old love, Virginia, who had not gone through the same process of feeling, ought to be ready to do so too and was to blame because she did not.

"You can go with papa, Virginia," she said with a warning look. "If he wishes it, certainly."

"In the early morning, mamma?" asked Virginia anxiously.

"Certainly. It is not for every morning; it will not be too great a tax on your strength, or take too much time from your sleep," the mother answered with a forced laugh.

Virginia's pale face flushed for a moment and then became still paler than before. The secresy enjoined on her by Sister Agnes had always been a trial and had sometimes been broken through; but this deliberate deception set forth by her mother was a heavier cross still. Yet by the law of obedience she must let it pass.

"When the day dawns Ladybird will be ready, I dare say," said her father good-naturedly. "And if she really does not wish to go with me, do not force her."

"Of course she will go with you, Richard, if you wish it," said Hermione hastily. "Say yes, Virginia."

"If I may," said Virginia hesitating.

"May! who is to prevent you, Ladybird?" he laughed.

She looked down and did not answer.

"Why! come here to me," he cried, holding out his hand. "I have never seen my Ladybird like this before! What has come to her? Come here, my pet, and let me feel your hand. Are you well?"

She rose from her place and stood for a moment without moving. Dinner and dessert both were over now, and they were going into the drawing-room. Hermione had risen and was standing a little apart. Richard was still seated.

"Come, my darling," he said fondly, turning round in his chair.

She went up to him, her pale, pure face quivering, her eyes moist and sorrowful.

"My darling!" he said tenderly. "What is it, my little Virginia?"

'She sank back fainting in her father's arms.'

She put her arms round his neck and kissed his upturned face, her tears falling down like rain.

"Oh papa, papa!" she sobbed. "If you would but become a Christian and be reconciled to the Church!"

"My little girl," he said gravely; "am I not the best judge for myself?"

"No, papa, you are blinded and led astray by Satan," she said. "He stands between you and me, you and mamma, you and Our Lord. I can see him now—there—there on one side. He has hold of you, papa, and the Blessed Mother cannot reach you though she tries. Oh, it is dreadful! dreadful! Poor lost papa!"

For the first and only time in her life, hysterical emotion overcame Virginia, and with a sharp cry she sank back fainting in her father's arms.

"That cursed brood!" said Richard bitterly. "There is no tie too holy for them to break, no lie too degrading for them to teach, if it can sap a pure love and establish their vile rule. The first use to which I would put my God, if I had him, would be to sweep all priests off the face of the earth as wild beasts who are man's worst enemies!"

"How dreadful it all is!" cried Hermione with strange passion, as she rang violently for aid. But whether it was the influence of the Sister over Virginia, or her pitiful vision and fainting fit, or the command of Mr. Lascelles to herself, or Richard's blasphemous denunciation that was dreadful, she scarcely knew. For the moment she hated the whole thing, and wished for the old sleepy loving tranquil life where was neither secresy nor excitement, and where, if they were dull, they were at least at peace and free from these strange disturbances.

CHAPTER XIII.

THE SNARE SET.

THAT strange fainting fit had no ill results so far as the health of Virginia was concerned; and, by somewhat frightening Hermione, it served to bring her and Richard for the time at least closer together than they had been of late; so that for the next ten days conjugal life at the Abbey ran on the smoothest casters to be found. Mr. Lascelles, holding that stone in his sleeve which he meant to fling with such a true aim at the dinner, forbore to interfere. This delusive brief St. Martin's summer did not trouble him, and would make the coming storm all the more effective by contrast. Wherefore, undisturbed by the subtle suggestions of her Director—suggestions which always cast so much trouble into her soul and so much sorrow into her life—made to feel at peace with herself and suffered to remain at peace with her husband, Hermione came back to her sweetest self, and was almost as happy as she had been in the first years of her married life.

Her very relations with Mr. Lascelles added to her happiness, because adding to the movement, the excitement, the interest, the affections of her days. Delicately flattered and spiritually caressed by him as she was —performing this little penance and that little task for him in pleasant obedience and constant remembrance— feeling him always as a warm and vital spiritual influence about her and living in a secret romance, not only negatively sinless but positively holy, and all the more delightful because it was secret—she had everything that she most desired; and, action and reaction operating according to their laws, her renewed tenderness for Richard was increased by her love for Mr. Lascelles, as her pleasure with the vicar added to her happiness with her husband. Thus, time flew fast on golden wings for the next ten days; and when the eventful evening came, the fair woman surpassed herself in beauty of person and sweetness of mood.

She had never looked so well, and had never been dressed with such a prodigality of wealth and luxury. Her dress was "moonlight" coloured satin—the palest shade of that blue which is as much green as blue and more grey than either—with a good deal of fine white lace and silver embroidery about it. She wore diamonds

in her hair and round her neck ; and their flash and play
of light lifted up into life what else might have been
delicacy refined into insipidity. She did not look more
than twenty-five years of age, with her fair innocent
face crowned by the curly golden hair among which the
diamonds shone and sparkled ; her beautiful arms,
with one diamond band on each ; her softly moulded
figure that had bloomed into generosity without losing
its grace, and of which the throat was as round and
smooth, the shoulders as finely modelled and as exqui-
sitely polished as when she was first Richard Fullerton's
wife, and the acknowledged belle of the county ; and she
looked as happy as she was beautiful—and felt what
she looked. She was the very ideal of a lovely woman
in her prime, possessing every quality which men most
admire and every virtue which they most adore. But
she had neither reasoning faculty nor self-reliance ;
which was no subject of regret to Mr. Lascelles ; while
Richard, who had dominated her by love, and had lived
their joint life in his own way, had never yet found out
that this sweet echo of his will was only an echo and not
a response, and that any one else who chose to take the
trouble could waken it as well as he had done—and it
might be even better.

This past week of happiness with her husband, her veiled romance with Mr. Lascelles, her conscience at rest and her imagination at fever-heat—all had brightened and embellished her to a marvellous extent; so that people looked at her twice, to see what she had done to herself; and Lady Maine, a hard-featured, stalwart kind of woman, five feet ten inches high and portly in proportion, stared at her curiously; then turning to Miss Molyneux, said, in not too discreet a whisper:—

"How wonderfully young Mrs. Fullerton looks to be the mother of that great girl there! It is almost indelicate; they look more like sisters than mother and daughter. Does she paint or dye? or what is it? It is quite unnatural!"

To which Aunt Catherine answered mysteriously: "It is the saints. Ever since she came over she has been like this. The saints do it for her at night. She looks as if she were fed on heavenly cream and roses; and so she is."

For her reward Miss Molyneux was set down in the great creature's mind as certainly insane; and with a smothered kind of groan, which the irreverent would have called a grunt, Lady Maine moved away.

She was afraid of mad people, she said when relating the occurrence to her friends; and, being a Protestant of the Protestants, would as soon have believed in the gods of Greece as in the saints of Christendom, and indeed thought reliance on the one no more idolatrous than faith in the other.

For the rest, Virginia, in her favourite white, with one row of pearls round her slender throat, and even more ethereal in appearance than usual, was the fair, sweet, natural nun, standing there as a spectator rather than an actor—looking on at the gay world, but not in it nor of it. She was not sad nor sorrowful, not pinched nor meagre, and still less censorious than either; she was simply out of place in what is called "society," and out of harmony with her present state of luxury. She was like some pure spirit lost out of its natural sphere, wandering for a while through the grosser world of men, waiting for the time when she might return home to the heaven she had left.

Aunt Catherine, still doing penance for her presumption in thinking that she, a wretched little potsherd, had been chosen as a vessel of grace for the reception of the divine essence, was in a black dress of sober cut, in imitation of the Sister's style. Hitherto she had been

noted for the multitudinous flounces and furbelows
with which she had hooped herself round, and for the
miniature market-garden that she had been accustomed
to pile on the top of her odd little bullet-shaped head.
And as she was short and very stout, with a round,
rosy face, and hairs so thinly planted as to show great
shining tracts of scalp beneath, her ornate fashions had
always been made occasion of much sarcasm and quiz-
zing from her friends.   But to-night she was just as conspicuous in another way. She had on a black alpaca
gown that was like a riding habit, scanty, perfectly plain,
and showing the lines of her rotund figure as distinctly
as her flounces and furbelows had exaggerated them ;
while, scorning ornament or disguise, she had braided
her poor little wisps of hair plainly on each side of her
head, and tied them up into a knot behind which a
small coffee-cup would have covered.

Theresa, looking thin and feverish, was also in
black, but of lighter material and more graceful form.
She had placed a few white chrysanthemums about her,
and looked as if in half-mourning.   Sombre tones
suited the state of her own feeling which was too intense not to be tragic ; and the scentless white flowers
were associated in her mind with the church decorations

on the day that had given her the fever which she mistook for ecstasy, the spiritual assurance which with her meant human love.

Pretty Beatrice in cream-colour—warmer than Virginia's dead white—had gold sequins round her head and neck. Her soft, clinging drapery, and the gold of the coins which gave life to the tender tone of that drapery, suited the sleepy oriental style of beauty which she had come by, no one knew how. But as nature never lies, there must have been some eastern graft somewhere in the family tree, for the large dark heavy-lidded eyes, the reddish-gold crisp and curly hair—every hair of which was as if alive and separate, making a misty cloud about her when she let it fall—the richly coloured carmine of cheek and lip set against the soft peach-like groundwork of her skin, the very hands and feet and unconscious grace of her indolent pose—all was eastern, without the possibility of denial; so was her placid temper, gentle, sympathetic, plastic, but traversed by a vein of potential passion which circumstances might call forth but which was as yet dormant.

Lady Maine had clothed her voluminous person in a much-befrilled dress of hard deep red; and Mrs.

Nesbitt, with her gentle face and matronly figure, was in grey covered down by black lace.

They made a pretty combination of colour and effect as they stood or sat about the room ; and though a holy man and an avowed celibate, Mr. Lascelles complimented most of them personally, and expressed his approbation of their appearance. By the way, he seemed to consider himself in some sort the master of the feast, and more than once, ignoring Richard as if he had not been in existence, went forward to greet the entering guests, whom he then took to Hermione. But how could any one resent the actions of a man with such a graceful bearing, such heroic self-possession, and such sublime unconsciousness of the possibility of giving offence as characterized the vicar of Crossholme ?

Going up to Hermione, he said that she was like a dream—" one of a dream of fair women, such as poets imagine and painters portray." Then, seeing her flush —she did not like to be one of many—he added in a whisper which no one but herself could hear : " But always the one to me in Crossholme or indeed all the world over—the fairest jewel in the crown of the Church, and the dearest to me personally."

" Thank you," said Hermione, with a rapid glance

to where Richard was standing on the hearthrug, leaning against the chimney-piece, one foot on the fender and his head resting on his hand, while he talked local politics with Mr. Nesbitt and thought the whole thing an unmitigated nuisance.

Of Theresa, whose thin hot hand he held longer and pressed more warmly than was at all necessary for friendly greeting or even clerical patronage, the vicar asked :—

"What have you done to make yourself so beautiful to-night, my dear child? Pomps and vanities—eh? This black gown and those white flowers become you wonderfully; and if they are pomps and vanities, they are simpler than most, and we must not be too hard on the young."

"If you are pleased, Superior—" answered Theresa, looking up into his face. Her eyes completed the sentence.

"Yes, I am pleased," he answered royally; "more than pleased"—lowering his voice: "and with your whole personality, my child, as well as with your dress. I shall see you at mattins to-morrow, of course? I have to speak to you afterwards."

By which the girl's cup of happiness was filled to

the brim and her very soul flooded with dangerous joy.

Even Beatrice was not left out in the vicar's tour of inspection and commendation, for all that she did not belong to the inner fold. He longed to count her among his flock of tender and obedient lambs, but he could not find the Archimedean point, nor how she could be moved from her present place. There was a baffling something that eluded his hand, try to hold her as he might. He could not say what that something was, he only knew that it existed. She was neither unimpressionable nor stupid—quite the contrary ; and she was both docile and sincerely affectionate. All the same she was impenetrable to his thrusts, and not to be moved from her quiet placidity, against which he raged as indifferentism and substantial heathenism. To-night he changed his tactics, thinking he would try what flattery would do.

"You are positively superb, Miss Nesbitt," he said, as he came to her in her turn, while making his tour of inspection and approbation round the room. He spoke in a tone of enthusiastic admiration, as if carried out of himself ; and yet those who knew him detected that well-known accent of satire which was the drop of vinegar in the honey. "You are the realization of Rebecca, in 'Ivanhoe;' or, better still, the type of some splendid young Heathen whose conversion will one day be the glory ·of her confessor:—of me?" he added, smiling with paternal benignity on the pretty dark-eyed creature.

Beatrice opened wide her sleepy long-fringed eyes, and with her eyes partly unclosed her handsome pleasure-loving mouth. She put on this look always when she was startled, or wished to show the "mild surprise and gentle indignation" which was her loudest expression of dissatisfaction.

"But I am neither a Jewess nor a Heathen," she said.

"And have no need of conversion?" he asked.

"No; how can I when I am a Christian?" asked Beatrice.

"And if I tell you that you, as we all, have this need because of sin?" he returned.

She shook her pretty richly coloured head, and the coins on her hair shook and jingled.

"I do not think I should quite believe you," she said with perfect inoffensiveness.

"So young and so strong in your conceit?" he

asked with a smile, wishing her to feel herself reproved, but tenderly as well as faithfully.

"I do not think it is being conceited not to feel a Jewess or a Heathen when I am English and a Christian," said Beatrice simply. "And, as for the confession you spoke of, I certainly should never do that. Fancy confessing—just like a Roman Catholic! How dreadful! Besides, I have nothing to confess; and it is not English, nor proper."

"Bee, dear, do not say that! We all have much to confess and much to be forgiven," said Virginia in a low voice; while Ringrove, who was sitting near and had heard what had been said, took up the parable hurriedly.

"The best confessor for a girl is her mother—for a woman, her husband," he said in a voice that was unmistakably harder and less cheery than his in general. "Any one else is worse than a mistake."

"Ah! but you are unconverted too—as yet—and speak according to the spirit that is within you," said Mr. Lascelles with a courtly but still paternal kind of air, smiling at the young man pleasantly and yet with some kind of friendly pity, as he moved away to speak to Sir Angus Maine. The General was as uncompromising a Protestant as his superior officer, my lady; and the vicar wanted to feel his ground, and see if he could not neutralize by personal influence the sectarian opposition of which he felt only too sure. But there was not much time for endeavour of any kind; for the dinner—which had been only awaiting the arrival of the inevitable laggards; this time two young officers from Starton—was announced in due form, and Richard, giving his arm to Lady Maine, led the way to the dining-room, the vicar, doing his best to fascinate Mrs. Nesbitt, following immediately after.

At the dinner-table the first hitch of the evening began. There were to be many before it should be ended; hitches all carefully prepared by Mr. Lascelles, who had laid his plans with the skill of a veteran used to the game and not nice as to the methods of success. He had undertaken, in his own mind, to cover Mr. Fullerton with confusion; to make him eat dirt before the strangers assembled at his table, to whom his objectionable opinions were as yet unknown; to convict him out of his own mouth of infidelity and consequently of immorality; and to hold him up before the world as a man to be shunned and despised, because he disbelieved in the Divine origin of the Bible, and was not prepared to assert positively, as of a thing which he knew and could prove, that man has an individual existence after death. All this had to be done before the last glass of claret had been drunk—and the first shot was fired at once.

Following the example of their graceless host, all the guests sat down, save Mr. Lascelles and the Moly-neux family. These stood—the ladies with bended heads and hands reverently clasped; Cuthbert in the exact attitude of an old monk in a certain illuminated missal which he had bought, and which it had taken his fancy to imitate; and Mr. Lascelles with his head held straight, his hands joined close together by the palms and fingers, but not interlaced. With a look of gentle reproof at Hermione who had seated herself in all innocence, he began an intoned grace in a loud official voice. It took every one but the Molyneux family by surprise; for even the Maines, used to the ceremony, were startled by the method. The servants stopped midway between the sideboard and the table; the ladies left off unbuttoning their gloves; the gentlemen ceased to unfold their dinner napkins; some rose confusedly and made a clatter as they did so; others kept their places, also confusedly, and bent their heads as if devoutly studying the monogram on their plates. Virginia, who, grace before meat being a novelty, had seated herself with the rest, rose with a precise imitation of Sister Agnes in the automatic movement of her body and the mediæval action of her hands. Hermione faltered between the two demonstrations, not wholly rising because of her husband nor frankly seated because of Mr. Lascelles; while Richard kept his place and did his best to look philosophically indifferent to what he considered superstition for the one part and impertinence for the other. But inwardly he chafed, not so much at the thing perhaps, as at the intention.

It was the first time that grace had ever been said at his table. Mr. Aston, who cared neither for bene-diction nor thanksgiving in comparison with the meats and the wines that came in between, had never troubled himself with a function which he knew would be un-welcome. If he chose to dine at the table of an in-fidel, he must take the consequences, he used to say to himself:—and Mr. Fullerton was master of his own house, and must be allowed to arrange his life as he thought best. But Mr. Lascelles was a different kind of man. What he held to be his duty that he would do,

in season or out of season, no matter what the obstacles
nor who the opposers. Those who did so oppose him
were in fault, not he who insisted; they were accursed,
but he was faithful. Wherefore he startled every one
with his High Church grace to-day, and flung the first
challenge into the face of his host.

Then Cuthbert Molyneux intoned the Amen; the
spell was removed; they all sat down or raised themselves up according to their attitudes; and the clatter
of preliminary serving began.

"I trust you are not displeased at my giving the
benediction unasked?" said Mr. Lascelles, in a loud
voice across the table to Richard, when the soup
brought a comparative lull.

Conversation between the two was easy, as each
sat facing the other, the length of the table having
been made the honourable place; so that Richard sat
between Lady Maine and Aunt Catherine, while Hermione opposite was between Sir Angus and Mr.
Lascelles. It had been "Superior's" wish to have
the table so arranged; and Hermione had of course
obeyed.

"It was official," said Richard quietly.

"Thanks for your patience; but I fancy that it is

not usual to say grace at your table?" persisted Mr. Lascelles with well-feigned embarrassment.

"No," said Richard; "it is not."

"Not say grace!" cried Lady Maine, with an air of personal offence. Orthodoxy and loyalty were with her personal matters, and she held herself justified in her wrath when she heard either assailed. "You don't say grace before meat, Mr. Fullerton?" she continued. "How very terrible!"

"Different people have different habits," he answered.

"But this is not a habit, like folding up your napkin or washing your hands—it is a duty," cried Lady Maine authoritatively. "I should expect my dinner to choke me if I did not say grace before it!"

He smiled.

"Mine does not; and I have an excellent digestion," he answered simply; then spoke suddenly of the weather, and how well the harvest had been got in, and the predictions made by the meteorologists of the coming winter.

By which Lady Maine was not a little annoyed. She was fond of laying down the law on things spiritual, and believed that she had got hold of the whole truth— that great, shifting, many-sided Truth, she held it all in the compass of one or two dogmatic sentences! But not to lose an occasion—and she found one everywhere—she cut Richard short a little abruptly, by saying, still in her authoritative commanding way :—

"It is very wicked to talk in that way, Mr. Fullerton. The Bible says 'the wind bloweth where it listeth,' and it is simple infidelity to try and find out things which the Almighty has mercifully hidden from us."

"I am afraid, Lady Maine, this argument would scarcely suit the present times nor advance the best interests of man," said Richard with a slight smile. "All that we know we have found out for ourselves, and you would scarcely have us go back to primitive ignorance ; nor can we stop where we are."

"There are limits, Mr. Fullerton—limits," she answered. "What we have to do is to believe in the Word and perform our religious duties."

"But, Lady Maine, Mr. Fullerton does not believe in religious duties," said Mr. Lascelles across the table.

"Mr. Fullerton must believe in religious duty !" said Lady Maine decidedly. "You are not mad, I suppose ?" she asked, turning abruptly to Richard.

"Not that I know of," he answered good-humouredly; "but my convictions are scarcely to the purpose at this moment. I will confess to you at some other time, Lady Maine."

"Ah! you see that is just the difference between us and you—the true and the false," returned Mr. Lascelles with odd persistency. "We are never ashamed to confess the faith we hold."

"So far to your honour," said Richard courteously but coldly ; and then broke resolutely away into the subject of the present Afghan war, on which Lady Maine held herself an authority, having been a baby in arms at Calcutta during the time of the last. The condition of India was a subject in which she took great delight ; and here too she never wearied of laying down the law. By which diversion full a quarter of an hour was lost before Mr. Lascelles found another opening.

Society was just then much interested in a certain case of wife-murder. The woman had led a loose kind of life ; the man was a hard-working, decent fellow who had borne patiently with her shameful habits, and had always hoped for better things. One day, exasperated beyond himself by her unfaithfulness as a wife and her drunken desertion of her duty as a mother, he had beaten her savagely ; and finally struck the fatal blow. It had been brought in murder and he had been condemned to death ; but the Society for the Abolition of Capital Punishment had taken up the case and was making strenuous efforts for a reprieve. Richard, who, like some others, thought that the worst use to which you can put a man is to hang him and that "extenuating circumstances" may sometimes be brought to bear in mitigation of the crude award as by law established, had signed the petition for commutation of the sentence, and had got "his men" to sign it too.

Mr. Lascelles had refused.

A pause in the general hum, and Lady Maine's ultimatum on the Afghan policy, gave the vicar the opening for which he had been waiting.

" I see you signed the petition for that man Westerton's reprieve—the murderer," he said across the table in a loud voice and one which commanded general attention.

" Yes, I did," said Richard.

" Will you get him off? "

" It seems likely.   I hope so," he answered.

"And I hope not," said Mr. Lascelles. "The man was a murderer, and the law should take its course."

"His provocation was great. He was more to be pitied than condemned," returned Richard mildly.

"'Whoso sheddeth man's blood by man shall his blood be shed,'" said Mr. Lascelles solemnly. "You cannot get over that, Mr. Fullerton."

"That is an argument which does not enter into the discussion," said Richard.

"The direct command of God is an argument that cannot be thrust out of any discussion," said Mr. Lascelles speaking loudly, his voice dominating the table. "It underlies all law and all duty."

"In which case we may as well pass on to another subject," returned Richard with perfect temper.

"Ah! pardon! I forgot!" said Mr. Lascelles, passing his hand over his face. "I remember now— you deny the Bible and its Divine authority. You see, it is so rare to meet with a man who rejects God's Holy Word, that I was off the track. As you say, it makes discussion difficult :—for if you take the Bible from us, what is left?—no solid foothold in law or morals anywhere!"

"You deny the Bible, Mr. Fullerton?" cried Lady

Maine. New to the place as she and Sir Angus were they had not learnt the social byways. " You deny the Bible ? " she repeated ; " and are not afraid that you will be struck dead like Ananias and Sapphira ? "

" Well, no; you see I have lived on till now," answered Richard drily.

" As a proof of God's infinite mercy—giving you time to repent ! " she said. " And may I ask what on earth do you believe, if you do not believe the Scriptures? "

" My faith cannot interest you, Lady Maine," he said gently. " Let us change the subject."

" Your faith, Mr. Fullerton !—your want of faith you mean ! " said Aunt Catherine with one of those odd gleams of quickness sometimes flashing from fools. " And want of faith interests all good Christians who would like to see the blessed saints allowed to work for the salvation of a lost soul."

" It is very kind of you to say so, Miss Molyneux, but I cannot see it in that light," answered Richard pleasantly. " And, at all events, it does not interest myself at this moment," speaking lightly.

" I think want of belief in the Bible the greatest sin in the world, except Popery," said Lady Maine stiffly.

She was displeased, and more than displeased, with

all round ; resenting the patent papistry of the vicar and
this silly little woman, who talked of the saints as if they
were personal friends, as much as she was horrified at
the confessed infidelity of her host; and sorely troubled
how to bear testimony which should be at once a
defence of religion and an attack on ritualism.

"Ah, but, Lady Maine, the new school to which
Mr. Fullerton, unfortunately for mankind, has dedicated
his splendid talents, makes it a principle not to recognize
faith in anything," said the vicar. "It believes only
in what it can weigh and measure—in what it can
demonstrate by mathematical symbols and record in
a series of experiments. Mystery exists nowhere for it—
only temporary ignorance of phenomena ; and faith, like
sin, like inspiration and forgiveness, is exploded. It has
put creation in the place of the Creator : for Deity it
has substituted force, and for the Divine ordering by a
loving will, dead mechanical laws. It does not believe
even the historical miracles of Scripture—does it, Mr.
Fullerton ?"

"The rationalistic school, if that is what you mean,
certainly does not believe in results without material
causes," said Richard quietly. "And you are quite
correct—it does believe in law."

"The miracle of Jonah is, I fancy, a typical stumbling-block to you all?" the vicar asked blandly.

"No whale could have swallowed a man," answered Richard; "not to speak of a man living three days and nights in a whale's body if he could have been taken into it."

"Not by God's power?"

"Not according to the limitation of a whale's anatomy and the necessities of a man's."

"And I believe it firmly," said Lady Maine emphatically. "For the Bible says, 'And God sent a great fish.'"

"Yes, we may rest assured all the miracles recorded were wrought," said Mr. Lascelles, addressing Lady Maine. "The speaking of Balaam's ass among them."

"Perhaps that is the least incredible of the series," said Richard drily.

"And the consuming by fire of the false priests of Baal!—that too we may believe," said the vicar with a cruel gleam in his sharp grey eyes.

"Yes; you priests of the dominant faith have always been ready with fire and slaughter when you were afraid of rivals," said Richard. "But this *aspic* is more to the purpose than theology at this moment. Will you not take some, Lady Maine?"

"Thank you, none," she answered disagreeably.

If she still continued to eat this infidel's food it should not be by his direct invitation, only under the compulsion of circumstances.

Mr. Lascelles did not intend to be put down.

"You cannot set bounds to the working of Omni-potence," he continued. "Where would you limit Almighty power, Mr. Fullerton?"

"Where you begin it," said Richard, looking him calmly in the face. "But this discussion strikes me as singularly out of place here, Mr. Lascelles. At any other time I will meet you as publicly as you will; but we have had enough of it now."

The loophole had been made.

"That we meet on the opposite grounds of faith and reason?" he asked eagerly.

"Yes, on these grounds."

"Which means Christianity or Atheism?"

"Make your own formula."

"It must be yours also," said the vicar, still speaking eagerly. "And therefore we must define our terms like our programme. I repeat, it is Christianity or Atheism."

"Christianity or Agnosticism," said Richard.

"Which is the same thing," said Mr. Lascelles. "At all events, let us understand this clearly :—I challenge you, Mr. Fullerton, to a public disputation. On my side I affirm a personal God, the inspiration of the Bible and the truth of revealed religion ; the separate and distinct acts of creation ; the miracle of the Sacrifice and the Atonement ; an immortal soul, to be judged at the Last Day according to the deeds done in the body ; and a future life of bliss or woe. And you deny all this—is it not so ? "

Mr. Lascelles spoke with a slow and measured utterance, his voice vibrating to the farthest corner of the room. All present had sunk into silence, and each held his breath, looking to their host, some with horror and some with pity.

He lifted his mild, fine, thoughtful face, looking straight into the eyes of his inquisitor.

"You have called on me for a confession of faith in a strange and somewhat unwarrantable manner," he said. "But I accept the challenge. I deny all these articles as set forth by you, but one—and that I neither deny nor affirm. It belongs to the domain of the Unknowable ; and neither you nor I know what comes after the death of the body—if anything, or nothing but the disintegration of the forces which made what we call life. Scientific analogy is against you—universal belief is with you ; but in this, as in many other things, the confession of ignorance is the greater wisdom and the truer modesty."

A shudder ran round the table. Lady Maine wondered why the earth did not open and swallow up this miserable sinner, this worse than Korah, Dathan, and Abiram. Sir Angus thought both the fellows mad alike, and longed to have the trying of them at drumhead court-martial; he would soon make short work of them ! Hermione sat paralyzed. It was as if her life had crumbled to pieces at her feet and she had lost for ever the husband of her youth and the man of her love ; while Virginia, the tears falling silently down her pallid face, called in her heart on the Divine Mother of God to convert her father suddenly—effectually—as St. Paul was converted ; to break down for ever the evil pride of intellect by which he had fallen into such fearful sin, and bring him as a little child to the gates of heaven and into the fold of the Church.

Mr. Lascelles smiled triumphantly as he looked round the table and saw the effect that had been produced.

He had shot his bolt, and it had hit the mark. Richard Fullerton was henceforth irretrievably damaged in the neighbourhood. For it is one thing to have it known that you hold "odd opinions," and another to deny the immortality of the soul and the inspiration of the Bible over a dinner-table; as he would find out before long.

"We will settle a convenient time and place afterwards," he said airily, feeling like a general who has prepared an ambush into which the foe has boldly marched.

"No time or place ought to be convenient for such a wicked discussion as this!" said Lady Maine. "The police ought to prevent it! It makes my blood run cold to think of such blasphemy as possible in our own happy land, where we have the light of the Gospel for our guidance!"

"We who value our privileges must pray for those who disdain them. The long-suffering of God knows no limit," said Mr. Lascelles nobly.

But Lady Maine seemed to think that it had come to its limit now, and that it was almost as wicked to hope for mercy for Richard Fullerton as for the ultimate restoration of Satan himself.

"Perhaps you will add a prayer to prove Galileo in error, geological records so many stone fables, the spectroscope a thaumaturge, and mathematics and the rest of the positive sciences mere moonshine. That would be more to the purpose than the conversion of my poor little insignificant soul," said Richard quite quietly.

To which Mr. Lascelles answered: "The wisdom of this world is foolishness with God, and your mole-like gropings in what you choose to call science leave the Rock of Ages untouched."

The dinner after this was flat and constrained. No one had liked the discussion which Mr. Lascelles had forced, and all but his own immediate adherents had felt it to be cruel and ill-bred. But even of those who were most annoyed with him, none went thoroughly with Richard ; and though some honoured him for his fidelity, yet even they wished that he had not testified. Mr. Nesbitt, with whom religion meant going to church once on Sundays, eating plum-pudding at Christmas-time and pancakes on Shrove Tuesday, being baptized, married, and buried according to the rules of the national Church, said it was untoward and embarrassing ; and condemned Mr. Lascelles roundly, if he did not quite exonerate Fullerton for his want of skill in fence. No man should force *his* hand, he said in an audible whisper to Ringrove from whom he was separated by Virginia; but the younger man not only exonerated but praised Mr. Fullerton, and answered back that he considered Mr. Lascelles' conduct simply infamous. Every one knew Mr. Fullerton's opinions, and it was the most scoundrelly thing he had ever known to force him in this way at his own table! If he had not been a clergyman, he, Ringrove, would have taken it up and have made him retract and apologize. He did not know what pain he was causing poor Virginia, nor how terrible it was to her to hear her father and Superior discussed and judged —her heart going with the one and her conscience with the other—and she unable to bridge over the gulf between them.

One of the young officers from Starton, to whom pretty Bee Nesbitt had been assigned, said to her quite aloud: "What a jolly queer conversation that has been for a dinner-table!—quite too funny altogether. Mr. Lascelles seems to be a tight fit, so far as I can judge; but Mr. Fullerton is plucky to the backbone. But I say," he continued confidentially, " what on earth does he mean by Agnosticism?"

" I don't know," said Bee, opening her big eyes.

Agnosticism, which she had so unconsciously explained, might be something to eat, if not to be afraid of in a narrow lane on a dark night. At all events, a right interpretation of what they had heard was as much beyond her not very extended mental range as it was beyond the young man's; and the two dark intelligences could not strike out a spark between them.

Lady Maine and Sir Angus blamed both Mr. Lascelles and Mr. Fullerton with impartial severity, and always spoke of this dinner as "their dreadful experience when they were between a Jésuit and an Infidel—a Papist and an Atheist;" and that nothing but their consideration for that poor little woman—"a deuced pretty creature," Sir Angus used to put in by way of parenthesis—kept them in their places; while Lady Maine invariably added :—

"I expected every moment to see the floor give way and swallow up that wretched creature before my eyes. And I was sitting next him too! I was never so frightened in my life. It was quite too dreadful altogether."

END OF THE FIRST VOLUME.

LONDON : PRINTED BY
SPOTTISWOODE AND CO., NEW-STREET SQUARE
AND PARLIAMENT STREET

Lady Maine and Hermione.

Under which Lord?

BY

E. LYNN LINTON

AUTHOR OF 'THE WORLD WELL LOST' 'PATRICIA KEMBALL' ETC.

IN THREE VOLUMES

VOL. II.

WITH TWELVE ILLUSTRATIONS BY ARTHUR HOPKINS

London
CHATTO & WINDUS, PICCADILLY
1879

' Because we have found not yet
Any way for the world to follow
Save only that ancient way;
Whosoever forsake or forget,
Whose faith soever be hollow,
Whose hope soever grow grey

Monotones : Songs before Sunrise

CONTENTS

OF THE

SECOND VOLUME.

LIST OF ILLUSTRATIONS

TO THE

SECOND VOLUME.

UNDER WHICH LORD?

CHAPTER I.

COMPENSATION.

FROM this time forth the Abbey was a forbidden book to most of the people round about Crossholme, and the comparatively mild disfavour in which Richard Fullerton had hitherto been held—the moral ostracism which had been so lightly written on the thinnest little egg-shells possible—changed its character from the date of this memorable dinner, and henceforth was a sentence of social banishment printed in broad black capitals on huge marble slabs. Up to now people had avoided all religious discussion with that pleasant-mannered, well-intentioned agnostic of theirs, and had tacitly agreed to ignore his infidelity so far as they could while accepting him as a good fellow—with a misfortune that a little spoiled him but did not wholly ruin. Such men as Mr.

Nesbitt and Ringrove Hardisty were always glad to have a private talk with him, to learn the precise ground where he was standing and how far his reasonings had led him; but the rest left him alone. Yet what even these bolder brains were glad to do, when strolling down the village or sitting with him alone in his study, they avoided when the world stood by and what was said by two was misinterpreted by many. Now however things were different ; if not with them, yet with all the rest; and Richard Fullerton passed from the mild condemnation of his former state into active social excommunication.

The ladies cut him openly ; and only Mrs. Nesbitt and Beatrice called at the Abbey after the dinner; the rest merely sent cards; and Hermione did not dare ask the reason why. She knew it without asking ; and resented her share of the social disfavour into which they had fallen because of her husband's iniquitous opinions, as Mr. Lascelles foresaw she would.

On his side, the vicar soon lived down the blame which at first had attached to him, as also in this case too, he knew that he should. He had trusted to time and his real manner to free him from the reproach of ill breeding; and his trust was not in vain. For after all, want of good breeding counts for very little when con-

trasted with want of faith in the Bible; and disbelief in
the immortality of the soul is total, wilful, wicked darkness, where impoliteness is a mere speck in the sunbeam.
And as the neighbours did not see that the whole thing
had been planned, they could not accuse the vicar of
cruelty or treachery, as else they might. So the matter
grew at last, by that queer distortion of truth which
takes place in all verbal reports, to be quoted as a gra-
tuitous insult to public decency in a shameful outburst
of passionate blasphemy on Richard Fullerton's part,
and a noble testifying of faith on the vicar's.

The effect of this social ostracism was to throw Hermione into still closer communion with the Vicarage.
This was the only place where she was received with
that special distinction which was so pleasant to her.
At Churchlands, and elsewhere among the community
of nominal "church workers" but practical adorers
of the vicar—his spiritual harem—there was too much
holy emulation, too much the sentiment of a race for
his favour and a struggle for the chief places of heaven
which he carried in his pocket, for that Christian cordiality which could give without grudging the supremacy necessary for Hermione's peace. And with out
siders, though she herself was personally liked, she was

always made to feel that she was the wife of an infidel
—to be pitied for her misfortune, if you will—but all
the same given to understand that it was a misfortune
which carried a taint with it as much as if she had been
the wife of a convict.

At the Vicarage she was the local queen ; the fairest
daughter of the Church; the brightest jewel in the
crown ; Superior's favourite friend—what about Theresa ?
—and honoured in proportion to the depths from which
she had risen and the strength of the evil influences which
she had resisted. And as love and praise had always
been as the breath of her nostrils, and were becoming
even more necessary as the confident assertions of youth
were changing to the uneasy doubts of maturity, and—
" Do I look well to-day ? "—the question more often
asked in her own mind than the self-approbation of old
—the distinction with which Mr. Lascelles received
her, and the adulation which he dealt out to her so
delicately yet so liberally, made the Vicarage like an
oasis in the desert;—the only place where, as she used to
say with tears in her pretty dark-blue eyes, she felt like
her real self or was treated as she ought to be.

But though it did really make up to her for the loss
of all the rest, Hermione, womanlike, was not minded to

forego her cause for grievance against her husband. She
was the victim and he was her executioner—intentional
or not, still her executioner. Things went very badly
with the poor fellow in these later times, when everything
was pressed into the service of her displeasure. If the
coffee was burnt or the chimney smoked, it was somehow
on account of his horrid opinions ; and, the swing of the
pendulum being a fixed alternation, her present estrangement exactly equalled her late return to tenderness. She
had never been so far from him as now, and never so
unjust, when only a few days and weeks ago she had
never been sweeter nor more delightful. Had Richard
been superstitious he might well have believed in Possession, so changed was this cold, irritable, discontented
wife of his from the mild, warm, loving creature whom he
had married twenty years ago and had loved without
doubt or break ever since. He could not quite understand it all, though in part it was only too clear. But
not knowing of the constant intercourse that existed
between his own family and the Vicarage—not dreaming
of the dangerous intimacy that had been established, the
inquisitorial authority exerted, and the overpowering influence which Mr. Lascelles had gained over Hermione
by means of that weekly confession, he was at a loss to

account for all the way that she had gone ; and he did
not choose to track it throughout its course.　He was too
loyal to confess to himself that Hermione, his faithful,
trusted wife, his beloved, his second self, had been warped
from him by another ; that she was less than wifely
to him because more than friendly to a rival.　And yet,
we feel what we do not formulate, and know what we
dare not translate ; and Richard felt and knew, and did
not dare to put into words.

In the midst of all this home discomfort news came
to Hermione that Lady Maine was giving a grand dinner,
to be followed by a ball, to which every one in the neighbourhood had been invited save themselves.　This was
the most patent sign of social disfavour which the pretty
woman had yet received ; and she took it to heart more
deeply than might have been expected.　It was not for
the loss of the mere pleasure, it was because of her husband's horrid opinions against which this exclusion was
simply the public protest, that she grieved so bitterly, as
she said to Mr. Lascelles, tearfully.

To which her Director answered with a strange
manner of repressed and concentrated bitterness :—

"You are right, my poor, dear child.　Your life is
essentially a martyrdom, and while you live with your

husband it can be nothing else." Then he added with a
smile : " Personally, I am selfishly glad that you are not
going, for I too am not invited ; and I like to feel that we
are included in the same circle, even if one of prohibition."

" But for what a different reason ! " said Hermione,
raising her eyes to the vicar's face with the same look of
pride in his personality that she used to have in Richard's.
" If I had been excluded because of too great love for the
Church, I should have been glad. As it is, I feel it so
dreadfully ! "

"Not while you have me to bear it with you,"
said Mr. Lascelles, speaking with the sweetest tenderness ;
and Hermione, dropping her eyes, felt suddenly warmed
and consoled, and as if the sun which had been hidden
had broken through the clouds once more.

The day after this little colloquy she was driving into
Starton. It was Virginia's day for visiting her district
with Sister Agnes, so the mother was alone. She met the
Maine carriage at the other side of the bridge, just outside the town, and passed it with a bow which pride
tried to make indifferent and mortification forced to be
offended. My lady pulled the check-string, and, leaning
backward, halloed to the Abbey coachman to stop ; then
made him a sign to turn round and come to her. She

had no idea of turning for her own part, and following the victoria till she came up to it. She was the wife of the commandant, and exacted deference.

"Mrs. Fullerton, I want to speak to you," she said in her loud rasping voice, as Hermione, looking pretty and fluffy and girlish and astonished, was whirled to the encounter.

"With pleasure," said Mrs. Fullerton stiffly.

"Get down, won't you? and we can walk a little way. I hate all the town hearing what I say," said Lady Maine authoritatively; and Hermione, whose plastic nature found mechanical obedience easy, submissively left her pretty little carriage and stood on the road-side till the large woman joined her.

"I am giving a dinner and a ball next week, Mrs. Fullerton," she began in her loud way. "Have you heard?"

"Yes," said Hermione, her voice trembling just a little.

"And I have not asked you," said my lady, coming to the point without further preamble, as rude people misnamed straightforward do. She was too coarse in grain for her own part to think it necessary to be tender of others ; and she was accustomed to boast that she always found the shortest way the best.

Hermione gave a conventional smile.

" It is impossible to ask every one," she said with fine magnanimity.

" Yes, it is," returned Lady Maine. " One has to draw the line somewhere, and I have drawn mine against Popery and Infidelity. I should expect to be found dead in my bed the next morning if I opened my doors to a man like your husband, who is not afraid to say that he denies the Bible and does not believe in Satan and the miracles ; or to one like Mr. Lascelles, who crosses himself in church, begins his sermon without a text, and bows down to stocks and stones."

" I think you can hardly class Mr. Lascelles with my poor unfortunate husband," said Hermione hastily. " The one has unfortunately gone astray in matters of faith, and the other is the sincerest Christian I know."

" My dear Mrs. Fullerton, you are no judge. The one is, as you say, a rank Atheist, and the other is as rank a Papist ; and there is not a hair's breadth to choose between them. So now you know why I have not asked you."

" It was quite unnecessary to enter into any explanation, Lady Maine," returned Hermione. " If you did not wish to have us, you were right not to ask us."

" Yes, but you see, that's where it is," said the lady.
" It was not that I did not wish to have *you*. On all
sides you yourself are a desirable guest—a nice ornament
in a room ; and Sir Angus would have liked it, for he was
greatly taken with your appearance ; and your dress was
sweetly pretty, I must say. You must give me the name
of your milliner. But as professing Christians we could
not ask that terrible husband of yours, and we could
not ask you, as a married woman, without him. You are
his wife, poor soul, and you have to make the best of it.
It is hard lines for you, I will say that ; but we cannot
help you. No one can, till it pleases God to take him ;
when I hope that he will repent in time and turn away
from his wicked ways before it is too late. I wanted to
say all this to you, that there should be no misunderstanding, and that you shouldn't feel hurt."

" You are very kind ; but really it was not necessary," said Hermione, choking back the tears which rose
to her throat before they came to her eyes.

" I think it was," said Lady Maine with her court-
martial air.

" I quite understand you, I assure you," returned
Hermione, with dignity arrived at by an effort.

" You do now. You couldn't be so dense as not ;

but you wouldn't if I had not spoken out," said Lady
Maine, elliptical as to grammar and rude as to manner.
Her Protestantism went right through her, and she was
nothing if not in opposition. "We are all very sorry for
you and that nice little daughter of yours," she continued. "Awfully sorry ; but the blasphemy of your
husband is too appalling to be borne."

"We must remember that he thinks he is right," said
Richard's wife gently. The denunciations of Mr. Lascelles were as holy as those of the prophet Jeremiah ;
but Lady Maine was only a woman like herself and had
no right to condemn.

"He thinks himself right ! Good heavens Mrs.
Fullerton ! do you excuse him !" shouted my lady, making
a dead halt. "We shall have you agreeing with him
next ; though from all I hear you have gone off on the
other tack, and that popish priest of yours has got hold
of you."

"I do not agree with my husband, and only say that
he thinks he is right ; and I know his motives."

"The motives of a son of perdition, of a second
Judas betraying his Saviour with a kiss !" said Lady
Maine. "What motives are they, I should like to know !
You might as well talk about the motives of Pontius

Pilate when he asked what was truth, or Peter when the cock crew."

Tears came into Hermione's eyes.

" There ! don't cry, you poor little woman," said my lady with gruff good-nature. " You cannot help it now, being the wife of an Infidel. But you must read your Bible and pray for him."

" I do," murmured Hermione dejectedly.

" Not in the right way," returned Lady Maine in the manner of one stating an unanswerable truth. " The Bible says, ' Ask, and you shall receive ;' and if you don't receive, it is because you don't ask as you ought. How can you, in that popery shop of yours?" disdainfully, " With lighted candles, crosses and incense and all, how can you expect your prayers to be heard ? "

" If they are not heard through the ways of the Church, they will not be by any other," said Hermione, repeating her lesson with fidelity.

" The Church ! rubbish ! Every professing Christian is a church in himself. We have the Bible, and we want no more—those of us who can read it in the vulgar tongue, and the rest can have it read to them. Anything else is man's invention," said Lady Maine ; "and that you cannot deny, Mrs. Fullerton."

Hermione did not answer, but, turning quickly, beckoned to her coachman. She did not want to enter into a religious controversy with the loud-voiced wife of the Starton commandant, and she was at no time apt in argument.

" I think I must go now, Lady Maine," she said, as the carriage drew up. " I have a great deal to do."

" And you are afraid of me," said her ladyship grimly. " And perhaps you are right. But you are a good little woman in yourself, only terribly badly led."

" And if it were not for such leading as I have, I should break down altogether," said Hermione, as, with her eyes full of tears and her face pale with emotion, she got into her carriage and drove off to Starton, where she really had something to do—for her indeed much.

She had to buy more house-linen and crockery for the Convalescent Home, which had been in working order for some time now and for which she supplied the greater part of the funds. Mr. Lascelles, unlike her husband, instead of sparing her trouble gave her all the occupation he could devise. It was in his plan to lead her to a certain kind of independence of action—under his own guidance—which should break down her reliance on Richard. He felt so sure of the hold which he himself had over her now, that he was not afraid of developing her love of freedom to an inconvenient breadth; and for the rest, it was all so much gained. Thus, he gave her things to do for the Home which she had never done for her own house, wishing to familiarize her with the details of domestic management so that she should presently take her own affairs in hand. Not that he particularly cared whether she were her own housekeeper or not; but it would be one other habit of life broken through, and so far one other blow dealt to Richard. And then, every task which he gave her to perform was an added link between them, and both drew her closer and kept her more secure.

When she had done all that she had to do, and bought linen that was far too fine and crockery that was far too fragile, she turned back on her way home; and when she was about a mile from the Abbey she overtook Mr. Lascelles walking with Theresa Molyneux. She stopped the carriage to speak to them, and at a glance Mr. Lascelles saw that something was amiss. He had learned her face better in these few months than Richard had after twenty years' possession. But Richard had not studied it with the same eagerness as he. The one believed that he knew all that the other had set himself to learn ; and when you have the whole poem by heart, why study the form of the letters? It is different when you are casting about for the formula of Abracadabra ; then the shapes of things are important ; but for the poem, all you want is the rhythm, the melody, the meaning ; and these poor Richard believed that he had in inalienable possession for ever.

Theresa's sensitive face changed when Hermione drew up. She had been having a delightful half-hour's walk with Mr. Lascelles—her time of holy enchantment —and she was sorry to be called back to prosaic life by the intrusion of the one woman whose claims on that beloved Superior's attention she instinctively felt clashed with her own. Not that she confessed to herself that she was jealous ; certainly not. The drama played among them all did not include the confession of human passions. It was all spiritual, all impersonal and godly. They were like creatures made of gas, without form or substance ; something in, but not of, humanity with its weaknesses and instincts. Mr. Lascelles, as a priest, was no longer a man ; his "penitents" had ceased to be women. So, at least, they said to themselves and among each other ; gravely ; and unlike the famous augurs, they did not laugh when they fastened on their masks and pretended that names change things, and that love, when it calls itself religion, puts off passion and knows nothing of temptation.

" How tired you are looking, Theresa ! " said Hermione, after she had shaken hands with both.   " Take my carriage, dear, and let Beech drive you home.   I can walk this little way to the Abbey."

Churchlands was about half a mile distant, on the old London road ; the Abbey road branched off to the right; the house itself was, as has been said, about a mile from here.

" Oh, no, I am not at all tired, thank you, dear Mrs. Fullerton," said Theresa, her manner as gratified as Hermione's had been kind.

" You look so ; does she not, Superior ? " asked Hermione, still sweet and gracious and apparently only solicitous to be of good service to the girl.   She thought so herself ; but she was not clever at introspection.

" It would be better for you to drive home," said Mr. Lascelles to Theresa, by way of answer.   " You have had a long walk, and you are not very strong."

" Indeed, I am not tired ! " she said eagerly, forgetting her obedience in her disappointment. She had expected that the vicar would have walked home with her, and

perhaps have stayed to four-o'clock tea ; and she was so
sorry to have her hope destroyed that she neglected her
manners.   Now he would probably go with Mrs. Fullerton, seeing that the Vicarage lay beyond the Abbey,
indeed between the Abbey and the village ; but there
was just the chance of his still walking with her, not
liking to leave her so pointedly, which her acceptance of
the carriage would destroy.

  " It would be better for you to be driven home, dear,"
persisted Hermione sweetly.   " But if you will not take
the carriage—can I set you down anywhere, Superior ? "

  Theresa's flushed face quivered and her eyes filled up
with tears.   Mr. Lascelles glanced rapidly from her to
Hermione and from Hermione back again to Theresa.
This little comedy amused him.   What a king he felt
among all these silly women prostrate at his feet, and
how easy it is for a man, who knows what he is about, to
dominate the inferior creature, now by its weakness and
now by its passions, if at times by its virtues !   Yet they
were useful.

  " Thank you," he said in an almost indifferent tone to
Hermione.   " You will do me a service.   I have to go to
the Home, and time presses.   This dear child here," with
a paternal smile to Theresa, " had something to say to

me, and you know a good pastor is the servant if also the protector of his flock. But I think it would be better if you were sent home first," he added to Theresa. "Indeed, I wish it."

He liked the feeling of ordering her movements and disposing of Hermione's carriage. No passion was so strong with him as the love of command.

Theresa said no more. She understood her sentence, and found in her obedience a sorrowful kind of solace for her banishment.

"Thank you," she said submissively; "I will take it, please."

But she did not look at Hermione while she spoke. She accepted the carriage as *his* gift, and obeyed *his* will in doing so; which made all the difference in her mind. She was not in the least degree grateful to Hermione though she kissed her and called her "dear," and thanked her in proper form as she got in and drove off. She felt as if the pretty woman had been some horrible old witch who had broken in on a scene of blessedness, and scattered all its glory into gloom; and when she turned her head and saw that beloved man walking by Hermione's side, leaning down as he had been leaning down to her, she gave a sob so irrepressible and deep that the groom turned round to look at her, thinking that she was ill or that she had called him.

This walking on the high road, with or without Mr. Lascelles, was of itself a strange innovation on Hermione's old indolent habits; but the vicar had been gradually breaking her in to more activity of body as well as more independence of mind, seeing the good to be gained in the future. He had dealt with her gently; it is only right to say this; and his "penitent" though she was, he had not as yet exacted daily matins from her, though he had of late enforced her attendance at Early Celebration; of which fact Richard, an early riser for his own part, had not been made aware. The Abbey study did not look on the drive nor the gate nor the road, but into the shrubbery where nothing ever moved save the squirrels and the birds; and as breakfast was not supposed to be ready before half-past nine o'clock at the earliest, Hermione had time to go down to church at eight and be at home again long before the gong sounded on Sunday morning. Virginia had been a regular attendant at matins ever since they began; but neither did her father know this any more than he knew what his wife was doing. Nor indeed did her mother at the first, and until she herself was prepared. Part of the power of the sect to which

Mr. Lascelles belonged lies in its secret dealing with women and the young, and the consequent gradual weakening of home authority which is to be replaced by clerical domination; and the vicar carried out this principle of secret dealing to its fullest extent.

"What is the matter with you, my dear child?" he asked, so soon as the little carriage had taken Theresa out of hearing. "That sweet, sensitive face of yours tells me that something has gone wrong."

(Not half an hour ago he had said to Theresa, looking up at him with feverish delight :—

"That sweet, sensitive face of yours tells me that you are happy, and my heart adds why.")

"I have just been insulted by Lady Maine," said Hermione; "and I think most cruelly."

"What can you expect from such a creature!" said Mr. Lascelles, with flaming eyes and angry disdain. "When was a Protestant other than brutal and ill-bred! It is the essence of the creed! But tell me what she has been doing to you, my poor child."

Hermione told him; perhaps with a little unconscious exaggeration; making a stronger case against her husband than was strictly true, and widening the borders of my lady's denunciations, which she need scarcely have done.

But she had come to the pass of wishing to make Richard not only responsible for all her vexations but patently her enemy; and she was not so much irritated against Lady Maine, by whom her latest blow had been given, as she was against Richard, as the cause why she had been struck at all.

"I am sorry for your annoyance. It must be hard for you to bear, with such a sweet and loving nature as yours and with your brilliant social position—which rightfully should have commanded the homage of the whole county and would, but for your miserable marriage," said Mr. Lascelles, rasping the sore which he appeared to soothe. "Of course, I do not much regret that you are not counted among the friends of such a woman as Lady Maine, sorry as I am for the cause," he continued, half seriously, half playfully. "Nor do I regret that you are not in the gay world, like those whose actions are unimportant because their lives do not furnish examples. Your actions are important because your life does furnish an example; and anything which separates you from the Protestant world is a gain to the Catholic cause."

"You are always so good!" said Hermione flattered. "Of course, you understand that I do not regret the dinner as a mere amusement. I was so much pained at the whole thing only because it was another instance of the disesteem in which my husband is held, and I in consequence."

" No, not you in consequence! Every one has but one word to say of you, and that a word of praise!" said Mr. Lascelles eagerly. "And what you are to me, you know well enough," he added in a lower voice, artificially broken.

"Thank you," said Hermione, speaking with some difficulty.

How handsome and well-bred and sympathetic he was! After all, her life was not so very pitiable if she could count such a friend as this among its chief treasures!

" For myself," continued Mr. Lascelles after a pause, " I would be glad to see you stand out yet more than you have hitherto done, as one of the most notable supporters of the Church. I want you to show the world that you have renounced it, with all its pomps and vanities, its infidelities and carelessness of divine things, and that you belong wholly to us, the living body of believers, who will give you more happiness if less pleasure, more peace if less pomp."

" I will," murmured Hermione.

" Even to public confession by means of dress and ornament ? " he asked, smiling.—

" By means of anything ! " said Hermione, with dangerous fervour.

He always dominated her when they were together. It was so sweet to follow as he directed !

" Some day then we will what the French call *parler chiffons* together," he said, still smiling. " I must not have you again as you were the other night at your own house. You were too lovely ! Lovely you will always be, my dear child, under any garb ; but I must have you simpler and less mundane in your attractiveness for the future. Will you let me guide you in your fashions as well as in all the rest ? " with courtly graciousness.

" Yes," said Hermione with mingled pain and pleasure ; the pretty woman's love of display warring with the tender woman's love of obedience and liking to be commended.

" You are such a sweet dear girl ! " said Mr. Lascelles, warmly, and, no one being in sight, he took her gloved hand from out her muff and laid it on his arm, pressing it against him tenderly.

"And now for another thing," he said, after a short pause. "We will make up for the loss of frivolous factitious gaiety by a closer affection among ourselves. We will organize social evenings once a week, either at the Vicarage or at Churchlands. This will bring some little brightness into your sad home life, and create a little diversion for your sorrowful thoughts. Would you like this?"

"Yes," said Hermione, looking up like a pleased child.

"Let us then begin next Sunday. We will spend the evening together; all our little band; and every Sunday evening, either at the Vicarage or Churchlands. Sunday duties do not include with us Sabbatarian severities, and the religious life, if it renounces the world, draws closer together those who have entered into it."

"It will be charming," said Hermione, rapidly considering that she was justified in this strange step by Lady Maine's exclusion, and that she was fortified so far against any discomfort with her husband should there be any to meet. She had been "cut" because of him, and she was in her right to find society elsewhere. Evil does sometimes work for good, she thought, and this was a case in point. Between a quiet evening at the Vicarage, with Mr. Lascelles making subtle love to her —love which it was against neither her honour nor her conscience to accept and return—and the most brilliant gathering elsewhere, there was not a doubt which to choose ; and the picture of the holy community bound together under his leadership was one that gave her both pleasure and courage.

Nevertheless, it was no more an agreeable moment than some others had been when she set herself to tell Richard on Sunday morning that he must dine alone to-day, as she and Virginia were " going to the Vicarage after evensong, where they would have supper." For a moment her husband made no reply. He looked startled, but that was all. It was the first time since their marriage that she had left him on such a plea ; but many things had happened for the first time of late, and he was getting sorrowfully used to novelties.

" Very well, my wife," he said, looking at her kindly. " I wish it had been to any other place ; but I will do my best without you and my Ladybird," turning to Virginia lovingly.

Virginia, mindful of Sister Agnes, did not look up. She knew that her father was looking at her, and longed to return his love, as of old ; but she had been forbidden, and must obey.

"We must go out sometimes," said Hermione a little peevishly. " Since the world has cut us because of you, we are thrown back, of course, on friends who like Virginia and me personally, and do not mix us all up as Infidels together."

" Has the world cut you? It is the first that I have heard of it," said Richard mildly.

"You never hear anything," returned Hermione disdainfully. "You are buried in those odious studies, and we might go to ruin before you would see that anything was wrong."

" I think not, my wife. I see clearly enough that things are going wrong now," he said. " But I confess that I lack the power to put them right."

" Yes. I am thankful to say you do," returned Hermione ; " taking the words as you mean them ; for that would be to cut us off from our religious privileges, and to forbid the new life into which Virginia and I have entered."

"You are right," he said. " Had I the power I would pull back you and our child from the path in which you are walking, as I would pull you back from any other that was leading straight to folly and false-hood."

"Oh, papa! don't!" cried Virginia, putting up her hands to her face.

"For shame, Richard! I wonder how you dare to talk such horrid blasphemy before Virginia!" said Hermione. "It is bad enough to say what you do to me when we are alone; but I think that you should respect her, at all events."

"Dear wife, you seem to forget that I speak as I think, and that what you call blasphemy I call reason and common sense," he answered.

"As if reason can judge of Divine things!" said Hermione with that disdain of intellect which piety assumes to itself as part of its sovereignty over nature and the natural man. "Reason, as you call it, has been the greatest curse of man since the Fall. We should have had no sin, no death, if the serpent had not reasoned and Eve had not listened," she added, quoting a phrase from last Sunday's sermon.

"I think I know a greater curse," returned Richard; "superstition and priestcraft; which have done the human race more harm than reason and knowledge have yet been able to make good."

"Than knowledge!—oh! that Tree of Knowledge!" said Hermione, still disdainful.

"What would you have in its place, wife—ignorance?"

"Faith!" she cried; "faith in God's Word. That is what we want, Richard, and obedience to the ordinances and commands of the Church."

"And you forget all the precious blood that has been shed, all the useful lives which have been cut short, and the unfathomable misery that has been occasioned to thousands, that a few old wives' fables might be upheld which the first breath of science has blown away? Yet your Divine Word set them forth as true, and your Infallible Church declared belief in them to be integral to salvation and right living."

"The Bible was not written to teach us science; it was written for our souls," said Hermione.

"I should think twice before I accepted statements which cannot be proved on the faith of an authority which has broken down so signally whenever it has been tested," said Richard.

"And I accept it all," cried Hermione. "And what I cannot understand the Church can explain. Both Virginia and I believe every word of the Bible, and every teaching of the Church, and you hurt and offend us both when you say the awful things that you do, and cast ridicule upon what is the most sacred thing in life to us."

"So! you and our child have really ranged your-selves on the side which produced the Inquisition and lighted the fires in Smithfield; and either killed those astronomers who denied the current figments of the day, or forced them, like Galileo, to recant under pain of death? You have gone over to the side which I have given my life to combat? If any one has cause to feel aggrieved, dear wife, it is I, not you. I stay where I was; it is you who have moved, and left my guidance for a stranger's."

"I can only say, Thank God, yes!" said Hermione bitterly but sincerely. "We have left you, and I am thankful for it. You are the enemy of the Church, and we are her faithful children. If we would be true to our Lord, we must be against you, Richard. You make us your enemies. It is your doing, not ours."

What was there in the words which touched him so deeply? stung him so painfully? His face became deadly pale, his lips quivered, and his eyes filled with sudden tears. They were unmanly, if one will, and unusual; but they were beyond his power to prevent.

"You and Virginia are my enemies?" he said very slowly, after he had conquered that sudden sweep of emotion. "Is there then enmity between us, wife?—on your side at least; on mine, you know, is only love! It is a strange word to my ears from you. Are you my enemy, wife?" he repeated, as if he scarcely realized his own words.

"Yes, I am," said Hermione hardily. She thought she was testifying.

He gave a little start, and his right hand, lying softly doubled on the table, clenched itself till the knuckles were white and strained. But he sat calm and to all appearance unmoved; and his still face and lowered eyes gave no sign.

"It is your fault. Why are you so irreligious?" said Hermione, looking at him with sudden soft regret.

She was a tender-hearted creature, and did not like to pain even her infidel husband, for all that she was so angry with him. She wanted him to be punished, but she regretted that his chastisement had been laid on her to inflict.

"You make me your enemy, Richard," she repeated more softly; "because you are the enemy of the Church."

He did not answer; but after another short pause got up from his chair and lightly touched her pretty golden head as he passed. His hand trembled, and his step was not quite firm.

"Bless you, old love!" he said, almost below his breath; then kissed Virginia on the forehead, half sighing as he murmured: "My little Ladybird—my own little child!"

And with this he crossed the hall and went back into his study, which somehow seemed to have become so desolate and empty! Here he sat, as he had sat once before, feeling that his treasure-house had been broken into and the jewel of his life stolen from him. Should he ever find it again? or was his life to be henceforth only a regret?—his happiness nothing but a lost dream?

This day was to him like the beginning of the day of death; and when in the evening Hermione and Virginia were at the Vicarage—the one happy in the attentions of her spiritual gallant, the other blessed in the society of her spiritual mother, and both, like all the rest gathered there, warmed and flushed by that mental excitement which goes by the name of religious fervour —Richard was trying to work off his dumb depression by a tough bit of philosophy which went to prove that

all matter is a function of mind and all emotion a function of matter. But he never got beyond the first page.
The image of his little daughter whom he so fondly
loved; of the wife who had been his second and dearer
self through all his manhood; of his trust and their one-
time faith, came ever between him and the words ;
and the thought that their love had gone from him, while
he was helpless to prevent or retain, obscured the reasonings by which human life was reduced to molecular
disturbance, and left him only the fact of mental suffering
which was so acute as to be almost bodily anguish.

CHAPTER II.

RECALCITRANT.

NEXT to Hermione who was won, and Richard who was impracticable, the conquest of Ringrove Hardisty, if it could be accomplished, would be the most important to the vicar. The Churchlands people were valuable, but the master of Monkshall would be more valuable still. He was richer and had more solid local influence than Cuthbert. As churchwarden elected by the parish he might, unless thus won over, be troublesome and something more; and, anti-ritualist as he was known to be, his conversion to "Catholicism" would be both an honour to his converter as the sign of superior mental strength, and the disarming of a formidable opponent.

As yet this conquest was no nearer than in the beginning. Where Cuthbert, already devoted to Bach and blue china, reverencing Botticelli and despising Raffaelle, had yielded without difficulty to the new régime of æsthetic piety and mediæval affectation—like ripe fruit falling by its own weight—Ringrove Hardisty,

practical rather than æsthetic, a citizen rather than a
sectarian, of the broadest section of the Broad Church
party, and by nature intolerant of personal interference,
had stood out firmly against all the pressure that had
been brought to bear on him; and had resisted both
the sensuous stateliness of the ritual and the spiritual
beseechings of Virginia with equal constancy. And the
vicar's favourite dream of the strong young man of the
parish brought low—the Samson of Erastianism with
his head in the lap of the Church—was still only a
dream.

How could it be realized? Arguments founded on
ecclesiastical assumption, on tradition and the Fathers,
were useless with a man who started with the proposition that the Church was only a function of the State,
and the clergy no more divinely inspired nor appointed
than so many soldiers or sailors. His strong English
good sense was of that hard granitic kind which no
sophisms could mould, no hysterical enthusiasm soften;
and it would be emphatically wasting time to assure him
that the Church has thaumaturgical powers as well as
the keys of heaven and hell, and that the transmuta-
tion of matter and the eternal destination of souls
belong to Canterbury all the same as to Rome.

Failing this conversion by reason there remained affection; and through his known love for Virginia the vicar thought there was a chance of leading Ringrove to obedience and submission. Further than this Mr. Lascelles specially desired that he should be made to feel the righteousness of true religion and the easiness of the ritualistic yoke :—so different from that which the Evangelical school lays on men's shoulders! With Catholics the whole thing was concentrated in Obedience. This given, the rest was easy. Thus—again taking the test of days—he thought it would be a step gained if he could show Ringrove that Sunday duties did not include Sabbatarian severities, as he had said to Hermione, but that, when the offices of the Church were over, good Catholics were free to enjoy themselves, like saints who had entered into their reward.

A short time before Christmas then, Mr. Lascelles told the Molyneux's that he wished them to ask Ringrove Hardisty to one of their Sunday suppers ; and at the same time he told Hermione that she was to bring him in her carriage. He was to be made much of, and his coming treated as a gentle kind of fête. He was to be made to feel that, notorious outsider as he was, the broad cloak of Christian charity covered him like the

rest—the Catholic fold was open for him as for all
other straying sheep—and he was to be shown that
the courtesy of high-bred gentlemen was as characteristic
of Churchmen as of worldlings. All this was as much
part of the game to be played as so many moves in
chess, and the vicar thought that he had arranged his
pieces to advantage.

"I hope greatly that he may be induced to become
one of us by your personal influence and his own
hope," said Mr. Lascelles to Hermione, in the manner of
one laying on her a work to perform. "We all know his
aspirations," he added; "and if he belonged to us, and
our dear child were not too decided in the holier way of
celibacy, it would be a good thing for the place; but as
it is—Never!" said Mr. Lascelles, closing his thin lips
firmly, conscious that here at least he held the keys and
could open or shut at his pleasure.

Wherefore, when Aunt Catherine received her instructions to ask young Hardisty next Sunday evening,
and Hermione received hers to bring him as specially
her friend though their guest, Virginia was again admonished by Sister Agnes to be very sweet and tender
to him, for the sake of convincing him that his best
friends were in the Church. She did not see that she

was being made use of as a lure—that she was trading
on the poor fellow's love for her. She was only made to
feel herself a vessel consecrated by the Church to be
the means of grace to another.

It was now close on Christmas, as has been said.
For the last three or four years Ringrove had dined on
this day at the Abbey, and he expected to be invited
this year again as before. But Mr. Lascelles intended
otherwise. It was his design that Hermione and
Virginia should dine with him at the Vicarage—his
desire that Ringrove should come with them. He
would not have it a "band" day; only such priests as
might have come to help him with the services, the
Abbey ladies, and the young fellow who wanted to
marry Virginia, but who should not unless he would
come over; and this Sunday evening at Churchlands was
to be the initiation. If he could bear this, he could
bear more ; and the certain hostility of his churchwardenship would be neutralized. If he could not
bear it, then he would stand out more openly than he
had hitherto done; he would range himself on Richard's
side, or at least would have the credit of doing so—
which would give room for much popular distrust ;
he would be called Atheist, like Richard; Hermione

and Virginia should cut him—so should all the Church party; his churchwardenship would be impotent, and his strength taken from him. The line of demarcation would be more broadly traced, and they would all shorten their swords.

Astute as he was, Mr. Lascelles had not forgotten those three important characteristics of Ringrove Hardisty, the man who was to be won over or forced into such a position as should weaken his hostility by reason of his allies—namely, his dislike to clerical domination, his possibilities of jealousy, and, for all his love for Virginia, his loyal friendship for Virginia's father. On the contrary, he had considered all three carefully; but there was always that "perhaps;" and love with young men is sometimes stronger than principle or self-respect. If he could be made to feel that submission to the Church would bring the reward of Virginia?—Love, if kept alive by hope, might work the miracle of faith here as elsewhere, thought the vicar; and to this end the child must be made to understand that kindness and sweetness to Ringrove were her religious duties now, whatever the future might be. This was cruel enough; but the priesthood of which the Honourable and Reverend Launcelot Lascelles was such a typical member does not trouble

itself much about human suffering. It seeks only for
ground whereon to sow its seed of supremacy; and blood
and tears fertilize the soil as well as anything else.

These Sunday suppers were so far secret that Ringrove knew nothing of them. Richard was not the man
to complain that his wife and daughter left him to dine
alone once a week and Ringrove was not the man to
whom gossip naturally gravitated ; and as he never went
to church in the afternoon or evening, he did not see the
Abbey carriage take up the vicar and his sister and drive
off to the Vicarage or Churchlands instead of home.
Hence he knew nothing of the new order of things, and
when Hermione said to him prettily : " I want you to go
with Virginia and me to Churchlands next Sunday,
after evensong—I know that you are invited," he had
no reason for refusing; especially as Virginia said, even
more earnestly than her mother : " Yes, you must come,
Ringrove ; we want you there so much."

On the contrary, far from refusing, he was boyishly
glad to go, seeing that he had been entreated by the girl
who stood with him as his ideal of womanly purity and
grace. He did not much care for the Molyneux's. He
thought Aunt Catherine slightly mad; Cuthbert more
than weak ; Theresa excitable beyond reason ; but Her-

mione was always delightful to him, and Virginia was his
beloved.

" Do *you* want me to go, Virginia ? " he asked in a
low voice and with marked emphasis.

" Yes ; you know that I do," she said softly and with
intentional kindness—was it not her duty to lead him
gently to the fold?

His heart beat fast, and he drew his chair a little
closer to where she was sitting always at work on her
rich quaint ecclesiastical embroidery.   She coloured and
looked embarrassed.

" You know we all wish that you were one of us,"
she said, involuntarily shrinking back.

" One of us ! Is there one party in the place
so distinctly marked as this ?   And are you of it
and I of another ? " he asked, the colour in his face
too.

" Surely," said Virginia, lifting up her eyes.   " We
belong to the Church."

" I am a Churchman too," Ringrove returned.

She shook her head.

" No ; you are a Protestant," she answered quite
simply.   " We are Catholics."

" The English National Church used to be Protestant

before the extremes of these later times became fashionable," said Ringrove manfully.

" It lapsed," answered Virginia ; " but we are trying
to bring it back to the right way ; and you must be one
of us, Ringrove," with one of her sweet rare smiles.

He smiled too, but incredulously.

" Submission to the clergy is not much in my line,"
he said. " If you put them in the place of power again,
we shall have lost all that our fathers fought for in olden
times—all the liberties that they won for us with their
lives."

" If only they were in their old place ! " cried Virginia
with enthusiasm. " If the Church, and by the Church
Christianity, were but the rule of one's life ! "

" Christianity is not necessarily the Church," said
Ringrove. " We are all of the Church—your father as
well ; like every man who is noble and faithful to his own
conscience. What more can we have than truth and
goodness ? "

" Faith and obedience," said Virginia.

" Yes, but obedience to what ? To my mind the
influence of such a man as your father is better than
that of a dozen churches," said Ringrove, thinking that
if he touched the right chord he might " do good " and

"make Virginia think." As if people become zealots for want of thought!—as little as they become free-thinkers and repudiators of the faith of their childhood for gaiety of heart!

Virginia looked away into the distance, and her eyes grew dark and moist.

"Papa follows his own way; but we must obey the higher law," she said sorrowfully.

"Is there a higher law than a woman's obedience to her husband—a daughter's to her father?" asked Ringrove earnestly.

"Yes," she said; "the Church is higher."

Ringrove could not answer. Turn where he would, he was always met by the one fixed barrier—the Church set in the place of God, nobler than humanity, truer than love. For a moment he was silent, realizing something of what Richard felt in the vagueness but unconquer-ableness of the influences that had so entirely changed both Hermione and Virginia. But he would not give up the struggle yet. Virginia was worth even a little misunderstanding of motives—a little false appearance; and if he kept close to her and her mother he might perhaps after all do that good of which he had already thought. Still, he must not let false appearances be too strong, and he had always his loyalty to Richard to remember.

"You will not think that I am taking part against your father if I go with you to Churchlands next Sunday?" he asked suddenly. "I know that they do not come here now—and why; and I should be more than sorry to seem to go over to the other side. You know how sincerely I love and respect him—as well as Mrs. Fullerton and you," he added in a moved voice; "and I should not like anyone to think that I had gone against him."

"We could never believe that you would take part against papa," said Virginia gravely. "No one does, Ringrove! He separates himself!" Tears came into her eyes, as they always did when she spoke of her father. As a daughter she loved him so tenderly, and until now had been so proud of him!—but as a Christian she was bound to hold him accursed and to steel her heart against him. She could only pray for him; perform penance in his intention; think how his heart, so hardened now against the truth, might be touched and opened;—but for communion or authority he was as one dead. Yet the sorrow of that death never quite passed from her consciousness.

"But, dear Virginia, you must allow his right of private judgment—in all fairness and common liberality you must."

"No, Ringrove—no one has the right of private judgment," she said gently but firmly. "We are the children of the Church, and our duty is to obey our Mother." With a sudden impulse she leaned forward and laid her hand on his shoulder. "And one day," she said, her eyes looking into his straight and full, tender and loving; "one day, Ringrove, you will be her dutiful son too, and we shall all make one family together."

She meant a family of good Catholics in Crossholme; Ringrove took it as a special household of themselves— of him and her together. His colour went and came, his breathing was oppressed, his heart beat fast and he trembled like a girl.

"Oh, Virginia!" he said, taking her hand and holding it between both his own; "will you not be my own— make one family with me?—for love's sake and because you know that you can trust me with your happiness? Let our minor points of difference go! You know that I love you, Virginia!—cannot you love me?"

She shrank away as before.

" Do not talk to me like that," she said. " I meant only that we should all be good Catholics, good Church people, here together—brothers and sisters—friends— whatever you like to call it. But I do not think of anything else, or want anything else; and unless I am commanded differently, I shall always live as I am now."

" Commanded by whom, Virginia ?" asked Ringrove jealously.

" By my Director," said Virginia gravely.

At this moment Hermione returned from a little business that she had been transacting with Sister Barbara, from the Home, and that had cost her just thirty pounds—"to go on with."

"You are coming with us, Ringrove ?" she asked, not noticing the flush on the face of the one, the pallor on that of the other, Virginia's shrinking attitude, nor his trouble and disappointment.

" Yes," he said, trying to speak cheerfully.

She smiled her pleasure.

" I will take you," she said. " Come to evensong, and then we can all go together. That will at least insure your coming to church once more than usual, you naughty person !"—glad as at a victory foredoomed.

"I think church once a day enough," said Ringrove quietly, but stealing a glance at Virginia.

Hermione shook her forefinger playfully.

"Such a heathen as you are!" she said laughing. "But you are to be reformed; so you might as well begin to set about it now," she added in her sweetest manner.

She was so happy at this moment! Sister Barbara had brought her a charming little note from "Superior" —a note of such mingled flattery and command, such subtle love-making and open confession of her "value to the cause," as had made her heart leap like a girl's, and dressed the grey dull winter's day in gold and rose colour throughout.

He shook his head half-sadly, half-playfully, to match her pleasant humour, and soon after took his leave, the matter standing as the vicar had arranged. So, next Sunday evening, Ringrove was carried off by Hermione to what might be considered one of the fore-courts of the sacred compound, and made the subject of the Crossholme hierophant's latest experiment.

"I am glad to see you here, Mr. Hardisty," said Mr. Lascelles, taking the lead as he always did when with his "band," and coming forward to receive the

Fullertons and Ringrove as if he, not Cuthbert, had been
the master of the house. He had preceded them by a
few minutes, having been taken by the Molyneux's. "It
is very good of you to come among us in this informal
way. It is the kind of feeling I wish to see established
among my flock."

"It was good of Miss Molyneux to ask me with Mrs.
Fullerton," said Ringrove stiffly, resenting the vicar's tone
of proprietorship in another man's house and "wondering
how that ass Cuthbert could stand it."

Cuthbert would have stood more than this had he
been put to it. One of those weak brothers to whom
the support of authority is essential, his strength was in
obedience as with other men it is in liberty. As it was,
he shook hands with Ringrove limply and said that he
was glad to see him tamely; and his halting, half-
hearted manner made the vicar's hospitable warmth still
more conspicuous, and threw himself, as the master of
the house, yet more in the shade.

"You know Virginia's friends, I think," the vicar then
said, as Ringrove, feeling somehow not quite as much at
home as he should be, looked round the room and saw
the little "band," at this moment mainly grouped about
two strange priests who had assisted Mr. Lascelles in the

service. He had a stock of wandering "brothers" always on hand, ready and glad to give their aid in this war which he was carrying on against freedom and Protestantism at Crossholme.

"Thanks, yes," he answered, shaking hands with those whom he knew ; after which the vicar presented him to " Father Truscott," and " Brother Swinfen," the one elderly and the other young, and both men of marked character in the cause which they had espoused. But Ringrove instinctively disliked both.   They were sincere without question ; but the Father was secret and the Brother was cruel; and each was, like Mr. Lascelles himself, a man with whom the end would at all times sanctify the means and who would never trouble himself about the deceptions that he might have to practise, the sorrow he might give, the promises to be broken, or the hope become certainty through his assurance that might be destroyed for ever.   They were Catholics, not men ; and human conscience was lost in sectarian partisanship.

" How did you like the Magnificat ?" Mr. Lascelles asked abruptly, when the little party had settled down and Ringrove's place had been assigned next to him.

" It was very fine," he answered ; "and new to me."

"Our sweet Mrs. Fullerton, who is always to the front in all good things, got it for me," said Mr. Lascelles, smiling as he looked at Hermione with a strange air of private proprietorship and secret mutual understanding. "She is always ready for every graceful duty. And that dear child of hers is following in her steps. Do you not see how charming she is becoming?"

"I have known Mrs. and Miss Fullerton all my life," returned Ringrove coldly, with a sudden flush that spoke of dangerous ground.

"What a privilege !" said Mr. Lascelles, still smiling. "How entirely then your appreciation must coincide with mine !"

"Perhaps it goes beyond yours," said Ringrove, stiffening his neck.

The vicar went on smiling.

"That is impossible," he answered ; and looked over to Hermione again as one who knew more than was confessed.

"What a splendid St. George that young Mr. Hardisty would make !" said Aunt Catherine in a whisper to Father Truscott, who stroked his ample beard and assented paternally, knowing the rift within that shaky lute which did duty for brain with the poor weak

creature. Always silly, her spiritual exaltation had
destroyed the little common sense that had hitherto been
just enough to keep her from absolute folly, and was fast
rendering her a fit inmate for a lunatic asylum.   Saints
and holy personages—she saw them everywhere; and
lived in an atmosphere of hagiology which made real life
less true to her than were these visionary existences.
Father Truscott was St. Peter, Brother Swinfen St.
Sebastian, and the vicar himself was St. Paul, and the
leader of all.

This was the strangest evening that Ringrove had
ever spent, and the most antipathetic. He, a rank
outsider, felt himself almost an impostor in being there
at all.   It was not his place, not his world, though he was
made much of by Mr. Lascelles and Hermione, and
flattered as he had never been flattered before and did
not like now.   Moreover the extraordinary attentions
paid to Mr. Lascelles by the ladies during the evening
revolted him even more than those paid to himself embarrassed.   The whole thing was a reversal of common
custom, and to him detestable.   Aunt Catherine placed
his chair—the vicar's armchair—sacred to him only—
which no one else was ever allowed to use and which
stood in one special place in the room, conspicuous by

its rich covering of some gold-embroidered red Venetian stuff. Theresa brought him a foot-stool, and arranged the fire-screen for his sole benefit. One lady brought a cushion which she was sure would make him more comfortable ; and another took off her own shawl to lay across his knees. Once he got up for a book, when Aunt Catherine and Theresa, and one or two more, all rushed forward in a scramble of white hands and floating folds to prevent his having the trouble; and even indolent, composed Hermione, looking at him tenderly, said : "Why did you not ask me to give it to you, dear Superior ?"

It was he who was ministered to and they who courted ; and to Ringrove, accustomed to think of women as, in a certain sense, sacred creatures whom it was a strong man's privilege to serve, this Eastern attitude of a lord in his harem, spiritual though it might be, was un-English, unmanly, and—let the word pass— loathsome.

Add to this the odd kind of familiarity that existed among them—the smiles and looks that passed from one to the other as allusions were made of which they only had the key—the jargon that they talked, and the shibboleth of "dears" and "sisters," "brothers" and "beloveds," which was their sign of fraternity—and it is easy to understand the state of Ringrove's mind; a state however which was not seen nor allowed for by the little band. They had been so much accustomed, for some months now, to treat the vicar among themselves like a living idol, a sacred personage, that they did not realize the natural disgust of an unconverted Samson, nor the natural jealousy of an old friend who had remained an outsider.

For the rest, Mr. Lascelles talked to him with less patronage and more conventional respect than was usual with him when seated in his chair of state as the private pope and autocratic director of his flock. He thought the young master of Monkshall possible, and worth the trial; and though it was not pleasant to come down from his semi-sacred heights and meet any man as an equal on level ground, yet to-night it was politic;—and the vicar was a man with whom policy was potent.

Among other things he said that he had formed his opinion of his flock greatly on what the Abbey ladies had told him, finding their judgment singularly correct as time had gone on and he had verified it by his own experience. "And this being so," he said graciously, seeming to think Ringrove was to be held by urbanity

above all things ; " I need hardly say what my opinion
is of you. I fear it would make you vain—as the reflection of theirs."

Ringrove looked over to Virginia, sitting in a low
chair close to Mr. Truscott, her face turned up to his
with even more than its usual saintly expression—with
something in it that was almost rapt—as the old priest
spoke to her with evident earnestness, but softly, so that
no one else should hear what he said. Then Ringrove
looked at Hermione who was on the vicar's right hand,
with the same tenderness in her dark-blue eyes as used
to be in them when she sat by her husband. More revolted than flattered by the vicar's words, not caring to
be assured of the good-will of people whom he had
known and loved all his life, by a man who was the
latest of their friends, hardened and irritated, not softened
and soothed, Ringrove slightly lifted his upper lip and
looked at the vicar coldly.

" I think I should rely on the good feeling of my
old friends without the need of assurance from anyone," he said slowly and with unmistakable haughtiness.
Then, turning to Hermione, he added affectionately :
" We have known each other so many years now we
scarcely need an interpreter, do we, Mrs. Fullerton ? "

" When you are good—no, " she laughed confusedly.

" Yes, I know all that," returned Mr. Lascelles tranquilly ; "but assurance can be made doubly sure for all of us. Is it not so ? It pleases me to hear that I have been spoken well of in my absence, and I like to pass on the good things."

" Dear Superior ! you are always so kind !" said Hermione, this time tenderly as well as confusedly.

" Our child seems interested," then said the vicar rather suddenly. "I wonder what Father Truscott is teaching her."

" Dear Father Truscott ! something good and precious," returned Hermione with an artificial intonation.

"Oh, that, of course !" answered Mr. Lascelles airily. Then laying his hand on Ringrove who half rose to interrupt the conversation which they pronounced good with so much certainty and which he feared was harmful with even more conviction, he said : " No, do not interrupt them, Mr. Hardisty. I think I do know what they are talking about. Shall I tell you ?—The best use to be made of riches. That is an important matter in the future with our young friend," he went on to say, speaking as if to one who was only so much interested in the matter as himself. " Her settlement in life will be a grave consideration with us all. She will have so much power, and the man who administers her fortune ought to be one of a character and conduct rare to find."

Ringrove flushed to the roots of his hair.

" Few men are good enough for her," he said with extreme embarrassment. " The best would have to make up in love and care for what he wanted in goodness."

" Yes, you are about right," said the vicar paternally. " But we must do our best to find him—a high-minded, well-principled man, and a staunch Churchman."

" We are all Churchmen," Ringrove returned.

" Most of you in a sense; but Nationalists rather than Catholics," said the vicar.

" English," replied Ringrove.

" You mean Protestant and Erastian. We do not call those Churchmen," said the vicar with lofty pity. " And that dear child yonder must be careful. Her guide and companion for life must be sound, whatever else he may be."

" I suppose her father will have a word to say in a matter so important as this?" said Ringrove, his head held high.

" Mr. Fullerton? a confessed Agnostic—in other words an Atheist?—he arrange or influence in any way

the marriage of one who, in the Ages of Faith, would
have been a saint in life and canonized after death?—
certainly not!" said Mr. Lascelles with vigour. "I am
thankful to say that Virginia, like her mother, would
obey the voice of the Church in any grave circumstance
that might arise, and that no one not in accord with the
great doctrines of the faith—no one not a true child of
the Holy Mother—would have the smallest influence
over either. I think we may consider that fixed and
settled. The man to whom Virginia Fullerton gives the
rich treasure of her love, the sweet and holy sanctities of
her home, will be a pronounced and decided Catholic :—
Such a man as our dear Cuthbert Molyneux, for instance,"
he added, lowering his eyes; "who indeed would be the
best husband for her of all within my knowledge."

"Cuthbert Molyneux and Virginia Fullerton!" cried
Ringrove with passionate disdain. "You might as well
choose out of Earlswood at once, Mr. Lascelles!"

"Ah, Mr. Hardisty," said the vicar with a compassionate air; "you have yet to learn that the weak things
of the world confound and overcome the strong, when
God blesses the one and the others trust only to themselves. Ah!" suddenly changing his voice, "I see that
supper is ready. May I take you?" to Hermione; and

to Cuthbert: "My dear boy, will you not bring Virginia?"

With which arrangement all were fain to be content, for the will of Mr. Lascelles at Churchlands was as the laws of the Medes and Persians, and when he had spoken no one dared to remonstrate. As for Cuthbert, he had no desire to remonstrate; and when Theresa was assigned by the vicar to him, Ringrove Hardisty dared not, for the sake of good breeding. But for his consolation he was placed between Virginia and Theresa at the table; and as on Theresa's other hand was the vicar—he at the head and Cuthbert at the foot— she on her side had no wish to complain.

What a great god Zeus the vicar was!—how he regulated and marshalled his little world of subordinates and lovers, and made each do as he desired! Even the strange priests—Father Truscott, an older man and a more notorious—were made to feel that he was the lord and they were his subjects, he was the sun and they were his satellites. Perhaps he a little surpassed himself to-night, wishing to prove to Ringrove where the power lay and what course it would be wisest for him to adopt.

"My child," he said to Virginia, whose glass was full of water; "drink a little wine to-night."

" Must I, Superior ? " she asked.

She disliked wine, as girls of her age and nature do ; and looked on it as a penance.

He smiled in his grand way, and for all reply said to Cuthbert :

" My dear boy, fill Virginia's glass. No, not claret— Marsala ; the small glass. You can put it into your tumbler of water," he added to Virginia ; and Virginia obediently mixed the wine with the water and drank the draught which, to her unsophisticated taste, spoilt the whole meal.

Also to Theresa—who was growing thinner and more feverish day by day, and who had now taken a rather severe cold and had a hard, dry, hacking cough—he prescribed her diet, as one whose dictum admits no denial.

" Aunt Catherine ! " he called out to the god-daughter of the saint, pouring her folly into the ear of Father Truscott and giving him too the sense of doing penance out of the ordinary course of his Director's ordering ; " Aunt Catherine ! "

She started as if from sleep.

" Yes, dear Superior. What is it ? " she said confusedly. Perhaps of all the group she was the one who was most afraid of the vicar.

" Where is Theresa's beef-tea?" he asked. " She must take it regularly. Have I not ordered it?" peremptorily.

" Please, sir, cook forgot it," said the servant respectfully; more respectfully than he would have spoken either to Cuthbert or to Miss Molyneux.

Mr. Lascelles frowned. Cook was one of his " penitents;" she would not have kept her place else; and by the look of things she would have a hard time of it when next she came to confess the thoughts which were suggested but had never been harboured, and keep back the tale of malpractices which were done and not suspected.

" I am sorry for that," he said with awful gravity. " You had better then take it to-morrow morning, instead of coffee for breakfast," he said to Theresa. " It is essential for your health—quite essential."

" Very well, Superior," said Theresa, flattered and delighted. " I will. What may I have for supper now?"

" Meat," said Mr. Lascelles ; "and—Aunt Catherine, have you any bitter beer in the house?—Yes? Meat and a glass of bitter beer, my child," to Theresa. Then looking at her kindly, he added : "I must have you looking better than this; I am not at all pleased with you !"

The girl flushed and brightened ; then coughed a little heavily; but she had concentrated on herself all his thoughts, all his attention, and for the rest of the evening she was too happy to realize how feverish she felt, nor how hard her breath was to draw when she tried to take a full inspiration—after coughing say, and when her lungs had become exhausted.   Only when he said to her, after one of these fits of coughing : " My dear child, you must take care of yourself, for all our sakes. You must give up mattins for a short time, and until you have got rid of this cold ; "—only then did her spirits droop and her courage break, as, with tears in her eyes, she said piteously : " Oh ! must I be cut off from this privilege, dear Superior ? Surely not, unless I grow much worse ! "

But Mr. Lascelles, who did not like opposition, answered in his most courtly but conclusive way : " You must do as you are told, my child. No mattins for a week, nor Early Celebration next Sunday."   Then seeing her poor sensitive face change almost as if her death had been announced, he added in a caressing voice : " You can come to the Vicarage on the fine afternoons, and if the weather is too bad I will come and see you.   I shall know how to appreciate your obedience."

This was but a sample of the vicar's position at

Churchlands and of his rule over the little band of
" workers " whereof he was titular Superior and practical
demigod. He was glad of the opportunity of showing
his power to Ringrove, and how necessary it was to conciliate him, the great clerical Zeus, if steps of a grave
nature were to be taken with Virginia or any other.
Perhaps he was rather ostentatious in the way in which
he made his living puppets dance as he desired, and cruel
in his indifference to the chance of hurting them when
he pulled this string or touched that spring, and played
on them as a man might play on so many instruments
from which none but himself could draw that note or
sustain that pitch. At all risks the master of Monkshall
must be convinced that this was the winning side, and he,
the vicar, the dominant power; and that the man who
would marry Virginia must put himself in accord with
the only authority which she recognized as absolute, and
conciliate those whom alone she would obey.

All this was quite well-reasoned and logical so far as
it went and for whom it would have suited; but it went
too far for Ringrove; and it did not suit him. As supper
went on, he grew colder and more silent. His fine strong
face, usually so bright and cheerful, became pale and
hard; his figure grew straighter in its lines and stiffer

in its forms ; his voice became deeper in its tones and rougher in its quality. He left off trying to speak to Virginia, who was listening with strange eagerness to " Father Truscott's " account of a certain Order—which he forgot to say was " Romanist," not " Anglican ; " he did not care to see her turn to him, when he spoke to her, with the pain and reluctance of one brought down from the beauty of holiness to the sordidness of earth. He did not like to feel that he, the old friend who had loved her so long and reverenced her as his ideal, who had hoped to make her his wife and waited for her consent with that patience which true love and manly strength alone make possible—that he was set aside in favour of these strange men, these Fathers and Brothers and Superiors who had come down like so many locusts on the green plain of Crossholme society, and had destroyed all that was sweet and precious. He felt as keenly as even his own position, the pain and the shame of Richard's ; and how these men had thrust themselves between the husband and the wife—had taken the daughter from the father. Let it be that Richard Fullerton had " unfortunate opinions " in some things—that did not make him less the good man, the faithful friend, the loving husband, the devoted father that he was; nor soften the guilt of those who had come into his tranquil home and blighted its happiness with the poison of their fanaticism. They had killed the fairest flower of all; and like ghouls they lived and fattened on their work.

These thoughts passed like fire through his brain as he sat there, stiffening and hardening in his pain and wrath. But what was to be done? How could all this iniquity, under the name of religion, be checked?—how could things be brought back to their old places? He asked himself this question twenty times, and never found the answer; but his main thought was the same :—

"I must speak to Fullerton. He ought to know how things are, and prevent them from going farther if he can. It is all horrible, unwholesome, unnatural, and will lead to worse evil unless it can be checked."

So the evening of initiation which was to bring Ringrove Hardisty nearer by his love, served only to fling him yet farther off, and to make him even more strongly than before the vicar's opponent at Crossholme and the partisan of Richard at the Abbey. But, for all that, he did not give up his hope of Virginia.

CHAPTER III.

FROM INFORMATION RECEIVED.

IT is one thing to resolve to "speak about it," and another thing to do it, when that speaking involves the chance of placing oneself in a false position and doing more harm than good ; as Ringrove confessed to himself when he thought on Monday morning how he should best tell Richard Fullerton of his last night's experience at Churchlands, and put into his hand this ugly end of a twisted and embarrassing clue. He felt sure that his friend did not know how things really stood between his own family and the Vicarage ; and it was only right that he should be told. But it was a difficult thing to do, and might be a thankless task when done. Besides, no honourable man likes to go into a house as a guest and leave it as an informer ; and yet the need for this small social treachery seemed to Ringrove to be imperative.

For very love's sake those dear women must be denounced to him who alone had power to stop their downward course. For their own good they must be hurt now that they might be saved from destruction hereafter ; brought back to right reason and self-respect before they had committed themselves irrevocably to the degradation of clerical despotism.

All the same, reason it out as he might, it was unpleasant ; and no one could have more disliked the office which he had imposed on himself than did poor Ringrove, who, the soul of loyalty and honour, had yesterday consorted as one of themselves with Richard's enemies and to-day was considering how to compass their defeat.

Riding along the road, he caught the outline of a well-known figure walking with an easy undulating movement, and at not too break-neck speed, between the frosty hawthorn hedges. It was pretty Bee Nesbitt, swathed in furs up to her dimpled chin and acting as chaperon to two of her younger sisters, inasmuch as she was taking them out for their morning walk in default of Miss Laurie the governess, who had gone home for the Christmas holidays. For Bee, as the eldest, was her mother's right hand and second self, and held capable of any amount of chaperonage and protection over the younger ones. And as she was a good, true-hearted girl, she justified her mother's expectations and answered to all the demands made on her.

When Ringrove came up to her he dismounted, took
the bridle on his arm, and joined the girl who, next to
Virginia, seemed to him one of the sweetest of her kind,
and who, if less his ideal, was more his companion. Of
all the girls known to him he always said that he would
have liked Bee Nesbitt best for his sister. She, on her
side, always said that Ringrove Hardisty was just like one
of her own brothers—her eldest brother, say ; more to be
trusted and less teazing than either Fred or Harry ; and
that she wished he had been in fact what he was in
feeling. They were certainly great friends :—and they
made a charming contrast together.

"Why, Ringrove, is that you ? " said Bee with affected
surprise ; arching so much of her eyebrows as could be
seen for the tangle of curls and fluff of fur that came so
low on her broad white forehead.

She meant to express the " mild surprise and gentle
indignation" of her present state of mind ; for news had
come to them even before breakfast to-day of Ringrove
Hardisty's appearance at Churchlands last night, and of
how he was now accounted a member of the new school.
No longer the sturdy defender of parochial liberties, the
champion of the independence of the laity, he was to be
henceforth ranked as a partisan of ecclesiastical domi

'The sweetest of her kind.'

nation, and might be expected to be soon seen carrying a "Mary" banner in the wake of Cuthbert Molyneux swinging his incense-burner. And though Beatrice knew that half of what they had been told this morning by their maid—who had heard it from the butcher, who had heard it from the Churchlands cook herself—was exaggeration ; yet that other half? or even that other quarter? The smoke might be excessive, but it argued some fire underneath ; and with Ringrove Hardisty, the Crossholme Samson of Erastianism and lay freedom, there should be neither smoke nor fire.

"Are you going to the Vicarage, or have you been to Mattins? You spell Mattins with two *t*'s in your school, do you not?" she asked, her not very profound sarcasm seeking to clothe itself in affected simplicity.

"The Vicarage? Mattins? No !" he answered, laughing and shaking hands with her cordially.

She was the person of all others whom he wished to see. He could open his heart to her more freely than to anyone else ; for she was one of those people who, without superiority of intellect, have the good judgment which comes from purity of character, ready sympathy, and the absence of disturbing passions ; and at this moment he wanted to tell her all about last night and the unpleasant impression which had been made on him.

"What makes you ask?" he added. "Why should I go either to the Vicarage or to Mattins, as you call it?"

"We heard that you had made it all up with the vicar, and become one of his penitents. I believe penitents is the right name?" said Beatrice demurely.

"Since when have you believed me mad, Miss Beatrice Nesbitt?" asked Ringrove, again laughing.

"Everyone is talking of it, so I thought there was something in it," was her not too direct reply.

"Talking of what? You must explain yourself. Conundrums were never much in my line."

"Of your being at Churchlands yesterday evening, at one of those famous Sunday suppers which scandalize the place so much. You have no idea what is said of those Sunday suppers, Ringrove! And now the last news is, that you were admitted a member last night—only I scarcely know what you are a member of at all—and that you are to be one of the vicar's most influential supporters."

"News flies fast and grows quickly at Crossholme," said Ringrove good-humouredly.

"Then you were not at Churchlands last evening?"

She asked this a little eagerly. How glad she would be if he should say No !

"Certainly I was there last evening," he answered. "Why not?"

"Oh !" said Beatrice.

She said only this; but this was eloquent.

"They asked me to go, and why should I have refused?" he went on to say.

"To a Sunday supper?" said Beatrice, arching her eyebrows.

"Well? and after? What about these Sunday suppers? Before this moment I did not know that they existed as an institution at all. I only went because Mrs. Fullerton and Virginia said they wished me to accept, and offered to take me with them if I would go. But the whole thing was as new to me as are your conclusions."

"I thought everyone knew all about these suppers," said Beatrice; "and that going to Churchlands, or the Vicarage, on Sunday evenings meant more than an ordinary invitation."

"I did not," he returned.

"Well, you are set down now as one of them, for only the 'body' goes. The Fullertons are there every Sunday, for one ; and it is really too bad of Mrs. Fullerton to leave that poor husband of hers as she does. Mamma is quite distressed about it, and says she does not know what to do. She longs to speak to her and Virginia, and yet she does not like to do so, as, of course, it is not our affair. I wish I was older! I am sure I would not mind then!" said this soft-voiced, large-eyed creature, sincerely believing that years would give her the pugnacity which nature had denied, and that at forty she would be able to fight with the strongest, when at twenty she could not stand against the weakest.

"I knew nothing of all this," said Ringrove, looking distressed.

"How should you? Men never do know anything of what goes on about them. It is only women who find out the truth," said Beatrice, with fine feminine advocacy. "And the truth of all this is, that Mrs. Fullerton is completely carried away by the vicar—taken off her feet, as nurse calls it; and she a married woman, too!—and Virginia is just as bad. Mr. Lascelles and that horrid sister of his twist them round their little fingers, and do what they like with both."

"You must not speak of either Mrs. Fullerton or Virginia as bad," said Ringrove gravely.

"How can I call it good?" she remonstrated. "They

go down to early service every morning, and to the communion before breakfast every Sunday; and Mrs. Fullerton
confesses to Mr. Lascelles every week in the vestry ; and
is not all that bad and dreadful enough ?"

"Are you sure, Beatrice ?" asked Ringrove with
half pathetic, half angry eagerness. " I can scarcely believe
that Mrs. Fullerton confesses to Mr. Lascelles—she, the
wife of a man whose opinions are so well known !"

"Yes, I am perfectly sure. Why ! she dates her letters
now the Feast of S. Michael and the Vigil of S. Thomas !
Such affectation !—it is not proper ! " said Beatrice Nesbitt
with disdain.

" There is nothing very improper in dating her letters
the Feast of S. Michael or the Vigil of S. Thomas," said
Ringrove hastily. " And that does not prove that she
confesses."

"Ringrove ! I think it all detestable !" cried this
pretty unconverted heathen, warmly. " It is bad all
through, and any one can see what mischief it is working.
Mrs. Fullerton used to be so sweet and nice, and now
she has changed as entirely as if she were some one else.
And how ill poor Mr. Fullerton is looking !—how sad
and heartbroken !—and he used to be always so cheerful
and bright. No wonder, poor fellow, that he is sad and

ill when his wife and daughter treat him as they
do."

"But things get so much exaggerated in a small place
like this," said Ringrove. "Mrs. Fullerton and Virginia
could not be unkind to anyone."

"Not unkind?—when they neglect him as they do,
and go their own way as if he did not exist? What
would you say if mamma and I left poor papa to dine
alone every Sunday, while we went off and enjoyed ourselves with his worst enemy? And after Mr. Lascelles
behaved to Mr. Fullerton as he did at his own table! It
is shameful from first to last!" said Beatrice indignantly,
her indignation making her even less compact in speech
and continuous in thought than usual. And she was
never noted for logical sequence of ideas. She was a
cowslip ball, not a steel blade—soft and fragrant, not
trenchant and conclusive.

"It is all the fault of that smooth-faced hypocrite!"
cried Ringrove, angry and unjust in consequence.

"It is as much the fault of those who worship him as
they do, and let him do just as he likes with them," returned Beatrice, holding the balance even and certainly
condemning according to reason. "Look at that poor
foolish Theresa! She is killing herself with fasting and

penance and going to church at all hours of the day and night. It is really too terrible! She washes all about the communion-table, kneeling on the floor and scrubbing like a housemaid, just to please Mr. Lascelles and make him like her—for she is as much in love with him as she can be. And Virginia does the same kind of thing too."

"No, no!" cried Ringrove, flinging up his head and involuntarily clenching his hands.

"She does, Ringrove! I assure you she does! I am awfully sorry to have it to tell you; but if you do not know, you ought. She cleans the candlesticks!— Virginia! who never did anything useful in her life; could not even sew on a button or mend her own gloves; and now she cleans those large heavy candlesticks with plate-powder and wash-leather, just as our footman cleans the plate. So now you can understand why we were so sorry to hear of your being at Churchlands last evening, and what grief it would be to us if you were to lose your head as they have done, and give in to all this absurd and wicked nonsense."

Tears stood in Bee's beautiful brown eyes. She was as earnest for Ringrove's salvation in her own way as were Virginia and Hermione in theirs.

Ringrove did not speak. All this came upon him, if
in some sense as a revelation, yet also as a painful confirmation of what he had seen last night; and more than
ever he felt that Richard ought to be told how things
were going, that he might exercise his authority as a
husband and father and stem the torrent which was
sweeping his beloved ones—where?

After a few moments' silence, not looking at Beatrice,
but half turning away his face, he asked, in a low
voice :—

"Does Virginia, as well as her mother, confess to Mr.
Lascelles?"

Beatrice stole a look full of compassion at him.

"She does not go to the vestry," she said. "If she
confesses at all, it is up at the Vicarage. All the rest go
to the vestry, but not Virginia. She does confess, though.
I feel sure of that from what she said to me ; but there
is a little mystery about her altogether, and no one quite
understands it. Mrs. Fullerton is always with Mr.
Lascelles and Virginia is always with Sister Agnes—that
dreadful woman !"

"Perhaps Virginia does not confess," said Ringrove,
half as if speaking to himself.

"I do not know," she answered; "but evidently

something is going on with her. No one knows what it is, but no one would be surprised whatever happened. If she went into one of those silly Orders, or took the veil, or preached to the people, I should not wonder. It is all horrible altogether," she cried, with an energy of reprobation rare in soft Bee Nesbitt.

"Mr. Lascelles is a scoundrel," cried Ringrove.

"And the Fullertons are weaker and blinder and sillier than I could have believed possible," said Bee.

He made an angry gesture: This gentle-mannered, sympathetic creature, who was so like a cowslip ball in his hand, rarely saw this look or roused this feeling in him.

"Don't be angry with me, Ringrove," she continued in a tender, pleading way. "I know all that you feel for Virginia, and you know how sincerely I have sympathized with you all through. But indeed she has shown herself so silly of late that I cannot pretend to feel any more interest in her, or to have any respect for her judgment. And that is just the truth!"

"Not a word against Virginia," cried Ringrove with a passionate burst. "All that she does is from the purest motives. If she has been carried away by these people, remember how young she is, and what a sweet saintly creature she is ! She is the kind of girl of whom saints and martyrs are made, and who fulfil one's idea of angels," he added, in a lower voice.

"Yes, I know," said Beatrice. "I know how sweet and good she is ; but that does not make her wise, Ringrove ! It would be far better for her if she were more commonplace and less like an angel, as you call her—or at all events less like a thing you read of. Virginia is not like an ordinary girl ; and really she and Theresa are too absurd with their fanaticism and excitement. For, after all, poor Theresa does as much as Virginia, and perhaps more. We ought not to forget that."

"Yes, but there is all the difference in the spirit," said Ringrove. "What Virginia does is from pure principle, and because she thinks it to be right ; and, by your own showing, Theresa mixes up with her religion a personal feeling for Mr. Lascelles which makes it another thing altogether."

"Poor Theresa !" repeated Beatrice compassionately. "She will kill herself if she does not take care. She looks in a consumption as it is ; and that dreadful cough of hers ! "

"And that scoundrel will be her murderer !" said Ringrove, looking straight into the sky. It was almost

as if he was invoking vengeance on the vicar's handsome
head. "He will be her murderer, as he has been the
ruin of the happiest home in England," he repeated.

"I wish he could be taken up and put in prison," said
unreasoning Bee Nesbitt; and then silence fell between
them, and they walked on between the frosted hedgerows
—the one gloomy and depressed by what he had heard,
the other wondering if she ·had done right to tell him
what she knew. She thought that she had; nevertheless she wondered and somewhat tormented herself in
secret.

"I am awfully sorry at what you tell me, Bee,"
then said Ringrove, drawing a deep breath. "I wish
I had known it all before; I would not have gone last
night if I had. But naturally I did not understand the
invitation as meaning more than any other would have
done, or that I ran the risk of being counted amongst the
vicar's partisans because I spent a few hours at Churchlands. The only feeling that I had was about Mr.
Fullerton. I scarcely liked to go because I knew that
they had cut him; and yet—it seems better not to mix
oneself up in local quarrels."

"It will soon be known that the whole thing is a
mistake, and that you have not been gained over," said

Beatrice. "No real harm will have been done. Papa said from the first that there must be some mistake, and that you could not possibly have changed so much and so suddenly; but mamma was a little frightened. She was afraid of Mrs. Fullerton's influence, she said; but you see papa was right!" triumphantly.

"After all, it seems making a great deal of a very little matter, does it not?" said Ringrove, trying to smile.

"It would be a very little matter indeed with anyone else, but it is Mr. Lascelles himself who makes so much of everything," Beatrice answered, sensibly enough. "He seems to lie in wait for one in such a strange manner!—and if he has the smallest chance, he pounces down on one as a cat pounces down on a mouse. Mamma and I would not think of going to the weekly services, for instance. I don't mean those papist-like 'Mattins,' but the Wednesday and Friday morning services which mamma says she would like to go to well enough. If we did, we should have Mr. Lascelles going about saying that we were Catholics, or some nonsense like that! So no wonder that they made a great account of you at one of their special institutions. By-the-by, how did you like it, Ringrove?" demurely.

" Not at all," he answered. "The whole tone was intensely disagreeable to me."

He did not say why.

" Poor Ringrove!" said Bee softly.

Their eyes met.

" How good you are to me!" said Ringrove, sighing.

If only Virginia would be as good to him as this sweet sister-friend!—if only she were as sensible and sympathetic !

On which he shook hands with her, at once sorrowful and indignant, and rode off, more perplexed than he had ever been before. For if Richard knew all this, there was no use in telling him ; and if he did not, it was not a pleasant tale to carry.

That evening Richard's lecture was on the influence of the imagination, and how far its lawful functions extended ; separating scientific prevision, based on the possible development of established conditions, from the assumptions of mere fancy which have no warranty in fact. To this he added a few words on authority ; and how far it was wise to trust to general opinion simply because general ; and how far it was better to hold one's judgment in suspense, and to refuse to believe the Unproved, even when one could not substitute a counter theory.

For him, he said, the mere consent of opinion had no weight as a ground of certainty. It expresses truly the mean distance to which thought has travelled and the average of the knowledge that has been attained; but it is only temporary and local, it is not fixed nor final. The delusions of witchcraft, of which the finest minds two and a half centuries ago were convinced as of an absolute certainty—a reality confessed by the Word of God and diabolically conducted—was a case in point; and Richard very naturally made the most of it. Then he made the usual application of his principles against Revelation, Christianity, the Church of England and Mr. Lascelles; and exhorted his hearers to test and try before accepting or believing.

At this some among the men whispered together, and said that it was all very well for Mr. Fullerton to speak as he did, but if he looked a little nearer home it would be better; and if he wanted his words to be taken by outsiders he should see that those of his own household did not go against them. The division of feeling in the Abbey had become by now the main subject of local conversation, and was doing mischief on both sides. Richard's views failed to obtain the respect which hitherto they had had, because of the public profession of ritualism made by his wife and daughter; and Mr. Lascelles was credited with more personal influence than was good for his reputation as a celibate priest, inasmuch as he had gained the women only and left the man's mind untouched. The whole condition of things was disastrous; and so everyone felt, to which side soever he might belong. The only excuse made for Mr. Fullerton by the men of the place was, that he could not possibly know how far his womankind had gone, and was therefore more to be pitied than blamed. Still to them, hard-headed, unemotional and destitute of æsthetic delicacy, it was a matter of manly honour that a man should be master in his own house; and he who let his womenfolk have their heads was wanting in one of the first duties of his state, and was but a poor creature, take him how you would. They did not formulate among themselves the way in which this headship was to be held. They only said that they would let their "missis" see who was master in their house, and make the parson understand which way to look on Sundays; but they did not say whether they would beat their wives or lock them up in Bluebeard's chambers, nor make it clear what they would do with them in any way if they became rebellious and recalcitrant, and determined on walking apart in freedom when they were bound by nature and good living to be fettered and to follow. Want of a settled plan of action on their own side did not however prevent their blaming Richard in that he did not " do something;" for even good men are not ashamed of cheap methods of self-assertion :— and to blame another is only the negative form of praising oneself.

Ringrove came to the lecture, as usual. He was almost as constant an attendant at these Monday evening parliaments as was John Graves himself; and he was certainly one of the most appreciative of the audience, By the way, that audience was thinning noticeably. Every week saw some one wanting in his accustomed place ; and by the defections here might be counted the vicar's successes. He had waited until he had established himself fairly well in the parish, before making withdrawal from the Institution imperative on all who would stand well with him or be admitted to the more sacred rites of the religion which some of them had neglected but not abandoned. And the members here were diminishing while those of his own congregation increased. But he left the gentlemen who upheld the place alone. Sincere as he was, rank and riches had their modifying influence with him as with all other

Englishmen; and if he did not believe with that profane old sinner, that "God Almighty would think twice before he damned a person of quality," he did think that a priest should not treat a gentleman with the ecclesiastical sans-façon with which he might lawfully treat a boor.

Nothing pleased Ringrove more than the way in which Richard Fullerton went straight to the root of things in these lectures. It was delightful to him to know that one man at least held the standard of independent thought so high and with so firm a grasp, though he might flourish it at times a little defiantly in the faces of the orthodox. And to-night it seemed to cheer him with a personal application when Richard spoke out so strongly on the question of authority, and classed the spiritual claims of the Christian priest with those of an Indian medicine-man or a Buddhist bonze. It made what he had to say easier, if only the opportunity would come. But it did not, to-night. Richard was not walking back through the park as usual. His trap was waiting for him at the door; so was Ringrove's horse; and the two parted without any private talk having passed between them. As they shook hands, however, Richard said: "Of course you dine with us as usual on Christmas Day?" to which

Ringrove answered "Yes;" neither of the men suspecting a hitch.

Hermione was in the drawing-room alone when Richard returned. She had miscalculated her chances of escape from her husband, and had remained too late, finishing a Christmas present for the vicar. Virginia had gone to bed. Richard came in, bringing the fresh scent of the frosty air with him, and suggesting the cold sharp night so vividly that the pretty woman shivered while she pricked her needle in and out the last leaves on the satin stole, and thought how beautiful it would look round Superior's holy neck on Christmas morning.

She glanced up once as her husband entered, truth to say annoyed that he had come home so early ; and when he said : "Well, my wife ! " tenderly, she answered : "Yes?" in a voice of studied commonplace, as if he had asked a question.

"I suppose the child has gone to bed?" he asked, looking round the room.

He would not allow it to himself, but he found conversation with that beloved wife of his difficult of late. She gave him the impression of being always on her guard against him, and as if waiting for a cause of blame.

"Yes," said Hermione, still stitching in her leaves. "She has been working hard all the day and is tired."

"Working hard—at what ?" he asked.

"The Christmas decorations in the school-house," she answered.

"Does she not do too much of this kind of thing, wife ?" he said gravely. "She is not strong and seems to me to try herself too far. She has been looking thin and pale and sadly depressed of late."

"Work is good for her," said Hermione.

"Not too much of it."

"She is carefully watched over," said Virginia's mother with the faintest little toss of her pretty head.

"I wish she could be watched over by one who had the right," said Richard with a sigh.

"She is," said Hermione, compressing her soft lips into a line like the vicar, and with an odd, half-defying look on her face.

"Not according to my ideas," he said.

"No ; but according to mine," she returned quite quietly.

"And you will not accept my view ?" he asked.

"I am her mother, and have the best right to judge for her," she said.

"I suppose you will be glad to have Ringrove to dinner on Christmas-day, as usual?" said Richard, not wishing to open dangerous ground to-night.

He knew that some day a tremendous moral earthquake would have to come ; but it was not on them yet.

"I am glad that he should come here for your sake," Hermione answered. "It will be pleasanter for you to have him than to be quite alone, as else you would be. Virginia and I shall be at the Vicarage."

Her hands, still busied on the vine-leaves of the white satin stole, trembled a little nervously as she said this ; but her voice was a capital imitation of indifference.

"On Christmas-day, my wife?" he asked, with a slight start.

"I did not suppose that the day had either value or meaning for you," she answered, looking up with feigned surprise.

This once perfectly simple and transparent creature was profiting with strange rapidity by the lessons of "reticence," "reserve," "second intention," and all the other phases of deceit so diligently inculcated in confession. With Mr. Lascelles, as with all his class, the end sanctified the means ; and the end of Richard Fullerton's final discomfiture was of such vital importance to the cause of the Church and the rescue of men's souls at Crossholme, as to sanctify any means whatsoever.

" As the commemoration of the birth of Christ it has none, as you know," he said ; " but as a point of family union—a time of social pleasantness—I have the English-man's natural regard for it, and I am sorry that you are leaving your own house for a stranger's on this day—so peculiarly the day of home life and home love !"

" The vicar and his dear sister are not strangers ; and both Virginia and I prefer tó dine where this most blessed day of all the year has its spiritual value, its religious consolation," said Hermione, repeating as she had been taught. " Here it means simply plum-pudding seasoned with infidelity. At the Vicarage it will be sanctified ; and we shall remember what act of Divine mercy it commemorates."

" My poor wife !" he said with pity; " how these thaumaturgists have bewildered you ! "

" And how your evil heart of unbelief has blinded you ! " returned Hermione with temper. " Before you pity me, Richard, be sure that you yourself are not an object for the deepest commiseration as a soul lost to all eternity ! "

" Wife ! where is all this to end ? " cried Richard.

" It is getting too painful to be borne! It is as if a spell had fallen on our lives!"

" You can end it all as soon as you like, Richard," said his wife, bending towards him with one of her sweet caressing movements, while she raised her blue eyes to his face and seemed to call him to her side as she used in the old days of irreligion and love. " Come over to the Church, make your peace with God, and there will not be a cloud between us! It lies with you, and you only."

" You might as well ask the river to run back to its source in the hills," cried Richard. " Wife! beloved! you know that I could not go back to a phase of thought which represents to me the grossest superstition and ignorance. Why do you urge me to become a Christian, knowing me as you do, and knowing too that what you mean by faith is not a mental state to be attained by voluntary effort? I could not believe in those old wives' fables which you call Scripture, even if I wished to do so. As soon could I accept a child's fairy tales for genuine history!"

" Then do not ask me to be what I was before I was converted," said Hermione, putting away her work hurriedly.

"Have I no influence over you by our long and faithful love?" he asked. "Do you not acknowledge my right of authority as your husband?"

She raised her deep-blue eyes, full to the brim with tears, and looked straight into his face.

"How can you? You are an infidel and I am a Christian. What influence ought you to have over me? The Church and the Bible both forbid it."

She said this distinctly enough, but quietly. Soft-hearted, weak, and with those memories of tender love behind her, she could be harsh only through the pressure of irritability. When it came to cold and stony determination she always broke down, at least in part.

"Wife! for the love of all that you and I both hold sacred, let this fearful misunderstanding end!" he exclaimed, going up to her and taking her in his arms.

She flung hers round him, and kissed him with her old tender passion; then shaking herself free, he scarcely knew how, she glided from him, saying in a broken voice :—

"You have only yourself to blame, Richard, for all that has come or will come."

Before he knew that she was at the door, she had left the room—one deep and sudden sob marking her passage through the hall; while Richard stood as one struck and dazed, conscious only that in this little conflict between love and fanaticism the latter had been victorious.

CHAPTER IV.

THE DAY OF GOODWILL.

VIRGINIA, neither fathoming the undercurrent of things nor suspecting what she did not see, knew nothing of Ringrove's feelings nor how the attempt to bring him over had simply resulted in flinging him so much the farther off. She was so completely absorbed in her new life, so entirely impersonal in her thoughts and feelings, that she was as if blind and deaf to things as they were. She had but one desire—that of doing the will of God as declared by the Church; while her sole pleasures were those found in the religious life—in attendance on the services ; in praying in her own room at stated times according to the directions of Father Truscott ; in working for the church ; in performing menial offices about the altar, such as cleaning the candlesticks and the like ; in reading religious books, and gaining courage from the lives of the saints and martyrs for her own constancy in the step which she was meditating.

And if she had but one desire, she had but one
sorrow—the lost condition of her father's soul and the
doubtful state of Ringrove's. She prayed daily for both;
performed vicarious penances for them, and made vows
which she hoped might be carried to the good of their
account with heaven; but the Fountain of Grace had as
yet remained sealed, and both Father Truscott and Sister
Agnes had begun to tell her that, so far as her father was
concerned, to hope for a miracle might be, in certain
circumstances, presumptuous; and that, if God had
abandoned that obnoxious infidel to the tender mercies
of Satan, to whose service he had bound himself, it was
not for her to seek to change the Divine decree.

For the rest the girl was in a different sphere of
thought and feeling altogether from that which the world
about her held; one that only Sister Agnes and Father
Truscott understood. Even Mr. Lascelles himself did
not know all that was going on in this young enthusiastic
mind; and the Father took care that he should not.
The "reserve" practised by the whole school to the
naughty world outside, not unfrequently translates itself
into double-dealing among themselves; and the elder
c ommunion has its emissaries in the heart of the body
which in fact proselytizes for that which it seems to

repudiate.   It was so with Father Truscott and Sister
Agnes; and Virginia was only one of many whom they
appeared to lead to one altar, while actually leading to
another.

The Father had assumed the Direction of the girl by
the consent and even desire of Mr. Lascelles, who
somehow did not care to make her his penitent together
with her mother and Theresa Molyneux;—but having
assumed it he kept his own counsel, and hers, and told
no one but the Sister—who was an old confederate of
his—which way things were tending.   The next act in
the clerical drama, as at present arranged, would be
Virginia's "retreat" prior to her confirmation at Easter;
but between this and then much would be done.

Among other things of secondary importance, the
Fullertons were enjoined to bring Ringrove Hardisty
with them to the Vicarage on Christmas Day, the vicar
having sent him a formal invitation to dinner.   And
Virginia was again bidden to use her influence, for his
soul's good, with the man who loved her, and for whom
she prayed often and performed penance for the good
of his account.   So she did; with unmistakable tenderness, but always with that far-away look in her eyes which,
if it made her like the child's dream of an angel, gave

her the appearance of being only half in earnest on any subject outside religion. She did not think it necessary to be specially pressing, however tender she might be ; for she did not imagine that Ringrove could be so ungrateful as to refuse what was, to her mind, the supreme privilege of present existence. Neither did she know of his engagement to dine here at the Abbey with her father ; her mother had not yet spoken of it. And even if she had known it, she would have thought it lawful to break through that for the greater good of communion with "the body," at the Vicarage.

"You will come, of course?" she said sweetly, after he had read the vicar's note which she had been commissioned to give him.

"No! never again among that set, as last Sunday evening!" he answered firmly.

She opened her blue eyes on him with reproach and astonishment.

"Oh, Virginia, if you could but see it all as I do—as it is," he went on warmly, his colour rising. "Theresa's unwholesome excitement—Cuthbert's unmanly submission—your own state, Virginia, good and sweet as you are, as unwholesome as poor Theresa's—the horrible familiarity among you all—the degrading adulation that

you pay to Mr. Lascelles—the unreasonable excess of
every religious practice; it is heart-breaking to a man
like myself, to whom the affectation of priests being
different from other men is abhorrent, and who sees in
the whole ritualistic movement just the selfish ambition
of unscrupulous men trading on the best feelings of
women, for their own purposes."

"Ringrove! I did not think you were so wicked as
· this !" cried Virginia, shrinking back.

"I am so sorry to hurt you !" he said affectionately,
"but I must ! How can you, a proud pure girl, submit
yourself as you do ! How can Mrs. Fullerton allow it, or
suffer it for herself !—or Cuthbert endure it for a moment
for his sister ! It made my blood boil to see the place
which was taken by Mr. Lascelles in another man's house
—and it made me blush with anger and shame to see
you and your mother give in to it—you two, whom I
have worshipped all my life, as my very ideal of what
women ought to be ! Forgive me, dear, I were no true
friend if I did not say what I feel and think in this
matter."

"You know nothing of what you are saying, and so
are to be forgiven as one sinning in ignorance," said
Virginia gravely, but with a deep flush on her sweet face.

"No outsider can understand the tie between a penitent and her confessor."

"Then you do confess!" interrupted Ringrove, speaking with agitation.

She raised her eyes.

"Of course," she said calmly. "Father Truscott is my Director, and my more than father. He is as if given me by God, and the very mouthpiece of God."

"Your own father would be a better director a hundred times over," said Ringrove hastily. "God did give him to you without an if!"

She sighed and turned away.

"My own is lost!" she said.

"Virginia! and they have taught you this!"

"Grace may work a miracle in his behalf," she went on to say, in a half-dreamy manner. "But how can we expect that it will when he hardens himself in his pride as he does, and refuses to accept the means of salvation held out to him?"

"He is a better man than any of those whom you place so far before him," said Ringrove steadily. "He does not spend his strength in making silly girls like Theresa Molyneux in love with him, nor in breaking down the natural pride and self-respect of such a girl as yourself, by putting her to the degrading work which you do for the church."

"Can that work which is done for the glory and beautifying of the House of God degrade a poor sinful creature like me? Ringrove! are you a Christian at all, and yet can say this?"

"Were it work for any real good—if it helped the great cause of humanity in any way—no! But simply to consolidate the power and gratify the whim of a man like Mr. Lascelles, I think it infinitely degrading!" said Ringrove passionately.

"To me it is infinite honour—infinite glory and consolation!" returned Virginia with a rapt look. "To kneel and pray while I do my work about the altar —what happiness! what sweetness! If I could do better by using my finest dress as a duster, by using my hair as a brush, I would, Ringrove!—I feel the glory of my work so deeply!"

"Oh, this is awful!" cried Ringrove with unspeakable distress. "No man with a man's heart in him could bear it! To see his wife or daughter or sister, or any woman whatsoever that he respected, brought to this point—with no self-respect, no pride left in her—no care for old friends or

natural ties !—it is frightful, Virginia ! it is hideous !—
maddening ! "

His eyes flashed, his lips quivered, his whole frame
seemed instinct with indignation, and he made a
passionate movement with his hands. Virginia had
never seen him so roused—had never seen that look
before in his eyes. She sighed heavily. Here was
another hope destroyed, and another human soul lost
and sinking deep into that awful Pit !

" I cannot listen to all this," she said coldly rather
than sadly, and as one bearing faithful testimony. " If
you will not hear the voice of truth, and will go over
to the wrong side, we can only pray for you and be
sorry. Superior has gone out of his way, and done all
that he could to win you over ; but if you will not be
converted—if you will cling to your errors and harden
your heart——." Tears came into her eyes, and her
voice broke.

" It is not I who am in error ! " said Ringrove,
whom her pain half maddened. " Virginia, sweetest
and dearest of all the earth to me, if I could but make
you see this frightful fanaticism as it is—all its horror—
all its danger ! "

He took her two hands in his, but she drew them away.

" Thanks be to our Blessed Lord and the Holy Mother I have found the truth, which I will keep through my life, and defend with my life ! " she said fervently. " It is all I care to live for ! "

" And your home affections—your duty as a daughter —your old friends—your social obligations—are these nowhere with you now ? "

" In comparison with religion ? no ! " she said. " Father Truscott himself absolves me."

" Father Truscott !—he absolves you !—and what the devil has he to do with you?" cried Ringrove, blazing out into sudden fierceness of passion. He could not be angry with Virginia herself, but he turned upon the first name presented the wrath which the very vagueness and unconquerableness of her tenacity excited.

Virginia rose. She was very pale, and her lips trembled.

" Good-bye, Ringrove," she said softly. " Some day you will be sorry."

Some day ! He had no need for the future :—he was sorry enough as things were in the present. He confessed this to himself bitterly, as he watched the girl's receding figure, and almost repeated Caligula's famous wish in favour of these enemies of the home who had crawled into this sweetest sanctuary of peace and love, and made it now a wreck.

They were obliged to content themselves with somewhat inadequate Christmas decorations this year at Crossholme. Service was held in the schoolroom now, the workmen having taken final possession of the church ; and though all was done that could be done in the way of draperies and vestments, decorations and processions, still the effect was not so imposing as it would have been had the church been available—as it would be next year when the restoration should be completed and the triumph of ritualism assured. Still they did what they could ; and Hermione's white stole played its part in the pageant and helped to make the vicar "lovely."

Ringrove was too much out of harmony with the whole thing to go to the service at all, "sidesman" as he was ; and only drove into Crossholme when he went to the Abbey to dinner, and braced himself to the painful task of putting Richard on his guard by telling him what he knew.

What a dinner that was for the two poor fellows who ate it together !—what a mockery of Christmas festivity !—what a ghastly pretence of seasonable jollity !

Both felt deserted and superseded; and each had the sense of the beloved woman's unfaithfulness. They talked of all subjects under the sun but the one which touched them nearest; and each tried to keep from the other the sorrow and shame of the wound from which both were smarting alike. Richard told Ringrove the latest discoveries in chemistry, in electricity, in biology; and the possible results on human life, as well as the changes sure to be wrought in human faith, from the new truths added to the store. And Ringrove told Richard this bit of local politics and that report of probable events, chiefly relating to a forthcoming election at Starton, where the contest between the Liberal and Conservative candidates would be close. But both knew that all this glib conversation was a fence and a sham; and that, if they had not been ashamed for sake of their manhood, they would have drawn together over the fire and bemoaned themselves aloud. As it was, the servants held them in due check; and for natural pride they kept up the farce bravely and made a show of quiet pleasure which deceived no one but themselves. But when the last glass of wine was drunk the play came to an end, and the two adjourned into the study, where at least they felt more natural and at home. And here Ringrove told his friend all that he now knew, including the early daily services and the weekly confession of Hermione to Mr. Lascelles—with the less evident but as sure confession of Virginia to Father Truscott.

When he had told all this, he laid his hand on his friend's arm and said earnestly :—

"You will not misjudge me, Fullerton? You know how much I love both Virginia and her mother; but it is for their own good I wish you to know what is going on, that you may stop it all before it is too late."

Richard held out his hand kindly.

"Thank you, my boy," he said in a low voice. "I know what this has cost you and you can judge what I feel ; but thank you for the effort."

After which there was a long silence between them ; and then Richard, taking up a plaster model of the brain, spoke of the increase in the convolutions which some say is taking place of Haeckel's "mind-cells," and the material conditions of thought.

Late in the evening Hermione and Virginia came home. They had hoped to find Ringrove gone and Richard too sleepy for much talk, when there would have been no meeting and no discussion ;—both of which, under present conditions and with Hermione's half-unconscious sense of treachery to her home, were awkward enough. There was no help for it however; and if she did not wish to be cowardly she must face the embarrassment which she had created for herself. Mother and daughter came in a little flushed and excited beyond ordinary wont—fresh from the intoxication of their spiritual dram-drinking, where subtle love-making and romance made up the charm for the one, for the other religious exaltation and the first beginnings of a secret purpose. Hermione's dress of bright deep-blue shone in the doorway like a strip of heaven, and Virginia's soft clinging robe of white was like a cloud lying against it. The men rose and went to greet these beloved women, glad that they had returned even at this late hour; yet both felt embarrassed—Ringrove as if he had committed an act of treachery against them, Richard knowing that he would so soon have to be their accuser and their judge.

Hermione, wishing to be charitable on this Day of Goodwill even to two outcasts like these, came forward with a cold artificial kind of smile. She thought herself very good to come into the study at all. It was like a Yezidi temple to her at all times; and at this moment, on this day, and as a contrast with what

she had left, it was more diabolical than usual. But
as she came forward she stopped suddenly and gave
a half frightened, half disgusted look at what she saw.
On the table stood three skulls, with the plaster
casts of the brains corresponding ; the one was that of
a chimpanzee, the other of a Bushman, the third of a
European—evidently ranged there to illustrate some
infidel point in comparative craniology. A book of
anatomical plates was lying open—horrid things suggesting an endless series of monster worms to the pretty
woman who thought that those portions of the living
human clock-case which custom left uncovered were
quite enough for an ordinary man's contemplation ; and
that to dive into the secrets of the works was abominable ;—save when a man was going to make medicine
his profession, and to receive money for his disagreeable
knowledge.   Specimens of rocks and fossils were
scattered about among odd bones and more complete
skeletons of fish and reptiles ; the microscope was
adjusted for use ; the electric machine was uncovered ;
all the objectionable furniture of this most objectionable seat of learning was in full display, and
the very air seemed tainted with materialism and
irreligion.

Ringrove had been smoking, as his contribution to the hatefulness of the local colour ; and two tumblers of punch mingled their fumes with the smell of the smoke, of the Russia leather binding of the books, of the chemicals, and the earthy taint of the rocks and old bones.

Hermione and Virginia had come from a feast informed by high Christian art and æsthetics—from sacred music and tender hymns; from fervent picturesque prayer and sweet comparisons· to earthly love, to give body as it were to spiritual aspirations ; from secret talks and hidden purposes ; from excitement and exaltation, and that kind of graceful and not too barren asceticism which charms a certain style of woman as a confession of her superiority and the reduction of the baser man's vile passions to the level of her own purer standard—like proud flesh eaten down to the surface of the healthy skin. They came from all this into an atmosphere of the earth earthy—an atmosphere that spoke to them of all manner of coarseness and unregenerate wickedness in these two heathens, whose very love for them made them wince and shudder. Though Hermione wanted to be charitable on this day and to hold out her hand over the gulf to her impenitent husband, if for only one moment, her tolerance could not quite compass this tremendous girth of sin. The fervid aspiration for the one and the refined love-making for the other, with the graceful asceticism for both, that they had had at the Vicarage, seemed so much the better and sweeter thing to each !

Hermione's fair face, already flushed with that rose-leaf kind of colour which went so well with her dark-blue eyes and golden hair, became a vivid crimson ; Virginia turned deadly pale ; and both men stopped midway in the room, restrained by the expression which came into the delicate faces looking at them with such evident abhorrence.

Also, what had those dear women done to themselves ? Hermione's golden hair, which used to stand about her head in fluffy rings and enchanting little curls, like the head of a wool-clad Ara Cœli bambino, was now braided plain and tight, without a fluff or a curl anywhere. Her dress of " Mary " blue was made with studied plainness —a plainness so evident that even men must notice it ; and she, who once used to hang herself about with chains and bracelets, beads and bands, like any Indian idol, had not one ornament save a large black cross that hung round her neck—the vicar's Christmas gift. Virginia was always simple ; but even her simplicity had taken on itself a strain

of severity which it had not had before ; so that she
looked truly nunlike as she stood in her plain and clinging
white stuff dress, with the black girdle, whence also hung
a large black cross, round her waist.   A thick white scarf
folded wimplewise about her face completed that graceful
but unwelcome likeness to a nun which struck both
Richard and Ringrove at the same moment.

" Welcome home, wife," said Richard with grave
courtesy as he went to meet her, conquering the moment's
hesitancy born of the expression on her face.

" Those horrid things ! how can you have them about ?
They are not fit for Virginia to see ! " she said.

Her impulse of goodwill had vanished.   The contrast
was too great, and really Richard was so unpardonably
wicked !

" These things are certainly not for you and our
child," he answered, quietly closing the book of anatomical plates.   " Let us go into the drawing-room.
Come, Ringrove."

" No ; you smell too strongly of smoke.   I cannot
have my drawing-room made so horrid," she answered
with strange decision ; and Richard noted the as strange
emphasis which she laid on the " my."   " How can you
indulge in such a vulgar habit, Ringrove ? "

"I am very sorry you caught me, Mrs. Fullerton," he answered boyishly. "If I had thought of it I would not have smoked at all. You know I am no slave to the habit."

"You will become so, and to something else too, if you do not take care," said Hermione looking at the steaming tumblers of punch expressively.

"Oh, wife! Christmas-day, and we poor deserted creatures left to our own base devices!" said Richard, forcing an air of playfulness.

But Hermione was in no mood now for playfulness, forced or natural. She had come in charitably inclined; but the shock had been too strong; and she had drawn back her hand now and let the gulf widen without an effort to bridge it over.

"And all this is perhaps the reason why you were left," she said. "We have no sympathy here—what conscientious woman could have sympathy with such habits as these, such pursuits? No one can wonder at our dislike."

She spoke as if Ringrove and Richard were men who led a coarse, rude, tap-room life, and that she and Virginia had been forced to banish themselves from their own home by the very need of womanly delicacy and refinement.

"I am sorry it should vex you," said Richard, not attempting more playfulness, but grave and quiet even beyond his ordinary self. "But after all, wife, neither Ringrove's cigar nor our obnoxious punch is of such heinousness, or so unusual, as to justify your anger. I think it was only so late ago as last year when we had the traditional bowl in the dining-room, and when my wife's own hands helped in the brew."

"This year is not last, and I did a great many things then that I would not now," she said.

"Ah! more's the pity for the change!" he answered with a sigh.

"Well, good night!" said Hermione abruptly. "Come, Virginia, it is late. Good night, Ringrove. I am sorry——"

She stopped.

"Sorry for what, Mrs. Fullerton?" he asked, retaining her hand.

"For a great many things," she answered evasively.

He looked at Virginia; Virginia was looking mournfully at him. Her melancholy eyes and half-parted lips echoed her mother's words, and he seemed almost to hear her say too: "I am sorry."

He was sorry enough for himself at this present

moment; but he had as little intention of making the
rough things smooth by giving in to the new régime as
had Richard—or as had the women themselves by coming
back to the old way.

"Many Happy Christmases and New Years to you,
Virginia," he said, going up to her.

"Thank you," she answered softly; but she did not
look as if she and happiness and Ringrove made a very
harmonious triad. Her whole figure was shrinking, nervous, uncomfortable. She felt out of place in her father's
house and with her own old friend; and she looked as
she felt.

"Good night, Ringrove," then said Virginia; "good
night, papa."

"Is my daughter going without a kiss to me?" said
Richard, holding out his hand.

Virginia looked at her mother, but her mother looked
at the wall over her head. She would not respond to
this mute appeal for counsel and direction. Though she
had her own personal dissatisfaction with her husband, by
reason of his infidelity and her new-born religious fervour
of which the groundwork was partly idleness and partly
the vicar's powers of fascination, she was half sorry that
Virginia had turned so entirely from her father. She had

so far her sense of justice left untouched by the sophisms which had warped all the rest. The daughter was as much the father's as the mother's; and there was a duty owing by Virginia to Richard from which she herself as the wife, the owner of the property and therefore more than his equal, was freed.

Wherefore, when Virginia looked to her for help in a difficulty of this kind and because of her father's loving claims to which she had been forbidden to respond, her mother forbore to give it. She would not counsel her to open disobedience, and she could not uphold him, infidel as he was, in any of his desires. This was about the only thing in which Hermione disobeyed the vicar; but the voice of nature, as it is called, was stronger than even the artificial godliness which was doing its best to stifle it, and she could not force herself to give poor Richard this, as it seemed to her, unwarrantable pain.

"No? not a kiss on Christmas night?" said Richard with tender reproach.

Virginia advanced reluctantly. Her father as he was, and once so dearly loved, she would as soon have received the kiss of Judas. Indeed, it was not very unlike a kiss from Judas; for was not Richard Fullerton a renegade to his baptismal vows, and a betrayer of the faith of which he was a born defender?

Her father took her cold and nerveless hands, and looked into her face.

"Look at me, Virginia," he said mildly but with unmistakable authority. "Look at me, my daughter!"

She lifted her eyes, dark with a kind of dread, then dropped them instantly to the floor, as one who saw something that repelled her and nothing that she loved.

"Is your heart so turned against me that you decline even to kiss me, even to look me in the face steadily as you used to do?" he asked.

She did not answer.

"Speak, Virginia; tell me the truth," he said, grave to sternness.

"While you are at enmity with God, you are excommunicated by the Church," said Virginia's clear voice lowered almost to a whisper, but fatally clear and audible still.

Her father let her hands fall, and Ringrove put his involuntarily before his eyes.

"My child!" said Richard; "do you think to please God by discarding all sentiment of love and duty to your father? By your own light has the fifth commandment no power over you, no significance for you?"

"He came to set the children against the father of those who believe and those who deny," said Virginia, still in that low clear voice, like one giving faithful evidence with the consciousness of death before her. "No one who loves the Church can love her enemy."

"Enough, my dear," he answered; "I know now what steps to take. Hermione," to his wife—it was years since he had called her by her name, since he had called her by anything but that which realized to him all human love and faith, the sacred name of wife— "you and I must have some serious talk to-morrow. It is too late now to enter on the matter that lies between us, but to-morrow both you and our child must listen to me."

Hermione bent her head with a half-frightened look.

"It will do no good," she said in a low voice, leaving the room with her daughter.

"Mamma!" cried Virginia, in a tone of terror and anguish, grasping her mother's arm in her slender hand that closed like a vice round the soft plump flesh; "you must help me with papa! you must get me away from home! I cannot bear it! and both Father Truscott and

Sister Agnes say that it is my duty to go into retreat. Mamma ! dear mamma, do help me ! "

" I will do what I can," said Hermione soothingly, "but you know, Virginia, that it will be difficult. You know how strong your father is in his own views, and how much opposed to us. Meanwhile, my dear," coaxingly, "try not to hurt him more than you can help. He has always been so fond of you, and he is your father after all; remember that, Virginia—he is your father," added the pretty woman softly, pleading with another for the morality which she herself did not practise.

" He is an atheist," said Virginia in a voice of horror, crossing herself as she spoke.

CHAPTER V.

THE NEW COMMAND.

THE next morning a cloud brooded over the Abbey household as heavy as that which hung against the sky. Hermione and Virginia had wakened, each with a sense of coming difficulty, Richard with a sense of present pain ; and all knew that the day was not to pass without a domestic cyclone of trouble and despair.

The snow had come down during the night and was falling fast now ; but mother and daughter had gone to morning prayers as usual; though partly from disinclination to face the driving snow, and partly because of Richard whom she did not wish to anger more than was absolutely necessary to please Mr. Lascelles, Hermione had taken the carriage. Virginia walked, as usual. This was a great concession to domestic peace on the part of the pretty woman whose daily penance of that cold early morning walk between the upper gate of the park and the church—or rather now the schoolhouse—was rendered sweet by the knowledge that Superior approved

the effort, and took her self-sacrifice as an expression of
personal attachment to himself as well as the faithful
performance of a religious duty. But to-day she wrapped
herself in her furs and took her penance easily ; knowing
what her husband would think, and dreading what he
might say if he found to what lengths her devotion
carried her. Had she been able, she would have
persuaded Virginia to go with her ; but boiling her peas
did not come into the girl's religious programme, and
personal discomfort made her prayers more fervent.

When "mattins" were over Hermione still lingered
in the schoolroom, outstaying even Aunt Catherine who
had brought a message from Theresa on some point of
conscience which she wanted solved—the wafer in which
she wrapped up her love.

"Let me speak with you alone," she said in an
anxious voice to Mr. Lascelles. "Can you give me a
moment ?"

"Sixty," he replied gallantly ; "twice sixty, if
necessary ! Come with me, dear child."

He led the way into the schoolmistress's private room
which had been assigned him as a "sacristy" during
the hours of service, and when he needed it as a
confessional.

"My time of trial has come, Superior," said Hermione with tears in her frightened eyes. "My husband knows something, and to-day is going, as he says, to talk to me—which means to oppose my present life and forbid Virginia's. What am I to do?"

"Be faithful to your creed," said Mr. Lascelles a little sternly.

She looked down. He could see her hands tremble and her delicate lips twitch nervously. She was evidently frightened at her position; and his exhortation to constancy, though what she had expected—and indeed though it was all that he could say—was hard to follow and full of unknown distress.

"I know how much you love your husband—how submissively you yield to him, and how in a manner you worship him," then said Mr. Lascelles with the frankest appearance of simple good faith and sympathy; "but you must remember that to uphold your religious liberty is a higher duty than to obey your beloved husband; and whatever anguish it causes you to go against his desires, you must bravely turn the knife in your own wound and offer your bleeding heart as the sacrifice."

He spoke with extremest softness of mood—tender, confidential, understanding; ostentatiously effacing himself, and making her feel that he purposely ignored his own claims and their mutual relations for her sake and to make things easier and plainer.

"I used to love him like this," said Hermione sadly, falling into the trap.

Mr. Lascelles, whose eyes had closed to a narrow line with a glittering kind of pencil-mark between the edges, smiled compassionately.

"Ah, poor child !" he said ; " if you only knew how much sorrow, sympathy, admiration I have for that passionate love of yours ! To see such a sweet and lovely nature devoted to one so unworthy that supreme affection ; to admire that affection, as I do, to my very heart, and to sigh over the object—you can hardly realize the mingled anguish and esteem of my feelings for you."

Hermione crimsoned. She shifted her pretty feet uneasily, examined the seams of her gloves, found one finger misfitting, and smoothed the fur of her muff. Then, as if she had taken a sudden resolution, she looked up into the vicar's face.

"I used to love Richard like this," she said again in a low voice ; "but I do not now."

Mr. Lascelles opened his glittering eyes wide and

met hers full and straight. There was a look in his which made her drop her own, shamefaced, to the floor. The insolent triumph that blazed from them seemed almost to scorch her as she looked, and the cruelty that lay behind that burning triumph filled her for a moment with pity and dread. She did not love Richard as she used ; granted ; but she did not wish him to be hurt. If she desired to be freed from her obligations to him as a wife, and from his control over her as a husband, she did not want to deliver him into the vicar's hands as his victim ; but she felt that she had done so, and for the moment repented her confession because afraid of its consequences.

Mr. Lascelles took her hands and drew her nearer to him. Gently but firmly he forced her to her knees, then bent over her and whispered something that made her blush and cower, turn pale and weep. Her trouble did not stir him.

"I command you," he said in a distinct voice. "You will be sinful and a castaway else."

"Oh ! I am sinful now. I should not have confessed this !" said Hermione, natural morality and womanly affection conquering for a moment the artificiality of her present piety.

"Not confess? to me, your Director?" said Mr.

Lascelles in a tone of surprise. "My poor child!" he added pityingly; "are you still so ill instructed in your duties after all the pains that I have taken with you?"

She heard his words and understood them clearly enough by her intelligence; but her heart was sore for the husband of her old-time love, from whom she had separated herself of her own act and motion, and she could not feel reconciled to herself—at least, not yet.

"Do not reproach yourself," then said Mr. Lascelles, reading her "It is well, and what must needs have come! You could not go on loving that impenitent atheist without denying Christ and dishonouring the Church. You had to choose your master. Which was it to be—God or man?—the Church or your home?—your Saviour or your husband?—me as your guide in the way of salvation or him as your leader into inevitable destruction? You have answered that question; proclaimed under which Lord you will take service, and renouncing the devil have bound yourself to God :—And now take comfort. This loss of love for your husband is the direct action of Divine grace on your heart; it comforts and rejoices me, and makes your way clearer and your cross so much the easier to bear."

All the same the tears still fell from Hermione's blue

eyes, and she dreaded the coming events of the day. She wished that she could have found out how to accomplish that impossible feat of serving God and Mammon at one and the same moment—blowing hot and cold with the same breath—pleasing Mr. Lascelles while not paining her husband—keeping all the privileges of her religious fidelity but bearing none of the penalties of her conjugal desertion. Steadfast opposition was so hard to her to keep up!—and the deception of silence and reserve had been so fatally pleasant and become so disastrously soothing to her easy-going, non-combatant temper! What a pity, she thought, that things had come to a crisis and that she was called on to take her part and stick to it!—what a pity that she could not have carried on her life according to her desire, while her husband continued blind as he had been! There was no help for it as things stood; and Hermione left the school-house in deep trouble and perplexity, fettered by her Director's command to bear her testimony without wavering, but in mortal dread of the trial.

With Virginia it was somewhat different. Though so much younger than her mother, and though a father's commands are so much more imperative than a husband's—though her nature was as gentle as Hermione's was soft—the trial of faith and constancy which awaited her was less difficult to meet if quite as painful to bear. She had no weak lingering wish to conceal what she was by appearing what she was not. She was sorry to have to vex her father, but she would have been more sorry to have to deny her faith. Her religion was so far more genuine than her mother's in that it had no admixture of personal feeling beyond the filial affection which she felt for Sister Agnes and Father Truscott. But even their influence over her sprang from their religion; it was not her affection for them which made her religious. They were to her the direct messengers of God—sacred, and therefore loved—not sacred because they were loved. Wherefore the issue of the contest that had to come with her father, however severe, however regrettable, was already foredetermined; and had it to end even in such mild martyrdom as the most severe of our nineteenth century intolerance is permitted to inflict, her constancy was assured.

For some months now—long before her mother had taken to the practice, and long before her mother had even known that she had done so—it had been part of Virginia's daily life to walk down to early morning prayers. Snow or shine, wind, rain, or hail, whether she

had a headache and was weary, or was brisk and ready
for exertion, she was ever at her post; and the walk,
being so often uncomfortable to the natural man, was,
as has been said, part of the religious exaltation in which
she lived. She would have felt a backslider had she
gone with her mother in the carriage to-day, though
she had a bad cold coming on, which this was not the
kind of weather to make better—which indeed it was
just the day to make very much worse, and from a slight
indisposition increase to a grave disorder. But when
she came home, her dark dress white with snow, her
hat encumbered, her feet soaked and sodden, her father
met her in the hall. Ringrove's information had set
him on the track of things hitherto unsuspected; and
he was waiting for the return of his wife and daughter,
wishing them to see that he knew of those practices
which hitherto they had concealed, and that henceforth
they had to oppose him openly, not to deceive him
secretly.

"Where have you been, Virginia?" he asked, as she
came in, shaking the snow from her dress and jacket at
the door.

"To mattins, papa," she answered, sounding the
double letter according to rule.

"Are you mad, my child, to go out such a morning as this, and when you are already indisposed?" he said, a little sternly.

"It does no one harm to go to church, and my cold is very slight," answered Virginia, by no means aggressively, only steadily and quietly.

"Hear me, Virginia; I forbid these morning prayers," he returned.

The girl turned pale, but she did not answer. This was only an outpost in the great battle of Armageddon to be fought to-day; and not worth the effort or the loss of even a skirmish. And as at this moment Hermione drove up to the door, while the servants flocked into the hall according to the duties of their several posts, the contest was postponed; and Richard contented himself by gravely handing his wife out of the carriage—both maintaining an ominous silence.

The breakfast passed in the same dead, dumb reserve; but when the last piece of toast had been eaten and the last cup of coffee drunk, Richard turned his face to his wife, sitting at the head of the table—a protest against the old love, a witness of the new command in her very appearance. In obedience to Superior she had put away all her curls and fluffs and jewels and ornaments, as so many circumstances of the unregenerate life with which she had no more to do. Her golden hair was braided as smoothly round her head as its natural frizziness would allow it to lie ; and her dress, of deep dark " Mary " blue, was as plain in its cut and style as Sister Agnes could desire or Aunt Catherine imitate.

" I have a word to say to you this morning about our child," began Richard, whom this change in his wife's appearance pained like a personal affront. " What we may speak of together will come best when we are alone. I find that much has been going on with our Virginia of which I have had neither cognisance nor even suspicion —and which I distinctly disapprove and as distinctly forbid."

He stopped. Hermione, balancing her teaspoon on the edge of her cup, did not look up.

" What do you disapprove of ? " she asked, knowing that she had to say something.

" This early daily church-going for one thing, and the child's having what I think you call a director, and plain people a confessor."

" Papa ! " said Virginia, " I cannot give up mattins ! Even if we had daily prayers at home I should feel it a loss to give up the dear service in the church ; but without even this, it would be wicked! I could not, indeed I could not, papa!"

"Your duty is to obey me, my child," he said. "I am your father, and the best director you can have, because the natural one."

"No, papa, my duty is to obey God and the Church," she said.

"I do not think you will induce Virginia to give up her religious privileges," said Hermione in an unsteady voice. "Life has been a different thing to her since, led by Sister Agnes she entered into holiness under Father Truscott's direction."

"This may be; nevertheless I forbid it all—with my whole authority as a father. No confessor shall stand between me and my daughter—me and my wife."

Hermione flushed, and Virginia looked across the table to her father, as if he had pronounced her sentence of death.

"Papa!" she said in a voice of almost agony; "you do not know what you are doing!"

"I know too well, my child," he answered. "I am protecting you from your own ignorance and the knavery of unscrupulous men—men who are neither more nor less than spiritual mountebanks, pretending to powers beyond nature and against all known laws. They, forsooth, can forgive sins and insure the reception into heaven of the soul!—they can transmute a bit of bread and glass of wine into so much flesh and blood!—from their hands comes some kind of divine emanation which carries on the trick and confers the same thaumaturgical powers to the remotest generation! This is the knavish nonsense, my child, that I wish to protect you from, and from all that it includes."

"Richard!" cried Hermione, revolted; "you have neither shame nor grace left in you!"

Virginia rose from her place with a bewildered air.

"Papa! it is a sin to listen to you," she said.

"Stay, Virginia," said her father sternly. "Keep your seat till I give you leave to go."

"Are you suddenly becoming a tyrant?" cried Hermione passionately.

"If you like to call me so—yes; a tyrant," he said. "At all events I am minded to use my power as the master of the household, the guardian of the family, to check these disorders which have crept into it. I wish you both to understand me—both you my wife, and you my child—I forbid this early church-going, and I forbid this weekly confession. I lay it on you, Virginia, as the duty you owe to me, your father, to obey my command; on you, Hermione, to enforce that obedience."

"I owe a higher duty still," said Virginia in a low voice. "And what the saints and martyrs of old did that must I do too. They had to suffer for their faith; and so must I, if you choose to make me, papa."

"You mean that you will disobey me, Virginia?" he asked.

Virginia looked down. She touched the crucifix within her bosom; murmured a prayer; then raised her clear blue eyes, not defiantly, only with the sorrowful constancy of one of those ideal virgin martyrs whose traditions she seemed to carry on into present life.

"You set yourself against the Church and are ac-cursed," she said. "I must disobey God or you:—but God is greater even than a father."

"Now go, my child," he said, after a few moments' pause. "Your answer is given—and my command."

He was taken aback and did not know how to bear himself. The girl's testimony to her faith was so clear and unwavering—so impersonal and placed on such high grounds, that he felt it useless to contend with it; and as difficult as useless. He could not make himself a tyrant—shut her up in her own room and treat her as a criminal or a prisoner. If she chose to defy him, how could he prevent it? Failing an appeal to her reason, to her love, to her duty, what remained? Fear? —physical inability to resist personal coercion? But he was hardly the man to use coarse personal threats or to coerce by force where he could not control by reason.

There remained however Hermione; and she, who had ever proved so plastic, might still be found amenable.

"Wife," he said when they were alone, "you must help me with our child. You must come back from all this folly, sweetheart, into which you have perhaps very pardonably fallen, and once more take your old place as my fitting wife and rational helpmate. The child's excitement can well be conquered and overlooked. She is but a child yet; and if you, her mother, take her in hand, all will come right."

"I cannot," said Hermione. "Virginia is right to live her religious life out to the end; and Father Truscott is a good and wise Director for her."

"My wife! I wish to be neither harsh nor unjust," he said; "but how is it possible that you can give in to this revolting practice of confession for yourself or for your daughter! What has such a girl as that to confess?

and what ought you to say to any man in secret—you who have a husband in whom you can confide all your thoughts and feelings?"

"All my thoughts and feelings in *you*?" said Hermione. "Can I confess to you my adoration of the Blessed Sacrament—my hope in the Divine Mother's intercession? Richard! the very idea is blasphemous!"

"You mean your practices are absurd," he said contemptuously. "Your adoration of a bit of bread—your belief in the intercession of a person dead more than eighteen hundred years, if indeed she ever lived!"

"You are too revolting!" said Hermione with anger. "It curdles my blood to hear you! I only wish that both Virginia and I could leave the house, at least till you got into a better frame of mind and did not insult us with your horrible infidelity."

"Is that to be the next move?" asked Richard, suddenly awakened into suspicion.

"It would be better for Virginia, if I am obliged unfortunately to remain," she answered. "Sister Agnes wishes her to go for a short time with her to C——. It will be a change for her, poor child; and as she is to be confirmed at Easter, a little time of study and preparation would be of infinite service."

"She shall not go with Miss Lascelles !" he said ; "and I will have no mummery of confirmation or the like in my family."

"Then you are really going to be a tyrant over your daughter ? With your principles of individual rights and liberties, it is strange ! "

She gave a short laugh.

"It is not tyranny to prevent a child from going to ruin, even if such prevention is against her will," he said. "Individual liberty does not include leave to commit worse than moral and intellectual suicide."

"That is your way of looking at it," said Hermione. "Ours is that we are living a higher life than what you and your materialism can give us ; that faith is superior to reason, and that we should deny our Lord if we obeyed you. I go with Virginia, and you cannot shake either of us."

" And I, the husband and father, have no influence ?"

"None," said Hermione, thinking of Mr. Lascelles and gathering strength by the thought. "You are an infidel."

"Has your love gone from me, wife ? "

He was very pale when he asked this question, standing up as one expecting the word of command.

Hermione was profoundly agitated. It was a hard thing to have to answer that question put so straightly, so uncompromisingly; but again she remembered Mr. Lascelles, and seemed to summon his spirit to help her.

"I do not love you so much as I did," she said in a low voice. "Your infidelity distresses and disgusts me too much."

"And the religion which rends asunder the holiest ties—which has broken up the happiest home in England, seems to you a good and holy thing?—and the man who leads you to this practical abandonment of your marriage bond seems a wise and noble leader? To me not! and you yourself would acknowledge that by 'their fruits ye shall know them' is a pregnant saying."

"Scripture from your mouth is too painful to me to listen to," said Hermione; "and for one such text as this I could bring forward twenty that would justify us and condemn you. We must serve God rather than man, and Divine Love is to be preferred to any form of human affection."

Always the same thing!—always the same vague but impenetrable barrier, and the circle turning round on itself, beginning where it ended and ending where it had begun! What was to be done? The world had suddenly become like an enchanted wood to Richard Fullerton, where was neither path nor issue, and where every footstep only entangled him the more.

" You tell me this calmly, my wife," he said, steadying his voice as best he could, but it shook and broke in spite of all his efforts. " Your love for me was once as certain in my mind as that to-morrow's sun would shine—mine for you as enduring as life itself. And now you have let this new man—a stranger here less than a year ago—come in between us and take you from me. You confess to him, you obey him, you believe in him, you strengthen his hands against me in the governance of our child. If you do not love him as no wife should love any man but her husband, it is because you are too good and pure to entertain an unholy passion ; but you give to him all the essential treasures of your love—all that redeems marriage from vulgar sensuality ; and you have despoiled me that you may make him rich. You see him with eyes blinded by a new excitement—dazzled by a strange fanaticism. The new ritual, the new order of things, has carried you away as it has carried away the child ; but, before it is too late, hear me !—hear your husband, your friend, your lover, your protector ! Come back to me, wife !—come back to your trust and your duty, to your happiness and your love. Wife ! my wife ! beloved ! come back to me ! Be your true sweet self once more, before you have broken my heart and fallen from your own purity ! "

He went up to her and took her to him, laying one hand on her forehead while the other was round her neck.

" Wife ! " he pleaded; " look into my eyes as honestly as you used !—let your heart speak for me before it has been too far warped ! "

But she lowered her eyes, took his hands from her neck—from her forehead—and trembling visibly drew herself gently away.

" It is too late now," she said, in a broken voice. " You are the enemy of the Church, and it would be a sin in me were I to love you as I did, or be to you what I was ! "

She hid her face in her hands and burst into tears. He took her to him again, and kissed her with the old boyish tenderness—kissed her head and neck and face and hands ; but the sweet caresses in which she had once found all her joy filled her now with dread and horror, and again she turned away from him shuddering.

" No ! " she said, flinging out her hands as if to ward him off; " we can never be the same to each other that we were. I have confessed to you to-day that I no longer love you as I did, and our whole lives must now be different."

Richard did not speak. The man's natural dignity came to his aid and checked the passion of sorrow else that would have overwhelmed him. He walked to the window and stood there for a while, looking out on the fast-falling snow and the grey dull sky. Then he turned back to his wife.

"Tell me," he said suddenly; "and tell me with your old candour—you were never yet a double-dealer, Hermione ; and your new religion has scarcely, I imagine, sanctified falsehood—is this separation of our lives of your own proper motion, or has it been suggested to you— perhaps commanded ? "

Hermione looked away, sorely tried and embarrassed. The doctrine of reserve had in truth eaten into her former candour so that she was less honest than she used to be ; but she was bound to be faithful now. Raising her heavy eyes by one supreme effort, she looked into her husband's face.

"My Director forbids me," she said.

"Mr. Lascelles ? "

"Yes : Superior."

"Thank you," said Richard, in a strange voice. "Now I know where I stand."

Again he went to the window looking out on the dreary landscape before him, his head leaning on his hand as he rested his elbow on the woodwork of the frame; and again he came back to her whose love had once made his happiness as her defection now made his despair.

"Do not be afraid, old love," he said gently; "I will not trouble you again with a fondness that has grown unwelcome to you. Only believe and know that I am the same to you as I was in the beginning, and have been all through. When you want me you will find me."

He held out his hand and pressed hers tenderly, looking into her face with a long long look as one bidding an eternal farewell. Then he left the room hurriedly, and in a few moments was out in the driving snow, ploughing his way—whither?

CHAPTER VI.

THE wind blew keen and the snow fell fast, but Richard, unconscious of all things outward and without the sense of personal discomfort, knew nothing of either as he walked hurriedly onward. The pain at his heart over-powered all other feelings, and what the day was like was as much a matter of indifference to him, writhing under his intolerable anguish, as it is a matter of in-difference to the tortured wretch at the stake whether it is in the gloom of the night, or under the glory of the noonday sun, that his limbs are racked and his flesh burned—as it is to the dying whether it is in the morning or the evening when the eternal farewell is given. He knew only these two things, which in fact were one :—that his life as it had been—that life of peace and love and honour—had come suddenly to an end ; and that his wife and child had withdrawn themselves from him at the instance of a stranger in whom they believed more than they believed in him. He confessed bitterly that his enemy had been stronger than he, and had carried the citadel of that dear wife's faith, that child's sweet reverence, which until now he had held as his own, impregnable against the whole world.

And now, what could he himself do?—poor crownless king whom love had once anointed, and whose dominion fanaticism and falsehood had taken from him! What could he do?—how recover what he had lost?—keep what he still held? Not knowing where he went nor how he walked, he ploughed his way mechanically onward; turning over scheme after scheme of action in his mind, and never striking on reasonable possibilities, never coming to satisfaction in any. Certainly he could leave the place; break away from his work; delegate to an agent his duties; and make a new life for himself and his family elsewhere; but what good would come from that? Those fatal ecclesiastical nets were spread on all sides; and wherever he turned he saw the same deadly influences besetting those who were dearest to him. East or west, there stood the priest between him and his honour, him and his happiness—there rose up the Church, the grim shadow of which hung like a cloud over his home and shut out the light of the sky. It was not to be supposed that all this change in Hermione and Virginia depended on Mr. Lascelles and Sister Agnes only; though they had undoubtedly been the prime movers in the "conversion" of which they made so much account, and were still the central points round which the rest revolved. Yet Richard could not hope that, even if he took them away from Crossholme, these dear blinded enthusiasts of his would unchristianize themselves and go back to their old attitude of toleration and indifference—tolerant to his atheism because indifferent to Christianity. To go abroad, say, and break the chain of continuity here, might be of use so far as interrupting the special influence of one man went; but it would not destroy their belief in the creed nor loosen the grip of the accredited professors of that creed. Therefore it would not restore the old order of life.

And again, if he decided to go and they refused? Influenced by Mr. Lascelles, who held her conscience in the hollow of his hand, Hermione well might so refuse both for herself and her daughter; and how could he compel them by main force? If they resisted quietly— passively—said they would not—made no arrangements —opposed simply the resistance of inertia—could he have them carried by men's arms to this carriage, that hotel, and treat them as refractory prisoners are treated by their gaolers?

What indeed could he do ? Should he speak to Mr. Lascelles ?—defy him ?—forbid him ?—argue with him dispassionately on the social inexpediency, the personal indelicacy of thus interfering in a man's house ? Should he forget his own pride and dignity, and stoop to a pitiful plea for compassion ?—a whining prayer, as of a conquered slave, suing the stronger master for mercy and forbearance ? Should he place the matter on the ground of elemental right and wrong ?—on the sacredness of the marriage tie, the inalienable rights of the father, the iniquity of filial disobedience, and the danger of conjugal estrangement ? Let him lay out the ground as he would, he saw no chance of good or profit. The vicar would join his long white hands together by the finger tips a little spread, lower his thin eyelids, put on his bland superior smile ; then in his smooth, artificial voice would say, with the correctest enunciation, that it was his painful duty to cause the unfaithful sorrow ; as a testifying minister of the Word he must draw the sword which his Divine Master, the Prince of Peace, had brought into the world, and use it against those ungodly ones for whose chastisement it had been sent and sharpened. It was his pastoral obligation, part of his ordination vows, to save from perdition those precious souls which agnosticism and modern science were

doing their best to destroy. He was in his right as a
priest and within the law as a citizen ; and remonstrance
would be as vain as prayer, as futile as threats. He
would look up at him, his thin lips curled into a smile
that meant a sneer ; he would say that he pitied a man
who stood in such a disagreeable position, and would
gladly help him out of it if he could—as he could; but
by one way only. Failing that one way he could do
nothing; and he, Richard, had not an inch of ground
whereon to stand against him. In his right as a priest
and within the law as a citizen, where was the place, and
where the foothold?

All this Richard knew by heart, and all this made his
action one of supreme difficulty. His field was so narrow,
his hand so weakened, and the enemy was so securely
entrenched! But things could not go on as they were,
and he must make one supreme effort to stop them before
he finally submitted—if submit he must. He felt the
shame and humiliation of his position in thus contending
with any man whatsoever, priest or no priest, for what
constituted the vital possession of the women of his
house. He, the husband and father, to contend, if by no
means more tangible than argument, discussion, anger,
opposition of will—still to contend for the preservation

of his wife's love, the enforcement of his daughter's obedience ! It was shameful, degrading, maddening. Philosophy was swept away in the great flow of his despairing wrath, as an Alpine storm sweeps away a summer châlet, beautiful to the eye and pleasant to inhabit when no tempestuous whirlwinds are about to show of what frail material it is made. His cherished principles of individual rights—of the liberty of each human being to develope according to his or her desires— of the sacredness of the conscience—of the equality of woman—all went to the ground before the hideousness of this present embodiment, this horrible translation into superstition, fanaticism, denial of natural duties, renunciation of natural affections. If absolute and brutal force could have brought back those dear ones into the way of truth and reason, as he held both, he would have used it: as he would have prevented a madman from committing suicide by binding his arms with cords ; or have stopped —if need be, harshly—a child running heedlessly on the edge of a precipice. Good as he knew them to be, but credulous and weak as they had proved themselves, according to his estimate of things, his authority would have seemed to himself only the rightful exercise of his natural function and what his place of guardian demanded.

But he could do nothing. While he was sleeping in security, trusting to the loyalty of the beloved as they might have trusted to his, they had suffered themselves to be led away, and had delivered him bound into the hands of his enemy. He was not angry with them, nor had his heart revolted against them for anything they had done. It was this stranger, this priest, who had invaded his home and brought him to shame as well as to sorrow, with whom he was offended and by whom he had been outraged. If he could have killed him, as any other reptile may lawfully be killed, he would ; but he was powerless. His hands were tied; and the iniquity which he could neither punish nor prevent must go on as it would. The world still consecrates some forms of tyranny and injustice—still demands that the victim shall salute the imperial Cæsar ; and this clerical executioner, this Christian Cain and worse than murderer, must live on to wreck more homes, destroy more lives, break the hearts of men and sap the essential virtue of women ; and no law could touch him, no hand must strike him !

Walking on, deaf and blind to all external life, following the road by instinct rather than clear knowledge of where he was, his eyes fixed on the white way before him but not seeing where it led, he was brought up

half-dazed by the door of the Vicarage—the door fronting
the little narrow path off the main street of the village,
which he had unconsciously taken. It was as if the necessity of the moment had led him there unawares ; if not
against his will, yet without his knowledge, his concurrence.
Void of superstition as he was, he yet accepted this act of
unconscious cerebration as if it had been intentional and
part of his plan ; and, without hesitating or staying to
reflect, he rang the door-bell loudly. Perhaps after all
this was the best thing to do ! Humiliating as it was to
him—perhaps all the same it was the best !

" I have come to see you, under protest," said Richard,
as he was ushered into the study, where he found Mr.
Lascelles sitting before the fire reading the day's news-
paper.

If plain and simply furnished, according to the law
of elegant asceticism under which the vicar lived, the
room was warm, home-like, sufficing ; and the handsome
priest himself, comfortably seated before the blazing fire,
was as well-ordered, as serene, and as elegantly ascetic as
his room. How unlike that pale and haggard man,
miserable, half-distraught, heart-broken, who staggered
in from the pitiless wind and snow, like some lone wreck
drifted upon placid shores !

Mr. Lascelles rose as he came in, mastering his surprise with an effort; and yet it was not surprise so much as a kind of catching of the breath at the triumph which, for some time foreseen, had now come at last.

"I am glad to see you," he said with perfect breeding and composure; but he did not hold out his hand. Had he done so, Richard would not have taken it.

"I want to say a few words to you," then said Richard slowly.

Both men were standing—Mr. Lascelles near the fire, Mr. Fullerton near the table.

"With pleasure," said the vicar blandly. "Take a chair."

"No," said Richard shortly. "I prefer to stand."

"As you please," returned Mr. Lascelles, seating himself; while there floated before his gratified eyes the image of Hermione's fair, flushed, upturned face, and the expression on it when she had looked shyly into his in the school-room this morning and had confessed that she no longer loved her husband as she used. And now that husband himself had come; and whether he had come to petition or to remonstrate, to oppose or to rebuke, it was equally a triumph and the sign of his victory.

"You are interfering in my house, Mr. Lascelles, in

a manner which no man of honour or self-respect could bear," began Richard with a slow heavy emphasis.

"I am doing what I can," returned Mr. Lascelles with a certain kind of dry humility, as one deprecating praise which yet he knew that he deserved.

" Doing what you can to detach my wife and daughter from me?—to weaken their love and to destroy my authority?"

" Just so," he answered.

" At least you have the merit, such as it is, of frankness that is cynicism," said Richard.

" In which I am like yourself," returned the vicar with his courtly smile.

"Let us understand each other, Mr. Lascelles."

The vicar crossed his legs, joined his hands together by their finger tips, and put on a gravely attentive look. Objectionable—a stronger word might be the truer epithet according to Mr. Lascelles—devilish, abominable, say, on all accounts as this agnostic was, and hopeless as was his errand let the substance of it be what it might, he should yet learn for himself the inexhaustible riches of Christian courtesy and how the saved can afford to be gracious even to castaways.

" I have only just now learnt the practices which you

'*Let us understand each other, Mr. Lascelles.*'

have induced my wife and daughter to adopt," Richard went on to say; "the daily public services, the weekly communion taken fasting, the degrading offices which you have imposed on them—or at least on my child—and the dishonouring, shameful, destructive habit of confession These are things which I am in no mood to tolerate. They must be stopped; and I forbid all further tampering with those for whose conduct I am responsible and whose actions touch my character and honour as much as their own."

"You cannot forbid my using my official influence over Mrs. and Miss Fullerton; nor can you prevent their yielding to it," said Mr. Lascelles suavely.

"I am master in my own house," said Richard.

The vicar smiled. He looked first at his white, well-washed hands; examined his nails, and rubbed back the band of his fourth finger; then he raised his eyes suddenly and fixed them on Mr. Fullerton's face.

"No," he said deliberately; "you are not master in your own house, Mr. Fullerton, for the simple reason that you have no house in which to be master."

"Are you mad!" cried Richard, making a step forward.

"Not that I am aware of; I am simply within the

limits of the case," returned the vicar in a quiet, half-mocking voice. " Is it necessary for me to remind you, Mr. Fullerton, that you have no legal status here in Crossholme?—not an inch of ground that you can call your own?—and no legal authority over your wife and daughter? Try it ! " he continued, raising his voice and hand to check Richard as he was about to speak. " Try it ! and so prove my case and ruin your own. If you attempt to interfere with your daughter in the exercise of her religious duties, her mother—guided by my advice —will carry her complaint into court, and you will be deprived of all authority whatever. The Shelley judgment stands unrescinded; and on that you will be cast. By the law you, an atheist who can be convicted of open blasphemy, and who would not—and so far I honour you—deny in public what you hold in private, or profess what you do not believe even to gain possession of your child—you, unchristian and infidel, have no voice in the moral education of your daughter ; as you have no claim on your wife's property beyond such bare maintenance as should prevent your becoming chargeable to the parish. It may be painful to you to hear these truths; but they are truths; and the deeper you take them to heart the less likely you will be to fall into difficulty on your own account, or to cause us embarrassment by forcing us into hostile action in self-defence. Turn which way you will, you have no foothold, no case. You have placed yourself out of the pale not only of the Christian communion, but out of the broader protection of the civil law. Your wife has the reins, if she has so far allowed you to hold them ; even your daughter is absolved from her natural duty of obedience ; and no one is to blame for either dilemma but yourself. And now let me end with one word of counsel —on your own behalf more than on ours."—It pleased Mr. Lascelles, cold, cruel, strong as he was, to see the reflection of this ostentatious union, this classification of himself with Hermione and Virginia, on the face of the tortured man before him. "Yield without opposition to the new order of things, and you will be generously tolerated and suffered to efface yourself without annoyance; fight, and you will be worsted. We have not only Divine command, but Parliament and the Law Courts, on our side ; and I warn you that the power which we possess we will use if you make it necessary. Fairness demands that I should tell you this, but fairness demands no more than this."

Mild, self-controlled, reasonable, philosophic—these were undoubtedly Richard Fullerton's prominent characteristics. He had educated himself in the exercise of all these qualities, and love and tranquillity had been his teachers. But those who could have read his heart at that moment would not have found much mildness or philosophic patience in it now. Nothing but the long-rooted habit of self-control and the self-respect of a gentleman, kept him from taking that insolent, smooth-voiced priest by the throat and strangling the life out of him as he sat there, rolling out the terms of his dishonour and defeat like a delicate morsel daintily caressed—a catalogue of insult pronounced in fair musical notes—a litany of damnation striking at all hope and set to a grandly-framed harmonious chant. He stood there, struggling with his passion and his shame ; half wondering why he might not kill that man as he would have killed a tiger crouching for its spring or a lurking savagefitting his arrow to the bow. In looking back over this moment, it was ever a mystery to him that he had conquered his natural instinct so far as to let that shameless assailant live. Silent, his broad chest heaving, his hands clenched, his mouth compressed till the full, kind lips were tightened into a bloodless line, his eyes on the ground, the lids narrowed as if the muscular contraction by which he restrained himself had touched even them, he stood there, the moral athlete wrestling with the wild beasts of rage and despair—with the man's natural sense of dishonour and instinctive desire of revenge. Mr. Lascelles, his eyes too half closed, watched him in this conflict, half wondering how it would end. Richard was a powerful man physically, and might easily be dangerous; and anguish has an ugly trick of making gentlemen forget their breeding, and of letting loose the natural passions which it is their social duty to control.

At last Richard conquered himself sufficiently to be able to speak.

"Your platform is well defined," he said in a constrained voice. "You do not hesitate in your terms."

"I knew that you would prefer candour," returned the vicar with a half-complimentary air. "Between men of the world the truth is always the best, and the shortest way the wisest."

"Perhaps you have left out one factor in the sum," said Richard, still in the same constrained manner, as if forcing himself by an effort to be calm.

"Yes? Which?"

"The affection of a loving woman, which will recoil from aiding in her husband's discomfiture."

Mr. Lascelles smiled. Again the image of that flushed,

half-tearful " penitent " of his, confessing to her own shame and his triumph, came vividly before him ; and he shook his head with undisguised satisfaction, if also with affected pity for the man whom he had over-come.

" In the days of her darkness, and before she had been called, yes, you might have believed in her acquiescence in your manner of life and in her refusal to join in any scheme of action which should disconcert you ; but now she is converted and gives her highest duty to God." He said this with clean and clear precision. He knew so much about Hermione Fullerton's soul, he could enlighten even her husband who had once known all and now understood nothing.

" God ! To your demon, you mean—to Moloch ! " said Richard with a bitter laugh.

" Blasphemy will not help you," said Mr. Lascelles quietly. " Call Him by what name you will, He is now her Master whose will she obeys, as expressed by the Voice of the Church."

" The Voice which teaches falsehood and superstition, enmity and deception, which is more cruel and no truer than that of Delphi and Cumæ ! " said Richard.

" Which teaches truth and righteousness," returned

the vicar; "and which, I am grateful to be able to say, your wife and daughter have heard—and obeyed."

"And this is the work in which you rejoice! The ruin of one of the purest hearts in England, your boast; the destruction of one of the happiest homes, your honour!"

"So speaks the unregenerate man; the Christian would say that I have cause for great thankfulness, inasmuch as I have been made the chosen means by which has been saved a precious soul, lost for all eternity until my advent." Mr. Lascelles spoke with the air of a man modestly taking the merit that was his due. "And for the rest," he continued—and his manner may be inferred from his words—"I can safely say that your wife, my precious penitent, had not a virtue in the past which I have not fostered by the discipline of the Church and strengthened by confession—not a grace which is not enhanced tenfold by religion. She has put on the beauty of holiness, and by so doing every natural beauty of her own shines with redoubled brightness. Between my creation and yours there is not a question which is the more admirable."

As Mr. Lascelles said this he got up and rang the bell. A certain sudden glare in Richard's eyes—a certain sudden movement—a little daunted him ; and the presence of a third person, if only a maid-servant, might be valuable.

"Wine," he said, as the girl entered suddenly.

The coming of Mr. Fullerton had excited the Vicarage household ; and if keyholes are not made for eyes and ears that wish to be informed, of what use are they?

"You will take a glass of wine, Mr. Fullerton? It is a cold day," he added with the nicest accent of sympathetic hospitality.

Richard turned away and stood for a few moments apart ; then faced Mr. Lascelles once more.

"There is no good in vulgar raving," he said slowly. "I understand you, without need of more words. You have played your game cleverly, and so far you have won. Craft and deceit generally do win against blind trust; and my trust was blind. For the rest I may try some of those points on which you have defied me, and strengthen my hands against you by the aid of the law where I can."

"Do so," said Mr. Lascelles cheerfully ; "and you will find that what I have said is true. You have no law on your side. You are an atheist, and the English conscience repudiates you. You have excommunicated yourself, and, like a felon—and you are a spiritual felon—

your crime has deprived you of your natural rights. Ah !
here is the sherry. Let me offer you some. It is dry,
and the day is wild."

" God! is such a man possible ? " said Richard, half to
himself. " This man is a model minister of Christ—this
man who almost makes me believe the devil possible ! "

Mr. Lascelles smiled.

" I should have fulfilled my duty had I made you
quite believe," he said. " It might have saved you a
rougher process in the future."

He spoke with admirable equanimity. To liken him
to the devil was but a stone cast by unblessed hands
that hurt him no more than those missiles cast at saints
which turned to rose-leaves as they fell. It was part of
that hypothetical "martyrdom" which these popular
dominators of souls, these petted inquisitors of men's
lives, are so fond of proclaiming that they undergo ;
glorifying themselves in that they are accounted worthy
to suffer for the truth, when all the time it is they who
burn and they who rack, they who destroy here and
consign to eternal perdition hereafter.

" Better hell with those wise and good with whom I
have cast in my lot, than heaven with such as you !" said
Richard with a gesture of repulsion.

"All right," said Mr. Lascelles; "it is well to be content with the bed which one makes for oneself. Really, you had better let me give you a glass of wine ! It will keep out the cold."

Richard did not speak, but turned abruptly and left the room ; and in the same state as he was in when he entered—blind and dazed, not clearly knowing where he was nor whither he was going—he passed through the hall, and once more set out into the cruel wind and driving snow of this bitter biting winter's day.

The interview had advanced nothing, done no good any way, he thought, as he walked onward. Some insolent truths had been said, some bitter words been spoken, but the main facts were rooted as before :—the love and obedience of his wife and daughter had been taken from him, and if he could not recover their love he could not enforce their obedience. The law had indeed made, in the one case the wife, in the other the Church, superior to the husband and father. Should Hermione so choose, he was as powerless in his dealings with her, through the terms of the will which gave her the sole possession of her fortune, as his natural authority over Virginia was nullified by those Acts of Parliament and decrees of judges which demand that every Englishman shall belong to some form of religious faith if he would receive the benefit of social conventions, or be confirmed in his natural rights :—Acts of Parliament and decrees of judges, thought Richard bitterly, which declare that learning, probity, goodness, self-devotion, shall count for nothing in a man's control over his children, if not backed up by belief in the Divine wisdom of a book which makes the universe about six thousand years old, and places the earth in the centre of the system. Yes, Mr. Lascelles was the stronger in this struggle for mastership over those two dear ones. He recognized that now, sorrowfully enough, but clearly. The law was on the side of the vicar; so was that large majority—those weak souls which must cling to something tangible and external if they would stand upright at all ;—" While I," he said aloud, "have only my own strength and the goodness of my cause, in the fight that I have made against superstition and credulity—in my endeavour to substitute for blind faith in legends which no man can prove and no ingenuity harmonize with known conditions, the study of facts and reverence for law."

But again—what could he do? Were he even disposed to command, he had no power to enforce; and a *brutum fulmen* only makes a man ridiculous. And of what use to attempt argument against blind faith in favour of reason, when reason itself was held to be a snare spread for souls by the Evil One, and this same blind faith was alone accepted as safe guidance because Divine illumination? Appeals to old affection, to the instinctive love the holy harmony of the family—these too would go to the wall before the firm if sorrowful assertion that martyrdom was the glory of the saints; and that it was better to serve the Saviour, who came to bring salvation into the world by setting the child against the father and the wife against the husband, than to attend even to the Ten Commandments which once represented the Word of God without appeal or comment. Everywhere he was met, baffled, defeated; and he felt like one round whom the iron cage is fast drawing in, leaving him neither hope of escape nor means of living.

It was as if years had passed over him since this morning, when he came home just as the short twilight was darkening into evening. He never knew where he had been nor how far he had walked. Had he been asked, he would have said that he had stood still for all these hours, searching for means of escape from a grievous spiritual prison, and finding none. But he knew that he must have walked far and fast, and been buffeted by the wind and snow in some exposed place; for he was dead weary when he reached his home, and soaked through to the skin. So far physical exhaustion had befriended him, by bringing him back to the consciousness of material things.

Also, his long absence on this fearful day had frightened both Hermione and Virginia, so that the ice of their late estrangement broke up under the pressure of their anxiety, and they were only eager to welcome back to his home the husband and the father whom their fanaticism had driven abroad. As time passed on and their fears deepened, they forgot all causes of displeasure which they had against this sinner, once so dear to both, to remember only that they loved him, that he was worthy of their love—mercy being infinite and the natural man a lineal descendant of Adam!—and that perhaps he was in danger, with no one to help him :—and they the cause of his peril.

CHAPTER VII.

ALMOST !

MOTHER and daughter had stood by the drawing-room window watching drearily, anxiously, for more than an hour before the small side-gate opened, and the weary master who was not owner passed through like one walking in a dream, and instinctively took the short wood-walk across the upper end of the park. Hermione's dark-blue eyes were full of tears which every now and then fell silently on her hands which she had clasped together against the framework of the window as a rest for her pretty, golden, self-accusing head. And Virginia's eyes too were full of tears ; but she had comforted herself by snatches of fervent, silent prayer ; and Hermione had not.

It had been a day of checkered emotions for the pretty woman whom nature had made for love and sub-mission, and whom the Church was fast transforming out of all likeness to her original self—or rather, was fatally transferring to another direction. At first she had been sorrowfully proud, mournfully elate, at the constancy with which she had borne her testimony, and the fidelity of her obedience to Mr. Lascelles. It had been hard at the moment, but when done it was well done ; and when she next saw dear Superior she would have a clean page to offer, which he would sign, smiling, with his approval. She was a little disturbed when she saw Richard dash out so heedlessly into the snow and wind ; and she thought that he was probably bound for the Vicarage, where he would see Mr. Lascelles, and either insult him by his unblushing atheism, or quarrel with him in some yet more terrible and ungodly fashion. This thought tormented her for a long while, now inclining her to anger for her husband and corresponding sympathy for the vicar ; now softening her to the former for fear of the hard things which the latter might say, and the telling blows that he might give. But as the day wore on and Richard did not return—when the luncheon had been announced, kept back, eaten, and finally dismissed, and yet he did not appear—then her thoughts became concentrated in one great sentiment of fear, and her imagination ran riot over all the possibilities of tragedy that it could create. Time passed ; and she grew sorry, self-censuring, penitent, humble. If only he would return ! She would be so glad to see him !—so glad ! so relieved ! As each successive

hour struck, her load of guilt grew heavier, her appre-
hensions more unendurable.   Restless and feverish, she
paced from room to room and wandered aimlessly about
the house, which seemed to have grown so large and
empty; but this fever of unrest passed into the stony
watching of extreme anxiety, and she stood by the window,
her eyes strained on the gravel walk of the garden up
which he must come, should he ever come back at all.

At last he came, rounding that clump of laurels in the
centre of the drive, which was the farthest point that could
be seen in the darkening evening and through the driving
snow.   How drooping and how weary he looked !   His
head bent and his step uncertain, she saw him through
the veil of the dusk and under the dimming shower of
driving flakes almost as if he had been the ghost of himself—something like but not real.   Yet it was he, truly
enough ; and with a little cry she ran from the window
through the room and into the hall, saying with a sob :—

" Richard ! At last ! at last ! "—crying out hurriedly
to her daughter—" Quick, Virginia ! come to meet dear
papa ! "

She herself opened the hall door, and stood out under
the portico ; the snow blowing over her and flecking her
dark-blue dress with momentary flakes of silver, while

the wind eddied round the hall and drove in light drifts
that soon made feathery heaps in all the angles. She
neither knew nor cared how things went. She thought
only of him, the beloved of her youth, the friend of her
maturity—was conscious only of her joy in his return.
The sweet, fond, self-forgetting wife had come back, and
the plastic creature of a spiritual seducer, masked as a
divine guide, had disappeared.

" Richard, my darling ! how wet and tired you look !
how cold and miserable ! You look half dead ! Darling,
come in and rest. Why, where have you been all this
dreadful day ?—and I so wretched, thinking of you ! "

She spoke with the incoherence of fear and tenderness
combined, going impulsively to meet him as he came
wearily up the steps of the portico. She laid her hand
on his arm, and seemed to lead him into the hall, where
she took both his hands in hers and chafed them
tenderly.

" My poor half-frozen darling ! " she said, looking up
into his face with her big blue eyes, soft and dark and
humid ; while Virginia said—she too with all her old
sweetness :—

" Let me help you with your coat, dearest papa. It
is wet through—do let me take it off ! "

Richard stood and looked from one to the other like a man rudely awakened from an opium dream—not seeing, not understanding, ignorant which was the truth—the dream or this. Was he mad now, or had he been mad? Was all that he had suffered the self-made anxiety of a disordered brain?—or was this hallucination and the feverish fancy of a despair so sick that it had taken on itself the very mockery of hope and happiness?—as men dying of hunger in the desert · see themselves set in gardens and fair places where they rest in happiness and delight. He passed his hand in a bewildered way over his forehead, looked round him vaguely, and turned to them with as much sadness as inquiry ; then he sighed heavily and closed his eyes.

Truly, this was home ; and these were his wife and daughter—the creatures whom he loved with every fibre of his being—whose soft touch he felt, into whose sweet eyes he looked, whose caressing voices he heard. Had he really been with that priest—that man who had boasted of his victory over these dear ones, and defied his efforts to bring them back to their duty of love—to subdue them again to his influence? Had they really spoken to him to-day as he thought he remembered that they had? Had his daughter pronounced him accursed? Had Hermione

taken herself from him? and were their lives to be henceforth based on a different plan and principle from what
had been formerly?

Uncertain, and shocked at his own entanglement of
thought—he whose perceptions were always so clear and
whose mind was so firm—he stood there for a while
silent, but trembling visibly, and almost breathless as the
dumb trouble of his suspense passed into the sharp pain
of reaction—the pleasure which makes pain.

" Wife ! my little Ladybird ! " he said at last in a
broken voice, drawing each to him lovingly, and kissing
each as he used in olden times.

Virginia's tears fell on his pale cold face as she met
his with lips almost as pale, almost as cold; but Hermione
clung to him with her old sweet touch, and felt him once
more her beloved—and her own.

Suddenly : " He is your destroyer—his love for you
is your soul's dishonour—yours for him a crime against
God," rang in her ears, as if Mr. Lascelles had been there
and was repeating this morning's denunciations, as well
as command ; and " I promise to obey you " was the echo
of her own voice sent by her wavering soul through her
memory. Yes; this morning she had promised to
withdraw herself, body and soul, heart and life, and to let

the Church divorce what the law had joined and love had
hallowed; and now, not twelve hours after her vow, she
was standing with her arms round the husband whose
expulsion had been decreed, her lips giving back the
tender touch of his. For an instant she shrank within
herself and recoiled; then she drew him closer to her
heart, saying to herself: " He is my husband and I am
his wife, and none shall come between us."

Still trembling—for indeed the reaction had been
almost too strong for him—silent, for he was afraid to
speak lest some new discord should break in upon this
divinest harmony—bewildered, but conscious of rest and
sweetest peace, Richard went slowly up the stairs—his
wife with him. With her own hands she drew the easy
chair before the fire in his dressing-room, and performed
all sorts of pleasant caressing little offices about him
before his man was summoned. He smiled and let her
do what she would. To have her thus about him rested
and refreshed him more than sleep or food would have
done. When she left him finally, promising to return in
half-an-hour, he was calm, peaceful, soothed, and she
herself was happier than she had been ever since that
fatal dinner. After all, he was her husband, fine and noble,
tender, just and true; and it was good to love him !

A note was put into her hand as she went into her own room. It was from Mr. Lascelles, and contained his photograph taken in the " sacrificial vestments " of which some part was her own work, accompanied by a beautifully bound manuscript in his own handwriting on the crime of disobedience to the will of the priest—representing God—and the awful authority given to him by confession and absolution.

Whether he had foreseen any strain of this present kind on the return of Richard, whose passage back through the village had been noted and reported to him, and so took the only means within his power to counteract the natural influence of a woman's pity and a wife's only half-destroyed tenderness, who can tell ? He had a faculty of prevision which embraced all possibilities ; and this might have been one of those occasions when his know-ledge of men and women made him prophetic. With the photograph to remind and the manuscript to recall, he thought that he had still his hand on the rudder, and that he need not fear the result of what he knew would be close sailing for the moment. Richard was the old, with the accumulated force of habit to back him ; but he was the new, with the keys of heaven and hell in his hand. As Jove held the thunderbolts, so had he the power

of excommunication from the Church and consequent
banishment from God ; and should the pretty woman
who was born to obey seek to rebel, she would have to
learn that lovers can become executioners at need, and
that a gentleman may court but a priest must compel.

If these gifts were potent as reminders, so was the
letter that accompanied them, going straight as it did to
the heart of the situation.   It recalled to Hermione the
exact terms of the sacred promise which she had made to
him the writer, her priest, her director, only so long ago
as this morning ; and bound it on her conscience to fulfil
to the letter all the conditions which he had imposed.
Those conditions were hard, and the words in which they
were set forth were strong and rasping; but he clamped
all together by the divine authority of which he was the
interpreter—the executant—and defied a child of Holy
Mother Church to disobey the supreme command.   He
seemed to have had magical insight into her poor, weak,
troubled soul; and he came on the scene of this probability of reconciliation like the spectre which stands by
the altar and with its fleshless hand forbids the marriage.
He had foreseen all this hesitation, this wavering, this
turning back like Lot's wife to the home that she had
abandoned, to the life which habit and love had endeared.

But the hand which held knew also how to keep ; and Mr. Lascelles was not the man to be discouraged by the feeble struggles of the victim which he had captured, and now was binding fast to the horns of the altar. He knew that until finally stilled the pendulum must beat, but its swing is ever shorter ; as the ebbing tide has waves which appear to advance, but the tide ever ebbs and the deserted shore is left dry, strewn with dead things and the wreck of what was once man's finest work. On pain of her eternal perdition, Hermione was commanded to continue steadfastly in holy opposition to this man of sin whom God had forsaken, and to withdraw herself finally from his hateful influence. Her love for him, she was told, was a sin against heaven, and to be in friendship with her husband was to be at enmity with God.

It was as if a voice from the Ark had spoken, calling back one wandering from the worship of Jehovah to the idolatrous temples of the groves—a voice which she dared not refuse to hear, a command which she dared not refuse to obey !

When she went back to her husband, she went back changed. She was gentle and sorrowful enough, but as if she had shrunk again within herself ; and if not cold nor repelling, yet she was no longer tender or expansive.

Again, the moral blight which already had destroyed so
much had fallen on her ; as subtle and as irresistible as
the blight which falls on the gardens and the cornfields.
In her fear for his safety, and her unregenerate self-
reproach for the pain that she had given him, she had
forgotten that Richard was an atheist, and had remembered only that he was her husband whom she had once
adored and still loved, and—despite herself—respected.
Now she had to remember rather that he was excommunicate ; and that the only tie between them was his name
which she bore, and the past which she could not undo
if she did her best to forget.

Richard held out his hand to her as she came in.
He was sitting thrown back in the easy chair as she had
placed it, weary in body but with the patient calmness of
mind, the sweet trustfulness, the happy uncriticizing love
which were essentially his. He had accepted all that had
come to him in this last hour as a full and complete reconciliation. He had his wife again, and their new life
would date from to-day. They would talk together, heart
open, as in olden times, and consult one with the other
how best to live in harmony and affection, even if it
should still be that their spheres of thought were different
and their objects of belief opposed. But at least they

had come together again, and no man stood between them.

He smiled and turned his head towards her as she came through the doorway—not that of communication with her room, but that which gave on to the corridor.

"Wife! dear wife! How good it is to see you!" he said in a low voice, caressingly.

The colour had gone out of her face, and she looked as pale under the lamplight as if she had been Virginia herself.

"I am glad you are safe at home. I was frightened about you," she said in a constrained manner.

"I do not like to have frightened you, sweet wife, but I love to hear that you were anxious," he answered, still smiling.

"I hope that you have not made yourself ill; you looked so tired when you came in, and were so cold and wet," she said in an odd jerky way; not looking at him; pretending to arrange the antimacassar with her dis-engaged hand. He held the other in both of his.

"It is all right now. I have your dear hand in mine," he said, kissing the soft pink fingers.

She turned away in desperate trouble. It seemed so cruel to hurt him afresh. But her vow—Superior's letter

—that manuscript of holy counsel—the divine guidance under which she lived—the commands which must be obeyed, let what human considerations there would oppose :—she dared not take her husband back to her heart, nor give herself to his as in the past. She dared not disobey the priest whom she had chosen as her spiritual guide in preference to this atheist, if once her beloved. It tore her own heart to part from him as much as it would tear his to lose her; but the command was greater than the pain; and though that pain should even kill, that command must still be carried out. The thing which somewhat comforted her at this moment was the knowledge that she herself suffered as much as she made her husband suffer. Hitherto she had yielded to the new law without much difficulty. It had even given her more than she lost, and she had often been more revolted by the atheist's infidelity than sympathetic with the husband's pain. Now she joined hands with him in sorrow, and regretted —how sincerely !—that she could not be at one and the same time a faithful daughter of the Church and a loyal and devoted wife.

After a time she turned her face to him again, and looked at him softly, but not caressingly as she had done.

"I love you as much as I ever did," she said in a low voice, believing her own words, while her tears began to flow; "but nothing has changed since this morning. You are an atheist, I am a Christian; and until you have made your peace with God I can be nothing to you. Our thoughts and ways are separate, and so must be our lives."

He raised himself in his chair and looked at her fixedly, then closed his eyes while his head sank forward on his breast. She thought he had fainted, and bent over him, breathless; but the twitching of his mouth, the quiver of his eyelids, and a look of anguish that was more sorrowful than tears, more grievous than a cry, showed her that here was no blessed relief of insensibility. He was suffering as few men could have suffered without failing under the strain; but he had been made strong enough by that short respite from torture to bear the rack again without giving way. Yet it was hard to have had the hope, the assurance, only to see it dashed again to the earth at the very moment when he thought himself most secure. Still, there it was; and his hope had been a fallacy. Her will—if set in motion by that other stronger, more determined, still always her will—decreed that they should be divided; and he could not help himself. And then, beside his inability, there came to his aid the man's self-respecting dignity which is even greater than the lover's love, and forbade him to continue what was essentially a fruitless rivalry with another for his wife's devotion.

"Things shall be as you will, wife," he said at last in a quiet voice, where were no suppressed tears but only the very stillness of submission to the inevitable, the very pathos of patience. "Some day you will come back to me of your own sweet will. Until then I will respect yours—and wait."

The extreme quietness of his renunciation touched Hermione more than if he had broken out into passionate despair. It was so like death! She seemed to realize in that moment all that she had voluntarily lost—all that she had killed with her own hands ; and sinking on her knees by his side, she buried her face in the arm of the chair and wept in a forlorn and helpless way that, more than anything else could have done, expressed all the weakness of her nature.

He laid his hand tenderly on her head. No longer soft and feathery with its multitudinous curls, but smooth and plainly braided, it was to him like the head of some one else—not his wife, his beloved. He missed the

elastic touch of those light rings and fringes which he had
so often caressed, and in which he took so much pleasure
of admiration ; and he thought, as one thinks of unimportant things in grave moments : " Even these are changed
with the rest."

He could say nothing to comfort her—nothing to
persuade her.   All this misery was self-made, and as
unnecessary as it was absolute.   She alone could break
the magic of the barrier that had been raised between
them, as she alone had half consented to and half
assisted in the weaving of the spell.   He stooped over
her and drew her face gently up to him, kissing her
forehead as one bidding an eternal farewell, while saying
tenderly:—" My poor wife !   What wretchedness for us
both—and all for what purpose ? "

" It is the will of God !" said poor Hermione sobbing;
and then slowly raising herself she stood by her husband's
side, half lingering before leaving him—as both felt for
ever.

Their eyes met ; he raised himself slightly and held
out his arms ; her fair face drooped towards his, and she
laid her hand on his shoulder.

" Wife ! wife ! " he whispered ; " my life ! my love ! "

Another moment he would have clasped her to his

heart ; but with a sudden spasm of fear and anguish she turned abruptly away and went back as if a blast of fire had struck her face.

"No, no ! you are an atheist !" she said.   "It is a sin to love you !"

"So be it !" he answered, and covered his face in his hands.

Sobbing, not daring to trust herself at this moment, loving him with all her old fervour, but afraid of God and bound by her promise to the priest, Hermione rushed from the room—again passing by the corridor, not through the door of communication—and kneeling at her faldstool before her crucifix, said some prayers which she tried hard to believe comforted her, and which she knew did not.   Her heart was full of the dear husband whom she had put away from her for ever ; and in her sorrow she found herself wishing that she had been left still unconverted, and not afraid to love one who had every virtue but that of Faith. But Richard passed through this Gethsemane without even the comfort of prayer—with nothing but his own strong heart to support him, and his love for her who had left him, to soften his despair at his bereavement.

CHAPTER VIII.

PLUCKED FROM THE BURNING.

IT was not all subtle spiritual courtship, the better to make idle women of means into devoted daughters of the Church, that employed the time and thoughts of Mr. Lascelles. He had the more masculine part of his parish-work to attend to, and the sturdy men of the people to convince, with their soft-hearted wives to win, as well as those idle women of means to interest. And, to do him justice, he was indefatigable in his activities of conversion on all sides alike.

He really did give himself without stint to the good work, as he euphemistically called his endeavour to break down mental independence and manly self-respect, and to render habits of thrift and foresight unnecessary. For the Church has doles for her obedient children that supply the place of lapsed wages ; and she makes it part of her duty to prove to the faithful that the time given to the service of the Lord is not time taken from the maintenance of the family, and that the cupboard need not go bare because the choir has its servitors and the nave its worshippers. The vicar set great store by this charitable bribery which to him represented righteousness: and put out his strength to effect the personal and economic demoralization of men by means of this lavish almsgiving which is so powerful an agent in the hands of a prose-lytizing priest.

By this time he and Sister Agnes had cut out for themselves far more than they could do without help. The Convalescent Home was now in full working order, with Sister Barbara as the Sister-in-charge, Sister Agnes as the Lady Superintendent, the vicar as Superior and Chaplain, and the ladies who had districts as Visitors. Affiliated to the Home was a Cottage Hospital which the ladies also visited on set days. Having to find a *raison d'être* for its existence at all, they did their best to fill it with "cases," whether of the right kind or no. If a man had a twinge of rheumatism or a woman an aching back, the district visitor would coax both the one and the other into the hospital, where ritualism and beef-tea, confession and a soft bed, the intercession of the Holy Virgin when entreated and human kindness without asking for it, prayers to the saints and presents to the children, went hand in hand; and the Church proved herself the mother whose service was endowment as well as salvation, and whose loving arms not only protected her faithful worshippers from the fiery darts of the Evil One, but sheltered them in the dark days of material trouble.

Then there were daily "mattins" and "evensong;" full choral services on Wednesday and Friday; "early celebration" and three services to follow on Sunday; the saints' days rigidly observed, and the vigils of the more important to boot; there were processions to arrange and methods of worship to teach; the Sunday-school to superintend; the choir to train; doctrine to develope; confessions to receive—secretly, but none the less actively; Bible-classes for men and those for women, taken separately, twice a week; weekly lectures to men to be given, and the lending library to look after; there were mothers' meetings, women's tea-drinkings, children's feasts on the one hand and cate-chizing on the other; the *crèche*, the infant-school, the clothing-club, the penny savings-bank, the coal club, the blanket fund, the shoe fund—what not!—to keep going. The days were indeed full!—and both time and strength were wanting for all this machinery for the subjugation of the parish by self-interest here and superstitious fear there. Hence it was absolutely

necessary that there should be parochial assistance, and
that too of a liberal kind.

There was no money in the living itself to pay for
curates or assistants; but the Molyneux's contributed a
large sum, and laid down one carriage, two horses, and
a man; and Hermione gave another large sum, and
laid down nothing, but got into debt instead; and
devoted friends at a distance lent a helping hand in
this war of Christian, in the person of the Honourable
and Reverend Launcelot Lascelles, with Apollyon as
Richard Fullerton, now carried on at Crossholme. For,
though Crossholme was only a quiet country parish,
of apparently no account in the world, yet the fight was
exciting the most ardent interest among the sect at
large; and poor Apollyon was destined to have a hard
time of it.

At first Mr. Lascelles had got on by himself, with
part local and steady, part foreign and spasmodic, help.
Cuthbert Molyneux had made himself his lay assistant
almost from the first, and was now reading for Orders,
when he would receive his title as Curate of Crossholme,
and devote himself also as consecrated economic de-
moralizer of the parish; and stray Priests and Brothers,
with an occasional Father—specially Father Truscott,

who was making his own little path down here, as yet
cleverly concealed—had come from their town parishes
and "missions" to see how things were going and to
help in the services. But now the regular staff had been
got together, chiefly by the help of the Molyneux's and
Hermione ; so that, with the vicar and his sister, they
had in all—counting nursing-sisters and Cuthbert
Molyneux—eight people specially devoted to the
manipulation of about fifteen hundred souls, all told.
With the staff of visiting ladies, and well-disposed
young men and maidens of the superior half of the
operatives and little shopkeepers, it made a formidable
body of workers for ritualism and against freedom.

There was one thing which perhaps expressed more
than all else the tremendous power that the vicar and
his sister had already gained over the women of the
place—their dress.

From Hermione downward—Hermione, who had
been notorious for her superb millinery, against which
the only thing that could be said was that it was too
beautiful for the country, and who had now gone into
the groove of simplicity with the rest—from her downward, the ladies and young women who had devoted
themselves to the work of the Church were all notice-

able for studied plainness of attire. So far Sister Agnes
had been a public benefactress. She allowed no gay
colours among those who came to the Vicarage to
embroider chasubles and stoles—no frills, nor furbelows,
nor fettering tying back of skirts, nor sweeping trains
eddying round the feet in embarrassing curves of graceful
entanglement; she forbad all jewelry, and cried out
against fluffy heads and fringed foreheads; she suffered
nothing but dark dresses plainly made, smooth braided
hair, linen instead of lace; and for gold and silver
ornaments, such as are worn by the unregenerate, she
substituted a big black cross or a small silver crucifix
which had been duly blessed by—the one who had
the power. A member of the Sister's " Band of Church
Workers " could be told at a glance; and, as was said,
nothing proved the power of her influence and her
brother's more than this ability to dominate the strongest
passion of womanhood, by reducing the luxury of fashion
to the simplicity of a uniform. Having done this, they
had fulfilled the hardest task of all.

It was strange how pauperism began to increase
under this rule of Faith and ceaseless ministrations. Up
to now Crossholme had been noted for its manly
independence as well as for its cleanliness of living.

Dead to all forms of religious enthusiasm, what had been wanting in spiritual aspiration had been made up in civic action, and morals were pure where belief was cloudy. Belief indeed had been even more than cloudy. Under Mr. Aston the parish church had been merely the symbol of parochial rights and national unity, where certain ceremonies were performed of common usage and legal obligation but of no vital benefit; and no dissenting missionary had succeeded in establishing a Little Bethel of any denomination. Methodist, Wesleyan, Baptist—all had been tried and each had failed. The seed had been cast on ground so stony, that not even chickweed or groundsel would grow there! For the last fourteen or fifteen years a body of men, inspired and directed by Richard Fullerton, had been gradually gathering together who had abjured the public-house and the church alike, and had lived the lives of honest, sober, self-respecting heathens. Little was done in the way of charity; less in the way of misdemeanour; nothing in the way of crime. To be on the parish rates was held here as next door to being in the county gaol; and the working men were content to be let alone by the rich, provided always they were not hindered. Ground game was free, and no one sought to poach the pheasants; compensation was made when the field went over the growing crops; and on all hands there was a friendly kind of feeling abroad, because the poor respected themselves and by so doing made the rich respect them too. To be sure, in the hard winter times there was a little relaxing of the high standard which else was so well maintained; and pannikins of good stout savoury soup were to be had in the Abbey kitchen by any who chose to come for them. But this was always given, as well as asked for, under a slight veil of pretence that appealed to human kindness and saved pride; such as—to warm the little children when they came home wet and half frozen from school; or to comfort this sick body or that aged person who could not eat meat and yet needed nourishment. And the independence of the men was maintained also by a kind of fiction, when occasion required:—as work being made for them which was not necessary to be done, but the doing of which earned money and prevented almsgiving. So that pauperism, like drunkenness, was almost rooted out of the place, and Crossholme cost the ratepayers less in relief than any other parish in the union, and was nowhere in the criminal statistics of the county; but also it was of no value to the revenue.

Now things were changing, and the place was
becoming church-going and pauperized at a hand gallop.
The women, won over by gifts and kindly talk, influenced
the men as they always have done. Between a bare
cupboard, with hungry children crying round the door,
and a full table and the gaping mouths well fed, what
mother would hesitate?—more especially when all the
price to be paid was going daily to a well-lighted, well-
warmed church, where were bonny things to see and
pleasant things to hear, with a heartsome chat with the
neighbours coming home and a good word from the
gentry! If Mr. Fullerton was a fine man and a good
master, so was Mr. Lascelles; and better every way
than the other. Mr. Fullerton exacted his pound of
flesh in labour; but the vicar, he gave freely, and asked
for nothing in return but what was good for their own
souls. For surely no one could deny that it was right
to go to church week-days as well as Sundays; for if it
was God's House on the Sabbath so it was on the
week-day. .So the vicar said; and he ought to know if
any one did—it came into his business. And then
surely, again, it was ever so much better for the
children to have stout shoes for school-going, and
themselves a warm blanket or a good gown, than that

Jack or Bill should maunder away his evenings listening
to a gentleman who, the vicar and his sister said, taught
a lot of things as were mere lies—as could be proved by
the Bible any day. And when you come to talk of
independence—well, it is all very well for folks who
have enough to be so high, but the Bible itself says
the rich ought to give to the poor; and that would
never have been said if it was a shame for the poor to
take what was given.

So the women argued; and the constant dropping
wore away the granite of self-respect, and by degrees
made the men as little averse from pauperization as
themselves.

Coincident with this more direct appeal to their
personal interests, carried on by means of the women,
the vicar did his best to sap Richard's influence over
the minds of the men by the way of the intellect. He
always spoke of him with a high-bred, archangelic
kind of pity, as St. Michael might speak of Lucifer, if
also with the satirical contempt of a scholar for a quack.
He was careful never to treat him as an intellectual
equal, when discussing him with those who were well
affected to agnosticism; only as a specious charlatan
who could be turned inside out by any thoroughly

well-read divine. For instance, Father Truscott, who preached to them last Sunday on the divine character of Authority—or Brother Swinfen, who proved to them the personal existence of Satan and the everlasting and material pains of hell, and besought them as reasonable men to conquer the one and escape from the other by the means held out to them by the Church and her ordinances—either could blow Mr. Fullerton out of the water in ten minutes, and prove him for what he was— an impudent, mendacious, presumptuous infidel. It grieved him, he said with fine manly pity—noble magnanimity and toleration for the innocently misled—it grieved him to see how, for want of some one to expose his errors, they, the honest men of Crossholme, not able to devote themselves to this poor charlatan's favourite subjects, had been led to believe in errors at which any really scientific man would laugh, and which, announced to-day as final and infallible, would be overthrown to-morrow by a new theory and a further discovery. He did not promise more than he could perform, he said at the Bible class where he mostly shot these bolts which were to transfix Apollyon ;—he would lay the two schemes of thought candidly before them, and leave them to judge between Divine Truth and Mr. Fullerton's falsehood.

In accordance with which promise he gave lectures on Richard's special night of Monday, and on his own ground of science. He got specialists down from London to do the hard work for him ; but whoever lectured, the proofs always went the opposite way of Richard's, and showed that all the conclusions to which that infidel had come were full in the teeth of evidence and in defiance of eternal fact. And then he fell back on the possibility of mystery and the impossibility of disproof, and challenged them to show where his explanation of things was less credible than Mr. Fullerton's. Both postulated the same thing, which he called God and the other Force—he a divine, living, beneficent, and all-wise Providence, the other dead, unintelligent law. And now, granting his view to be the truth—as it was—there was nothing in the Bible that should disturb or perplex them. Miracles were as much an order of the Divine rule as ordinary law ; for it was absurd to suppose that the Power which had made could not control, and that the creature might not be regulated by the Creator.

This was the back-bone of all his arguments : Who shall limit ? ever clinched by the exhortation to believe Christianity and the Bible at all events. " If not true, no harm is done ; but if true, and you reject it, where

will you be then ? Consigned to eternal perdition and
the never-ending torments of hell ! "

These lectures were always accompanied by tea and
buns, by music and singing, and enlivened by pretty
pictures hung against the walls and often changed. The
women were encouraged to come and bring their knitting
or sewing with them ; and all that remained over of the
tea and cake was slipped into maternal pockets for the
little ones left at home. There was nothing to pay for all
this as at the Institution, which, respecting their independence, Richard wanted his men to feel more their own
property than his gift. But Mr. Lascelles gave everything
and demanded only obedience in return. One clause
in this charter of obedience touched on the matter of
literature, which was to be limited to such books as were
approved of by him. Nothing whatever was to be taken
out of the infidel library of the Institution, and only such
works read as were supplied by the lending library pre-
sided over by the vicar. Then, his demands growing as
he felt his way onward and made his footing more secure,
the men were required to absent themselves altogether
from the Institution ; and the members sensibly
diminished, as did that of the agnostic's Monday
hearers. All but those thoroughly committed and in

earnest began to drop in only shyly and at rare intervals, instead of constantly and boldly; some looking half afraid of being seen there, with the sentiment of breaking the law and being trounced for it, if caught ; and others with a false courage which betrayed them as much as the franker discomfort of the more timid. Then the vicar got up village sports, such as cricket and football, but only for his own party—thereby breaking up the teams which hitherto had played together. For he allowed no one in his field who was not a regular churchgoer and communicant; whereby he won over not a few from among Mr. Fullerton's men, when the play had become stinted for want of players. He gave large donations too, for every conceivable purpose, ecclesiastical or secular, social or intellectual—but only for communicants—rigidly excluding all who went to that infidel shop over there by the Abbey Park gates.

All of which recruited so many for the army of the Church Militant that brother and sister, when they reckoned up their gains as they often did at the Vicarage, were justified in saying between themselves that the infidel stronghold was thoroughly invested by now, and that Apollyon would soon be brought low.

It may be remembered that John Graves and George

Pearce, his son-in-law, were tenants on the Molyneux estate ; that Tom Moorhead's shop and forge belonged to the Abbey ; and that Adam Bell's shop was on part of the glebe. The vicar had soon made short work of the little chandler, or rather he himself had made short work of his own coquetting with infidelity ; for, as we know, long before pressure had been put on any from without, Adam Bell had executed his manœuvre of retreat, and had faced round with his back to Mr. Fullerton and his eyes on Mr. Lascelles. He therefore was safe in his holding ; but John Graves, his brother Ben, George Pearce, Dick Stern and others in the little street called Church Row, were in danger ; and Tom Moorhead's lines too would have to be changed, if he did not reform before it was too late. What Richard had feared in the beginning was preparing now to be an accomplished fact, and if these men would not come over, then should they be driven out. There were others beside these who were as clearly committed to Richard and agnosticism ; but they need not be brought on the scene, which they would encumber not illustrate.

Though Mr. Lascelles was, by the very necessities of his position, revolted by the presumptuous independence of these recalcitrant members of the Christian community, he was all the same determined not to lose a chance of bringing them into the fold; and from the first treated the three chief misdemeanants with special consideration. He listened with stately courtesy to their arguments, halting and broken as they were—arguments which had more of the result than the method, and which showed, as with all the ill-grounded, that they believed because they had been told, not because they had found and proved; and he did his best to destroy their confidence in themselves and their instructor by sudden, sharp, and searching questions which they were by no means ready to answer; such as those crucial tests of all anti-evolutionists: How about the missing link? and the bridge between two diverse kingdoms, whereof no man has yet found the exact moment nor the precise form; while— may not Life be the work of a Divine Intelligence, external to things, as well as be the inherent property of brute matter slowly evolving itself into consciousness? Even Mr. Fullerton was obliged to stop at the Unknowable: why then not one form of mystery which was comforting rather than another which was dreary?

But though the men could not meet him with scholarly arguments, and though they were neither to be bribed by favour nor bent by fear, yet some among them a little wavered, and confessed that science did not give them everything. George Pearce was the one who was cooling to the doctrine of Law and the self-consciousness of matter in favour of spiritual insight and Divine influence, while Tom Moorhead was only the more strengthened in bull-headed opposition by the vicar's arguments against him.

And now, having exhausted his stock of forbearance, Mr. Lascelles drew on that other fund—his righteous indignation; and resolved that· the Church should no longer be vexed by the continued presence at her gates of these her enemies. John Graves and his son-in-law were tenants-at-will whom a month's notice would dispossess at any time, but Tom Moorhead had a lease terminable at three months' notice. The vicar, of course, had Cuthbert's consent in his pocket; and he was going to make the blacksmith's holding a test of his power over Hermione.

George's sickly wife was scarcely well over her trouble, when the vicar called one day at the house. She was sitting over the fire nursing her baby, whose poor little flickering life, after having almost cost her own, was evidently not destined to remain long in a world which is intolerant of weakness and where the

poor have to work. It had been a bad time all through
for Nanny, but the vicar and his sister had been that
dutiful, she said with tears in her eyes, as she could
never forget; and Sister Barbara from the Home had
been like a mother to her. If it had not been for all of
them indeed, she would never have held on ; but they
had wrought for her main grandly, and she and her child
had been spared.

When George, mindful of his independence, had
wished to reject their help and send them back with
their pannikins unemptied and their jellies untouched,
they had put aside his scruples with such true honest
human feeling—they had been so Christian, so com-
munistic if you will, so earnest only to preserve a new-
born life for the world, and to be of service to a sick
creature needing care—there had been such a marked
absence of all proselytizing—when he was by—that his
pride and his fears alike had been set at rest; and he
was fain to be thankful for help which saved his wife and
child, and asked nothing in return but the leave to serve.

Even the vicar had not bothered him with religion ;
though he had, unknown to him, prayed with Nanny
lying there between life and death—and touched her
heart once and for ever, as he knew he should.   He

had left George to events which, he calculated rightly, would do the same work for him through his affections; and now he came to drive in the nail and see how great a weight he could hang on it.

When he went into the cottage Nanny rose with unconscious grace and intentional reverence. The vicar's handsome person, courtly manners, and high-priestly assumptions had taken possession of her imagination, as much as his condescension, and the human kindness of the whole body of High Church workers, had softened her heart and aroused her gratitude. She smiled all over her poor wan face when he stooped his fine head and came in with that grand mingling of the gentleman and the priest which was so essentially his characteristic. And she smiled still more and blushed, when he shook hands with her so paternally, and looked at the baby and patted its face with his fore-finger, and told her to be seated, and inquired minutely how things went with her and her child—"as if he had been an old wife himself," she said to George with animation; "and he such a grand gentleman!"

And then, sitting down by her, he opened fire cautiously, and told her what had to be done.

He was very sorry, he said; no one more so; and

he had kept young Mr. Molyneux quiet until now, always hoping, like Moses, that God would soften the stubborn hearts of those who were now His enemies, and turn them to grace and truth ; but now he could keep their landlord back no longer. He was determined, said Mr. Lascelles with an air half pitying half approving, not to give longer tenancy to a set of men who defied God and denied His Holy Word, and despised all that he and every other Churchman held most dear and sacred. And Nanny could see for herself, he said, that it was scarcely fitting for a man like Mr. Molyneux to harbour those who were on the road which her father and husband, and some others in the Row, had taken. Would she like to give shelter to a man who slandered her mother, and did all the harm that he could to her husband, and would kill her child if he had the chance ? Would she not rather bid him begone and shut the door hard and fast against him, than keep with him on terms of friendship and even give him a house near to her own ? And this was just what they who were Christians felt for those who crucified Christ afresh by their infidelity. So that she could scarcely be surprised if Mr. Molyneux did not want to keep that lot as tenants, and preferred, on the contrary, men who would, at the least, not hinder nor blaspheme the work of the Church in the parish.

To which poor Nanny assented sorrowfully, not able in justice to deny.

Well then, what was to be done? the vicar went on to say. Her father was too much set on his own way for any hope of his giving in, but George—might he not be influenced? He would not be the first unbelieving husband who had been saved by a believing wife. Winter too was on them. She was delicate and not able to bear the wear and tear of a flitting, and the child was too weakly to be taken into a new cold house, with all the draughts about and nothing warmed. Could she not prevail on George to give up going to Mr. Fullerton's lectures, and to take his name off the list of members of the Institution?—that hot-bed of infidelity which did no good here and would ruin him for everlasting! It was not much to ask; and then he would keep his home and not expose her and their little one to certain danger and probable death.

The vicar pleaded with Nanny long and eloquently, and when he left he had got her promise to influence her husband—if she could; and if she could win over her father, then would her crown of glory be complete.

This, however, was not likely. John found in the darkness of agnosticism more comfort, because less contradiction, than there was for him in the light of revelation—which leaves things in the same state as the other, he used to say, but entangled by the admission of a Power which could set them all straight if it would ; sin, misery and ignorance all to be done away with by a breath—Satan pardoned—hell abolished—and the reign of virtue and happiness begun to-morrow, if only it would ! He was a strong-headed, noble-minded kind of man who could suffer without need of comfort ; but George was of a slighter mental make, younger and not habituated yet to pain ; and sorrow broke him up as it breaks up women, and made him yearn for external support. Nanny's near skirting by death had stirred him deeply. It had sent him to his knees for the absolute want of some one to whom to cry aloud in the darkness—for a Father to lay hold of—a Saviour to redeem him. Man's philosophy was all very well as a quiet mental speculation, but it fell dead and dry on his soul when in pain ; and when the vicar told Nanny, and Nanny repeated it to him as of her own notion, that God was leading him through sorrow—chastening him as a sinner before receiving him as a son—he let the

words sink into his heart ; good seed, said the vicar,
which would germinate and bring forth fruit in
abundance.

Yet it was misery untold to him to feel that men
would have the right to say he was a turncoat—ratting
like Adam Bell, or the like of him, and leaving the ship
for fear of its sinking. Never in his life before had there
been a breath against his character ; and though he
should go into the more powerful camp, if he went out
from his own, yet he dreaded that men should say how
he had failed his word. Nevertheless, there was his
own conscience with which he had to reckon, and that
terrible word : " If it be true ? " that haunted him night
and day.

At Nanny's earnest request, he had just been reading
an old copy of Bunyan's " Pilgrim's Progress " which
had belonged to her mother, and to which, be sure, she
did not know the vicar would have objected; and he felt
like Christian before his way had been made clear, while
still knocking at the little wicket-gate and carrying that
heavy burden of unforgiven sins at his back. And then
he loved his wife dearly, and she had influence over
him—such as good, tender, modest women have over
good and somewhat feminine-natured men. So indeed,

for the matter of that, had his father-in-law influence;
and so had Richard Fullerton. But all the same, in
spite of the arguments of this last, "If it be true?" stuck
like a leech, and disposed him to listen—and more than
listen—when Nanny pleaded recantation of his errors
and the abandonment of Richard Fullerton for the
Church and Christianity.

She got so much of her own way that he consented
to her public churching next Sunday; and also to the
public baptism of the child. The vicar had told her
plainly that, should it die unbaptized, he would not
allow it to be buried in the churchyard nor have any
funeral service read over it. And he had added with
compassionate emphasis: "Poor little frail lamb! It
seems scarcely able to live through to-day; and that it
should be deprived of eternal life by man's cruel
blindness!"

This was the argument that finally moved Nanny,
and through her secured George. He consented to her
prayer, partly because it was her prayer and partly
because "there might be something in it." That "sort
of a something" might be real after all!—and he said
that he would go with her and face the neighbours like
a man. It was too, only what he owed the vicar for his

kindness—he confessed to that; and Mr. Fullerton was not the gentleman to object to an act of gratitude, looking at things all round.

Wherefore next Sunday, those who knew how matters had been with the carpenter and his father-in-law were edified or scandalized, according to their feelings and what they thought consistent, to see George Pearce and his wife at church ; where she was churched, their child baptized and publicly received into the body of the Anglican Church. The next day John Graves and a few more had notice to quit at the month's end; and Nanny, while crying bitterly for her father's trouble, felt as if the Lord had interposed to save her and her own house from destruction.

But if only John would have flown out at him ! thought George, as they sat in a little group about the younger man's fireside. It would have been a relief if he would have turned against him and called him a few hard names—undeserved in fact, but by the look of things only too well merited ! His gentleness was the poor young fellow's heaviest cross ; but railing was not much in John's way, and he knew that George had become a convert for conscience' sake and not because he was a rat and afraid of consequences.

Still, it had come at an awkward moment. John felt that as much as George did himself. It had a bad look, and looks go as far as things sometimes; and people must be less given to evil-thinking than most are, if they can accept such a coincidence as this as accidental, and not see in it the best way of escaping a forfeit after having played on the chance of winning. Tom Moorhead was not of that liberal kind, nor was Uncle Ben, nor Dick Stern, nor Allen Rose, nor any one else who had received his notice to quit. Each had his word to fling at George when the papers came in, and he was left undisturbed; and when, for the first time for ten years or more, John went off to the lecture alone, he felt as if he had left a death behind him, and had lost for ever the son who had been dear to him. Poor George felt badly too, when he saw his friend and father go without him; but he was acting according to his conscience and giving his new thoughts a chance; and though the direction had been in every way different he had been trained by Richard Fullerton in self-reliance and courage towards his own convictions.

How different indeed it all was! Instead of the Great Stone Book of Geology from which Mr. Fullerton was wont to recite his lessons for the day, Nanny made

her husband read aloud some parts of the New
Testament which Mr. Lascelles had indicated; and she
herself kneeled down and prayed for faith and forgiveness out of a little Manual of Devotion which also he
had given her, at the very moment when that defiant
lecturer was proving to his hearers not only the inutility
but also the presumption and rebelliousness of prayer,
on either hypothesis of, in the one case absolute law, in
the other an omnipotent and beneficent Power as the ruler
of the universe.

"Where is George?" asked Richard, who knew
nothing of yesterday's testimony in the church.

John Graves looked away, embarrassed and distressed.

"Not ill, I hope?" he asked again.

"Not in body, sir," said John.

"In trouble? What is amiss, John?"

"He has been got hold of, sir. Nanny's illness
troubled him, you see, and made him feel lonesome and
like in the dark. He said to me the day when she was
at the worst, 'Oh, father! if I could but pray and believe
that I should be heard!' and now you see, sir, it has
come. He had the child baptized yesterday in church,
and he was there himself to see it done. I doubt
if he'll come here again; and I'm sorry; but a man's

convictions must be respected, however far adrift they may be."

"I am sorry, too," said Richard gravely. "I can see it all. Mr. Lascelles hit the right moment. They are all clever in that."

"Yes," said John, with a slight sigh; "what between coaxing and bullying, working on men's fears and their affections, their self-interest and their superstition, they get hold of a vast more than would ever go over of themselves. They have got hold of my daughter through George, and I am sorry that it came at this moment, of all others in the year."

He stopped, and looked down on the ground, rubbing his chin thoughtfully.

"Why now?" asked Richard, with a sudden flush.

Had his own miserable story leaked out? Was the world made free of his humiliation—his despair?

"Well, you see, sir, we are all warned," said John;— "all of us in the Row as belong to the Institution, and George is the only one left unmolested. I know the lad, and I know that he is as pure as a child from any under-hand dealing; but some of the men misdoubt him; and looks are ugly—there's no doubt of that!"

"I am sorry to hear that you have to leave your

house," said Richard. " Where are you thinking of going?"

The tailor shook his head.

" There's ne'er a place would suit me for my work," he said; "and Mr Molyneux knows that. I've been a tenant on the estate these thirty years for my own hand, and my father he had the place for as many years before me. It seems hard; but new men and new measures!— that's about the size of it now, here away in Crossholme."

" If you are harassed and want a place, I will build one for you and for your brother Ben, and all who are dispossessed," said Richard. " I should like to have the lot of you as my tenants."

John Graves looked up and smiled.

" Thank you, sir," he answered heartily; "and not a man among us but would rather have you for his landlord than any other." Then, in rather an anxious tone, he added, " I hope you do not feel yourself poorly this evening, sir? You are looking what one may call a little out of sorts."

"No," said Richard quietly; "I am all right, thank you, John."

"Glad to hear it, sir. Keep well; for you are our main prop, you know, Mr. Fullerton," said the tailor, looking into the other's face with frank sympathy and undisguised friendliness. Whereupon the two men shook hands and parted, and Richard went back to his desolate home, and felt, as did John Graves, that death had taken those most beloved from him.

CHAPTER IX.

THE NEW DEPARTURE.

THE threatened eviction of the men in the Row stirred the village greatly. This was only what might have been expected, and what indeed Mr. Lascelles had foreseen and provided for. He knew that the action was harsh, and that to turn out of their homes a body of hard-working, sober, respectable men because they did not go to church and believed in science rather than revelation, was as close on persecution as the times will allow. But he calculated on the natural respect of humanity for force and thoroughness—if also its natural abhorrence of tyranny had to be considered as well— and he thought that he would make the bold stroke boldly and abide by the issue.

He heard, of course, that it was Richard Fullerton's intention to build cottages for the dispossessed; and he smiled when he heard it. He would suffer the houses to be built, sure enough; but who would be the tenants was another matter. The weather was such however, that nothing could be done for the present beyond marking out the ground and digging the foundations; and meanwhile Mr. Fullerton managed to lodge John Graves and his brother Ben in a house of largish size which happened to be vacant; while Ringrove, in spite of what he knew would be Hermione's displeasure and Virginia's distress, found places for many—Dick Stern and Allen Rose among the number; and the rest were housed by Mr. Nesbitt and the local Laodiceans. Thus, as things turned out, the break-up was not so disastrous as it had threatened to be, and the men were not ruined, while the Church had shown her power. She meant to show more yet before the end of all things; but for the present this preliminary blow was enough.

Meanwhile, though much was said, nothing was done; and that burning in effigy, discussed at Tom Moorhead's, never came off. Tom would not have been sorry to have had a hand in it, and would have given his best hat with a free heart if it would have made the likeness closer; but on the whole they thought better of it. Mr. Fullerton, they said among themselves, would be main sure to object, and the notion died out as some others had done. The village talked over the eviction— which they persisted in taking to be rather the work of

the vicar than of that softy, young Molyneux—as men on
'Change talk over the imperial war that chances to be on
hand; and some said one thing and some another; but,
save here and there a half-hearted malcontent 'taking
pet' with the Church and absenting himself for a few
Sundays from the services—to go back when his temper
had cooled—no action was taken. On the whole—
though everyone said it was a shame and a sin, and Mr.
Lascelles was no better than the Pope of Rome, and
they would have to look sharp if they didn't all want
to be made into slaves—yet, in spite of all that, the
Englishman's veneration for strength carried the day,
and if the vicar got ill-will from some he got respect
dashed with fear from more.

At the Abbey that kind of lull which follows on a
storm fell on the household after the discussion between
the two men, and the rearrangement of their lives
between Hermione and her husband; and for a few
weeks things were apparently tranquil—as death is
tranquil. No bystander could have seen that the love
which had been so deep and true had received its
death-blow, and that there was as little real peace as
happiness in this well-ordered, well-mannered family.
Hermione, secretly dissatisfied with herself, and, like all

women, regretting the love which she had finally repulsed, at the first did not care to aggravate her secession
by unnecessary bitterness; and the vicar, satisfied with
his substantial gains, left off for the moment grasping at
the fringes. Knowing that weakness is always an uncertain holding, and fearful lest Hermione should go back
on her old self if the tension were too strong—aware
that crafty angling gives length of line, and that rest
must sometimes be taken even in a struggle—Mr.
Lascelles took things quietly for the time, and let the
present fetters wear themselves easy before he put on
new ones. He even seemed to give his adversary some
slight advantage by a relaxation of Church observances,
which, by the way, Nature herself commanded.

The winter had set in with exceptional severity;
snow-storms were of frequent occurrence, and the frost
did not break in between. The short days were sunless
and dark, and "mattins" and evensong were perforce
given up for want of attendants. Both Hermione and
Virginia had rather bad colds; and the vicar was afraid
of too much austerity in the discipline which yet was
necessary for the maintenance of his influence. Had
the daily services been continued he would not have
allowed either to join in them; and without them, if not

quite the play of Hamlet with the part of Hamlet left out, they would have been something like it. Theresa Molyneux, with her increasing thinness, her hollow cough and constant fever, was out of the bounds of possibility in weather which tried strong men and killed off the weak and aged ; and Mr. Lascelles did not think the soul of tough Aunt Catherine of so much importance that he should arrange daily service mainly for her benefit. Others of the female members of his congregation were also ill and disabled ; so that, after deliberation, he thought it wiser to abandon early daily prayer until the weather should change, than to go on in spite of the elements, and make the Magnificat include bronchitis, and the Grace culminate in pneumonia.

All that was required for the present of the faithful who were in tolerable health was attendance on the Wednesday and Friday services, early celebration on Sunday, and that all-important weekly confession which gives the priest supreme control of the family, so that he can break up a dangerous love and an opposing unity if he will, as the seed of a upas tree planted in a clay pot would soon split it into fragments. These duties were imperative on all who would stand well with their local pope and be sure of their place in heaven; but these led to no domestic collision at the Abbey.

For though Richard kept more with his wife and daughter than he had ever done before, yet he could not constitute himself either their gaoler or their spy; and so long as he knew that certain things were not done, he had to content himself with the rest. When he asked Virginia, as he almost always did at breakfast: " Have you been out, my child?" and she answered: " No, papa," he was satisfied that, so far, the spoke of common sense had been put into that murderous ecclesiastical wheel, and that the car of Juggernauth had been stopped to this extent in its destructive course. He did not know of all the notes which passed in the day between the Abbey and the Vicarage; of the exhortations, the confessions, the constant spiritual presence that was never suffered to fade from their consciousness. He only knew that for about a fortnight those two dear ones of his, whom he was believing to guard, did not do anything monstrously unwise, and that neither Mr. Lascelles nor any other of the clergy entered the house. But this was only the outside of things; the core remained the same.

His keeping so much nearer to them, and seeing so much more of their actions, did not in the end advance

Richard's cause with either wife or daughter. Kind and gentle as he was to both, he was all the same a hindrance —an overseer and controller in one, whose companionship must not be suffered to bring pleasure and which hindered what it did not give. Had they not been warped and held as they were, this new frequency of association would have been infinite joy, but now it had come too late :—" too late ! " sighed Hermione, looking back to the old shrine with its withered flowers and defaced god, while borne away by a stronger will than her own to the temple where that god was accursed and his worship the un-pardonable sin.

While the weather was so bad that they were perforce kept so much in-doors, to have Richard coming in and out continually, now with a scrap of news from the day's paper, now with a beautiful bit of fairyland revelation by the microscope, if sometimes embarrassing when notes had to be written, and the like, yet sometimes was not wholly unpleasant—at least to Hermione, whose humour varied with the hour. To Virginia, more intense and less personally swayed, her father's presence was always now a pain. But when the worst of the winter broke and their lives were ordered back into the old groove of religious activity, while Mr. Lascelles resumed his command, it became an unmitigated torture to both alike.

How could they go to the Vicarage daily—that ark of their peace!—as they had been accustomed to do, when Richard smilingly proposed to accompany them in their walk or asked to be taken with them in the carriage? They might say that they had parish work to attend to once or twice in the week, perhaps;—but every day? Impossible! Unless they wished to bring things to a premature crisis, they must be "well and wise walking" as the Khans of the legends; and how devoted soever they might be in spirit, yet, as they were told by their respective Directors, they must be wary in action.

How unhappy they all were! Mr. Lascelles and Sister Agnes bitterly resented this slight obstruction to the completeness of their control; and their bitterness reacted in rather spiteful castigation of the two who suffered most. The Sister's coldness nearly broke Virginia's heart and sent her to her knees in agonies of grief, whereby she was made colder and yet colder to her father as some sort of expiation; while Hermione— now chafed by the vicar's satirical congratulations on the evident peace established between her and her husband -- now excited to spasmodic self-assertion by his allusions to her rights of property and sighing regrets that she could not take back her gift of control—"not being strong against the man whom she had loved so fervently" —roused to feverish unrest of vanity by his praise, to unwholesome excitement by his half-checked words, his suddenly averted eyes, his ostentatious self-control— discontented with herself and her life, her past and her present alike—soon slipped into the state and place from which that fortnight's rest had apparently rescued her. Her heart torn between those two opposing influences— now longing to throw herself into her husband's arms, beseeching him to forgive her sin against his love and to take her to himself as of old—now kneeling to Mr. Lascelles, confessing her most intimate feelings, her most secret thoughts, and giving herself to his guidance ; oscillating between wifely love and ecclesiastical fana- ticism—old affections and new excitements—it was scarcely to be wondered at if her humour became varied and uncertain beyond what it had ever been before. Neither was it to be wondered at, seeing how things really were with her too, if Virginia had an anxious kind of look, restless and searching, like a caged creature looking for means of escape.

This closeness of companionship which was to guard,

unite and reclaim, was daily becoming insupportable to both Hermione and Virginia ; and consequently daily more disastrous to Richard's own interest. It threw the charm of difficulty and the fascination of the forbidden into the scale with the other attractions found at the Vicarage. Hermione's interviews with Mr. Lascelles —Virginia's with Sister Agnes and Father Truscott— were briefer and seldomer than before, but they were more fervid and intense in consequence. So much had to be packed into a small compass ; and certain feelings, certain resolves and wishes, like gun-cotton, gain force by compression. Do what he would Richard felt the ground giving way under his feet, and the hands which he strove so hard to retain, slipping cold and limp from his. An evil fortune seemed to pursue him which made all his efforts useless, and worse than useless. The force that opposed him was as irresistible as electricity, as overpowering as gravitation ; and he was as relatively weak as Thor when he stirred the foundations of the earth and wrestled with that feeble-looking crone whose name was Age. And what was true on its own side with Hermione was as true with Virginia, if the threads here were of a slightly different complexion from those which wove the tangled web there.

When convinced that no good was coming to him or to them by the present method, Richard one morning broached the subject of foreign travel, saying with transparent pretext :

"Would you not like to escape the hard winter, Hermione? The weather is really terribly trying ! I long for the sunshine and blue skies of Italy. What do you say ?—shall we pack up and go ?"

This was much for him to propose, pretext as it was. He had no travelling blood in him, and he loved both his home and his work, his bodily quiet and mental activity, too well to like the idea of knocking about foreign towns where was as little repose as duty.

"Travel ? no indeed!" said Hermione with a made-up shiver, as she turned her head to the window and the dreary prospect lying before her. She seldom looked at her husband in these later days ; never when she could avoid it, met his eyes.

Virginia looked at her mother wistfully.

"Would you not like to go to Italy, mamma ?" she asked—"not go to Rome ?"

"No, not even to Rome," answered her mother with a forced laugh. "We are best at home."

"If you and the child like it I am ready, and should

be glad to go," said Richard turning to Virginia as an advocate unexpectedly retained.

" Certainly not !" said Hermione with a nervous cough. " It makes me cold to think of it."

Mr. Lascelles had prepared her for the chance of this proposal. He had foreseen it, and had warned her so that she should not be taken by surprise.

" A very few days of easy travelling in well-warmed carriages would take us out of all this snow and frost and bring us into summer sunshine and spring flowers," said Richard, drawing on his imagination liberally.

" Yes, mamma," urged Virginia ; " it would be so lovely at Rome now ! "

Her mother gave her a warning look.

" If you like to go with your father, do my dear," she said. " I will not hinder you. I shall not go. I would not dream of leaving home at this time ; but you can if you like, of course."

"Virginia would be a very sweet travelling companion," said Richard fondly ; " but without her mother, I doubt if either she or I would like it."

Hermione blushed and looked embarrassed.

" You are very good," she said shyly, like a great girl receiving a compliment from her lover. "I dare say

Italy would be very pleasant just now—I am sure indeed that it would—but for many reasons I am best at home, and it is only waste of time to talk about going."

On which she got up and left the room, on pretence of attending to some domestic duty which did not exist and which she would not have attended to if it had existed.

For her reward, Mr. Lascelles assured her that all the heavenly hierarchy were well pleased with her constancy, and, what was more to the purpose perhaps, that he himself was entirely content. But he warned her that the infidel against whose wickedness they were both arrayed would spread his snare again; and he prepared her with her weapons of defence against those "innumerable devices of Satan" of which this objectionable agnostic was supposed to be the chosen executant. Wherefore it came about that, when Richard went back on the same subject—this time emphasizing his own wish by complaining of not feeling well;—and indeed he was looking miserably ill;—of suffering from the weather, craving for sunshine, wanting change, excitement, movement—Hermione took up an argumentative tone, saying with a kind of unnatural firmness and indifference which showed clearly enough what was the unconquerable strength of will behind her :

"If you really require change, Richard, go abroad by all means. We shall take no harm and you will get good."

"But will you not come with me?" he asked.

She shook her head.

"Impossible," was her only answer.

"I should not care to go without you," he said with grave tenderness.

"Oh, that is childish," she answered with mock primness. "Old married people as we are we can afford to be separated for a few weeks without breaking our hearts."

As she said this she suddenly crimsoned, then turned aside with a little laugh as affected as the rest.

"And if I laid it on your duty as a wife?" asked Richard with a smile, but conscious that he was trying a dangerous experiment.

"I should then oppose you with my duties as a proprietor," said Hermione, repeating her lesson. "If you left, I should stay behind to look after my affairs."

She spoke in a level, artificial voice, her heart misgiving her. But Superior had told her what to say, and she was bound to obey him.

Reading between the lines Richard understood so far.

" Morse "—the bailiff—" would attend to all the business details," he said quietly.

" I should not choose to give everything up to Morse. I would prefer to superintend them myself," she answered.

He smiled. Her words called up one of the sweet images of the past.

" It would be pretty to see you over the books," he said, remembering her old-time inability to add up a page in a day ledger with tolerable exactness, and her general confusion between pence and shillings which made the total not a little misleading.

Hermione flushed.

" It is your fault that I can do so little," she said with petulance. " I think it is very hard that I know so little of my own affairs ; and I must say I do not like to be so entirely in the dark as I have been kept all my life."

This was the first card of the new lead, the first indication of the new departure.

Richard looked at her full and straight in the face— his own was grave rather than stern.

" You shall be enlightened on all that concerns us at any moment when you will give me your attention," he said. " I have no wish to keep you in the dark."

" It is very odd then that you have done so,"
said Hermione. Then repenting of her injustice, she
added impulsively : " No, I should not say that after
all ! It has been the fault of my own wretched
indolence."

" Less that than the result of your loving trust," said
Richard. "Where one can do all single-handed, is it
not a waste of force to employ two? But for my own
part I shall be delighted to show you all the mysteries of
book-keeping and lease-letting. When will you come
for your lesson? "

He smiled again as he spoke. The vision of her
pretty golden head bending over the accounts in his
study, as she used in the first days of their marriage,
when she thought that somehow her money had grown
in the night because she put down an account of fifteen
pounds in the shilling column and was the triumphant
possessor of so much more than she had a right to expect
—the vision of her certain mistakes and their pleasant
correction came before him as perhaps the beginning of
a new life between them and the sweeping away of those
wretched misunderstandings by which they were kept
asunder.

" When will you come, wife? " he asked again,

forgetting the terms on which they were living, and leaning forward with sudden eagerness.

She felt the false move that she had made. What would Superior say if he heard of this monstrous proposition of friendly intercourse with her excommunicated husband? and what would he do were she to assent to it? The thought made her shiver.

"If you go from home I will find it all out by myself," she said hurriedly, in the tone of one half-frightened. "And, as you say, 'while you have the management of things, I am not wanted.''

And then the conversation dropped. Richard went wearily into his study while she, stifling her heartache by first reading a page or two of *De Imitatione,* turned to an illumination which the vicar had begged her to do for his own private room. It was to be a secret between them; and secresy gave it a greater charm and carried with it a deeper danger. But even though the work pleased her, and Superior was the centre of her holiest feelings and highest life—so she was for ever repeating to herself—a tear dropped on the vellum, which gave her infinite trouble to work over.

After this nothing more was said about leaving Crossholme. Here too Richard's aim had been taken— and had failed.

Things went on in this uncomfortable way, the gulf between this infidel father and husband and his converted beloved growing deeper and wider day by day, till suddenly on a certain Wednesday morning Hermione and Virginia appeared at the breakfast-table, dressed in black, and with a generally austere air that Richard must have been blind not to have seen. They had been down to " mattins," and Hermione had evidently been weeping; while Virginia was even more serious than usual, and with more of that perplexed and feverish expression which had lately taken the place of her former calm intensity. Religion with her had been neither fear nor doubt nor yet division of feeling. It had been one straight path which she was called on to follow, and which she would have died rather than forsake. Now something had sprung up within her soul of which even her mother, even Superior was ignorant—and must remain so until she had seen her way once more clearly. But during this time of fighting through her difficulties, she was almost as unhappy as her father, almost as torn and tossed and hesitating as her mother. And her face on this Wednesday morning was the mirror of her mind.

Richard looking at them curiously—manlike not at the first understanding how the change in their general appearance had been made—noticed that neither took more for breakfast than a small cup of coffee without milk, and a small square of toast without butter. He let the eccentricity pass without comment. Truth to say he was growing afraid of troubling the waters which he could not control when he had stirred, and which healed no one who went down into them. Luncheon he had by himself; and when he asked where the ladies were he was told they were at church. The rusty little bell of the schoolroom had been tolling lugubriously all the morning—this soft, mild February morning, with the first breath of the future spring stealing out from the banks and bushes. But Richard did not know what was afoot. He only saw that something more than ordinary was on hand in the ecclesiastical world, and wondered what superstitious vagary it might be.

At dinner, things were as odd as they had been at breakfast, and as dreary as at his solitary luncheon. The flowers and table ornaments had all been removed; and the soup which would have been familiar enough to a Frenchman in his " meagre " days, was unfamiliar to Richard Fullerton. The salt-fish too was not a frequent dish at his table, and he himself disliked it. So did Hermione and Virginia ; but they took nothing else, and of this sparingly; and the meats which followed were manifestly prepared for one person only, and placed before him alone.

It was a solemn and essentially funereal dinner; and, though of late their meals had been silent and dull to an embarrassing extent, to-day things surpassed themselves, and the self-evident mortification of the flesh of the believers made the personal indulgence of the heretic seem gross and shameful.

"Why do not you and Virginia eat?" asked Richard of his wife.

Love-names and tender epithets had dropped between them. Hermione had repulsed them too often to make it possible for any man with self-respect or dignity to continue what was so evidently unwelcome; and Virginia's shrinking from her father when he spoke to her tenderly was as visible as used to be her former delight in his fondness.

"It is Ash Wednesday," said Hermione with a reproachful accent.

"But if it is Ash Wednesday, why should you not eat your dinner?" he returned, helping himself to the fricassee of pigeon which formed his sinful entrée.

"It is fast-day with us," said Hermione, emphasizing the pronoun.

Richard looked up with a sudden flash of scorn.

"So!—you are pleasing the Great First Cause by eating sparingly of a very disagreeable kind of food, and letting your gastric juice play the mischief with your mucous membrane !" he exclaimed.

"Richard ! what a horribly gross way to put it !" said Hermione.

"It is the true way," he answered. "What rational relation can you make between salt-fish and the higher life, parsnips and the Unknowable ?"

"These things are nothing in themselves," said Hermione. "The value is in obedience to the Church."

"It is a comfortless kind of thing," returned her graceless husband. "For my own part I cannot see the ethical value of indigestion or the religious sublimity of hunger."

"The strait way is not the way of pleasure, and we were not sent into the world to seek heaven by our senses."

Hermione said this with the oddest kind of demureness possible—odd, because so evidently this was a lesson learnt and a doctrine superimposed on the original material, and was in no wise spontaneous or real.

"I don't know about that," said Richard. "Good

digestion and happiness, prosperity and virtue, are often interchangeable terms in life. The worst crimes known to humanity have come from the most rigid ascetics; and insufficient as well as improper food disorders the liver, and in consequence the brain, quite as much as over-indulgence."

"And the rich man and the needle's eye?" she asked with weak sarcasm.

"Oh! that is all humbug," he answered hastily. "The Kingdom of Heaven spoken of there meant simply communism and self-impoverishment. We have the right to suppose that the rich young man was wise enough to understand that almsgiving demoralizes more than it helps, and that the conscientious capitalist, using his wealth for wages, is the best providence which the working man can have. Rich men, as a rule, are infinitely more virtuous than the poor, because they are better educated and have fewer temptations. We do not find the dangerous classes among the rich, any more than we find the diseases induced by want and misery among the well-housed and well-fed. So why go back to conditions from which it is the end of civilization to escape?"

"I prefer the way of the Church and her teaching,"

said Hermione stiffly. "And, if you please, we will drop the conversation. When you can call the Bible humbug it is time."

"I did not mean to offend you," said Richard. "But I confess with shame that I lose patience at times when I see a book which dealt with quite a different condition of civilization and range of thought from our own, used as the eternal obstacle to progress and reason; and in my own life made the destroying agent of my happiness. The idolatry which you deprecate when applied to Vishnu and Siva is nowhere so absolute as in this blind worship of myths and axioms which might suit the childhood of society, but which the science of a maturer age checks and refutes at all points."

"If you say another word in the same strain I will leave the table," said Hermione severely; while Virginia, her pale face full of colour, rose abruptly and left the room without speaking. "It is useless to talk to you," she continued with temper. "Let us speak of something else—or not at all—which, perhaps, would be best."

"No; let us speak of something else—of your new dress," said Richard, feeling that he would rather have it all out now at once, and thinking that perhaps a little personality of application might shame his poor wife into some return to common sense. "What are you and Virginia wearing to-day? You look as if you had been to a funeral."

"We are in Lent," said Hermione, severely.

"Mourning?"

"Yes; the Church, our mother, is in mourning, and we are her children."

"The modern milliner's version of the Eastern filthy dust and ashes? Forty days of sombre ugliness! Hard on unregenerate men like myself, who love bright colours and who take pride in the wife's beauty, the daughter's grace!"

He spoke with sadness, dashed with mockery as the salt which lifted it up from the deadness of mere sorrow.

"If you want bright colours look at the new house-maid," said Hermione with a scornful accent.

"Yes? I have never taken much notice of the housemaids or their dresses," he returned quietly. "But I fervently hope that all my household is not going into black because of Lent, and the fables of Greek and Syrian mythology which it has incorporated?"

"If they wish to remain in my service they will," replied Hermione with strange emphasis. "Have you

finished? If so, I will go to Virginia. Your coffee will
be brought to you. Good night. Do not disturb
yourself for us again."

"Am I not to see you or the child again to-night?"
asked Richard, not raising his eyes. He could not
accustom himself to this painful estrangement; and
every fresh proof, every new phase, increased the bitterness of his sorrow, till he sometimes wondered how he
lived through the agony of his days.

"No," said Hermione, she too not looking up, but
trying to remember all that Mr. Lascelles had said to her
this morning—trying to realize Richard's iniquity so that
her heart might harden itself against him. "Virginia and
I wish to end this solemn day in peace and holiness. We
do not wish all our sacred associations to be disturbed by
the blasphemies of which you are so liberal."

"As you will," said Richard. "It is but one more
sacrifice to your Moloch!" He sighed heavily. "When
and where will it all end?" he said half to himself.

"That lies with you alone," replied Hermione.
"Truth is unchangeable, and we are in the way of
truth. Good night. I will wish Virginia good night from
you."

"Good night," was his reply made with a faltering

voice. " This Lent—this time of mourning—at which you are playing is too sorrowful a reality for me ! "

She made no answer. What could she say? She knew it all only too well ; but he was an atheist, and it was his own fault if he suffered. He had cut himself off from peace as from light, as from truth ; and the hideous master whom he was serving was but dealing with him according to the law of his being.

With a sigh as sad as his own she turned from him silently. As she closed the door, he crossed his arms on the table, and laid his face on them wearily. If only he could see the end of it all! He would wait in patience and in love, he would be forbearing, and he would not use his rights if only he might hope that one day he should recover what now he had so strangely lost. But things were growing worse, not better ; and his hopes were dimmer and his heart heavier as the days passed one after the other, each bringing some new triumph to his enemy, some new discomfiture to himself. And he—he could no more arrest nor improve than if his beloved were at the point of death, and he called on the Primal Force to bring them back to life!

As he sat thus, a sudden gasp, a sudden spasm at his heart, brought him back from regrets to consciousness.

He had had much discomfort about his heart of late, and more than once these sharp pains had startled him as now. But the faintness which followed soon passed ; and when Jones brought in the coffee he saw nothing save that his master was deathly pale, and with a look of pain on his mild fine face that made the man's heart ache for sympathy ; and that made him, too—being by no means really " converted," though he seemed to be so to please his mistress—swear silent oaths against " that black rascal," as he called the vicar, which would have got him a decent penance had they been repeated in confession.

The severities which began on Ash Wednesday were continued through Lent ; and the slight relaxing of discipline that had been permitted during Advent was now exchanged for the strictest austerities that have been as yet formulated by the ritualist party. During this time of sacred mourning and holy mortification, the strain on the relations between Richard and his wife and daughter was increased almost beyond bearing. Never had the Church been made so prominent in his household ; never had the defiance which it inculcated been so openly flung in the face of his authority, so passionately proclaimed. Every ecclesiastical observance that had been given up for the time was resumed, and more were superadded.

Wednesday and Friday fastings with abstinence-days to boot; "mattins" and evensong, and full services on every possible occasion ; confession, with more severe consequences of penance and forced abstention from innocent enjoyments not connected with the Church than had even hitherto been the rule ; Sunday spent wholly in the schoolroom and the Vicarage ; an ostentatious display of piety and devotion all round, coupled with a coldness like death to Richard the agnostic, excommunicated and infidel—these were the commands of Mr. Lascelles—these Father Truscott's directions ; and the two women under their control fulfilled them to the letter.

It was in vain that Richard remonstrated, in vain that he reasoned, that he ridiculed, that he forbade. His wife and daughter opposed that silent stubbornness of women who cannot be coerced and will not be influenced, and went their own way, no matter how much he opposed. And as Hermione said when he was more urgent than usual because of Virginia's increased pallor and her own feverish unrest, unless he absolutely locked them up and they were unable to get out, they would go on disobeying him, bound by a higher will than any that he knew or could impose.

What could he do? Nothing. Mr. Lascelles had

spoken the truth—the law had tied his hands. Because
of his speculative opinions, the rights which Nature herself had given were disallowed by men's convention ;
and one day his wife, at the instance of her confessor,
told him that if he persisted in interfering with either
herself or Virginia, she would apply to the Court of
Chancery for protection, and make *her* daughter a ward
whose religious life the law would respect and for the
unfettered exercise of whose duties it would provide.
Then, as Mr. Lascelles had done, she offered him the
alternative of submission to the new order of things, when
he would be let alone and his abominable infidelity so
far tolerated ; or, if not this, and he chose to fight them—
well ! she would meet him at his desire, and let the
Master of the Rolls judge between them !

So there the thing stood, and Richard could not
change it ; as little as could Ringrove, who yet tried his
best, casting in his lot with his friend. Hermione and
Virginia lived their lives, and the reprobate husband and
father lived his. They met at meal-times and at no other ;
and those meals were the least painful when there was
least said. Discussion was sure to breed increase of
bitterness, and to bring additional sorrow on all concerned. Silence was safe, just as dead men strike no

blows ; and silence therefore was the order of the day at
the Abbey.

But though the clerical power had carried the day, the
two Abbey ladies were always spoken of at the Vicarage,
and by the Church party generally, as persecuted witnesses for the truth—domestic martyrs for whose sufferings the faithful were called on to intercede fervently and
frequently, and whose constancy they were bidden to
admire, and if need be imitate.   It was a proud position
into which the wife who had forsaken her vows, the
daughter who had abjured her obedience, were exalted ;
and with the self-deception of their kind they accepted
the martyr's palm as if it honestly belonged to them.
And while Richard Fullerton was slowly breaking his
heart under the blight that had fallen on him, the man
who had conquered and the women who had deserted
him, asked a blessing on their methods of destruction,
and bemoaned themselves for their own unmerited misfortunes.

CHAPTER X.

THE BURNING FLAX.

IF Hermione and Virginia were the more interesting converts, because of domestic difficulties to be overcome and substantial gains to the Church to be secured for the future, the Molyneux family were the more advantageous possession in the present. Over them Mr. Lascelles was absolute, without the need of exercising tact or care in his own conduct, and with no fear of counter influence over theirs. He disposed of their time, their property, their persons, their actions, as if independence and self-respect were words without meaning in English life ; and they obeyed him as if they had been born into slavery and knew nothing higher than the docility of dogs following at the heel of the master.

If he wanted more money than he thought well to ask from Hermione—whom however he was leading deliberately into debt, to have a still better purchase over her—he applied to Cuthbert. If Cuthbert had run dry— as often happened now—he came on Aunt Catherine who had private funds beyond those which were thrown into the common stock ; and if these funds were exhausted, then he drew on Theresa's personal allowance out of her share of the estate—also thrown into the common stock—limiting her own expenditure to five pounds a quarter and taking the rest as a loan to the Lord. From one or the other of these human sheep he managed to shear sufficient wool for the parish ; and the vestrymen, who knew to a fraction what the vicarage yielded, marvelled at the lavish outgoings which were like the cruse of oil and measure of meal that increased with the using.

When priests and brothers came down in such numbers as he himself could not house at the Vicarage, he told Aunt Catherine how many beds he wanted, and gave her the names of his guests as coolly as if she had been the hotel porter hired to register arrivals. He did not ask, be it understood, for this hospitality to his friends, these gifts to the poor. He ordered what he wanted without preface beforehand or thanks to follow. When he wished this sick man to have so many pounds of beef, he wrote the order on Churchlands, as if making use of a banking account which he did not trouble himself about overdrawing. If he wanted the carriage, he sent down his man with a message giving the hour ; if he had not enough forks or spoons, glasses or crockery, for the occasion, his housemaid went to Churchlands with a basket, commissioned to bring back so many. He disposed of his three proselytes body and soul ; and they knelt at his feet and found their pride in the extremes to which they carried their submission.

Aunt Catherine, besides her personal respect, which was of the most slavish kind, had an abject fear of this handsome vicar of theirs, as the arbitrary dispenser of spiritual pains and privileges, of eternal penalties or rewards; and dreaded nothing so much as his displeasure. The sacred powers of binding and loosing, which he claimed as Priest, her superstitious fancy accorded even more liberally than he himself demanded; and she often lost herself in a dreamy kind of haze wherein the Honourable and Reverend Launcelot Lascelles was identical with St. Peter, with qualities and attributes inextricably intermixed. More than once she whispered to her friends her own conviction that the vicar of Crossholme was an avatar of the Apostle ; and she added her advice to pay the price of humility and submission now for the sake of getting good places hereafter. Like all unreasoning people, she enlarged the permitted

borders by exaggeration; and like all weak ones she was
a fetish-worshipper under the name of a Christian.
"Superior" was the talisman by which she was ruled,
and her credulity that by which he conjured; and the
result of all was that her weak brain was becoming daily
weaker, until it was only too evident that she would soon
degenerate into confessed imbecility, and dribble out the
remainder of her life as a harmless lunatic, passing her
days in close companionship with the demigods of the
Christian Olympos.

But if Aunt Catherine was still his creature, through
all the subjugation enforced and submission rendered,
something of a disturbing kind had of late traversed
Cuthbert's mind, which Mr. Lascelles, proud and confident as he was, scarcely noted, still less set himself to
analyze. But there it was; and the question was, what
was it? Was it love for Virginia? and by that love the
faintest possible wearing away from his former holy zeal?
—looking back after his hand had been put to the plough?

Plain in feature, weedy in frame, awkward in gesture,
poor Cuthbert was little likely to please a fastidious taste.
He was of the kind, when extraordinarily animated, to
make short butts and dashes at the object of his
affections; to take her hand somewhere about the wrist,

then drop it after a moment's limp holding as if he
had burned his fingers ; to laugh insanely at small jokes
whereof no one but himself could see the fun ; and to
ask her advice as to the thickness of his coat according
to the day, and whether he should put on his woollen
scarf or no. If "high" he would present her with
copies of Fra Angelico and Botticelli ; if "low" he
would make the Bible do service for his Ovid, and quote
texts that should give his earthly passion a voice but
keep his soul in the right way. 'If poetically mediæval
he would follow his beloved at a respectful distance as
her servitor devoted to the joyful task of submission to
her will and the glorification of her graces ; he would
stand in sloping lines like the pictures of pages and
squires in skin dresses and plumed hats ; and when she
spoke he would reply to her with exaggerated courtesy
and respect ; he would make weak verses, wherein
his lute and my lady's garden would often occur ; and
he would think that he had copied to the life the early
Italian poets whose stately methods of courtship had
touched his fancy. This he would do when of the kind
which aims to live up to its blue china, and parodies the
noble school with whom passion is not sense so much
as thought.

But he had not got to the length yet of any of these self-committing expressions. He contented himself with nourishing for Virginia a washy, feeble sort of sentimental admiration which was his version of the magnificent insanity of which Romeo died—of the passionate religion for which Tasso suffered. He made love—if he made it at all—by looks only. He wanted nothing more than he had—which was to see Virginia every day, and often more than once in the day; when he would plant himself where he could watch her pure and passionless outline; his light grey eyes fixed on her as if there was nothing else to look at. It was like a mask staring at her—the lips wide apart, and the pale face, dashed here and there with unhealthy streaks of colour, set in long lines of solemn feebleness. But he never said anything to her. It was all dumb watching, voiceless approval, and no attempt at anything more ardent. And yet there was a certain mute understanding between them which might mean—anything.

Though he gave the idea his sanction, and preferred it infinitely to any chances with Ringrove, the vicar was not much interested in this tame wooing of his spiritless acolyte. He felt as sure of him as of Virginia, and counted on both as his own devoted personal friends

as well as the loyal children of the Anglican Church,
who would never diverge from the strict line of his
guidance and his teaching. If they were to be married,
he would then have to consider the chances of such
changes as might result from their new relations. A
bold demand for the recovery of some of that property
of which the hypothetical ancestor had robbed Holy
Mother Church might be needful, seeing that earthly
love does sometimes weaken ecclesiastical devotion, and
the claims of a family have the trick of setting themselves against those of a priest. And he did not think
that he should fail in his appeal when the time came
wherein to make it. But as yet nothing pressed, if some
things had changed.

In the beginning of his zeal for vestments and
incense, Cuthbert had often declared to the vicar that
nothing would give him so much ease of conscience as
this sacred restitution of sacrilegious wealth. They had
even gone over the map of the estate together, and,
with Theresa's consent as joint heiress, had decided
on the farms and fields that should be sold and the
proceeds applied to the endowment of the Church. Of
late however he had rather fenced with the subject when
either Superior or Theresa spoke of it. Nothing definite

was done anyhow ; and he laid the blame of the delay on the broad shoulders of those mysterious sinners, the lawyers. He professed himself disgusted, and even went to the length of a feeble lie by saying that he had written letters of inquiry ; which he had not done ; but the act of restitution was none the nearer completion, and the rent skirt of the Mother was still wanting that godly patching.

Also, the young man had a little wavered about going up for his ordination at Easter ; sometimes saying that he was not prepared intellectually, and the examining chaplain would never pass him ; sometimes pleading moral humility, and that he was not worthy to under-take the sacred office which only holy men should fill. But he always ended by saying that he would probably go up at Easter as originally proposed, and if not then, yet certainly he would eventually. All the same he fenced with the one question and drew back on the other. But though Mr. Lascelles was often irritated, he was never afraid. He smiled as he thought how firmly he held this weak brother in the grip of his strong hand, and how entirely he had dominated his feeble nature ; and he believed that this hesitation was really due to what Cuthbert himself said—the scruples of a supersubtle conscience, which made him feel unworthy.

In this state of things Lent passed into its middle term—the *mi-carême* of Romanism. It was settled that Virginia was to be confirmed at Easter. Father Truscott was preparing her, and Richard's opposition did not count. Confirmation comes into the ordinary life of respectable Protestants, and the objections of an infidel father would go no way in law. This matter was safe enough; that in doubt was the girl's visit to C—— for her "retreat" prior to confirmation. To this Richard would certainly never consent; and as this is no part of ordinary respectable Protestantism, the infidel here would prove the stronger should it come to a collision between father and daughter—agnostic and Christian.

All the same that retreat should be arranged and accomplished, let it cost what it would in the way of domestic peace and filial duty. So Father Truscott and Sister Agnes decided; and Mr. Lascelles and Hermione approved.

Father Truscott had almost taken up his abode now at Crossholme, where he made himself useful and did more work than anyone else. He helped the vicar manfully in the parish and with the services, and took many of his penitents off his hands. Of these, Virginia Fullerton was of course the most important. He was carrying on a secret spiritual tillage with her that so far had borne no outward fruit, but of which the harvest was none the less growing—if silently and secretly, yet always growing. He brought her books and beads and odds and ends of queer things which he called relics, and which he gave to her alone, with much pomp of reverence, requesting her to keep them hidden. She was not to show them even to her mother. Sister Agnes was the only person who might handle them, making the sign of the cross as she did so—press them to her forehead, her lips—kneel before them with outstretched arms, invoking the protection of the saints whereof these curious bits of dusty decay were said to be the sacred remains. She was the only one who knew all that was going on behind the scenes, and what it meant and was to end in. And her countenance strengthened Virginia—that once pure and transparent soul—in what was substantially a living lie. But for this countenance the girl would have found her position unendurable; with it, double dealing and falsehood masked as religion became only too fatally easy. The Sister had taken over her the same kind of control as that which the vicar had taken over Hermione, and had so completely usurped the place of mother that the actual mother and daughter were simply friends, not confidantes. Sister Agnes was Virginia's real mother, as Father Truscott was her real father ; and her conscience was at rest when these two approved what mamma and the vicar would have disallowed, and that poor lost servant of Satan at home would have forbidden. Whither this little quartette of secret Illuminati were tending, and what was being hidden from the face of day among them all, time alone would reveal.

If Aunt Catherine feared Superior as a vicegerent who could punish, Theresa adored him as a god who could bless, whose worship was in itself ecstasy and whose service was its own reward. She was never so happy as when she was being used for the glory of the Church and the conversion of the parish. But it must be under his direction, else would the salt have lost its savour and piety its holiness. Without his words of encouragement, his smile of approval, his counsel, his very remonstrance—ah ! how well she knew that tender joy of the loving who kiss the rod by which they are chastised !—she would have found religion but a tame affair ; and her soul would have drooped those ambitious pinions which had carried it to such giddy heights of enthusiasm, and would have fallen down to the safer

levels of " reasonable service," as with so many others
when the overruling personal influence is withdrawn.
While however, things continued as they were, Theresa
touched the confines of insanity in her now ecstasy, now
despair ; and her very life was consumed by the fervid
passion with which she made love to a man under the
form of serving the Church and worshipping God.

In one thing only was she disobedient to her hiero-
ophant ; she would not refrain from the devout imprudences which made her happiness and destroyed her
health. Now that Lent had come in she fasted and
abstained with a very fierceness of self-abnegation, though
she was in the state which required generous living and
frequent nourishment. Whatever the day might be, she
was to be found punctually in her place at "mattins"
and "evensong," and she would have felt herself as reprobate as unhappy had she missed Early Celebration—of
course fasting. She was forced to give up her pleasant
task about the temporary altar in the schoolroom, as she
was forced to give up all of personal activity of serving.
Her failing strength compelled even her ardent mind ;
and when she had fainted two or three times over her
task, she had nothing for it but submission to her weakness.

Miss Pryor, the schoolmistress, who cherished for the

handsome vicar one of those hopeless passions from a distance which make the romance of some humble women's lives—whereof the reality is to marry the draper —took the girl's work on herself, and did it better. This enforced renunciation was as much as Theresa could bear. More would have broken her down, even though Superior himself would have approved. She could not bring herself to renounce her holy imprudences, more especially that of attendance at the offices. Her highest moment of happiness was when she could see that beloved priest standing between her and the Divine— himself to her the Divine; when she could hear his voice; let her soul be carried as it were in the arms of his spirit up to the gates of heaven by his prayers; and take her especial share of the benediction which had so much more significance when given by him than by any other; when she could pour out her love and call it now a hymn and now a prayer.

She could not give it all up. Her temperament was of that imperious kind which is " founded on absolutes," in matters of love demanding personal communion for happiness. She was no female Rousseau to leave her lover for the pleasure of writing to him and receiving his letters in return. She could not make herself content

with memory or imagination. Anticipation to be sure
did something for her, but anticipation without fulfilment
was only so much additional pain. If she had expected
to see Superior and been disappointed, her anguish became intolerable ; and a sleepless night spent in passionate
weeping, in feverish despair, was by no means the best
kind of thing for a girl whose life was hanging by a thread
so frail that it might snap from one week to another.

Unless one of two miracles should be wrought in her
behalf, things would evidently go ill with poor Theresa.
If she could not force herself back to common sense
and self-control—or if a ritualist clergyman, who found
his advantage in celibacy, would not break through his
misogamous vows and marry one who was of some slight
advantage to him as a penitent and would be none as a
wife—there would be one grave the more in the old
churchyard before the year was out. Failing either
alternative, the only chance for her safety lay in her
immediate removal ; when perhaps a change of scene
might induce a change of interest, and her health might
be restored because her heart would be healed.

The vicar saw all this clearly enough and determined
to act on it. Her hysterical emotion troubled him by its
impetuosity, and very little more was wanted to make a

scandal to the Church by some public display which
should reveal to the world all that it was most important
to conceal, and tell even more than the truth. Her
presence at the services embarrassed him in more ways
than one. Those dangerously bright eyes fixed on him
with such intensity when he was performing the most
sacred functions of his holy office disturbed his thoughts,
distracted his attention, and filled him with dread of what
might come. Her tempestuous tears now distressed, now
irritated him ; her self-accusations of imaginary sins, to
excuse the hysterical passion which she could not control,
taxed his ingenuity to soothe with becoming gravity and
tenderness combined ; her despair when he checked her
over-zeal, her perilous exaltation when he encouraged,
perplexed his powers of management ; and he was anxious
to remove from the place one whose religious ardour was
so evidently the mere cloak for the disorders of human
passion.

More than once before in his career he had made
devoted daughters of the Church by first making devoted
adorers of himself. A dangerous game at the best, it had
never been so full of peril as now ; and though as yet it
had always ended in the sacrifice of those poor victims
and his own gain—their forfeiture and his coming off

scot-free—he could not be quite so sure in this case. Theresa's nature was more impassioned as well as more brittle than most Englishwomen's—more easy to inflame, more difficult to subdue, and of an intenser quality all through. But the work of subjection after stimulation had to be done; and the vicar was the man to do it.

That dreaded display came just before Mr. Lascelles had decided on removing this inconvenient worshipper. It was on a Sunday, at morning prayers, while the Litany was being intoned. Weakened by her insidious illness— her ardent imagination still more excited by the super- fluous fastings, the frequent acts of adoration, the personal austerities, the disturbing confessions which made the peril and the joy of her present unwholesome state— Theresa went into a kind of hysterical trance, something like that which she had had on the day of the Harvest Festival after her first confession in the sacristy. She had been much moved during the service, weeping bit- terly during the confession, the psalms, the hymns; she was oppressed by a sense of spiritual sin which only Superior could remove—of her lost condition wherein only Superior could save. But he was so far off!—he was like the Holy Mother whose protection she invoked —like that Dread Being Himself whose wrath she depre cated. The schoolroom and all that was in it faded into darkness—only the vicar's figure stood out in light as he knelt by the reading desk and read the clauses of the Litany, to which the congregation and the choir responded. Gradually she lost all sense of where she was; time flowed into eternity and circumstance was swallowed up in feeling. She knelt, with eyes strained on this beloved man whom fancy and fanaticism had rendered more beautiful than before, but had also made awful and to be feared; the responses died on her lips, the sound of them died from her hearing, and when the service was over and all rose from their knees she was kneeling still, rigid, white, over-wrought, lost to all outward sense and reason alike.

Aunt Catherine touched her.

"Theresa!" she whispered; "are you asleep?"

At the first the girl did not answer, but on the second touch her wandering senses returned, and with a shriek that startled all in the room, she cried out:

"Superior! Beloved Superior! Save me! Oh save me! I am lost without you! God has forsaken me—my God in man do you save me!"

Then she fell backwards in an uncontrollable fit of hysterics; shrieking, sobbing, screaming, beating the air

with her hands, fighting off imaginary foes, calling again
on the vicar to save her, and going through all the
degrading phases of this terrible temporary madness.

The women sitting nearest to her gathered round her.
Aunt Catherine, herself in hysterics of a milder kind,
screamed out that she was possessed and besought
Superior to exorcise the demon and restore her niece to
reason and calmness.   Miss Pryor, shedding tears, chafed
her hand and called her "poor dear" and "afflicted
lamb;" while Sister Agnes, who had some common sense
in spite of all her fanatical follies, tried what severity of
voice would do ; and Mrs. Nesbitt said : "Carry her out
into the fresh air and dash cold water in her face."

Virginia, pale and trembling, prayed fervently to the
Blessed Virgin as her contribution to the healing methods
of the moment ; and Cuthbert mechanically took up the
thurible and swung a cloud of incense into the room.
But nothing of this was of much avail till Ringrove,
leaving his place, strode a little grimly to the agitated
group, and taking up the screaming girl in his arms carried
her, still struggling and crying out like one in agony,
into the open space of playground before the schoolroom.
There he laid her on the gravel, and before any one knew
what was being done, Mrs. Nesbitt dashed a few cupsful

of cold water in her face, and by degrees restored her to her senses.

But it had been a horrible exhibition—to be remembered against the vicar, both now and when the time of reaction should come—if indeed it ever should !

The next day the vicar went to Churchlands, armed with the scourge which it was his duty to use.

He found Theresa lying on the sofa, looking flushed and breathing painfully. As he came into the room she started up with feverish delight yet dread, afraid that he would scold her for the scene of yesterday, but too happy to be in his adored presence under any conditions to conceal her joy.

"My child! you have grieved me," he said paternally, gravely, with a fine mingling of sorrow and rebuke. And it cost him something to speak to her gently. He placed her back on her pillows, and took her hot thin hand in his. "Now I have come to talk to you," he continued. "I must have something done for you. You will break all our hearts else."

"How good you are, and to such a wretch as I am !" murmured Theresa, her large eyes filling with tears.

He smoothed her dark and shining hair, as was his paternal habit when they were alone ; but somehow his touch was different to-day from what it always was. A woman's love has strange sensibilities, and Theresa's nature was as sensitive as a mimosa plant; but though her perceptions were not obscured, she was in the state which makes those who love, shamefully grateful for even insulting notice.

"Dear Superior!" she said, lifting her eyes to him with that rapt look which told all that her lips were forbidden to speak.

"I am very unhappy about you, Theresa," said the vicar in his sweetest voice, and how sweet he could make it when he chose!

"Dear Superior!" she said again.

Her heart was too full for more than these half-sobbing interjections; and that he should be unhappy when he might have been angry was too delightful to her soul for any pretence of deprecation.

"I have been thinking earnestly of what would be best for you," he went on to say, looking away from her— at the window opposite—like a man in deep consideration, only thinking of what he is saying, and not seeing that at which he is looking. "All last night I was awake thinking of you and praying for you. Your painful attack cost me more anguish than I can well express. No; do not

speak, child! Listen to me in humility and silence"—
this with sudden severity. "I have a plan for you. It
is that you leave Crossholme for a while, and try a milder
climate. I should like you to go to Penzance. I have
friends there who would look after you ; the place is
lovely, the air delicious, and you would thus avoid the
cold east winds which are so pernicious here in the
spring."

"Oh, Superior ! I could not leave Crossholme," cried
poor Theresa trembling and with a sudden rush of
tears. "The dear services, my district, Sister Agnes—I
could not give them up !"

A sarcastic smile crossed the vicar's thin lips. That
bead-roll of reasons why, and the governing cause left
out!

"You would at my desire ; I am sure of that," he
said with emphasis.

She covered her face.

"Your wishes are sacred to me," she said, the hot
tears forcing themselves through her wasted fingers ;
"but indeed it will be such a pain to me to leave home
that I am sure I shall be far worse than I am now ; and
I am not ill, dear Superior. I am not indeed. I am
much better than I was."

She raised her face as she said this, pitiful, pleading, eloquent with the passion of her grief, of her love. It was a face that might have excused any man's yielding to the weakness of compassion, but to Mr. Lascelles at that moment it was hideous and hateful.

"You think yourself stronger than you are, as do all invalids in your condition," he said coldly in spite of his wish to simulate kindness. Could nothing take the fire out of those burning eyes? "Your friends know better than you how much you need care at this time. A few weeks in a favourable climate will probably restore you to your usual health, and make us all happy about you again."

"Do not send me away, Superior," she half whispered, laying one hand on his arm in entreaty. "Let me stay with you all. I will submit to any restrictions you please, if only I may stay at home. I shall get quite well when the spring comes, and I get rid of this horrid cold; and then you will give me back my work in the dear church when it is opened. I have been very good, Superior," forcing a smile that was meant to be playful and that was instead of the saddest pathos. "I have obeyed you so faithfully in all that you have ordered; now let me have my own way for once—let me stay here; do not send me from home."

" For your own good, Theresa," said the vicar with his sweetest smile and in his softest voice, but with his eyes at their hardest. " It will be no pleasure to me to lose you out of my congregation; but for your own sake you must go. Remember that dreadful, that awful scene of yesterday. We must not have that repeated."

He said this with a fierce uncontrollable burst of indignation, half rising from his place while he flung her hand from his arm.

" It was such a mere accident. I do not know what came to me. It never happened before, and it never would again," stammered Theresa, penitent and distressed.

" It might, but it shall not," returned Mr. Lascelles with cruel meaning. " You little know all the mischief that it has done. No; you must leave home for a time, without question; if only as part of your penance for your sinful folly."

" But home is so much the best place when one is not well," pleaded the poor girl, shifting her ground with unconscious inconsistency.

" Change of air is better," said the vicar.

" If it broke my heart?" she asked beseechingly.

" The Church breaks no hearts that obey her. Peace comes best by the way of duty and obedience," he

answered sententiously.   Then in a different voice he
said, sternly as well as sharply : " The question is not one
on which to argue, Theresa.   It is my will that you go.
Need I say more ? "

She did not answer, but taking his hand kissed it
with feverish reverence.

" Your will is the will of God to me," she then said
in a broken voice.   " I will obey you, if it kills me."

At this moment Cuthbert came into the room.

" You must help me, Molyneux, with your dear sister
here," said the vicar, glad of the diversion, and in a more
friendly manner than he had used before, but it was an
artificial friendliness.

" What can I do, dear Superior ? " asked the Crossholme future curate humbly.   " I should think you
wanted no help with her.   Sister is dutiful," he added,
writhing himself into an attitude.

" Induce her to submit cheerfully to the inconvenience
of leaving home for a little while," Mr. Lascelles answered.

" Why should sister leave home ? " asked Cuthbert
who had lately adopted this somewhat quaint form of
speech as sounding simple and antiquated.

" Because of the dear child's state of health, which
distresses me," said Mr. Lascelles, looking above

Theresa's head compassionately. "Change to a warmer climate will do her good till the spring has really settled."

"It will be hard to go," said Theresa ; but she added submissively, though the words almost strangled her : "but of course Superior knows best, and, if he wishes it, I am ready to obey."

An odd expression came on Cuthbert's face. Humble and downcast as it always was when he was dealing with Mr. Lascelles, it was not quite sincere. There flitted over it too the reflection of the thought : If so submissive, what need of help from me? and what does this pretence of impotence hide? Aloud, he said hesitatingly :

"Sister can scarce go alone."

"I have provided for all that," answered the vicar, master of all the points. "I have friends who will look after her at Penzance, where I wish her to go ; and she must take Drusilla."

Drusilla was the maid.

"I think that our aunt will hardly like sister to go alone," said Cuthbert returning to the charge with the tenacity of his kind.

"Not if I undertake the responsibility?" asked the vicar with a seriousness which a turn of the scale would dispose to menace. He liked blind obedience from his creatures ; and this future curate of his, what was he but the chief of his creatures?

Cuthbert shuffled his feet uneasily.

"You are always kind and thoughtful, dear Superior," he said, submissive, craven, flattering as ever, but with the same odd accent of insincerity as before running through his blandishments. "Still, we have always been so much to each other, sister and I and our aunt. I think it will be a trial to our aunt to let sister go alone ; and with her cough, too."

"Trials are the saints' methods of perfection," said the vicar.

"Under authority, yes," said Cuthbert, lowering his eyes.

"As now," said Mr. Lascelles emphatically.

Cuthbert bent his head and joined his hands together like a Founder receiving the benediction of a saint.

"As now," he echoed reverentially; but his loose lips crisped a very little and the voice was dry and hard.

"The question then is settled, and Theresa goes to Penzance next week," said the vicar.

"If you wish it, Superior," replied Theresa, giving up her love for love's very sake. But a look of such despair came into her face that even Mr. Lascelles was touched to the point of compassion if not to that of relenting.

"If you are good and get well soon you can return soon," he said kindly. "You need however more care than you yourself believe, and I must provide for your having it. We have not so many faithful daughters of the Church, that we can afford to lose such a one as you."

"Thank you," said Theresa with a swift upward glance of adoration. "When you approve, Superior, my conscience is at rest. I know no higher authority."

Again Cuthbert shuffled his feet uneasily, but he echoed his sister's words, and said: "Our highest," like a parrot repeating a lesson.

He was sitting in his favourite mediæval attitude, his eyes on the ground and his hands joined together flatwise, resting on his knees.

"The highest is the best," said Mr. Lascelles enigmatically.

"Yours is the highest. It is the same as God's!" said Theresa.

"I do my best to make myself a faithful interpreter and a safe guide, but I often fail like others. I am only a man after all," said the vicar with a smile of graceful humility.

" To me more than a man ! " murmured Theresa; and then she closed her eyes and her head sank deeper into the pillow ;—again, as so often before, Semele over whom the breath of her God has passed !

If the man's heart waxed fat for gratified pride, what wonder ? True, folly, fanaticism, vanity, passion, credulity, are not the noblest set of motives by which a man gains influence over his kind. But when that influence is gained?—when he can induce a loving wife to repudiate her husband and transfer to himself the duty and obedience which were rightfully that other's ?—when he can inspire a good girl with a frantic passion, and turn the current of her youth from the sweet modesty of maidenhood to the self-destroying violence of a Mænad ?—when he can uproot the influence of a tender father over his once adoring child ?—ruin the position of a noble-minded man in his own country, and cut the ground from under his feet closer and closer till soon there will be nothing left for him but the final fall?—when he can carry all before him and subdue every stronghold that he assaults ?—what marvel that he should be proud and assume the quasi-divine and personally infallible power which no one has the courage or the common sense to deny? The position of a ritualist " priest " is about the proudest of all in the

world of human leaders. Freed from the close organization, the authority of the Romish Church, he is absolute
in his own domain ; and no one understood this better
than the smooth-voiced fiery-souled Honourable and
Reverend Launcelot Lascelles, Vicar of Crossholme, and
Richard Fullerton's conquering foe.

When he had gone, Cuthbert, unbuckling himself as
it were from his mediævalism and slouching into the
commonplace, took up the parable and spoke tartly to
his sister, saying that she gave way too much to the vicar
—he did not call him Superior, but simply the vicar—
and paid him a vast deal too much honour.

"How can I ?" said Theresa. "Too much honour !
my Director, a priest, and in authority over me !"

"To a certain extent," hesitated Cuthbert.

"What do you mean, Cuthbert ? Are you cooling
towards Superior ?" cried Theresa, half rising in her horror.
This was of a truth bringing sacrilege into the house.

"No, I am not cooling to him at all," he answered
shuffling ; "but his assumptions are a little extreme. He
has not authority for all that he says and does."

"No one would have more over me," said Theresa, a
little beside his meaning.

He left her dark, but returned, as perhaps a slight lead :

" I think that dear Father Truscott would support my
view if I laid it before him for decision. I think he would
give it as his opinion that your submission to Superior
savoured a little of idolatry, which is a sin against the
Church that ranks with witchcraft. You yourself say that
Mrs. Fullerton's submission is extreme and not quite
wholesome."

"She is married," replied Theresa hastily ; " I am
not. That makes all the difference."

So it did ; but neither brother nor sister saw clearly
the full significance of this bit of naïve reasoning on the
girl's part, who thus unconsciously showed the direction
of her own feelings, and perhaps the shadow of her
hopes.

The end of this, as of other conversations of the like
kind, was that, over-excited, distressed, and disappointed
—she did not understand why—Theresa cried and sobbed
so violently that she broke one of the smaller vessels
and dyed her handkerchief with blood. There had been
a good deal of this alarming hæmorrhage of late, but no
one knew of it save Drusilla; and she was bound over to
secresy. More than half in love as she was on her own
account with the handsome vicar, and reading only too
clearly the state to which poor Theresa had reduced

herself, she kept all that she knew a close secret. She did not wish to distress her young mistress, nor to bring harm or confusion to the dear vicar; and she was right in thinking Aunt Catherine too weak and Cuthbert too silly to be of use had she told them all she knew— right too in feeling that Theresa must fight it out by herself and be lost or saved—" as God wills," said Drusilla piously, mistaking folly for fate.

CHAPTER XI.

AND THE SMOKE THEREOF.

THINGS always enlarge themselves in the telling, and this hysterical attack of Theresa was exaggerated out of all likeness to its real self. Every kind of shameful thing was said, every kind of infamous reason given for what was really only the physical break-down of a sickly girl weakened by fasting and disease, and excited by religion and love in one. Everyone was astir, everyone felt personally outraged on which of the two sides he or she stood ; and the whole neighbourhood was as busy as a nest of ants when its secret ways are laid bare. Even Mr. Lascelles, though he had foreseen much, had not fully realized to what extent the fire of scandal would run on the dry stubble of credulity and love of gossip ; and for a moment he stood aghast at the mischief which his ardent and devoted penitent had unwittingly wrought him. She, who would have given her life for him, had herself lighted this fire which was to scorch if not consume him—had herself let loose the howling pack of detractors and contemners who were to harass and afflict if not to utterly destroy him ! He was sorry for her, but he was more sorry for himself ; and though in the depths of his consciousness he was vexed with himself, on the surface of things, and so far as self-acknowledgment went, he blamed her only and held himself more sinned against than sinning.

The news spread as far as Starton, and reached Lady Maine's unreluctant ears. By this time it had bulged considerably, and had lost almost all its original form ; but my lady accepted it as it was, greedily, and rubbed her hands at the chance it gave her. Hating ritualism as she did, it was a joyful day to her when she could hit a blot in the professors, and pounce down on a weak place in the humanity of those ghostly fathers and spiritual daughters. And on this occasion her satisfaction was complete. She believed implicitly all that the outlying world proclaimed. There was no doubt about it ;—there never is any doubt about things of which we know absolutely nothing and whereof we never examine the evidence ;—and it was sure as the indubitable four made up of two and two, that Mr. Lascelles had been flirting with Theresa Molyneux, and now had jilted and thrown her over. And if the girl had been

silly enough to fall in love with him, and was breaking
her heart at the disappointment, he ought to be made
to marry her, said Lady Maine; or else, she added, her
sense of retributive justice as strong as her knowledge
was weak, his gown ought to be taken from him. She
had no patience, she said, with these Pharisees who go
about among silly women and devour widows' houses;
and if she had the management of things she would
make all that kind of thing penal.

Alas for the main body of clerical proselytisers if
the Lady Maines of Protestantism had it all their own
way, and the personal love of their female disciples were
accounted to them for sin !—and good-bye to the
influence of the priesthood if it might deal only with the
intellect of man and not trade on the heart of woman !—
that heart with all its strength and weakness, its hopes,
its fears, its passions, its desires on which they build
their stronghold and found their empire. That would
indeed be the lamp without the oil, the thorns laid
beneath the pot and no fire at hand to make them
burn.

But though Theresa had been worse than silly to
have fallen in love with Mr. Lascelles, and more than
reprehensible to have shown that she had done so in

public—and at church too, of all places in the world !—
still she was motherless ; and Lady Maine was one of
those by no means necessarily maternal women to
whom an orphan girl is the fit object for all kinds of
impertinence and bullying under the head of " giving
advice, because, poor thing, she has no mother to tell her
any thing."

And now, though she abhorred the whole nest of
Papists, as she called the congregation at Crossholme,
yet this was an occasion when sectarian consistency must
yield to womanly duty ; and Lady Maine felt it to be an
imperative duty to go over to Churchlands and " speak
to that silly little owl plainly. Poor foolish thing ! "
she added, holding herself erect; " she has no one to
guide her ; for that weak-brained old aunt of hers, with
her saints and her rubbish, is no better than a magpie
about the girl. I doubt if she knows the head of a
leech from the tail, or how a mustard-plaister should be
put on !—and I dare say if the thunder turned the milk
sour she would say that some saint had done it for
punishment ; though, for the matter of that," said Lady
Maine, her thought making a sudden return, " it might
be Satan who had had a hand in it. For we know that
he goes about like a roaring lion seeking whom he may

devour. So why not the milk as well as anything else?"

Prompt and decided, Lady Maine drove off at once on this mission of "rallying" Theresa Molyneux; and of course found her at home—and visible. With the feverish obstinacy that characterizes her disease, the poor girl insisted on it that she was not really ill—that she was getting better daily, and as soon as the spring came she would be quite well. Meanwhile she would give up nothing that she could possibly retain, and she would not give up seeing those who might call. For this week she was forbidden to leave the house; but Superior had not interdicted visitors, of whom Lady Maine was the first.

She came into the room with her usual martial stride and military bearing. Her thickly-wadded mantle of black velvet, trimmed with broad bands of Russian sable, made her look bigger than she really was; and her sweeping train of heavy silk and high bonnet surmounted by a plume of hearse-like feathers, increased her apparent stature by at the least eight or ten inches. Truly she was a formidable creature to look at; and her deep-toned voice, with the uncompromising directness on which she prided herself, made her as formidable to **listen to.**

She stood over the flushed and attenuated girl lying on the sofa as if she had been a nightmare in bodily substance ; and Theresa knew instinctively that she had an ordeal to face. She was so sorry that this rasping creature had been let in and both Aunt Catherine and Cuthbert out ! But as the thing was on her it had to be gone through, and Lady Maine could not take root there and grow ;—and the dinner-hour is at the end of the day.

"Well, Miss Molyneux," began my lady severely, " and how may you be to-day ? "

"Very well, thank you, Lady Maine," said Theresa.

"You call this being very well, do you ? I don't; and I don't see how you could be much worse, you foolish child, to be alive there on that sofa at all."

" I am getting better," said Theresa ; and then she coughed with what Lady Maine, in speaking of this interview, called " that churchyard cough of hers—and she saying she was quite well indeed ! It was downright impiety and flying in the face of Providence ! "

" And what have you to say for yourself, making that precious scene that I heard of in church, last Sunday ? " asked my lady as severely as before. " Pretty goings-on indeed when a young woman like you can go shrieking and screaming in the middle of the Litany, and accuse herself of goodness knows what sins and wickednesses! It is time the Bishop looked you all up here in this blackhole of Papistry—that is my opinion; and the sooner a stop is put to all this impiety and idolatry the better for every one concerned. It isn't decent, Miss Molyneux; and now you see where all your High Church vagaries have led you!"

"I do not suppose I am the only one who has been taken ill in church," said Theresa, plucking up a spirit; "and I do not see what the High Church, as you call it—what our Anglicanism has to do with it."

"Listen to the poll-parrot!" cried my lady disdainfully. "No; and you are not the first silly girl who has fallen in love with a smooth-tongued, designing priest!" she added.

"Lady Maine!" said Theresa, raising herself in her indignation.

"Oh yes! it is all very well to say, 'Lady Maine' here and 'Lady Maine' there, but Lady Maine knows what she is about as well as any one can tell her; and this is just the simple truth, Miss Molyneux—you are madly in love with that good-for-nothing parson of yours, and the whole county knows it and is talking of it.

And if your brother does not take it up and bring it into court, he ought.   That's all I have to say!"

"My brother! do you think he believes such an infamy as this!" cried Theresa violently agitated.

"Of course you deny it; all girls do when things are as plain as this scarlet shawl of mine.   But others must be allowed to judge," said my lady grimly.   "And as far as I myself go, I have no doubt on the matter.   You have fallen head over ears in love, I tell you; and you are a foolish girl for your pains.   That kind of man never marries, bless you!" with supreme contempt. "He would lose half his power over girls like you if he did. Cannot you see that for yourself?   So take my advice. The wisest thing you can do is to wipe all this folly out of your mind and begin afresh.   Make a clean sweep of it—your ritualism; playing with the fire of Romanism you mean!—your abominable practice of confession, Mr. Lascelles, hysterics, and all the rest of it; and take shame to yourself that you have been so foolish hitherto, and resolve to be wiser for the future.   You may be forgiven as far as you have gone, because you have no mother to tell you things and keep you in the right way—and that aunt of yours is little better than a child herself; but now that I have spoken to you, you have

T 2

no excuse. You cannot say that you have not been told the truth and put right."

" I do not see what you wish me to give up, Lady Maine," said Theresa, whose answer was delayed because of a terrible fit of coughing, during which Lady Maine patted her back rather forcibly, as if she had been choking, and nearly killed her on the spot. " Would you wish me not to go to church ?   What is it you think so wicked in our lives ? "

" What do I think wicked, child?   Your putting your faith in stocks and stones instead of in the precious Scriptures—your worship of the creature instead of the Creator, and letting Mr. Lascelles carry you off your feet, as you do.   It is not decent, I tell you !   You an unmarried girl too !   And that pretty little Mrs. Fullerton with a husband ! It is downright iniquity and the abomination of desolation ; that is what it is, and so I tell you !"

" I do not know what you mean," said Theresa wearily, and turned her face inwards to the pillow.

" Why ! don't you confess, and take the sacrament every week, and have saints' days and processions and vestments, and spend more than half your time in church ?" the lady said in a surprised way.   " And then you say you don't know what I mean, indeed! What more could I mean, and what more could you all do? Would you make that parson of yours a pope at once? You have done the most you could; if you did more, you'd have to carry him about as a gilt idol with diamond eyes! I dare say, if the truth was known, you kiss his foot, as those benighted Romans do with their Pope. It would be only like you all if you did."

"He is worthy of it," said Theresa with strange passion.

Lady Maine rose.

"I see that you are given over to your witchcrafts and idolatries," she said in her deep, bell-mouthed way; "and I see that my kindly Christian endeavour to bring you back to the truth of the Gospel has not been met in the spirit which it deserved. I, a Christian mother, come to offer you, a motherless girl, good advice; to show you where you have done wrong, and how you can repent. You put up your shoulder, and turn a deaf ear to me. Don't say however, that you have not been warned. At the Last Day remember you will have to give an account for all your means of grace misused; and this visit of mine to-day will be one of them."

"I should have to give an account if I neglected the

means held out to me by the dear Church," said
Theresa. still too much roused to know the cooling
influence of social fear.

"Poor misguided girl ! I will pray for you," said my
lady with acrimony. "I will pray that you may be led
into the way of Gospel truth."

"Rather ask the prayers of the Church for yourself,
that you may be made one of her children," retorted
Theresa.

"You are obstinate and impertinent !" said my lady
angrily. "I am wasting my time here."

"I must always love the Church and obey her
teaching, through her priests," said Theresa.

"May God forgive you !" said Lady Maine, turning
from the couch by which she had been standing, and
striding out of the room like one who has discharged her
conscience of a heavy burden, and now is free to harbour
in its stead a due amount of righteous indignation.

And when she had gone, Theresa had another fit of
coughing, which ended again in that fatal red line—the
measure that told how life was wasting.

Lady Maine was not the only woman who came to
play the part of a chastising mother to the child of many
and daughter of none. Sister Agnes also took on herself

the office which indeed was hers by right of place, according to her rank in the local theocratic executive, and came to administer correction and rebuke in her own manner.

If my lady was rough as granite, the Sister was sharp as steel, and spared this poor erring Sappho of ecclesiasticism no more than did the coarse-grained, military-minded lady of Starton. Certainly she spoke to her smoothly, even smilingly, and with her best breeding. She asked after her health down to the minutest symptoms, with a pathological kind of sympathy that would have made the fortune of a hospital nurse. Then she touched on the scene of last Sunday; said it was a pity and a grievous offence that must be atoned for; that she ought to have asked for help against the temptation and to be supported in her weakness.

And when Theresa averred that she had—that she had prayed and prayed till all grew dark about her, and she felt as if God had deserted her and given her over into the clutches of Satan—the Sister bent her eyes on her with a look so searching, so steady, that Theresa quailed before it, while she said in her gentlest voice, her stillest manner :

" You did not ask in the right way, my child, else

grace would have come to you. You make the Eternal Promise of no avail if you do not see this."

" I did my best," said Theresa weeping.

"Ah !" said the Sister, bland, imperturbable, hard, severe; "some fly was in the ointment, and it was some earthly film of your own corrupt nature that had come between you and eternal light."

Going on, she said in the same way of personal smoothness and intrinsic cruelty :

" I must tell you now, dear Theresa, how greatly Superior was shocked at the whole scene. I know how good and kind he is, and that in all probability he would not tell you what he felt when he called. You are in a delicate state of health at this moment, and he would wish to spare you. He is never one to break the bruised reed ; but he was revolted and distressed beyond all measure. Nothing but the grace which surrounds him could have borne him through that painful trial with the dignity and patience so peculiarly his own—the ideal of the Christian gentleman as he is ! "

She watched Theresa narrowly while she praised her brother so enthusiastically. It was part of the punishment that she had devised for the girl, with whom indeed she was so irate that it was with great difficulty she could control herself even to this outward seeming of quiet-ness.

"I am so sorry!" cried Theresa, her ready tears flowing fast. "And he is so splendid—so great! To think that I, of all people, should have vexed him!"

"It was a grievous pity," said the Sister. "To a man like Superior, so essentially pure-minded and self-controlled, these wild excesses of undisciplined nature in a woman—these mad, screaming hysterics, for nothing—are beyond all things hateful. Women are to him in a certain sense sacred creatures; as they are to all men with his principles. He wishes to see in them only the virtues and perfections of saints and virgin martyrs; and anything else pains and disgusts him, oh! more than I can say! And you see I know him," she added with meaning.

"Yes," said Theresa dejectedly. "How sorry and ashamed I am!"

"A man who has vowed to devote himself to the service of the Church—who will never marry, never!—never!" repeated Sister Agnes with an intensity of emphasis which, in a less holy person, one would have said was passionate feminine spitefulness—"a man who has a horror of all coarseness and publicity, to be

appealed to in the midst of his holy office by a girl in
the crowd of his congregation going into a shrieking fit
of hysterics ! It was most unfortunate—most lamentable
on all accounts ; and will give the enemy cause to rejoice
over him !" said Sister Agnes, with a tight and nervous
clasping of her hands together to prevent the irritable
flicking of the fingers of less subdued people.

"If I could do anything——" murmured poor
Theresa, between sobbing and that dreadful cough !

"No, you can only perform penance for your own
sin," said the Sister severely. "The public shame and
hindrance Superior must live through as he best can.
It will be a hard trial, but God will strengthen him to
bear it.   But we scarcely looked for such a stumbling-
block to our work here from *you*, Theresa.   You have been
one of our dearest and most cared for ; yet and from you
has come this cutting insult, this terrible wrong-doing !"

"Sister Agnes ! have mercy !" cried the poor girl,
holding out her arms and catching at the Sister convulsively.

The Sister unclasped her hand with her strong
vice-like grip.

"I will have no scenes, Theresa," she said severely.
"Be quiet, this instant, or I shall leave you."

She might as well have commanded the waves of the sea to be still. Sorrow and shame for what she knew—unexpressed anguish for what she did not know,—overpowered her, weak as she was; and when Sister Agnes rang the bell and summoned Drusilla to her tortured mistress, she and the maid both thought that she would have died in their hands.

"Faugh!" said the Sister brushing her dress hastily, as she left the house; "it is full of her shameless love! I feel unclean—as if I had been sitting with a leper! Ah, this leprosy of passion—this vileness of earth that clings about such girls and women! And my brother, who encourages it all—who has made both this little fool and Mrs. Fullerton, and half a hundred more, in love with him—it is shameful! hideous! I will have no more of it. My soul turns against it all. I hate this place and all the work that goes on in it, and I hate myself that I ever gave in to the scheme of helping it forward. It is insincere, personal, vicious, earthly. The very pivot is Launcelot's dangerous power over Hermione Fullerton; and though she is right to discard that atheist husband of hers, she is infamously wrong in her motives."

While thinking all this bitterly, she suddenly came

upon Virginia, walking alone, in her Lenten robes of
solemn black relieved only by the blue scarf which she
wore in token of the Heavenly Mother whose child she
was.

"Here at least is one whose touch is pure !" she said
to herself ; "and who abhors as much as I do the follies
of the sillier sex and the vices of the viler !"

In which brief catalogue the Sister summarized the
whole of that portion of humanity which loves according
to nature, and does not waste in visions and reveries the
forces given for humanity and reality.

"My Mother!" said Virginia with fervour as they
met.

And when the Sister answered back, "My good
child, well met !" the girl's happiness was complete—as
complete as was at any time Theresa's when Superior
made her understand that he loved her like a man while
directing her like a spirit; made her understand, mark
you; but never committed himself by one word or
gesture which he could not explain away on the score
of paternal guidance, and as having no more special
meaning than if she had been a child, or both a pair
of china images.

The whole place continued in an uproar, and in

spite of the vicar's partisans and their unwearied activity of explanation, things looked ugly for this handsome celibate who had introduced ritualism and confession. Even Father Truscott was moved to speak a little by the by, and by no means in a straight line, to his friend round whose feet all these waves of scandal surged ; and to recommend to him, allusively, a little more discipline and a little less fascination.

Speaking in general of the best method of conducting a congregation, and specially the female part of it, Father Truscott said quietly that he, for his part, had always fought shy of hysterical temperaments, however precious their zeal when won. He found them the most difficult of all to manage, and always capable of doing as much harm as good.

" They personify too much," he said, looking at the ceiling as if studying the map of fine cracks that had come into the whitewash. " A priest, however holy, becomes a man to them, and their Director is their personal and private friend. Sometimes, wretched creatures, they even permit themselves to love !—and the priest suffers in his office for their miserable inconsistency and want of vital religion."

" Yet we must brave all dangers for the sake of the

gain that may accrue to the Church," said Mr. Lascelles gravely. "It is an incessant fighting with wild beasts ; and this is only one of the herd."

"It is delicate work—needs cautious handling," said the Father. "For myself I have always avoided the whole range ; and those women whom I have sought to influence were eminently safe by temperament as well as principle. And when I was a younger man I was even more careful. The Church will never be safe from misadventures and misunderstandings," he continued, "until the celibacy of the clergy is made part of the legal condition of Orders, so that no false hopes can be possible. Then, if women love they will love with their eyes open and to their own shame and damnation."

But Mr. Lascelles objected, and said he thought that this, like many other things, should be a matter of choice and individual will ; and that enforced celibacy would deprive of its grace and benefit that which was voluntarily undertaken.

"Ah !" said Father Truscott smiling ; "it is always the same thing with you, Superior. You boggle at discipline outside yourself, and want to be at the head of all organization and authority. You must be commandant—you will not be lieutenant ; and your position has not only its spiritual danger but its organic weakness—as any close reasoner could point out."

It was a bold thing to say, even from a Father; but the vicar did not resent the liberty. On the contrary he smiled too, joined his hands together according to his wont, beat his clean, well-kept taper finger-tips lightly against each other, and accepted his rebuke as meekly as if he had been a little girl at the knee of her mother. A rebuke according to Father Truscott, it was his title to honour to Mr. Lascelles. In this war with the Bishops, as well as with the law of the land, which the ritualist clergy are carrying on in England, and where each man is leader, general, bishop, pope to himself, the very charm of the contest lies in the fact that while all make the freedom of the Church to exercise tyranny over the laity the main object, each fights in his own way, and pays no obedience to any authority whatsoever, other than that which he chooses to elect for his own particular guidance. Bashi-bazouks of ecclesiasticism as they are, only the sincere and the humble go over to Rome, where rightfully they belong; because they only will give up this terrible fascination of personal power—this seductive snare of spiritual autocracy—for the sake of what they believe to be the truth. And Mr. Lascelles was not of these.

"We must do what we can, left by our leaders without guidance as we are," said the vicar in reply, with perfect urbanity. "We must pray against vanity and self-sufficiency; but until our beloved Church has taken to herself her own unfettered rights of organization, we must each act for the best according to the light vouchsafed."

They looked at each other searchingly; but neither read what the other wished should be kept hidden. Each man was sincere in his aims, hypocritical in his methods; crafty, self-controlled, secret and clever. They were well matched in their game; but between the two it was Mr. Lascelles this time who was the dupe.

Not only the blatant exaggerations of the world which knew nothing and the strictures of his friend who knew too much, the frosty displeasure of his sister and the embarrassed annoyance of Hermione, troubled the vicar's peace at this time, but anonymous letters flew about like tongues of fire, and made that which was already bad still worse than need be. More than one was sent to the vicar accusing him of shameful deeds that would not bear translating into speech; and more than one was sent even to poor Theresa, ill and perhaps even now dying as she was known to be. An expert might have made out a family likeness to the little chandler's weekly bills for soap and oil and candles ; but the writing was cleverly disguised, and there were no caligraphic experts at Crossholme. As it was they came in with the general difficulties and disagreeables of the time ; and though they chafed the proud nature of the English gentleman as well as the autocratic priest, yet they had to be borne ; and all things are "lived down" at last, thought Mr. Lascelles.

Meanwhile the talk grew and grew, and the feeling raised thereby was more bitter and yet more bitter in the minds of those who had not given in to the new movement, though it brought the phalanx of believers into apparently a still closer, more compact, more solid body. But to those who were against the whole thing these vile reports and shameless commentaries were a weapon which they did not scruple to use. Things went so far that one day when the vicar was passing Tom Moorhead's forge a word came hissing out with the sparks from the iron that struck his ear with a sense of burning ; and some one standing by the fire laughed brutally. He stopped, turned back, and stepped inside the threshold.

"Good day, my men," he said with clerical abruptness. " Is there anyone here among you that belongs to God?"

It was a bold thing to do ; but boldness takes in England, and some of the men answered him respectfully enough ; if Tom himself, standing there in the ruddy light, with his bushy red beard turned to flame and his brawny arms bare to the shoulder, gave the horse-shoe which he was forging a vicious blow as if he had had the vicar's head between and answered bluffly :

" I don't know what you mean by belonging to God, master. If you mean do we belong to that rag and doll shop of yours, I take it that we don't, and we don't wish to neither."

" All in good time, Tom," said the vicar cheerily, standing there in the doorway erect, unruffled, speckless, the beau ideal of the high-caste priest !—" You are too honest a fellow in your own way to be let to go to perdition. The grace which turned Saul the persecutor into Paul the Apostle will some day draw you too from the darkness to the light."

" No, sir, it won't. I'm a fossil, I am," said Tom with a jeering laugh. " You can't change a fossil !"

" No," returned the vicar quickly. " You can only clear him from his crust. That is something, is it not,

'A word came hissing out with the sparks.'

my man?—clean him round the edges, scrape away all that mass of limestone and chalk in which he is embedded, and make him come to his best. Even fossils, you see, Tom, can be done something with by care; and the Power which created can restore."

"Ah, the jingle goes well!" said Tom, turning his back rudely; "but it don't get over me. Come mates, bear a hand! I have my work to do, and can't stand chopping logic with this gentleman all day."

"Well, I will not detain you any longer," said the vicar with perfect composure. "You are busy now, I see. Good day, Tom. Good day, my men. Remember what I always have to tell you—the awful choice between good and evil, time and eternity, heaven and hell, that you are called on to make and are now making. Let each man among you put this question to himself solemnly :—'What have I chosen? which am I choosing?' Good day. God be with you all."

"Come mates! dang it all!" cried Tom impatiently, "this balderdash has lasted long enough. It may do for a few foolish wenches as have nothing else to think of, but it won't go down with us. We are men, and have learned in quite another school. Here, Jim, bear a hand and look sharp!"

But some of the men said : " Good day, sir,"
humanely, as the vicar turned ; and no one again flung
out that shameful word as he passed—so far recognizing
his English courage in bearding the surliest lion of them
all in his den.

END OF THE SECOND VOLUME.

LONDON : PRINTED BY
SPOTTISWOODE AND CO., NEW-STREET SQUARE
AND PARLIAMENT STREET

'They were seated side by side on the couch at the feet of the bed.'

Under which Lord?

BY

E. LYNN LINTON

AUTHOR OF 'THE WORLD WELL LOST' 'PATRICIA KEMBALL' ETC.

IN THREE VOLUMES

VOL. III.

WITH TWELVE ILLUSTRATIONS BY ARTHUR HOPKINS

London

CHATTO & WINDUS, PICCADILLY

1879

' Because we have found not yet
  Any way for the world to follow
  Save only that ancient way;
Whosoever forsake or forget,
  Whose faith soever be hollow,
  Whose hope soever grow grey

Monotones : Songs before Sunrise

CONTENTS

OF THE

THIRD VOLUME.

LIST OF ILLUSTRATIONS

TO THE

THIRD VOLUME.

UNDER WHICH LORD?

CHAPTER I.

THE LAST APPEAL.

ALL this disgraceful turmoil about Theresa Molyneux
and the Honourable and Reverend Launcelot Lascelles
was perhaps more painful to Ringrove Hardisty than to
any other. He had the honest Englishman's sensitive
pride in the purity of the women who were his friends;
and the fair fame of girls whom he had known from their
infancy and who were in a manner like his sisters—the
only version of sisters that he had—was specially dear to
him.

To make it the harder for him now, a few years ago
there had been certain tentative little passages between
him and Theresa. She had fancied herself in love with
him when she came home from school; and she had
shown what she felt too clearly to be mistaken. He had

been struck by her prettiness, flattered by her preference, and in consequence had wandered round her for a short time, asking himself if it would do, and was she really his assigned half? Finally he decided that she was not; and that a temperament which gave before being asked to give, was not that which he most desired in his wife. Still, he always had for her that certain tenderness and secret sense of possession which a man feels for a woman of whom he has dreamt; and his indignation was the more bitter now because of that short time of hesitation and virtual ownership, when he had laid a few flowers of thought and fancy on the altar where the vicar had lighted such a consuming fire.

Like everyone else, he understood the true state of things, and how the religion which expressed itself in hysterics and nervous exaltation was simply the passion of love under another name. And also like everyone else not committed to ritualism blindfold, he knew that Theresa had been led into this state of semi-madness by the spiritual philandering with which a celibate priesthood enforces dogmatic teaching, and that Mr. Lascelles had made love to her after his own manner. Whether that manner had been crafty and undeclared, or open and confessed, it had been love-making all the same; and to

Ringrove and some others the vicar stood as the responsible author of all the mischief.

But this was too delicate a thing for him to touch.
Women, maternal and other, may take girls to task for
their folly; and fatherly men may say a word in season,
of not too direct a kind, against that sleeve-wearing of
the heart which attracts the daws; but what can a young
fellow do? especially if the lines are not laid in his own
country—if the one implicated is out of his beat both
for age and knowledge, so that he cannot drop hints
about undesirable habits and knows nothing of any
damnatory antecedents, both of which well handled may
be made useful as checks and refrigerators? A young
man cannot go to a girl of his own age and say: "My
dear, you are making a fool of yourself with the vicar or
the curate—the captain or the lieutenant, and all the
world is laughing at you." And even straightforward
Ringrove felt this, and knew that it was not possible for
him to lecture Theresa or advise her, to reprove or to
enlighten her.

But if he could not do this, he could speak to Hermione
and Virginia; and under cover of deprecating their friend's
folly and deploring the scandal that it had occasioned,
perhaps he might do them some little good, and open

to the hateful truth, as he saw it, the dear eyes which were so fast shut now,

He saw very little of either mother or daughter in these sad later times ; only at the Sunday morning service. When he called at the Abbey as he still did—often—they were sure to be out or engaged, and he had to content himself with Richard's company only. The two men indeed were discarded with impartial severity by the women to whom fanaticism was dearer than love ; and if Richard was held to be the Man of Sin, Ringrove took rank as his younger brother.

But a man's love bears a tremendous strain when put to it ; and to Ringrove as to Richard, these beloved ones were not so much to be blamed as pitied. It was to both as it would have been had they believed in possession. A grievous thing truly, that those fair bodies should be made the strongholds of fiends ; but it was by no fault that they had been so disastrously invested. It was only a question of relative strength and weakness ; and the Evil One is so strong !

It was just about noon when Ringrove entered the drawing-room of the Abbey, and sent in his name to Mrs. Fullerton and Virginia who were in Virginia's room upstairs.

"Shall we see him?" asked Hermione, looking perplexed and a little frightened.

At this moment they were seated side by side on the couch at the foot of the bed; watching the maid who was packing a small portmanteau of Virginia's with linen; only with linen. No girlish possessions dating from childish times and sacred as the first beginnings of private property were added; no pretty trinkets nor personal adornments; no favourite books of poetry, nor photographs of home or friends, nor any vestige of finery:—only linen. The crucifix before which those fervent daily prayers were said with so much holy zeal, so much mistaken application—some books of devotion and that queer collection of sacred rubbish which even her mother must not see nor handle, given her with such pomp of reverence by Father Truscott— this was all that was being packed up in the little portmanteau which her father had given her two years ago; everything else was renounced and left like the old loves and the old life.

"Yes, mamma," said Virginia after a short pause: "let us see him. It can do no harm, and I should like to say good-bye to him and to part good friends."

"Oh! we must be always good friends with him, in a way—unless we are forbidden; I hope though that we shall not be. It makes so much talk in the place when things come to a public breakdown," said Hermione with an unwonted burst of good sense.

"We ought not to mind that," returned Virginia, always on the side of uncompromising sincerity.

"After all, Ringrove is a good fellow!" said Hermione, with a strangely kind accent. "Had he been a good Churchman he would have been a splendid creature!"

"Yes; but it is just that if!" said Virginia with a sigh.

Mother and daughter were in an abnormal state to-day; and both were of softer mood towards outside sinners than their Directors allowed, or they themselves thought right. Though no tears had come to their eyes they were very close with each; and had they not been restrained by the sense of sinfulness and the carnal creature, should they mourn for the joyful event that was now at hand, they would have clung to each other weeping with the illogical sorrow of women who have wilfully undertaken to carry an unnecessary cross by which they give pain to themselves and to others, under the mistaken idea that what is unnatural and disagreeable is right, what is loving and pleasant is wrong.

The maid, less controlled and on a lower level of holiness altogether, was weeping bitterly; and it did not mend matters when Virginia, laying her hand on her shoulder, said in a low sweet voice, while her face was as it were illumined by a kind of inner light:

"Don't cry, Mary. Why should you? I am going away only for the sake of truth and holiness. There is nothing to make anyone unhappy in this?"

"But the first time as you have left home alone, Miss, and no one to do your hair or see to your things!" said Mary, crying more because of the exhortation. "You will be lost, away by yourself. It seems as if you would never come back again!"

"As for doing things for myself I shall not have much to do, as you know, Mary," answered Virginia kindly. "And my hair—that is very easily done now!"

"Yes, indeed it is!" sighed Mary ruefully; grudging the conversion which had cost her young mistress all that artistic elaboration which would have made her "look so pretty." "As you say, there's not so much to do now, the way you wear it; still, I like to have the handling of it myself."

"So you will, Mary! Miss Fullerton will be home again in ten days from this," said Hermione, looking to her daughter with a smile; but Virginia had turned away at that moment and was arranging something on the table.

"Well! I suppose we must go down and see Ringrove," then said Hermione. "You know what to do, Mary. Come, Virginia!—it is getting nearly luncheon-time. Shall I ask him to stay, dear? I will do just as you like."

"Yes," said Virginia. "It will be better for papa."

Her lip quivered as she said this; but she mastered herself by that strange power which had come to her of late—the power by which all feeling was controlled, all expression repressed, all thought concealed; and then they went downstairs—to receive as an act of Christian liberality the man who had once been the familiar friend and favourite guest of the house; by the wishes of the parents and the fitness of things appointed to be one day the holder of all, Virginia herself included.

"How glad I am to find you at home!" said Ringrove joyously, going forward to meet them as they came into the room, his face aglow with pleasure and his look and bearing that of old times, rather than belonging to the new order of things. "I have seen so little of you of late!" he added with the loving regret which is such sweet flattery when received by love!

"That is not our fault," said Hermione gently, but with meaning in her reproach.

"Nor mine," he answered. "I have called here so often!—but you were never at home."

"We have so much to do out of doors," she returned.

"I wish I saw more of you—as I used in old times before I had offended you," said Ringrove, looking at Virginia.

"Then why do you not?" asked Hermione. "It is your own doing, Ringrove. You have cut yourself off from us. If you had been good and what you ought to have been, there would never have been this separation. And if you had liked us as much as you used to say, you would not have deserted us as you have done. Had your friendship been what I once believed it was, you would have gone with us in our new life, and have become a good Churchman as you ought. It would have given both Virginia and myself so much real happiness to have counted you as one of us. But you had not enough friendship for us even to make the trial!"

"Dear Mrs. Fullerton, this is scarcely just! You know how truly I have always loved both you and Virginia!"

Ringrove spoke with more agitation than he could conceal.

"Then why did you not come over with us?" asked Hermione. "We did not wish you to do anything wrong. We only wanted you to become a good man and lead a religious life, as you ought to do."

"But how could I make one of a party which I look on as the enemy of national liberty and intellectual progress?" he said. "I could not join the clerical party here, dearest Mrs. Fullerton. All the manly conscience and English feeling that I have are dead against it. I think and always have thought priestly domination the most disastrous of all the tyrannies that the world has ever seen. So how could I, as you say, go over to your side?"

"Conscience!—your pride and want of faith, your self-will and undutiful disobedience, you mean. Call things by their right names, Ringrove. We shall understand each other better then."

Hermione said this harsh-sounding speech in the sweetest voice and with the tenderest face and accent possible. It was an established formula rather than a personal accusation—something that she had been taught rather than had reasoned out for herself; as when believers say generally that men become sceptics that they may have freer license to do evil—that they may give way to their passions without fear of punishment—

banishing God out of their world because they are afraid of Judgment.

He smiled.

"Not quite so bad as that!" he said lightly; then more gravely : "Do you seriously think, Mrs. Fullerton, that any man who knows the world can give in to a system which produces such results as that of last Sunday?"

"Ah, poor Theresa!" she answered compassionately, but with unmistakable contempt. "We must not judge of things from her. She has always been excitable and hysterical, and lately she has been overworking herself and taxing her strength too heavily. And after all, Ringrove, an hysterical attack even at prayers, lamentable as it is, is not like a sin of intention, and must not be laid to the charge of the Church."

"No, but it supplies the answer of those who refuse to give in to the new order of things," he said. "When we see, as we do, these priests as you call them, making women in love with them under the name of religion, you cannot expect that men like myself, for instance, should be desirous to strengthen their hands."

He spoke boldly, but all the same he knew that he was touching the shallows, skirting perilously close to danger.

Virginia flushed painfully, and a look partly of repulsion, partly of terror, came on her face.

" It is horrible to hear you say such things, Ringrove," she said. " Because one sick girl is over-excitable, is the whole faith and practice of holiness to be slandered? To speak of these vile things in connexion with the Church and her priests is worse than shameful! Do you give these unholy thoughts and motives to us all? Oh it makes me weary of the world!" she added with strange passion, clasping her hands to her forehead—" this wicked and slanderous world, where even the saints are not respected!"

" I ascribe nothing to *you*, Virginia, but what is perfectly sweet, pure, and holy," answered Ringrove with indescribable tenderness, but always bold and direct. " But then you are not as other girls. You know that I think this; and you know this too, Mrs. Fullerton," turning to Hermione ; " I have never hidden from you my hope in the future, nor the depth and truth of my love for Virginia."

" Hush ! hush !" cried Virginia. " It is a sin for me to hear this !"

" How can it be a sin?" asked Ringrove. " Why should you not be loved, Virginia, as any other woman, and told so like any other? The faithful love of an honest man cannot be a sin, nor yet a degradation!"

"You may not care to hear it, dear, but there is no sin in poor Ringrove's love for you. Superior himself did not say there was!" Hermione said this with a flash of her old self—her old sympathy with romance and human passion. She was stirred more than she herself knew by Ringrove's honest fervour, and wished for the moment that Virginia would listen to him. There was no harm in it, and there might be good.

"It is a sin to me," said Virginia with a kind of horror which even her mother did not understand and which to Ringrove was simply like madness.

"Oh! that I could clear your mind of all this terrible hallucination!" he said passionately. "There is no reason in it, Virginia! it is not worthy of your good sense! That you do not love me, and do not care to listen to me, I can understand; that it should be a sin to you my saying how much I love you—that surely is the mere folly, the mere pedantry, of reserve!"

"You do not understand," she said, turning away in a hopeless manner. "No one understands!"

"Perhaps only too well," he answered with a sigh. "But hear me, Virginia. I have loved you too long and faithfully not to have earned the right to speak, and you need not be afraid of me. What I have borne for all these years I can go on bearing, if it is your absolute will;—for you have been the one central thought of my life for a longer time than you know of. I shall never forget you as I first saw you when I came home from the Continent, coming up the steps while I stood at the door, holding your blue frock back from your feet, your face a little raised—looking at me with pleasure then !—your shining hair like gold about your head—exactly like the little Virgin at Venice! I knew then what a lovely womanhood yours would be; as pure and beautiful as hers ! "

Virginia shuddered and hastily crossed herself.

" This is blasphemy ! " she said in an awestruck voice.

" Why do you say that, dear? Whatever else your belief makes her, was she not a woman like any other ? " he asked. " What blasphemy is there in saying that an innocent little girl reminded me of a picture of her own girlhood, or that a lovely womanhood is of the same type as hers ? "

"She was more than woman," said Virginia in a reverent voice. " She was the Divine Mother, and it is a sin to liken anyone to her."

"Ah Virginia ! what a world of fanciful sin you make for yourself !" he said with manly pity. "There is no harm in this, at least not in my eyes, or those of anyone not bound and fettered by false reverence. I would not say it if I thought it wrong, but I will not again if it pains you. I want only to tell you now, before your mother, what I have felt and thought for all these years. No ! do not turn from me, Virginia ! Let me speak straight to the point, if for the last time ! "

"Let him speak, dear," said Hermione in a low voice. "He is a good man, Virginia ; and if he does love you so much, you may yet win him over to the Church."

Virginia mentally repeated a prayer to the Holy Virgin as a safeguard against what she felt to be the sin of the moment, and when she had finished she raised her mild eyes with a half-sad, half-weary look.

"You can say what you like, Ringrove," she said with the feeling of one performing penance. "I will listen to you patiently. Perhaps, as mamma says, I ought."

"Thank you !" Ringrove answered tenderly ; not seeing below the surface and only grateful for the opportunity of speaking. Perhaps too—for who can limit the miraculous power of love ?—he might turn her heart to him by the very force of his own love for her. "What you were as a young girl," he went on to say, " made me believe that when you were older you would be as you are, dear—my ideal of what a true woman should be. I knew that if you were I should love you as I do love you; and I hoped, and at one time believed, that you would learn to love me. I watched you as you grew up, and saw you always the same—gentle, patient, conscientious, truthful, without a particle of vanity or pretence in you, and only desirous to do what was right; and I thought that if I were not good enough for you—what man would be!— I could still make you happy, and be a true and loving husband to you. Your father was on my side, and so at one time was this dear mother; and with two such advocates it did not seem to me that the thing was hopeless. You should have been so happy! I would have lived only for you, and to keep you from all sorrow. I would have loved you so well! And the faithful love of an honest man is worth something to a woman, even though he may not be so good or pure as she," said Ringrove Hardisty with that noble simplicity of self-assertion which belongs to manly men conscious of their power, and which for the most part charms womanly women.

"I would have been glad at the time—very glad," said

Hermione softly ; " and I would be glad now, Ringrove, if you were a good Churchman."

" I am a Churchman," said Ringrove ; "what else can you call me ? "

" A Protestant !" murmured Hermione, in a voice of plaintive condemnation.

" Whether good or not, is another question ; but, such as I am, I would have guarded her from every breath of evil as carefully as I would have kept her from all sorrow. She should never have known more of the world's sins than she knows now, and less of artificial evil. You should have been surrounded by love and honour," he continued, turning again to Virginia ; " and all that was best in myself should have been my tribute to your purity. I would have been your protector and you should have been my good angel. We should have done the best thing that anyone can do for the world—have made a perfect home and lived a noble life ; and we should have been happy in each other, and would have done more good to our kind than we can fairly compute. You would have been an example to the whole county, a standard of womanly excellence, living the true life of woman in the quiet activities of home. Your influence would have been unbounded; for who can limit the influence of a pure woman living the honest natural life of wife and mother? And I should have been a better man than I shall ever be now without you! And all this hope—all this grand life—has been destroyed, for what? If you had been born a Roman Catholic I should not have wondered so much, however sorry I might have been. You would then have been, in all probability, a nun by choice ; but, as it is, yours is a lost life "——

"No, no ! gained !" murmured Virginia.

" —When it might have been one as beautiful, as perfect, as anything that the noblest poet could imagine ! "

Virginia turned pale and red by turns.

" You allow that it would have been my vocation to be a nun had I been a Catholic?" she asked in a strange voice.

" Yes ; and as a Catholic I would have respected your choice," he answered ; " though as a Catholic I should have deplored the false view of goodness which takes from active life the purest and finest natures to shut them up in a living tomb where they can do no good to anyone ! "

" We are the last in the world to uphold the Romish Church with all its errors of doctrine and superstition," said Hermione speaking as she had been taught. " But

you must in fairness allow us Anglicans the same vocation."

He shook his head.

"No, I do not," he said gently. "A woman can do
better for herself and the world than by incarcerating
herself and renouncing all practical usefulness. A
mother is of more value than a nun."

For a moment Virginia did not speak; then she
turned to Ringrove with a certain kind of decision in
her very frankness that was more convincing than her
mere words.

"Thank you for all your goodness to me," she said,
her voice low and calm without a quiver of faltering in
it; "but no man could have ever had my deepest love :
—that belongs only to God and my Church. I have
always liked you, as you know, but I do not think I
could have ever loved you had things even remained as
they were ; and now we are as far as the poles asunder."

"Virginia, is it quite impossible?" said Hermione, in
a moved voice.

"This is your last deliberate word, Virginia? You
reject my love and all that it would give you—all that
you could do for me and society as my wife—for this
pale imitation of Papistry—this playing at Roman

Catholicism?" asked Ringrove, standing like one who expects the death signal.

"Mine is not a pale imitation, nor a mere play," she answered, lowering her eyes.

"How can it be anything else?" he said with his naïve frankness and ignorance of esoteric meanings. "You are not a Roman Catholic, and what else but imitation and mockery is all this assumption of Roman Catholicism by the High Church party?"

"Let that part of it alone," Virginia answered again, speaking more hurriedly than was usual with her. "You were talking of yourself not of me. All I have to say is, I do renounce all that you have offered me, as all that the world could give me anywhere, for the greater gain of my choice."

"For ever, without hope of change, Virginia?"

"For ever, and I can never change!" she returned. She held out her hand. "We part as friends, Ringrove," she said; "but we do part. This is good-bye."

Ringrove did not answer. He took her hand and carried it reverently to his lips; then abruptly left his seat and went to the window, looking out into the garden. A dead silence fell among them all, and Hermione, who was crying, found herself wishing that Virginia had just one little corner left unconverted—one little corner which Ringrove Hardisty might have possessed.

Soon after this Ringrove left, though Hermione asked him to stay quite affectionately and like her old self, having for the moment forgotten all her artificial displeasure with him, and only sorry that Virginia was so set in her renunciation ; and though Virginia too said : " Will you not ? " kindly and as if she really meant it.   He felt that the strain would be more than he could well bear, and one which it was of no use to bear ; so he put aside both entreaties, and took his hat from the table where he had laid it.

" Another day, not now," he said huskily ; but when he said this Virginia did not look up, though her mother, glancing at her with slight surprise as well as a kind of entreaty to unbend for just this once, smiled in his face and repeated prettily :

" Yes, another day ; after Virginia is confirmed."

The luncheon to-day was slightly less miserably dull than was the law with all the meals—that is, the meeting times of the husband and father with his wife and daughter.   Certainly Virginia was scarcely able even to pretend to eat, but she was not so deadly cold in her manner to her father, and Hermione, secretly much dis-

turbed in spite of her Director's influence, was more
gentle and less reserved to her husband than was usual
with her of late. Not much was said however; only the
spirit of the hour was different, owing to that certain
perturbation which somewhat marred the consciousness
of triumph and successful wilfulness—that weak feeling
of natural compassion for the sinner for whom the thong
had been so cleverly knotted.

"Are you inclined to come with me to Starton? I
am riding over; will you come with me?" asked Richard
of Virginia. Keenly alive as he was now to every change
with these two beloved rebels, he felt the softer mood of
the moment; and he was weak enough to think he could
profit by it.

Mother and daughter exchanged looks.

"I do not think I can, papa, to-day," said Virginia,
not looking at him.

"I want Virginia to come with me," said Hermione,
also not looking at him.

"I am sorry. It is a fine day, and a ride would do
Virginia good," he said. "You seldom use your horse
now," he added to his daughter. "Seldom?—never, I
should say."

"I do not care for riding," said Virginia evasively;
"and I have to go with mamma."

"Where are you going?" he asked.

It was not suspicion which prompted this question; it was only interest.

"We have business that you would scarcely feel any sympathy for," said Hermione, quite gently and amicably.

He sighed.

"I suppose not," he said; "if it is the old thing."

"When are you going to Starton?" his wife asked, as if she too were merely interested in a friend's movements.

"In about half an hour's time. I have first to go to Lane End to see the new cottages, and then I shall ride over to the town. Is there any chance of meeting you and Virginia there?" a little eagerly.

"I do not know yet; we may," she answered, while Virginia turned pale and crossed herself faintly.

"Well, I must be off, I suppose," said Richard, rising reluctantly. This small approach to a new spirit was very precious to him. He did not like to break up a meeting that had more of the flavour of old time about it than had been the case for many weeks now.

"Yes, it is time too that we were going," said Hermione, looking at the clock, and rising. "Good-bye till we meet again."

She spoke quite softly, and Richard's face, which of

late had grown thin and worn and haggard, turned to
her with a sudden gladness that almost transformed it.

"Good-bye, my dear," he said ; "till we meet again.
Good-bye, my Virginia."

"Good-bye, papa," answered Virginia.

Impulsively he held out his hand to her. He
had never been able to reconcile himself to the
child's coldness, almost less than to Hermione's
withdrawal.

Virginia went up to him and put her hand in his.

"Have you come to give me a kiss?" he asked, a
little taken out of himself by this sudden surrender. He
had lived so long now in such strict excommunication by
wife and daughter that their gentleness to-day went near
to unman him.

"Yes, papa," she said, and held up her face as she
used when a child.

He caught her to his heart and kissed her forehead
tenderly.

"My Ladybird ! my little darling !" he half whispered.
" Ah then you have still some love left for your father ! "

"And my prayers, papa !" she answered, flinging
herself into his arms with a passionate pressure as strange
as all the rest.

" Your prayers will do me no harm, my darling," he said ; "but your love will give me new life ! "

" Papa ! say that you value my prayers for your soul!" she pleaded as if for very life.

"As expressions of your love for me? yes, my darling ! " he answered.

"No ! no ! as possible means of grace and true en- lightenment ! " she said.

He smiled a little sadly, and shook his head.

" Your love is all I want, my Virginia—yours and your dear mother's. That is the best means of grace that you can offer me. Give me back all that you have taken from me—or seemed to have taken from me of late—and you will do more for me than any number of prayers could do ! "

"I do love you, papa," said Virginia with strange solemnity. "But because I love you, I must pray for you ! "

At this moment Jones came into the room.

" Please, sir, the horse is at the door, and John Graves is in the study and wants to speak to you for a moment," he said.

" I will come," returned Richard quietly ; but he was sorry for the interruption ; and as the men began to clear the table, no more was to be said or done at that moment.

He turned his mild kind thoughtful face once more to his wife, and from her to their child.

"Till we meet again," he said smiling.

Virginia did not answer. Had she tried to speak her voice would have failed her ; and Hermione, whose eyes were full of tears, made a little inclination with her head and murmured something that stood for a friendly fare-well—till they all should meet again. And then in a short time, John Graves and his business being ended, they watched the poor unconscious victim of coming sorrow mount his horse and ride slowly down the avenue.

"Poor papa! I hope he will not be very angry," said Hermione compassionately. "I am afraid he will; but it is only for a short time. You will be home in eight days from this."

"I hope it will not be very sad for you, mamma," said Virginia, clasping her mother's hand with a close nervous pressure.

"I will do my best, dear," said her mother; "and you will be back so soon! It is not worth making a fuss about; but, of course, I shall miss you and the Sister terribly. Still—a week soon passes, does it not?"

" Yes," said Virginia constrainedly.

" And it was what Superior so much desired," continued Hermione. " As soon as your confirmation was decided on he had set his heart on your going into Retreat:—and so had Father Truscott."

" Yes," said Virginia, still more constrainedly.

" So now let us go upstairs. It is a pity that papa is going to Starton too to-day ; but we will take the low road—he always takes the high ; and perhaps we shall not see him. It would be awkward if we did."

" Let us go now ! He will not have finished at Lane End yet," said Virginia. " And perhaps the Sister and Father Truscott are waiting for us."

" Very well! come !" said Hermione briskly, as if trying to shake off the depression which would cling in spite of herself.

They went upstairs together and dressed themselves quickly. The small portmanteau was already packed, and in a few moments' time the carriage would come round.

" Superior wished me to say this prayer, dear," said Hermione, coming into her daughter's room with a written paper in her hand.

Virginia was already kneeling at her faldstool, praying earnestly, but like one in the very extremity of pain.

Had she been a martyr enduring the worst conceivable agony for the truth's sake, she could not have looked more grievously tortured, more pitifully anguished.

" Don't, Virginia ! don't look like that ! " cried Hermione, falling into a sudden passion of tears. " It is only for a week, darling ! " she repeated. " Think how soon a week will pass ! and how much spiritual good you will get at C——."

" Mamma ! pray to our Lord to help me ! " cried Virginia, clinging to her mother convulsively.

" Yes, let us both ask for help ! " was the answer ; and in a broken voice Hermione recited the prayer which Mr. Lascelles had sent her, asking the Divine blessing on the step which her daughter was taking—that step of obedience to a Director and disobedience to a father—of adhesion to a creed and deception to her parents, which was assumed worthy of special approbation. Then, the prayer ended, they both rose, and still clinging hand in hand went down the stairs and entered the carriage where the portmanteau was already stowed.

" To the Starton station," said Hermione to the astonished man. " Go by the low road, and drive fast."

Not a word was spoken for the whole five miles. Each had to keep up her courage and to quiet her natural conscience which would make itself heard only too clearly in spite of the artificial sophistries that had done so much to obscure its native purity. To each, falsehood, deceit, treachery was abhorrent; yet at this moment both were dealing deceitfully, both were false and treacherous alike. Taught by that fatal school which maintains that the end justifies the means—that the faithful must perfect their work at all cost of morality, of humanity—that infidels and atheists are accursed and to be dealt with as the enemies of God and man alike—that honesty is sinful, while crooked dealing is holiness if that honesty would check superstition and that crooked dealing encourage it—both had become warped from the first uprightness of their lives; and now when they stood face to face with certain consequences they were sorrowful and secretly ashamed. Hermione was betraying her husband, Virginia was betraying both father and mother; but the Director of each had assured his penitent that she was doing well, and that God and the Church approved; and with this assurance each was now striving to quiet her conscience and content her soul—and finding the task hard.

The time passed, and the station was at last reached, without mishap of undesirable meeting by the way; and at the station they found Mr. Lascelles and Sister Agnes, Father Truscott and Cuthbert Molyneux waiting to receive them and to ensure the carrying out of the design on hand.

" Just in time ! " said the courtly vicar smiling, when the two pale, half-frightened women came on the platform as the train rounded the curve.   " But a near thing ! "

" Good-bye, dear Virginia ! " said her mother, kissing her hastily.   She dared not show any feeling before those who were watching her so closely.   " In a week's time, remember ! I shall be very dull till you come back ! "

" But you do not grudge her? " asked Sister Agnes slowly and with meaning.

" No ! no ! indeed not ! but she must come back in a week's time ! " repeated Hermione, finding comfort in the definiteness of the time allotted.

Virginia kissed her mother, but neither spoke nor wept. The Sister held her cold hand firmly, almost cruelly clasped ; and Father Truscott whispered in her ear : " For the Blessed Virgin and her honour ! "

After she had, as it seemed, wished her good-bye finally, Virginia turned back to her mother as if to speak to her—to kiss her once again ; but the Sister, ever watchful, drew her with a firm hand to the carriage.   " No looking back, child ! " she said ; while Father Truscott, under guise of help, lifted her bodily from the ground and set her in the carriage. Then the doors were shut, the bell was rung, the whistle sounded, and the train moved out of the station.

" Our Mother's chosen child ! " said Sister Agnes with her silky smile.

" Child, you have left the darkness of error and are now going into the light and the truth ! " said Father Truscott with more sincerity of fervour ; while Virginia, feeling as if her heart would break, carried her sin as a cross and her sorrow as a sin, and asked to be supported through the one and forgiven for the other. It was for the good of souls—her own and others—and for the glory of God that the thing had been done. The Father of Lies was draped in shining garments for the occasion ; and the life of deceit through which she had been led for so long now was, according to her instructors, a pious fraud which the wickedness of others had necessitated and the holiness of the end justified.

CHAPTER II.

TO ITS LOGICAL CONCLUSION.

"AND the child—where is Virginia?" asked Richard, as his wife came into the room alone.

Since the new order of things mother and daughter kept· always together, with a certain sense of mutual support and countenance against this soul-destroying infidel of theirs, whose influence they feared with the fear of old-time love and indestructible respect ; and to see one without the other was strange.

"She is with Sister Agnes," said Hermione, trying to speak with indifference.

She was very pale, and her indifference was a little too strongly accentuated to be real.

"I am sorry," he returned slowly. "Will she be late?"

"I do not know exactly," answered Hermione from among the music-books where she was making·believe to search for something, so that her face should not be seen, and the nervousness in her voice might be somewhat veiled by distance.

Of course she knew that her husband must be told the truth sooner or later ; but, as she and Mr. Lascelles had agreed, the later the better. If he could be kept quiet for this evening it would give the pious runaways a still longer start should he determine on following them ; for by the time he could reach London Virginia would be safely homed in the House of Retreat at C——, whence she must be taken by main force and the police if taken at all ; and Richard would naturally think twice before he made such a scandal as this.

"Are you sure that Virginia is quite well?" he asked after a short silence and when Hermione, thinking the times now safe and the subject dropped, had come back from turning over the music-books.

"Dear me, yes!" she answered, still trying to speak with light indifference.

"To my eyes not. She is as changed in body as in mind," he said with a deep sigh. "Her new friends and their absurd practices, of which I probably know less than half, have had a disastrous influence on her."

He looked at his wife with some reproach. She did not answer. She was thinking with dread of the time when he would have to know that other half of the truth.

"What is she doing to-night?" he asked. "Any new vagary?"

"Not that I know of," said Hermione, not resenting the phrase as she would have done had her conscience been clear. But her face betrayed the trouble of her mind, and seemed to show that more was hidden than had been expressed.

With a sudden flash of what was real terror Richard remembered Virginia's strange emotion, Hermione's unwonted softness of this afternoon ; and now this studied indifference, which of itself confessed embarrassment. What did it all mean? What new disgrace was in store for him? what further sorrowful perversion for them?

"Something is wrong with you and the child," he said suddenly. "Tell me what it is."

"There is nothing wrong," she answered with a deep blush.

"Look at me, Hermione," he said gravely and sternly.

She raised her eyes and tried to meet his, but she could not. She looked just up to the knot of his cravat.

"How can you be so silly, Richard?" she said with a nervous little laugh, her delicate lips strained and quivering.

Deceitful as she had become through the fatal doctrine of "reserve," she was still candid at heart ; and when closely pressed, as now, her nature asserted itself.

" There is something wrong," said Richard again. " You cannot look in my face, Hermione, and I know yours. Tell me the truth frankly. This double-dealing is so strange in you who were once the very soul of honour and sincerity, I cannot reconcile myself to it. Come, speak to me honestly. What is this about Virginia ? Why is she not here to-night ? "

" I suppose I had better tell you now at once," returned Hermione, her confusion deepening, and her inability to stand examination overcoming her promise to Superior. " It is all the same whether I tell you now or after," she continued, arguing the matter aloud ; " and really there is nothing so very much to tell. Virginia has only gone away with Sister Agnes for a week's Retreat at C—— ; that is all. Nothing so very formidable, you see."

Again she laughed affectedly, and again her small sweet lips were strained and quivering.

For the first time in his life Richard felt something like contempt for this dearly loved wife of his. Hitherto his love had been of that quiet unobservant kind which

is characteristic of a constant temperament and an
occupied mind.   He loved her ; and there he stopped.
He asked himself why, no more than he asked himself
why the sunshine was delightful to him or the flowers
were beautiful.   She was part of his life, her perfect beauty
of mind and body part of the existing order of things ;
and not to love her, not to believe in her without further
examination, not to imagine her free from fault or blemish,
would have been until now impossible.   Her worth and
moral loveliness were as absolutely settled, as arbitrarily
proved in his mind, as the revelations of the spectroscope.
It was not a thing to debate about ; it was a question
closed and done with.   But now at this moment there
swept across his mind a bitter kind of disdainful pity for
her weakness and duplicity, which at one time would
have been as impossible for him to feel as that he should
have deliberately injured or publicly insulted her.   As he
looked at her she seemed to be almost some one else.
Was she indeed Hermione, the beloved of his youth,
the trusted of his maturity ?   She who could not look in
his face, who could not even lie bravely and who dared
not tell the truth ?—she who had lent herself to this pitiful
farce of kindly pretence at the very moment when she
knew that she was doing that which would stab him to

the heart? He did not know which was the more painful
—his daughter's disobedience or his wife's falsehood.

"So! this was the meaning of the little comedy played
off on me to-day," he said with a bitter laugh, as strange
from him as was Hermione's duplicity from her. "I
might have known that it was only a blind for something
even worse than had yet been done. I ought to have
known; and yet I was weak enough to hope that you and
the child had come back to your better selves, and did
really feel something of the tenderness you were pretending. Well! you have had your laugh against me;
and I bear the sting of the disappointment and the shame
of the insult."

"You have no right to speak like this," said Hermione
half in tears, and as much pained that he should doubt
her when she had been sincere as if she had never
betrayed him when he had trusted her. "Both Virginia
and I were really grieved to be obliged to deceive you,
though only for a few hours. But we knew that you
would not have given your consent had we asked it, so we
thought it better to say nothing about it till it was done.',

"And the knowledge that you were offending me
counted for nothing with you? You never stopped to
ask yourselves whether you were doing right or wrong in

thus defying as well as deceiving me? You, my wife, had no scruples in helping my child to disobey me?"

Never in her life before had Hermione been spoken to by her husband in this tone and manner. If the sudden revelation of her duplicity had transformed her to him, this bewildering severity did the same for him to her.

"It was for the good of her own soul and in the service of the Church. That makes everything lawful," said Hermione, looking down.

"You are right, Hermione! In the service of a lie, falsehood—in the service of tyranny, cruelty—in the service of superstition, ignorance. You are quite right! I see you understand your formula and can state it with admirable precision. You do credit to your teacher!"

"I do not understand you," said Hermione with a curious mixture of fear and anger.

"How should you?" he answered with the same manner of bitter mockery, of angry scorn. "You understand Mr. Lascelles; and I can scarcely credit you with such catholicity of sympathy as would enable you to compass the two extremes of character. Naturally you do not understand me; you are in too close sympathy with him for that. And if I regret the change in your feelings

I do not regret the apportionment. Whatever else I may be I am at least an honest man, and scarcely desire to run curricle in your esteem with such an incarnate lie as Mr. Lascelles ! "

" Richard ! " she exclaimed with indignation in her tone, her look, her attitude. But whether it was indignation at hearing Superior spoken of so disrespectfully, or at being told, for her own part, that her husband did not care for her esteem—which with him meant affection —it would have been hard for her to say. She only knew that she was indignant and that Richard was very disagreeable ; how much she wished that she could have added "unjust" as well !

" Where has Virginia gone ? " he then asked suddenly, still cold and contemptuous as well as stern. " Can I trust you to tell me the truth in your answer ? It seems strange to me to have to say this to you, Hermione ! Not so very long ago I would have staked my life on your perfect sincerity; now I find myself doubting whether you can give as straight an answer to a simple question as might be expected from a Jesuit, or even Mr. Lascelles himself."

" If you think so ill of me, it is scarcely worth while my answering at all," returned Hermione, wavering between wrath and tears.

"I think you will answer," he said sternly. "The child is under age, and I have a right to know where she is and what she is doing!"

"I have told you. She has gone for a week's Retreat to C—— with Sister Agnes, before her confirmation."

Hermione tried to speak with offended dignity, but she found it hard. She had never respected her husband so much as when he made her understand that he did not respect her. Though her happiness lay in being made romantic love to—in being courted, flattered, petted, and all the rest of it—she was a woman who needed a master and with whom a certain amount of fear was wholesome.

"Where is this Retreat?" he asked again.

"At C——."

"Not far from London?"

"No, not far."

He looked at the clock.

"There is time to catch the up train to-night. I shall bring her home to-morrow."

"No, Richard, you will do nothing so shameful!" rising too in her agitation. What would Sister Agnes say, what would Superior think, if she let him go on such an errand! After she had promised that she would hold him as a blood-hound in leash to have set him so prematurely loose on their traces! "Why should you make all this horrible fuss and confusion for nothing? Such a mere trifle as it is! Virginia has gone only for a week's quiet prayer and contemplation before the solemn rite of confirmation; she is quite safe with Sister Agnes, who is also in retreat; and you cannot go to a house full of holy women and ramp and rave about as if you were searching for a thief! It will be too disgraceful to make such a scandal!"

"You should have thought of that in time," he said. "I have been patient and forbearing with you up to a certain point, but now that point is passed and I will bear no more. You have proved yourself an unfit guardian for your daughter. You have sacrificed her to your infatuation, as the mothers of old sacrificed their daughters to Moloch. She has no true friend but me her father, from whom you and your advisers have done your best to separate her; and it is my duty to snatch her from destruction."

"To snatch her from salvation, you mean," put in Hermione, a little below her breath and more as a formal protest than a real opposition. Her soft soul was impressed by her husband's unwonted energy; and though at all times a godless infidel, yet, after all, he was the recognized head of the house, the rightful controller and manager of things, and to themselves—the husband of the one and the father of the other.

For all answer Richard rang the bell; and when Jones came in ordered the carriage hastily, peremptorily, in a manner so unlike his own, with such an odd return on the young officer commanding his squad, that the man looked at him curiously as if he too found the general aspect of life changed.

"Good-bye, Hermione," he said, not even shaking hands with her—standing at some distance from her.

"Good-bye, Richard," she answered humbly. "Then you are really going?"

She made a step towards him. This was their first separation since they married.

"Yes. I will bring her home to-morrow."

She made another little step forward.

"I shall be very lonely till you return," she said, and looked into his face. She had forgotten Mr. Lascelles for the instant, and wanted her husband to kiss her before he went—if indeed he must go at all.—In her heart she wanted to cajole him to stay.

" I scarcely think so," he said; " I am so little to you now, others are so much ! "

" You are always Richard," she said with the sweetest air, the tenderest voice.

He caught her to his heart, but put her from him as suddenly as he had taken her.

" I must save my child," he said in an altered voice, and turned away abruptly as if he distrusted himself as well as her; and in a short time was on his way to Starton, to just miss the train, the last train that night, which steamed out of the station as he drove up.

Thus the religious runaways had a yet longer start, and premature detection was made so much the more difficult.

Telegraphing to London and to C—— brought no good results. No one answering to the description of any of the four fugitives had got out at either place. To be sure, a Sister had alighted at C——, but she was well known at the Home there, and she was moreover alone ; so that her arrival only occupied the telegraph wires for a short time and created a still further delay. Foreseeing all chances, the little party had divided into two couples, and had changed the route. While being looked for in London they were making for Southampton ; while the telegraph was clicking at C—— they were passing the Needles on their way to St. Malo. Everything had been arranged with the most consummate skill; and Richard was again weaker than his adversaries—craft and cruelty were once more triumphant.

The whole thing remained a mystery to everybody alike. Richard went up to London by the first train in the morning, not returning to the Abbey at all, and the detectives did what they could to help him; but the scent was lost, and the four had disappeared as completely as if they had vanished into space. No endeavours could hit on their traces, and by the end of five days Hermione's courage and endurance failed. She had never been left alone before, and in spite of Superior's attentions she was too unhappy to bear herself. Solitude and anxiety together broke down her strength, as the snow and hail break the tender twigs of garden shrubs ; and, half in hysterics, she drove over to Starton on the fifth day and telegraphed to her husband to come home at once. She was ill, she said, and wanted him ; so Richard had nothing for it but to leave London and abandon the faint hope of finding Virginia, that he might minister to the wife who was in chief part to blame for all the misery that had befallen them.

It was a curious spasm of reaction that made Hermione send for her husband—unknown to Mr. Lascelles.
Not exactly the rekindling of her love, it was yet that
imperious craving of habit which comes into marriage—
crystallizing the old forms so that even when dead they
look like life. She was so accustomed to have Richard
as part of her daily life—once the pivot of the whole and
now the obstacle which it was part of the play to circum-
vent—that it felt to her as if a death had taken place and
she was surrounded only by ghosts and shadows. Even
the greater liberty granted by his absence took away half
the charm of her pious naughtiness, because all the
secrecy and therefore all the romance. It vulgarized
the whole thing ; and she felt less elation than disturbance
when the vicar came boldly up to the house, now purified
by the absence of its agnostic master, and made a new
place of master for himself. Then, she did not like to
have those lonely mornings, those solitary meals, those
long dull evenings ; nor to know that she slept alone in
the house, with only the servants to trust to in case of
danger. If Sister Agnes had been at home it would
have been different, she thought. She could have gone to
the Vicarage—which she would have liked better than
that Superior should come to the Abbey—and at the

Vicarage she always felt homed and happy. But as it was she was miserable; and poor Richard too must be so wretched in London, alone and in such anxiety! And then again she thought twenty times in the hour: What on earth has become of Virginia!

She was not afraid of any disaster. She was sure that the child was safe; four people do not come to grief without some one hearing something about it;—but where was she? what had the Sister done with her? why was the plan changed, and why had they not gone to C—— as arranged from the first? The mystery of it all per-plexed and worried her, and woke up vague and uneasy suspicions as she remembered Virginia's look of pain when she found her kneeling at her faldstool; her almost passionate farewell to her father; and again her excess of emotion and distress at leaving home which had been visible all through, though so well controlled. It was a horrible fear that came across her every now and then; and Superior, to whom she confided it, though he laughed it down for the moment, looked grave afterwards and seemed to be secretly as much disturbed as herself. And then, not able to bear the situation longer, Hermione telegraphed to her husband to come home; and herself went to the station to meet him.

If only Mr. Lascelles had died then ! But the noble lives that are taken and the worthless ones that are left ! —the peace which would come were these gone, the ruin that follows on the loss of those !—the enemies that cling far into old age, the friends that drop off in the early years !—what a tangle it all is, and what a hopeless confusion of circumstance and providential design ! If only Mr. Lascelles had died, the two, now so fearfully estranged, would have gone back to their old places and one victim at the least would have been spared. As it was, nothing was changed. The tremendous power given by the fatal practice of confession made Mr. Lascelles absolute master of the situation all round, because the supreme controller and director of Hermione. Everything was in his hands—her soul and Richard's happiness— her essential virtue and her husband's essential honour. He knew her every thought and regulated, or punished, her every action. If she gave the reins for a moment to her natural affection, and allowed herself to be even compassionate to the man whom the priest had set himself to crush, she was frightened back again to her assigned attitude by all the terrors of wrath and judgment of which he had the irresponsible dispensation. She was his, not Richard's ; and he made her feel this when he set her

that long list of penitential tasks to purge her soul of the
sin of disobedience which she had committed in sending
for her husband because she wearied for him.

"This man of sin, this accursed infidel!" said Mr.
Lascelles, flaming with holy wrath; "and that you, a
good Churchwoman, should have *asked* him to come
back! Why did you not let him go for ever—and why,
when he was once safe away, did you not keep him
away!"

But when he said this, Hermione turned so white—
was in such deadly terror lest indeed this should be
imposed on her as her next act of renunciation and
obedience—that Mr. Lascelles, in his turn, was afraid of
going too far and too fast. He laughed off his suggestion
so pleasantly, so playfully, that he soothed her and made
her forget what he had said. But he held her to her
penance all the same, and made her feel that she had
been both unrighteous and indelicate.

Meanwhile a letter came from Sister Agnes to her
brother—enclosing a few words from Virginia to her
mother, saying simply: "Do not be uneasy. We are all
well, and will write in a few days." The two letters were
identical in the wording, and the postmark was Paris.

This note was something to show to Richard, who

was still keeping Scotland Yard and the telegraph wires busy; and so far was a comfort. For though it brought no help to him on the point which most nearly touched him—the Sister's influence and Virginia's fanaticism—it proved that the child was at least alive and not yet made the victim of ecclesiastical foul play, though she was still that of ecclesiastical superstition. He could not hear more than what these few unsatisfactory words told him ; not even what the postmark of the letter had been, nor what the postage-stamp.

"Mr. Lascelles had burnt the envelope," said Hermione when she was questioned ; "and she had not taken any notice of either the stamp or the postmark ;" and Richard had to content himself with this in the best way he could, and to wait for the further unrolling of the page whereon this pitiful family history was being written.

It came at last, and then they knew all. In a long letter written by Virginia to her mother the mystery was revealed, the seal of secresy broken. She had carried out her intention to its honest logical conclusion, and had become in name the Roman Catholic which she had been taught to be in fact. She and Sister Agnes, Cuthbert Molyneux and Father Truscott, had all gone over publicly, and had been received as acknowledged

members of the Church to which they had either gravitated by force of direction from without, or to which, like
Father Truscott, they had already for some time secretly
belonged, doing its work while seeming to be devoted
to a rival cause.

It was a letter full of the stock arguments put forward
at such times. Authority and tradition ; the validity of
these Orders with the invalidity of those; historical evidences; the divine mark of miracles ; the absolute and
perfect organization of the Romish communion ; the
value of belonging to a Church the dominion of which
extended over all the earth and was supreme both in
heaven and hell; the loveliness of the conventual life,
and the joy found in following the example of those holy
men and women, the cloud of witnesses, who had lived
for the truth and died for its glory; the rest found in
unqualified submission to authority and in the total destruction of all independent judgment ;—all the reasonings which had been so craftily instilled into her by
Father Truscott were reproduced in her letter ; and she
ended by beseeching her mother to reconsider her present position and to make one of the True Church.
Anglicanism, she said according to her Director's direction, was a fair kind of gateway to those born worshipping

under its shadow.   If more than this, and not made the
gateway to the true Temple, then was it a prison-house
for the soul.   The letter went on to say that she, Virginia,
was now with Sister Agnes at the convent of the Pregatrice, where she had entered as a postulant to be received
as a member when her novitiate should be ended.   She
had found her true sphere at last, she said, and had never
known so much happiness as she knew now.   She was
to be one of those perpetual adorers of the Blessed
Sacrament whose lives she had vaguely imagined before
she knew either the reality or what led up to it ; and she
was more than ever grateful to the Sister who had first set
her in the right way and then carried her step by step to
the end.   Then she sent her love to papa, and told him
that she would pray for him without ceasing and in full
faith that her prayer would be heard and his heart turned,
before too late, to God.

The letter was an exact counterpart of the one written
by Sister Agnes to her brother, save in the personal para-
graphs.   For these the Sister substituted a few sharp
stinging sarcasms on Theresa's shameless passion and
Hermione's sinful infatuation ; on the heat and excitement and individual flavour of all that which was being
done at Crossholme, and which revolted her now when she

thought of it as much as at the time. And at the time
how much she had suffered! She had sometimes felt
as if she must have stood up in the midst of these
spiritual odalisques, and have reproached them for their
criminal self-deception, their hideous sacrilege in mask-
ing their love for a man under the guise of devotion to
the Church. And in saying this of them, she wished to
add her supreme condemnation of him, her brother, who,
instead of putting down this unwholesome excitement
among the women, encouraged it and so made himself
a party to the sin. She thanked God that she had now
reached the haven of absolute purity where man did not
enter ; and where her soul would be no more vexed with
the vanity and frivolity, the passion and the impurity, that
had spoilt the work down at Crossholme.

This then was the end of it all, and the downfall of
more card-houses than one. To Mr. Lascelles the blow
was especially severe. The sum of money which he had
hoped to get for the Church from the Molyneux estate was
now an impossibility; for Theresa and Aunt Catherine
without Cuthbert could do nothing. Virginia's perversion
also had destroyed his hope of future restitution from the
Abbey ; and the cause of Anglicanism, which was his
own—the pedestal of his influence and supremacy—had

received a severe shock by the desertion of these two
young people, and of his sister and Father Truscott. If
this was where an advanced ritual was to land them all—
he knew so many would think—the less they had to do
with it, and the closer they clung to their barren Protestantism, the better. If indeed ritualism is only a bridge
to Romanism, they would say, let us break it down before
more have gone over; and if what seems to be the endeavour to obtain free development for the national
Church is only fighting for our old enemy the Pope, then
let us force these masked foes to marshal themselves
under their proper banner, and let our own flag be distinct—and Lutheran. He knew all these arguments so
well; and felt some of the pain of Sisyphus when he has
rolled the stone to the top only to have it fall back again
to his feet.

Then again, the solitude in which Hermione was left
by the absence of her daughter was bad, inasmuch as by
it she would be cast into so much closer communion with
her husband; and the difficulty of his own intercourse
with her, through the loss of his sister as the mistress of
the Vicarage, was both annoying to him personally and
embarrassing to him officially. Take it all round it was a
heavy blow to him, and he felt decidedly illtreated; and

then, more than all this, they had gone into deadly error
and left the true for the false.

For nothing is farther from the thoughts of certain of
the ritualistic school than to go over to the Church of
which they are the mimics—to take service in the army
of which they are the irregulars. Romanism is official
suicide for the despotic Anglican priest who despises the
bishops, breaks the law of the land, flouts the courts, and
snaps his fingers at Parliament. The exchange of individual power for the comparative self-effacement of an
organization where he is only a subordinate member, under
orders like any little curate of his own, does not suit the
man whose aim is to be irresponsible ruler, neither paying
obedience nor acknowledging superiority; but the honest
and sequential do go over before the end of all things,
and so far justify their faith. Mr. Lascelles was not one
who would ever leave the English Church, where he was
everything, for Rome where he would be only a unit.
He loved power too well to give it up for the sake of
consistency; and he had reasoned himself into the belief
that the Anglican position is logically sound and honestly
tenable. Hence he was in his right, he thought, to feel
sore and illtreated and to hold those recreant four as
perverts from the truth and traitors to the cause.

The whole neighbourhood felt the news as the shock of a crime; and to Ringrove it was as if Virginia had committed self-murder. Nothing that had ever happened in his life had given him so much pain. He would rather that the girl whom he loved had died than that she had done this thing: and he mourned her as one dead, but dead with a strange obscure stain of sin on her former purity.

To Lady Maine however it was the brightest bit of news that she had heard for many a long day. It was just what it should have been, she said with jubilant condemnation. The cloven hoof had at last shown itself; and if those poor wretches were sinful they were at least self-confessed. It was what she had prophesied all along; and now who was right? and ought not that popish vicar of Crossholme to be drummed out of the parish like the rogue he was? Protestantism, in the person of Lady Maine, had a tremendous lift by this secession; and had anything been wanting to complete "Superior's" annoyance it was this triumph of his loud-voiced enemy, and the Io pæans which she shouted over his discomfiture.

If mere friends and acquaintances felt all this, what was the blow to Richard, whom indeed it struck on every side? As a landowner who had hoped to leave this important estate in proper hands, and to die knowing that his daughter was carrying on the traditions of her mother, and that Ringrove was as faithful a steward, as devoted a husband, and as true a liberal as he himself had been; as a father, great part of whose happiness had been bound up in his only child; as a philosopher working for the good of his kind, hating imposition and falsehood, and living only to extend knowledge and give minds light and liberty;—on all sides he was wounded to the heart, and—he scarcely acknowledged this to himself—found himself unable to forgive Hermione. Her own defection, horrible to him as it was, maddening, humiliating in every sense, was more specially a personal offence, therefore easier to be borne; but that she should have proved herself such a bad care-taker of her child was a crime; and he could not pardon her the destruction of the life which it had been her assigned duty to protect.

"It is the logical outcome of all this pitiful mummery in which you have wilfully indulged," he said bitterly, when Hermione handed him the letter and he read in it Virginia's painful announcement. "The child is the only honest person among you all!"

"No! it is a dreadful mistake!" said Hermione. "To go into the Roman Church, so loaded with error, is a sin."

" What matters a few grains more or less of dust to those who are in the sandstorm ? " he said. " You are blinded, choked, destroyed, one as well as the other, and the details are of very little moment. The Pope's infallibility or Mr. Lascelles' ! For my own part I should prefer the former if I must have one. The child is dead to us now for all time, and you, her mother, who should have protected her——"

He checked himself, got up and went to the fireplace, where he stood, leaning his face on his arm.

" I am so sorry, Richard," she said penitently, creeping nearer to him as she spoke ; and indeed she was very sorry and ashamed as well.

He did not answer. He could not comfort her and he did not wish to reproach her.

" I had no idea of what was going on," she continued after a short pause, wondering at his silence. " I never could have believed that Sister Agnes could have been so deceitful or that Father Truscott was such a hypocrite. You believe me, don't you, Richard ? "

She laid her hand on his shoulder and intentionally allowed her fingers to touch his hair. She expected that he would turn and take her to him as he had done on the night when he went away. Judging of the present by the

past she thought that he would be overjoyed, penetrated
with gratitude, for this slight caress, this half-timid act of
familiarity—that he would be responsive even beyond
what she would have dared to encourage. But he did
not move. His face was turned downwards on his arm,
and his hands were clasped in each other.

"Richard," she said softly, trying to unclasp his hands.
"I knew nothing of it all!" she pleaded. "I had no
suspicion of what was going on, and would not have
believed it if I had been told ; nor had Mr. Lascelles.
I am so sorry, dear! so grieved! what can I do to help
you? I know how much you suffer; and I am so unhappy, too—so lonely! so wretched!"

Here she broke down and burst into tears. She was
indeed at this moment most unhappy, and scarcely knew
what would give her comfort.

Her husband raised his head, and in his turn laid
his hand on her shoulder.

"There is only one thing that you can do," he said,
in an unsteady voice ; "renounce all this present folly
and come back to your better self and your true duty.
We have lost our child, but we can yet piece together our
own lives so that they shall be honourable and loving.
It depends only on you, Hermione. I am what I was,

and where I was—it is you who have moved from the old ground. Come back to me and right reason, wife, and let us forget this miserable time of estrangement in a new and happier union."

" I cannot give up the Church nor make myself an atheist," said Hermione with a frightened look ; " I will do anything else for you, Richard, but I must keep to my own religion."

" Then you cannot help me," he said, taking his hand from her shoulder. " Religion with you means being the subservient creature of Mr. Lascelles ; and while you are that you can be no comfort to me ; you can be no more to me than what you are ; and that is— nothing ! "

" Am I really nothing to you, Richard ? no comfort ? no help ? " she said, lifting her blue eyes to him softly, tenderly, full of reproach as for harshness unmerited. " Do you say that I am nothing to you now ? " she repeated.

" What should you be ? " he answered slowly. " Neither wife nor friend, neither companion nor sym- pathizer, what are you, Hermione, but the witness of another man's triumph and my own defeat ? "

" Do not speak of Superior as a man—he is a priest and my Director ! " said Hermione.

He turned his eyes on her with a flash of scorn and indignation.

" Salve over your conscience with such transparent pretence, if you will ! " he said contemptuously; " but leave me the bitter and humiliating truth ! "

His look and tone made her tremble. She was a woman whom a man's anger terrified ; and like all long-suffering people, Richard's wrath when roused was terrible. And then, sophisticate as she would, her conscience was inwardly uneasy; for, though Mr. Lascelles was a priest, Richard was her husband; and a husband is, or ought to be, a sacred circumstance in a woman's life, not to be removed at another man's bidding. Still, side by side with all this was the tremendous fact of confession, whereby she was indeed made Mr. Lascelles' creature and slave by her belief in his spiritual power:—and above all, there was Richard's hideous agnosticism.

" Then you will not give up that mock papist priest for me?" he asked again, after a short silence. " It is one or the other ; you must choose between us."

" It is not Mr. Lascelles whom I will not give up; it is the Church," exclaimed Hermione.

" Confession—absolute obedience—suffering another man to come between husband and wife—to rob the parents of their child—giving to another man, call him priest or what you will, the most sacred feelings of your heart, the deepest and strongest of your love—you, a wife, submitting to the indelicacy of inquisitorial questions, to the indignity of regulations—is all this part of the Christian religion, Hermione?—all this necessary to your church life?"

"Confession is necessary," she said faltering. "Without confession there is no absolution, and without the absolution of the Church no pardon or salvation."

"My poor child!" he said with sudden softness. "And they have brought you to such pitiful absurdity as this! Can nothing be done for you? Between us both, wretched as you have made me, you are more deserving of compassion."

"Not for my faith—that is my only consolation," said Hermione, weeping.

"Then we need say no more," he returned. "While you cling to your faith as you call it—I your error!— we remain as we were, divided. I do not care to share your love with Mr. Lascelles—such miserable fragments as he allows ; and until you can come back to me wholly it is better that you should stand as you do, aloof. Good night. The loss of the child is only the natural conse-

quence of the loss of the wife. But it is your own will—
so let it stand. Good night."

She stood as if irresolute, when he turned to go to his
solitary study, the scene of his present anguish as it had
once been of his purest pleasures. As he passed through
the doorway, she made a few steps forward.

" Richard ! come back ! " she whispered softly.

But he did not hear her ; and when he had fairly
gone and the door was shut between them, Hermione
gasped, as at a danger safely got over. What would
Superior have said had she become reconciled to her
infidel husband, and consequently false to him, her spiritual
Director ? When she thought of the confession which would
have had to be made she literally trembled ; but when
she realized the state into which she had suffered her
home to be brought she cried ; and between the two
irreconcilable opposites felt herself the most miserable
woman in the world.

CHAPTER III.

THE times were hard for Mr. Lascelles, but he kept a firm front through his difficulties and gave the enemy no cause to rejoice by any confession of weakness or even of dismay. His official indignation rose to the height of the occasion, and on the Sunday following the public defection of his sister, his friend, his disciple, and the child of his most important penitent, he preached against the errors of Rome and the sin of perversion to her communion as strongly as if he had been preaching against Richard Fullerton's infidelity and the presumption of scientific inquirers in general. The only one whom he spared was Virginia ; and her he excused under the guise of the innocent young seduced by the false guides in whom they had placed their trust. But for the mature who had known the blessed truth of Anglicanism, and now had gone over to the Romish falsehood, he had no strictures that were too severe.

The personal application of his fiery discourse was of

course easy enough to make ; and it sounded outspoken
and sincere ; but it did not reconcile the Protestant part
of the community to the existing state of things. As they
persisted in seeing in ritualism the first step to Romanism,
and the vicar as nothing but a Jesuit in disguise, they could
not understand the hostility of the mimic to the original,
and doubted the sincerity which sounded so well.   The
opposition of the more sober-minded men of the parish
to the covert papistry of their parson—as they believed
it to be—had never threatened to be so severe as now
when he was fulminating against the Church to which
these three important members of his own community had
seceded, and of which he denounced the deadly errors
while running his own ecclesiastical lines exactly parallel.

But they could do little or nothing now. Wait till
the church should be opened and the services conducted
therein according to the new code, and then see what
they would all do !

Undoubtedly the times were unpleasant ; and the
Honourable and Reverend Launcelot Lascelles needed
all his courage to tide him over the discomfort of the
hour.

What was his loss the unconverted counted as their
gain ; and the Laodiceans of the place—notably the

Nesbitts—thought this a good opportunity for winning back Hermione Fullerton to safety and common sense. Now that she had lost the incitement of Virginia's pure if mistaken intensity, they thought she must have lost the main impulse to her own religious life. They could not believe that she had suffered the influence of Mr. Lascelles to become the mainspring of her actions. Religious fanaticism was bad enough, but personal fascination was worse. The one was a folly but the other was a crime; and they would not charge her with this. So now when she had proved by sad experience whither ritualism logically tended, she would surely be frightened and take refuge from herself and her dangers in the society of her wiser friends. Surely the vicar's spiritual staff was broken, and the beginning of the end at hand !

"It is such a pity, dear ! I am so sorry for it all !" said Mrs. Nesbitt with friendly sympathy, when she went to pay her visit of condolence to the bereaved mother, whose case she considered worse than that of one who had lost her child by death.

The words might be trivial enough ; but the kind sweet face and softened voice of her who uttered them gave them a charm which redeemed them from their intrinsic poverty.

" Yes," said Hermione, her eyes full of tears.   " It is an awful perversion ! "

" But what might have been expected," said Mrs. Nesbitt sighing.   " Sorry as I was to hear it, I cannot say that I was taken by surprise."

" I was," returned Hermione.   " And I knew more of Virginia than anyone else."

" But sometimes those who stand nearest see least," Mrs. Nesbitt said sensibly; "and to us who do not go all the way with you, that Ritualism should lead to Romanism seems just as natural as that seeds should bring forth flowers.   Yours is the seed ; and the Romish Church knows that as well as we do."

" If you understood our faith you would not say such a thing as this," said Hermione.   " We abhor the errors of Rome ; and while we recognize the good that is in her, and the measure of grace which she contains, we hate her perversions and refuse her traditions.   *We* have gone back to the truth in its purity, and she has gone aside into superstition and error."

" I do not see much difference between you," persisted Mrs. Nesbitt, with a woman's pertinacity of assertion and a passing wonder at Hermione's polemical fluency.   "The great difference is that Rome is consistent

and you are not; and that those who have been born
into the Romish Church have excuses for their superstition which you have not. But do not let us talk of all
this, dear; we shall never agree, and it is not necessary
that we should. What can I do to help you? You and
I were young wives and mothers together; and I feel as
if you were my sister. If such a thing were to happen
to one of my children, I think it would break my
heart !"

"It would break mine but for the help that I get
through the beloved Church," said Hermione cou-
rageously.

She must not let them think her less than dutiful
because Virginia had been seduced from the right way.
She must still hold fast to the truth and Mr. Lascelles :—
was she not his penitent, and had she not given him
possession of her very soul?

"I wish I heard you say, dear, that you got help
from that dear good husband of yours," was Mrs.
Nesbitt's characteristic rejoinder.

"Poor Richard! he can do nothing for me, and
nothing for himself, while he thinks as he does," she
answered, a certain wifely softness breaking through the
hard spiritual superiority of her tone. "If he did not

hold such dreadful opinions as he does perhaps this would
never have happened. Virginia would have been able
then to have confided in him, when she first began to
waver ; and he would have directed her and have saved
her."

"She did not confide in you, her mother," said Mrs.
Nesbitt.

" I am only a woman," said Hermione simply.

" But now that you are alone at home, and, as Miss
Lascelles is not there, you cannot be so much at the
Vicarage, I do hope that you will come and see us, and
that we may come and see you as in old times," said
Mrs. Nesbitt. "Such old friends as we are, we ought to
see more of each other than we do, and our friendship
should not be allowed to die out as it seems to have done
of late. If there had been even a quarrel or a misunderstanding we ought to have made it up, but for a mere
difference of opinion to have drifted apart as we have
done—it is not neighbourly, not Christian ! And you
know, dear, that the coolness has not been on our side."

" Friendship with the world is enmity with God," said
Hermione, as Mr. Lascelles had more than once reminded
her.

" But I am not the world," returned Mrs. Nesbitt,

smiling. " I am only a quiet, easy-going, home-staying wife and mother—and your old friend. Come, dear! do not let this estrangement go on. It has lasted too long already, and there is not the slightest reason for it. Come to us as you used. Come to dinner with us to-morrow, as in the dear old days—you and your husband. Though we cannot change this awful affliction for you, still we can make a few hours pass less painfully; and, at all events, there is nothing with us to remind you of poor Virginia's dreadful mistake. At the Vicarage now, or with the Molyneux's, you must be reminded at every turn by the things that first gave her this fatal direction."

" You are very, very kind," said Hermione in a hesitating manner.

She knew that Superior would be ill-pleased with her if she went to the Nesbitts'; but at this moment she was so sorely in need of comfort that she did not know how to put this kindly temptation from her.

" Then you will come?" cried Mrs. Nesbitt with friendly warmth. " It will give us all so much pleasure. It will be a real gala day at home!" Seeing that she still hesitated, she added : " If Mr. Lascelles cuts you off like this from your old friends, how can he reconcile it to his conscience? Christianity is charity with all men, not this Pharisaical exclusiveness."

"Still, we must obey the Church, and we must not question her commands," put in Hermione, and she then added plaintively : "It is not our fault that you will not join us! I wish you would!—it makes everything so difficult!"

"I do not know what you and Mr. Lascelles want," said Mrs. Nesbitt, opening her eyes. "We are all good Christians at Newlands, and what more would you have?"

"That you should be good Church-people," said Hermione, looking, dear soul, as if she believed what she was saying and understood what she meant.

Just then Ringrove Hardisty was announced. It was the first time that he had called at the Abbey since the fatal day when he had unconsciously assisted at Virginia's leave-taking of the world; and he felt like a man who goes into the room where the corpse of his beloved is lying. He was very pale, very sad, very much changed in these last few weeks; for not even Richard himself had grieved more than he had done for that which was substantially the death of Virginia. Though he did not feel it a sin yet he did hold it for shame that Virginia

should have done this thing, and done it with so much
duplicity and want of candour. Lost to them for ever as
she had become by her act, he would rather that she had
died in reality. It would have been less terrible than the
knowledge of this living entombment in the heart of
superstition—this dreary culmination of falsehood and
fanaticism.

"And you will come too, Ringrove?" said Mrs.
Nesbitt with intentional abruptness as he came in.

She guessed how things were with him and Hermione,
and that this first meeting would be painful.

"Where?" he asked, holding Hermione's hand but
looking at Mrs. Nesbitt.

"To dine with us to-morrow. This darling here and
Mr. Fullerton are coming," was Mrs. Nesbitt's positive
assertion of a vague possibility.

"With pleasure. Mrs. Fullerton knows how much I
value her society, and nowhere more than at your house,"
said Ringrove, a strange huskiness in his voice as he
pressed the soft hand held in his and looked at her with
his frank blue eyes, softer and darker than usual.

Hermione turned aside her head.

"You are very good to us," she said with a little sob.
And Mrs. Nesbitt, putting her comfortable arms

about her, more like a mother than a woman not much older than herself, believed that the conquest was assured, and that Mrs. Fullerton was now saved from ritualism and Mr. Lascelles.

By the look of things at home the belief was not quite so wild as might have been thought. For nothing stirs a woman so much as indifference—except it is opposition ; and since Virginia's flight, and that last futile attempt at full reconciliation on his part, Richard had been indifferent—inasmuch as he had made Hermione understand that he accepted their present arrangements as final and would not again attempt to disturb them. Always courteous he had ceased to be loving—always gentle he was never tender. Now that she was alone he made it a matter of duty to be much with her ; to go out with her—when his presence was not too patently displeasing ; to sit with her in the evening ; to talk to her during meals ; but all this was only as a friend. No word, no look betrayed more than the courteous good-breeding of a pleasant acquaintance ; while running through it all was a curious thread of manly dignity, as if what he did was as much for the self-respect of a gentleman in the fulfilment of his duty, as from affection for the woman whom he had once loved better than his pride or his life. He never touched on any subject that interested him ; spared religion his girds and science his advocacy ; and he never alluded to Virginia nor the past —not because he wished to forget or to banish her, but because her name was a standing reproach against his wife ; and to speak of his daughter was, with him, to condemn her mother. It was the dullest life that could be imagined, and the most unsatisfactory ; but if Richard had studied how best to touch his wife and incline her to him again, he could have hit on no better plan.

Ashamed, sorry, lonely, her life shorn of its former full intensity, and the natural pride of her womanhood piqued now in earnest where formerly much had been made up and more wilfully imagined, she felt the indifference of her discarded husband almost as acutely as if she had never transferred her allegiance from him to Mr. Lascelles, and had never found the excitement of religious romance more satisfying than the monotony of married security. His security had made her discontented and uncomfortable ; his acquiescence in the severance which she herself had decreed, made her long to bring him back to her as of old.

" I suppose Richard will have no objection," she said, returning to the question of that dinner to-morrow.

" Perhaps I had better send to ask him," she added with her old manner of girlish deference, as in the days when only one will was between them, and that will was his.

" I will go to him," said Ringrove, also in his old manner of the son of the house—that place which had ever been his by mutual understanding, and which, curiously enough, founded on Virginia as the original *motif,* was now restored to him by her loss.

" What a good dear fellow that is ! " said Mrs. Nesbitt, as his firm step was heard clanking through the hall.

" Yes ! " said Hermione with a sigh. How ardently she wished at this moment that Virginia had seen with Mrs. Nesbitt's eyes !

Older, greyer, a little bent in the shoulders, thinner, haggard, the former calm repose of his face changed to a fixed unwavering sadness, the quiet self-restraint of his manner become now the resignation of despair, Richard showed only too plainly how deeply he had been struck —how mortally wounded. Mrs. Nesbitt felt her heart swell and sink with sudden pain when she looked at him, so terribly changed as he was ; and how bitterly she hated Mr. Lascelles and the whole school to which he belonged, .for the mischief and misery they had wrought !

" Dine with you to-morrow ? no, I thank you," he said in a weary way. " I am scarcely in tune for a dinner."

" Only your two selves and Ringrove Hardisty," urged Mrs. Nesbitt. " It is like your own home, you know, Mr. Fullerton, and you have not been for so long."

"Will you not go, Richard?" said Hermione, half timidly.

" If you wish it, go by all means," he said with a slight air of surprise.

" Not without you," she returned. " I should like to go very much, but only with you," she added, raising her pretty eyes with a soft and sweet expression that once would have taken the heart out of him.

Ringrove looked at him anxiously; Mrs. Nesbitt full of compassion.

" If you would like it, certainly I will go with you," he said gravely, after a moment's pause; but no light came into his face, no love into his eyes; he yielded out of respect for her wishes, but only as a gentleman yields to a lady—not as a loving man to a beloved woman.

Hermione flushed painfully. She felt the difference which both Ringrove and Mrs. Nesbitt divined; and thought her husband cruel and unkind to be so cold when she would fain have been on more friendly terms. She had all the modern woman's belief that it belongs to her alone to set the lines between herself and the man whose name she bears ; and that hers is the commanding voice while he repeats only the echo. She had discarded him when pressed by Mr. Lascelles to do so ; now, when she would have drawn nearer to him in her loneliness, she was to her own mind an injured wife in that he kept in the place which she had assigned to him.

She gained the day so far however, that they both went to the house of Laodicea as if they had been the friends they were long ago ; and Hermione, carried back to her former self by a sudden sweep of old-time emotions, said when she left that she had not been so happy for years. This was a long pull on the part of the pretty woman ; but it was the truth in substance if beyond the mark in distance.

When Mr. Lascelles heard of this act of virtual, if not literal, disobedience, he showed so much manly pathos of personal sorrow, and he expressed so much righteous indignation at the falling away from grace of one whom he had believed secure, that Hermione was partly softened and partly frightened, and made to feel that she was a backslider who had to be contrite and penitent if she would be restored to favour and forgiven her offences. Mr. Lascelles fulminated against that dinner as if it had been the unpardonable sin and that quiet moral wholesome English family a mere Sabbath of witches, in whose unholy revels she, a vessel of grace, had participated. He brought her to her knees, as a child asking forgiveness ; and when he had sufficiently humbled her, he held out the olive-branch once more, and put the rod back into its corner. She must do penance for the past as well as promise better things for the future ; and part of that penance, embodied in an Act of Contrition, was to give for the use of the church a cheque for five hundred pounds. This made rather more than a thousand beyond her assigned allowance ; and for this sum she was in debt to the bank.

The effect of that cheque was to make the bank write to her, reminding her that her account was overdrawn by that amount, and desiring a renewal of deposits before further business could be done. At the same time certain accounts which ought to have been settled months ago began now to pour in, and Hermione, who could not add up a day-book correctly, for the first time in her life felt herself in a financial difficulty which she

dared not confess to her husband, and could not face by
herself; and wherein Superior was of neither help nor
comfort.   It was part of his play to get her into this
entanglement, that he might have yet an additional hold
on her.

This matter of the dinner set Mr. Lascelles thinking.
Coupled with the difficulty of private meetings and a
certain subtle reserve in confession as well as a certain
subtle shrinking from that bitter wholesale condemnation
of her husband by which he, as her Director, had
done his best to make wifely loyalty appear a sin and
mental infidelity a virtue, it made him plan out a new
combination.   Things could not go on as they were
now.   She was too weak to be trusted to herself, and
would slip from his hands into those of her husband if
she were not held by main force.   Reconciliation with
her infidel would be her newest excitement unless she
was well watched and prevented; but by the absence of
his sister and Virginia, his own close guardianship was
interrupted, and consequently his influence and authority
were weakened.   This must not be.   Punctual still in
her religious duties, the inner fire had a little damped
down, and she was acquiescing with more Christian
resignation than he liked to see in the unavoidable

slackening of their intercourse. Without question the fever-fit had a little subsided, and her heart was wavering back to her husband. He saw it, felt it, knew it, in every line and movement of her body, every look of her eyes, every word of her mouth. The shock of Virginia's defection had set the pendulum swinging to the other side, and he knew that, unless he bestirred himself, his days of power were numbered. Wherefore he drew out his new plan of attack, and laid it on his penitent to accept his scheme.

" A very precious friend of mine," he said to her one day abruptly after confession ; "a good Churchwoman, and I need hardly tell you a most valuable person all through—Mrs. Everett ; Edith Everett—wants to come here. I told her that you would receive her at the Abbey. She knows all about your trials and sufferings, and I shall be glad for you to have her. She will be invaluable to you, lonely and needing comfort as you are !"

"Thank you, dear Superior," said Hermione, with feigned cordiality. In her heart she wished that he had not made this arrangement. She was not so lonely now as she had been at first. She saw a good deal of Mrs. Nesbitt, whom she could not help loving in spite of her want of soundness, and Ringrove and Bee were almost as often at the Abbey as they used to be a year or more ago. And then she was sure that this Mrs. Everett would not be congenial to Richard. Poor Richard! he had suffered so much already, she really did not like to give him any more pain.

Mr. Lascelles looked at her sharply. He evidently expected her to say more than that mere bald word of thanks, and he seemed to understand her thoughts.

"What is she like?" asked Hermione hurriedly and with a woman's instinctive jealousy.

"She is beautiful," replied Mr. Lascelles with fervour.

The pretty woman's soft pink cheeks flamed into a sudden red, and she held her slender neck a trifle stiffly.

"In mind if not in person," continued her Director. "Spiritually, she is as near perfection as a sinful mortal can be; and when you know her you will say so and love her as well as I do."

"I am sure I shall," she returned in a constrained voice, looking down and feeling that she should hate her instead. And after all, though Superior was—Superior —it was rather a liberty that he had taken, was it not? seeing that now—What?—Seeing that deep down in that foolish heart of hers was the unacknowledged wish to become reconciled to her husband, and the moral certainty that if left alone she would become thus reconciled. But she did not put this into words. After all that had been between her and Superior—after the holy love which they had mutually confessed : a love so holy as to be without sin or shame—after the authority that he had claimed and the obedience that she had paid —after the assignment to him of her conscience and the gift which she had made him of her wifehood—it was impossible to refuse an arrangement proposed for her benefit ; or to do other than accept it with apparent gratitude and real dismay ; smiling up into his face while saying to herself with ill-suppressed tears : " How shall I ever be able to break it to Richard ! "

" If you will be guided by me," said Mr. Lascelles, from whom nothing was concealed—" will you, my child ? "—he put in smiling, as if he playfully doubted and seriously trusted.

" Of course, dear Superior," she answered, also smiling, but with an odd little quiver of affectation in her eagerness.

" Well, then, take my advice. Say nothing to Mr. Fullerton until the hour of Mrs. Everett's arrival. Then tell him that she is coming, and that you are going to Starton to meet her—as of course you will do."

"And you do not think this will be too abrupt?" she asked anxiously.

"Oh! if you wish to spare his feelings so very much you had better ask his consent and abide by his decision," said Mr. Lascelles with rough contempt. "I thought you had regained enough self-respect by now to be able to ask a lady friend to stay with you for a short time without going on your knees to your husband for his permission. And such a husband!—to whom all things godly and of good repute are abhorrent. But I do not wish to guide you against your inclinations. Do as you think best. I have but one desire — your temporal happiness and spiritual well-being. And when this desire oppresses you I will withdraw my care."

"No, I do not wish you to withdraw your care. You are my best friend," said Hermione, humbled to the point where he wished her to be brought. "I will do as you tell me, and say nothing about Mrs. Everett till I go to bring her from the station."

He smiled and leaned forward to look the better into her eyes.

"Sweet child!" he murmured tenderly; "the world would be a blank to me if, after having known the truth, you were to become a backslider and lapse into error.

But you will keep firm, will you not? You will not give the enemy of souls power over you by any sinful weakness for the infidel to whom the law has given the name of your husband? Remember again what I have said to you before—it is God or man, salvation or eternal destruction, Divine guidance or Satan and your husband. You cannot have the two together any more than you can breathe pure air in a foul pit. You must make your election—as you have; and abide by your decision—as you will."

"Yes," said Hermione. "I will always be guided by you."

He took her hand.

"You vow that on the Cross?" he said, at once sternly and eagerly. "You will always be guided by me?"

"Yes," she answered, trembling.

"I will soon put you to the test," he said, letting her hand fall suddenly. "When I do, remember your oath, your vow of obedience sworn on the Cross!"

CHAPTER IV.

HER GUIDE AND FRIEND.

" A LADY is coming to stay with me for a few weeks.   I
am just going to the station to meet her."

Hermione made this announcement with an attempt
at ease that was undeniably a failure, her eyes looking
just about her husband's scarf-pin and her voice husky
for all its artificial carelessness.

Richard looked at her with surprise.   What was the
meaning of this announcement?   Why was the coming
of this stranger so suddenly sprung on him?

"Who is she?   Where have you met her?" he
asked.

" She is Mrs. Everett and I have not seen her yet,"
was the answer.

" Her name tells me nothing.   Who and what is this
Mrs. Everett?—and why is she coming here?" he
returned.

"She is a friend of the vicar's, and wants to come to
Crossholme to see the work," said Hermione.   " As she

could not go to the Vicarage now, unfortunately !"—
sighing—" I offered to take her in here"—with a characteristic little fib to save Superior and appearances.

" I hope she will approve of the work and like
her quarters," said Richard, a touch of sarcasm in his
voice.

" You do not object to her coming, do you?" she
asked, tempting Providence.

She was one of those women who are not satisfied
with having their own way, but demand also that others
should approve as well as acquiesce.

" That has nothing to do with it," he answered.

" Yes, it has. I should be very sorry to displease
you," said Hermione impulsively.

" I fear you went beyond your record there," was his
grave rejoinder. " Unhappily, sorrow for my displeasure
has long ceased to be a restraining influence over you,
Hermione."

Tears of genuine feeling came to her eyes.

" You misjudge me cruelly," she said ; and at the
moment she honestly believed in her own words.

" No, I am not cruel," he said quietly ; " I am only
on my guard. I do not care to fall into another
mistake."

" And perhaps you are more mistaken now than you were before," said Hermione, holding out her hand and looking up at him with sudden softness.

He took her hand and held it without speaking. What indeed could he say? He knew that all this was only a passing mood, not a vital change of feeling ; and that to-day in one form, to-morrow she would be in another, according as the influence of Mr. Lascelles or her own natural instinct had the upper hand. These passing moods, these fleeting, flitting changes, were not to be trusted ; and even that evident desire to draw a little closer to him, which she had shown since Virginia's departure, was as fallacious as the rest. It was no real reconciliation that was offered. There was but one way for this ;—to renounce Ritualism and Mr. Lascelles and return to her wifehood in the perfect love and obedience of the past—that love which made obedience unity. Failing this, her half-hearted efforts at a partial peace were in vain. They were due rather to weariness of herself than to any true reawakening of love for him, he thought with the straightforward courage of a man who prefers pain to self-deception—because she was lonely, not because she was repentant.

" Of course," Hermione went on to say, womanlike,

giving reasons that should exonerate her when she had
not been accused;—" Of course it is very lonely for me
now; and it will be nice to have a companion. I feel
that."

Richard sighed heavily. By whose fault and folly
was it that she had lost the best companion a woman
can have, in her own child, and was now forced to seek
the association of a stranger to relieve her desolation?

" I hope we shall like her. I dare say we shall," she
continued, speaking rapidly, for her husband's face was
not encouraging and she was nervous and uncomfortable.
" Mr. Lascelles knows her very well, and says that she is
charming; and beautiful as well. That will make it
pleasant for you, Richard!" she added, attempting a
playfulness that failed as much as her composure had
failed a short time since.

" If you are satisfied, that is sufficient," he said.

" But you must be satisfied too," she persisted, sincere
at the moment and piqued by his quietness.

"I have no part in the matter," he said. " It is idle
to talk of me in connexion with your actions, Hermione!"

" How unkind you are!" she said, raising her big
blue eyes reproachfully.

He turned away. It was all too painful to him. He would rather have her honestly estranged because of false principles sincerely held, than humiliated to what was substantially coquetry. It jarred on every feeling of truth and self-respect that he had, and distressed him more than her petulance and ill-temper had ever done.

"Well!" said Hermione, sighing, and feeling deeply ill-used; "I hope that you will not dislike her, Richard, and that she may make you a little happier than you have been of late."

"The presence of a stranger cannot possibly make me happier," he said. "She cannot give me back my lost child nor my wife's love."

"It is very hard on me—you are always vexed and irritated with me now!" cried Hermione with a look of angry sorrow. "The more I try to please you the less I succeed."

"I am never vexed nor irritated with you, Hermione," said Richard; "I have only learnt a new reading of you; and the lesson is painful. But that is not the present question. The thing before you to-day is the reception of Mrs. Everett; and it is time you were setting out."

"You are horribly cruel!" cried Hermione, who

longed to fling herself into his arms, and felt as if she had done so and been repulsed.

He made no answer, but with a little farewell movement of his hand left her to herself and the half-dreaded task of welcoming the strange lady whom Mr. Lascelles had pronounced perfect.

A tall and graceful woman, with a clever face but not in the least handsome, got out of the train at Starton, set all the officials astir in their attendance on her, and looked about her curiously. She was a woman of a singularly unembarrassed manner, but as gentle as she was composed ; a woman who bore her womanhood as at once a weapon and a shield, and who held herself as a kind of sacred creature whom the world was honoured in respecting. She had light, almost flaxen hair, without the faintest tinge of gold or red to redeem it from insipidity ; her eyes were a greenish hazel; her skin was of exquisite colour and clearness; her nose was short, blunt and kid-like. Her address was good; as artificial in its own way as had been that of Sister Agnes, but less sanctimonious. She was evidently a woman of the world who had added religion as an extra ornament ; a Ritualist on the outside of her and a woman of the world all through. She was also one who, while

appearing to be frank, held all her real self in absolute
reserve, and while soft and supple and caressing in her
ways, had a will of iron and a grasp of steel. The velvet
glove was never more fully exemplified than with Mrs.
Edith Everett ; and the current verdict of those who
knew her only superficially was : "What a sweet woman
she is ! "—but her children feared her, and her servants
never stayed beyond the conventional year.

Forewarned, she took Hermione from the first as one
to be compassionated, coerced, scourged, encouraged
and praised all in one. Backsliding to the extent of
making even the hollowest kind of peace with her infidel
husband was a sin of which the possibility was not to be
contemplated ; and Mrs. Fullerton was to be made to
feel that in Mrs. Edith Everett she had a jailor of
godliness who would stand no paltering with evil,
however craftily disguised as conjugal affection or
womanly tenderness. The renunciation which had been
ordained and carried out so far was not to be repented
of ; and in the drive home Mrs. Everett touched without
disguise on the sorrow which so faithful a daughter of
the Church must endure through the companionship of
a godless and depraved husband like Mr. Fullerton. It
was public property in the sect to which both belonged,

and there was no indelicacy in speaking of it—so at least her manner seemed to say.

"Superior has told me all about you, and explained how I can best comfort you and be of use to you," she said, at once ranging herself with Hermione as joint allies against a common foe. "He has told me of your heavy trial, and how nobly you bear it."

"I do my best," answered Hermione confusedly.

"Yes ; Superior says you are grand—and understand so wisely how impossible it is in your case to be both a good Churchwoman and a fond wife ! It is hard on you, poor lady ; but you cannot serve God and the devil, and you must make your choice."

"My husband is good in everything but his opinions," faltered Hermione, shrinking at the uncompromising condemnation of her husband, for whom since the loss of Virginia she had felt so much more kindly, and with whom she had been trying to establish a little line of closer relationship. It was painful enough sometimes to hear poor Richard so harshly judged by Superior ; but by this stranger, Superior's perfect woman, it was un-endurable!

Mrs. Everett smiled. What a babe in the world of truth the pretty creature was after all !

"Why! that is just the heart of everything," she said. "What is anything without right doctrine? Superior would tell you the same, I know;—is it not so?"

"Yes," said Hermione, like a catechized child.

"I have often heard Superior preach on that very subject," continued Mrs. Everett;—"'The nothingness of natural virtue and the absolute necessity of right doctrine.' I do not think Superior holds anything more necessary to salvation than this belief. It opens a wide door else, dear Mrs. Fullerton—the door which leads to eternal perdition! Is this your place?" suddenly changing her voice as they drove through the lodge gates. "How pretty it is! What a paradise! and," sighing, as she added a little below her breath but quite audibly, "with the serpent here as well as in Eden!"

Her introduction to the serpent, which took place just before dinner, was rather awkward in more than one direction. Hermione, conscious that she had brought into his house an enemy to her husband as declared as Mr. Lascelles himself, and sorry that she had been forced to do so, was neither natural nor at ease. Mrs. Everett, faithful to her programme, was cold and scarcely courteous to this confessed son of perdition; and the master of the house himself, catching the tone of the moment, offered the mere skeleton of hospitality—no more. When introduced to Mr. Fullerton, Mrs. Everett made a cold bow, and, afflicted with sudden myopy, did not see the hand held out in conventional welcome. When dinner was announced, she refused Richard's arm, saying with a smile as she took Hermione's hand : "You and I will go together, and then there will be no distinction ; " and all through dinner she kept to the same *rôle.* She never let the talk flag for a moment ; but she spoke exclusively to Hermione, and when Richard put in his word, answered him only through his wife. She never looked at him save when he was not looking at her, and then by stealth as it were; scanning him with the same kind of curiosity as she would have had in looking at some monster. From him she turned her eyes slowly to Hermione; and then she changed from the curiosity of horror to pity and tenderness. And Hermione saw all this facial byplay, as it was intended she should. Whatever Richard said Edith Everett contradicted and persistently turned the conversation on theology and the Church. She spoke of themselves— the Anglicans or Catholics—as persecuted by such as Richard—"the strong ones of the earth "—whose

wickedness they must endure for a while to triumph with
the saints in the end. To hear her one would have
imagined that fire and faggot, the thumbscrew and the
scavenger's daughter, were still in active use, and that
she and hers went in daily fear of their lives from Richard
and the law. Their steadfastness to the truth was,
according to her, a service of peril for which they
suffered gladly ; while infidelity had all the good things of
life and was the tyrant who ruled the land and did despite-
fully to the faithful. She candidly acknowledged this
tremendous power of evil, and did not soften the iniquity
of the present visible wielder of the diabolical flail,
sitting there at the head of the Abbey table; but her
manner, taken by itself, was free from active insolence.
She was like a calm superior being recognizing, but not
fearing, the might of the Evil One, as embodied in this
his living emissary. Her frank and unconditional condemnation made Hermione wince ; but Richard, refusing
the challenges flung one after the other into his face, let
all pass without debate or comment. Spiritually crucified
as he was, did it signify to him if a casual passer by railed
at him ? Neither did he care to argue as to the wood
of which his cross was made, nor on the name of the
forge where the nails which held him were made.   But

the quiet constancy with which he refused to be roused did not tend to make Mrs. Everett more his friend or less his appointed and willing enemy.

For her own part, Hermione soon found that it would not do to defend her agnostic husband when she and her new friend were alone.   She tried it once when Superior's perfect woman was more than ordinarily severe and unjust ; but Mrs. Everett, looking at her with her clear penetrating eyes—eyes that neither flashed nor melted, neither drooped nor dilated, but that simply—looked— looked—as if they would read and dominate her very soul—answered in her soft and rather monotonous voice :

" You must not make excuses for him, dear Mrs. Fullerton, else I shall think Superior's fear is justified."

" What does Superior fear ? " asked Hermione with a half-frightened look.

"That because of your almost criminal love for your husband, you should fall from grace and become a cast-away," said Mrs. Everett, as quietly as if she were speaking of an old gown to be discarded.

" I hope not that," said Hermione with a superstitious shiver.

" Then do not tempt Providence by defending such

a dreadful man. You might as well defend Judas Iscariot," was the calm rejoinder.

"I do not defend his opinions. No one can condemn these more than I. I only say that he is not bad all through," replied Hermione with the courage of irritation.

"My poor soul! not bad all through!" said Mrs. Everett sweetly. "How can an infidel be anything but bad all through? You might as well say that a man dying of cancer is not diseased all through! Mr. Fullerton's infidelity is the cancer that taints every part of him, and you make yourself one with his sin when you defend him or even apologize for him. I grant you it is natural," she went on to say with a generous concession to human weakness. "Considering the regrettable amount of love that you have for him, I can understand your wanting to put him in the fairest light possible. But it is not right. There are times when even the love of a wife for her husband is unholy : and in your case, dear, yours is undoubtedly unholy, and at all costs must be subdued. It is a terrible trial to you ; but you must suffer and resist."

This was the tone taken by Mrs. Everett, under direction. She assumed on the part of Hermione an

all-devouring passion for her husband which brought the
blood into the pretty woman's face for shame, and made
her afraid to show the smallest kindness to this infidel
whom the Church had given her and now wanted to take
from her. Whenever she spoke to him Edith Everett's
clear hazel eyes fixed themselves on her steadily until she
had ended; and she was made to feel unrighteous if she
spoke to him gently or when not absolutely obliged.
He was the outcast, and she the rebel against divine
authority when she recognized that he had human claims.
But her chances of backsliding were carefully curtailed.
Wherever she went, Mrs. Everett was by her side—
whatever she said or did, Mrs. Everett was there as
auditor, witness and judge. Her life gradually passed
from her own control; and one by one, quietly, stealthily,
craftily—never offering the point where Hermione could
resist nor the moment when she could refuse—this soft-
mannered guest took into her own hands all sorts of little
duties and activities, which made the mistress of the
house daily more dependent on her and daily under
closer control. And above all, she brought her into
constant communication with Superior, and made all
things as possible and proper as in the days of Sister
Agnes and a free Vicarage. She was the occasion, the

duenna, if need be the scapegoat ; and Hermione had
no more chance against her than the fly has against the
spider when once caught in the net.

Yet for all this Hermione was unhappy.   Flattering
her in speech, protecting her in appearance, coercing
her in reality, Mrs. Everett seemed somehow to stand
between her and Superior on the one hand, and between
her and her husband on the other ; that husband with
whom, now that she was prevented, she longed secretly
to make peace.   She was too much her interpreter ; and
Hermione would rather have been allowed to interpret
for herself.   She did not like to hear her thoughts and
feelings and desires explained to Superior, and her soul
made as it were into a set of copybook headings which
Mrs. Everett wrote out and she had only to sign.   But
she was powerless.   Mr. Lascelles had established a
spiritual " mousetrap," after the manner of the great spy ;
and Hermione was not only watched and reported on,
but was made to feel that Mrs. Everett was but another
name for Superior, while Superior himself was the consecrated interpreter of the Mind of God.   Between the
two the soft, weak soul had not the thinnest fibre of
independence left her, and was bent hither and thither
just as they most desired.   If that strong hand which held

her with so firm a grasp was the crutch for her weakness, it was also the band and buckle of restraint, the lash and the goad that coerced ; and nothing but the superstitious dread of offending Superior, and, through him, Eternal Justice, kept her in the state of moral thraldom from which one word to Richard would have relieved her. But that one word ! It was just that which she dared not say. For would it not have been calling on Satan to deliver her from the holy hands of the Church ?

And all this while both Mr. Lascelles and Mrs. Everett despised the weakness of which they made their account and to Hermione herself extolled as grace.

A clever woman with a keen sense of the ridiculous and a strong love of power—also with very clear and decided views as to what she wanted out of life and meant that it should give her—Mrs. Everett found much in the state of things at Crossholme to laugh at and more to condemn. The feminine worship paid to Superior revolted her for more reasons than one ; and she satirized it so unsparingly that Mr. Lascelles him-self became ashamed, and thought that perhaps it was after all a little in excess of his rightful spiritual due. To those whose love for the man ran into their reverence for the priest she was as bitter as she was unscrupulous

in her denunciations; and she did not even spare
Theresa, dying as she was.   Miss Pryor and all the
humbler sisterhood who fed on Superior's words and
looks as the hungry Chosen fed on manna, were never
so sharply rallied as by this tall, smiling, blunt-nosed
woman with the soft voice and the keen wit, who
said the cruellest things in the blandest manner, and
made them all cry in secret and blush in public.   What
her own feelings were for this man who stood as the
target for so many feminine arrows no one could divine.
Surely, said some, she was too clever to imagine that he
would marry her—a widow without beauty or fortune—
though she had all those social qualities by which a
wife gets her husband on in the world.   Yet she was
evidently a power with him, and had more influence over
him than anyone else.   She had the oddest way possible
of laying down the law on matters; when she would
look over to Mr. Lascelles and say: "Superior, I am
sure that you see it as I do;" and Superior would
invariably see it as she did, and say so.   In any
controversy or dispute that might be on hand between
her and anyone else, he "gave her reason" though she
had none; and said she was right when she was
manifestly wrong.   People talked of it, as of course.   In

small communities where there is but one masculine sun
of any account and a great many feminine satellites, a
few rays of benevolence more or less are jealously
weighed and measured; and what is no one's business
becomes everyone's, like a riddle given to the public to
guess. But whatever Mrs. Everett's own thoughts might
be, or wherever Superior's inclinations tended, the work
undertaken by the one after the design of the other
was plain and clear enough—the absolute prevention of
anything like relapse in Hermione's relations with her
husband, and the separation between them widened, not
narrowed. Richard was an infidel to be crushed ; and his
wife should be made to crush him. It was infamous
that an atheist should hold this large property which
was not his own ; a scandal to justice and Christianity
both, that he should apply to the spread of infidelity
funds rightfully belonging to the Church ; and it must be
put an end to now as speedily as might be. Though the
great hope of permanent restitution had been frustrated
through Virginia's perversion, pretty pickings might
still be gathered from the liberal table of the present
proprietor if only that wretched obstructive could be
removed.

This, then, was the ultimate point—Richard must be

ousted from his place of power and Hermione must take on herself the administration of her own affairs. The train had been well laid ; now was the time for prudent firing.

Mrs. Everett smiled as she listened to Superior declaiming with such scathing irony on the weakness of women and the folly of love, while trading on the one and living by the breath of the other. But she understood her lesson and practised it faithfully. From the day on which she entered the Abbey Richard had no recognized status in his own house ; and, in spite of his evident displeasure, Mrs. Everett's conversation alternated between religion and the Abbey estate.

" *Your* house, *your* fields, *your* farms," she used to say with emphasis to Hermione, of whom she asked questions concerning this and that, to which the pretty woman could give no reply save in a helpless appeal to her husband.

" Do not you know your own affairs ? " asked Mrs. Everett one day. " How dreadful ! "

" Why ? " said Richard gravely. " What more is needed than that the husband should act for the wife ? "

" You hear what Mr. Fullerton says," returned Mrs. Everett, still speaking to Hermione. She never addressed

Richard directly. " Do you too, think that marriage merges a woman's individuality so entirely as to make her no longer responsible for what may be done in her name with her means? I confess I do not ; and the doctrine seems to me as dangerous as the practice is indelicate. We are all directly responsible for the use or abuse of our powers and privileges ; and to say, ' My husband did this or that,' ' My husband forbade this or commanded that,' will not exonerate us if things are done which tell against the glory of God and the influence of the Church."

Hermione coloured and looked down. Richard turned from one to the other, his sad face set into a certain proud sternness which, once an expression entirely strange to him, was now becoming only too mournfully familiar.

" My wife's principles were different from yours," he said quietly. " When we married our wills, our hearts, our interests were the same, and one interpreter was sufficient."

" Shifting one's responsibilities does not lessen the guilt of misused power," said Mrs. Everett, adjusting her tucker. " Don't you think so, dear?" to Hermione. "You are not afraid to speak openly, are you?" in a low, sympathetic voice.

"No, she has no reason to be afraid," said Richard ; and ; "No, I am not afraid," said Hermione, both together in a breath.

"Then, do you really think that a woman, because she is married, has no direct responsibilities?" asked Mrs. Everett, pursuing the theme. The opportunity for striking a few nails into the coffin of conjugal affection was too good to be lost.

"No, I do not think that," Hermione answered.

"Yet you act on what you do not believe?"

Hermione laughed nervously.

"We all do that at times, I fancy," she said with affected levity.

Mrs. Everett smiled.

"That will be but a poor excuse at the Last Day," was the reply made with perfect urbanity. "Bone of my bone and flesh of my flesh will have a bad time of it, I fear, if the one bone has taken service under Satan, and the other lets itself be dragged into the same ranks —knowing better."

"Your Last Day must be a ruthless kind of spiritual butchery, if a poor soul is punished for not having learnt, when in the body, what farms belonging to her were let, and for how much and to whom," said Richard. "How you Christians can imagine such a Divine Being as He whom you worship I cannot conceive. Your God of Love is more cruel than Moloch—your Divine Reason more insensate than Juggernauth!"

"Richard! don't!" cried Hermione in despair.

Why would he say such dreadful things at the very time when she was doing her best to defend him against Mrs. Everett, and honestly trying to think a little less ill of him than she had done of late!

"I do not wonder at your husband's sentiments, detestable as they are," said Mrs. Everett, still addressing Hermione. "If I held one part of his vile opinions, I should the other. Naughty children always think the chastising parent cruel and the punishment hard. And so it is with sinners."

"If I had compared the action of your God to that of a man, you would have called it blasphemous," said Richard, who was determined to have it out with her.

Mrs. Everett turned on him.

"And so it would have been," she said passionately. "What can a blasphemer be but blasphemous! It is a sin to discuss such subjects with you!" she added, rising in an agitation that was partly real and partly feigned. Then, as if she had recovered her serenity by an effort,

she turned back from the window where she had gone as
if for refuge, and said to Hermione amiably : " I am
going out now, dear, though it is raining. Shall I tell
Superior that you were afraid of the weather?"

"No," said Hermione, rising also in agitation. "I
will go with you. I am not afraid of the weather."

"I wish you would not go out, Hermione. It is not
fit for you to-day," said Richard, coming up to where she
stood and laying his hand on her shoulder.

Mrs. Everett averted her eyes as from something unholy ; Hermione dropped hers, and her lips quivered with
nervous shyness. What a frightful position ! It would
have been so pleasant to have done as Richard wished ;
but there was Mrs. Everett—and then Superior ! She
dared not anger them ; and to please him would be to
anger them.

"I can take any message that you like to send to
Superior," said Edith Everett in a cold voice and with an
unpleasant smile. "I can tell him that Mr. Fullerton
would not allow you to come, and that you were too
good a wife to disobey. He expects you, I know; but
that is no matter. He will live over his disappointment."

"How silly it all is !" said Hermione nervously.

"Of course I will go; I am not made of sugar, Richard"—to her husband with false playfulness; "and," to Edith Everett, "I always keep my engagements when I can."

"Do not be angry with me, dear, for speaking as I did just now," said Mrs. Everett when they were alone. "I was carried out of myself for the moment; but I ought to have remembered your feelings, and for your sake should have spared the blasphemer. It is so hard to me to realize that you, Hermione Fullerton, love a man whom every good Christian should abhor, and who in the Ages of Faith would have been excommunicated and burnt. You so good and earnest—I cannot understand this indifference to the Church and the truth!"

"I see my husband's faults as clearly as anyone can, and suffer from them more," said poor weak Hermione faltering.

"Yet you go on living with him—go on putting all the power into his hands! You give your whole fortune to him, and he uses half of it to make men infidels and destroy in them the blessed hope of salvation and the belief of immortality;—and then you say you see his faults and are a loyal daughter of the Church!"

She spoke severely; Hermione's spiritual state was

evidently one of grievous peril to her mind. Even
Superior himself, inimical to Richard as he was,
had less harshness towards this wifely weakness
which kept the conjugal tie, though strained, not
wholly broken.

"My position is difficult," said Hermione.

Edith Everett smiled.

"'He who would save his life shall lose it,'" she said;
"and you know, my dear, we cannot carry our darling
sins on our backs if we would enter in at the strait gate.
Your husband is your darling sin and you will not free
yourself from him; but I am afraid—I am afraid—that
strait gate is terribly narrow!"

"What ought I to do?" asked Hermione, with a kind
of desperate courage.

Mrs. Everett came close to her and took her two
hands in hers.

"Shall I tell you?" she said in a clear metallic voice.
"Take back the management of your own affairs; forbid
him to use your money as he does for the spread of
infidelity; make him an allowance and have a deed of
separation. You will never be a true Christian or a good
churchwoman, Hermione, until you do all this; and
Superior knows this as well as I do."

'*You do not know what you are saying.*'

"No, I cannot do all this. Poor Richard!" said Hermione.

Mrs. Everett let her hands fall.

"Then you can never hope to go to heaven," she said. "You prefer the creature to the Creator, and sensual passion to holiness and faith. Your love for your husband is simply sensuality and a shameful sin, call it what you will."

"You do not know what you are saying," cried Hermione, strongly agitated.

"I think I do," said Mrs. Everett in a superior kind of way. "It is you, poor thing, who do not know what you feel! Neither I nor Superior will ever think differently until you take your courage in both hands and do as I say—and as he says too :—rid the place of this infamous atheism which your husband teaches, and free yourself from the declared enemy of the Church and your priest. There is no second way. It is this, or consenting with sinners and making yourself responsible for their sin. There! don't cry! Tears do no good unless they are tears of repentance; and you are only crying because you are weak and worried and cannot make up your mind to do bravely what is right."

She went to her and kissed the grieving woman as if she had been a child.

"I have said enough for the present," she thought, watching her. "Things must go gently."

After a moment she spoke again.

"You poor darling!" she said; "I am so sorry to make you unhappy. But I must, until I make you good. Don't fret any more just now. Put on your bonnet and come with me to see dear Superior. He will comfort you and tell you that I am right."

"I don't see how that will comfort me," said Hermione irritably.

At this moment Mrs. Everett was the most hateful person in all creation to her whom she had been appointed to guide and befriend.

CHAPTER V.

THE TERRORS OF JUDGMENT.

MR. LASCELLES and Mrs. Edith Everett stood by the parting of the ways, she to return to the tedium of her duennaship at the Abbey, he to the discomfort of his bereaved Vicarage; both a little rasped by the unpleasant conditions of the present moment, but drawn closer together by the common need of sympathy rather than driven apart into unfriendliness because of irritated nerves and ruffled temper. They had been talking of many things connected with the parish, and had touched at last on the relations of Hermione with her husband, and how far she might be counted on in the final struggle which Mr. Lascelles was preparing to make. Both knew that she was profoundly impressed with faith and fear—that she believed in the truth of Christianity and was afraid of the power of the Church; but both knew also that her love for her husband was not dead, and that since Virginia's defection it had undergone an undeniable revival; and both were anxiously watching

the alternate rise and fall of these two antagonistic forces,
and speculating as to which would finally overcome.

"Do you think she will be permanently influenced
for good?—you see so much more of her than I do!"
said Mr. Lascelles, careful not to show too much
personal interest in Hermione.

"Well, you see, she is so weak!" replied the pretty
woman's friend and guide, speaking with tranquil contempt. "There is no certainty with weak people; and
as for her, you never know where to have her. You
think you have brought her to a right view of things one
day, and the next she has taken a new start and is as
far off as ever. She is terribly fatiguing. I hope she is
worth all the trouble taken about her!"

"She is very impressionable," said Mr. Lascelles,
steering between praise and blame.

"That is a meek way of putting it, Superior. I
should call her miserably feeble-minded," returned Mrs.
Everett, still with that same calm, mocking contempt.
It was her method of asserting her own superiority.

"Her will has been crushed so long. It is the para-
lysis of disuse," said the vicar, wishing to be charitable
as well as just, yet not caring to champion Hermione
Fullerton too warmly to Mrs. Everett. Those hazel eyes

of hers were not pleasant to meet when they looked as if they were reading the secret writing of the soul ;—and somewhat despising the literature.

"She need not have been crushed. She need not have given in to that vile husband of hers if she had not liked it," she said. "Really, no excuses are to be made for her, Superior ! She is just a child with nice manners and a pretty face and nothing whatever in her. When you have said that she is kind-hearted you have said all for her that you can. Of mind she has not a trace."

"You, at least, will not strain the truth for charity. I honour your uncompromising spirit," said Mr. Lascelles, with a courtly smile.

"No," she answered, ignoring the sting and accepting the blandishment. "It is never my way to strain the truth for false charity. I like to see things as they are, and to speak of them as I see them."

"Yet submissiveness has its uses, my dear friend," he said pleasantly.

"I am not clever enough to see them in the case of Mrs. Fullerton," she answered. "Jelly-fish and that dreadful protoplasm have their uses too, I suppose ; but I confess I do not know what they are."

"As an agent inspired by others," said Mr. Lascelles. "The docility which has made Mrs. Fullerton submit so readily to her husband will make her as obedient to the Church."

Mrs. Everett looked into vacancy and put on, as she could do at will, a perfectly stolid, stupid, mindless look.

"She believes—that is the great thing gained," continued Mr. Lascelles ; and then waited for an answer.

"But she is one of those emotional people who require so much personal influence !" she said. "It is not as if she had any intellect, any will, any force that could be trusted to. She has to be always held in hand—always guided."

"She has that influence in Direction," replied Hermione's confessor demurely.

"To forget everything that she has promised as soon as she is at home !" retorted Mrs. Everett cruelly. "She must be an enormous trouble to you, Superior, if she is honest."

"I allow that. She does give me infinitely more trouble than some others whom I could name—some others who are at once stronger and yet more submissive."

The vicar smiled as he said this, his smile giving his words their application and meaning.

Mrs. Everett smiled too, and adjusted her bonnet-strings with the automatic coquetry of a woman who, though she knows that she is not beautiful, also knows herself admired. Truly she had no cause to fear Hermione! There was no rivalry here that should make her afraid. Blunt nose; small, greenish, hazel eyes; a face that had not one redeeming feature save its transparent skin, on the one side—on the other loveliness as fresh and fragrant now as at eighteen; but still no rivalry that should make her afraid! For had she not brains by which she was enabled to be a clever man's still cleverer manipulator as well as coadjutor?—while Hermione was but a child to be petted and cared for—loved if you will and admired—but neither trusted to in moments of difficulty nor confided in when clear counsel was needed —a mere doll-wife, dainty, sweet, caressing, loving;—and that was all! With such a man as Superior brains would count for more than beauty, and sweetness was less necessary than sense. He wanted some one by his side who had intelligence enough to understand his own mind and act with independent accord—strengthening his hands while freeing him from the trouble of direction; not a mere machine, however pretty, to work when guided but sure to fall into disorder if left to itself.

No ; Mrs. Everett saw nothing to be afraid of and much to hope for. But she must not let Superior understand her too clearly, and she must manage things in her own way; which was not exactly that in vogue at Crossholme.

"Some men like troublesome women," she said.

"Do they?" asked Mr. Lascelles with affected innocence of inquiry.

"Yes; pretty little creatures whose inferiority is a perpetual witness of their own supremacy," she said. "It gratifies their self-love to feel themselves always on a pedestal, and to see the relative silliness of the dear little things!"

"So! And who are these men?" he asked, still with that innocent air as of one wanting to know.

"Well, I do not think that you are one, Superior!" said Mrs. Everett with frank confession. "You are too wise to like the dangerous honour of being the head-centre of an association of pretty simpletons. You would feel more in your right place if surrounded by those who understood and could help you as interpreters of your mind, rather than by mere dummies acting only according to minute orders; is it not so?"

"Surely!" said Mr. Lascelles with a peculiar smile. "But where are such to be found? So few women

understand the deeper thoughts of men! Some sup-
plement us," he added courteously ; " but it is given
to very few to really understand us."

" I know that, being one of the few," she said carelessly. "I do most thoroughly understand them and
society too. Had I been born a man I should have
gone into diplomacy. And I would have made a name.
As it is I shall make my son's, when he is old enough.
My husband died just as I had laid the train of his success," she went on to say. " Had he lived he would
have been distinguished. I know that he would have
been made a bishop. The whole thing was ripening
when he was taken."

" I know you are invaluable," said Mr. Lascelles with
earnestness that was more flattering than passion. " But
in the matter of your husband, now—I, who uphold the
celibacy of the clergy as a necessity of Church discipline,
can scarcely be expected to feel entirely satisfied."

He lowered his eyes as he said this, and put on an
official look.

" Yes, as a principle, their celibacy is best," returned
Mrs. Everett. " But when we have so much to work
against any help is valuable. And a wife may be looked
upon as a lay worker—like a district visitor, for instance.

I think the thing would be lawful if her own heart was in the right place, and she could be really of use to the Church by the social advancement of her husband. Women have power, Superior!"

"You have," he said.

"Yes; I know that I can be of use where I am trusted," she answered. "As I hope you will find in this matter of Mrs. Fullerton," lightly, as if to put the other aspect of the subject from her.

"And you really think she will be induced to take the estate out of her husband's hands?" he asked, also anxious to drop that slight discussion on the value of diplomatic wives to ambitious ritualistic priests.

"I think so," said Mrs. Everett; "and would say 'yes' without hesitation if she had the smallest pretence to a moral backbone. But one can never be quite sure of such a fluid creature as she is."

"The scandal of the present state of things is unbearable," said the vicar angrily.

"My only wonder is how you have not put an end to it before this," returned Mrs. Everett. "I think I should have found the way had I been here. Your sister ought to have managed it ; for this is just one of those cases where a woman's aid is required, and where no man can act satisfactorily by himself."

"I count on you now," said the vicar with emphasis.

"I will do my best," she answered. "Poor Superior!" she added with a sympathetic little smile. "What a dreadful set you have fallen into! Hermione Fullerton—Theresa Molyneux—your sister who deceived and deserted you—all these silly gaping creatures setting their caps at you and each hoping to be the Honourable Mrs. Lascelles, while not one has the smallest qualification for the place. You are to be pitied!" She shrugged her shapely shoulders and laughed.

"But with Edith Everett to put all straight—" he said.

"You are to be congratulated in having one serviceable head among the dummies!" she answered quickly; bidding him farewell and leaving him to digest what she had already said. It was enough for one day.

By this time the cottages in Lane End were almost finished, and the men had been told by Richard that they might take possession when it suited them. Naturally the news got abroad; as indeed why should it not? An open check to the vicar, there was no secrecy in the matter from first to last; and neither Richard nor the men cared who knew it.

They were charming little cottages, built with all modern appliances and conveniences, and each standing in its own pleasant plot of garden ground; and they were architecturally ornamental and made a pretty feature in the landscape. They were not set at a fancy price either up or down in the scale; but the rent was calculated on a just basis, as a fair and equitable interest on the capital expended. Thus, no eleemosynary character tainted the benefit which they undoubtedly would be to the tenants; and a few architectural flourishes were not reckoned as of exorbitant value because pleasing to the eye. They were dwellings built with humane thought and generous intention, but with the common sense of a good business man as well. Parcelled out among the men from the first, they had been all along looked on as their certain homes; and each assigned occupier had made this and that suggestion for his own fancy or convenience while his house was in course of erection, and had determined where this and that should go, and what he would do here and there. They were all highly delighted with their prospective dwellings, and looked forward to taking possession with pleasure and eagerness. If there was one thing more than another that might be considered

certain in this shifty life of ours, it was that Richard
Fullerton's new cottages would be inhabited by the men
for whom they were designed. Failing the sudden death
of the intended tenant, there was surely nothing that
could step in between—earthquakes and tornadoes not
being things of ordinary occurrence in England.

This then was the moment for which Mr. Lascelles
had been waiting. When most secure the blow that
shatters all comes with greatest force; and if he could
strike that blow now he should have accomplished the
larger half of his great endeavour. Could he? Would
Hermione do as directed? Though her mind, never
strong nor self-reliant, had become weakened through
superstitious belief, yet her affections were not dead.
Had she been an intelligence only, with no interrupting
emotions, the thing would have been easy; but side by
side with her superstitious belief in the power of the
priesthood—in the sinfulness of reason—in the lost
condition of that soul which dares to doubt and hesitates
to obey—was the strength of her natural affectionateness,
her hatred of giving pain, her indestructible respect for
her husband;—that respect which still lived beneath the
superincumbent mass of reprobation that had been
heaped over it ;—and her sense of injustice in offering

him this unmerited affront. Step by step she had been
led up to this, the final blow; and now when she was
commanded to give it, she quailed and refused.

When the vicar told her what he wanted her to do,
she cried and shrank within herself, saying No ! she
could not.! indeed,. indeed, she could not ! Richard had
had so much sorrow of late ; she dared not give him
any more! It would kill him if she did, and she would
be his murderess. She besought Superior to spare her
this trial ; to be merciful as he was powerful ; to be gentle
to her and humane to her husband. He might have
been a God before whom she knelt, so abject was she, so
humble, so passionate in her pleading ; and she might as
well have sued to the tempest, sought to soften the rock
by her tears, as pray thus passionately to him ! The
vicar was not the man to defer his triumph for a woman's
tears ; and when crosses had to be carried he objected to
too great an outcry.

" It is your bounden duty, your obligation to God
and man," he said sternly. " You are the real owner of
the property, and to allow your husband, your agent, to
openly affront me and offend the Church by harbouring
these men who are my enemies and the Church's rebels,
is to make yourself one with his sin. And what is this

ostentatious harbourage of men whom I have driven out but an act of direct hostility to me—of open defiance of my authority? And you uphold this—make yourself one with it—you my chosen friend and dearest daughter!"

"He has always managed the estate, and he promised to befriend those men," she faltered weakly.

"A nest of infidels!—You wish them fostered here in this parish where we of the true faith are giving our very lives to establish religion and sound doctrine?— where I am straining every nerve, and submitting myself to every indignity to recall these lost sheep; and where you are all-powerful for good or evil, as you choose to make yourself? At present you are all-powerful for evil; but you might be my bravest, best, most valuable assistant, if you would shake yourself free from this sinful subservience to your infidel husband—this infamous obedience to the enemy of the Church!"

One strong irresistible wave of feeling swept over Hermione. The vicar's brutality, nicely calculated as it was, stirred her loyalty rather than shamed her love. Her heart turned back to the husband of her youth, to the man of her girlish passion, and she forgot all that level tract of dull content which lay between. He was her husband, the father of her child, the one true guide and centre of her life. The Church and the Revelation which he had so systematically outraged and denied faded away into the dim distance of her consciousness, and only feeling, affection and old-time loyalty remained.

"He is my husband," she said, lifting her eyes and speaking, though still gently, with a certain warmth that smote on the vicar's ear as if she had uttered blasphemy.

He almost gasped. It was the traditional worm turning against his heel—the legendary dove roused to self-defence—the return-blow of a slave thought to be subdued to passive non-resistance for life ; and for a moment astonishment checked his speech. But only for a moment. Looking at her as if she had been some curious insect :

"My dear child, I thought I had explained away your superstitious regard for the mere words of a promise which Satan has broken and defiled," he said with compassionate contempt. "You cannot be a true daughter of the Church and an obedient wife ; and if you hold by your husband, you must of necessity abjure your Saviour. Must I go over the whole ground again?"

"I know all that you would say, but I cannot act up to it," said Hermione with a certain helpless patience that would have touched anyone but Mr. Lascelles. "Sometimes you seem to be right; but when you want me to do such a thing as this, I do not think you are— and I cannot!"

She covered her face with her hands. He took them away, not too gently.

"No; you shall look at me," he said sternly. "Your defiance shall at least be open and confessed!"

"It is not defiance, Superior," she pleaded, lifting up her soft eyes to his yet not giving way—keeping to her point through all her gentleness. Was this really Hermione Fullerton—the plastic creature whom he had manipulated with so much trouble, whose divorce he had managed so easily, and whose very soul he had won, as he once believed, so thoroughly? Was this really Hermione Fullerton? He could hardly believe it.

"No?" he sneered. "It is not defiance? By what euphemism then, would you call it?"

"My duty as a wife," she said humbly.

"No! no! A thousand times no!" he answered, in a low, concentrated, hissing kind of voice. "It is not duty; it is *lâcheté*; it is base and craven cowardice; it is shameful self-indulgent sloth of soul—more shameful self-indulgent passion for a man whom you should regard as an emissary of Satan, a Judas re-incarnate. Go back to your husband in all the infamy of your former love ; go back in open infidelity to Christ ! Do not dignify your sin by fine words, Mrs. Fullerton ! Confess it for what it is, and take your part with the enemies of God and the Church ; range yourself with Satan and his agents with something like whole-heartedness ! Leave the Church ! leave me to my arduous fight against the devil, whose visible power your husband strengthens by your means ! Go back to the practical atheism of your former state ; but do not stand here neither in the pale nor out of it, neither a true daughter of the Church nor an open foe, confessing Christ with your lips and dishonouring Him by your deeds ! Lukewarm adherents like you do us more harm than declared enemies ; and were you twenty times Mrs. Fullerton of the Abbey, I would excommunicate you from among us ;—and will—if you are not obedient to Direction."

She crouched like one who has been struck, kneeling on the floor.

" You frighten me !" she said with a little cry.

" Because I shame you !" he answered. " It is your conscience which makes you afraid, not I. I am but the mirror in which you see the hideousness of your guilty soul."

" Superior ! Superior ! have mercy !" she cried.

A crucifix was standing on the table by which he sat. For the second time he took her hands from before her face, and made her look at the sacred emblem of her faith and the divine source of his power.

" You swore on this to obey me when I com= manded," he said. " What was the value of your oath then? Where will it land you if you break it now ?"

Hermione did not speak ; she could not. This was the concentration of all the anguish that life could give. The spiritual insolence and harshness of the priest in place of the high-bred courtesy and soft philandering to which she was accustomed, at once terrified and revolted her. The pride of her womanhood, of her gentle ladyhood, was outraged ; her personal delight in this handsome Director was wounded ; her submission, which had already cost her so dear at home, was returned with ingratitude. She thought of Richard, of his patient tenderness, of his very dulness by reason of loyal security—and now this tyranny ! this insolence ! She made a movement as if to rise from her knees, swung by the impulse to go back to Richard and shake all this from her as too degrading to be borne.

As she moved, half raising herself, Mr. Lascelles took her hand and placed it on the crucifix.

"Take this," he said in a deep voice. "Honour it or renounce it. Obey me, the appointed interpreter of Him who died for you, or crucify Him afresh by your misdeeds. You shall do one or the other before you leave this place. You shall be cast out from our midst or you shall be faithful and obedient. Will you swear to do as I command and refuse to harbour these men on your estate?"

"Superior!" she cried.

"Will you? One word—yes or no?"

"How can I say this to my husband! Have pity on me, Superior!"

She clung to him, grasping his coat; but he tore away her hands with contemptuous passion.

"Do not touch me!" he said. "You are perjured and accursed. You have denied your Lord; and until you repent and obey, you are excommunicate from the Church!"

He turned away abruptly and left her still kneeling on the floor; that accusing crucifix before her on the table, and "excommunicate from the Church" ringing in her ears.

CHAPTER VI.

'TWIXT HAMMER AND ANVIL.

THE day passed, and yet nothing was done. Hermione, in disgrace with the vicar and denied absolution, was still further exercised by Mrs. Everett, who made her understand that she considered her more sinful than even her atheist husband, in that, having put her hand to the plough, she had turned back from the work— having made one of the household of faith, she had gone over to the service of Satan. She spoke of the spiritual peril of such a state as hers, and what would come to her after death if she died in her sins, with the commonplace conviction of one who affirms that dynamite will explode if sharply struck, or that a ship will sink if scuttled. She told her in plain words without gloss or circumlocution that she was cast out by the God whom she had practically denied, and in the grasp of the Evil One whose work she was doing—as she had done for so many years now ! But with this difference, to her shame, that whereas formerly she was unawakened and unconscious, now she knew the full heinousness of her guilt. Were she to die at this moment—and whose life is safe even for an hour?—she would go headlong to perdition ; down, down to that eternal pit, as surely as a stone flung into the water sinks to the bottom. She was doomed. So long as she maintained her present attitude of rebellion to the divine authority of the Church, there was no hope for her in heaven, no peace for her on earth.

All this was said again and again, now with indignation at her wickedness, now with wonder at her weakness, and again with pity for her tragical fate ; but it was said incessantly ; and Hermione felt girt round with fire turn which way she would, whether she resolved to obey Superior or protect Richard, all the same doomed to suffer.

And it must be remembered that she believed implicitly in all this fuliginous theology. It was no vain image to her when the awful condition of lost souls was painted in words of fire and flame ; Satan was no turnip-headed bogie dressed up to frighten the ignorant, but a very real and actual presence, acknowledged now to be known by visual demonstration hereafter ; heaven and hell were tangible realities, the one in the eternal light of

the sky, the other somewhere in the dark; and according
to our actions we were carried up into the ineffable glory
of the one or dashed down into the unfathomable misery
of the other. When Edith Everett reminded her of all
these fearful perils which she was braving because of her
cowardice—"for what else is it but cowardice?" asked
her guide and friend scornfully—she trembled as if she
were already in the grasp of that hairy-handed fiend
to whom she had given herself by her sin. Her
Christianity had none of that robust eclecticism which
chooses the sunny places where the soul may dwell in
comfort and leaves the shady corners as unpleasant
lodgments; which eats its fill of sweet fruits and leaves
the bitter herbs to rot in the ground which brought them
forth. She accepted all legends, all fables, without a
glossary or index expurgatorius; and the power of the
Church was the coping-stone of the building. Hence,
judging herself by her creed, she knew that she was at
this moment, as Edith Everett said, accursed because
unabsolved—in the power of Satan because in disgrace
with the vicar. She realized the sinfulness as well as
the danger of her disobedience to her Director in this
weak return to wifely deference and wifely pity, as clearly
as she realized the fact of the antipodes; but she was

unable to nerve herself to the self-crucifixion demanded
by the Church. And even when exhorted to pray for
strength so that she might be able to perform this act of
immolation, she wept instead, in her heart not wishing to
be so strengthened.

So the day passed, and nothing was done.

In the evening Mr. Lascelles sent up a note to Edith
Everett, telling her to say to Mrs. Fullerton that he
begged she would not present herself at Early Celebration to-morrow, as he should feel himself compelled to
refuse her ; and that in the existing state of things he
would rather she did not come to the services at all.
It would be painful to him and an increase of condemnation to herself ; and in very tenderness for her he must
deny her false consolation. He was determined to make
her excommunication complete until her unqualified and
entire return to submission. He was not a man of half-
measures, and this was a case wherein apparent harshness
was the truest kindness.

This note, written for Hermione to see, was handed
to her so soon as read ; and as she gave it to her
Mrs. Everett realized the joy which a woman feels when
her rival is humiliated. But she expressed herself as
deeply, sincerely grieved ; grieved that things should be

as they were; but, being as they were, Superior was in the right, and she, poor sinful weak-hearted Hermione, was wrong! Did not the Service itself say that the impenitent eat and drink their own damnation? And until she had repented of her obstinacy and turned again to the right way of obedience and sincerity, Superior had nothing for it but to cut her off from the body of the faithful, lest worse should befall her. Would she then do as she ought? Would she forbid those infidel men the use of *her* cottages? Might she, Mrs. Everett, write and tell Superior that she had come at last into a proper frame of mind, and that she was penitent and obedient?

To which poor Hermione answered despairingly :

"Not yet! not yet! Give me a little more time to make up my mind!"

"To dally with sin, you mean," said Mrs. Everett severely. "Remember, Hermione! each hour's delay strengthens Satan by so much extra power, and makes your return to grace so much the more difficult."

"I must think of it. I cannot to-night. Richard looks so pale and ill. I think another blow would almost kill him; and this will be such a blow!" said Hermione, turning her eyes wistfully to the door.

" If he is the man of sense he passes for, he will not let it be a blow or a surprise to him in any way," said Mrs. Everett. " He must know, if he reflects at all, that it is impossible things can go on like this. When you were unconverted and as careless of God as he himself, you did not trouble yourself as to what was done with your money and in your name. But now, when you have become a faithful Churchwoman—are you a faithful Churchwoman after all?—it is monstrous to suppose that you will allow your fortune to go in propagating infidelity and making scandalous favourites of notorious infidels. Mr. Fullerton must see it all as clearly as we do ; and if he is really liberal, he must allow you to act according to your conscience."

" But this will not make the pain any the less," said Hermione.

" And until he is pained your soul is in deadly peril, and the consolations of religion are denied you," returned Mrs. Everett. " For my own part, I would do anything in the world rather than stand in your present position. The marvel to me is how you can bear it for an hour, when you yourself can put an end to it, now this very instant if you will. Excommunicate ! You ! Denied the holy Eucharist—even forbidden to attend the

public offices of the Church ! And you suffer all this that
you may not wound the self-love, the base human pride,
of the most notorious soul-destroying atheist in the
country ! What a farce to call yourself either a Churchwoman or a Christian ! "

" I am both—but I am a wife as well," said Hermione, too sharply stung for patience.

Edith Everett's long upper lip curled contemptuously.

" Do you call such a union as yours 'marriage'? " she
said. " To us of the true faith it is legalized sin, and a
shame that you should speak of it ! Do not shelter
yourself behind that poor little pretence ! There is no
marriage where there is no blessing by the true Church.
And you know that the Church neither could nor does
sanction such a union as this ! To sacrifice the Church
to Mr. Fullerton on the plea of his being your husband
is simply to add to your sin, because bringing into it one
guilt the more."

" I am very, very unhappy ! " said Hermione, letting
her hands fall on her lap.

" Yes," replied Mrs. Everett; " of course you are !
We are always unhappy when we are doing wrong. Then
I am not to tell Superior that you submit ? "

"No, I will tell him myself—when I do," said Hermione, turning wearily away.

The next day, Sunday, all things were as Mr. Lascelles had decreed. The Lady of the Manor was for the time excommunicate, and her place among the worshippers was kept conspicuously vacant. For though the theory was that all places were free alike, the practice was different; and the great ladies of Crossholme were never incommoded by the jostling of the little people. Everyone looked and wondered at this strange vacancy of Mrs. Fullerton's accustomed chair; and when service was over everyone crowded round Mrs. Everett, and asked : Was Mrs. Fullerton ill? what was amiss? why had she not come? had she had bad news of Virginia? was Mr. Fullerton laid up, and she at home nursing him? what was it that had kept her away? what did it mean?

To which questions Mrs. Everett gave cautious, yet in a manner suggestive, answers. Mrs. Fullerton was not ill in body, she said, with a slight emphasis that pointed the alternative so obviously as to set the congregation wondering what ailed her mind—and had she gone out of it? as more than one scoffer had prophesied she would.

But her guide and friend having said this, said no more; and always smiling, took her way back through the park and so to the Abbey—calculating her chances as she went. Not handsome, without money, and the mother of four children—could it be done? If he believed in her capacity to help him on in his work and with the world, yes. And the first test of this capacity would be to succeed where he had failed ; to influence to the point of unqualified submission that tender soul, which he, with all his powers of fascination and authority combined, had not quite controlled. If she could do this, he might then perhaps be brought to credit her ability to make him a bishop, if she were his wife. And as a bishop how much wider would be his sphere of action, how much more impressive his authority and more effective his influence ! As for his principles on the celibacy of the clergy—other men who held the same views have found their better part in matrimony when the thing came to them rightly presented, so why should not he ? The question had been asked before at Cross-holme, with as yet no satisfactory reply; but then Edith Everetts were scarce ; and it would take one as clever as she to win such a man as Mr. Lascelles.

This dead, dry, soulless Sunday passed like all other uncomfortable times, and Monday came in its course. No action had yet been taken, and the men were pre-paring to move in ; John Graves was already in pos-session, and Dick Stern's wife had promised him his new home by night. Hermione stood at the fork, still hesitating—not brave enough to go resolutely on either road ; temporizing, doubting, fearing, hoping against hope and vaguely looking for a miracle which should save her from her trial and Richard from his pain, yet put things square with the vicar's desire. She sent messages and notes of abject humility, beseeching Superior to pardon her, but not promising obedience ; but as he could not bend her he would not forgive her ; and each hour that passed only deepened her sin and added to his demands. At first he had ordered her merely to refuse the men possession of the new cottages built for them at Lane End ; but now, raising the price of his forgiveness, like that of the Sibylline Books of old, he demanded that she should not only do this but also take the Institution out of her husband's hands ; and then, not only the Institution but the whole management of the estate. On these terms only would he receive her back into the Church as a penitent absolved from her sin. It was this or excommunication, both from his friendship and the sweet consolations of the Church.

It was a bold stroke that he played ; for all or nothing; but the moment was ripe. If he let this occasion slip he might never have another so favourable.

And now the final struggle had come. Love or religion—her husband's control or her Director's authority —the obligations of marriage or the ordinances of the Church—which would win? Under which Lord would she finally elect to serve?

To add to her present personal perplexity, the bills which she had incurred for the restoration of the church, and other things connected with the parish and Mr. Lascelles, were sent in to her in a mass, and instant payment was peremptorily demanded of some; and to add yet more to the pressure put on her on all sides, dear Superior fell ill, and sent for Edith Everett in terms which would have suited a dying man sending for his best friend to receive his last wishes.

"Let me go with you!" pleaded Hermione, when her guest told her the news.

"I am sorry, but it is impossible," she answered; and showed her a little postscript, wherein Mr. Lascelles had written in a very unsteady hand: "On no account allow Mrs. Fullerton to accompany you, unless she has repented of her sin and is prepared to obey."

"How can I do it! how can I!" murmured Hermione, hiding her face in despair.

" You must answer that to the Eternal Judge at the

Last Day," said Mrs. Everett coldly. "There will be no half-measures then, and no plea of 'how can I?' allowed."

On which she turned away and went down to the Vicarage, where she sat for about two hours with Superior, who had really a slight attack of feverish cold, and whose notes she wrote, and all his other business transacted, with the most delightful assumption of necessary assistance as well as with charming facility and help.

"She is an uncommonly clever woman!" thought the vicar as he lay back in his easy-chair, watching the long lissome fingers moving so swiftly over the paper. "And though she is not handsome at first sight, it is a face that satisfies one more on acquaintance than many others of perfect beauty. She has mind and character; and is such a thorough woman as well!"

If Mrs. Everett could have read the vicar's mind, would she have called this an advance in her secret project?

When she returned to the Abbey after her two hours of tranquil business-like assistance, she went into the drawing-room with deep melancholy, unspeakable dejection imprinted on every feature, expressed in every

gesture. Dear Superior was very ill indeed, she said ;
his distress of mind at Hermione's lost condition and
strange recalcitration was such that he could not sleep
nor eat—he could only pray with tears for the recovery
of the dear lost soul now given over to Satan.

"He is sick for your sin," said Edith Everett with
mournful solemnity. "If he dies you will be the
cause. He is in a high fever and is really very ill,"
she added, falling into commonplace almost without
knowing.

"May I not go down and see him?" asked Hermione
anxiously.

"No," Mrs. Everett answered. "He begged me to
forbid any such attempt on your part. Even Theresa
Molyneux has to be given up, though this is her day ;
and you know how punctual he is in his parochial duties;
so that I am sure he is not able to see *you*."

"But I am so much more his friend than Theresa
has ever been !" said Hermione jealously.

"And for that very reason your visit would be so
painful as to be impossible," she returned. "You know
how many hopes he built on you, and what a holy joy it
was to him to think that he had been privileged to save
you from perdition—and now, to see you so utterly a

castaway ! It would be more than he could bear in his critical condition !"

Tears came up into those clever eyes and over-flowed the lids with a decent kind of passion. Hermione turned away in trouble that she could neither control nor conceal. It touched her soft heart to think that Superior should be so sorry for her as this ; it pricked her conscience that she should be so undutiful to the Church ; it probed her pride that her visit should be refused—she who had been supreme up to now, to be set aside while Edith Everett was exalted in her stead ! Her whole moral being was disturbed ; and beyond and above all was that abject fear of the Judgment to come, which both Mrs. Everett and Superior said she had provoked and which her own conscience, as informed by Church teaching, told her she deserved.

"What can I do ?" she cried, wringing her hands.

"Do as you are commanded," said her guide and friend. " Take the management of your affairs into your own hands and out of those of your infidel husband ; refuse to allow your money to be any longer used for the spread of atheism and the ruin of immortal souls ; and refuse to allow your land to be turned to the use of infidels who spend their lives in trying to destroy the

Church. It is childish to ask what you are to do ! Your duty is plain before you, and until you do it you can have no peace."

" I shall have no peace any way, do what I will," said poor Hermione, speaking sincerely in her sorrow.

" No peace in doing the will of God ? Are you too an infidel ? " asked Mrs. Everett severely.

" The flesh may be weak, however willing the spirit," said Hermione.

" If your spirit were really willing you would soon find strength for your duty," returned her friend. " How you can think of your present state, and keep in it, I cannot understand ! " she continued. " It would send me mad ! I would do anything in the world to get out of it—cut off my hand, pluck out my eye ! "

" I believe you would; but then you do not feel giving pain so much as I do," returned Hermione.

Mrs. Everett turned herself square to her friend and faced her angrily.

" I do not feel giving pain so much as you do ? " she said. " To a sinful man who has brought countless souls to perdition, perhaps not ; and I thank God for it ! But I feel more than you do the crime of giving pain to my Director, of causing scandal to the Church, of crucifying Christ afresh by my sin. If I were in your horrible position I certainly should not mind giving pain to the man who had done so much to hurt our Mother ; and if you were a true Churchwoman you would not have two thoughts on the subject."

"I am a true Churchwoman, and I have a great many thoughts," said Hermione petulantly.

Mrs. Everett looked at her with undisguised contempt.

"You are a mere child !" she said. "I shall never take your part with Superior again. He may think of you what he likes, and I shall not trouble myself to defend you."

"Superior has no right to speak against me. I have been his best friend here, and have helped him to the utmost of my power," said Hermione with spirit.

"You have—granted ; but what are you doing now ? You were a help to him, but now you are a broken reed and have pierced his hand when he most leant on you ! I think Superior is quite right in all he says ; and I will do what I can too to help him to make an exchange. Crossholme is not a fit place for him. He is lost here, and would be far better off elsewhere ; and better appreciated too !"

Hermione started and looked at Edith Everett with a sudden spasm of fear on her face.

"He told me to-day," continued the widow carelessly, "that he could not bear the strain here any longer. And I can understand it. A conscientious priest has difficulties enough when he is helped on all sides. The sins of unregenerate humanity are hard enough in themselves to cope with; but when it comes to a person in your position helping infidelity, giving confessed atheism all the influence of your money, all the prestige of your position, then the thing becomes impossible! And Superior is quite right to shake the dust off his feet and leave you all to yourselves and destruction. Perhaps the next vicar will be a Protestant"—contemptuously— "or a cloaked infidel calling himself a Broad Churchman; or one of those heretics who pride themselves on being Evangelical"—still more contemptuously. "I hope so. He will be better fitted for the congregation, so far as I can judge, than a devoted priest like Superior, with his faithful band of followers and helpers."

"Does he talk seriously of going?" asked Hermione in dismay.

"Certainly he does," Mrs. Everett answered as calmly as if she had been telling the truth. "He told me to-day that if you continued impenitent he would give up the living. After the shameful disgrace in which your daughter took such a prominent part, I must say, Mrs. Fullerton, I think you owe him more consideration than you show."

"That is just what I feel about my husband," she returned. "His distress about Virginia is so great; and, after all, she was the youngest of them, and entirely under the influence of Sister Agnes."

"How blind and mad you are!" cried Mrs. Everett with temper. "As if her father's awful infidelity was not the primary cause of your daughter's perversion! You speak as if he was to be pitied, when it is by him alone, in the first instance, that this awful crime was committed! I look on him as the ruin of your child, not in any sense as the sufferer. As Superior says, that man is the direct agent of Satan, and all his natural good qualities, which we do not deny"—"We!" thought Hermione jealously— "are so many more snares set by the enemy of mankind for the destruction of souls. You know all this as well as I do, and yet you uphold him, and do your utmost to strengthen his hands. Never call yourself a Christian, still less a good daughter of the Church, again! You are the comforter and abettor of infidels; and I only hope that Superior will leave Crossholme and carry his precious ministrations where they will be better appreciated and do more good."

" Don't ! " cried Hermione, covering her face.

" Then repent of your sin and do your duty as you ought," said Mrs. Everett, going back to her point with the cold insistance of an automaton.

'Twixt hammer and anvil in truth, and no one able to save her ! Faithless to the Church or cruel to her husband, on no side could she find comfort or get rid of that awful difficulty—opposing duties ! Here called by natural feeling, there commanded by ecclesiastical authority—she scarcely knew which voice to obey since it was impossible to reconcile the two. If only her duty to the Church could have been harmonized with humanity to her husband !—if only Superior would absolve and bless her once more, yet poor Richard be saved from further suffering ! What could she do ? What could she do ? She must not let Superior leave the place, abandon his work, his congregation, his mission, because of her. That would be a sin for which she could never hope to be pardoned. And just now too, when the church, in the restoration of which he had taken so much pride and pleasure, was so nearly finished and

ready for reopening ! And then he was ill, on account
of her ; and in such deep mental distress because of her
sin ! Things could not go on in their present state ; and
yet she had not the heart to free herself from her
difficulties by dealing so hardly with her husband. And
yet again, if she did not, she must confess all that mass
of debt to him, and what she had undertaken to do for
the church ! There was no way of escape for her, turn
where she would. Girt round with fire—'twixt hammer
and anvil—there was nothing for her but pain and
penance, and the anguish, as it was to her, of making
others suffer.

In the midst of her desperate trouble Richard came
into the drawing-room where she and Mrs. Everett sat—
the one writhing, the other torturing.

"Could I have a word with you, Hermione ? " he
asked.

His manner was as quiet, his face as calm and sad
as ever, but he did not look more than usually disturbed.

"Yes," said Hermione in an embarrassed voice.
"What do you want with me, Richard ? "

"It is to look at the leases of the new cottages at
Lane End," he answered. "They are ready for your
signature."

"Now is the moment. Be firm to the Church, or by your own deed expel Superior from the parish. If the men get those houses he will not stay; it all depends on you," said Mrs. Everett in a low tone of voice, preparing to leave the room, but bending over Hermione before going.

"Perhaps it will be more convenient to you to come into my study? I do not wish to disturb Mrs. Everett," said Richard.

" It will not disturb me to go upstairs for an hour," said Mrs. Everett, answering Richard through Hermione, as was her wont.

"I would rather go into the study," said Hermione, trembling.

She felt as if the sight of those iniquitous skulls of Esquimaux and Andaman Islanders, those atheistic casts of brains and blasphemous anatomical plates, those soul-destroying microscopes which, with the photographs of the moon and a chart of Fraunhofer's lines, were the visible witnesses of Richard's infidelity—she felt as if all these things would strengthen her in dealing the blow, if it had to be given, as she feared must needs be ! She must not sign those leases; she must not let Superior leave the place and imperil the eternal salvation of her own soul and all the parish because of her weakness in the face of pain. And yet, poor Richard! Poor Richard was so good in spite of everything! And at one time how much she loved him; and would now, were it not a sin!

"Remember, Hermione! God sees you, and Superior will have to be told," were Edith Everett's last words, spoken in a whisper as the miserable Lady of the Manor walked slowly away.

CHAPTER VII.

THE DIE CAST.

THE country was looking its best to-day. A morning shower had washed the air and brought out the full fragrance and colour of the flowers in the garden, of the trees and turf in the park, of the. beanfield to the right, of the tangled thorns and resinous pines in the woods to the left. By the afternoon, as it was now, the clouds had lifted and the sun was shining ; so that the Abbey and the grounds, lying full to the south, were literally flooded with light, and the whole place looked as if newly minted to-day. From every voice and circumstance of nature stole out that subtle hope, that sense of possibility in the future, which fills the heart with undefined pleasure; as if our sorrow had passed with the winter weather and we were left free to love and enjoy. It was a day when the owners of lands and the dwellers in fair places feel doubly the delight of life and the graciousness of fortune ; and Richard, for all his pain, recognized the influences of the moment as keenly as of old.

He looked out with the pride of the owner, mixed with the loving understanding of the naturalist and the deeper thoughts of the philosopher, as he and Hermione passed the open window to the table beyond. What a grand day for the land, he thought; and how well he knew those thousand sounds and scents which were ever to him like the voices of friends whom he could trust! How glorious was this thing which man calls Nature! —what a mine of truth and knowledge! And then he sighed, and looked again on the papers in his hand and Hermione by his side.

Her husband's study was a strangely unfamiliar place to Hermione. For the last five or six years now—since first that vague dissatisfaction with his pursuits which had grown of late to such overpowering height had begun to germinate in her mind—she had not much affected it, and had always sniffed a little disdainfully at the uncongenial things which lay about. But now those uncongenial things were actively sinful to her eyes; the place was infected throughout; and had she come here when not absolutely compelled, she would have felt like a second Naaman bowing in the house of Rimmon—but a Naaman without a dispensation. She had not been here since that fatal Christmas night when her husband and Ringrove had represented to her and Virginia all imaginable personal coarseness and spiritual darkness; and, as she had rightly judged, the renewal of the impression was useful, on Superior's side, by shocking her sense of intellectual propriety and making her realize yet more keenly the gulf between her and that infidel whose name she bore—though she bore it set so far in the shadow of her own. Still, though the skulls and bones, the flints and fossils, the maps of the moon and spectroscopic diagrams that were about were so many accusers, setting forth Richard's scientific presumption and abominable atheism, she was agonized by what she had to do. The fresh sweet time had softened her even beyond her wont—of the kind as she was to be softened through her senses, delicately touched. For some time now her heart had wavered back to her husband, and nothing but the tremendous power which Mr. Lascelles had over her by confession kept her steady to the point to which she had been brought; nothing but her fear of eternal damnation, should he refuse to absolve her, held her to the stake where she was to undergo torture and inflict what she endured. What a dreadful moment it was for her!—she who knew what was to come, and poor dear Richard who knew nothing! She was quite unlike herself as she crossed the room with him in a tumult of conflicting feelings, hating his atheism and her own action about equally ; loving and condemning him ; fearing Mr. Lascelles yet fascinated by him ; and unable to see her way clear before her, save in unqualified submission.

Richard drew the chair to the table and laid the paper before her, courteous and tender as he always was, and to-day something more. He dipped the pen in the ink and held it ready for her use.

"These are the leases of the Lane End cottages," he said. "They only want your signature."

Though he had supreme authority in the management of the estate, according to the terms of the power of attorney given to him at Mr. Fullerton's death, he had always kept up this little formality of joint signature when leases were granted. He had begun it in the early days of their happiness, not as an act of homage to the Lady of the Manor and the recognition of her rights so much as a declaration of unity between husband and wife and the association of her privileges with his duties ; and he had continued it ever since. But Hermione, indolent and satisfied, had neither asked nor cared to know any particulars of the papers she signed ; and more than once had stopped his mouth with a kiss when he wanted to explain. What did she know about business !—she used to say with a pretty laugh—he knew and she did not; but she liked to see her name bracketed together with his. To-day however when she sat down she did not take the pen as usual, but, looking at the endorsement, asked : " What leases did you say ? " with an affectation of interest as well as ignorance that was as new as her Ritualism—and his pain.

" For the houses at Lane End," he repeated.

" Are these the men who were turned out by Cuthbert Molyneux ? " she asked again, fluttering the leaves and making believe to read what she saw.

" Yes," said Richard.

She glanced at the door. It was open by about an inch, and she distinctly saw the outline of a face and the gleam of eyes watching her.

" They ought not to have these houses," she then said in a faint voice and trembling.

" No !—why ? "

He had been leaning over her up to this moment, pointing out with one hand the place where she was to sign—the pen in his other hand. Now he laid down the pen, took his finger from the paper, and straightened himself.

"They are infidels," said Hermione.

"Is that a reason why they should be homeless?" he asked, still quite quietly.

"It is a reason why they should not have houses on *my* estate," she answered after a pause, her manner by no means so decided as her words.

He was silent, feeling the ground before him.

"I have pledged myself to them," he then said rather slowly. "These cottages were built expressly for them and have been assigned from the foundation-stone. Some of the men indeed are already in possession. John Graves, for one, moved in on Friday; and others are moving to-day. They trusted to my word in the matter of the leases, which came from Starton only to-day."

"I am sorry, of course; I do not like to distress you or to disturb them. I hate interfering in things; but they ought not to have these houses; I ought not to harbour them."

Hermione spoke in short interrupted phrases, her breath often failing her, her colour coming and going, her whole being in disorder.

"It is my doing, not yours," he answered, watching her.

"I am responsible to God—it is my estate," she returned with difficulty, again glancing at the door.

"Why does your responsibility to God make you refuse these men as tenants?" he asked. "They are industrious, sober, well-conducted; they stand at a fair rent, and are sure to pay punctually. You could not have more desirable tenants."

"They are the enemies of the Church," she answered.

"I also," said Richard, with emphasis.

Again she trembled, but she did not speak. She only sighed, and her lips began to quiver. It was a heavy burden laid on her, and she felt as if Superior had been needlessly cruel. After all, what did it signify? Even infidels must live somewhere; and then she checked herself as in the commission of a sin, and remembered her primary duty of Obedience.

"I cast in my own lot with theirs," then said her husband, after another slight pause, still keeping his eyes on her, studying her every movement, her every look and change of colour.

"How can you do that? You have not built a cottage for yourself," she answered simply, not taking his meaning.

"No, but I have given my word and must keep it— or fall with it," he said.

She made no answer; still fluttering over those

fatal leaves where she seemed to read all but knew
nothing.

"Surely this is a mere passing fancy!" then said
Richard. "Are you serious, Hermione? Do you really
mean to use your moral rights—my legal powers would
count for nothing against your will—and forbid these
houses to my friends?"

"What an extraordinary thing to say, Richard! As
if a gentleman can make friends of blacksmiths and
tailors!" was her childishly disdainful comment, glad of
an escape into another question, like one in pain shifting
the position for a moment's ease.

"My wife! The Man whom you have deified made
His friends of publicans and sinners, of lepers and
castaways," said Richard, with one of his old tender but
half-playful smiles—the sign of remonstrance usual with
him when Hermione was wont to be more than commonly
illogical and wide of the mark. "If the teaching of
Jesus means anything at all it means democracy carried
to its ultimate limits, and far beyond my standpoint.
His democracy was out-and-out socialism traversed by
class enmity to the rich and respectable—*quâ* rich and
respectable—and mine is only the recognition of human
worth wherever found, independent of social condition."

"We leave the Church to explain all that," she said

hastily and with a freer manner. Argument was not so painful as action. "Of course Protestants who go to the Bible for themselves fall into error and make what was given us for our salvation their destruction instead. But we who are good Church people are better taught."

"Taught the value of class exclusiveness?—of strict caste?"

"Of ordained degrees of dignity and obedience to authority," she answered, using the vicar's own words spoken for her guidance not so long ago.

Her husband looked at her with a smile, this time of infinite sadness.

"Yes, you have been well taught enough!" he said with a sigh. "I scarcely recognize your mind as the same sweet simple intellect it used to be, as innocent of dialectics as of evil. You are now as clever in casuistry as one would expect the pupil of—Mr. Lascelles—to be."

She blushed and looked uneasy.

"I have had to be taught everything," she answered. "My mind was a blank sheet of paper when Superior— Mr. Lascelles—first came."

"Across which he has written, in bolder characters than I care to see, words which are of all others the most painful to me," he said. "But," rousing himself,

" we are wandering from the subject on hand, and this matter of the leases must be settled.   What do you really mean to do?   Will you sign, or refuse to grant them ? "

She was silent for what seemed an eternity to her, tossed as she was from side to side, and coward as she naturally was to pain.   She held the leaves between her fingers, and the dead silence which had fallen between her and her husband seemed to have reached out into the world beyond.   She heard nothing but the beating of her own heart and the half-checked breathing which a little more would turn to tearless sobs; then the figure behind the door rustled audibly and the schoolroom bell rang out for prayers.

" I cannot sign them," she said in a low voice and with effort, letting her hands fall nervelessly on the desk.

Richard caught his breath, and a slight quiver stirred his lips.   The blow had fallen, and so far reality was better than suspense.   But he did not give up the contest yet.   It was not for himself, but for those whom he called his friends, that he was striving—and not against Hermione but against Mr. Lascelles.

" You do not see the cruelty of this refusal ? " he asked, after a pause.   " You do not see that it is essentially an act of persecution, and as unjust as it is—what shall I say?—tyrannical? I, your husband, hold and teach the doctrines for which you punish these men, yet I possess your estate, enjoy your fortune, live in your house, and you forbid them to be even your tenants?"

"It is not by my wish nor with my consent that you do teach these awful doctrines," she said half timidly. Again there was a slight movement at the door, and the schoolroom bell seemed to ring out yet more imperatively, more loudly:—"and I am wrong to allow it," she added, her colour coming again, and her breath almost as much disturbed as if she had been running.

He looked at her narrowly.

"I always must teach them," he said slowly. "I shall teach them to the last hour of my life, and only death shall stop my mouth. Christianity represents to me darkness and falsehood, science and Agnosticism light and reason ; and under all penalties I must remain true to the faith that is in me."

Now was the crucial moment. All that Superior had said, and all that he had done by right of his office— his exhortations, his commands, his anger, and that awful prohibition !—all that Edith Everett had urged, and all that she herself believed, came in one huge wave of spiritual terror over her mind. It was her final moment

of choice, her unalterable decision between a love which
they had taught her to regard as unblessed and shameful,
and the Lord who had died for her and whom she
would crucify afresh if she did not sacrifice her husband;
between the Holy Catholic Church, whose priest held the
keys of heaven and hell, and the infidel who, himself
eternally doomed, would drag her along with him to
the place of everlasting torment; between Mr. Lascelles
and Richard—the rights given by confession or the
duties owing to marriage. Which was it to be?—with
the bell sounding for prayers and Edith Everett watching
through the half-opened door, seeming to repeat her last
warning words: "Remember! God sees you, and Superior
will have to be told."

"No," then said Hermione in a low voice, scarcely
able to articulate.

"What do you mean, dear? 'No' to what?—in what
sense?" he asked.

"Your infidel doctrines—you must not go on teaching
them—not here—not in the Institution," she faltered.

"I built the Institution for that very purpose," he
said.

"You must not any longer," was all that she could
say; and the woman behind the door smiled.

" Be explicit, my wife," he said, for the second time going back to the old phrase of the past, which he had given up ever since that terrible day when she had withdrawn herself from him. He took a chair and sat down by her, speaking with intense tenderness and the very pathos of patient dignity. " I do not want you to give yourself more pain than is necessary," he said, laying his hand on hers as it rested on the table. " I only want to have your meaning clear. Have your friends counselled you to take the administration of the estate out of my hands?—and do you mean to take their advice?"

" You must not preach blasphemy in the Institution," she said evasively.

"But that amounts to a prohibition ; and prohibition means that you dispossess me. Speak plainly, dear—you have never found me a harsh husband, and will not now. I only want to have your real wishes, so that we may not make a mistake."

He laid his other hand gently on her shoulder.

" You are an infidel," said Hermione. " You use your power here against the Church."

Then she covered her face in her hands, too broken and bewildered even to pray.

" And if I do not conform to the creed in which I do

not believe, you take the power of administration from me?   Say it all out now—yes or no!"

"Yes," said Hermione, almost in a whisper.

Surely now the sacrifice was complete!

Richard passed his hand over his forehead and cleared his eyes.   Then he rose from his seat and went to the window, leaning against the frame, looking out on the view before him.   But it was as if a veil had been drawn between him and all that he looked at—as if nature, so long his friend, had suddenly shut herself away from him, and was now indifferent and silent.

"Your will is my law," he then said quietly, coming back to her side.   "I will not press you further.   Poor child!   I know what it has cost you to come to this!"

"Oh, yes! it has! it has!" she said eagerly, grateful that he should believe her less cruel than she seemed to be, and glad that he should recognize her suffering rather than blame her for his pain.

"Things have gone too far now to be patched up," he continued, "and I have nothing for it but to yield." He was silent for a moment.   "Morse knows all that you have to do and can keep things straight for you," he then went on to say, speaking in a more composed, more business-like tone.   "You will find the books and accounts quite clear and intelligible. The whole of your affairs are in perfect order; no outstanding debts beyond the necessary current expenses; nothing confused or obscure anywhere. And you can always write to me if you want further information."

At the words, "write to me," Hermione looked up with a start; as at the words, "no outstanding debts," she had thought with a pang of her own entanglements which she would be so much ashamed to confess, yet which she did not know how to arrange unaided; but notwithstanding her sudden terror she did not speak. She laid, instead, her hand on her mouth to stifle her sobs and repress the recantation of all that she had just now professed and ordained.

"I do not think I have anything to tell you more than this," he continued. " It has been an easy property to manage, and everything is in perfect order."

She turned to him suddenly and raised her blue eyes to his. It was the impulse of a caress; but she remembered herself in time and fell back to her former drooping attitude and tortured air.

" Good-bye, old love," he went on to say, pitying her pain and for her sake wishing to get it all over now at once. "You have made me the happiest of men for all our lives together until now when you have suffered these strange influences to come between us and take you from me.   But I do not forget the past because of the present; and though I pity you I do not condemn you ; not for anything, sweet wife—except for the loss of our child."

His voice changed as he said this, and again he turned away to the window, where he stood leaning against the frame.

Hermione rose from her place and went up to him.

" Why do you speak as if you were going away ?" she asked, her natural weakness conquering her unnatural strength.   " You are not going to leave me, Richard?"

" Can you expect anything else, dear?" he asked, always gentle, always patient, but with dignity as well as tenderness.   " Can you even wish that I should stay here to bear witness to my enemy's triumph ?   You have preferred Mr. Lascelles to me, and I have no choice left me."

" Not Mr. Lascelles to you, but my Director," she stammered.

" Man or Director, it is all one to me," he answered. " I make no difference between the two.   But in any case, ask yourself whether the position to which you have reduced me is one which the man whom you once loved, and who is the father of your child, ought to hold. I cannot believe that you wish to humiliate me to the point of keeping me here as a kind of footstool for Mr. Lascelles to buffet at his pleasure."

"You are only asked to give up your lectures, and not use my money to spread infidelity and befriend atheists," she answered wildly, preaching peace where there was none. She wrung her hands as she spoke, and looked round the room as if trapped and scared.

"Do not try to salve over hard facts by soft words," he said. "That is unworthy of us both."

"No! it is only that!" she cried.

"Ah! my wife, do not lay flattering unctions to your soul," he said. "You have dispossessed me simply in obedience to Mr. Lascelles. Had it not been for him I might have taught what I liked to the end of time. Well—so be it. You have the power and I have no remedy. There is nothing for me but to submit, and leave you. The law is on your side; on mine only the love which has at last failed to touch you."

"But what shall I do alone? You cannot go! I cannot live alone!" she said.

"If you want me you can send for me," he answered. "You will always find me where you left me. Nothing will ever change with me; and when you have flung off this hallucination, with all its crookedness and want of truthfulness, you have only to call me to your side again, and I will come—you know how gladly."

"Richard, you must not go!" she cried hysterically, clinging to his arm.

"It is this or your own full and unconditional return to me," he answered. "There is no alternative. If you are sincere in not wishing to separate, you will come with me and leave all this pain and horror till you have got beyond its danger. Will you come, Hermione? Shall we go back to the old happiness and union? Speak, my wife, old dear love—say, shall we?"

He drew her closer to him, and kissed her forehead.

What was that small sound which came through the half-opened door? Richard heard nothing, but to Hermione it was audible and intelligible enough.

"Oh, why are you an infidel?" she cried, with a terrified look, freeing herself from his arms with a gesture of despair.

"It is too late to ask that now," he answered, again passing his hand over his face and clearing his eyes. "It is too late all round! Good-bye, old love! It is useless to give you or myself more sorrow. The die has been cast. I recognize my fate. Good-bye!"

He turned for the last time, and was half-way through the room, when she called him with a cry as if she were in fearful pain.

"Richard!" she cried, her face convulsed with anguish.

He stopped.

She made a sudden rush forward.

"You must not go!" she exclaimed. "Richard! my husband! my beloved!"

The door opened abruptly, and Edith Everett came quickly into the room.

"I am afraid I am intruding," she said, with a cold, sarcastic smile. "But the bell is ringing, Hermione, and we shall be late for evensong."

Hermione shrank back as if she had been detected in a crime. Richard stood his ground quietly.

"With whom do you elect to go, Hermione?" he asked; "with Mrs. Everett or myself?"

"I can answer that," said Edith, taking the poor, weak, unresisting hand and drawing it within her arm. "You will come with me, Hermione; because if you do not, you will deny our Lord, defy the Church, and sink your soul to the lowest depths of hell. You are bound to obey as the Church has ordained."

"Is this your deliberate choice, my wife—with all that depends on it? Will you forsake me for these cruel destroyers of happiness and love? Oh, Hermione! shake off this hideous nightmare once for all! Come with me—with your husband, your friend—and leave these heartless fanatics to themselves! Come! come, wife !"

He laid one hand tenderly on her head, and passed the other round her soft, fair shoulders.

Mrs. Everett shuddered.

"These sinful familiarities !" she said. "My sister, how can you, a pure-hearted woman, endure them ? The caresses of the devil, and you a child of our Mother !"

Hermione hid her face on her friend's shoulder.

"Speak, my wife ! speak, old love !" said Richard, with inexpressible tenderness. "Will you come with me, or go with her?"

"The Church commands you to come with me," said Mrs. Everett. "If you do not, you worship Satan, not our Lord."

"I cannot disobey the Church," said Hermione, in a suffocated voice.

"Now you are answered!" said Mrs. Everett triumphantly. "She has saved her soul alive, and the gates
of hell have not prevailed. You have done well," she
whispered to Hermione caressingly. "Our Lord and His
Blessed Mother are looking down on you from on high,
and the Church will give you absolution and blessing!"

Then, half carrying her, she bore her away from the
room, leaving Richard alone, conquered, humiliated and
dispossessed.

The victory gained with so much effort was not
endangered by negligent holding. All that day Hermione
was kept at the Vicarage in a state of spiritual intoxication
which prevented her from feeling or thinking. Superior
received her back into the bosom of the Church as
joyfully as if she had been the traditional prodigal who
had repented of her sins and returned into the way of
grace from that of destruction. He received her confession, and gave her absolution with a fulness of assurance that made her feel as if already accepted into
heaven. He drew vivid pictures of the beaming satisfaction felt by Divine Personages, and the joy passed
round among the angels on account of her recall. He
painted with a generous palette and a juicy brush the
pains of that place of eternal torment which she had

escaped; and made her thrill with terror as she seemed almost to hear the gnashing of teeth and the cries of unclean and impotent despair from which she had just escaped. It was like the loud music and strong drugs, the intoxicating perfumes and delightful finery with which a Hindù woman is surrounded on her sacrifice, reconciled to her loss and assured of her gain. Her conscience drugged and her vanity excited—her superstition roused to the highest point, here of hope, there of fear—her affections turned from their natural course and poisoned at the source—her very weakness made a fulcrum for the strength of those who had overcome her—she was helpless in their hands. They were crafty, and she was simple ; they were clever, and she was credulous ; they were cruel, and she was timid ; and, above all, they believed in themselves and their doctrines, and so had the extra leverage of sincerity against her.

All day long and far into the evening they kept up this spiritual music and incense, these drugs, this finery, by which their victim and widow was cajoled into completing the sacrifice already begun—prevented from leaping off the funeral pyre which they had laid for her best womanhood, her highest fidelity, her purest love. They intoxicated her as thoroughly as if they had given her strong wine to drink or Indian hemp to smoke; and made her as incapable of clear thought or honest reflection as if she had been physically insensible. She was in the spiritual ecstasy of the spiritually drunk, and knew nothing beyond the devout joys of holy imagination. She was one of the Accepted; and her unresisting obedience to Superior was the price which she had paid for the assurance of that acceptance. She had no sense of morality, no conscience beyond obedience, and was in that state wherein women have sacrificed their children to Moloch, flung their darlings to the lions when commanded by the high priest, who to them was the voice of their god. The victory was absolute, as complete in all its circumstances as the warmest advocate of lay submission could desire; and when the two women left the Vicarage, Edith Everett said in a hurried tone to Mr. Lascelles, as he handed her into the carriage:—

"Did I not promise that I would bring her to reason? Now will you trust me again?"

"The cleverest woman I know anywhere!" he answered warmly, looking right into her eyes. "And one of the most faithful daughters of the Holy Mother," he added in a prim voice, dropping his own demurely.

CHAPTER VIII.

THE CONQUERED AND THE CONQUERORS.

THE Institution chanced to be more than usually crowded to-night, for the subject of the lecture was attractive. It was to be a rapid survey of salient points showing the homogeneity of our planetary system as proved by the spectroscope, and of life on the earth as proved by evolution. And certain of the Laodiceans among the congregation, who subscribed neither to Ritualism nor to the upsetting theories of science, but who liked to keep well with their parson and to learn exciting facts when they could, had agreed among themselves to turn a deaf ear to the anti-scriptural applications so sure to be made, and go to the lecture to hear what Mr. Fullerton had to say about the unfinished condition of Jupiter and the telluric analogies of Mars—the development of man from an ascidian and the close chain of likeness running through the whole race of the vertebrates.

It would be rare fun too, said some, to hear how all these data would be found to prove one thing in his

hands when they had just been made to prove another in
those of an orthodox popularizer of science whom Mr.
Lascelles had lately had down at Crossholme to refute
the local Apollyon and hoist him with his own scientific
petard. Yes, it would be rare fun, said those who were
lazily indifferent to the contradictions between fact and
faith; rare fun, said the presumptuous ignorant who think
it fine to sneer at the know-nothingness of philosophers,
because, while they all acknowledge the same facts, they
all make irreconcilable deductions. They and some
others promised themselves a fine treat ; wherefore the
room was fuller than it had been of late, since Mr.
Lascelles had christened it the Devil's Shop, and made
abstention therefrom a *sine quâ non* of Church acceptance
and a share in the good things dealt out to the faithful ;
and, with the contradictiousness of fate, on the very
night when Richard would have been glad to have met
only his handful of sympathetic friends, to whom he could
speak freely and without pain, he was encountered by a
host of the curious, the indifferent, the semi-inimical—
and one active enemy in the person of Adam Bell, the
vicar's colly-dog and spy.

Mild and quiet as ever, but as pale as if his veins had
not a drop of red blood left in them, Richard gave his

lecture in his old manner and with his old care. The
bold word said in the calm voice, so peculiarly his
characteristic ; the richness of illustration to fix attention ; the choiceness and yet simplicity of language to
raise the literary taste and insure the self-respect of his
hearers, so that they should not feel themselves spoken
down to, and yet should perfectly well understand all
that was said to them and be in no wise addressed over
their heads; all the tact and thoroughness, the delicacy and
thoughtfulness, which made him such a consummate lecturer for working-men, were as evident to-night, during his
agony, as they had ever been at his best and freest moments.
Nothing could have shown more clearly the nature of the
man whom his wife had been induced to repudiate as
an emissary of the Evil One ; nothing could have proved
more conclusively his conscientiousness, his patience, his
self-control, his high idea of duty and what each member
owes to the community of which he forms a part. It was
only when all the facts came to be known that the men
who listened to him now with pleasure, remembered him
as he was to-night with reverence. Even Adam Bell
confessed, in that small cynical " mind-cell " which other
men call their souls, that Humanity in its highest
development is a thing rightly worshipped ; and that

Mr. Fullerton was a man who made one somehow believe pretty clearly in a God.

When the illustrative and physical part of his lecture was finished, Richard went back on his old argument—the untrustworthiness of the Bible wherever it can be tested, and the consequent untenable pretensions of the priesthood whose fundamental claim is based on scriptural infallibility. It was all false throughout, he said; and the chain of reasoning, however logical in itself, which gives spiritual power and insight to the clergy, falls to pieces when we examine the starting-point—like those conjuror's chains which can only be undone by pulling out the first link. But that first link had been pulled out —some generations ago now. So soon, he said, as it was proved that the sun is the centre of our system and the earth only one of many planets revolving round it; so soon as it was proved that we and all these other worlds were of the same identical substance as the sun, and that this was only one of many systems like our own; so soon too as the doctrine of evolution in nature became established as a scientific fact, true in substance if in parts faulty in detail—so soon did the Bible become a simply human record of puerile fables mixed up with lofty thought— interesting as an historical study, but a dead letter as

Revelation. They could judge of its infallibility by the difference between proved cosmic facts and the explanation of things given in its pages. They could judge whether the importance assigned by it to man, and all that followed on that importance, was likely in view of his relative position in the universe ; and if the groundwork thus failed them, what became of the superstructure? —if the Bible was proved untrustworthy in its facts, where did they stand, those ecclesiastics who offered themselves as its divinely inspired interpreters? Of those ecclesiastics, he said, he must again and again warn his hearers to beware. Men who thought it within the range of their duty to take the children from the parents, to sever husband and wife and destroy the peace of families, were not of the kind to be welcomed into English homes or encouraged as the leaders and guides of society. No human affection was sacred to them if it stood in the way of ecclesiastical aggrandisement; no morality was of value if in opposition to their dogma. They cared only to consolidate their power and deepen the influence which superstition had allowed them to gain over the lives and minds of men. And with their confessed principle of the end justifying the means, they knew neither remorse nor fear in the methods adopted to secure that end.

He besought them to lay to heart all that he had said
to them for some years now; and to understand clearly
that they were at this moment in the thick of the fight
between knowledge and superstition, tyranny and freedom.
The new vicar had resolved to carry Crossholme, and he
had spared no pains to insure the victory. He gave
them fine sights and good music in the services to charm
their senses, and he would do more in this way when the
church should be reopened; he sought to terrify them
with old wives' fables of eternal damnation for being
what they were born to be, unless they would go to him
and the Church for safety; he roused their imagination,
subjugated their intelligence, damped their energies,
soothed their sorrows—yes, he soothed their sorrows!
and got his tightest hold when they were weakest!—by
promises of a heaven where they should be compensated
for the sufferings and shortcomings of their lives on
earth; and he attacked them still more closely by
charities which degraded them to accept. The whole
thing was a net closely woven and craftily cast, and
meant in all its circumstances, simply and solely, power
to the Church; which in its turn meant loss of liberty
to the laity. Let them beware of all that was now
offered to them, and be brave to bear loss, if that should

be included in steadfastness to their birthright of mental
freedom and manly independence.   This was his last
word to them—at least for the present.   He was leaving
Crossholme to-morrow, and it would probably be long
before he should see them again, if ever.   The Institution
was to be shut against the old members, and would pass
into other hands, and be used for other purposes; (his
pale face flushed when he said this, and his lips twitched
visibly beneath his moustache); and this was the last
lecture which he should give them here from this place.
And so he bade them all heartily farewell and trusted
that he had not been their fellow-worker—their fellow-
seeker after truth—for so many years in vain.

His voice a little failed him, when he thus bade them
farewell; but he recovered himself before he had betrayed
his emotion too plainly, and bore himself through his
trial as manfully as he had borne himself with Hermione
—accepting with the patience of strength the pain from
which neither energy nor courage could free him.

As he came down from the desk to the floor of the
room, the more intimate of his friends gathered round him.

"What is that you say, sir?" asked John Graves
anxiously—"you are leaving us? and the Institution is
to be given up?"

Tears stood in the man's eyes. He had had many a hard fall in life, but this was one of the worst. This touched more than himself — it wounded truth, the progress of thought, and the good of humanity, which were more to him than even his own private affections; for he had learnt his lesson of "altruism" well, and was the fitting lieutenant of such a captain as Richard.

"Come aside with me, my friends," said Mr. Fullerton, turning to those to whom had been promised the cottages—about ten men in all.

He indicated Ringrove Hardisty as well, but when the sharp face of the little chandler pressed in behind Tom Moorhead's brawny shoulders, he said quietly:—

"No, not you, Adam—you are out of it!"

"Hope it's nothing good, sir!" said the former pedlar, sniggering; "I don't care to be out of the swim when there's fine fish afloat."

"So it seems," said Richard; "but your net is cast in other waters, and you have no business now in ours. Here, Dick Stern! do you come up here—I have a word to say to you. And I have something painful to say to you all," he continued, when he had collected them in a group, standing about him amazed and a little breathless, as men knowing that a shock was to come and that they

were in some unknown danger. "The leases of your
cottages are refused, my friends. Mr. Lascelles has
induced Mrs. Fullerton to reject you as tenants on her
estate. You know, of course, that this is her property.
I have been merely her steward; though sometimes I
believed I was master where, when it comes to the pinch, I
have to remember that I have only been the agent, to be
dispossessed of my power at pleasure. Now she wishes
to manage things on her own account, and we must not
think hardly of what is done by her. She has become a
warm convert to Ritualism—this is no news to anyone;
consequently she does as she is directed by the vicar, who
advises her not to give tenements to men not in accord
with the Church. I am grieved to have this to say to
you. I know that you have counted on my word as if it
had been a lease duly signed and sealed; you John, above
all, are on my heart. You can understand, all of you,
what it has cost me to give this lecture and to tell you
this bad bit of news. And you know for yourselves what
it includes. But it had to be done."

"And you were never greater than now, sir," said
John Graves with a tender kind of respect that had in it
all the essence of loyalty to the fallen—the respect of a
disciple who would not deny his master, but who stood

firm to share in his martyrdom, whatever form that martyrdom might take. "I know what you must be suffering just now—we all can realize that; but Mr. Fullerton, sir, a brave man like you stands above humiliation. The man in you is a deal sight higher than anything that can happen to you; and you can't be brought down, you can't be humiliated, let them try their worst!"

"There's nought for us, then, but to leave the old place," said Dick Stern. He was the naturalist of the little band, and for years had found his highest pleasure in noting the various dates:—when the first primrose was to be seen, the first ashleaf, the first ear of wheat; when the first cuckoo was heard and the first swallow appeared, and so on;—which dates he then sent to a local paper, and, humble as it was, felt that he had done something for knowledge by contributing this little brick to be set in the great temple. "I thought to have lived all my days here," he continued, "but it seems that's not to be. As the master says—it has to be done; worse luck!"

"Yes, worse luck, indeed!" said Allen Rose. "It's hard lines to make a new place and find new friends at the age of most of us; when we've rooted, so to say, and have nothing beyond the old home."

"It's enough to rouse the country side!" cried Tom Moorhead's thundering voice. "If any brave lad would put an ounce of lead into that"—objurgation—"parson's skull he'd be doing a good day's work, though he swung for it! It wouldn't be so bad as shooting a dog fox!"

"Softly, Tom! softly!" said Richard. "We have nothing to do with bullets and the gallows here! We are quiet, law-abiding, truth-loving men, who want to know the best kind of life that we may follow it ourselves and teach it to others. We are not assassins or felons!"

"Mr. Fullerton, sir, you are too soft!" cried Tom passionately. "You are too good for the like of them, and they just prey on you—that's where it is, sir! If you had kicked that priest there out of your house the first moment he set foot in it, and forbidden anyone as belonged to you to follow after him, it would have been a precious sight better for us all! You'd have been master to the end, and we'd not have been the laughing-stock of the country."

"Silence, Tom!" said Allen Rose angrily. "Another word of the same sort and I'll kick *you* out of the place!"

"Hold your noise, you big mooncalf!" said Dick Stern, shoving the blacksmith aside. "As if things were

'*We'll have no words among ourselves to-night.*'

not bad enough without your bellowing to make them worse !"

" Come, my friends ! no wrangling among yourselves," said Richard. " We all know Tom—a good heart and a fiery temper which is apt to run away with him before he knows where he is. But we'll have no words among our-selves to-night. That would, indeed, be a triumph to the other side !"

"And look here, my men," cried Ringrove, in a loud voice, so that all in the room, who had gathered nearer by degrees and had already heard Tom's views of things, were fully aware of what was going on, " you shall stand at no loss by this. I am sure I am doing what my friend here would have approved, had I consulted with him on this subject before speaking, when I say that I will give you each what Mr. Fullerton would have done—that is, a roomy house and a plot of garden ground, man for man of you. I will put the plans in hand to-morrow. Hold on till the houses are ready. While I am alive, no priest shall have it all his own way here in Crossholme ; and for the sake of my friend, Mr. Fullerton, I will befriend all of you whom he has stood by."

" Thank you, sir."—" Thank you, Mr. Hardisty."—
" A chip of the old block."—" Mr. Fullerton's second

self."—"Things won't go far amiss while we've got such a man at the head of them."—"The vicar 'll have his match, I'll go bail;"—dropped from the men, and culminated in a ringing cheer "for the master of Monkshall," while Richard grasped the young fellow's hand warmly, and said:—

"Thank you, my boy, you are what I always knew you to be."

"Thanks, Mr. Hardisty, to the example set you by Mr. Fullerton here," said John Graves, faithful to the old flag and turning still to the setting sun.

But even with this break in the clouds there was sorrow enough about at this moment—specially that sorrow of the parting. Many of the men wept like children as they shook hands for the last time with him who had been their guide, their friend, their teacher and example. Tears stood in Richard's eyes too, and his good-bye to John Graves was like the parting from a brother. But all these things were simply details. The great grief and origin of all lay behind; and these were only so many turns of the knife in the wound through which his life-blood was slowly flowing. They were painful enough; but they were secondary pains—the counting up of individual relics gone down in the shipwreck in which had been lost wife, child, and fortune.

It came to an end however at last, and Richard and Ringrove were left alone. Then the strength which had borne him up so well failed the dispossessed master of the Abbey. He sat down on one of the chairs, and bent his face on his crossed arms, hiding his anguish even from his friend.

After a time he controlled himself so that he could look up.

"Give me a bed to-night, my boy," he said. "I shall leave by the first train to-morrow morning, but I could not sleep in the Abbey to-night. It would be only an unnecessary pain. You understand it, do not you? My life is over there, and my wife will be best left alone."

"Yes, yes ; I see it all !" said Ringrove excitedly. "I cannot talk of it ! I should say what I should regret after. Yes, come home with me. My house is yours— my purse is yours; you are my friend, my elder brother, and I have nothing which is not yours, if you like to have it."

"Thank you, my boy," Richard answered simply. "I knew what you were. All that I want from you however is a bed to-night, and that you will be my agent when I am gone. Befriend my men and give a look now and then to *her*. And do not judge her harshly,

Ringrove. She has not done me this wrong of her own will. She has been overcome."

His words came abruptly to an end, and he got up and walked to the fireplace. For the moment he had forgotten Virginia and his bitter cause of grief against her mother, and remembered only Hermione—his wife, the woman whom he had loved with such calm intensity of trust, such fondness of faithful affection, and whom he had lost, in truth he scarcely knew how!

After a while he turned back.

"Now let us go," he said. "This is simply losing strength."

"Let me only say that you may trust me as you would yourself," said Ringrove in a low voice. "I love her too well and believe in her real goodness too thoroughly not to treat her with deference and respect, as much for her sake as for yours; and I may perhaps do a little good," he added.

"You will do no good," said Richard. "Things have gone too far, and she believes too much."

"Tom Moorhead was right, brutal as he is—that man is good only for killing!" said Ringrove passionately.

"Better kill the superstitious ignorance whence he

draws his power. The people who mislead are as much
to be pitied as those who are misled. They believe
what they teach," was Richard's characteristic answer,
wishing to be just even to Mr. Lascelles.

Then they passed out into the soft, sweet, fragrant
evening air, and drove home by the highway to Monkshall—the Abbey left for ever.

That night Hermione woke with a start from a
confused and troubled dream. As she woke up more
thoroughly she felt that someone was in the room, and,
half dreaming as she was, she thought it was her
husband—old habit stronger than new conditions.

" Richard, dear !" she said in a tender sleepy voice.

Only semi-conscious, the excitement of her spiritual
suttee had passed away, and she had come back to her
living natural self.

" Richard, darling !" she said again in that sleepy,
warm, caressing voice.

The curtain of the bed drew slowly back, and Edith
Everett stood white and tall by her side.

" My poor sister, you are dreaming !" she said in
her smooth tones, through which penetrated the cold
smile that made that smoothness glacial. " Wake
up, Hermione ! Satan has inspired this vision. Shake
off this horrible possession."

"Give me my husband! give me back Richard!" cried Hermione with an hysterical cry, spreading out her arms and flinging her head wildly on the pillow.

Edith took the soft round dimpled arm in her strong and nervous grasp. She forced the frightened woman back to her former position, and laid the crucifix, which she snatched from the little table by the side, as a kind of exorcistic charm on the heaving breast.

"Do you want to become a castaway?" she said in a low stern voice. "Your love for your atheistic husband is a crime, a sin against your womanhood! You shall not go back to him. I will keep you sacred to our Lord even against your will!"

"You frighten me! you hurt me!" cried Hermione, half rising and trying to struggle herself free. "Richard! Richard!"

"Fool!" said Mrs. Everett, flinging her back roughly and holding her down as harshly. "You are too contemptible! But you *shall* submit! You shall not have your own will!"

It was the old story—the whip of Mr. Lascelles and the scorpions of Edith Everett—tyranny, contempt, and cruelty, when the end had been attained and there was no longer need of flattery and cajolery!

The next morning when the gong sounded for breakfast no one appeared save Mrs. Everett ; Hermione was in bed with headache and fever, and Richard was already on his way to London, finally conquered and driven out. The fight had been fought out to the end—if indeed that can be called a fight which had been active on one side only, on the other the mere passive resistance of one whose hands had been tied and his weapons of defence taken from him from the first. Such as it had been however it was now over, and the way was cleared of all obstruction. The new brooms might sweep where they would—"the besom of destruction," said Mr. Lascelles, smiling with that saintly waggishness of his kind when they base their humour on the Old Testament, for which they have at the best but a problematical kind of respect. And the besom of destruction set to work pretty sharply—grass growing under the horses' hoofs not being to the liking of Mr. Lascelles.

On the receipt of a note from Edith Everett the vicar came up to the Abbey by ten o'clock, ostensibly to comfort Hermione in this undeserved affliction of her husband's cruel desertion.

" Had he been really the unselfish creature he passed

for, he would have kept by you to help you in your
new duties," said Mr. Lascelles.   " He knew how helpless he had made you for his own purpose ; and now to
leave you in the midst of your difficulties !—It is too
cruel ! "

"The dear little woman need not fret about that,"
said Edith's calm smooth voice.   "You and I, Superior,
have both good business heads, and we can help her.
Would you like us to look at the things to-day, dear ? "
to poor, flushed, feverish Hermione.   " If we do, we
shall be ready for you to-morrow.   And something
must be done legally about those leases.   The men
already in possession—there are two, I think you said,
Superior ?—must have their notice to quit properly given.
You must be careful to be on the right side of the law.
Shall we see to all this for you ? "

"Yes," said Hermione, too ill and unhappy to care
much what she said or what was done.

"Then we will leave you, dear, to get a little sleep,"
answered Edith, with a look at Mr. Lascelles.   "Shall
we go down at once, Superior, while you have the time
to give ? "

" It will be best," said the vicar, unconsciously
falling into the second place while appearing to hold

the first —acting as was suggested while seeming to keep
the command. " I have an hour free for this painful
but necessary duty. Our friend here must not feel herself
deserted or without help. Now sleep, and be at rest ! "
he added, making the sign of benediction over her while
he repeated the words. " Sleep ! knowing that the Church
holds you as her dearest daughter, and that Our Lord is
well pleased with you ! "

But, for all that, her husband was banished, and she
knew in her own heart that she had broken his.

Then the two, going downstairs, went into the
study, and began their work of inquisition. Such and
such a thing in this infidel collection of natural science
Mr. Lascelles resolved to take down to the Vicarage,
for his own purposes. Turned to atheistic uses as they
had been—to the proving of " ontogenetic evolution,"
the demonstration of " mind-cells," and all the other
soul-destroying principles to which Richard had devoted
himself—in his hands, and in that very Institution which
hitherto had been the Temple of Satan, he would make
them evidences of Divine Intelligence and the mystery
of creation. He would transfer the furniture and
transpose the image so that what had hitherto been
dedicated to blasphemy and idolatry should now become

aids to the Church and true religion. Such, and such, and such, he said ; and Edith Everett, looking over his shoulder, said : "Yes, do take them, Superior;" but nevertheless she resolved that she herself would have a close study of them all before they went. She was a clever woman and had the curiosity of her sex.

When this preliminary survey was made they then turned to the books and private accounts ; and before noonday came they had so far mastered the details of the Abbey estate, that Mr. Lascelles could judge for how much Hermione, now her own mistress, might be held good in the way of tribute :—"loans lent to the Lord," said the vicar with the euphemistic hypocrisy of his calling, when the laity are called on for funds wherewith to build their own intellectual prisons and forge their own mental chains :—"loans lent to the Lord," and so much left for her own uses. "If she has a thousand a year she may think herself well off," he thought, smiling as he reckoned up his future funds.

CHAPTER IX.

THE DAY OF TRIUMPH.

CONDEMNED as a soft, foolish thing not fit for her place nor worthy of the good stuff she had, by the men who loved her husband and who regarded Hermione's choice much as Hamlet held his mother's :—Indignantly wondered at by Mrs. Nesbitt, who failed to recognize her old friend in this new presentation, and who refused to accept any other alternative but "mad or bad:"—By virtue of his manhood more tenderly judged by Ringrove, who not only saw Virginia in her mother and Richard in his wife, but who honestly loved Hermione for herself— and yet, though he loved her well and judged her tenderly, he could do nothing stronger for her than apologize and throw the blame of the "first hand" on the vicar :—The object of confused displeasure on the part of Lady Maine, who, jubilant at the atheist's overthrow, yet thinking the papist who had dismounted him every whit as abominable, was unwilling that Mr. Fullerton, infamous as he was, should be scourged by those who

O 2

themselves deserved the lash :—Held by Mr. Lascelles
as his creature and his conquest, ranked as so much
pecuniary gain to the Church, to be quietly let drop when
exhausted :—Despised by Edith Everett for her weakness—as if feminine weakness has not been the universal
pabulum of spiritual dominators in all times and all
climes !—and her Ritualism laughed at for all that she
herself, clear and far-sighted, had joined the extreme
section of the party; but then Edith Everett knew
what she was about, and Hermione did not :—Compassionated only by Theresa who once had feared her,
but who now, with the keen *flair* of the dying, knew
that since the clever widow had come to Crossholme
that beloved priest of theirs had ceased to care for
either of his favourite penitents as he used formerly,
and that she in her own person, destroyed by obedience,
burnt up by love, was now only a trouble and an
embarrassment :—Held by all as criminally attached to
Mr. Lascelles and therefore insincere in her conversion
and infinitely blameworthy all round ;—this was the net-
work of commentary and condemnation that Hermione
had woven about her name by what was, after all, only
the righteous logic of her principles. Granting those
principles true, neither she nor Mr. Lascelles nor yet

Edith Everett was to blame for what had been done. As the egg so the chick; and the chick is not in fault. An eagle chips his shell here, a vulture struggles into light there, and kites are hatched by brooding mothers as well as doves and nightingales. It is by the direct action of that brooding mother what kind of creature is added to the forces of life; but it all depends on man what kind of egg he chooses shall be hatched. If he has a fancy for kites and vultures, he cannot expect to save his lambs and ducklings.

On one point however Mr. Lascelles was sedulously careful:—Hermione must not be allowed to feel the chill breath of public disfavour. She must be surrounded too closely by the clerical chorus bound to sing her praises, for a discordant note to be heard above their louder melodies. The rapping of the tom-tom and the intoxication of drugs and incense must go on till that voluntary suttee was completed and the wealthy victim—widow of love!—had no more to give. Until that hour should come she was not to be given time to think; and he carried out his design. The Abbey was like a Roman seminary for all the priests and brothers and fathers who swarmed there at all hours, like locusts fluttering down on a green cornfield; and even at night no dangerous solitude was allowed. Edith Everett slept in her room, under pretence of kindly guardianship, and read her to sleep every night out of ecstatic books wherein the Church was always spoken of as the Great Mother in whose arms all sins and sorrows were abandoned, and in whose service no crime could be committed when the action was of holy intent. Her debts too, which were really the most important matters in Hermione's present life, were not suffered to press on her. Mr. Lascelles undertook to settle them, if dear Mrs. Fullerton would be guided by him ; and dear Mrs. Fullerton, naturally enough, was guided by him. She was unable to cope with difficulties of any kind ; but pecuniary difficulties were so many algebraic problems which no amount of figures set down on paper could make clear to her. So the vicar, who was anxious to be able to say in his discourse on the day of the opening of the church that not a fraction of debt encumbered the building, put the affair into the hands of his own lawyer, raised a considerable sum of money in a hocus-pocus kind of way that was almost like a con- juror's trick, paid off what was owing to the last farthing, and then told Hermione that she had so much to the good in the bank.

It was a piece of charming legerdemain to the pretty

woman who could not calculate—something like that mysterious fructification of old time, when an item had been put down twice over and the pounds had multiplied to that extent ; and she expressed her gratitude as warmly as if the pious juggler had made her a present of the whole sum. To her mind indeed he had.

Edith Everett too praised dear Superior for what he had done so warmly and incessantly that Hermione was almost bankrupt in gratitude, and could not be sufficiently sweet and humble.

" So kind ! so generous ! " she said twenty times a day; and the clever widow now led and now echoed her.

Meanwhile the two pious confederates had no scruple in thus misleading their dupe. It was not for themselves but for the Church; and for Her even exploitation and *escroquerie* were lawful.

The opening of the church was close at hand now; but before the day really came the vicar had one or two things to do. For one, he had to scatter the band, if he could, now that the leader had been discomfited. Acting on the information given him by Adam Bell, and by nature one of those who never forgive, he had Tom Moorhead up before the magistrates at Starton to answer to the charge of using threatening language and inciting to a breach of the peace. By a refinement of cruelty, all the men of Richard's special following were made to give evidence against their comrade, and Tom, whose personal recognizances were refused, and who on his part declined to let his friends go bail for him, was marched off to the lock-up as a dangerous character best out of the way.

From that moment the blacksmith was a ruined man, in conduct, character, and estate ; and Adam Bell's chances with pretty Janet were not so desperate as they had been. He had calculated on this temporary removal of her father as a powerful agent in his favour; and his calculations were not so far out. This too was another instance of the unseen influences which govern life and action, the personal motives by which we are stirred when seeming to be acting only on the broad principles common to society. If it had not been for Janet, and because he was angry at her father's opposition, Adam Bell would in all likelihood not have " split " on Tom ; and Tom would not have been sent to the lock-up, to come out a reckless, ranting demagogue, fearing no man and honouring no law, ungoverned by reason and to be kept in bounds solely by the brute strength of the majority.

The vicar did his best to spoil the lives of the other men as he had spoilt Tom Moorhead's, honestly believing that he was doing God service in thus showing of what flimsy stuff their virtue was made; but here Ringrove stepped in, and took such as would come to him into Monkshall itself, until their own houses were ready. Both John Graves and Dick Stern went up to the house, but some of the rest either declined the further fight and shifted into Starton or migrated farther away still to London or America. Those who were left however Mr. Lascelles sought to starve out; and to have employed one of these excommunicated sinners would have cost the members of his own party more than any among them chose to pay. He was in the saddle now; and they should learn the strength of the hand which held the reins.

He took the Institution for his own purposes, and, as he said, made the place which had so often echoed with Mr. Fullerton's blasphemies resound now with true Church doctrine. Some of the most objectionable books he burnt; the rest he sold, and got what he called sound literature with the proceeds. He made Adam Bell custodian and librarian, partly because it is politic to reward ratting, and partly because he was a sharp spy and a valuable reporter; and the vicar believed that a government is best carried on when there is no opposition, or when what there is is muzzled.

But by all this he roused Ringrove who kept a firm front and helped the remnant of the beaten band where he could. The master of Monkshall did not go so far as Richard in speculative opinions certainly, but all this high-handed tyranny drove him in that direction, and alienated him from the Church. He was as strong as Richard had been in urging the men to remain free and self-reliant, and even more passionate in his denunciations of priestly domination, because with him it became mixed up with that element of jealousy which was one of his sins and was not one of Richard's. He spent a good deal of money on Secularism, as he called it; and Mr. Lascelles had done so far good in his life in thus making the master of Monkshall decidedly public-spirited, and pre-venting his sinking into the mere country gentleman of pleasure. And with all Ringrove's good qualities this possibility had been on the cards. He often went to see Hermione, painful as those visits were. But he thought it right to her in her spiritual bondage, giving her the chance as it were of freeing herself when she would—and it was his duty to Richard, to whom he wrote two or three times in the week telling him how things stood both at the Abbey and elsewhere. He had little to tell that was comforting to the poor exile. Hermione never mentioned him; she had been forbidden to do so by Superior, and Edith Everett never left her alone to make disobedience possible. Richard had written once, saying in his letter that if she did not answer he would understand her silence as meaning her desire not to hold any communication with him; and Hermione had not answered. The reason was simple: she had not received the letter, which had somehow found its way to the Vicarage, and from the hands of Mr. Lascelles to the fire. She fretted a good deal at this complete abandonment—so unlike Richard, she used to think—but she had no chance of learning the truth, and perhaps in the mental thraldom in which she was held it would have changed nothing if she had learnt it.

Ringrove often went to see the Nesbitts too. He thought pretty dark-eyed Bee the sweetest girl of her kind to be found within the four seas, and that kind, if not so lofty, not so ideal as Virginia's, yet infinitely beautiful, infinitely restful to a man like himself—good, generous, manly, but a little high-handed and more than a little prone to jealousy. He knew what would come—not just yet, but presently; and he knew that when that moment did come, soft, gentle-hearted Bee would look up into his face with tears of sweet surprise in her large, deep, humid eyes, and would learn in one swift moment what she did not know now, how that she loved him, and had loved him for long months, unacknowledged to herself if seen and rejoiced in by him. He would never suffer her or her mother to say a slighting word of either Hermione or Virginia ; and by his own steadfast honesty performed that difficult task of keeping well with common friends who have split asunder and gone into opposing camps.

The most miserable man in the place at this time was George Pearce. " Traitor and coward " Tom Moorhead called him, and yah'd at him like a gorilla when the young carpenter passed his forge on his way to morning prayer. Sometimes he called himself the same, if at others he knew that he had sacrificed what was dearest and easiest to give that " sort of a something " a chance, and to bear witness to the truth as it had slowly manifested itself to him. Nevertheless he was always downcast and forlorn, and with the sense of dishonour and exile about him. His father-in-law was ever the same to him ; but when these darker days came all but John turned still more wrathfully against him ; and even Dick Stern, moderately mild as he was by nature, spoke for his benefit the parable of the cuckoo and how the rats leave the sinking ship.

Nanny was miserable too. Her father's misfortunes preyed on her heart; her husband's incurable sadness made their well-ordered little home no better than a place of wailing, and neutralized the happiness that love and prosperity and virtuous living would else have given them; the baby was weakly and kept her always in a state of restless anxiety; this in its turn hurt her health which had never been sound, and made the melancholy of her home deeper and more pronounced. When the little creature slipped through her hands, in spite of all her care, and died just at that time of dawning intelligence which most endears a child to its mother, then poor Nanny felt as if her cup was indeed full, and life too truly a valley of tears without sunshine now or joy to come. To be sure Mr. Lascelles and all the clerical body told her that she ought to rejoice, not weep; for that her little one had been taken up straight into heaven where it was one of the blessed angels ever singing the praises and glory of God. It was far better off, they assured her, than if it had lived to grow up a prince; but the mother's heart bled if the Christian's faith was assured, and she shed as many tears, poor woman, as if her babe had gone to the Bottomless Pit:—As it would have done, said the vicar, laying down the chart of the Unseen with a firm hand and a broad brush, had it died unbaptized.

So things went on till the day came of ecclesiastical triumph in the reopening of the church—the culmination of all things for the present moment.

Restored and beautified, this church of St. Michael and All Angels was like a cathedral of small dimensions, and was fitted with every kind of ornament, lawful and unlawful. It had painted windows, saints in niches, carved stalls for the choir, a reredos and a rood screen, a magnificent organ, a superb lectern, an irremovable crucifix on the altar, lighted candles, and a lamp ever burning in honour of the Real Presence. It had open benches, and no seats assigned to anyone, though so many " seats in the parish church " went with the leases of all lands and houses ; a finely carved confessional stood at the north-east side ; the altar was adorned with flowers, recalling that Day of Thanksgiving now, to judge by events, so long ago ; and it seemed as if Mr. Lascelles had determined to try the question with his parishioners and understand now at once what they would bear and how far he could go.

The bishop of the diocese, being Moderate, had not been asked to honour this reopening. Mr. Lascelles,

preaching unqualified submission to the laity, paid neither
obedience nor respect to his own superiors unless they
carried the same flag as himself; and he had in especial horror this diocesan of his, who, he maintained,
had been wrongfully appointed and was unfit to be the
Church's ruler, because he was a Protestant, an Erastian,
and a loyal citizen as well as a cleric. Hence there was
no kind of check on the day's demonstrations. Processions and banners, genuflexions and incense, vestments
and candles—everything was there; and the travesty of
Romanism was complete. The party sent its chief men
as sympathisers and representatives, and the clerical array
which they made was both imposing and important. The
organist who came down to open the organ was the best
man in London; the Sisters who had suddenly found it
necessary to visit the Convalescent Home were among
the richest members of the most extreme Orders. Every
possible ritualistic adjunct had been made use of, every
available wandering light had been got hold of; and
since Crossholme had been a parish at all it had never
seen so gorgeous a display of ecclesiastical finery or of
clerical magnificence.

Whatever, in the way of splendid sensuousness of
ritual, the service had been on the Day of Thanksgiving

for the Harvest, this, on the reopening of the restored church, surpassed it as much as the sea surpasses a mountain lake. There were no temporary bazaar-like print and calico substitutes for the real thing to-day; no young ladies' offerings of perishable prettiness and questionable ecclesiastical taste—all in use for this opening service was solid, enduring, costly ; and the needle-work alone represented a small fortune. Banners and vestments, altarcloths, eucharistic linen, offertory bags, were of the finest material and the most elaborate embroidery ; the chalice and paten were of gold set round with precious stones ; the crucifix of the fairest ivory on the closest-grained ebony was a superb work of art. No expense had been spared to make the display supreme ; and whatever objection might be raised by certain heretical Protestants, Mr. Lascelles took care that for this day at least he would display his power and suffer no stint of splendour in ritual or appointments.

The whole parish had assembled to take part in the ceremony, and among the rest the Nesbitts and Ringrove Hardisty—the churchwarden on the side of the parish. This was not a sectarian matter, they argued, and it was parochial ; and their presence there—the most notorious objectors to the new order of things as they were—

betokened assertion of their rights rather than deference
to the vicar or acceptance of his programme. But Virginia and Sister Agnes, with that poor foolish mediæval
ape, Cuthbert Molyneux, were absent; and both to
Ringrove and the Nesbitts it seemed as if the want of
that fair, sweet girl who had knelt beside her mother at
the Harvest Festival, made all the rest cold and poor.

They looked at Hermione to see whether any memory
of what she had lost flitted across her face, but they could
read nothing there save the bewilderment of spiritual
intoxication, the stupor of a drugged conscience, the
feverish delirium of the widow voluntarily performing
suttee. She had been presented to all these wandering
ecclesiastical lights as the most shining beacon of the
day. It was she who had done this, she who had done
that: she who had emptied these jewels into the treasury
of the Lord, and who was an example to her generaticn
for faithfulness and devotion. She had had to go through
trials and persecutions of all kinds, but she had stood
firm to the Church and true to her baptismal vows; and
now she had conquered and was at peace. Satan had
left her to the Lord who had supported her, and her day
of triumph had come.

At which all the clerical sympathizers had congra-

tulated her, while flinging holy stones at Apollyon's head ;
and the loud blare of their trumpets had for the moment
drowned the still small voice which yet they could not
wholly stifle. Small chance then that—kneeling there
as a kind of ecclesiastical Queen, the Eldest Daughter of
the Church, spoken of by name in the vicar's sermon,
conscious all through that she was the great lady of the
day, and that her name would be handed about from
one to the other as that of a sincere Churchwoman who
had done these good deeds for the party in the face of
persecution and contumely—small chance that, through
all this glittering haze of vanity and self-deception, ugly
thoughts and sad memories would intrude, haunting her
soul like ghosts in the moonlight. No—she remembered
nothing ; she was what she had been made—bewildered,
drugged and intoxicated.

When the service was about to begin, and just as the
organ had sounded the note which announced the arrival
of the procession, a slight bustle at the side-door turned
all heads to see what it was. It was poor Theresa,
carried in on the couch which she had discarded now
for some time for her bed. The vicar had never dreamed
of forbidding her to come to this Church festival, because
he had never dreamed of her attempting what was

apparently impossible—practically suicide; but, borne up by that strange flickering fever of the last days, she had determined on making the one supreme effort, and now was carried in, hoping that if she had to die she might die now and here.

Aunt Catherine, whose face had become rounder and sleeker and more fatuous than before, walked by her side, smiling serenely. She had made no opposition to the girl's proposal. On the contrary, she had approved of it ; sure, as she said, that the saints would support her and give her strength for the exertion ; had she not prayed to them and promised them public honours if they would ? And the serenity on her mindless face was perhaps the most shocking thing in the whole tragedy.

A thrill of horror passed through the congregation as the girl was brought in, lying there on her couch like a dying devotee before the shrine of Siva—the god who had been her destroyer ; but no one felt the pain of the situation more than Mr. Lascelles. He had not seen much of Theresa of late. She had ceased to be his tender care, and had become only a " case " which it was part of his pastoral duty to attend—he or another priest ; and, for the most part, that other. But he him-

self had gone past her, as he would have said had he
discussed his state of feeling; and she had fulfilled her
purpose. She had given him all that he had desired—a
study of feminine nature, an example of implicit obedience, a handsome window for the church, and as much
money as he could squeeze out of her; and now she
was of no more use than an orange that has been sucked
dry. She might depart and be at peace when she would;
why should life be prolonged when all that made up its
practical value is done for? To Mr. Lascelles, the devoted priest, men and women were circumstances rather
than individualities, and valuable only so far as they were
useful to the Church. Nevertheless, he felt it keenly, like
a loud reproach or a blow in the face, when he saw the
wasted, ghastly face of the poor girl lying there in the
church where she could see the altar and him, and
gaze up into his face during his sermon. It was not
pleasant to look at her and know that this was his work;
but he had had to meet the like unpleasantnesses before
now; and was he not protected as well as sanctioned
by his sacred office? If women would be fools, and
take him as a man when he offered himself as a priest, on
their heads be the sin, the shame, and the punishment!
His, surrounded by the halo of his office, was clear.

This was his rapid thought as he walked round the church with joined hands held before him ; his eyes, which saw everything, cast humbly on the ground ; his shining satin vestments glistening in the sunlight as he passed the open door and across the light of the windows ; his heart swelling with pride, as one part of his great object was thus magnificently accomplished. Fortunately for the peace of the congregation Theresa was too weak to make any hysterical outbreak. She lay during the service in a kind of trance, conscious only of the heavy clouds of incense which rose up about the altar, touched by the sun to gold, and enveloping the officiating priests in a glory that likened *him* to Moses or to One yet more divine —conscious only of the thrilling music that now sighed in supplication, now swelled in triumph through the church, stirring up vague, delightful images of a love which was at once human and divine, and creating that kind of ecstasy which satisfies all desires and pérfects all emotions. She heard his voice, of which in her half-unconscious state the music seemed only the continuance ; she saw his face transfigured in glory, half-revealed, half-hidden, in the golden cloud that seemed to lift him from the gross material earth and carry him midway to heaven. It was all indeed like heaven visible and entered for her; and as she looked at the window which she had given—Magdalen worshipping at the feet of Christ—she lost herself in her dreamy and delicious delirium, and was herself the woman while he was the god.

So the service passed, without a break or hitch. Many women wept, and many young men were carried out of themselves by that passionately sensuous emotion which a splendid ritual excites. Aunt Catherine was smiling all over her round, fresh-coloured, apple face, while tears of ecstatic imbecility ran down her cheeks; and Hermione was always the Queen who had done great things for her people—the Daughter of the Church who had honoured her Mother.

When the service came to an end and all who would went up to the Abbey for breakfast, as they called what was substantially luncheon—the triumph of the day was complete. Mr. Lascelles took the foot of the principal table; and for the moment Hermione did not remember that he was in her husband's place. In the midst of such guests, such circumstances as surrounded her, the presence of that husband would have been too incongruous for his absence to be regretted; and in truth she did not remember him at all. The drums were too loudly beaten, the stupefying drugs too liberally

used for thought or reflection to be possible. She was
surrounded by a crowd of courtiers, each of whom
vied with the other in praises, flatteries, congratulations.
Mr. Lascelles, in his speech, likened her to all the
gracious women of old, and made her fair face flame
with the lusciousness and strength of his praise; needy
priests with " cases" and close-fisted or impecunious
congregations, with gaunt unfurnished churches and
scant ecclesiastical finery, buzzed round her as flies round
the honey-pot, wondering if they could get anything out
of her for themselves, and, if anything at all, how
much ;—the whole thing was like a bridal day with a
shadowy bridegroom somewhere in the distance. She
had never been so happy, she thought to herself—indeed,
until now she had never known true happiness at all !
She was in a state of blessedness that almost rivalled
Theresa's passionate ecstasy—the state in which, whether
the occasion be right or wrong, the sentiment true
or false, the human nature to which we give such fine
names is completely satisfied, leaving us no more to ask
of fate or fortune.

All day long this delicious excitement was kept up.
Breakfast over, there were more splendid and intoxicating services in the church, where Hermione was

always the Eldest Daughter of the sacred Mother. The services over, there was again adjournment to the Abbey, where she was the beautiful and bountiful Queen of the Land, hemmed round by her obsequious courtiers, her sweet-voiced flatterers. But all things come to an end in time, and so must this glorious day of ecclesiastical triumph. When the last great chord from the organ had died away in sighing whispers through the empty aisles— when the last glass of wine had been drunk in the Abbey—then the company began to depart, melting away like spring snow on the meadow; and Mr. Lascelles himself was forced by good manners to go too, accompanying his own friends. It was like the fading of a dissolving view, when one after the other left—and left the place peopled with images and ghosts. How strangely silent and empty it was! thought Hermione; and yet how confused and disturbed her mind! She felt as we do when we suddenly pass from a deafening noise to intense stillness, and by that stillness realize how great the noise has been.

A certain Sister, one Sister Monica, had stayed the last of all. She was Edith Everett's especial friend, and the two had been upstairs when the last priest had shaken hands with this fair-faced Mother in Israel, and

had laid his parting contribution of flattery at her feet.
Now they came down—Edith as well as the Sister in her
cloak and bonnet.

"I am going to Starton," she said to Hermione.
"Sister Monica cannot stay here for the night, I am sorry
to say."

"No," said the Sister. "Our dear Edith was good
enough to ask me, but I must get back to C—— to-
night."

"I have ordered the carriage; it is at the door now,"
said Mrs. Everett quite tranquilly. "Come, dear Sister,
you will be late if you do not make haste."

"Good-bye, Mrs. Fullerton. I am sure you must
feel happy to-night," said the Sister, smiling.

"Good-bye, Sister; yes, I do," answered Hermione
with a troubled face. "You will come back soon,
dear?" she asked of Edith, turning to her anxiously.

Her guide and friend—her guest and mistress—
smiled contemptuously.

"I shall not run away," she said smoothly but
coldly, as she hurried out of the room.

And now Hermione was alone. That delicious
turmoil was over—that intoxicating excitement had
passed—the day of her triumph had come to an end, and

she was once more herself and alone. The solitude to
which she was unused, and naturally disinclined, touched
her to-night with double force. The silence hung about
her like some grim companion from which she could
not free herself; thoughts which had been pressed
back in her mind by the invading influences of the day
gathered with greater volume, more loud insistance to
be heard. All was so empty—everything so distant!
In this large house even the very servants might have
been miles away; and not a sound crept out of the
stillness to break the loneliness and gloom of the
moment.

She wandered up and down the room, restless,
nervous, in dumb distress and vague, unreasoning terror.
She went into the dining-room whence all had been
cleared and put in order—not a chair displaced to
mark the stations of her triumphal course and bring
back the living memory like a presence; she crossed
the hall, intending to go upstairs to her own room, but
dragged as by a secret influence—a "spirit in her feet"—
she turned aside and took the passage that led to the
study.

Half frightened, half longing, she opened the door,
with a wild kind of childish hope as if she could possibly

expect to find Richard there. All here too swept and garnished!—all evidence of that infidel's contaminating presence gone! It was the first time since her husband's departure that she had visited the room, and the shock of its changed aspect was almost beyond her strength to bear, overwrought and weakened as she was by all that had happened in the day. How much rather than this cold spiritual cleanliness would she have preferred to see those sinful evidences of his abominable atheism!—how she would have welcomed even a hideous skull, or the godless, soul-destroying portraits of a nosed ape and a flat-faced savage set side by side as shameful parallels. All gone!—even that criminal accessory to infidelity, the microscope—and those dumb witnesses of agnosticism, the spectroscopic diagrams and the maps of the moon! It was like going into a mausoleum where she had looked for signs of pain and horror; and found only emptiness more painful, more horrible still.

At last, lying half hidden by some papers in a corner of the bookshelf, she saw the cast of a two-headed fish and a sheet of paper whereon her husband himself had figured the development of the bird's skeleton from that of the reptile. No one was there to see her, no one to ridicule or condemn her. She took the cast of that ugly

two-headed fish and kissed it, and her tears fell on that
rudely drawn picture, from which she well knew some
abominable conclusion had once been drawn. The reaction was as sudden and violent as a physiologist might
have foreseen ; and she stood by the bookshelves weeping
for her lost love, for the banished lord of her past life—
the man whom she herself had driven out—weeping passionately and bitterly. Then she went and sat down in
his chair by his writing-table—where she had sat when
he asked her to sign those leases, and whence her refusal
had banished him for ever.

Had she done right, after all ? He was her husband,
and, though an atheist, such a good man ! and so true to
her ! How she wished that she could see him again !
Oh, if she could but once more throw her arms round
his neck and feel his round her ! No one loved her as
he had—as he did. Superior was charming and delightful, but to everyone alike, and in reality more devoted to
Edith Everett than to her ; but her husband had been
hers, and she his, in such perfect oneness, such unbroken
fidelity, till—— Till what, Hermione ?—his agnosticism
or your defection ?

Here at last, at this melancholy moment, in this
deserted room, her conscience answered truthfully ; and

the widow realized her sacrifice and the horror of the
suttee she had been so craftily persuaded to perform.
The glittering heights had been won, but the poor, weak,
foolish heart turned back to the warm and leafy hollows
where she had lived and loved ; and the wife regretted
what she had lost more than the Churchwoman rejoiced
in what she had won.

When Edith Everett came home she found her still
sitting there weeping—Nemesis having at last come up
with her and overtaken her.

" Poor child ! " said Mr. Lascelles with artificial
tenderness, when this was reported to him ; " she needs
firm handling and incessant care."

" Yes," said Edith Everett with as artificial smoothness ; " and she shall have both."

" At your good hands ?—of that I am convinced," he
said.

" And at yours," she answered. " But "—in another
voice—" she will go back to her husband, Superior.
Believe me, I know the kind so well ! "

" You are too timid, dear friend. I think she will
be faithful," he replied.

" And you are too sanguine, dear Superior ! Remember my words when the time comes ! And take my

advice : Make her do now what you wish her to do at all. The day will come when your reign will be over."

He smiled at this.

" My reign will never be over, because it is the reign of the Church," he said with humility. " And I have assured that here ! " he added with triumph.

At that moment the servant brought in a letter. It was from Ringrove, giving him notice that he, the churchwarden and Aggrieved Parishioner, would carry a complaint to the bishop, objecting to the vicar's papistical observances.

Mr. Lascelles slightly snapped his well-kept fingers.

" Worth just that ! " he said with a calm smile, flicking a speck of dust from his sleeve.

CHAPTER X.

QUENCHED.

A CHANGE was gradually creeping over things at the Abbey ; and as time wore on the relations between Edith Everett and Hermione entered on a new and unpleasant phase. Subtle, secret, like a venomous blight that burns unseen, this change was of the kind when those who feel aggrieved cannot seize one salient point of offence, cannot halt at the moment when nor challenge the reason why. But there it was ; and Hermione was conscious of covert insolence and thinly-veiled tyranny, which she had neither the courage to resent nor was given the opportunity to resist. She longed to get rid of her guest, who seemed to have taken up her permanent abode at the Abbey. But the good breeding of a gentlewoman forbade her to say crudely, Go ; and so long as it suited her purpose, it was very evident that Mrs. Everett would continue to stay, and not trouble herself either about the length of her visit or her manners as a visitor.

The danger of conjugal backsliding passed, it was un-

necessary to watch Hermione as in the beginning ; and
Edith, to whom dry-nursing, as she once said to Superior,
was especially distasteful, was once more free to live her
own life.   As her own cleverness had delivered her from
her task, she thought herself privileged to profit by her
liberty ; and she did not stint herself.   In some incom-
prehensible way she was always with Superior, and
Hermione was not.   Even when the pretty woman's turn
came round, and the business of her district, to which
she was kept close, demanded a conference, even then
Edith stood between them as the careful guardian of
appearances and picked her traditional gooseberries with
bland fidelity.   Save at confession—which somehow had
become rather meagre and unexciting of late—she was
never suffered to be alone with Mr. Lascelles ; and more
than once she had been plainly admonished by Edith
as to the need of greater caution in her manners and
actions, with hints, not always gentle, of secret proclivities
to be carefully repressed.

" For you know, dear," she said one morning, when
they were sitting together in the Abbey drawing-room—
Hermione embroidering, Edith illuminating—"a separated
wife cannot be too particular ; and though Superior is so
pure and holy, the world is so censorious and people are

so wicked! They will be sure to talk if you go so much
to the Vicarage as you do, and are not more indifferent
in your manners to Superior."

"No one could be so wicked as to talk of me in
that way," said Hermione hurriedly. "Everyone knew
how much I loved poor dear Richard, and how I nearly
broke my heart because he would be an infidel. Besides,
I am not a girl now—forty next birthday!"

"Yes, of course forty is forty; and a woman of that
age must be a downright fool if she cannot take care of
herself. But then you see some women are downright
fools. Not that I mean you, dear," said Edith Everett
with an odd smile; "but you are not always guarded in
your ways, and you might, you know, get yourself talked
about; and then think what a scandal it would be! You
really are quite good-looking still, and sometimes don't
look above thirty-seven or -eight, I assure you. Superior
said yesterday how wonderfully well you wore;
but then he thinks you much older than you say
you are. Are you really under forty, dear? At
any rate, whatever your age, you are wonderfully well-preserved and at times look extremely
nice. And then, you see, Superior is not an old man,
and everyone must allow he is a very handsome one.

Besides, although he is a priest, he is perilously fascinating
to some women," she went on to say in her smooth,
artificial, monotonous voice, which had begun to grate
on Hermione's nerves as much as if it had been made
up of rusty iron rods. "I could tell you such stories of
the follies that I have known of—quite too disgraceful
altogether."

"I do not see what that has to do with me," said
Hermione with a sudden flush. "I am not aware of
any special folly that I have committed."

"No, dear, I do not say you have ; but you must
remember you discarded your husband only after you
came under Superior's influence.   Looking at things from
the world's point of view, there is enough here to get you
into trouble unless you are very careful.   You must
indeed, Hermione, be more particular now than when
Mr. Fullerton was living with you.   A husband is such a
shield, even when the wife is light and people are disposed to be ill-natured !   But you see you have deprived
yourself of this defence, and now you must mind what
you are about with everyone—but especially with Superior."

" It seems odd that you should say all this, Edith, when
you were the most earnest in the matter," said Hermione,
opening her blue eyes very wide.

" Say all what, dear?—that you should be careful of your conduct now that you have discarded your husband and are a separated wife?"

" No ; but to speak in that tone, as if I had done something wrong," said Hermione. "To discard one's husband—to be a separated wife—what horrid expressions ! They are scarcely proper, Edith ; they certainly are not ladylike !"

"Ah ! I see you like periphrases, and I don't," replied Edith calmly. "Spades should always be spades, my dear ; and when a woman 'chassé's' her husband, no matter what the cause, she is none the less a separated wife. What a little goose it is !—Honey and butter ! nothing stronger or sharper than honey and butter !" she added with a careless smile, glancing at the clock and putting down her brush. "Will you send for me to the Vicarage at one o'clock ? and shall I bring back Superior with me?" she then asked as she rose from her seat.

" Are you going out now ? You were away all yesterday !" said Hermione, colouring with displeasure.

" Superior wants me," said Edith.

" You are always at the Vicarage !" cried Hermione petulantly. " I am sure if people were inclined to talk of Superior with anyone it would not be with *me*, Edith !"

"You mean they would with me? I dare say," said the guide and friend tranquilly. "But then you see I am free, and you are not. That makes all the difference. If Superior and I were in love with each other there would be nothing to prevent our marrying, excepting our principles about a celibate priesthood. But these would prevent our falling in love in the first instance. And the world understands this. It is quite another matter with you. And the practical result is—I can do things which you must not."

"So it seems," said Hermione crisping her small lips.

"Besides, I am of real use," continued Edith in a lounging kind of a way. "I can add up his accounts and keep the district books in order, and all that; and you know, dear, you are not strong in that line," with a little laugh.

"Why do you make all these apologies, dear?" returned Hermione, with a rapid change of front. "If I am old enough to take care of myself I am sure you are too; and it cannot signify to me whether you go to the Vicarage every hour of the day or not. I have plenty to do at home, and of course I do not want you to feel tied to me in any way, or that I am responsible for your actions."

" Of course not ; I know all that, dear," replied her friend. " So, good-bye. Do not expect me home before dinner then, unless you send the carriage for me and Superior to come back to luncheon. By the way, won't you come for me yourself?"—graciously, as if giving an invitation.

" No, I should be in your way," said Hermione disagreeably.

" Think so? Please yourself, dear," answered Mrs. Edith Everett.

" No, I keep away to please you," retorted Hermione.

" Why? How silly of you ! I am sure Superior would be glad to see you. I know you are quite a favourite of his," said Edith with a little insolence. " However, do as you like, dear ; I must go at all events. *Au revoir*, little woman."

She made a French salute with her hand, smiling, and glided from the room with the satisfied feeling of the duellist who has drawn the first blood.

" She is perfectly odious ! I must get rid of her ! I will tell Superior that I will not keep her any longer ! insolent wretch !" were Hermione's passionate thoughts so soon as her friend had closed the door. " She is of no use to me ; none in the least ! She leaves me all day alone, and is staying only to flirt with Superior. How can he ! a plain thing like that—with her small ferret eyes and insignificant nose, and that hideous upper lip ! I thought he had more taste. Poor Richard saw through her from the first, and hated her ! And I am sure I do not wonder at it. She behaved in the most insolent way to him, and now she is beginning the same kind of thing to me. But I will not bear it ! and will tell Superior of her. It is too bad, and when I am so miserable and lonely. Dear Richard ! my poor Virginia ! "

The indignant tears which had gathered into the big blue eyes changed from anger to self-pity, and Hermione suddenly realizing her full loss turned her face downward to the sofa cushion and sobbed aloud.

Always that grim shape of Nemesis on her traces— always that deep sense of disappointment in the Paradise to which her Act of Sacrifice was to be the gateway—and now, the dawning perception of ingratitude as the reward of her abject submission. It was a bitter moment for her ; and yet she had not fathomed half the possibilities of cruelty in a woman like Edith Everett, or a man like Mr. Lascelles ; both strong-willed and unscrupulous—

the one devoted to a cause which had for its object the
subjugation of humanity, the other to making her own
way clear through the brake; and both indifferent as to
the means by which they should gain their ends.

Like all his kind, using his personal graces to excite
the love of those women who would be useful to the
Church, Mr. Lascelles never faltered because of the
sorrow to come, when, having given all that they had to
give, he should throw them aside as no longer of use.
When they had done their work they were as dead to
him as seeded plants, and he thrust them back that their
place might be taken by the fruit-bearing members as
yet ungarnered. He did not care to spend his strength
in ornamental attentions. Life lies before us, not behind,
he once said; and when things are done with it is a
man's duty to go past them and press forward to new
duties. This was just what he was gradually doing with
Hermione Fullerton. Now that the contest was over
between himself and her husband, and he declared victor
at every point; now that he was sure of getting all he
wanted in the way of money for his own parish and the
ragged congregations of his friends; now that the Abbey
was a kind of hostelry for him, where he could invite whom
he would, and which he could use as his own private pro-

perty ; now that Hermione was committed too deeply to
retract ;—he was glad to give up the close attention and
dangerous spiritual flirtation by which he had accomplished
his purpose.   It was the repose of conquest, the security of
possession, and thus left him free for fresh exertion—
specially for that most important of all, the coming contest
with Ringrove Hardisty.   Also, it was only wise, as Edith
Everett suggested, to be very much on his guard, and
while giving Hermione nothing of which to complain, to
be careful not to give the world anything of which it could
take hold.   Hence the same kind of subtle change crept
into his relations with the pretty woman as already
existed in those between her and Edith.   He saw very
little of her at all, and never alone ; and he made her
understand, at first with regret but now with resignation,
that he must be careful for her sake, and she submissive
to restrictions for his.   The less she was seen at the
Vicarage, or he at the Abbey, the better ; the more she
was among the sick, at the Home, the schools, the
women's meetings, without him, the better still.   The
roaring lion of calumny must find no weak place in the
defence set up by prudence round her good name and
his ; and though as she well knew, he said with suggestive
tenderness and well-defined sorrow at the stern neces-

sities of things, no soul given to them by Our Lord was
so precious in his sight as hers—yet, that wisdom of the
serpent ! Compared with it, the innocence of the dove
was nowhere !

With Mrs. Everett, of whom Hermione now spoke
with sudden bitter self-betraying jealousy, things were
different. No one could mistake matters with *her*, he
said, looking at Hermione with undisguised admiration
in his eyes, and speaking of Edith Everett with fine contempt for her womanly attractions conveyed in his voice.
And Hermione was reassured and her fears set at rest,
at least for this time. The vicar had no need to quiet
his own fears. He had none. Edith's place with him
was distinctively her own, and he wished nothing
altered. He did not make love to her, nor she to him—
at least, not of that open fulsome kind in use at Crossholme. She was the one woman whom he could trust
to carry out his wishes without that silly exaggeration which was so fatally compromising to him, and
who could translate even his silence according to its
meaning. She was astute, quiet, prompt; the most
valuable coadjutor in the world, and he was more
dependent on her than he knew. She was quite as
helpful to him as his sister had been, and he was as much

at ease with her. Wherefore she was welcome at the
Vicarage at any hour, because she was always practical
and useful ; and while slowly yielding to her influence
Mr. Lascelles was congratulating himself on the possession of a friend—a dear sister in the Church—on
whom he could rely as on a second self, without the
necessity of godly flattery or crafty love-making.

As if the cleverest man in the world is not as helpless
as a babe when the right kind of woman, who knows
how he ought to be managed, takes him in hand :—and
manages him !

Poor Theresa had also been shunted in these change-
ful later times. There had never been more real love
for her than for Hermione, though the vicar had so
often simulated the half-suppressed signs to both. With
Hermione it had been the honest desire of good and gain
to the Church in the destruction of her infidel husband ;
with Theresa, professional zeal in securing converts had
been mixed up with the psychological curiosity which
makes a man tempt a woman to show her love that he
may study the process. It improves his knowledge of
human nature ; and experiments in moral vivisection
cause no outcry. But the real basis of all that had been
said or done to both had been the establishment of

Ritualism here in Protestant Crossholme; and now, when the Ritualistic Church was established four-square, and apparently not to be shaken, he was released from further trouble.

Besides, things had got too hot with Theresa to make a continuance of any show of personal interest—even of his private ministration—advisable. Wherefore he had, for some time now, given up to Brother Swinfen—who was no spiritual philanderer even for the sake of the Church—the daily attendance proper to her state; alleging as his excuse the multiplicity and importance of his occupations, and the impossibility of the pastor of a flock devoting so much time to one, even though that one was sick unto death.

This also was the effect of Edith Everett's clever manipulation. She had the art of suggesting a course of conduct by assuming that Superior had already determined on it, and praising him with decent warmth for his wisdom and common sense; but indeed there was no other way, she would say, as he had evidently seen. Hence it was that by her advice, conveyed as commendation, he had yielded the daily care of Theresa to the Brother, reserving to himself only special occasions and the more sacred offices.

Meanwhile Hermione, weary of the dull parish work, to which she was held so close, without reward ; missing the flattery, the acknowledgment of personal supremacy which had hitherto been hers in such full measure ; missing too the excitement of opposition to her husband which had been a factor in the sum while it lasted ; and not fitted by nature to take her place as a simple member of the congregation, of no more account in the celestial calendar than Miss Pryor, say, or Nanny Pearce ; —was beginning to feel tricked and sore ; and Theresa's last day was drawing on apace.

The dying girl was making a hard fight of it. It was beyond pathos—it was terrifying, awful—to watch her fierce struggle for life, the passionate tenacity with which she clung to hope, her angry refusal to recognize her danger, her rebellious determination to contest every inch of the way, and to live, whether it was God's decree that she should die or no. It was as if her will was stronger than disease ; as if she lived because she would not die. But at last she was conquered. All her desire of life, all the feverish love for Superior which had been such an overwhelming passion, had to give way before the one great King. The last strand was frayed to the breaking-point, and the sands of the hour-glass had nearly run out. Then, and then only, she accepted the terrible truth, and confessed that this was Death.

Hermione had seen much of her of late. Superior had intimated that he wished Mrs. Fullerton to undertake Theresa as her special care, and a strong sympathy had sprung up between them during these last weeks, very unlike the mutual jealousies and pretensions of the earlier days. Now they were both in the same position —practically abandoned by the man to whom they had sacrificed, the one her marriage and the other her life.

If Hermione had not yet fully confessed to herself how things were going, Theresa had the clear vision of the dying to whom further deception is unnecessary, and who see the truth sharply cut and without disguise. But up to now she had held her peace and kept faithful to the man whom she loved. Now however the moment had come when she had done with life and all that life means; when weakness had conquered resolution, and her brain had at last yielded to the terrors and conviction of her state.

She was lying there, gasping painfully, the death-damps already on her. All day long there had been an unwholesome excitement about her bed; a coming and going of priests and Sisters; a perpetual succession of religious offices, of prayers and exhortations; her last confession; the last Celebration; extreme unction; the crucifix to kiss; the spiritual presence of all the Divine Personages in the Christian drama asserted as an incontestable fact which she would soon realize for herself—excitements infinitely mischievous and disturbing, hurtful to the peace of the passing hour and making the agony still more terrible than need be—excitements which the doctor from Starton had vainly tried to check. Now things were quieter. The doctor had gone; he was wanted elsewhere. Here he was of no more use; he had done all that he could, and that all was substantially nothing; there he might save life. He pressed her hand for the last time; said a few words of honest, manly comfort; and with him passed her last earthly hope.

Brother Swinfen also had left her for the time; it was his hour of private prayer and meditation, and a man must attend to his own soul though occupied in trying to save another's. No one was in the room save Aunt Catherine, Drusilla, the faithful, foolish maid, and Hermione. The evening was wearing on. Would Theresa live into the night? She had always been at the worst in the evening, and it would be a hard time for her now.

All knew this but Aunt Catherine, who never lost her imbecile cheerfulness, and who smiling placidly said she was sure the dear saints would come about her so that her passage should be swift and the process ecstatic.

"So faithful as she is, she must pass in glory," said the weak-brained creature, thinking of the picture where Saint Catherine is carried up to heaven by angels, and sincerely believing that this would be Theresa's experience—as in time her own.

Too weary to care much about men or angels, just living and no more, Theresa lay with half-closed filmy eyes and pinched mouth, breathing hard and heavily. All was still; that heavy breathing the only sound which broke through the silence of the death-chamber. Feebly she motioned to Hermione to take her hand, and made a sign for water to moisten her lips.

"Take care of Mrs. Everett," she then said in a hoarse whisper, and with difficulty; "she is not your friend; has not been mine; is here for no good; Superior will marry her."

She closed her eyes again as she said this, and

seemed for a while to doze. Suddenly she opened them wide and started. The filmy glaze that had been over them before seemed to be withdrawn, and they blazed out as if a fire were behind.

" Send for him ! send for him !" she said in a wild unnatural voice. "I cannot die till he comes. He must bless and pardon me."

" Dearest, you have already been pardoned. He gave you absolution and the Blessed Sacrament this morning. Don't you remember, dear? You are waiting only for heaven—you are sure of salvation," said Hermione's soft voice tenderly.

" No, no ! send for him ! I am in the torments of hell already !" cried Theresa again, passionately beating the air and plucking at the bedclothes. " I cannot die like this. He must release me !"

" Pray to the dear saints, my darling !" said Aunt Catherine. " The dear saints will hear you ! "

" We had better do as she wishes," said Hermione ; and, writing on a slip of paper : " Pray come at once; Theresa is in agony," she sent it off to the Vicarage at speed.

Her message found the vicar at home with Edith Everett at work in the study; and both came back in the Abbey carriage to Churchlands together.

And now began that terrible scene which occurs so often and is so seldom confessed in the horror of simple truth—the scene when the reason is extinct, when hope has died, and only spiritual fear and the physical agonies of death are left. Here was no poetic euthanasia—no sweet spirit leaving the body to the music of angels' harps and the vision of the opening heavens, but a tortured woman writhing in the agonies of superstitious terror, realizing the wrath of the God whom she imagined she had dishonoured, and believing herself already in the power of the Devil to whom she had given herself by the secret sin of her thoughts.

Her blackened lips drawn back from her teeth—her thin face set into a mask of horror, terror, passion, despair—her eyes opened wide, flaming with the awful fires of a distracted brain—disturbed by unwise excitement in what should have been the peaceful passage from life unto death, and roused by all the spiritual turmoil of the day into a temporary spasm of strength—she poured out her last powers in the terrible delirium of her dying agony. Her love for Superior had been idolatry, she said—a sin that was not nor could be forgiven. Not all the power of the Church could absolve her; the Eternal Mercy could not reach her;

and the Evil One had already his sharp talons in her heart. She was going down to hell, and her love had sent her there. When she had prayed it had been to Superior—he had been her God, her Saviour, and she had worshipped him instead of the Lord. She had loved him more than her own soul, and now she was to suffer for her sin. She had loved him till she had died of her love, and now she was to be sent to eternal torture for punishment.

"But," she said in a hoarse shriek, "you made me love you, Superior. You made me think you loved me ; and when you kissed me in the sacristy you took my heart out of my body and put one of fire in me instead. I was never the same after. I thought no man would have kissed a girl if he did not love her, and that you would have married me after that. It was cruel ! cruel ! You sold me to Satan then, and now he is claiming me. He is there ! at the foot of the bed waiting for me ! Save me, Hermione ! Aunt Catherine, save me ! "

She started up with superhuman strength ; beat off something with her hands ; her ghastly face, on which the lamplight fell with strange black shadows, fixed in horror ; her eyes wide open, fixed and staring ; then with one loud shriek she fell back on the pillow, but for her breathing to all appearance dead.

Hermione trembled and turned sick with terror. She threw herself on her knees almost fainting and scarcely praying; Edith Everett's clever face looked blank, but her keen eyes stole one sharp glance at Mr. Lascelles. Brother Swinfen, whose "hour" had passed and who had now stolen back into the room, felt outraged and shocked, but more on account of the scandal that would result to the Church should any. word get about than because of Superior. Like Father Truscott, he had long seen this astute priest's propensity for playing with edged tools, and he was not surprised at what he had just heard. But Mr. Lascelles himself, standing there smooth, tall, bland, priestly, sublimely self-possessed, bent over the dying girl with the angelic pity, the un-ruffled serenity of innocence.

"My poor, poor child!" he said softly, making the sign of the cross over her. "Theresa, do you not know me—your priest, your Director?—These terrible deathbed hallucinations!" he added, looking round on the little group behind him with a soft compassionate smile.

Theresa's eyes opened once more. All the darkest passions of humanity burnt in them in one last expiring flame. There was no softness, no womanhood, no love left in her. It was hate and rage, scorn and despair; the best already dead and only the worst left still alive.

" Hypocrite ! " she said fiercely; then her body collapsed, her jaw dropped, and her glazed eyes turned.

Mr. Lascelles knelt and began to intone the Office for the Dying—his voice interrupted by the stifled sobs of the women and the hoarse death-rattle from the bed. By degrees this terrible sound grew fainter and fainter, then ceased; a few shuddering gasps—one last deep sigh, and all was over. Then the vicar rose from his knees, closed the glassy eyes, and repeated in an artificial voice the prescribed formula for the dead. Yes, she was dead and he was in a sense her murderer ; but to his own soul he was the sinless priest who had not gone beyond his rights when he had bound this poor victim to the horns of the altar by the compelling force of love, and offered her as a living sacrifice acceptable to the Lord and useful to the Church.

This last clause was doubtful. Stories got about, no one knew how ; and the deathbed scene of Theresa Molyneux was exaggerated with every repetition. The vicar, as one justified by the truth, met the whole thing fairly and manfully with those whom it more specially concerned ; and those whom it did not concern he passed by with the lofty disdain of conscious rectitude. He was specially anxious that Hermione should be set right, and her mind disabused of any lingering doubt ; and at last, after some difficulty, his cleverness prevailed, and he succeeded in making her believe that the poor girl's dying words had been pure delusion and that he had given her no cause to mistake him.

"She was never more than a fragile enthusiastic kind of child to me," he said with the finest accent of sincerity ; "and that story of the kiss—I blush to repeat it !—was a simple hallucination—a vision conjured up by the Devil to bewilder her dying moments and set a stumbling-block in the way of the Church. Have I ever shown *you* that I was this kind of man ?" he added, fixing his eyes on her with meaning.

"No," she answered uneasily, with a deep blush. Was that "No" perfectly honest?

"Then, if not to *you*, of all women in the world, certainly not to her ! Do you not believe me ?" gently.

"Yes," said Hermione, frankly holding out her hand.

He said the same thing to Edith Everett, using precisely the same words ; and the widow answered smoothly—

" Of course it was hallucination from first to last! We all know that!"

She smiled incredulously as she spoke. He did not feel quite sure whether it was incredulity of the assertion made by Theresa or the denial made by himself; and he thought it wiser not to ask. There is such a thing as probing too deep.

" It is always so difficult to deal with hysterical girls!" then said Edith quietly, as Father Truscott had said before her. " Really an unmarried priest is placed in a very dangerous position. He must do his work, and yet he may be brought into such trouble by his penitents!"

" It is our cross," said Mr. Lascelles, with his most sanctimonious air.

" Yes," she answered, catching his tone. " But the worst of it is, that it sometimes brings so much scandal on the Church when women are silly and fanciful, and have nothing better to do than dream themselves into love for the priest! It is really very difficult to know what is best for the Church in the end!"

" That, Wisdom must decide," said Mr. Lascelles enigmatically ; and Edith Everett smiled again and said " Yes," without further comment.

The world however was not so easy of belief as

Hermione nor so complaisant in its incredulity as Edith; and the vicar's name got rough handling among all classes. Yet, after all, it was one of those reports which, the nearer they are looked at, the farther they recede and the more shadowy they become. It was hardly fair to count it for sin to the vicar that an hysterical girl had fallen in love with him and killed herself by severities undertaken to please him and as the expression of her love. Nevertheless the flavour of his spiritual philandering remained like a bad taste in the mouth of the public, and so far helped on the astute widow's designs by making it evident to the vicar himself that his celibacy was a cause of offence and a temptation to evil speakers.

Everyone was talking of the affair; some doing their best to sift the truth from the falsehood, others piling up the romance without regard to either. Among the former were the Nesbitts, being of the kind to whom scandal is not pleasant food and charitable interpretation comes easy. All the same they blamed the vicar to a certain extent; and thought, not unreasonably, that "there must have been something in it," and that Theresa had not made it all out of her own imagination. He must have flirted with her to some degree, even if she had been silly, poor dear, and believed that he meant more than he did."

Ringrove said the same, and added a few masculine epithets that were more forcible than polite. No one wondered at this. It was well known how the young fellow felt for Mr. Lascelles and with what good reason—owing indirectly to him the loss of his own great hope and love, and more directly the destruction of his friend's happiness.

They were all walking up the garden at Newlands, on their way back from church the Sunday after Theresa's death, when the vicar had preached her funeral sermon with saintly quietness, speaking of her as now a soul in glory—the middle passage having been mercifully shortened in consideration of her good deeds done to the Church.

" How could he stand there and preach that sermon when he knew how much she loved him, and that she had killed herself by all that she did for the Church!" said Bee as her rather disjointed contribution to the talk going on.

Tears of confused feeling rose in her big brown eyes, and she was unstrung and unlike herself. She and Ringrove were a little behind the rest.

He turned and looked at her with a strange fixed look that made her blush and confused her yet more. He looked as if he forgot that she had eyes and could see him, as if he had somehow the right to look at her, smiling with the masterful security of a man who neither doubts nor fears.

"Bee! how glad I am that you never gave in to all this detestable folly!" he then said suddenly.

She laughed nervously, but did not answer. She wished he would take his eyes away. It was not like Ringrove to look at her like this—to make her feel uncomfortable and confused.

"Do you know why I am· glad?" he said again abruptly, turning into the shady shrubbery walk.

"I suppose because you do not belong to it yourself," she answered in a voice that was not quite her own, and making an heroic but totally useless effort to appear at ease.

He stopped in their walk, and quietly put his arms round her.

"Not only that," he said; "I am glad because, if you had been one of them, you would never have been my dear wife. And now you will be—will you not, sweet Bee?"

"Oh, Ringrove!" said Beatrice, turning away her face; but involuntarily, instinctively, she not knowing what she did, her own arms were round him, and her pretty head was laid on his shoulder as if a resting-place there was natural.

He pressed her to him and whispered tenderly : " Kiss me, darling, and then I shall know that you love me. Do you love me, Bee ? "

" Yes," she said softly, lifting her face with the sweetest mixture of shyness, love, submission, and offering her fresh lips with the innocence of a child.

" My own darling ! " he said fondly. " You are just what you ought to be. You were made for me, my Bee ; and now I am perfectly happy."

" And I, too, Ringrove," whispered Bee, raising her soft eyes to his, worshipping.

Surely a better ending to her girlhood than Virginia's immolation or Theresa's self-destruction—the one for devotional enthusiasm, the other for religious excess ! Surely too a better kind of confession, warm, loving, natural as it was, than those made so often in the church where casuistry creates sins that do not exist in fact, and superstition bends its neck to acts of penitence that have neither warranty in reason nor cause in nature!

CHAPTER XI.

EBB AND FLOW.

THE Samson of Erastianism, Ringrove Hardisty, church-warden and aggrieved parishioner, made a gallant fight of it with their local Pope ; but things came to but a lame conclusion when all was done. The ecclesiastical law is not too explicit in its regulations touching the uniform conduct of public worship ; and the Church of England boasts of her elasticity. That she can give tenable lodgment to the Ritualist priest who is a Romanist in all save submission to authority superior to his own ; to the Evangelical minister who is a dissenter from her organization in all save his appreciation of her endowments ; to the Broad Church clergy-man who coquets with Socinianism, denies eternal punishment, and rationalizes the miracles ;—is her title to honour. She calls it catholicity, and glories in that she sweeps the sea with so wide a net, and so generous an arrangement of closely-meshed pockets. If this is incom-modious, perhaps that will hold you safe. Between the supreme power of the Church which admits of salvation only through obedience to her commands, and the doctrine of free grace by faith and the Bible; between the daily recurring miracle of Transubstantiation, and the bland endeavour to find an intelligible meaning in the story of the dispossessed devils sent into a herd of swine;— there is surely some possible abiding-place where the most fidgety soul may find rest! And at the worst, if you are a spiritual nomad, as some are, and go through states and doctrines as people go through climates and diet, you can travel from one pocket to the other, yet always remain in the net of the Church of England as by law established.

What is true of the doctrines is also true of the ritual. Catholicity of formula goes into diversity of practice; and it is as difficult to define what is lawful and what is forbidden in the way of observance as to state the leading colour of a chameleon. Mr. Lascelles knew every inch of the ground whereon Ringrove Hardisty had ventured; and knowing his way he had no fear. He followed in the footsteps of some of his predecessors, and bought his crown of martyrdom cheap. He simply ignored the right of the law to deal with things ecclesiastical, and proved his foresight when he snapped his fingers and said: "Worth just that!"

He made no reply when called on for his answer to
the charges brought against him ; put in no appearance
when summoned ; let judgment go by default, and then
paid no heed to the sentence of prohibition. He still
swung his censer, lighted his candles in broad noonday,
offered up the Sacrifice of the Mass, kept the crucifix on
the table, bowed and knelt at strange places in the
service and before strange objects of adoration. He
performed the service just as he had performed it before
the suit had been instituted and the decree pronounced ;
and the Court of Arches might have been an Aristophanic
city in Cloudland for any respect paid to it by the
Honourable and Reverend Launcelot Lascelles. Only
when the voice of the law found a hand, and these
" fond and superstitious " fancies were removed by main
force—only then did he give way, always under protest,
and to prevent, as he said, an unseemly riot in the sacred
edifice.

These indignities were worth something to him,
and brought him in a pleasant little solatium. The
subscription got up by the faithful of the congregation, and headed by soft-hearted Hermione, as a
salve for poor dear Superior's wounded feelings, was of an
amount for which many a man would willingly have
undergone an hour in the pillory or a twist with the

thumbscrews, and held himself well paid ; but according to his own account of things and the relative value of salve and suffering, money was but scant comfort to the vicar for all that he had endured. Posturizing as a martyr, and preaching as if the Church were on the brink of persecution—as if *Christianos ad leones* were the popular cry against conscientious Catholics, and the winnowing process had begun—he made the women weep for sympathy, shudder with dread ; while he, grand, calm, handsome, hierophantic, solemnly exhorted all men to constancy and courage so that the wicked might not prevail nor the Holy Mother be aggrieved.

The prosecution, which he and some others were careful to call persecution, had one evident result—good or bad as people may think ; it divided the parish sharply into placets and non-placets, and did away with the indefinite fringe of neutrals. Those who went with Ringrove got up a written address to him, which all signed boldly ; those who went with the vicar got up a subscription for him, to which all gave liberally ; and the two factions mutually spread evil reports, falsified facts, ascribed unworthy motives, and made ducks and drakes of neighbourly sociability and Christian charity.

But the vicar was the stronger on the whole. He

had the women and the purse-strings, and beat the
liberals on the rubber if he lost here and there a
point.

While the action was going on, and for some time
after the decision, the two parties were not on speaking
terms together. Mrs. Everett wrote to Ringrove in
Mrs. Fullerton's name, formally forbidding him to come
to the Abbey; and Mr. Lascelles intimated to him, the
Nesbitts, and some others that he would prefer not to
see them at Holy Communion, as he did not consider
them in a fit state to receive that blessed consolation.
They tried the question however on its merits; and
forced him to recognize their rights as Christian citizens,
to whom the services and solemnities of the Church
were part of their national inheritance, and who had
done nothing worthy of disinheritance according to the
provisions of the rubric—the only code of denial to
which they would pay obedience. The bishop, to
whom they appealed, decided in their favour; and the
vicar here again received an open check. He was very
wrathful, but he had to give way; and for the special
Sunday when those abominable Erastians presented
themselves, found himself obliged to be from home.
But, in spite of this little discomfiture, he was essentially

the victor. A few ornamental adjuncts had been removed, but the core was left untouched. Confession, prayers for the dead, the worship of the Blessed Virgin, obedience to the Church as synonymous with obedience to God, the vital principle of the power of the priest to regulate the lives, limit the knowledge, and order the thoughts of the laity—all these were left. And by these the manly spirit of the parish was subdued, the essential purity of the women sapped, the right of intellectual freedom denied, the progress of true education stopped, and the law of the land stultified and defied.

All the same the vicar still complained of the wickedness of an unbelieving generation, and preached on the theme of a glorious martyrdom with an air of saintly courage that made the soft hearts of the women bleed for sympathetic pain.

Meanwhile the more secular portions of local history were being followed to their appointed end ; and among these came that unfinished chapter on Mr. Fullerton's men, whom Mr. Lascelles had found it imperative by the law of Christian duty to ruin.

Ringrove Hardisty had housed them, as has been said, and had done his best to befriend them all round ; but somehow things had not gone well with them. It is always difficult to help high-spirited workers when their work will not keep them and they object to unearned gratuities. Even the faithful had suffered with the recalcitrant in one way, if not in another, and George and Nanny were as hardly holden as the rest. Nanny, always in delicate health and now frailer than ever, pined away after the death of her child, and gradually sank into her eternal sleep ; while George, thrown off his balance by grief, gave himself up to religious enthusiasm and the realization of the Promise, as the only assuagement he could find. Full of the restless energy of proselytism, desirous that all should experience the blessed Hope that had come to him, and feeling his place as a member of a ritualistic congregation, where his highest virtue was quiescent obedience, too narrow for his burning zeal, he went out into the open, became a free-lance in the general army of the Lord, and gave himself to preaching in the highways. He took a solemn leave of all his old friends and associates, of whose eternal perdition he was only too sorrowfully sure, and told them with many tears that he should never see them again, neither in this world nor the next, for where he went they could not come ; he did his faithful best to convert the vicar on another count, and to prove to him the scriptural apostasy of his papistical doctrines which put anything of man's invention before free grace and the naked Bible ; and then he went out, as another St. Francis Xavier, and made his scanty daily bread by hawking tracts among the unsaved, while preaching the doctrine of Faith, and getting up small village Revivals.

"I would rather have seen him laid by the side of my poor girl," said John Graves, with something that was more pathetic than tears in his eyes. " He is lost, not only to me, but to all reasonableness and manliness ; and a turn more would land him in Bedlam."

So it would; but wanting that turn he was free to tramp about the country, preaching salvation by faith, and the sin of priestly mediation, just as Mr. Lascelles was free to go into the pulpit and preach salvation for Englishmen by the Anglican Church only, with the priest the appointed agent of God, and the sin of heresy less pardonable than that of murder.

Like the rest of the men John was painfully poor in those dark days. Custom fell off from him, no one but Mr. Lascelles quite knew how. A new tailor set up in Crossholme and prospered apace. He came from London and was a devoted Churchman ; but his work was not as good as John's ; and devoted churchmanship gave neither a fair fit nor satisfactory stitching. All the same, he got the best part of the local custom ; and only those few old-fashioned carles who disliked the vicar's doctrines, and preferred the old stagnation to the new movement, stuck to John for the sake of the lang syne and stitches that would hold together when they had a strain.

Tom Moorhead's case was the worst, for he lost more than house or money. He had not the fine fibre of John Graves, nor that kind of manly philosophy which would keep him straight under pressure. He had always been a ramping, violent, hard-mouthed Son of Thunder, who, at the best of times, had needed careful handling, and to be deftly guided, not harshly driven. Richard Fullerton had had supreme influence over him, and had kept him pretty well to the right point of the moral compass ; but since the fatal evening when the old Adam had blazed out in those fiery words, and the vicar had taken such revengeful note of them, Tom's demoralization had begun ; and it had continued ever since at a hand gallop.

His work left him, and he left his work. He had always been sober in fact, with possibilities in him of a loose life if things went wrong ; and now these possibilities had become actualities. His pride crushed, he took refuge in forgetfulness, was seldom out of the public-house and ever " on the rampage." With his great personal strength and furious passions, he was a formidable element in the little village society; and the vicar had his eye on him, as had many others, prepared to fling him heavily at his first legal trip—which everyone felt sure would come in its own good time.

As Tom went down Adam Bell went up. It was the old seesaw, and this time craft and a shaky past had the best of it. Adam had prospered right over the borders. The man had a jackdaw's faculty for accumulation, and money seemed somehow to grow in the night with him. He had left off scheming out his mechanical revolutions since he came to Crossholme, and had applied himself with a will to the more profitable occupation of making more than the two ends meet. Evidently he had suc- ceeded ; and the lap over was considerable. He had put a fine new front to his little shop, and his plate-glass window was the admiration of the village ; his goods were well chosen, and he was always bringing in some novelty of which use made a necessity ; he was secretary here and treasurer there ; and his energy, obliging man- ners, and neat handwriting had their share in the garner- ing of his goodly harvest. Whatever might lurk in the

shadows of the past, here in the present he was all square
and above-board ; and really, as some said, it seems
scarcely fair to mistrust a man because he came out of
the dark of yesterday without a character pinned to his
back or a certificate from his last place, when he had
lived so long as Adam Bell had lived at Crossholme, and
not a soul had a bad word to say of him ! It was only
a reasonable argument, as most confessed ; and the little
chandler got the benefit of it. People had left off dis-
trusting him, and had begun to think him no worse than
his neighbours ; in which they were about right; and at
all events they paid him the wage for which he had been
working.

Thick-headed, bull-necked Tom Moorhead was not
one of these kindly ratters. Once a blackamoor always
a blackamoor with Tom ; and he scoffed at the theory
of leopards changing their spots. To him Adam Bell
had always been a sly cat of a man who had come mous-
ing here from the Lord knows where, and who shall say
with what kind of soot on his muzzle ?—and let him get a
character by half a century of industry and solvency,
Tom would still have that apocryphal parish register to
fling in his face, and those two unanswered questions to
ask : " What workhouse bred you ? " and " What gaol

held you?" Pretty Janet took a different view of things.
Pretty Janet saw no fun in a bare cupboard and patched
gowns, with a drunken father staggering home at night,
half mad from bad liquor and a worse conscience, and
fit to take the house if so much as a cricket chirped, as
she used to say. Adam Bell, a clean-shaven, smart,
smug little man, as sharp as a needle and with a repute
for good gear, had followed her for many a day now,
and so far showed his disinterestedness. Young men
here-away were scarce ; so she made up her mind to
take Adam for good and all, and run for shelter under
the vicar's wing should her father " turn rusty."

The result of all this was, that one moonlight night
Tom, coming home a trifle earlier than usual and not so
drunk but that he could see, caught the pair of them
standing just under the haystack, with Adam's arm round
Janet's waist, and their lips too close to each other for
his taste. He took the little chandler with one hand,
and almost thrashed the life out of him with the other.
It was a near thing ; and for two months the one lay
in prison, while the other hovered between life and
death—the issue to determine whether Tom was to be
tried for murder or only aggravated assault and battery.

Thanks to the wiry thread that ran through him

Adam lived over his broken bones; and as soon as he could turn himself about he and Janet were married at the parish church and the vicar himself officiated. So that Tom when he came up for trial had the additional smart of knowing that he was to serve out his term, with hard labour, for the man who was now his son-in-law, and who had his daughter as well as justice and public opinion on his side.

But nothing much signified to him now, he said. He was a broken man from the day when he had been put into the Starton lock-up for inciting to a breach of the peace anent the vicar; and he took his punishment so sullenly, that it was no matter of wonder to the authorities when they found him hanging in his cell by an ingenious contrivance of rope made out of his bedding. So perhaps it was a wise instinct in Janet to make her own nest warm, seeing that her father's house would never more give her comfort.

Soon after this, the marriage of Ringrove and Bee Nesbitt came to the point, and with it arose a certain difficulty. In the relations in which they stood to the vicar and his party they did not wish that he or any of his curates should perform the cere-mony; but he, also because of those relations and

to punish their disobedience, refused to lend his church
to a stranger for this or any other purpose. Ringrove,
as his solution of the difficulty, proposed the Registrar
and said he thought it would be better to fling over the
Church altogether. It was the law which made the marriage, he said, not the priest. The law suffered the Church
to run side by side with it in this matter—allowed her to
be exponent, lieutenant, a second self; but it was always
the law that had to be satisfied ; and if the Church married you against the law it would be a dead form, null
and void for all the purposes of marriage.

At first Mrs. Nesbitt, who represented conformity to
established custom, shook her head, more than a little
scandalized by this audacity of her prospective son-in-
law, and said : "No, certainly not ! Bee must be married
from home and at her own parish church, like any other
lady." She would not dream of allowing such an indignity as a marriage at the Registrar's office. If they were
not married in church it would not be like a proper wedding at all, and she would never feel that things were as
they should be. No ! the meagreness of Ringrove's proposal had no kind of support from her, and even Mr.
Nesbitt said it would scarcely do.

For Bee herself, she would have been married at a

police court if Ringrove had wished it. He was her lord,
and his will was her desire; but he convinced Mrs.
Nesbitt at last, and proved to her that for him in his
position the Registrar's office was the most suitable
kind of thing, as evidencing the majesty of the law,
and being another blow dealt to the supremacy of the
vicar.

It was a hard struggle; for conformity is like lifeblood
to the normal Englishman, and still more to the normal
Englishwoman; but Samson conquered at last, and put
the finishing touch to his iniquity by making his marriage
simply a civil contract, and flinging overboard the blessing of the Church as a caligraphic flourish not vital to the
bond.

They did not do themselves much harm by their rebellion to forms. People said: "How very odd of the
Nesbitts!" and mothers declared they would not have
allowed such a marriage with their daughters; but by
degrees the little tumult subsided and the reaction set in
—when it was called plucky, and just what that papist
in disguise deserved.

"And this is the man for whom you designed your
sweet Virginia!" said Edith Everett, in a tone as if Hermione were personally responsible for all that Ringrove

had done or was designing to do, from the "persecution" of the vicar to this infidel and ungodly marriage.

"Oh! he was much better then than he is now," said Hermione simply. "He was a very dear fellow then, and I was very fond of him."

"What an extraordinary expression! How much I dislike to hear a married woman use it!" answered her guide and friend suavely. "A married woman should never say she is fond of any man whatsoever. It is indelicate and not nice."

"I do not see anything either indelicate or not nice in saying that I used to be fond of Ringrove Hardisty," retorted Hermione with spirit. "I knew him when he was a little boy, and I hoped at one time that he would have married my daughter; so I think I am entitled to say that I was fond of him. You have such strange ideas, Edith; and such an uncomfortable way of putting them."

"Now don't lose your temper, dear. I speak only for your own good," said Mrs. Everett, with amiable equanimity.

"You are always doing and saying disagreeable things for my good," said Hermione. "I must be very bad to want so much putting to rights."

"You certainly want a great deal of putting to rights, my dear," returned her friend with an amiable smile. "Whether you are very bad or no is another matter."

"I know what *you* would say; so we need not discuss that part of the question," Hermione answered hastily.

She had come to the pass when all that Edith Everett said or did seemed harsh and cruel—Edith to that when all that Hermione said or did seemed contemptible and quite beyond the need of courtesy. It was getting time for them to part if they were to keep even the lifeless husk of friendliness between them; and Edith was only waiting for the moment until she felt that she had made herself so useful to the vicar as to be eventually indispensable.

"In that case silence is golden, dear," returned Edith.

Hermione put her head on one side a little defiantly.

"You can scarcely wonder at my feeling an affection for Beatrice Nesbitt and Ringrove," she went on to say, as if there had been no break in that part of the conversation. "They have always been so sweet and affectionate to me! It seems quite another life when I look back and remember how good Mrs. Nesbitt always was, what care she took of me, how kind she used to be, and how respectful and attentive Ringrove was!"

"What a soft, sugar-loving baby it is!" said Edith. "I do believe, Hermione, you care for nothing in the world but flattery and attention! It never seems to occur to you that people are valuable or reprehensible for themselves and what they are—only whether they are what you call kind to yourself or not. Cannot you raise your thoughts a little higher than this, dear? It is distressing to see such immaturity of mind in a woman of your age!"

"I don't wish to become one of your cold, hard, strong-minded women," returned Hermione, crimsoning to her very temples. "I hate that kind of woman—so cruel and self-sufficient as they are! I would far rather be what I am, and care whether people liked me or not."

"Well! live on sugar-plums to the end of your life, if you like, dear; I prefer a nobler kind of food," answered Edith, shrugging her shoulders. "I like to make friends with people I respect, not only because they take it into their heads to be what you call kind to me; and I think mine is the nobler view of life, dear."

" Mine is the more natural, and I should not care to live as you do, dear, with no one to love me," was Hermione's seemingly artless reply.

To which Edith Everett made answer by a laugh, and a sudden announcement of going to the Vicarage, " where Superior had something of great importance to tell her."

" And that is the flattery I care for," she said in a drawling kind of voice. " When such a man as Superior, with his mind, tells me his troubles, confides to me his most secret affairs, and asks my advice, then I feel that I am of some use in the world and that I am more cared for than if I were just a pretty little doll, flattered and caressed because good for nothing else ! "

" Thank you," said Hermione.

" Oh, I did not mean you, dear," said Edith Everett blandly. " You are of use, you know. You have got rid of the parish atheist and restored the church !—two titles to honour of no mean value. Well, good-bye, little woman. I see Sister Barbara coming up the drive, so you will have a companion. When we meet again I hope you will be radiant. Smiles become your pretty face more than frowns ; and you are undeniably frowning at this moment."

She gave the round dimpled chin a little "chuck" as she passed; but Hermione drew herself away, saying crossly—

"Don't be so silly, Edith! You treat me just like a child."

"Do I, dear?" said Edith, laughing, as she left the room; while Hermione was soon immersed in tiresome details with Sister Barbara, who came to her from the Convalescent Home, and worried her almost into tears about uninteresting matters which took up her time and prevented her from doing what she wished to do, and gave her no satisfaction from thanks or *kudos* when they were done.

At last the big, fat, smiling Sister left, and then Hermione ordered the carriage and drove straight to Newlands.

She was so irritated, so disturbed altogether, that she felt as if she must do something desperate and insubordinate. She knew nothing worse than to show favour to the Nesbitts and Ringrove, who were now almost as typical for ungodliness as Richard himself had been. And she thought that, although she was very angry with Ringrove, of course, still dear pretty Beatrice had done no wrong, and they had once been such friends together!

She did not like that the girl whom she had known from her infancy should marry without some little token from her; so she put up in a little parcel the row of pearls which she and Richard had given Virginia on the last birthday spent at home, and which had been worn only once, at the fatal dinner. She wrote a few kind words, accompanying the gift; and felt so much the happier because of her generosity, her delicate thought in connecting Ringrove's wife with Virginia, which she knew would please him so much,' and her disobedience to Superior and Edith Everett! Mild mutiny was in her way, and she thought that to be easily lost when not carefully held was something for a woman to boast of and quite within the range of righteous self-assertion. "Qui me néglige me perd" had been one of her favourite mottoes when she had been a girl; and a bird escaping from the unguarded cage her device.

She had not intended to go in at Newlands, but when her carriage was seen coming up the drive Ringrove and Beatrice both rushed out to the door; and it touched her soft heart to see the evident delight with which the young lovers, and presently Mrs. Nesbitt, received her.

"Ah, this is nice of you! this is like you, Mrs. Fullerton," said Ringrove enthusiastically; and before

Hermione well knew what had happened she found herself in the Newlands drawing-room, where Mrs. Nesbitt kissed her like a sister, and Bee made much of her with cushions and footstools, and words as sweet and soft as her own dear eyes. Her visit was made quite a fête by all, and she was surrounded by the pleasant and affectionate little fuss which was what she liked better than anything else.

"You are only a great boy yet, Ringrove," she said, smiling in spite of her endeavour to look grave, when he insisted on kneeling at her feet. "You will never be what the children call grown up."

"If to be grown up means to become indifferent to you, I certainly never shall be," laughed Ringrove. "Bee knows that."

"Yes, indeed," echoed Bee. "Not a day passes when we do not speak of you, dearest Mrs. Fullerton. Ringrove seems to care more for you than anyone in the world."

"Bar one," said Ringrove, with the folly of happiness ; and Bee gave back a happy, soft, foolish little laugh, as she said : "I don't think even 'bar one,' as you call it."

"Ah, my dear, you know where your true friends

are," said Mrs. Nesbitt patting the pretty woman's round shoulder. "Never any change here, dear Hermione !—always the old affection when you care to take it !"

"I know that," said Hermione, with a sudden feeling of choking at her throat.

What a pity that these bad Church-people should be so nice as friends, so good as the natural man ! If they had but come over how much pleasanter everything would have been !

"You have always been a kind of Queen among us, you know," then said Ringrove. "Our beautiful Mrs. Fullerton was the crown of our society."

"You must not flatter," said Hermione, with a kind of frightened pleasure.

It was delightful to hear all these caressing words once more ; but what would Superior say when he knew she had been here and listened to them ? She must not let herself be carried away, and she must cut the whole thing short.

"I dare say you wonder at my coming, dear," she then said to Mrs. Nesbitt ; "but I could not let Bee marry without a little present from me, and I have brought you "—to Beatrice herself—"what I am sure you and Ringrove both will like better than anything else—this row of pearls which we gave our dear Virginia on the last birthday she spent with us. She wore them only once, at that awful dinner party," with a shudder; "but perhaps you will like them none the less for that. It was only once; and they are really great beauties."

"They are all the dearer for that," said Beatrice heartily; and Ringrove, taking them from her hands, kissed them reverently, then fastened them round Bee's soft throat and kissed her after he had done so.

"I am glad that your wife will wear those pearls," said Hermione impulsively.

"And I am glad that my marriage will connect me with you by even this little link," he answered with grave tenderness.

"Poor, sweet Virginia! these pearls will be a sacred treasure in our house," said Mrs. Nesbitt lovingly; and Beatrice half whispered, "Yes;" with tears in her eyes.

Then Hermione rose to leave, and Ringrove took her to her carriage.

"Have you heard from your husband lately?" he said abruptly but quite naturally, as if Hermione had been in the habit of hearing from him every week.

"No," she replied, with painful embarrassment.

"I shall see him when I pass through London on

my way to Paris next week. Shall I say anything from you?"

"Give him my love, and say I hope he is well," answered Hermione in a low voice; "mind you say this, Ringrove."

"Willingly. Nothing more?"

"No, nothing more—only my love, and I hope he is well. Good-bye, Ringrove; God bless you and make you happy, and do not think harshly of me;" she said impulsively; "and give Richard my love," she repeated for the third time as the carriage drove away.

When she reached home she found a certain odd bustle of preparation about the house. The servants were discomposed and the hall was encumbered with luggage.

"What is the matter?" she asked; and the man, with a broad smile, answered—

"Mrs. Everett, ma'am. She is leaving by the next train."

"I have had a telegram," said Edith with perfect tranquillity of conscience, when Hermione went into her room to ask what it all meant. But if she had it must have been by a private wire and special service. "My boy wants me."

T 2

"Is he ill?" inquired Hermione anxiously, her dislike subdued by sympathy.

"A little out of sorts," answered Edith. "At all events it is my duty to go to him."

"I am so sorry! You will let me know how he is, and you will come back again," the soft-hearted creature said with a pitying accent; but at the same time drawing a deep breath. It was as if a prison door had been suddenly opened and the fresh mountain air had blown in on the dust and darkness.

Edith smiled sarcastically. She understood too well the difference between impulse and conviction not to see the rootlessness of Hermione's invitation.

"Thanks," she drawled; "thanks for all your great affection and generous hospitality. I hope, however, I have been of use to you. I think I have; but you must not fall back when you are left to yourself, Hermione. And above all things keep clear of those dreadful Nesbitts and Mr. Hardisty."

This she said with a little laugh, and Hermione became crimson. It was a chance shot, but it had the look of a true aim; and when the pretty woman changed colour in that tell-tale manner, her inquisitor knew that somehow she had hit the mark, though the how was not quite clear.

" You are so weak, you see, dear," she added amiably,
" that one never knows what you may not do. But you
will be shamefully wrong if you make friends again with
these people who have persecuted poor dear Superior and
the Church so bitterly."

"One cannot quarrel for ever," said Hermione at
once evasive and apologetic.

Edith Everett curled her lip.

"You are impossible !" she said contemptuously ;
and turned to her own affairs with the manner of one
who has renounced further communion.

Even when she took her final leave she still kept up
this manner of renunciation and severance ; and hastily
brushing Hermione's cheek with her own, as the only
kind of embrace she could find it in her heart to give,
she hurried into the railway carriage and did not even
look up from her travelling bag for the last orthodox
salute.

" Gone at last !—how glad I am !" was Hermione's
thought as she turned away ; and : "What a relief to have
got rid of that awful fool !" was Edith Everett's, doubled
with : " I wonder what Superior will do without me. I
am sure he will miss me awfully. I hope so ; else I have
done foolishly to go !"

CHAPTER XII.

RING DOWN THE CURTAIN.

THE loss of Edith Everett was more severely felt by Mr. Lascelles as time went on than even it had been in the beginning ; and more severely by far than had been that of his sister.   A certain sympathy of nature between the vicar and the widow, which had not been between the brother and sister, had given a special charm to all that came from her hands ; and though Sister Agnes had been clever, Edith Everett was cleverer still.   With as much devotion to the Church, she had more tact with out-siders ; and then she was just those five years younger which make all the difference in a woman's life—those five years which leave the gate still open and keep the roses blooming within—over-blown and damaged by wind and weather, if you will, but all the same roses and in bloom.

The vicar bemoaned himself bitterly on the loss of his faithful friend.   He felt desolate, oppressed with tire-some minutiæ, and not able to gather up the multifarious threads which she had quietly taken into her own hands, and had now thrown down in a tangled heap at his feet.

It was exactly the result which Mrs. Everett had foreseen, and for which she had played. To make him feel first her value, and then her loss, was about the best card in her hand ; and if this did not win the game, she knew of none other that would. Had she seen him now fuming over insignificant details from which she would have freed him—besieged by hysterical penitents whose consciences could be soothed only by his writing to them or their calling on him ; had she seen him with his sacerdotal calmness laid aside and an undeniably petulant humanity manifest in its stead, she would have glorified herself in the success of her stratagem, and would have thought, as so often before, that no matter how much intellect a man may have, he is nothing but a lump of plastic clay when an astute woman undertakes to mould him.

When Mr. Lascelles heard that Hermione had been to Newlands even while Edith was still at the Abbey, and speculated on what wrong use she might now make of her dangerous freedom, he was swept into a torrent of wrath that made him ashamed of himself when it was over. Adam Bell had told him—for there was very little

that Adam did not know—and he had sworn aloud when
he was alone ; but he curbed himself so far as not to send
the scathing letter he rapidly wrote out, and contented
himself with passing on coldly and hurriedly after evensong, when he came out of the church and found
Hermione as usual loitering slowly up the road hoping he
would overtake her.   He did overtake her—he and all
his curates and choristers, whom he generally shook off
long before he came to this point.   This afternoon,
however, with a curt : " Beautiful day it has been ! " as
his only greeting, he passed on at speed.

" Superior is angry ! " thought Hermione, as he and
his following strode on.   " He has heard of my going to
Newlands, and means to punish me.   What a tyrant he
is ! " was her next thought.   " How unlike poor dear
Richard in everything ! " her last, ended with a sigh.

Should he marry her ?   This was the question which
evening after evening the vicar asked himself as he sat in
his solitary study, turning the thing over and examining
it on every side.   Should he marry her ?   She was eminently the right kind of wife for him if he should take
one at all ; and those things which some men might consider drawbacks were so many points in her favour with

him. She was not handsome, therefore the ungodly could not say that he had sacrificed principle to the temptations of the flesh; she was not rich, therefore the cry of Mammon and mercenary motives would be a failure; she had four children—four witnesses of his Christian patience and philanthropy; and she was capable, intelligent and devoted to the Church. Perhaps she would be more useful to the cause as a wife than as merely a friend! The world is so censorious, so unwilling to believe in purity, so set against innocent friendships between men and women! A celibate priesthood is undoubtedly the ideal of ecclesiastical organization, and in certain circumstances gives the most power. In others, the reverse obtains. Was this one of those others?—and, here at Crossholme, would a married vicar be of more solid benefit than one, like himself, unmarried, fascinating, and consequently a living target at which all women aimed their erotic darts and calumny let fly her poisoned arrows? Poor Theresa had been a case in point! Unless something supremely good offered he should remain at Crossholme. The church made attractive by its appointments and splendid ritual, the benefice enriched by the offerings which he had induced the wealthy faithful to give, the majority submissive and the recalcitrant

minority impotent:—yes, he would keep the living ; for
all that he summed up on the other side of the account :
—the Abbey funds almost exhausted, Ringrove Hardisty
sure to prove troublesome if he had the chance, and
Churchlands reported sold to a Roman Catholic who
would draw away more than one weak vessel when the
opposition mass was in working order.   But he would
stay, in spite of all this ; unless indeed he were called
away by an offer of so much gain or dignity as it would
be impiety to refuse.   And being here, a country vicar
—so different from a town incumbent—would it not be
better for him to marry ?

He had no doubt of Edith herself. Though she did
not give him the idolatrous love of poor Theresa, nor
had he over her the same kind of rootless personal fascination that he had over Hermione, still he knew that
she would marry him if he asked her.   The tie between
them was stronger and tougher than that of personal
affection.   It was the tie of intellectual companionship.
They mutually supplemented each other, he said to himself ; and she was a wonderfully intelligent executant.
He little thought that, while he thus patronized her as
the worthy handmaid of his power, she knew herself his
manager.   Every time she led him by that invisible

thread of suggestion was a triumph of which she understood the full value. He was strong, but she was
stronger ; and however brilliant his intelligence, hers was
the governing influence. " The cleverest man is not
equal to the cleverest woman." This was her axiom,
and her own life justified her.

And still, while he pondered and hesitated, those
matters which she could best regulate pressed more and
more heavily on him, and Hermione's practical uselessness was more and more evident by force of contrast in
this hour of need. Then he decided on what to do,
and wrote to Edith Everett the letter which was to determine all.

When the answer came, as he expected, in the
affirmative—a grave, sensible, judicious answer, for which
he had been made to wait many days, and wherein was
expressed no jubilation, no personal affection, nothing
but a rational review of their joint circumstances, and
how the Church could be best served—he went up to
the Abbey, where he spent several hours with Hermione
alone. He did not tell her what he had done. He had
in his pocket the letter by which the whole programme
and meaning of his life would be changed ; but he kept
his own counsel and made no confidences—at least, for

the present.   Time enough to proclaim this sudden re-
volution in his principles when secrecy was no longer
possible and public avowal had to be made.

It was long since he had been so delightful to Hermione as he was to-day.   The return on the original Mr.
Lascelles, whom somehow she had lost since she had
performed her final act of sacrifice at his instance, was
as complete as it was fascinating.   Never had his manner
been so tenderly suggestive, his personal devotion, purified by pastoral care, so satisfying.   It was like some
one lost and now found again ; and she welcomed his
return with pleasure that passed from gratitude to self-
abasement.   It pleased him, strong and cruel as he was,
to act out this last scene in the drama where he had all
along played under an impenetrable mask, and she,
poor soul ! with not even the flimsiest rag as a veil
between her innermost heart and his keen eyes.   It
flattered his sense of power to see her sensitive face
change from the discontented sadness that had lately
settled on it into something of its former girlish softness
and shy delight ; to watch her colour come and go as
he skilfully mingled priestly exhortations and lover-like
flatteries together ; to see her blue eyes brighten when
he spoke to her in parables, wherefrom she might, if she

chose, infer that had she been free he would have made himself her slave, but which he knew she would not dare to interpret too closely. It was a pleasure, and in existing circumstances no peril; and this was the last time that he should know it.

So the hours passed; and when he went away he carried with him, in the same pocket as that which held Edith Everett's letter, a cheque of four figures, which he knew too well it was simple robbery to take from her cruelly diminished income.

"It may be the last," said Mr. Lascelles to himself, as he took the paper with effusive thanks and delightful praise. "I am wise to take what I can get and when I can get it; and by rights it all belongs to the Church."

For some time yet the vicar kept his secret; but at last one evening he wrote to Hermione, telling her that he was leaving Crossholme to-morrow for a short time. After having recommended to her care this case and that house, and planned out her work during his absence, he said: "And now I am about to communicate to you, my dearest and most faithful friend, a fact wherein I am sure of your loving sympathy. When I return, it will be with Edith Everett as my wife. This will, I am sure, be good news to you. It will not only render my ministrations here at Crossholme more effective than at present, but it will also be of benefit to you. It will give you a sister in her, as well as a more efficient protector in myself. Else I should not have taken a step to which, I am sure you will believe me when I say, the consideration of your gain has most powerfully impelled me. Let me have your prayers and congratulations ; my cup of happiness will then be full."

It would have been difficult for Hermione to have put into words what she felt when she read this letter. Anger, disappointment, sorrow, the sense of having been duped and played with, of having been badly used, of having had something taken from her that she believed was hers—all sorts of confused and embittered feelings came like tumultuous clouds, unstable, intangible, but evident and real. And yet, why should she feel as she did ? Why should this marriage make her loneliness so much more barren—her widowhood so much more burdensome ? What did it take from her ?

When she tried to reason it out fairly she had no self-justification in fact or common sense ; but none the less she felt so much the poorer and more desolate on account of it as to be substantially wrecked—as also, in some obscure way, insulted, jilted, and aggrieved.

She was very foolish to take it so much to heart, she thought, as she sat there with the letter in her hands and the sensation of utter ruin and collapse about her. But, after all, it was a shameful thing to do! Superior had so often spoken against marriage for the priesthood; he had so often said that a celibate clergy was the only righteous body; and now he himself had broken through his own rules and falsified his own principles! Yes, now she had made it clear to herself:—it was because he was false to his own teaching, not because he was false to her. Of course that was impossible! She was married, and it could not make any difference to her, as a woman, whether he took a hundred wives or no. But on that other ground he could not expect anything else than her displeasure. After he himself had taught her that a married priest is a sacrilegious anomaly, to go and marry on his own account—and of all women in the world that odious Edith Everett! Anyone but her! Poor Theresa Molyneux, a thousand times rather; even that ridiculous Miss Pryor, with her sidling airs and wasp's waist, would have been better; but Mrs. Everett, so ugly as she was, and such a hypocrite as she had been!—it was horrible to think of! Her sister, indeed!—no sister of hers! She should never come to the Abbey as Mrs. Lascelles—

never! never! Whatever happened, this should not
come into the list of her trials to be undergone for the
sake of the Church and her Director! It was shameful,
it was impious! Superior married, and Edith Everett
his wife! She wondered he did not expect to be struck
dead before the altar the next time he celebrated the
Sacrifice of the Mass!

And then her mental ravings ended, as of course
they must, in a passionate burst of despair, in a wild cry
of " Richard! Richard! why did I ever leave you?"

All this happened just before the return of Ringrove
and Beatrice from their wedding trip. They had made a
long journey on the Continent and had been over more
than the stock touring-ground. Now they came back to
begin the life that Ringrove had once pictured with Virginia; and the county prepared to do them honour.
But the first who called on them was Hermione
Fullerton.

Conscious that she had been played with, deceived,
and *exploitée* by the vicar for his personal ends—whether
connected with the Church or no, still personal—she was
feverishly anxious to show him that she had thrown off
her allegiance. She was still a good Churchwoman;
that she would always be—must be, indeed, by the nature

of her mind, unless she should go deeper still and follow in Virginia's steps ; which was not impossible—but she must make it clear that she was no longer under his special domination, and that the individual priest was nothing if the organization was still omnipotent. All that delightful haze of feeling, that half-flattered, half-reverential homage which had given the whole thing its special power, making it religion and fascination, worship of the Divine and tenderness for the man in one— all that had gone ; and she must show that it had. She had never been really in love with him ; looking back, she could say that. But he had had a greater hold on her by her imagination, by her belief in his esteem and sympathy for her, and by her instinct of obedience, than was perhaps wise. When the spell was broken, she recognized so much of the truth, and knew now, when he was about to marry Edith Everett, how much of her religious zeal had been due to the splendid personality of the priest who had converted her. The man had endeared the creed ; as must ever be in those religions which give the priesthood powers beyond nature and supreme authority over the consciences and lives of men.

From this date however all was to be changed ; and she would take up again so much of her old life as she

could reconcile with her conscience. She would find
out Richard and bring him back in triumph to the
Abbey. Or if he liked it better, they would make a new
home for themselves somewhere else. Perhaps she could
yet reclaim him from his errors. God might still work
a miracle on her behalf, and strike him with the blinding
light of truth before it was too late. He was so good !
—though an infidel, still so good ! She wanted him
too in matters of business. Her affairs were in frightful
confusion and she could not put them straight. She
would give them all into his hands again, and he might
do as he thought best. She would ask no questions ;
and ignorance would absolve her from the guilt of parti-
cipation should he use her money as he used it before—
for the spread of infidelity. Anything was better than
the present wretched state of things, where she did not
know what she had to spend nor what she had to pay ;
when bills on which she had never calculated were
always coming in, and interest on loans which she never
remembered was always going out. And really cottages
let for so much rent, even to infidels, would be better
for her in the state of her finances than these same cottages given now to this and now to that purpose of the
Church for no rent and some outgoings. These loans to

the Lord, so perpetually negotiated by Mr. Lascelles, were terribly heavy, all things considered, and, since the treachery of the negotiator, unendurable.

Full of these thoughts, she drove over to Monkshall to call on the young people just returned, and to make the first step in that backward path which was to redeem the past. She had heard nothing of her husband since Ringrove's letter from London, two days after his marriage, telling her that he had seen Richard ; that he was not looking well, but would not confess to feeling ill ; that he was occupied at a certain Institution where he gave lectures and made experiments and investigations ; and that he had gone back to his own name, being now simply Spence—Richard Spence. Ringrove did not give the address either of the Institution or the lodgings.

This abandonment of her name had hurt Hermione at the time more deeply than she could explain to herself. She thought it cruel, insulting, a repudiation that she had not deserved, taking her at her worst ; for she was of that large class of women who think it a shame that they should be made to pay their forfeits, or have a return in kind when they do wrong to others. She had withdrawn herself from her husband, but he had no business to drop her name. She had been misguided, but he had been actively to blame. Her anger however had died by now, and had left only a faint feeling of a wrong somehow done her; so that when she resolved to seek out Richard, and offer him reconciliation and reinstatement, it was pleasant to believe that she had something to forgive. It strengthened her purpose and gave her courage.

Weary, pale, depressed, over-taxed with work, and disabled by disease, Richard Spence, the popular lecturer at the —— Institution, came back to his meagre lodgings early in the afternoon of an off-day at the laboratory. That old pain at his heart scarcely ever left him now ; he had often fits of sudden faintness and general loss of power ; he was soon tired, and no rest refreshed him—always exhausted and unable to eat. But he still went on doing his day's work manfully, though his life was drawing to its close—and he knew it. He was lying back in the easy chair, not sleeping, but in that half-doze of weakness which looks like sleep, when the door softly opened, and Hermione, trembling, shamefaced, eager, came in.

By an instinct of pure womanliness she had dressed herself as of old in a certain grey silk gown, touched here and there with pink, which had been a favourite of his. She had arranged her hair in the fluffy frivolous way that he liked, and put on her rings and chains and bracelets. She was as she used to be in the days before her divorce—the dream of his youth, the wife of his manhood, the woman whom he loved, and, because he loved, believed in and trusted.

For a moment he thought that he was dreaming and this a mere cheat of his brain; but when she came up to him and laid her hand on his, and half sobbed half whispered his name, then he knew that it was true, and that his weary exile had come to an end.

He raised himself from his reclining position with the difficulty, the faintness, of overpowering gladness; hung over her and held her to his heart as she knelt by his side—just as he had held her and just as she had knelt on the evening of the day when Mr. Lascelles had successfully defied and she had divorced him. Neither spoke; only her quick sobs and his laboured breath told how with her contrition was greater than joy, how with him joy was so great as to be pain.

At last he lifted her face and held it back with his hand on her forehead.

" Let me look at you," he said in a low voice. **"Ah,**

this dear face of my wife—how sweet to see it once more! My own again! My wife, my love! Sweetest and dearest of all women on the earth—Hermione!"

"Say first that you forgive me," she sobbed.

"Love has nothing to forgive," he answered with infinite tenderness. "You have come back to me, and the past is forgotten. You are mine, my own, my second self, my soul. I have nothing to forgive, I can only love!"

"Do you love me, Richard, after all that has happened?" she asked, stealing her hand half timidly up to his neck.

"Could I live without loving you?" he answered. "A man's love is not to be cast aside so easily, sweet wife. As soon could I live without breathing!"

"But you are ill, darling! You are so pale, and your hands are burning. Why did you not tell me that you were ill?" her blue eyes raised to his full of loving reproach.

"Why should I, my wife? I did not wish to trouble you. If you had not come to me I should have passed away in silence and left you in peace for ever."

"That would have been cruel! It is cruel to think this of me," she said with all her old fondness and inconsequence.

" No, wife, it would not have been cruel," he answered, smiling.

" But I wanted to see you; I wanted to know all about you; and I knew nothing till Ringrove told me yesterday."

" You are here now, let us forget all the rest," he said hastily. " I do not want the shadow of painful memories to lie on the brightness of this day. See! the very sun comes out to welcome you," he added, smiling as a sudden burst of sunshine poured through the window and fell over Hermione like a golden glory.

" And now we will never part again," she said, cling-ing to him.

A spasm passed over his face as he pressed her to him fondly. Never? For how long would that symbol of eternity run?

" And I will make you quite well, Richard," she went on to say, smoothing back his thick gray hair.

He smiled a little sadly.

" If anything can make me well, it will be this dear hand in mine," he said.

" Why do you say 'if,' Richard? You are not really ill —only out of health ; there is nothing really wrong with you, is there ? " she asked in sudden fear.

" I am not quite myself, sweet wife," he said, " but well enough to know all the happiness of your return," he added with kindly haste.

" Well enough to live for many, many years in this happiness.   You shall be so happy, Richard !—I will be always so good to you ! " she returned.

" For your sake I will try, dear love," he said still smiling, but this time even more sadly than before.

" And if you die I shall have killed you ! " cried Hermione with a burst of unaffected agony.

He stopped her mouth with a kiss.

" Let the past be buried between us," he said.   " We must bury our dead, sweet wife ; and all this sorrow is dead.   Leave it where it lies, undisturbed."

" I never knew how good you were till now ! I never appreciated you as you deserved ! " said Hermione, raising his hands to her lips.

" Hush ! you were only too good to me, and you were my joy and delight," said Richard softly.

" And will be again.   The old life will come back just as it was," she returned.

His eyes filled up with sudden tears. Just as it was ? The unity of his happiness ?—the continuance of his work ?—the well-being of the men who had been ruined because of him ?—and, above all, that beloved child, fettered in the prison-house of superstition, and dead to him and humanity alike—could any of this be given back? Herself and all the happiness lying round her love, yes; but the old life as it was, never!

Nothing of all this fashioned itself into words; and though Hermione caught the reflection of his thought on her conscience neither did she speak. She only laid her face, which suddenly burned as if with fire, on his breast, while he passed his fingers through her golden feathery hair—glad to forgive because of love's sake, and the godlike power of magnanimity.

The next day they went down to the seaside to wait there until Richard should be strong enough to travel. Then they were to go abroad; for when Hermione had asked him with many tears and blushes, and shamed, shy looks: Would he not go back to the Abbey? he had answered: No; at least not yet. His work was now elsewhere, and the Abbey had passed from him.

She did not tell him that it had well-nigh passed from her too; and that she would soon have to give it up altogether, because she had been *exploitée* to the extent of not being able to keep it. She would reserve all that till he got well; meanwhile, the first thing before them was to get back his health.

By the seaside Richard seemed at the first really to

rally by this return to peace and love ; but it was only the delusive stimulus of happiness. After that first burst of apparent strength he fell rapidly back and grew steadily weaker day by day ; but she shut her eyes to the truth, and opened them only to the sweet flatteries of hope. She would not believe in his danger. He was her lover once more, as dear as in the early days, and she could not let him go. Now that they were so happy again, how could he die ? And again, so good as he was, how could he die, still unbelieving and impenitent ? As yet she had carefully abstained from all attempts at conversion, though she kept up her own devout habits and went, if not daily, yet often, to church. Still, she had let the question lie untouched between them ; but one day, from what the doctor had said, heartbroken for herself she had become infinitely distressed about his soul, and oh, how anxious to win from him one word of recognition for the solemn truths which were so real to herself ! But every tentative little effort that she made fell dead. He would not take up her more timid challenges, and when she grew bolder and insistent he kissed her with a quiet smile, saying:—

"Let sleeping dogs lie, sweet wife ! You and I must never have a theological discussion again."

" Only this once, Richard ! " she said, anxious, yearning, caressing, lovingly pertinacious. " Let me send for a clergyman. One word from him might clear your mind. God may manifest Himself at last ! "

It was about noonday when Hermione said this. The sun shone bright and warm, and the quiet lapping of the sea, just at the ebb, came with a pleasant, soothing sound through the open window. Pretty trifles and vases full of flowers were set about the room—that peaceful room !—where Hermione, like. some dear treasure recovered from the spoiler, sat by the side of the couch, her husband's hand in hers, looking at him, as both knew too well, for the last days. At the best he could not hold out much longer, and he might die at any moment.

It was strange how Richard's own dignity of patience had reacted on Hermione. Something seemed to have passed into her that had strengthened and ennobled her as nothing else had ever done. Her very religion was more rational than before—less a superstition and more a sentiment; but always lying on her heart was the desire that Richard should confess and be converted, even at the eleventh hour.

" Let me send for a clergyman ! " she pleaded again,

and mentioned one well known in the place where they were. "Darling! one little act of faith in the Christian Sacrifice—one word of Hope in God!"

His calm face looked into hers steadily, but with inexpressible tenderness.

"Belief in the creed founded on a lie and maintained by craft and cruelty?—where the fiction of a God-man, because of God's love for the earth, is made the weapon which destroys human happiness and love?—No! I am what I have been, dear wife—an Agnostic, knowing nothing, and refusing to affirm what I cannot prove."

"But when we die, Richard?" Tears drowned her voice.

"We go into the light of knowledge or the darkness of annihilation," he answered calmly. "It must be one or the other, sweetheart, and the laws of the universe will not be altered because one man believes in immortality and another is content with doubt."

She sobbed bitterly.

"You are lost!—we shall never meet again!" she said in pathetic condemnation.

He drew her to him.

"If the God in whom you believe is true, you dishonour Him by your distrust," he said. "Why should my soul be sent to an eternity of suffering because I am unable to believe contradictory and imperfect testimony? —testimony which stultifies all experience, and is disproved by every scientific truth?—which makes of Omnipotence a bungler and of Omniscience a dupe? If your faith be true, has not your God power to enlighten me now at the last moment?"

"You have neglected the means of grace offered to you, and we have no right to expect miracles," she said.

He smiled.

"Let me die then in peace, dear love!"

"This is not peace—it is enmity with God," she said.

"It is the best I know :—peace with man ; forgiveness even of him who was my enemy, and of those who stole my child from me. They acted according to their lights ; and it is not they but the creed which makes such crimes as theirs possible against which I have set myself. I have done my work. I can do no more now—only remain steadfast to the end."

"And you do not even confess God?" said Hermione.

"I confess the Unknowable," he answered with quiet solemnity. "Now kiss me, old love," he said with a smile, "and stand in the sunlight, just as you are. You are made for the sunshine, sweet wife. That glorious light! source of all power and life! shall we ever know what lies beyond?" he murmured, looking up to the sun. "Will humanity ever be delivered from superstition and set fairly in the light?"

He kept his dying eyes still fixed on the sun—his face irradiated with a kind of divine glory, as before his mind, marshalled in grand and long procession, passed thoughts of the noble victories over superstition and the glorious truths made manifest, the peace of nations, the spread of knowledge, the abolition of vice and misery and ignorance, the sublime light of universal freedom and the unfettered progress of humanity which should inform and govern the future through the supreme triumphs of True Knowledge.

"Man the God incarnate!" he said; "yes, the myth was true."

Presently he looked at his wife, but scarcely as if he saw her as she was, rather as if he saw her and something more.

"Sweet wife! my little Ladybird!" he said softly with a smile. "Good-night!"

He closed his eyes and his head sank back among the pillow as if he were sleeping. Hermione bent over him, her tears falling silently on his face. He did not seem to feel them. So quiet, so placid, so pale and peaceful as he looked he might have been already dead but for his faint breathing, and once a little smile that crossed his face. Once, too, she heard him say in a low murmur: " My men, seek out the Truth : " and again: " Refuse to believe a lie, my friends. If it cost you your lives, refuse."

After this he said no more, but continued to sleep so quietly that she dare scarcely breathe for fear of awakening him.

His noble face was verily sublime in its grand tranquillity. His thick grey hair was spread on the cushion in shining locks that stood away from his broad brow like an aureole of silver ; his full lips were slightly parted ; one hand was quietly lying on his breast, the other in his wife's. The whole attitude was one of perfect peace, of untroubled, dreamless repose. Presently a change came over him ; subtle, undefined, to be felt rather than seen —a change which showed that something had gone. His life—and what beside?

She stooped to listen to his breathing—to feel his heart :—all was still and silent. She laid her head on his breast—no answering throb of love welcomed her to her old resting-place ; she took his hand—it lay powerless in hers ; she kissed his lips—no warm response came from them ; and when she carried his head to her bosom and held it clasped there for long long minutes, no colour came. back to the pale cheeks beneath her kisses, the closed eyes did not open to her voice. Hushed, almost tearless, with strange and reverent patience, she laid him down again as tenderly as if a rough movement would have wakened him, and sank on her knees beside the couch. Passion and the violence of despair would have been a desecration about that quiet death ; it must be only love and patience in harmony with the life that had passed away. But she lifted up her eyes to heaven and said aloud, with a strange kind of belief that her prayer would be answered : "O God, receive the soul which wanted only Thy Light to be made perfect ! "

And yet it was a perplexing mystery to her for years to come when she remembered the agony and torment in which Theresa, a fervent Catholic, had died after receiving the Blessed Sacrament and Absolution ; while Richard, an infidel professing Agnosticism to the last, passed away with the serenity of Socrates or a saint already in glory.

And now to reckon up the loss and gain of this tragic

barter. For herself she had lost husband, child, money, place, and the finest flavour of her womanly repute. But she had gained the blessing of the Church which denies science, asserts impossibilities, and refuses to admit the evidence of facts. For Mr. Lascelles, what had he gained as the equivalent for the misery he had occasioned? Not so very much, when all was told. After his marriage, things went back into the old groove, and the excited zeal of Crossholme came to an end. The women, with no special desire now to win Superior's favour, took up again their fluffs and flounces, their glaring colours and frivolous ornaments. The salt waters of worldliness stole gradually back upon the redeemed lands, and Edith, as Mrs. Lascelles, had no power to speak of. The men, no longer pressed on by the women, fell off in their church duties; but, demoralized by the lavish use of pious bribes, the parish lost its former manly spirit, and the break-up of such a body as Mr. Fullerton's had been helped to bring things still nearer to low water-mark.

Cuthbert sold his estate to a Roman Catholic who brought his clerical staff to pick up the Anglican stragglers;—of whom Aunt Catherine was the first. She entered a convent, where she was treated kindly enough

—an imbecile, good-natured nun, who saw visions and dreamed dreams that never crept beyond the convent walls, not being out of line, and affording something to talk about in the cloisters. The Abbey was let to a Protestant who gave his countenance to the Nesbitts and Ringrove, and helped in putting on the break whenever it was possible. But, in truth, after his marriage, Mr. Lascelles himself modified his more extreme practices. He was looking for preferment, as enabling him to be more useful to his party; and he recognized the wisdom of drawing in so far as not to be counted with the Irreconcileables. When he reckoned up his gains—bought by the death of Richard and Theresa, the perversion of Sister Agnes, Virginia, Cuthbert, and Aunt Catherine, the destruction of Richard's men, the impoverishment and life-long loneliness of Hermione— he found :—a church far too magnificent for the population ; a Convalescent Home and sundry ritualistic establishments which could not be kept up and were abandoned by his successor ; and, as the permanent good, an increase of endowment which raised the value of the living to over fifteen hundred a year.

When all was over, Hermione went abroad, and in due time found herself in Rome. The day after her

'Her hands outstretched to her child.'

arrival, she went to the church where the Pregatrice for ever adore the Holy Sacrament, and where Virginia was now a professed nun.

As she was kneeling by the grating, two nuns came in to replace those whose function had ceased. The one was dressed in pale blue, the other in black; the one was Virginia, and the older woman by her side was Sister Agnes. Did they recognize Hermione kneeling there, in her heavy widow's mourning? Did they hear her sudden sob, her startled cry, and see her hands outstretched to her child, as she came with bent head and clasped hands to her station? Who knows? No sign of recognition was made; only Virginia became suddenly paler even than before. But she went through her prayers and psalms with an ecstatic passion of devotion that seemed to wrap her very soul away. Home and parents were alike forgotten; her father's death, her mother's tears—nothing touched her, absorbed as she was in the adoration of a mystery—the worship of the Divine Sacrifice. She was as dead to Hermione as was Richard himself; and her mother felt she would almost rather have known her to be in name what she was in essential fact.

Hermione knelt before the altar till Virginia's function

was over, and she and Sister Agnes had left. Then she
rose from her knees and turned to go. The darkness
of the early winter evenings had come on, and she stood
by the church door uncertain which way to take. How
desolate she felt—a solitary woman, childless and a
widow, alone in this strange, solemn city—alone in this
wide, empty world ! Had she done well after all? She
had given the victory to the Church ; had the conditions
imposed by the victor been righteous? Love, home,
happiness, her husband and her child—these had been
the forfeits claimed, the tribute cast into the treasury of
the Lord under whom she had elected to serve. Had
it been a holy sacrifice of the baser human affections to
the nobler spiritual aspirations? or had it been the cruelty
of superstition? the inhuman blindness of fanaticism ?

THE END.

LONDON : PRINTED BY
SPOTTISWOODE AND CO., NEW-STREET SQUARE
AND PARLIAMENT STREET